JUDE THE OBSCURE

JUDE THE OBSCURE

Thomas Hardy

edited by Cedric Watts

broadview literary texts

Canadian Cataloguing in Publication Data
Hardy, Thomas, 1840-1928
  Jude the obscure

(Broadview literary texts)
ISBN 1-55111-171-3 (softcover)   1-55111-313-9 (hardcover)

I. Watts, Cedric, 1937- . II. Title. III. Series.
PR4746.A2W37 1999   823'.8   C99-930392-9

Broadview Press Ltd., is an independent, international publishing house, incorporated in 1985.

North America:
P.O. Box 1243, Peterborough, Ontario, Canada K9J 7H5
3576 California Road, Orchard Park, NY 14127
TEL: (705) 743-8990; FAX: (705) 743-8353;
E-MAIL: 75322.44@compuserve.com

United Kingdom:
Turpin Distribution Services Ltd.,
Blackhorse Rd., Letchworth, Hertfordshire SG6 1HN
TEL: (1462) 672555; FAX (1462) 480947; E-MAIL: turpin@rsc.org

Australia:
St. Clair Press, P.O. Box 287, Rozelle, NSW 2039
TEL: (02) 818-1942; FAX: (02) 418-1923

www.broadviewpress.com

Broadview Press gratefully acknowledges the financial support of the Ministry of Canadian Heritage through the Book Publishing Industry Development Program.

Broadview Press is grateful to Professor Eugene Benson for advice on editorial matters for the Broadview Literary Texts series.

Text design and composition by George Kirkpatrick

PRINTED IN CANADA

Contents

Acknowledgements and Editorial Note

I gratefully acknowledge the co-operation of Sussex University in granting me leave to complete this volume. In preparing this work, I have been particularly helped by Michael Millgate's *Thomas Hardy: A Biography* (1982); and I have drawn on various previous writings of mine, including *The Deceptive Text* (1984) and a critical study, *Thomas Hardy: "Jude the Obscure"* (1992). Several friends and colleagues have kindly provided useful information: they include Dr. Hugh Drake, Dr Roger Ebbatson, and Professor A.D. Nuttall.

For the reasons given in the "Note on the Text", this edition represents the text of the first edition of *Jude the Obscure*. The annotations silently correct some errors promulgated in previous editions and identify certain quotations or allusions which previously have not been identified. The appendices set the novel in a wide critical and cultural context.

Introduction

In the sequence of Thomas Hardy's novels, *Jude the Obscure* (1895) is the last, and the fiercest, work. It is variously realistic and expressionistic, ironic and elegiac, symbolic and documentary; indeed, the list of its paradoxical attributes can be extended at length, for it is understated and strident, Victorian and modernistic, clumsy and adroit, benign and bitter, subtle and blatant. Its ferocity and ruthlessness mingle with its keen sensitivity, compassion and modes of comedy. Depicting a strife of ideas, beliefs, traditions and prejudices, it is a wounded and wounding novel. Hardy denied that *Jude the Obscure* was autobiographical; but, in all its tensions and conflicts, which it both describes and enacts, it is more intimately (if obliquely) autobiographical than the entirety of the lengthy autobiography which Hardy published in the guise of a biography written by his second wife. That *Life of Thomas Hardy* often voices reserve, prudence, detachment and circumspection; the novel voices the passion, anguish, anger and division of the deeper self. Through the mask of fictional identities and narration, Hardy speaks more vitally and comprehensively. W.B. Yeats wrote: "We make out of the quarrel with others, rhetoric, but out of the quarrel with ourselves, poetry."[1] Out of the quarrels with others and with himself, Hardy made *Jude the Obscure*. To understand those quarrels, it is useful to recall Hardy's early years, for they find significant reflection in the novel.

1. Biographical Matters

Thomas Hardy was born on 2 June 1840 in a thatched cottage in Higher Bockhampton, a village about three miles from Dorchester in Dorsetshire, a rural county of southern England. His father was a mason employing bricklayers; sometimes business was bad, sometimes it prospered. He was a smallholder, too, growing vegetables and fattening a pig for slaughtering each autumn. (Already there are glimpses of Jude, the mason appalled by the necessity of slaughtering his pig.) Hardy's mother was a former maidservant and cook who had

---

1 W.B. Yeats, *Mythologies* (London: Macmillan, 1959), 331.

known poverty but retained a strong, resilient personality, furthering her ambitions through her son in a way that anticipated D.H. Lawrence's maternal upbringing. Thus Thomas Hardy was born into an artisan "caste" (as he termed it) which was in everyday contact with the humbler workers.

Rural life had its traditions, pastimes and festivities, but also its poverty, squalor and hardship. Not far from the Hardys' home, the "Tolpuddle Martyrs" had been sentenced to transportation (six years before Hardy's birth) for their attempts to organise a trade union. Hardy saw both the harshness of the countryside and its consolations: the beauties of the natural cycle, and the pleasures of local music, whether folk-song, carols or hymns. His parents were keenly musical, his father playing the violin, and in course of time Hardy himself became an adroit, energetic fiddler at village dances. He was also intensely moved by the hymns and rituals of the Church of England during the family's regular attendance at Stinsford Church. "As a child," he later recalled of himself, "to be a parson had been his dream":[1] another link with Jude, who, in addition, is similarly responsive to ecclesiastical music.

One of the great achievements of Victorian England was its establishment of a nationwide educational system. Hardy entered the local National School when it opened in 1848. His early reading included popular novels by Lord Lytton, poems by W.J. Mickle, and Bunyan's *Pilgrim's Progress*. Walking home from school one day, he was so frightened by Bunyan's description of Apollyon "that he hastily closed his book and went on his way trembling, thinking that Apollyon was going to spring out of a tree whose dark branches overhung the road."[2] His fears thus recalled those of the young Jude, who "started homewards at a run, trying not to think of giants, Herne the Hunter, Apollyon lying in wait for Christian....." There were also three volumes given to Hardy by his mother. One of these was John Dryden's translation of Virgil's works, which initiated his lifelong study of the classics; and another was Samuel Johnson's *Rasselas*, that stoically pessimistic novel which declares, in tones which might be those of the disillusioned Jude, "Human life is everywhere a state in which much

---

1 F.E. Hardy, *The Later Years of Thomas Hardy 1892-1928* (London: Macmillan, 1930), 176.
2 *Later Years*, 260.

is to be endured, and little to be enjoyed."[1] The third volume was a translation of J.-H. Bernardin de Saint-Pierre's *Paul et Virginie* and of Sophie Cottin's *Élisabeth, ou Les Exiles de Sibérie*. A wise man in the former tale offers this unintentionally ironic advice:

> "My son! talents.....cost dear; they are generally allied to exquisite sensibility, which renders their possessor miserable.....He who, from the soil which he cultivates, draws forth one additional sheaf of corn, serves mankind more than he who presents them with a book."[2]

Many years later, Hardy's Jude, disillusioned with Christminster, would feel that humble artisans do more to serve mankind than do the scholars within the cloisters. Furthermore, as Phillotson will note, Cottin's depiction of the intense romance of Paul with Virginia provided a precedent (as did Shelley's *The Revolt of Islam*) for the relationship of Jude with Sue: "They remind me of Laon and Cythna. Also of Paul and Virginia a little."[3] Those literary lovers (the former being siblings, the latter virtually so) were exceptionally dedicated to each other.

Hardy's next school, the British School at Dorchester, gave him a grounding in Latin and French, while providing practical exercises in mathematics and letter-writing of a kind appropriate to boys entering trades. After his years here, Hardy was articled to John Hicks, a local architect, to be instructed in architectural drawing and surveying; and he frequently surveyed and measured churches that were to be "restored" or modernised to suit Victorian tastes. Again like Jude, who, as a monumental mason, provides Victorian Gothic refurbishments, Hardy experienced misgivings about alterations that might be regarded as destructive of tradition. Near the opening of *Jude the Obscure*, the narrator remarks that the old village church has been replaced by a building "of German-Gothic design" erected by "a certain obliterator of historic records who had run down from London and back in a day."[4]

---

1 Samuel Johnson, *Rasselas* (London: Oxford UP, 1887), 67.
2 Sophie Cottin, *Elizabeth; or, The Exiles of Siberia* (London: Noble, 1850), 74-5.
3 The first edition erroneously rendered "Cythna" as "Cynthia."
4 F.E. Hardy's *The Early Life of Thomas Hardy 1840-1891* (London: Macmillan, 1928),

A further connection between Hardy and Jude was that, while working for the architect, Hardy found time to pursue a study of Greek, concentrating on the Greek New Testament (both men used Griesbach's edition). If Jude was inspired by Phillotson to dream of the intellectual life of Oxford University, Hardy's friend Horace Moule (who had studied at both Oxford and Cambridge) imparted similar visions of the cultural riches of a university education. Hardy never enrolled at a university, and always retained part of that sense of deprivation which is so marked in Jude; although, like the fictional character, Hardy knew that much of his own learning was deeper and more conscientiously acquired than that of many undergraduates whose wealthy circumstances had gained them unjustly-easy access to the collegiate cloisters. His ambition of taking a Cambridge degree followed by a country curacy died in 1866, when he told his sister Mary: "I find on adding up expenses and taking into consideration the time I should have to wait, that my notion is too far fetched to be worth entertaining any longer."[1] While working as an architectural draughtsman, however, he pursued his studies of literature and experimented with journalism, poetry, and novel-writing. The late nineteenth century was a golden age for authors, as the education system was producing a large popular readership, technological advances were reducing the production-costs of books and magazines, and the burgeoning of systematic advertising increased the viability of numerous periodicals.

Hardy's first published novel, *Desperate Remedies*, appeared in 1871. This was a luridly melodramatic suspense-narrative incorporating an explicit lesbian encounter, the concealed killing by a husband of his alcoholic wife, a mistress later masquerading as that wife, and the last-minute rescue of the heroine from her honeymoon-night with her villainous spouse. The reviews of this vivid thriller were mixed: some were hostile, but others extended high praise. The response was sufficiently encouraging for Hardy to exchange the career of a draughts-

---

104, says of the modernisation of St Juliot's Church in Cornwall: "Hardy much regretted the obliteration in this manner of the church's history, and, too, that he should be instrumental in such obliteration....." (In 1997, thieves vandalised St. Juliot's and stole its altar.)

1   R.L. Purdy and M. Millgate, eds., *The Collected Letters of Thomas Hardy*, vol. 1 (Oxford: Oxford UP, 1978), 7.

man gradually for that of a full-time fiction-writer. There followed *Under the Greenwood Tree* and *A Pair of Blue Eyes*. By the time of *Far from the Madding Crowd* (1874), Hardy was famous and acclaimed; sales, too, were good, particularly as the author was able to command high fees for serialisation in magazines in addition to good royalty-rates on his books. For *The Hand of Ethelberta* (1876) he was paid over £1,250, at a time when the average earnings of an adult male in England were approximately £60 a year.[1] *Tess of the d'Urbervilles* (1891) proved highly controversial; but controversy (particularly concerning a novel's sexual contents) was then, as it is now, commonly a guarantor of large sales. Hardy had given the provocative sub-title "A Pure Woman" to this novel of the rape, suffering and lethal revenge of his heroine. R.G. Cox reports:

> Of the three-volume edition of *Tess* two further impressions of 500 each had succeeded the first 1,000 within four months. The one-volume reprint at 6s [six shillings] ran to five impressions totalling 17,000 between September 1892 and the end of the year.[2]

The novel was soon translated into numerous foreign languages, and between 1900 and 1930 was reprinted some forty times in England alone; Macmillan published 226,750 copies between 1895 and 1929; furthermore, 100,000 copies of the paperback by Harper were issued. The scandalous *Tess* ensured Hardy's prosperity.

Although Hardy thus enjoyed burgeoning success as a novelist, his works tended increasingly to express pessimism and social criticism. One reason for this development was the failure of his first marriage. In 1874 he had married Emma Gifford, daughter of a solicitor who felt that she had demeaned herself by marrying a "churl" with a Dorsetshire accent. The marriage proved childless, and after many years Emma complained to a friend that

1 A.L. Bowley, *Wages and Income in the United Kingdom since 1860* (London: Cambridge UP, 1937), 5, 6. In 1883 Jude, as a mason, might earn about £80 a year: see Leone Levi, *Wages and Earnings of the Working Classes* (London: Murray, 1885), 107.
2 R.G. Cox, ed., *Thomas Hardy: The Critical Heritage* (London: Routledge & Kegan Paul, 1970), xxvii–xxviii.

at fifty, a man's feelings too often take a new course altogether. Eastern ideas of matrimony secretly pervade his thoughts, and he wearies of the most perfect, and suitable wife chosen in his earlier life.[1]

Hardy said that when he first knew Emma, she was an agnostic (it might be truer to say that she wore her religion lightly); later, she became an Evangelical, and eventually was obsessively devout. Again, there are glimpses of *Jude the Obscure* here: Hardy's movement towards greater scepticism clashed with Emma's increasing piety, anticipating that discordant counterpoint of scepticism and piety in the relationship between Jude and Sue. Indeed, the unhappiness of Hardy's marriage evidently influenced the treatment of Jude's marital wretchedness and the text's rather jaundiced view of matrimony in general. Emma said that if she had read the manuscript, "it would *not* have been published, or at least, not without considerable emendations."[2] When *Jude the Obscure* appeared in 1895, it proved to be as controversial as *Tess*, and one of the reviewers claimed that Hardy belonged to the "Anti-Marriage League". The novel was attacked for its sexual frankness, "sordid" realism and impious satire. Hardy claimed that this outcry persuaded him to abandon novel-writing for poetry; but it was also the case that the sales of both *Tess* and *Jude* were so large that (when the continuing success of earlier novels was taken into account) he had no further financial obligation to pursue the career of a fiction-writer. In England alone, 20,000 copies of *Jude* were marketed within three months, and between 1896 and 1929 Macmillan sold over 109,000 copies; sales in the United States were also large.[3]

Hardy stated that the "scheme" of *Jude the Obscure* had been prompted partly by the death in 1890 of his cousin, Tryphena Gale (née Sparks), with whom he had a love-relationship in 1868. After her death, Hardy called on her daughter;[4] thus he anticipated Jude's re-

---

1 Denys Kay-Robinson, *The First Mrs Thomas Hardy* (London: Macmillan, 1979), 175.

2 Alfred Sutro, *Celebrities and Simple Souls* (London: Duckworth, 1933), 58.

3 *Thomas Hardy: The Critical Heritage*, xxviii; Simon Gatrell, *Hardy the Creator* (Oxford: Oxford UP, 1988), 251-2, 241.

4 Carl J. Weber, *Hardy of Wessex* (London: Routledge & Kegan Paul, 1965), 202. Tryphena was also commemorated by Hardy in the poem "Thoughts of Ph —a/At News of Her Death" (March 1890) and in the accompanying drawing which (in *Wessex Poems*) depicts a draped female corpse on a bier.

flection: "If at the.....death of my lost love, I could go and see her child.....there would be comfort in it!" Another factor was that when Hardy's sisters, Mary and Kate, had studied at the Teachers' Training School at Salisbury, he had visited them there; and this doubtless contributed to his hostile description of that "species of nunnery known as the Training School at Melchester" which Sue attends. Arabella was based partly on a "village beauty" referred to as "Rachel H—" in Hardy's journal: he recalled "her rich colour, and vanity, and frailty, and clever artificial dimple-making."[1] Hardy's sense of social deracination and insecurity has influenced Jude's situation as one who is sufficiently educated to be culturally superior to the folk of his rural origins, yet lacks the means or manners to be readily accepted in middle-class circles. Even the childhood fears of adult life as ominous and disruptive ("If he could only prevent himself growing up!") are common to Jude and his author.[2] In addition to being bookworms who study Clarke's Homer and Griesbach's Greek New Testament, both make telling quotations from Buckley's translation of Æschylus. Jude shares Hardy's view that Salisbury Cathedral is "the most graceful architectural pile in England"; and both men find the Book of Job all too appropriate a commentary on their disappointments in life.

More important than such local details, however, is the fact that the ideological tensions and conflicts which energise the novel derive so evidently from Hardy's personal experience of class conflict and injustice, of religious aspiration and disillusionment, of the moral hypocrisies and double standards in late Victorian England, and of "a deadly war waged between flesh and spirit"[3] within the evolutionary hybrid, man: a creature so often divided between noble idealism and demeaning desire.

2. Thematic Tensions and Sources

Henry James once referred patronisingly to the author as "the good little Thomas Hardy";[4] but, in his responsiveness to sexual, political and cultural matters, Hardy possessed a range compared with which

---

1   *Early Life*, 270.
2   Cf.: "He came to the conclusion that he did not wish to grow up": *Early Life*, 19.
3   From p. viii of the revised version (published in 1912) of the 1895 Preface.
4   Percy Lubbock, ed., *The Letters of Henry James*, vol. 1 (London: Macmillan, 1920), 194.

James seems, very often, parochially limited. Understandably, given his social and cultural situation, Hardy experienced inner divisions. He thus became a Janiform writer: one whose tutelary deity appears to be Janus, the two-faced deity of thresholds who looks in opposite directions at the same time. We can relate Hardy's tensions partly to his social position: he was a man from the class of rural artisans who moved amongst the intelligentsia and gentry of the city; a scholar and autodidact who could look critically both on the philistinism of the labouring class and on the prosperous life of the university-educated gentry of London; a man who yet anxiously sought acceptance in fashionable social circles, while harbouring fierce resentments at the injustices of the system which gave easy advantages and privileges to a favoured few. He was receptive to some of the most radical ideas of his time, but preserved a defensive scepticism and resilient pessimism.

A concise list of the resultant tensions in *Jude the Obscure* might be this:

1. Society is gradually becoming more liberal and tolerant; yet society increasingly oppresses the sensitive.
2. In the future, life may be better for the aspiring Judes and Sues; yet, in that future, such people may be extinct.
3. Aspirations express enlightenment; yet they are symptoms of the modern vice of unrest.
4. Sexuality may bring joyous fulfilment; yet sexuality tortures and demeans the idealistic.
5. Culture is desirable and liberating; yet culture is a false god nurtured by privilege.
6. Reflectiveness brings wisdom; yet ignorance is bliss.
7. Evolution is progressive; yet evolution engenders woeful awareness.
8. There is no transcendent deity; yet a callous or stupid Will ordains events.

Jude the Obscure, accordingly, is a Janiform text: in important areas it is not merely ambiguous or complex but moves towards paradox and even self-contradiction. Vigorously structured in its narrative patterns and powerfully sombre in its general tenor, the novel nevertheless displays an ideological volatility. The author is entangled in some of the confusions which he seeks to describe and explain. Thus *Jude*, for all its architectural symmetry of plotting, reveals marked variability in its moral and philosophical outlook. The following sections discuss that variability.

2.1. Evolutionary Theories

Sir Charles Lyell's *Principles of Geology* (1830-33) was potently influential. Its geological findings tended to undermine the Christian beliefs that the world was of relatively recent creation (4004 B.C., according to Bishop Ussher), that man was a special creation and that the creative process was overseen by a benevolent God. The resultant sense of loss and dismay was eloquently voiced in Tennyson's *In Memoriam*, with its horrific evocation of "Nature, red in tooth and claw." There followed Charles Darwin's *The Origin of Species* (1859) and *The Descent of Man* (1871), which provided evidence of man's simian ancestry: man was no longer lord of the creation but was merely a reflective part of the animal world. Of course, some writers sought to put an optimistic gloss on theories of evolution by suggesting that the process was progressive, gradually yielding improvements. Tennyson had done so in the closing section of *In Memoriam*, Darwin in the peroration of *The Origin of Species*.

Hardy said that he had been "among the earliest acclaimers of *The Origin of Species*",[1] and his works display his keen interest in the implications of evolutionary theory. In *Jude the Obscure* there is an element of tension or contradiction created by the tug of meliorist notions against a dominant pessimism. One meliorist suggestion in *Jude* is that both Jude himself and Sue are, in terms of human and social evolution, "ahead of their times": if they could have lived in a future era, they would have been less beleaguered and society would have been more hospitable. "Our ideas were fifty years too soon," reflects Jude. "It takes two or three generations to do what I tried to do in one." Against this, the novel suggests that in the future there may be no Judes and Sues, for the sensitive will prefer to perish. Here the novel reflects the bleak pessimism of Arthur Schopenhauer. That philosopher had argued that, in view of the widespread human distress, pain

---

1 *Early Life*, 198.

and suffering, it would have been better if there had been no life on earth. If the act of procreation were preceded by rational consideration, "[w]ould not a man rather have so much sympathy with the coming generation as to spare it the burden of existence?"[1] This dismal notion seems to be echoed in *Jude* when a doctor suggests that the death of the siblings portends "the coming universal wish not to live." The young Jude, we are told, seemed "born to ache a good deal before the fall of the curtain upon his unnecessary life should signify that all was well with him again."

Hardy was deeply divided in his judgement of sexual desires. Consider again his prefatory claim that the novel deals with "the strongest passion known to humanity": sexual desire, that combatant in the mortal conflict between "flesh and spirit". Jude's spiritual and educational aspirations are disrupted by his seduction by Arabella; he reproaches himself bitterly for letting his sexual desires overcome his higher ideals. It is as though he is an evolutionary hybrid, mentally advanced in humanity yet biologically chained to the bestial world. Yet, when Jude suffers agonies of frustration during his relationship with the coy Sue, the matter becomes highly ambivalent. Partly, the narrator's viewpoint is sympathetic to Jude, who is given some telling lines of expostulation; and, partly, it is sympathetic to Sue. There are many possible explanations of her sexual "inhibitions"; one is that in an evolutionary scale she has advanced further than the menfolk in her world, so that she is less governed by the carnal than they, who repeatedly demean what might be a "higher," "purer" kind of love. In some respects, the novel advocates a sexually liberated time, when the desires are not fettered by conventional ties of "holy wedlock" and lovers may live freely together; or, as Sue puts it: "I said it was Nature's intention, Nature's law and *raison d'être* that we should be joyful in what instincts she afforded us – instincts which civilisation had taken it upon itself to thwart." William Blake and D.H. Lawrence, not to mention many people in subsequent "permissive" societies, would have approved her claim. Nevertheless, in opposition to this liberal advocacy of spontaneity in sexual commitment, the novel places heavy emphasis on the betrayals, the quarrels and the coercions caused by the sexual impulses, which form part of that meshwork of

---

1 Arthur Schopenhauer, *Studies in Pessimism*, tr. T. B. Saunders (London: Swan Sonnenschein, 1891), 15.

"gins and springes" (traps and snares) which captures struggling individuals; and Jude's children perish wretchedly, as if to confirm Phillotson's grim assertion that "Cruelty is the law pervading all nature and society."

2.2. Religion and Scepticism

In religious matters, Hardy's attitudes include the agnostic, the atheistic, the antitheistic, the nostalgic, and what he termed "the churchy"; and, furthermore, he conceived an evolutionary theology which was both distinctively Hardeian and clearly of its times. Agnosticism, the belief that human beings cannot know whether there is or is not a God, has been available for many centuries; but the term "agnosticism" itself was first coined in 1869 by Thomas Huxley, a leading advocate of Darwinism. Hardy referred to himself as "a harmless agnostic", but that claim is repeatedly belied by the vigour with which he voiced atheistic and antitheistic sentiments. (Whereas the atheist denies that there is a God, the antitheist affirms that God exists but is uncaring or malevolent instead of benevolent.) Indeed, the context of Hardy's claim aptly illustrates this point:

> To cry out in a passionate poem that (for instance) the Supreme Mover or Movers, the Prime Force or Forces, must be either limited in power, unknowing, or cruel – which is obvious enough, and has been for centuries – will cause them [i.e. "the vast body of men"] merely a shake of the head; but to put it in argumentative prose will make them sneer, or foam, and set all the literary contortionists jumping upon me, a harmless agnostic, as if I were a clamorous atheist, which in their crass illiteracy they seem to think is the same thing...[1]

Here, in the very act of describing himself as an agnostic and not an atheist, he concedes that the ideas which he wishes to "cry out" include the idea that "the Supreme Mover" is "either limited in power, unknowing, or cruel" – a range which includes the antitheistic.

---

[1] *Later Years*, 57-8.

In Appendix D of this book appears Hardy's famous poem "Hap." That short poem is atheistic in its argument that human woes are caused not by "some vengeful god" but by "Crass Casualty" and "dicing Time" (stupid chance and the random changes); but even there the personifications tend to make these forces resemble the hostile God. In a letter to Alfred Noyes, Hardy denied claiming "that the Power behind the universe is malign": "the said Cause is neither moral nor immoral, but *unmoral*"; "The Scheme of Things is, indeed, incomprehensible."[1] Nevertheless, his journal entry for 10 December 1888 had blended the notion of the *unknowing* Cause with that of the *sinning* Cause:

> He, she, had blundered; but not as the Prime Cause had blundered. He, she, had sinned; but not as the Prime Cause had sinned. He, she, was ashamed and sorry; but not as the Prime Cause would be ashamed and sorry if it knew.[2]

In the nineteenth and early twentieth centuries, the religious heritage in Europe was so powerful that even those thinkers who sceptically rebelled against religion often experienced difficulty in emancipating themselves from religious conceptions. Both Bertrand Russell and Albert Camus, for example, sometimes confused the notion of the non-human universe with that of the inhuman (i.e. cruelly hostile) universe; anthropomorphism enters their reflections. Scepticism may still retain some vestiges of religious thought; and, in a society where institutional religion remains potent, the sceptic may revert guiltily to the arms of faith. As the narrator says in *Jude*: "affliction makes opposing forces loom anthropomorphous". Sue, in her bereavement, gains "a sense of Jude and herself fleeing from a persecutor". She has sought to be intellectually liberated, but her suffering convinces her that a wrathful God is punishing her for her sins, and she undergoes an appalling penance. Hardy was fond of quoting Gloucester's lines in *King Lear*: "As flies to wanton boys are we to the gods:/They kill us for their sport." In *The Return of the Native*, Eustacia Vye cries: "O how hard it is of Heaven to devise such

---

1 *Later Years*, 217, 217, 218.
2 *Early Life*, 282.

tortures for me, who have done no harm to Heaven at all!"[1] Most significantly, the plot-structures of Hardy's major novels (particularly *Tess* and *Jude*), with their notorious coincidences and ruthless ironies, may seem to imply less the non-existence of God than the existence of a deity actively hostile to the sensitive, idealistic and well-meaning: a "President of the Immortals" who indeed enjoys cruel sport.[2]

The idea which most commanded Hardy's intellectual and imaginative assent, however, was more sophisticated than this. We are told that in those youthful days "when her intellect scintillated like a star", Sue Bridehead had held

> that the First Cause worked automatically like a somnambulist, and not reflectively like a sage; that at the framing of the terrestrial conditions there seemed never to have been contemplated such a development of emotional perceptiveness among the creatures subject to those conditions as that reached by thinking and educated humanity.

These ideas are not Sue's only; they were ideas long held by Hardy. He formulated and re-formulated them in his notebooks over many years; they were versified in such poems as "God's Funeral", "The Sleep-Worker", "New Year's Eve", and "God's Education"; and they would gain their fullest literary expression in his great verse-drama, *The Dynasts*. His preoccupation with evolutionary ideas suggested to him a "First Cause" or "Creative Will" which creates blindly, so that there have evolved human beings who exceed in awareness their creator; humans are conscious and reflective amid an unconscious and alien universe. As Darwin had shown that reflective awareness dawns in creatures after æons of evolution, so Hardy envisaged a tardy growth of awareness in the creative force. At the end of *The Dynasts* we are offered the hope that the "Will" may at last evolve into consciousness, see what a mess it has made of the creation, and put matters right – "Consciousness the Will informing, till it fashion all things fair!" Hardy claimed this "evolutionary meliorism" as his own idea

---

1   *The Return of the Native*, vol. 3 (London: Smith, Elder, 1878), 200-201.
2   "'Justice' was done; and the President of the Immortals, in Æschylean phrase, had ended his sport with Tess." (*Tess of the d'Urbervilles*; London: Osgood, McIlvaine, 1891; vol. 3, 277.)

"entirely", though it owes debts to Æschylus, Shelley, Hegel and Schopenhauer.

In 1890, Hardy had written: "I have been looking for God 50 years, and I think that if he had existed I should have discovered him."[1] On his deathbed in 1928, he asked his wife to read to him the following verse from the *Rubáiyát of Omar Khayyám*:

> Oh, Thou, who man of baser Earth didst make,
> And ev'n with Paradise devise the Snake:
> For all the Sin wherewith the Face of Man
> Is blacken'd – Man's forgiveness give – and take!

Hardy's "pilgrim's progress" thus concluded with a defiant, pessimistic and partly-antitheistic stanza. He had once declared: "Pessimism ... is, in brief, playing the sure game. You cannot lose at it; you may gain. It is the only view of life in which you can never be disappointed."[2] One of the most obvious causes of the pessimism which is so marked a feature of the late Victorian cultural climate was the loss of religious belief. Matthew Arnold, in "Dover Beach", spoke of the "melancholy, long, withdrawing roar" of the sea of faith. Scientific discoveries in geology, physics and biology, the evident progress attained by empirical procedures, and new historical analyses of the books of the Bible: all these had served to erode religious convictions. *Essays and Reviews* (1860), by seven distinguished scholars, caused scandal by its sophisticated analyses of the Bible's implausibilities. Sue Bridehead reflects the new sceptical, critical spirit when she derides the traditional marginal glosses of the Song of Solomon: glosses designed to tame as pious allegory the patent eroticism of the original verses. Nevertheless, the pervasive power of the church and of religious reference-points for conduct remained strong.

When Hardy described himself as "churchy", he meant not only that he had long been preoccupied with religious matters, not only that he could relate present problems readily to biblical texts (Job, Corinthians, Numbers, Judges, Ecclesiastes, the Song of Solomon, Revelation and the Gospels being cited in *Jude*), but also that all his

---

1   *Early Life*, 293.
2   *Later Years*, 91.

life he liked to attend church services and was profoundly moved by particular hymns and anthems. There was a strong aesthetic element here, and also a form of cultural nostalgia for a church with which his father, grandfather and their friends, as musicians of the "quire", had for so long been associated. Hardy also entertained the apparently illogical hope (influenced by Comte's "religion of humanity") that the Anglican Church might so dilute its doctrines, purging them of "preternatural assumptions", as to open its gates to agnostics.[1] Tennyson had written:

> There lives more faith in honest doubt,
> Believe me, than in half the creeds.[2]

Hardy's hope for a church of "honest doubt" was almost fulfilled in the late twentieth century as the Anglican Church successively diluted its doctrines; indeed, influential priests (among them, Don Cupitt and various members of the "Sea of Faith" movement) denied the Resurrection and the objective existence of God.[3] Sue shares Hardy's nostalgia and his love of Swinburne's poetry when she says:

> To be sure, at times one couldn't help having a sneaking liking for the traditions of the old faith.....; but when I was in my saddest, rightest mind I always felt,
> "O ghastly glories of saints, dead limbs of gibbeted Gods!"

In the suffering heroes of the Old and New Testaments – Job,

---

1 "Apology" to *Late Lyrics* in *The Complete Poems of Thomas Hardy*, ed. James Gibson (London: Macmillan, 1976), 561; *Collected Letters of Thomas Hardy*, vol. 1 (Oxford: Oxford UP, 1978), 136-7. Hardy felt that Auguste Comte's "religion of humanity" would be more persuasive if Comte had included Christ among the worthies in his calendar: this "would have made Positivism tolerable to thousands who.....now decry what in their heart of hearts they hold to contain the germs of a true system" (*Early Life*, 189).

2 *In Memoriam*, section 96, lines 11-12. Compare Hardy's poem "The Impercipient/(At a Cathedral Service)," in which the narrator regrets that he is an "outcast", as "faiths by which my comrades stand/Seem fantasies to me."

3 In 1997 it was reported that more than seventy serving Anglican priests were members of the "Sea of Faith" movement, named after Don Cupitt's controversial television series. Though paid to teach that God has objective existence, those priests believed that God is only a concept produced by the human imagination. (*Sunday Times*, 30 November 1997, section 1, 7.)

Samson and Jesus (particularly the Jesus who said, "My God, my God, why hast thou forsaken me?") – Hardy found reference-points and exemplars for aspects of the characterisation of Jude. Indeed, *Jude the Obscure* could be regarded as a *Pilgrim's Progress* rewritten by a sceptic: a progress not towards salvation but towards the nirvana of death, under heavens that seem sometimes empty and sometimes the stronghold of an uncaring or hostile force. *Jude the Obscure*, the story of an orphan, is a lament for the metaphysically orphaned, for all those abandoned by a mortally mythical Father.

2.3. Hebraism and Hellenism

In *Culture and Anarchy* (1869) Matthew Arnold influentially analysed culture in terms of "Hellenism" and "Hebraism." "The governing idea of Hellenism is *spontaneity of consciousness*; that of Hebraism, *strictness of conscience*."[1] By Hebraism he meant the Judaeo-Christian religious tradition, with its emphasis on sin and on the importance of virtuous conduct in the world; Hellenism, in contrast, he saw as the tradition of "sweetness and light," the appreciation of beauty, and the desire to let "a free play of thought live and flow around all our activity." He suggested that in his time, in the nineteenth century, Hebraism was too dominant and needed to be tempered by a Hellenistic openness to life. Arnold's discussion was often abstractly vague, but at least he was helping to extend the challenge which had been made more incisively by J. S. Mill in *On Liberty* (1859): the challenge to a dominant religious ideology by liberal, sceptical thought which sought to extend individual liberties. Speaking of Christianity, Mill declared:

> Its ideal is negative rather than positive;..... in its precepts (as has been well said) "thou shalt not" predominates unduly over "thou shalt". In its horror of sensuality, it made an idol of asceticism.....[2]

The person who is guided by convention and tradition instead of thinking for himself or herself "has no need of any other faculty than the ape-like one of imitation," asserted Mill; and, in *Jude the Obscure*,

---

1 *Culture and Anarchy* (London: Smith, Elder, 1869), 92.
2 J.S. Mill, *On Liberty* (London: Longman, Green, Roberts and Green, 1865), 29.

Sue fervently repeats his observation to the hapless Phillotson. The protest against Hebraism gained fervently lyrical expression in the poems of Swinburne, most notoriously in his "Hymn to Proserpine," which says:

> Thou has conquered, O pale Galilean; the world has grown grey
> from thy breath;
> We have drunk on things Lethean, and fed on the fullness of
> death.

With some pride, Hardy noted in his journal that the literary furore occasioned by *Jude the Obscure* was the greatest since the publication of Swinburne's *Poems and Ballads* in 1866. Hardy was familiar with Matthew Arnold's works; J. S. Mill was one of his cultural heroes; Swinburne and his mentor Shelley were among his favourite poets; and he relished the ironic scepticism of Edward Gibbon. All these authors are cited in *Jude the Obscure*. (Gibbon, for instance, is epitomised as "the smoothly shaven historian so ironically civil to Christianity.") Unlike the bland diplomacy of Arnold's discussions, Part Second of the novel (Chapters II, III and IV) sets forth the contrast between Hellenism and Hebraism with an abrasive starkness.

At her workplace, Sue is obliged to toil in the service of Hebraism, painting Christian texts and slogans, but her inner Hellenism is shown by her purchase of the statuettes of Apollo and Venus. She sets them on her chest of drawers as if they were tutelary deities while (in contrast to Jude's close study of the Bible) she reads Gibbon and Swinburne. When Miss Fontover, the abbess-like guardian of the ecclesiastical workplace, enquires which statuettes Sue has purchased, the reply is "St. Peter and St. – St. Mary Magdalen." Eventually, Miss Fontover identifies and smashes the figures. Sue Bridehead's intellectual revolt against Hebraism is contrasted repeatedly with Jude's Christian preoccupations; and when she visits the exhibition of the model of Jerusalem, her comment to Phillotson is typically Hellenistic:

> "I fancy we have had enough of Jerusalem," she said, "considering we are not descended from the Jews. There was nothing first-rate about the place, or the people, after all – as there was about Athens, Rome, Alexandria, and other old cities."

She delights in educating Jude in modern heresy, and the combination of her ideas and adverse circumstances leads him towards scepticism. Of course, as Hardy designed, Hebraism then achieves a cruel victory over her Hellenism when, shattered by the deaths of the children, she is overtaken by religious guilt and returns to Phillotson.

2.4. The "New Woman"

In the 1912 "Postscript" to the "Preface" of *Jude*, Hardy reported that a German reviewer of the novel had told him that Sue Bridehead was "the first delineation in fiction" of

> the woman of the feminist movement – the slight, pale "bachelor" girl – the intellectualized, emancipated bundle of nerves that modern conditions were producing, mainly in cities as yet; who does not recognize the necessity for most of her sex to follow marriage as a profession, and boast themselves as superior people because they are licensed to be loved on the premises.

The German reviewer did not, apparently, read widely. The characterisation of Sue was not the "first delineation" but was already part of a tradition: the tradition of representation of the "New Woman", the proto-feminist, the young woman who is educated, intelligent, emancipated in ideas and in morality, and who is resistant to the conventional notion that marriage and maternity should be the goal of any normal female's progress.

The question of women's rights, so fiercely debated in the second half of the nineteenth century, had gained fresh publicity from the *succès de scandale* of Ibsen's play *A Doll's House* (1879, but first performed in London in 1889). In the early 1890s, the "New Woman" appeared in plays by Shaw (particularly *Mrs Warren's Profession*, 1894), and in numerous novels and tales, notably *The Heavenly Twins* (1893) by "Sarah Grand" (Frances McFall), *Keynotes* (1893) by "George Egerton" (Mary Chavelita Clairmonte, who would praise *Jude*), Mona Caird's *The Daughters of Danaus* (1894) and Grant Allen's *The Woman Who Did* (1895). In *Mrs Warren's Profession*, Vivie Warren, Cambridge-educated, successfully wards off her suitors and becomes dedicated to her career as an actuarist. More usually, though, the New Woman's revolt ends either tragically or in conformity. Herminia, the heroine of *The Woman Who Did*, eventually commits suicide; Gypsy of *Keynotes* succumbs to the claims of maternity; and Evadne, in *The Heavenly Twins*, emerges from a mental breakdown to acquiesce in a second marriage and motherhood.

Sue Bridehead has the intelligence, vivacity and unconventionality of the New Woman; she has a capacity to earn her own living, being gifted as a teacher; and she is resistant to the sexual claims of men. Partly the text sympathises with her; partly the text depicts her as a flirt, a teaser who likes to lead men on, and who is hoist with her own petard when the sexual realities of marriage impose themselves on her. The text is oddly ambivalent about marriage itself. *Jude the Obscure* depicts divorce as easily obtainable by ordinary people (at least when they resort to collusion or deception), if not by the eminent. Jude remarks that "obscure people" can be dealt with "in a rough and ready fashion," whereas "patented nobilities" would have "infinite trouble."[1] Nevertheless, rather inconsistently, Hardy depicts marriage as a snare which durably entraps people whose feelings for each other may not be so durable; and the author breaches realism in order to maintain a satiric animus against wedlock. For instance, we are told that their landlord suspects, on seeing Arabella kiss Jude, that they may be living in sin:

> and he was about to give them notice to quit, till by chance overhearing her one night haranguing Jude in rattling terms, and ultimately flinging a shoe at his head, he recognized the note of ordinary wedlock; and concluding that they must be respectable, said no more.

Previously Arabella, seeing Sue and Jude together at the Agricultural Show, had remarked: "How she sticks to him!..... O no – I fancy they

---

1   The 1857 Divorce Act had made divorce less expensive, though in 1891 there were only 369 divorces in the whole of England and Wales. Arabella reminds Sue that marriage provides legal protection for the wife. In addition to help provided by the Married Women's Property Acts (1870, 1874, 1882), the Maintenance of Wives Acts (1878 and 1886) "allowed a battered or deserted wife to obtain a temporary maintenance order from a local magistrate". See Lawrence Stone, *The Road to Divorce: England 1530-1987* (Oxford: Oxford UP, 1990), 386, 389-90, 435 (quotation, p. 386); see also Appendix G.

are not married, or they wouldn't be so much to one another as that....."

Gail Cunningham has rightly noted some elements of conventionality in the workings of the plot:

> Sue's career follows a pattern made familiar by the New Woman writers: theoretically emancipated to start with, she suddenly and almost inexplicably marries the wrong man, makes an initially successful bid for freedom and then collapses into crushing conformity. This is an exact parallel to the sequence of Hadria's life in *The Daughters of Danaus* and bears general similarity to the plots of other New Woman novels. Almost all New Woman heroines break down at the end, most go through some period of nervous prostration if not madness, and both Evadne and Hadria anticipate Sue in turning back to the Church in their defeat.[1]

Even Sue's elusive variability was a familiar characteristic. Gypsy in *Keynotes* (studied by Hardy) says of women:

> "At heart we care nothing for laws, nothing for systems.....Perhaps many of our seeming contradictions are only the outward evidences of inward chafing.....A woman must beware of speaking the truth to a man; he loves her the less for it. It is the elusive spirit in her that he divines but cannot seize, that fascinates and keeps him."[2]

Hardy was not, then, as original as the "German reviewer" had suggested, for the New Woman was already a well-represented type when *Jude* appeared in 1895. George Bernard Shaw claimed that discussion of the New Woman was at its height in 1893, and in 1896 the *Saturday Review* declared that the topic had expired a year previously.[3] The ambivalence of Sue's revolt – a revolt which, though sympatheti-

---

1   Gail Cunningham, *The New Woman and the Victorian Novel* (London: Macmillan, 1978), 106.

2   George Egerton, *Keynotes* (London: Mathews and Lane, 1893), 28-9.

3   George Bernard Shaw, "Preface" to *Plays: Pleasant and Unpleasant*, vol. 1 (London: Grant Richards, 1898), xii-xiii; *Thomas Hardy: The Critical Heritage*, 279.

cally depicted, is also shown to meet its nemesis – was certainly a common ambivalence in literature of the time. The reviewer who complained that a female novelist "would never have allowed her to break down at the end" was clearly wrong, for such females as Mona Caird, George Egerton and Sarah Grand had described such breakdowns, whereas male playwrights (Ibsen and Shaw) had shown successful revolts. Given the extent of the repressive forces in the society of that time, there may well have been numerous real-life counterparts of the defeated New Woman.

In *Jude the Obscure*, the author's allegiances veer markedly between, on the one side, sympathy for the independently-minded young woman who seeks to elude stereotyping and, on the other, endorsement of some traditional stereotypes. When contemplating the women sleeping in the dormitory of the Training School, the narrator observes sombrely that they are inscribed by nature as "The Weaker [Sex]" and must inevitably endure years of injustice, child-bearing and bereavement. Sue, we are told, is "essentially large-minded and generous on reflection, despite a previous exercise of those narrow womanly humours on impulse that were necessary to give her sex." Nevertheless, when *Jude the Obscure* is compared with other novels of that time which depict the New Woman, Hardy's novel is generally more vivid, intense and moving than they. Sue is given sharp memorability by a wealth of fine specific details. These include Aunt Drusilla's cameos of her tomboyish and precocious childhood (the pond-wading, the ice-skating with the boys, the recitation of Poe's "Raven" when "she would knit her little brows and glare round tragically" at the empty air); then there is her intermittent preference for speaking obliquely, from behind some barrier or defence, whether it be a window-sill, a quotation, or the distance lent by written messages. Above all, her temperament and physical presence are rendered by many convincing particulars, ranging from her "nervous motion", her quick affectionate spontaneity, her "apple-like" breasts and "liquid, untranslatable eyes", to her very handshake, in which her hand merely "flits" through the other's. She lives.

3. Conclusion

Jude the Obscure is vivid and intense, but certainly flawed. Hardy himself told Edmund Gosse:

> Of course the book is all contrasts – or was meant to be in its original conception. Alas, what a miserable accomplishment it is, when I compare it with what I meant to make it! – e.g., Sue and her heathen gods set against Jude's reading the Greek Test[amen]t; Christiminster academical, Chr[istiminster] in the slums; Jude the saint, Jude the sinner; Sue the Pagan, Sue the saint; marriage, no marriage; &c. &c.[1]

One obvious flaw of the novel is that Hardy's anti-Christian, anti-providential animus has induced plotting in which coincidences repeatedly operate to maximise misery for the sensitive; a plotting, furthermore, in which the parallels and symmetries repeatedly induce cruel ironies: for instance, as Jude embraces fully Sue's scepticism, Sue regresses towards morbid piety. When Hardy is writing at his best (in, for instance, the scene of young Jude's chastisement by Troutham, or the scene of the pig-killing), the moral indignation is implicit in the plausibly detailed rendering of the situation. Sometimes, however, the action or characterisation seems to be the puppet of the indignation. Thus, notoriously, Jude's son, Time (already implausibly dismal as a character), kills his siblings and himself in a melodramatic catastrophe. Elsewhere, the narrator seems embarrassed by the concession that Jude and Sue did have their moments of happiness, and little is said of such moments. Within the narrative, there is a pressure of willed pessimism (and possibly vicarious self-pity) which accounts for its more strained and implausible features. In the latter half, particularly, some events seem rushed or weakly realised; the siblings have little substance; their very existence is inconsistent with Sue's character;[2] and Jude's drunken re-marriage to Arabella appears a defeat of plausibility by ironic symmetry. G. K. Chesterton was mischievous but acute

---

1 *Collected Letters of Thomas Hardy*, vol. 2 (Oxford: Oxford UP, 1980), 99.
2 Sue tells Time that childbirth is inevitable ("a law of nature"); but in real life her intelligence and "fastidious" sexuality would probably have led her to use a contraceptive device (e.g. the widely-publicised contraceptive sponge). See Joan Perkin, *Women and Marriage in Nineteenth-Century England* (London: Routledge, 1989), 281-7.

when he said that in Hardy we see "a sort of village atheist brooding and blaspheming over the village idiot."[1] By over-statement and manipulation, Hardy made less persuasive his indictments of orthodox religion, holy wedlock and repressive Victorian conventionalities. Though he endeavoured to achieve tragedy, by his heavy ironies and insistent disasters he sometimes rather produced scenes of melodrama and pathos.

His achievement remains great; and *Jude the Obscure* proved to be amply influential. It was "ahead of its times" in so many respects: in its sympathetic treatment of a young working man and his frustrations, and of a young emancipated woman and her sufferings; in its frank depiction of sexual desire and an extra-marital sexual relationship; and in its restlessly critical probing of a wide range of ideas and principles. D.H. Lawrence provides ample illustration of that influence. Much of Lawrence's writing can be seen as a creative quarrel with Hardy, on Hardy's own ground: the interaction of rural and urban life during the great transition from the mid-Victorian to the early modern era; the relationship of new knowledge to old beliefs; and that conflict between flesh and spirit. Lawrence's book-length "Study of Thomas Hardy", written in 1914 and published posthumously in *Phoenix* [Vol. 1], 1936, offers an analysis of *Jude* which is characteristically intense, perceptive and eccentric. It stresses Hardy's inner divisions. Any work of art "must contain the essential criticism on [sic] the morality to which it adheres," says Lawrence; so, while Hardy intends to denigrate the body and the physical, his text reveals a deep "sensuous understanding" which subverts that intention. We see that "Arabella was, under all her disguise of pig-fat and false hair, and vulgar speech, in character somewhat of an aristocrat"; she "makes a man" of Jude. As for Sue, she "was not the virgin type, but the witch type, which has no sex." She is almost pure consciousness, and she awakens Jude to full mental being. Their tragedy is that Jude demands a sexual response which is alien to her nature; he effectively violates her, and is drained rather than fulfilled as a result. Finally,

> this tragedy is the result of over-development of one principle
> of human life at the expense of the other; an over-balancing; a
> laying of all stress on the Male, the Love, the Spirit, the Mind,

---

1   G.K. Chesterton, *The Victorian Age in Literature* (London: Oxford UP, 1913), 143.

the Consciousness; a denying, a blaspheming against the Female, the Law, the Soul, the Senses, the Feelings.[1]

In reading Lawrence's account of Hardy, one repeatedly senses links between *Jude* and Lawrence's own works, notably *Sons and Lovers* and *Women in Love*. Lawrence's sense of cosmic vitality opposes Hardy's sense of cosmic fatality, but the continuities remain. Both writers conceive central characters as locations of paradox, contradiction, struggle and fluctuation. In descriptions, Hardy and Lawrence display a kindred sense of scenic montage: they like realistic yet symbolically-suggestive groupings of two or three characters and some central object. Both writers protest against the fetters imposed by conventional morality; both advocate greater sexual liberty; and both, while deeply preoccupied by religious ways of appraising the world, oppose the established Church's taboos, denials and repressions.

In short, the connection with D.H. Lawrence is a reminder of the extent to which Thomas Hardy, in various works but most notably in *Jude the Obscure*, was a challenger and an innovator; a writer whose embodied ideas helped to bring about widespread cultural change. But that adjective "embodied" should be stressed. At its best, *Jude the Obscure* has qualities of articulate intelligence, imagination and sensitivity which ensure that its effects combine the rational and the emotional in the probing manner of durable fiction. As we journey through the novel alongside Jude, we learn diversely not only of the stresses and strains of the late nineteenth century but also of ways in which, even today, there continues "a deadly war waged between flesh and spirit."

---

1   D.H. Lawrence, *Phoenix* [Vol. 1] (London: Heinemann, 1936), 509.

A Note on the Text

For this Broadview publication of *Jude the Obscure*, I have used the text of the first British trade edition, published in London in 1895 by Osgood, McIlvaine and Company. Instead of reprinting the text of a later edition, or amalgamating readings of various editions produced at various times and places, I have privileged the text which corresponds to the historic date of the novel: the version which would have been seen by its first British readers and reviewers. My procedure gives this edition clear credentials for critical and contextual discussions. The present reader can see the text which was, at the time, so controversial, and which, as Appendix A indicates, differs significantly from that of later editions of the novel. (Extracts from some of the early reviews are given in Appendix C.)

My editorial emendations are, deliberately, limited; and all of them are listed below, so that readers may, if they wish, reconstitute the first edition virtually "warts and all." Page numbers in the list refer to this Broadview Press edition; the 1895 reading follows the oblique stroke. (The Broadview "house style" requires that where the original text used single quotation-marks, this text normally uses double ones, and *vice versa*.)

45 *thus?"* / *thus?*
72 preferred / perferred
117 "How / "How [*a misprint of* 'How]
122 inside those / inside. Those
170 "To-morrow / To-morrow
182 draped,'" / draped,'"
183 lightly. "I / lightly. I
185 *protégée* / *protegée*
210 unpredictable / unpredicable
264 Cythna / Cynthia
272 me." He / me. He
275 fidgeted / fidgetted
284 may I?" / may I?
304 Cartlett.'" / Cartlett.'"
316 matrimony. / matrimony.'

317 multiplied,' / multiplied,
371 men!' / men!'" [*a misprint of* men!"]
396 junketing / junketting
402 "Well – now / Well – now
425 thinking ——." / thinking ——.

I have allowed various inconsistencies to remain (notably "Delphine" and "Delphin", "Ridge-way" and "Ridgeway"). Hardy's transliteration of Greek in Part Second, Chapter III, has been preserved, though my footnote specifies the corrections that he made to it for the 1903 edition. His two footnotes are identified as such; all the others are mine. In passages quoted in the editorial matter, a sequence of five points (.....) represents an omission that I have made, whereas a sequence of three or four points represents an ellipsis already present in the material being quoted. Apart from the five-point omissions, all editorial changes to quoted matter are enclosed in square brackets. Quotations from Shakespeare are from *The Complete Works*, ed. Peter Alexander (London and Glasgow: Collins, 1951; reprinted 1966).

Thomas Hardy: A Brief Chronology

1840   *2 June:* Thomas Hardy born at Higher Bockhampton, a village in Dorsetshire.

1841   Birth of his sister Mary.

1848   Attends village school.

1849   Attends school at Hatfield.

1849-56 Attends school in Dorchester.

1851   Birth of his brother, Henry.

1856   Becomes articled trainee (until 1860) of John Hicks, a Dorchester architect. Birth of sister Katharine.

1860   Becomes Hicks's clerk.

1862-7   Lives in London, working as architectural draughtsman for Arthur Blomfield.

1863   Apparently becomes engaged to Eliza Nicholls, a lady's maid.

1865   Satirical essay, "How I Built Myself a House", published in *Chambers's Journal.*

1866   Decides not to seek entry to Cambridge University.

1867   Returns to Bockhampton, working part-time for Hicks.

1867-8   Writes *The Poor Man and the Lady,* a novel rejected by publishers.

1868   Love affair with his cousin, Tryphena Sparks, a trainee teacher.

1869   Based at Weymouth, writing fiction and supervising ecclesiastical rebuilding.

1870   In Cornwall meets and falls in love with Emma Gifford, a solicitor's daughter.

1871   *Desperate Remedies* (novel) published to mixed reviews; a financial loss for Hardy.

1872   *Under the Greenwood Tree* (the first of the "Wessex" novels) published; moderate critical and commercial success. Leslie Stephen befriends Hardy.

1873   *A Pair of Blue Eyes* (novel) published as serial and book: very good critical reception. Horace Moule, a friend and supporter, commits suicide.

1874   Hardy marries Emma Gifford in London, and begins to enter fashionable circles. *Far from the Madding Crowd* (serialised in *Cornhill* magazine) published as book; high acclaim and rapid sales.

1875   £1,250 (a great sum then) promised for British book version and U.S. and British serialisation of the forthcoming *The Hand of Ethelberta*.

1876   *The Hand of Ethelberta* (novel) well received. The Hardys travel to Germany.

1878   Elected to Savile Club. *The Return of the Native* (novel) criticised for "gloomy fatalism".

1880   Meets Matthew Arnold. Visits Paris. *The Trumpet-Major* (Napoleonic novel).

1880-81 Hardy bed-ridden for months.

1881   *A Laodicean* receives laodicean but respectful reviews.

1882   *Far from the Madding Crowd* (play) performed. *Two on a Tower*.

1883   "The Dorsetshire Labourer" (essay) in *Longman's Magazine*.

1884   Hardy becomes Justice of the Peace (magistrate) at Dorchester.

1885   Max Gate (near Dorchester), a house designed by Hardy and built by his father, becomes the author's main residence.

1886   *The Mayor of Casterbridge*. Meets R. L. Stevenson. Death of William Barnes, poet and friend.

1887   Tours Italy. *The Woodlanders*.

1888   *Wessex Tales*.

1890   Death of Tryphena.

1891   *A Group of Noble Dames* (tales). *Tess of the d'Urbervilles* provokes controversy and sells very well.

1892   Hardy's father dies. *The Well-Beloved* (novel) serialised. Attends Tennyson's funeral.

1893   In Ireland meets and becomes friend of Florence Henniker.

1894   *Life's Little Ironies* (tales).

1895   *Jude the Obscure* proves highly controversial and financially successful.

1895-7   First collected edition of his novels (published by Osgood, McIlvaine and Co.).

1896   "The Spectre of the Real", by Hardy and Florence Henniker, published in her collection *In Scarlet and Grey*. Hardy resolves to concentrate on poetry and abandon novel-writing.

1897   *The Well-Beloved* (in book form). Both Hardys tour Switzerland.

1898   *Wessex Poems*, Hardy's first book of verse (illustrated by himself), has mixed reception.

1901   *Poems of the Past and the Present*; generally favourable reception.

1903   Macmillan "Wessex Novels" edition.

1904   *The Dynasts* (verse drama), Part I. Death of his mother.

1905   Receives honorary doctorate from Aberdeen University. Visits Swinburne.

1906   *The Dynasts*, Part II. Meets Edvard Grieg. Bicycle journeys in Dorset and Somerset.

1907   Hardy's wife in suffragist demonstration. Hardy meets Gorky, Wells, Shaw, Conrad. Both Hardys attend King Edward's Garden Party at Windsor Castle.

1908   *The Dynasts*, Part III, generally acclaimed. Hardy edits poems by Barnes. Declines knighthood.

1909   Death of Swinburne. Operatic version of *Tess*. *Time's Laughingstocks* (poems) very well received.

1910   Awarded Order of Merit.

1911   Film version of *Far from the Madding Crowd*.

1912   Death of Emma, his wife.

1912-14 Collected edition of his works ("Wessex Edition") published by Macmillan; augmented in later years.

1913   Cambridge University confers an honorary Doctorate (Litt.D.) on Hardy; later he becomes Honorary Fellow of Magdalene College. *A Changed Man and Other Tales*. Film version of *Tess*.

1914   Marries his assistant, Florence Dugdale. *Satires of Circumstance* (poems).

1915   Death of his sister Mary. Another film of *Far from the Madding Crowd*.

1916   *Selected Poems of Thomas Hardy*.

1917   *Moments of Vision* (poems).

1919   Siegfried Sassoon presents Hardy with a tribute from many poets.

1919-20 37-volume *de luxe* "Mellstock" edition published by Macmillan: Hardy is paid £2,775.

1920	Oxford University confers an honorary Doctorate of Letters on Hardy. The University's Dramatic Society performs scenes from *The Dynasts*. Royalties, film and other rights earn him over £4,400 (a huge sum then).
1921	Film of *The Mayor of Casterbridge*.
1921–2	Hardy's royalties, July 1921–June 1922, about £2,300.
1922	*Late Lyrics and Earlier* (poems). Hardy elected to Honorary Fellowship at Queen's College, Oxford.
1923	Prince of Wales has lunch with Hardy at Max Gate. *The Famous Tragedy of the Queen of Cornwall* (verse drama) published; performed at Dorchester.
1924	Another film of *Tess* appears. Hardy's dramatisation of *Tess* performed at Dorchester.
1925	Hardy receives £1,100 for serialisation of *Tess* in *John o'London's Weekly*. Play of *Tess* has 131 performances at Garrick Theatre, London. *Human Shows* (poems).
1927	Visits "Egdon Heath" with Gustav Holst.
1928	*11 January*: Hardy dies after heart attack. *16 January:* Hardy's heart is buried at Stinsford Church; the ashes of his cremated body are buried at Westminster Abbey, the Prime Minister (Stanley Baldwin) heading the pall-bearers. *Winter Words* (poems). *The Early Life of Thomas Hardy* (ostensibly by Florence Hardy, but almost entirely by Thomas Hardy).
1929	*Chosen Poems of Thomas Hardy*.
1930	*The Later Years of Thomas Hardy. Collected Poems.*
1937	Death of Florence Hardy.

Hardy's Preface (1895), Revised Preface and Postscript (1912)

For the first edition (1895) of *Jude the Obscure*, Hardy provided a short preface. In 1902, for the 1903 edition published by Macmillan (in the "Wessex Novels" series), he expanded its penultimate paragraph. The original wording, "and to point, without a mincing of words, the tragedy of unfulfilled aims", became "to tell, without a mincing of words, of a deadly war waged with old Apostolic desperation between flesh and spirit; and to point the tragedy of unfulfilled aims". In 1912, for the new Macmillan "Wessex Edition" of the novel, he not only added a "Postscript" but also (still without indication of the fact) again altered the first preface for its reprinting together with that postscript. In view not only of the evidence that Hardy was prepared to "rewrite history" but also of the significance of one of the alterations (the presence of the much-quoted phrase "of a deadly war waged between flesh and spirit"), both the 1895 and the 1912 versions of the prefatory material are given below. The woman whose death in 1890 is mentioned is Tryphena Gale, the teacher who was Hardy's cousin. The "fantastic tale" noted in the "Postscript" is "The Spectre of the Real", by Thomas Hardy and Florence Henniker, first published in *To-Day* magazine, 17 November 1894, later reprinted in *In Scarlet and Grey: Stories of Soldiers and Others* (London: Lane, 1896). The irate bishop is William Walsham How, the Bishop of Wakefield, though he did not specify that the book by Hardy which he had burnt was *Jude the Obscure*. (Incidentally, How had graduated from Oxford University with a third-class degree after lamenting: "I.....don't think reading would hurt me, do its worst! And then I find I *can't*.") The horrified female reviewer is Jeannette Gilder. The Diderot reference is to his remark, "the civil law should only be the enunciation of the laws of nature", as quoted in Havelock Ellis's *The New Spirit* and noted by Hardy in 1890. Ruskin College (originally Ruskin Hall) was founded at Oxford in 1899 for the higher education of working-class men. "Bludyer" was originally the name of a ruthless reviewer in Thackeray's novel *The History of Pendennis*. The "poor lady in *Blackwood*" was Margaret Oliphant, whose review is quoted later in this volume.

PREFACE [1895]

THE history of this novel (whose birth in its present shape has been much retarded by the necessities of periodical publication) is briefly as follows. The scheme was jotted down in 1890, from notes made in 1887 and onwards, some of the circumstances being suggested by the death of a woman in the former year. The scenes were revisited in October 1892; the narrative was written in outline in 1892 and the spring of 1893, and at full length, as it now appears, from August 1893 onwards into the next year; the whole, with the exception of a few chapters, being in the hands of the publisher by the end of 1894. It was begun as a serial story in *Harper's Magazine* at the end of November 1894, and was continued in monthly parts.

But, as in the case of *Tess of the D'Urbervilles*, the magazine version was for various reasons abridged and modified in some degree, the present edition being the first in which the whole appears as originally written. And in the difficulty of coming to an early decision in the matter of a title, the tale was issued under a provisional name – two such titles having, in fact, been successively adopted. The present and final title, deemed on the whole the best, was one of the earliest thought of.

For a novel addressed by a man to men and women of full age; which attempts to deal unaffectedly with the fret and fever, derision and disaster, that may press in the wake of the strongest passion known to humanity, and to point, without a mincing of words, the tragedy of unfulfilled aims, I am not aware that there is anything in the handling to which exception can be taken.

Like former productions of this pen, *Jude the Obscure* is simply an endeavour to give shape and coherence to a series of seemings, or personal impressions, the question of their consistency or their discordance, of their permanence or their transitoriness, being regarded as not of the first moment.

T.H.

August 1895.

PREFACE TO THE FIRST EDITION
[as silently revised in 1912]

THE history of this novel (whose birth in its present shape has been much retarded by the necessities of periodical publication) is briefly as follows. The scheme was jotted down in 1890, from notes made in 1887 and onwards, some of the circumstances being suggested by the death of a woman in the former year. The scenes were revisited in October 1892; the narrative was written in outline in 1892 and the spring of 1893, and at full length, as it now appears, from August 1893 onwards into the next year; the whole, with the exception of a few chapters, being in the hands of the publisher by the end of 1894. It was begun as a serial story in *Harper's Magazine* at the end of November 1894, and was continued in monthly parts.

But, as in the case of *Tess of the d'Urbervilles*, the magazine version was for various reasons an abridged and modified one, the present edition being the first in which the whole appears as originally written. And in the difficulty of coming to an early decision in the matter of a title, the tale was issued under a provisional name, two such titles having, in fact, been successively adopted. The present and final title, deemed on the whole the best, was one of the earliest thought of.

For a novel addressed by a man to men and women of full age; which attempts to deal unaffectedly with the fret and fever, derision and disaster, that may press in the wake of the strongest passion known to humanity; to tell, without a mincing of words, of a deadly war waged between flesh and spirit; and to point the tragedy of unfulfilled aims, I am not aware that there is anything in the handling to which exception can be taken.

Like former productions of this pen, *Jude the Obscure* is simply an endeavour to give shape and coherence to a series of seemings, or personal impressions, the question of their consistency or their discordance, of their permanence or their transitoriness, being regarded as not of the first moment.

August 1895.

POSTSCRIPT

THE issue of this book sixteen years ago, with the explanatory Preface given above, was followed by unexpected incidents, and one can now look back for a moment at what happened. Within a day or two of its publication the reviewers pronounced upon it in tones to which the reception of *Tess of the d'Urbervilles* bore no comparison, though there were two or three dissentients from the chorus. This salutation of the story in England was instantly cabled to America, and the music was reinforced on that side of the Atlantic in a shrill crescendo.

In my own eyes the sad feature of the attack was that the greater part of the story – that which presented the shattered ideals of the two chief characters, and had been more especially, indeed almost exclusively, the part of interest to myself – was practically ignored by the adverse press of the two countries; the while that some twenty or thirty pages of sorry detail deemed necessary to complete the narrative, and show the antitheses in Jude's life, were almost the sole portions read and regarded. And curiously enough, a reprint the next year of a fantastic tale that had been published in a family paper some time before, drew down upon my head a continuation of the same sort of invective from several quarters.

So much for the unhappy beginning of *Jude*'s career as a book. After these verdicts from the press its next misfortune was to be burnt by a bishop – probably in his despair at not being able to burn me.

Then somebody discovered that *Jude* was a moral work – austere in its treatment of a difficult subject – as if the writer had not all the time said that it was in the Preface. Thereupon many uncursed me, and the matter ended, the only effect of it on human conduct that I could discover being its effect on myself – the experience completely curing me of further interest in novel-writing.

One incident among many arising from the storm of words was that an American man of letters, who did not whitewash his own morals, informed me that, having bought a copy of the book on the strength of the shocked criticisms, he read on and on, wondering when the harmfulness was going to begin, and at last flung it across the room with execrations at having been induced by the rascally reviewers to waste a dollar-and-half on what he was pleased to call "a religious and ethical treatise."

I sympathized with him, and assured him honestly that the misrepresentations had been no collusive trick of mine to increase my circulation among the subscribers to the papers in question.

Then there was the case of the lady who having shuddered at the book in an influential article bearing intermediate headlines of horror, and printed in a world-read journal, wrote to me shortly afterwards that it was her desire to make my acquaintance.

To return, however, to the book itself. The marriage laws being used in great part as the tragic machinery of the tale, and its general drift on the domestic side tending to show that, in Diderot's words, the civil law should be only the enunciation of the law of nature (a statement that requires some qualification, by the way), I have been charged since 1895 with a large responsibility in this country for the present "shop-soiled" condition of the marriage theme (as a learned writer characterized it the other day). I do not know. My opinion at that time, if I remember rightly, was what it is now, that a marriage should be dissolvable as soon as it becomes a cruelty to either of the parties – being then essentially and morally no marriage – and it seemed a good foundation for the fable of a tragedy, told for its own sake as a presentation of particulars containing a good deal that was universal, and not without a hope that certain cathartic, Aristotelian qualities might be found therein.

The difficulties down to twenty or thirty years back of acquiring knowledge in letters without pecuniary means were used in the same way; though I was informed that some readers thought these episodes an attack on venerable institutions, and that when Ruskin College was subsequently founded it should have been called the College of Jude the Obscure.

Artistic effort always pays heavily for finding its tragedies in the forced adaptation of human instincts to rusty and irksome moulds that do not fit them. To do Bludyer and the conflagratory bishop justice, what they meant seems to have been only this: "We Britons hate ideas, and we are going to live up to that privilege of our native country. Your picture may not show the untrue, or the uncommon, or even be contrary to the canons of art; but it is not the view of life that we who thrive on conventions can permit to be painted."

But what did it matter. As for the matrimonial scenes, in spite of their "touching the spot," and the screaming of a poor lady in *Black-*

wood that there was an unholy anti-marriage league afoot, the famous contract – sacrament I mean – is doing fairly well still, and people marry and give in what may or may not be true marriage as light-heartedly as ever. The author has even been reproached by some earnest correspondents that he has left the question where he found it, and has not pointed the way to a much-needed reform.

After the issue of *Jude the Obscure* as a serial story in Germany, an experienced reviewer of that country informed the writer that Sue Bridehead, the heroine, was the first delineation in fiction of the woman who was coming into notice in her thousands every year – the woman of the feminist movement – the slight, pale "bachelor" girl – the intellectualized, emancipated bundle of nerves that modern conditions were producing, mainly in cities as yet; who does not recognize the necessity for most of her sex to follow marriage as a profession, and boast themselves as superior people because they are licensed to be loved on the premises. The regret of this critic was that the portrait of the newcomer had been left to be drawn by a man, and was not done by one of her own sex, who would never have allowed her to break down at the end.

Whether this assurance is borne out by dates I cannot say. Nor am I able, across the gap of years since the production of the novel, to exercise more criticism upon it of a general kind than extends to a few verbal corrections, whatever, good or bad, it may contain. And no doubt there can be more in a book than the author consciously puts there, which will help either to its profit or to its disadvantage as the case may be.

T.H.

April 1912.

JUDE THE OBSCURE[1]

Thomas Hardy

"The letter killeth."[2]

---

1   *the title*] St Jude is the patron saint of lost or hopeless causes. In the Bible, the General Epistle of Jude is very short, was once of dubious status, and offers warnings against "*filthy* dreamers" who "defile the flesh." See Appendix E.
2   "The letter killeth"] "For the letter killeth, but the spirit giveth life": 2 Corinthians 3: 6.

PART FIRST

AT MARYGREEN[1]

"Yea, many there be that have run out of their wits for women, and become servants for their sakes. Many also have perished, have erred, and sinned, for women....O ye men, how can it be but women should be strong, seeing they do thus?" – ESDRAS.[2]

I.-I.

THE schoolmaster was leaving the village, and everybody seemed sorry. The miller at Cresscombe lent him the small white tilted[3] cart and horse to carry his goods to the city of his destination, about twenty miles off, such a vehicle proving of quite sufficient size for the departing teacher's effects. For the school-house had been partly furnished by the managers, and the only cumbersome article possessed by the master, in addition to the packing-case of books, was a cottage piano that he had bought at an auction during the year in which he thought of learning instrumental music. But the enthusiasm having waned he had never acquired any skill in playing, and the purchased article had been a perpetual trouble to him ever since in moving house.

The rector had gone away for the day, being a man who disliked the sight of changes. He did not mean to return till the evening, when the new school-teacher would have arrived and settled in, and everything would be smooth again.

The blacksmith, the farm bailiff, and the school-master himself were standing in perplexed attitudes in the parlour before the instru-

---

1   *MARYGREEN*] based on the village of Fawley, Berkshire, where Hardy's paternal grandmother, Mary Head, had lived.
2   *"Yea..... thus?"*] Apocrypha: I Esdras 4:26, 27, 32.
3   tilted] canopied.

ment. The master had remarked that even if he got it into the cart he should not know what to do with it on his arrival at Christminster,[1] the city he was bound for, since he was only going into temporary lodgings just at first.

A little boy of eleven, who had been thoughtfully assisting in the packing, joined the group of men, and as they rubbed their chins he spoke up, blushing at the sound of his own voice: "Aunt hev got a great fuel-house, and it could be put there, perhaps, till you've found a place to settle in, sir."

"A proper good notion," said the blacksmith.

It was decided that a deputation should wait on the boy's aunt – an old maiden resident – and ask her if she would house the piano till Mr. Phillotson should send for it. The smith and the bailiff started to see the practicability of the suggested shelter, and the boy and the schoolmaster were left standing alone.

"Sorry I am going, Jude?" asked the latter kindly.

Tears rose into the boy's eyes, for he was not among the regular day scholars, who came unromantically close to the schoolmaster's life, but one who had attended the night school only during the present teacher's term of office. The regular scholars, if the truth must be told, stood at the present moment afar off, like certain historic disciples,[2] indisposed to any enthusiastic volunteering of aid.

The boy awkwardly opened the book he held in his hand, which Mr. Phillotson had bestowed on him as a parting gift, and admitted that he was sorry.

"So am I," said Mr. Phillotson.

"Why do you go, sir?" asked the boy.

"Ah – that would be a long story. You wouldn't understand my reasons, Jude. You will, perhaps, when you are older."

"I think I should now, sir."

"Well – don't speak of this everywhere. You know what a university is, and a university degree? It is the necessary hall-mark of a man who wants to do anything in teaching. My scheme, or dream, is to be a university graduate, and then to be ordained. By going to live at Christminster, or near it, I shall be at headquarters, so to speak, and if

1 Christminster] corresponds mainly to Oxford.
2 historic disciples] At Jesus's crucifixion, "All his acquaintance..... stood afar off" (Luke 23: 49).

my scheme is practicable at all, I consider that being on the spot will afford me a better chance of carrying it out than I should have elsewhere."

The smith and his companion returned. Old Miss Fawley's fuelhouse was dry, and eminently practicable; and she seemed willing to give the instrument standing-room there. It was accordingly left in the school till the evening, when more hands would be available for removing it, and the schoolmaster gave a final glance round.

The boy Jude assisted in loading some small articles, and at nine o'clock Mr. Phillotson mounted beside his box of books and other *impedimenta*,[1] and bade his friends good-bye.

"I sha'n't forget you, Jude," he said, smiling, as the cart moved off. "Be a good boy, remember; and be kind to animals and birds, and read all you can. And if ever you come to Christminster remember you hunt me out for old acquaintance' sake."

The cart creaked across the green, and disappeared round the corner by the rectory-house. The boy returned to the draw-well at the edge of the greensward, where he had left his buckets when he went to help his patron and teacher in the loading. There was a quiver in his lip now, and after opening the well-cover to begin lowering the bucket, he paused and leant with his forehead and arms against the frame-work, his face wearing the fixity of a thoughtful child's who has felt the pricks of life somewhat before his time. The well into which he was looking was as ancient as the village itself, and from his present position appeared as a long circular perspective ending in a shining disk of quivering water at a distance of a hundred feet. There was a lining of green moss near the top, and nearer still the hart's-tongue fern.

He said to himself, in the melodramatic tones of a whimsical boy, that the schoolmaster had drawn at that well scores of times on a morning like this, and would never draw there any more. "I've seen him look down into it, when he was tired with his drawing, just as I do now, and when he rested a bit before carrying the buckets home! But he was too clever to bide here any longer – a small sleepy place like this!"

A tear rolled from his eye into the depths of the well. The morning

---

1 *impedimenta*] (Latin:) baggage.

was a little foggy, and the boy's breathing unfurled itself as a thicker fog upon the still and heavy air. His thoughts were interrupted by a sudden outcry:

"Bring on that water, will ye, you idle young harlican!"[1]

It came from an old woman who had emerged from her door towards the garden gate of a green-thatched cottage not far off. The boy quickly waved a signal of assent, drew the water with what was a great effort for one of his stature, landed and emptied the big bucket into his own pair of smaller ones, and pausing a moment for breath, started with them across the patch of clammy greensward whereon the well stood – nearly in the centre of the little village, or rather hamlet.

It was as old-fashioned as it was small, and it rested in the lap of an undulating upland adjoining the North Wessex[2] downs. Old as it was, however, the well-shaft was probably the only relic of the local history that remained absolutely unchanged. Many of the thatched and dormered dwelling-houses had been pulled down of late years, and many trees felled on the green. Above all, the original church, hump-backed, wood-turreted, and quaintly hipped,[3] had been taken down, and either cracked up into heaps of road-metal in the lane, or utilized as pig-sty walls, garden seats, guard-stones to fences, and rockeries in the flower-beds of the neighbourhood. In place of it a tall new building of German-Gothic design, unfamiliar to English eyes, had been erected on a new piece of ground by a certain obliterator of historic records who had run down from London and back in a day. The site whereon so long had stood the ancient temple to the Christian divinities[4] was not even recorded on the green and level grass-plot that had immemorially been the churchyard, the obliterated graves being commemorated by ninepenny cast-iron crosses warranted to last five years.

---

1 harlican] (dialectal corruption of "harlequin":) "wild-looking urchin" (Hardy).

2 North Wessex] the northern part of the south-to-southwest region of England. In ancient times, Wessex was an Anglo-Saxon kingdom. William Barnes, Thomas Hardy, and George Eliot (in that order) applied the old name "Wessex" to the region in the nineteenth century.

3 hipped] having a roof with inclined ends extending from the ridge to the eaves.

4 Christian divinities] a sly suggestion that Christianity (with its God the Father, God the Son, and God the Holy Ghost) resembles polytheistic religions.

I.–II.

SLENDER as was Jude Fawley's frame he bore the two brimming house-buckets of water to the cottage without resting. Over the door was a little rectangular piece of blue board, on which was painted in yellow letters, "Drusilla Fawley, Baker." Within the little lead panes of the window – this being one of the few old houses left – were five bottles of sweets, and three buns on a plate of the willow pattern.[1]

While emptying the buckets at the back of the house he could hear an animated conversation in progress within-doors between his great-aunt, the Drusilla of the signboard, and some other villagers. Having seen the schoolmaster depart, they were summing up particulars of the event, and indulging in predictions of his future.

"And who's he?" asked one, comparatively a stranger, when the boy entered.

"Well ye med[2] ask it, Mrs. Williams. He's my great-nephew – come since you was last this way." The old inhabitant who answered was a tall, gaunt woman, who spoke tragically on the most trivial subject, and gave a phrase of her conversation to each auditor in turn. "He come from Mellstock, down in South Wessex, about a year ago – worse luck for 'n, Belinda" (turning to the right) "where his father was living, and was took wi' the shakings for death, and died in two days, as you know, Caroline" (turning to the left). "It would ha' been a blessing if Goddy-mighty had took thee too, wi' thy mother and father, poor useless boy! But I've got him here to stay with me till I can see what's to be done with un, though I be obliged to let him earn any penny he can. Just now he's a-scaring of birds for Farmer Troutham. It keeps un out of mischty.[3] Why do ye turn away, Jude?" she continued, as the boy, feeling the impact of their glances like slaps upon his face, moved aside.

The local washerwoman replied that it was perhaps a very good plan of Miss or Mrs. Fawley's (as they called her indifferently) to have him with her – "to kip 'ee company in your loneliness, fetch water, shet the winder-shetters o' nights, and help in the bit o' baking."

---

1 willow pattern] a traditional design in Chinese style.
2 med] (dialectal:) may, might.
3 mischty] (dl.:) mischief.

Miss Fawley doubted it.... "Why didn't ye get the schoolmaster to take 'ee to Christminster wi' un, and make a scholar of 'ee," she continued, in frowning pleasantry. "I'm sure he couldn't ha' took a better one. The boy is crazy for books, that he is. It runs in our family rather. His cousin Sue is just the same – so I've heard; but I have not seen the chile for years, though she was born in this place, within these four walls, as it happened. My niece and her husband, after they were married, didn' get a house of their own for some year or more; and then they only had one till – Well, I won't go into that. Jude, my chile, don't *you* ever marry. 'Tisn't for the Fawleys to take that step any more. She, their only one, was like a chile o' my own, Belinda, till the split come! Ah, that a little maid should know such changes!"

Jude, finding the general attention again centering on himself, went out to the bakehouse, where he ate the cake provided for his breakfast. The end of his spare time had now arrived, and emerging from the garden by getting over the hedge at the back he pursued a path northward, till he came to a wide and lonely depression in the general level of the upland, which was sown as a corn-field. This vast concave was the scene of his labours for Mr. Troutham the farmer, and he descended into the midst of it.

The brown surface of the field went right up towards the sky all round, where it was lost by degrees in the mist that shut out the actual verge and accentuated the solitude. The only marks on the uniformity of the scene were a rick of last year's produce standing in the midst of the arable, the rooks that rose at his approach, and the path athwart the fallow by which he had come, trodden now by he hardly knew whom, though once by many of his own dead family.

"How ugly it is here!" he murmured.

The fresh harrow-lines seemed to stretch like the channellings in a piece of new corduroy, lending a meanly utilitarian air to the expanse, taking away its gradations, and depriving it of all history beyond that of the few recent months, though in every clod and stone there really lingered associations enough and to spare – echoes of songs from ancient harvest-days, of spoken words, and of sturdy deeds. Every inch of ground had been the site, first or last, of energy, gaiety, horse-play, bickerings, weariness. Groups of gleaners had squatted in the sun on every square yard. Love-matches that had populated the adjoining hamlet had been made up there between reaping and carrying. Under the hedge which divided the field from a distant plantation girls had given themselves to lovers who would not turn their heads to look at them by the next harvest; and in that ancient corn-field many a man had made love-promises to a woman at whose voice he had trembled by the next seed-time after fulfilling them in the church adjoining. But this neither Jude nor the rooks around him considered. For them it was a lonely place, possessing, in the one view, only the quality of a work-ground, and in the other that of a granary good to feed in.

The boy stood under the rick before mentioned, and every few seconds used his clacker or rattle briskly. At each clack the rooks left off pecking, and rose and went away on their leisurely wings, burnished like tassets of mail,[1] afterwards wheeling back and regarding him warily, and descending to feed at a more respectful distance.

He sounded the clacker till his arm ached, and at length his heart grew sympathetic with the birds' thwarted desires. They seemed, like himself, to be living in a world which did not want them. Why should he frighten them away? They took upon them more and more the aspect of gentle friends and pensioners – the only friends he could claim as being in the least degree interested in him, for his aunt had often told him that she was not. He ceased his rattling, and they alighted anew.

"Poor little dears!" said Jude, aloud. "You *shall* have some dinner – you shall. There is enough for us all. Farmer Troutham can afford to let you have some. Eat, then, my dear little birdies, and make a good meal!"

They stayed and ate, inky spots on the nut-brown soil, and Jude enjoyed their appetite. A magic thread of fellow-feeling united his own life with theirs. Puny and sorry as those lives were, they much resembled his own.

His clacker he had by this time thrown away from him, as being a mean and sordid instrument, offensive both to the birds and to himself as their friend. All at once he became conscious of a smart blow upon his buttocks, followed by a loud clack, which announced to his surprised senses that the clacker had been the instrument of offence used. The birds and Jude started up simultaneously, and the dazed eyes

---

1 tassets of mail] metal plates used in thigh-armour.

of the latter beheld the farmer in person, the great Troutham himself, his red face glaring down upon Jude's cowering frame, the clacker swinging in his hand.

"So it's 'Eat, my dear birdies,' is it, young man? 'Eat, dear birdies,' indeed! I'll tickle your breeches, and see if you say, 'Eat dear birdies,' again in a hurry! And you've been idling at the schoolmaster's too, instead of coming here, ha'n't ye, hey? That's how you earn your sixpence a day for keeping the rooks off my corn!"

Whilst saluting Jude's ears with this impassioned rhetoric, Troutham had seized his left hand with his own left, and swinging his slim frame round him at arm's-length, again struck Jude on the hind parts with the flat side of Jude's own rattle, till the field echoed with the blows, which were delivered once or twice at each revolution.

"Don't 'ee, sir – please don't 'ee!" cried the whirling child, as helpless under the centrifugal tendency of his person as a hooked fish swinging to land, and beholding the hill, the rick, the plantation, the path, and the rooks going round and round him in an amazing circular race. "I – I – sir – only meant that – there was a good crop in the ground – I saw 'em sow it – and the rooks could have a little bit for dinner – and you wouldn't miss it, sir – and Mr. Phillotson said I was to be kind to 'em – O, O, O!"

This truthful explanation seemed to exasperate the farmer even more than if Jude had stoutly denied saying anything at all; and he still smacked the whirling urchin, the clacks of the instrument continuing to resound all across the field, and as far as the ears of distant workers – who gathered thereupon that Jude was pursuing his business of clacking with great assiduity – and echoing from the brand-new church tower just behind the mist, towards the building of which structure the farmer had largely subscribed, to testify his love for God and man.

Presently Troutham grew tired of his punitive task, and depositing the quivering boy on his legs, took a sixpence from his pocket and gave it him in payment for his day's work, telling him to go home and never let him see him in one of those fields again.

Jude leaped out of arm's reach, and walked along the trackway weeping – not from the pain, though that was keen enough; not from the perception of the flaw in the terrestrial scheme, by which what was good for God's birds was bad for God's gardener; but with the awful sense that he had wholly disgraced himself before he had been a year in the parish, and hence might be a burden to his great-aunt for life.

With this shadow on his mind he did not care to show himself in the village, and went homeward by a roundabout track behind a high hedge and across a pasture. Here he beheld scores of coupled earthworms lying half their length on the surface of the damp ground, as they always did in such weather at that time of the year. It was impossible to advance in regular steps without crushing some of them at each tread.

Though Farmer Troutham had just hurt him, he was a boy who could not himself bear to hurt anything. He had never brought home a nest of young birds without lying awake in misery half the night after, and often reinstating them and the nest in their original place the next morning. He could scarcely bear to see trees cut down or lopped, from a fancy that it hurt them; and late pruning, when the sap was up and the tree bled profusely, had been a positive grief to him in his infancy. This weakness of character, as it may be called, suggested that he was the sort of man who was born to ache a good deal before the fall of the curtain upon his unnecessary life should signify that all was well with him again. He carefully picked his way on tiptoe among the earthworms, without killing a single one.

On entering the cottage he found his aunt selling a penny loaf to a little girl, and when the customer was gone she said, "Well, how do you come to be back here in the middle of the morning like this?"

"I'm turned away."

"What?"

"Mr. Troutham have turned me away because I let the rooks have a few peckings of corn. And there's my wages – the last I shall ever hae!"[1]

He threw the sixpence tragically on the table.

"Ah!" said his aunt, suspending her breath. And she opened upon him a lecture on how she would now have him all the spring upon her hands doing nothing. "If you can't skeer birds, what can ye do? There! Don't ye look so deedy![2] Farmer Troutham is not so much better than myself, come to that. But 'tis as Job said, 'Now they that

---

1   hae] (dl.:) have.
2   deedy] (dl.:) serious.

are younger than I have me in derision, whose fathers I would have disdained to have set with the dogs of my flock.'[1] His father was my father's journeyman,[2] anyhow, and I must have been a fool to let 'ee go to work for 'n, which I shouldn't ha' done but to keep 'ee out of mischty."

More angry with Jude for demeaning her by coming there than for dereliction of duty, she rated him primarily from that point of view, and only secondarily from a moral one.

"Not that you should have let the birds eat what Farmer Troutham planted. Of course you was wrong in that. Jude, Jude, why didstn't go off with that schoolmaster of thine to Christminster or somewhere? But, O no – poor or'nary[3] child – there never was any sprawl[4] on thy side of the family, and never will be!"

"Where is this beautiful city, aunt – this place where Mr. Phillotson is gone to?" asked the boy, after meditating in silence.

"Lord! You ought to know where the city of Christminster is. Near a score of miles from here. It is a place much too good for you ever to have much to do with, poor boy, I'm a-thinking."

"And will Mr. Phillotson always be there?"

"How can I tell?"

"Couldn't I go to see him?"

"Lord, no! You didn't grow up hereabout, or you wouldn't ask such as that. We've never had anything to do with folk in Christminster, nor folk in Christminster with we."

Jude went out, and, feeling more than ever his existence to be an undemanded one, he lay down upon his back on a heap of litter near the pig-sty. The fog had by this time become more translucent, and the position of the sun could be seen through it. He pulled his straw hat over his face, and peered through the interstices of the plaiting at the white brightness, vaguely reflecting. Growing up brought responsibilities, he found. Events did not rhyme quite as he had thought. Nature's logic was too horrid for him to care for. That mercy towards one set of creatures was cruelty towards another sickened his sense of harmony. As you got older, and felt yourself to be at the centre of

---

1 'Now.....flock'] Job 30:1.

2 journeyman] workman hired on a daily wage.

3 or'nary] (dl.:) mediocre.

4 sprawl] (dl.:) vigour.

your time, and not at a point in its circumference, as you had felt when you were little, you were seized with a sort of shuddering, he perceived. All around you there seemed to be something glaring, garish, rattling, and the noises and glares hit upon the little cell called your life, and shook it, and scorched it.

If he could only prevent himself growing up! He did not want to be a man.

Then, like the natural boy, he forgot his despondency, and sprang up. During the remainder of the morning he helped his aunt, and in the afternoon, when there was nothing more to be done, he went into the village. Here he asked a man whereabouts Christminster lay.

"Christminster? O, well, out by there yonder; though I've never bin there – not I. I've never had any business at such a place."

The man pointed north-eastward, in the very direction where lay that field in which Jude had so disgraced himself. There was something unpleasant about the coincidence for the moment, but the fearsomeness of this fact rather increased his curiosity about the city. The farmer had said he was never to be seen in that field again; yet Christminster lay across it, and the path was a public one. So, stealing out of the hamlet he descended into the same hollow which had witnessed his punishment in the morning, never swerving an inch from the path, and climbing up the long and tedious ascent on the other side, till the track joined the highway by a little clump of trees. Here the ploughed land ended, and all before him was bleak open down.

I.-III.

NOT a soul was visible on the hedgeless highway, or on either side of it, and the white road seemed to ascend and diminish till it joined the sky. At the very top it was crossed at right angles by a green 'ridgeway' – the Icknield Street[1] and original Roman road through the district. This ancient track ran east and west for many miles, and down almost to within living memory had been used for driving flocks and herds to fairs and markets. But it was now neglected and overgrown.

---

1 ridgeway.....Street] Ridge Way: a pre-Roman road along the Berkshire downs. Icknield Street: another, longer, pre-Roman road, to the north of Ridge Way.

The boy had never before strayed so far north as this from the nestling hamlet in which he had been deposited by the carrier from a railway station southward, one dark evening some few months earlier, and till now he had had no suspicion that such a wide, flat, low-lying country lay so near at hand, under the very verge of his upland world. The whole northern semicircle between east and west, to a distance of forty or fifty miles, spread itself before him; a bluer, moister atmosphere, evidently, than that he breathed up here.

Not far from the road stood a weather-beaten old barn of reddish-gray brick and tile. It was known as the Brown House by the people of the locality. He was about to pass it when he perceived a ladder against the eaves; and the reflection that the higher he got, the further he could see, led Jude to stand and regard it. On the slope of the roof two men were repairing the tiling. He turned into the ridgeway and drew towards the barn.

When he had wistfully watched the workmen for some time he took courage, and ascended the ladder till he stood beside them.

"Well, my lad, and what may you want up here?"

"I wanted to know where the city of Christminster is, if you please."

"Christminster is out across there, by that clump. You can see it – at least you can on a clear day. Ah, no, you can't now."

The other tiler, glad of any kind of diversion from the monotony of his labour, had also turned to look towards the quarter designated. "You can't often see it in weather like this," he said. "The time I've noticed it is when the sun is going down in a blaze of flame, and it looks like – I don't know what."

"The heavenly Jerusalem,"[1] suggested the serious urchin.

"Ay – though I should never ha' thought of it myself.... But I can't see no Christminster to-day."

The boy strained his eyes also; yet neither could he see the far-off city. He descended from the barn, and abandoning Christminster with the versatility of his age he walked along the ridge-track, looking for any natural objects of interest that might lie in the banks thereabout. When he repassed the barn to go back to Marygreen he

---

1   heavenly Jerusalem] "the holy city, new Jerusalem, coming down from God out of heaven" (Revelation 21:2).

observed that the ladder was still in its place, but that the men had finished their day's work and gone away.

It was waning towards evening; there was still a faint mist, but it had cleared a little except in the damper tracts of subjacent country and along the river-courses. He thought again of Christminster, and wished, since he had come two or three miles from his aunt's house on purpose, that he could have seen for once this attractive city of which he had been told. But even if he waited here it was hardly likely that the air would clear before night. Yet he was loth to leave the spot, for the northern expanse became lost to view on retreating towards the village only a few hundred yards.

He ascended the ladder to have one more look at the point the men had designated, and perched himself on the highest rung, overlying the tiles. He might not be able to come so far as this for many days. Perhaps if he prayed, the wish to see Christminster might be forwarded. People said that, if you prayed, things sometimes came to you, even though they sometimes did not. He had read in a tract that a man who had begun to build a church, and had no money to finish it, knelt down and prayed, and the money came in by the next post. Another man tried the same experiment, and the money did not come; but he found afterwards that the breeches he knelt in were made by a wicked Jew. This was not discouraging, and turning on the ladder Jude knelt on the third rung, where, resting against those above it, he prayed that the mist might rise.

He then seated himself again, and waited. In the course of ten or fifteen minutes the thinning mist dissolved altogether from the eastern horizon, as it had already done elsewhere, and about a quarter of an hour before the time of sunset the westward clouds parted, the sun's position being partially uncovered, and the beams streaming out in visible lines between two bars of slaty cloud. The boy immediately looked back in the old direction.

Some way within the limits of the stretch of landscape, points of light like the topaz gleamed. The air increased in transparency with the lapse of minutes, till the topaz points showed themselves to be the vanes, windows, wet roof slates, and other shining spots upon the spires, domes, freestone-work, and varied outlines that were faintly revealed. It was Christminster, unquestionably; either directly seen, or miraged in the peculiar atmosphere.

The spectator gazed on and on till the windows and vanes lost their shine, going out almost suddenly like extinguished candles. The vague city became veiled in mist. Turning to the west, he saw that the sun had disappeared. The foreground of the scene had grown funereally dark, and near objects put on the hues and shapes of chimæras.[1]

He anxiously descended the ladder, and started homewards at a run, trying not to think of giants, Herne the Hunter, Apollyon lying in wait for Christian, or of the captain with the bleeding hole in his forehead, and the corpses round him that remutinied every night on board the bewitched ship.[2] He knew that he had grown out of belief in these horrors, yet he was glad when he saw the church tower and the lights in the cottage windows, even though this was not the home of his birth, and his great-aunt did not care much about him.

Inside and roundabout that old woman's "shop" window, with its twenty-four little panes set in lead-work, the glass of some of them oxidized with age, so that you could hardly see the poor penny articles exhibited within, and forming part of a stock which a strong man could have carried, Jude had his outer being for some long tideless time.[3] But his dreams were as gigantic as his surroundings were small.

Through the solid barrier of cold cretaceous[4] upland to the northward he was always beholding a gorgeous city – the fancied place he had likened to the new Jerusalem, though there was perhaps more of the painter's imagination and less of the diamond merchant's in his dreams thereof than in those of the Apocalyptic writer.[5] And the city acquired a tangibility, a permanence, a hold on his life, mainly from the one nucleus of fact that the man for whose knowledge and purposes he had so much reverence was actually living there; not only so, but living among the more thoughtful and mentally shining ones therein.

---

1   chimæras] mythical beasts combining parts of various creatures.
2   Herne.....ship] Herne the Hunter: legendary hunter said to haunt Windsor Forest (see Shakespeare's *Merry Wives of Windsor*, IV. iv). Apollyon the monster awaits Christian in Bunyan's *Pilgrim's Progress*. The captain, corpses, and bewitched ship derive from Wilhelm Hauff's tale, "Die Geschichte von dem Gespensterschiff."
3   tideless time] uneventful period.
4   cretaceous] chalky.
5   Apocalyptic writer] author of Revelation, who says: "And the foundations of the wall of the city *were* garnished with all manner of precious stones" (21:19).

In sad wet seasons, though he knew it must rain at Christminster too, he could hardly believe that it rained so drearily there. Whenever he could get away from the confines of the hamlet for an hour or two, which was not often, he would steal off to the Brown House on the hill and strain his eyes persistently; sometimes to be rewarded by the sight of a dome or spire, at other times by a little smoke, which in his estimate had some of the mysticism of incense.

Then the day came when it suddenly occurred to him that if he ascended to the point of view after dark, or possibly went a mile or two further, he would see the night lights of the city. It would be necessary to come back alone, but even that consideration did not deter him, for he could throw a little manliness into his mood, no doubt.

The project was duly executed. It was not late when he arrived at the place of outlook, only just after dusk; but a black north-east sky, accompanied by a wind from the same quarter, made the occasion dark enough. He was rewarded; but what he saw was not the lamps in rows, as he had half expected. No individual light was visible, only a halo or glow-fog over-arching the place against the black heavens behind it, making the light and the city seem distant but a mile or so.

He set himself to wonder on the exact point in the glow where the schoolmaster might be – he who never communicated with anybody at Marygreen now; who was as if dead to them here. In the glow he seemed to see Phillotson promenading at ease, like one of the forms in Nebuchadnezzar's furnace.[1]

He had heard that breezes travelled at the rate of ten miles an hour, and the fact now came into his mind. He parted his lips as he faced the north-east, and drew in the wind as if it were a sweet liquor.

"You," he said, addressing the breeze caressingly, "were in Christminster city between one and two hours ago, floating along the streets, pulling round the weather-cocks, touching Mr. Phillotson's face, being breathed by him, and now you be here, breathed by me – you, the very same."

Suddenly there came along this wind something towards him – a message from the place – from some soul residing there, it seemed. Surely it was the sound of bells, the voice of the city, faint and musical, calling to him, "We are happy here!"

---

1   forms.....furnace] The "forms" in the fiery furnace were of Shadrach, Meshach, Abed-nego, and one like "the Son of God" (Daniel 3:12-30).

He had become entirely lost to his bodily situation during this mental leap, and only got back to it by a rough recalling. A few yards below the brow of hill on which he paused a team of horses made its appearance, having reached the place by dint of half an hour's serpentine progress from the bottom of the immense declivity. They had a load of coals behind them – a fuel that could only be got into the upland by this particular route. They were accompanied by a carter, a second man, and a boy, who now kicked a large stone behind one of the wheels, and allowed the panting animals to have a long rest, while those in charge took a flagon[1] off the load and indulged in a drink round.

They were elderly men, and had genial voices. Jude addressed them, inquiring if they had come from Christminster.

"Heaven forbid, with this load!" said they.

"The place I mean is that one yonder." He was getting so romantically attached to Christminster that, like a young lover alluding to his mistress, he felt bashful at mentioning its name again. He pointed to the light in the sky – hardly perceptible to their older eyes.

"Yes. There do seem a spot a bit brighter in the nor'-east than elsewhere, though I shouldn't ha' noticed it myself, and no doubt it med be Christminster."

Here a little book of tales which Jude had tucked up under his arm, having brought them to read on his way hither before it grew dark, slipped and fell into the road. The carter eyed him while he picked it up and straightened the leaves.

"Ah, young man," he observed, "You'd have to get your head screwed on t'other way before you could read what they read there."

"Why?" asked the boy.

"O, they never look at anything that folks like we can understand," the carter continued, by way of passing the time. "On'y foreign tongues used before the Flood, when no two families spoke alike.[2] They read that sort of thing as fast as a night-hawk will whir. 'Tis all learning there – nothing but learning, except religion. And that's learning too, for I never could understand it. Yes, 'tis a seriousminded place. Not but there's wenches on the streets o' nights....

---

1 flagon] jug or bottle for liquor.
2 spoke alike] Genesis 11:7-8. For the 1912 text, Hardy changed "before the Flood" to "in the days of the Tower of Babel".

You know, I suppose, that they raise pa'sons there like radishes in a bed? And though it do take – how many years, Bob? – five years to turn a lirruping hobble-de-hoy chap[1] into a solemn preaching man with no corrupt passions, they'll do it, if it can be done, and polish un off like the workmen they be, and turn un out wi' a long face, and a long black coat and waistcoat, and a religious collar and hat, same as they used to wear in the Scriptures, so that his own mother wouldn't know un sometimes.... There, 'tis their business, like anybody else's."

"But how should you know ——"

"Now don't you interrupt, my boy. Never interrupt your senyers. Move the fore hoss aside, Bobby; here's som'at[2] coming.... You must mind that I be a-talking of the college life. 'Em lives on a lofty level; there's no gainsaying it, though I myself med not think much of 'em. As we be here in our bodies on this high ground, so be they in their minds – noble-minded men enough, no doubt – some on 'em – able to earn hundreds by thinking out loud. And some on 'em be strong young fellows that can earn a'most as much in silver cups. As for music, there's beautiful music everywhere in Christminster. You med be religious, or you med not, but you can't help striking in your homely note with the rest. And there's a street in the place – the main street – that ha'n't another like it in the world. I should think I did know a little about Christminster!"

By this time the horses had recovered breath and bent to their collars again. Jude, throwing a last adoring look at the distant halo, turned and walked beside his remarkably well-informed friend, who had no objection to tell him as they moved on more yet of the city – its towers and halls and churches. The waggon turned into a crossroad, whereupon Jude thanked the carter warmly for his information, and said he only wished he could talk half as well about Christminster as he.

"Well, 'tis oonly what has come in my way," said the carter unboastfully. "I've never been there, no more than you; but I've picked up the knowledge here and there, and you be welcome to it. A-getting about the world as I do, and mixing with all classes of society, one can't help hearing of things. A friend o' mine, that used to

1   lirruping hobble-de-hoy chap] (dl.:) slovenly, clumsy young man.
2   som'at] (colloquial:) something.

clane the boots at the Crozier Hotel[1] in Christminster when he was in his prime, why, I knowed un as well as my own brother in his later years."

Jude continued his walk homeward alone, pondering so deeply that he forgot to feel timid. He suddenly grew older. It had been the yearning of his heart to find something to anchor on, to cling to – for some place which he could call admirable. Should he find that place in this city if he could get there? Would it be a spot in which, without fear of farmers, or hindrance, or ridicule, he could watch and wait, and set himself to some mighty undertaking like the men of old of whom he had heard? As the halo had been to his eyes when gazing at it a quarter of an hour earlier, so was the spot mentally to him as he pursued his dark way.

"It is a city of light," he said to himself.

"The tree of knowledge grows there," he added a few steps further on.

"It is a place that teachers of men spring from and go to."

"It is what you may call a castle, manned by scholarship and religion."

After this figure he was silent a long while, till he added:

"It would just suit me."

I.-IV.

WALKING somewhat slowly, by reason of his concentration, the boy – an ancient man in some phases of thought, much younger than his years in others – was overtaken by a light-footed pedestrian, whom, notwithstanding the gloom, he could perceive to be wearing an extraordinarily tall hat, a swallow-tailed coat, and a watch-chain that danced madly and threw around scintillations of sky-light as its owner swung along upon a pair of thin legs and noiseless boots. Jude, beginning to feel lonely, endeavoured to keep up with him.

"Well, my man! I'm in a hurry, so you'll have to walk pretty fast if you keep alongside of me. Do you know who I am?"

"Yes, I think. Physician Vilbert?"

---

1 Crozier Hotel] the Mitre.

"Ah – I'm known everywhere, I see! That comes of being a public benefactor."

Vilbert was an itinerant quack-doctor,[1] well known to the rustic population, and absolutely unknown to anybody else, as he, indeed, took care to be, to avoid inconvenient investigations. Cottagers formed his only patients, and his Wessex-wide repute was among them alone. His position was humbler and his field more obscure than those of the quacks with capital and an organized system of advertising. He was, in fact, a survival. The distances he traversed on foot were enormous, and extended nearly the whole length and breadth of Wessex. Jude had one day seen him selling a pot of coloured lard to an old woman as a certain cure for a bad leg, the woman arranging to pay a guinea, in instalments of a shilling a fort-night, for the precious salve, which, according to the physician, could only be obtained from a particular animal which grazed on Mount Sinai,[2] and was to be captured only at great risk to life and limb. Jude, though he already had his doubts about this gentleman's medicines, felt him to be unquestionably a travelled personage, and one who might be a trustworthy source of information on matters not strictly professional.

"I s'pose you've been to Christminster, Physician?"

"I have – many times," replied the long thin man. "That's one of my centres."

"It's a wonderful city for scholarship and religion?"

"You'd say so, my boy, if you'd seen it. Why, the very sons of the old women who do the washing of the college can talk in Latin – not good Latin, that I admit, as a critic: dog-Latin[3] – cat-Latin, as we used to call it in my undergraduate days."

"And Greek?"

"Well – that's more for the men who are in training for bishops, that they may be able to read the New Testament in the original."

"I want to learn Latin and Greek myself."

"A lofty desire. You must get a grammar of each tongue."

"I mean to go to Christminster some day."

---

1   quack-doctor] (coll.:) unqualified and fraudulent doctor.
2   Mount Sinai] the mountain on which Moses received God's commandments (Exodus 19-34).
3   dog-Latin] crude Latin.

"Whenever you do, you say that Physician Vilbert is the only proprietor of those celebrated pills that infallibly cure all disorders of the alimentary system, as well as asthma and shortness of breath. Two and threepence a box – specially licensed by the government stamp."

"Can you get me the grammars if I promise to say it hereabout?"

"I'll sell you mine with pleasure – those I used as a student."

"O, thank you, sir!" said Jude gratefully, but in gasps, for the amazing speed of the physician's walk kept him in a dog-trot which was giving him a stitch in the side.

"I think you'd better drop behind, my young man. Now I'll tell you what I'll do. I'll get you the grammars, and give you a first lesson, if you'll remember, at every house in the village, to recommend Physician Vilbert's golden ointment, life-drops, and female pills."

"Where will you be with the grammars?"

"I shall be passing here this day fortnight at precisely this hour of five-and-twenty minutes past seven. My movements are as truly timed as those of the planets in their courses."

"Here I'll be to meet you," said Jude.

"With orders for my medicines?"

"Yes, Physician."

Jude then dropped behind, waited a few minutes to recover breath, and went home with a consciousness of having struck a blow for Christminster.

Through the intervening fortnight he ran about and smiled outwardly at his inward thoughts, as if they were people meeting and nodding to him – smiled with that singularly beautiful irradiation which is seen to spread on young faces at the inception of some glorious idea, as if a supernatural lamp were held inside their transparent natures, giving rise to the flattering fancy that heaven lies about them then.[1]

He honestly performed his promise to the man of many cures, in whom he now sincerely believed, walking miles hither and thither among the surrounding hamlets as the physician's agent in advance. On the evening appointed he stood motionless on the plateau, at the place where he had parted from Vilbert, and there awaited his

---

1   heaven.....then] "Heaven lies about us in our infancy!" (Wordsworth's "Immortality Ode").

approach. The road physician was fairly up to time; but, to the surprise of Jude on striking into his pace, which the pedestrian did not diminish by a single unit of force, the latter seemed hardly to recognize his young companion, though with the lapse of the fortnight the evenings had grown light. Jude thought it might perhaps be owing to his wearing another hat, and he saluted the physician with dignity.

"Well, my boy?" said the latter abstractedly.

"I've come," said Jude.

"Who? who are you? O yes – to be sure! Got any orders, lad?"

"Yes." And Jude told him the names and addresses of the cottagers who were willing to test the virtues of the world-renowned pills and salve. The quack mentally registered these with great care.

"And the Latin and Greek grammars?" Jude's voice trembled with anxiety.

"What about them?"

"You were to bring me yours, that you used before you took your degree."

"Ah, yes, yes! Forgot all about it – all! So many lives depending on my attention, you see, my man, that I can't give so much thought as I would like to other things."

Jude controlled himself sufficiently long to make sure of the truth; and he repeated, in a voice of dry misery, "You haven't brought 'em!"

"No. But you must get me some more orders from sick people, and I'll bring the grammars next time."

Jude dropped behind. He was an unsophisticated boy, but the gift of sudden insight which is sometimes vouchsafed to children showed him all at once what shoddy humanity the quack was made of. There was to be no intellectual light from this source. The leaves dropped from his imaginary crown of laurel; he turned to a gate, leant against it, and cried bitterly.

The disappointment was followed by an interval of blankness. He might, perhaps, have obtained grammars from Alfredston, but to do that required money, and a knowledge of what books to order; and though physically comfortable, he was in such absolute dependence as to be without a farthing of his own.

At this date Mr. Phillotson sent for his pianoforte, and it gave Jude a lead. Why should he not write to the schoolmaster, and ask him to be so kind as to get him the grammars in Christminster? He might slip a letter inside the case of the instrument, and it would be sure to reach the desired eyes. Why not ask him to send any old second-hand copies, which would have the charm of being mellowed by the university atmosphere?

To tell his aunt of his intention would be to defeat it. It was necessary to act alone.

After a further consideration of a few days he did act, and on the day of the piano's departure, which happened to be his next birthday, clandestinely placed the letter inside the packing-case, directed to his much-admired friend; being afraid to reveal the operation to his aunt Drusilla, lest she should discover his motive, and compel him to abandon his scheme.

The piano was despatched, and Jude waited days and weeks, calling every morning at the cottage post-office before his great-aunt was stirring. At last a packet did indeed arrive at the village, and he saw from the ends of it that it contained two thin books. He took it away into a lonely place, and sat down on a felled elm to open it.

Ever since his first ecstasy or vision of Christminster and its possibilities, Jude had meditated much and curiously on the probable sort of process that was involved in turning the expressions of one language into those of another. He concluded that a grammar of the required tongue would contain, primarily, a rule, prescription, or clue of the nature of a secret cipher, which, once known, would enable him, by merely applying it, to change at will all words of his own speech into those of the foreign one. His childish idea was, in fact, a pushing to the extremity of mathematical precision what is everywhere known as Grimm's Law[1]– an aggrandizement of rough rules to ideal completeness. Thus he assumed that the words of the required language were always to be found somewhere latent in the words of the given language by those who had the art to uncover them, such art being furnished by the books aforesaid.

When, therefore, having noted that the packet bore the postmark of Christminster, he cut the string, opened the volumes, and turned to the Latin grammar, which chanced to come uppermost, he could scarcely believe his eyes.

---

1 Grimm's Law] the set of rules devised by Jakob Grimm (1785-1863) for the permutation of consonants in the Indo-European languages. (The rules, being flawed, were later revised.)

The book was an old one – thirty years old, soiled, scribbled wantonly over with a strange name in every variety of enmity to the letterpress, and marked at random with dates twenty years earlier than his own day. But this was not the cause of Jude's amazement. He learnt for the first time that there was no law of transmutation, as in his innocence he had supposed (there was, in some degree, but the grammarian did not recognize it), but that every word in both Latin and Greek was to be individually committed to memory at the cost of years of plodding.

Jude flung down the books, lay backward along the broad trunk of the elm, and was an utterly miserable boy for the space of a quarter of an hour. As he had often done before, he pulled his hat over his face and watched the sun peering insidiously at him through the interstices of the straw. This was Latin and Greek, then, was it, this grand delusion! The charm he had supposed in store for him was really a labour like that of Israel in Egypt.[1]

What brains they must have in Christminster and the great schools, he presently thought, to learn words one by one up to tens of thousands! There were no brains in his head equal to this business; and as the little sun-rays continued to stream in through his hat at him, he wished he had never seen a book, that he might never see another, that he had never been born.

Somebody might have come along that way who would have asked him his trouble, and might have cheered him by saying that his notions were further advanced than those of his grammarian. But nobody did come, because nobody does; and under the crushing recognition of his gigantic error Jude continued to wish himself out of the world.

I. - V.

DURING the three or four succeeding years a quaint and singular vehicle might have been discerned moving along the lanes and by-roads near Marygreen, driven in a quaint and singular way.

In the course of a month or two after the receipt of the books,

---

1 labour.....Egypt] Exodus 1:13-14.

Jude had grown callous to the shabby trick played him by the dead languages. In fact, his disappointment at the nature of those tongues had, after a while, been the means of still further glorifying the erudition of Christminster. To acquire languages, departed or living, in spite of such obstinacies as he now knew them inherently to possess, was a herculean performance which gradually led him on to a greater interest in it than in the presupposed patent process. The mountain-weight of material under which the ideas lay in those dusty volumes called the classics piqued him into a dogged, mouselike subtlety of attempt to move it piecemeal.

He had endeavoured to make his presence tolerable to his crusty maiden aunt by assisting her to the best of his ability, and the business of the little cottage bakery had grown in consequence. An aged horse with a hanging head had been purchased for eight pounds at a sale, a creaking cart with a whity-brown tilt obtained for a few pounds more, and in this turnout it became Jude's business thrice a week to carry loaves of bread to the villagers and solitary cotters[1] immediately around Marygreen.

The singularity aforesaid lay, after all, less in the conveyance itself than in Jude's manner of conducting it along its route. Its interior was the scene of most of Jude's education by "private study." As soon as the horse had learnt the road and the houses at which he was to pause awhile, the boy, seated in front, would slip the reins over his arm, ingeniously fix open, by means of a strap attached to the tilt, the volume he was reading, spread the dictionary on his knees, and plunge into the simpler passages from Cæsar, Virgil, or Horace, as the case might be, in his purblind[2] stumbling way, and with an expenditure of labour that would have made a tender-hearted pedagogue shed tears; yet somehow getting at the meaning of what he read, and divining rather than beholding the spirit of the original, which often to his mind was something else than that which he was taught to look for.

The only copies he had been able to lay hands on were old Delphine editions,[3] because they were superseded, and therefore cheap.

---

1 cotters] dwellers in "tied" cottages belonging to a farm or estate.
2 purblind] partly or nearly blind.
3 Delphine editions] classic texts in editions produced in France between 1670 and 1682, reissued by A. J. Valpy between 1819 and 1830. ("Delphine" is a variant of the more usual "Delphin".)

But, bad for idle school-boys, it did so happen that they were passably good for him. The hampered and lonely itinerant conscientiously covered up the marginal readings, and used them merely on points of construction, as he would have used a comrade or tutor who should have happened to be passing by. And though Jude may have had little chance of becoming a scholar by these rough and ready means, he was in the way of getting into the groove he wished to follow.

While he was busied with these ancient pages, which had already been thumbed by hands possibly in the grave, digging out the thoughts of these minds, so remote, yet so near, the bony old horse pursued his rounds, and Jude would be aroused from the woes of Dido[1] by the stoppage of his cart and the voice of some old woman crying, "Two to-day, baker, and I return this stale one."

He was frequently met in the lanes by pedestrians and others without his seeing them, and by degrees the people of the neighbourhood began to talk about his method of combining work and play (such they considered his reading to be), which, though probably convenient enough to himself, was not altogether a safe proceeding for other travellers along the same roads. There were murmurs. Then a private resident of an adjoining place informed the local policeman that the baker's boy should not be allowed to read while driving, and insisted that it was the constable's duty to catch him in the act, and take him to the police court at Alfredston, and get him fined for dangerous practices on the highway. The policeman thereupon lay in wait for Jude, and one day accosted him and cautioned him.

As Jude had to get up at three o'clock in the morning to heat the oven, and mix and set in the bread that he distributed later in the day, he was obliged to go to bed at night immediately after laying the sponge;[2] so that if he could not read his classics on the highways, he could hardly study at all. The only thing to be done was, therefore, to keep a sharp eye ahead and around him as well as he could in the circumstances, and slip away his books as soon as anybody loomed in the distance, the policeman in particular. To do that official justice, he did not put himself much in the way of Jude's bread-cart, considering that in such a lonely district the chief danger was to Jude himself, and

---

1   woes of Dido] Dido, deserted by her lover Aeneas, committed suicide (Virgil: *Aeneid*, Bk. IV).

2   sponge] soft fermenting dough.

often on seeing the white tilt over the hedges he would move in another direction.

On a day when Fawley was getting quite advanced, being now about sixteen, and had been stumbling through the "Carmen Sæculare,"[1] on his way home, he found himself to be passing over the high edge of the plateau by the Brown House. The light had changed, and it was the sense of this which had caused him to look up. The sun was going down, and the full moon was rising simultaneously behind the woods in the opposite quarter. His mind had become so impregnated with the poem that, in a moment of the same impulsive emotion which years before had caused him to kneel on the ladder, he stopped the horse, alighted, and glancing round to see that nobody was in sight, knelt down on the roadside bank with open book. He turned first to the shiny goddess, who seemed to look so softly and critically at his doings, then to the disappearing luminary on the other hand, as he began:

"Phœbe silvarumque potens Diana!"[2]

The horse stood still till he had finished the hymn, which Jude repeated under the sway of a polytheistic fancy that he would never have thought of humouring in broad daylight.

Reaching home, he mused over his curious superstition, innate or acquired, in doing this, and the strange forgetfulness which had led to such a lapse from common-sense and custom in one who wished, next to being a scholar, to be a Christian divine. It had all come of reading heathen works exclusively. The more he thought of it, the more convinced he was of his inconsistency. He began to wonder whether he could be reading quite the right books for his object in life. Certainly there seemed little harmony between this pagan literature and the mediæval colleges at Christminster, that ecclesiastical romance in stone.

Ultimately he decided that in his sheer love of reading he had taken up a wrong emotion for a Christian young man. He had dab-

---

1 "Carmen Sæculare"] Latin poem ("Hymn for the Games") written in 17 B.C. by Horace.
2 "Phœbe.....Diana!"] "O Phœbus, and Diana, Queen of the Forests!" (the opening of the "Carmen Sæculare").

bled in Homer, but had never yet worked much at the New Testament in the Greek, though he possessed a copy, obtained by post from a second-hand bookseller. He abandoned the now familiar Ionic[1] for a new dialect, and for a long time onward limited his reading almost entirely to the Gospels and Epistles in Griesbach's text.[2] Moreover, on going into Alfredston one day, he was introduced to patristic literature[3] by finding at the bookseller's some volumes of the Fathers which had been left behind by an insolvent clergyman of the neighbourhood.

As another outcome of this change of groove, he visited on Sundays all the churches within a walk, and deciphered the Latin inscriptions on fifteenth-century brasses and tombs. On one of these pilgrimages he met with a hunchbacked old woman of great intelligence, who read everything she could lay her hands on, and she told him more yet of the romantic charms of the city of light and lore. Thither he resolved as firmly as ever to go.

But how live in that city? At present he had no income at all. He had no trade or calling of any dignity or stability whatever on which he could subsist while carrying out an intellectual labour which might spread over many years.

What was most required by citizens? Food, clothing, and shelter. An income from any work in preparing the first would be too meagre; for making the second he felt a distaste; the preparation of the third requisite he inclined to. They built in a city; therefore he would learn to build. He thought of his unknown uncle, his cousin Susanna's[4] father, an ecclesiastical worker in metal, and somehow mediæval art in any material was a trade for which he had rather a fancy. He could not go far wrong in following his uncle's footsteps, and engaging himself awhile with the carcases that contained the scholar souls.

As a preliminary he obtained some small blocks of freestone, metal

---

1 Ionic] the most important of the three main branches of the ancient Greek language (the others being Doric and Aeolic).

2 Griesbach's text] Johann Griesbach's critical edition of the New Testament (used by Hardy), first published in 1774-7.

3 patristic literature] theological writings by the "Church fathers" in the early centuries of the Christian era.

4 Susanna] Hardy associated this name with the story of Susanna and the Elders (Apocrypha: Daniel and Susanna).

not being available, and suspending his studies awhile, occupied his spare half-hours in copying the heads and capitals in his parish church.

There was a stone-cutter of a humble kind in Alfredston,[1] and as soon as he had found a substitute for himself in his aunt's little business, he offered his services to this man for a trifling wage. Here Jude had the opportunity of learning at least the rudiments of freestone-working. Some time later he went to a church-builder in the same place, and under the architect's direction became handy at restoring the dilapidated masonries of several village churches round about.

Not forgetting that he was only following up this handicraft as a prop to lean on while he prepared those greater engines which he flattered himself would be better fitted for him, he yet was interested in his pursuit on its own account. He now had lodgings during the week in the little town, whence he returned to Marygreen village every Saturday evening. And thus he reached and passed his nineteenth year.

I.-VI.

AT this memorable date of his life he was, one Saturday, returning from Alfredston to Marygreen about three o'clock in the afternoon. It was fine, warm, and soft summer weather, and he walked with his tools at his back, his little chisels clinking faintly against the larger ones in his basket. It being the end of the week he had left work early, and had come out of the town by a roundabout route which he did not usually frequent, having promised to call at a flour-mill in that direction to execute a commission for his aunt.

He was in an enthusiastic mood. He seemed to see his way to living comfortably in Christminster in the course of a year or two, and knocking at the doors of one of those strongholds of learning of which he had dreamed so much. He might, of course, have gone there now, in some capacity or other, but he preferred to enter the city with a little more assurance as to means than he could be said to feel at present. A warm self-content suffused him when he considered

---

1 Alfredston] corresponds to Wantage (a market town in Berkshire), the birthplace of King Alfred.

what he had already done. Now and then as he went along he turned to face the peeps of country on either side of him. But he hardly saw them; the act was an automatic repetition of what he had been accustomed to do when less occupied; and the one matter which really engaged him was the mental estimate of his progress thus far.

"I have acquired quite an average student's power to read the common ancient classics, Latin in particular." This was true, Jude possessing a facility in that language which enabled him with great ease to himself to beguile his lonely walks by imaginary conversations therein.

"I have read two books of Homer, besides being pretty familiar with passages such as the speech of Phœnix in the ninth book, the fight of Hector and Ajax in the fourteenth, the appearance of Achilles unarmed and his heavenly armour in the eighteenth, and the funeral games in the twenty-third.[1] I have also done some Hesiod, a little scrap of Thucydides, and a lot of the Greek Testament.... I wish there was only one dialect, all the same.

"I have done some mathematics, including the first six and the eleventh and twelfth books of Euclid; and algebra as far as simple equations.

"I know something of the Fathers, and something of Roman and English history.

"These things are only a beginning. But I shall not make much further advance here, from the difficulty of getting books. Hence I must next concentrate all my energies on settling in Christminster. Once there I shall so advance, with the assistance I shall there get, that my present knowledge will appear to me but as childish ignorance. I must save money, and I will; and one of those colleges shall open its doors to me – shall welcome whom now it would spurn, if I wait twenty years for the welcome.

"I'll be D.D.[2] before I have done!"

And then he continued to dream, and thought he might become even a bishop by leading a pure, energetic, wise, Christian life. And what an example he would set! If his income were £5000 a year, he would give away £4500 in one form and another, and live sump-

---

1   speech of Phœnix.....twenty-third] These were also Hardy's favourite passages from Homer's *Iliad*.
2   D.D.] Doctor of Divinity.

tuously (for him) on the remainder. Well, on second thoughts, a bishop was absurd. He would draw the line at an archdeacon. Perhaps a man could be as good and as learned and as useful in the capacity of archdeacon as in that of bishop. Yet he thought of the bishop again.

"Meanwhile I will read, as soon as I am settled in Christminster, the books I have not been able to get hold of here: Livy, Tacitus, Herodotus, Æschylus, Sophocles, Aristophanes –"

"Ha, ha, ha! Hoity-toity!" The sounds were expressed in light voices on the other side of the hedge, but he did not notice them. His thoughts went on:

"– Euripides, Plato, Aristotle, Lucretius, Epictetus, Seneca, Antoninus. Then I must master other things: the Fathers thoroughly; Bede and ecclesiastical history generally; a smattering of Hebrew – I only know the letters as yet –"

"Hoity-toity!"

"– but I can work hard. I having staying power in abundance, thank God! And it is that which tells....Yes, Christminster shall be my Alma Mater;[1] and I'll be her beloved son, in whom she shall be well pleased."[2]

In his deep concentration on these transactions of the future, Jude's walk had slackened, and he was now standing quite still, looking at the ground as though the future were thrown thereon by a magic lantern. On a sudden something smacked him sharply in the ear, and he became aware that a soft cold substance had been flung at him, and had fallen at his feet.

A glance told him what it was – a piece of flesh, the characteristic part of a barrow-pig,[3] which the countrymen used for greasing their boots, as it was useless for any other purpose. Pigs were rather plentiful hereabout, being bred and fattened in large numbers in certain parts of North Wessex.

On the other side of the hedge was a stream, whence, as he now for the first time realized, had come the slight sounds of voices and

---

1   Alma Mater] (Latin:) "bountiful mother": a nurturing educational establishment.

2   I'll.....pleased] "And lo a voice from heaven, saying, This is my beloved Son, in whom I am well pleased" (Matthew 3:17).

3   characteristic.....barrow-pig] A barrow-pig is a castrated hog; its "characteristic part" is the penis.

laughter that had mingled with his dreams. He mounted the bank and looked over the fence. On the further side of the stream stood a small homestead, having a garden and pigsties attached; in front of it, beside the brook, three young women were kneeling, with buckets and platters beside them containing heaps of pigs' chitterlings,[1] which they were washing in the running water. One or two pairs of eyes slyly glanced up, and perceiving that his attention had at last been attracted, and that he was watching them, they braced themselves for inspection by putting their mouths demurely into shape and recommencing their rinsing operations with assiduity.

"Thank you!" said Jude severely.

"I *didn't* throw it, I tell you!" asserted one girl to her neighbour, as if unconscious of the young man's presence.

"Nor I," the second answered.

"O, Anny, how can you!" said the third.

"If I had thrown anything at all, it shouldn't have been such an indecent thing as that!"

"Pooh! I don't care for him!" And they laughed and continued their work, without looking up, still ostentatiously accusing each other.

Jude grew sarcastic as he wiped the spot where the clammy flesh had struck him.

"*You* didn't do it – O no!" he said to the upstream one of the three.

She whom he addressed was a fine dark-eyed girl, not exactly handsome, but capable of passing as such at a little distance, despite some coarseness of skin and fibre. She had a round and prominent bosom, full lips, perfect teeth, and the rich complexion of a Cochin hen's egg.[2] She was a complete and substantial female human[3] – no more, no less; and Jude was almost certain that to her was attributable the enterprise of throwing the lump of offal at him, the bladder, from which she had obviously just cut it off, lying close beside her.

"That you'll never be told," said she deedily.[4]

---

1 chitterlings] intestines.
2 Cochin hen's egg] light-brown speckled egg of a richly-plumaged domestic fowl. (In 1888, Hardy noted that W. E. Gladstone had a healthy "Cochin-china-egg" complexion.)
3 female human] For the 1903 edition, Hardy changed the phrase to "female animal".
4 deedily] (dl.:) earnestly.

"Whoever did it was wasteful of other people's property."

"O, that's nothing. The pig is my father's."

"But you want it back, I suppose?"

"O yes; if you like to give it me."

"Shall I throw it across, or will you come to the plank above here for me to hand it to you?"

Perhaps she foresaw an opportunity; for somehow or other the eyes of the brown girl rested in his own when he had said the words, and there was a momentary flash of intelligence, a dumb announcement of affinity *in posse*,[1] between herself and him, which, so far as Jude Fawley was concerned, had no sort of premeditation in it. She saw that he had singled her out from the three, as a woman is singled out in such cases, for no reasoned purpose of further acquaintance, but in commonplace obedience to conjunctive orders from headquarters,[2] unconsciously received by unfortunate men when the last intention of their lives is to be occupied with the feminine.

Springing to her feet, she said: "Don't throw it! Give it to me."

Jude was now aware that the intrinsic value of the missile had nothing to do with her request. He set down his basket of tools, raked out with his stick the slip of flesh from the ditch, and got over the hedge. They walked in parallel lines, one on each bank of the stream, towards the small plank bridge. As the girl drew nearer to it, she gave, without Jude perceiving it, an adroit little suck to the interior of each of her cheeks in succession, by which curious and original manœuvre she brought as by magic upon its smooth and rotund surface a perfect dimple, which she was able to retain there as long as she continued to smile. This production of dimples at will was a not unknown operation, which many attempted, but only a few succeeded in accomplishing.

They met in the middle of the plank, and Jude held out his stick with the fragment of pig dangling therefrom, looking elsewhere the while, and faintly colouring.

She, too, looked in another direction, and took the piece as though ignorant of what her hand was doing. She hung it temporarily on the rail of the bridge, and then, by a species of mutual curiosity, they both turned, and regarded it.

---

1   *in posse*] (Latin:) in potentiality.

2   conjunctive.....headquarters] sexual urgings of nature.

"You don't think I threw it?"

"O no."

"It belongs to father, and he med have been in a taking[1] if he had wanted it. He makes it into dubbin."[2]

"What made either of the others throw it, I wonder?" Jude asked, politely accepting her assertion, though he had very large doubts as to its truth.

"Impudence. Don't tell folk it was I, mind!"

"How can I? I don't know your name."

"Ah, no. Shall I tell it to you?"

"Do!"

"Arabella Donn.[3] I'm living here."

"I must have known it if I had often come this way. But I mostly go straight along the high-road."

"My father is a pig-breeder, and these girls are helping me wash the innerds for black-puddings[4] and chitterlings."

They talked a little more and a little more, as they stood regarding the limp object dangling across the hand-rail of the bridge. The unvoiced call of woman to man, which was uttered very distinctly by Arabella's personality, held Jude to the spot against his intention – almost against his will, and in a way new to his experience. It is scarcely an exaggeration to say that till this moment Jude had never looked at a woman to consider her as such, but had vaguely regarded the sex as beings outside his life and purposes. He gazed from her eyes to her mouth, thence to her bosom, and to her full round naked arms, wet, mottled with the chill of the water, and firm as marble.

"What a nice-looking girl you are!" he murmured, though the words had not been necessary to express his sense of her magnetism.

"Ah, you should see me Sundays!" she said piquantly.

"I don't suppose I could?" he answered.

"That's for you to think on. There's nobody after me just now, though there med be[5] in a week or two." She had spoken this without a smile, and the dimples disappeared.

---

1 med.....taking] (dl.:) "might have been angry".

2 dubbin] grease used for waterproofing leather.

3 Arabella Donn] Commentators speculate that the name suggests to Hardy "Arable Bella Donna": the "ploughable" beautiful woman; and "belladonna" is a poison.

4 black-puddings] black sausages made from pigs' blood, suet, and other ingredients.

5 med be] (dl.:) might be.

Jude felt himself drifting strangely, but could not help it. "Will you let me?"

"I don't mind."

By this time she had managed to get back one dimple by turning her face aside for a moment and repeating the odd little sucking operation before mentioned, Jude being still unconscious of more than a general impression of her appearance. "Next Sunday?" he hazarded. "To-morrow, that is?"

"Yes."

"Shall I call?"

"Yes."

She brightened with a little glow of triumph, swept him almost tenderly with her eyes in turning, and throwing the offal out of the way upon the grass, rejoined her companions.

Jude Fawley shouldered his tool-basket and resumed his lonely way, filled with an ardour at which he mentally stood at gaze. He had just inhaled a single breath from a new atmosphere, which had evidently been hanging round him everywhere he went, for he knew not how long, but had somehow been divided from his actual breathing as by a sheet of glass. The intentions as to reading, working, and learning, which he had so precisely formulated only a few minutes earlier, were suffering a curious collapse into a corner, he knew not how.

"Well, it's only a bit of fun," he said to himself, faintly conscious that to common-sense there was something lacking, and still more obviously something redundant, in the nature of this girl who had drawn him to her, which made it necessary that he should assert mere sportiveness on his part as his reason in seeking her – something in her quite antipathetic to that side of him which had been occupied with literary study and the magnificent Christminster dream. It had been no vestal[1] who chose *that* missile for opening her attack on him. He saw this with his intellectual eye, just for a short fleeting while, as by the light of a falling lamp one might momentarily see an inscription on a wall before being enshrouded in darkness. And then this passing discriminative power was withdrawn, and Jude was lost to all conditions of things in the advent of a fresh and wild pleasure, that of

---

1   vestal] pure maiden (originally, virgin priestess devoted to the goddess Vesta).

having found a new channel for emotional interest hitherto unsuspected, though it had lain close beside him. He was to meet this enkindling one of the other sex on the following Sunday.

Meanwhile the girl had joined her companions, and she silently resumed her flicking and sousing of the chitterlings in the pellucid stream.

"Catched un, my dear?" laconically asked the girl called Anny.

"I don't know. I wish I had thrown something else than that!" regretfully murmured Arabella.

"Lord! he's nobody, though you med think so. He used to drive old Drusilla Fawley's bread-cart out at Marygreen, till he 'prenticed himself at Alfredston. Since then he's been very stuck up, and always reading. He wants to be a scholar, they say."

"O, I don't care what he is, or anything about 'n. Don't you think it, my child!"

"O, don't 'ee! You needn't try to deceive us! What did you stay talking to him for, if you didn't want un? Whether you do or whether you don't, he's as simple as a child. I could see it as you courted on the bridge, wi' that piece o' the pig hanging between ye – haw-haw! What a proper thing to court over! Well, he's to be had by any woman who can get him to care for her a bit, if she likes to set herself to catch him the right way."

I.-VII.

THE next day Jude Fawley was pausing in his bedroom with the sloping ceiling, looking at the books on the table, and then at the black mark on the plaster above them, made by the smoke of his lamp in past months.

It was Sunday afternoon, four and twenty hours after his meeting with Arabella Donn. During the whole bygone week he had been resolving to set this afternoon apart for a special purpose, – the re-reading of his Greek Testament – his new one, with better type than his old copy, following Griesbach's text as amended by numerous correctors, and with variorum readings in the margin. He was proud of the book, having obtained it by boldly writing to its London publisher, a thing he had never done before.

He had anticipated much pleasure in this afternoon's reading, under the quiet roof of his great-aunt's house as formerly, where he now slept only two nights a week. But a new thing, a great hitch, had happened yesterday in the gliding and noiseless current of his life, and he felt as a snake must feel who has sloughed off its winter skin, and cannot understand the brightness and sensitiveness of its new one.

He would not go out to meet her, after all. He sat down, opened the book, and with his elbows firmly planted on the table, and his hands to his temples, began at the beginning:

Η ΚΑΙΝΗ ΔΙΑΘΗΚΗ.[1]

.   .   .   .   .   .

Had he promised to call for her? Surely he had! She would wait indoors, poor girl, and waste all her afternoon on account of him. There was something in her, too, which was very winning, apart from promises. He ought not to break faith with her. Even though he had only Sundays and week-day evenings for reading he could afford one afternoon, seeing that other young men afforded so many. After to-day he would never probably see her again. Indeed, it would be impossible, considering what his plans were.

In short, as if materially, a compelling arm of extraordinary muscular power seized hold of him — something which had nothing in common with the spirits and influences that had moved him hitherto. This seemed to care little for his reason and his will, nothing for his so-called elevated intentions, and moved him along, as a violent schoolmaster a schoolboy he has seized by the collar, in a direction which tended towards the embrace of a woman for whom he had no respect, and whose life had nothing in common with his own except locality.

Η ΚΑΙΝΗ ΔΙΑΘΗΚΗ was suddenly closed,[2] and the predestinate Jude sprang up and across the room. Foreseeing such an event he had already arrayed himself in his best clothes. In three minutes he was out of the house and descending by the path across the wide vacant hollow of corn-ground which lay between the village and the isolated house of Arabella in the dip beyond the upland.

---

1   Η ΚΑΙΝΗ ΔΙΑΘΗΚΗ] (Greek:) The New Testament.
2   suddenly closed] changed in 1903 to "no more heeded", as the book is open when Jude returns.

As he walked he looked at his watch. He could be back in two hours, easily, and a good long time would still remain to him for reading after tea.

Passing the few unhealthy fir-trees and cottage where the path joined the highway he hastened along, and struck away to the left, descending the steep side of the country to the west of the Brown House. Here at the base of the chalk formation he neared the brook that oozed from it, and followed the stream till he reached her dwelling. A smell of piggeries came from the back, and the grunting of the originators of that smell. He entered the garden, and knocked at the door with the knob of his stick.

Somebody had seen him through the window, for a male voice on the inside said:

"Arabella! Here's your young man come coorting! Mizzel,[1] my girl!"

Jude winced at the words. Courting in such a business-like aspect as it evidently wore to the speaker was the last thing he was thinking of. He was going to walk with her, perhaps kiss her; but "courting" was too coolly purposeful to be anything but repugnant to his ideas. The door was opened and he entered, just as Arabella came downstairs in full walking attire.

"Take a chair, Mr. What's-your-name?" said her father, an energetic, black-whiskered man, in the same business-like tones Jude had heard from outside.

"I'd rather go out at once, wouldn't you?" she whispered to Jude.

"Yes," said he. "We'll walk up to the Brown House and back, we can do it in half-an-hour."

Arabella looked so handsome amid her untidy surroundings that he felt glad he had come, and all the misgivings vanished that had hitherto haunted him.

First they clambered to the top of the great down, during which ascent he had occasionally to take her hand to assist her. Then they bore off to the left along the crest into the ridgeway, which they followed till it intersected the high-road at the Brown House aforesaid, the spot of his former fervid desires to behold Christminster. But he forgot them now. He talked the commonest local twaddle to Arabella

---

1   Mizzel] (dl.:) Hurry away.

with greater zest than he would have felt in discussing all the philoso-
phies with all the Dons in the recently adored University, and passed
the spot where he had knelt to Diana and Phœbus without remembering that there were any such people in the mythology, or that the
Sun was anything else than a useful lamp for illuminating Arabella's
face. An indescribable lightness of heel served to lift him along; and
Jude, the incipient scholar, prospective D.D., Professor, Bishop, or
what not, felt himself honoured and glorified by the condescension of
this handsome country wench in agreeing to take a walk with him in
her Sunday frock and ribbons.

They reached the Brown House barn – the point at which he had
planned to turn back. While looking over the vast northern landscape
from this spot, they were struck by the rising of a dense volume of
smoke from the neighbourhood of the little town which lay beneath
them at a distance of a couple miles.

"It is a fire," said Arabella. "Let's run and see it – do! It is not far!"

The tenderness which had grown up in Jude's bosom left him no
will to thwart her inclination now – which pleased him in affording
him excuse for a longer time with her. They started off down the hill
almost at a trot; but on gaining level ground at the bottom, and walking a mile, they found that the spot of the fire was much further off
than it had seemed.

Having begun their journey, however, they pushed on; but it was
not till five o'clock that they found themselves on the scene, – the
distance being altogether about half-a-dozen miles from Marygreen,
and three from Arabella's. The conflagration had been got under by
the time they reached it, and after a short inspection of the melancholy ruins they retraced their steps – their course lying through the
town of Alfredston.

Arabella said she would like some tea, and they entered an inn of
an inferior class, and gave their order. As it was not for beer they had
a long time to wait. The maid-servant recognized Jude, and whispered
her surprise to her mistress in the background, that he, the student,
"who kept hisself up so particular," should have suddenly descended
so low as to keep company with Arabella. The latter guessed what was
being said, and laughed as she met the serious and tender gaze of her
lover – the low and triumphant laugh of a careless woman who sees
she is winning her game.

They sat and looked round the room, and at the picture of Samson and Delilah[1] which hung on the wall, and at the circular beer-stains on the table, and at the spittoons underfoot filled with sawdust. The whole aspect of the scene had that depressing effect on Jude which few places can produce like a tap-room on a Sunday evening when the setting sun is slanting in, and no liquor is going, and the unfortunate wayfarer finds himself with no other haven of rest.

It began to grow dusk. They could not wait longer, really, they said. "Yet what else can we do?" asked Jude. "It is a three-mile walk for you."

"I suppose we can have some beer," said Arabella.

"Beer, O yes. I had forgotten that. Somehow it seems odd to come to a public-house for beer on a Sunday evening."

"But we didn't."

"No, we didn't." Jude by this time wished he was out of such an uncongenial atmosphere; but he ordered the beer, which was promptly brought.

Arabella tasted it. "Ugh!" she said.

Jude tasted. "What's the matter with it?" he asked. "I don't understand beer very much now, it is true. I like it well enough, but it is bad to read on, and I find coffee better. But this seems all right."

"Adulterated — I can't touch it!" She mentioned three or four ingredients that she detected in the liquor beyond malt and hops, much to Jude's surprise.

"How much you know!" he said good-humouredly.

Nevertheless she returned to the beer and drank her share, and they went on their way. It was now nearly dark, and as soon as they had withdrawn from the lights of the town they walked closer together, till they touched each other. She wondered why he did not put his arm round her waist, but he did not; he merely said what to himself seemed a quite bold enough thing: "Take my arm."

She took it, thoroughly, up to the shoulder. He felt the warmth of her body against his, and putting his stick under his other arm held with his right hand her right as it rested in its place.

1 Samson and Delilah] Jude will later be termed Arabella's "shorn Samson." (See Judges 16.)

"Now we are well together, dear, aren't we?" he observed.

"Yes," said she; adding to herself: "Rather mild!"

"How fast I have become!" he was thinking.

Thus they walked till they reached the foot of the upland, where they could see the white highway ascending before them in the gloom. From this point the only way of getting to Arabella's was by going up the incline, and dipping again into her valley on the right. Before they had climbed far they were nearly run into by two men who had been walking on the grass unseen.

"These lovers – you find 'em out o' doors in all seasons and weathers – lovers and homeless dogs only," said one of the men as they vanished down the hill.

Arabella tittered lightly.

"Are we lovers?" asked Jude.

"You know best."

"But you can tell me?"

For answer she inclined her head upon his shoulder. Jude took the hint, and encircling her waist with his arm, pulled her to him and kissed her.

They walked now no longer arm in arm but, as she had desired, clasped together. After all, what did it matter since it was dark, said Jude to himself. When they were half way up the long hill they paused as by arrangement, and he kissed her again. They reached the top, and he kissed her once more.

"You can keep your arm there, if you would like to," she said gently.

He did so, thinking how trusting she was.

Thus they slowly went towards her home. He had left his cottage at half-past three, intending to be sitting down again to the New Testament by half-past five. It was nine o'clock when, with another embrace, he stood to deliver her up at her father's door.

She asked him to come in, if only for a minute, as it would seem so odd otherwise, and as if she had been out alone in the dark. He gave way, and followed her in. Immediately that the door was opened he found, in addition to her parents, several neighbours sitting round. They all spoke in a congratulatory manner, and took him seriously as Arabella's intended partner.

They did not belong to his set or circle, and he felt out of place and embarrassed. He had not meant this: a mere afternoon of pleasant walking with Arabella, that was all he had meant. He did not stay longer than to speak to her stepmother, a simple, quiet woman without features or character; and bidding them all good night plunged with a sense of relief into the track over the down.

But that sense was only temporary: Arabella soon reasserted her sway in his soul. He walked as if he felt himself to be another man from the Jude of yesterday. What were his books to him? what were his intentions, hitherto adhered to so strictly, as to not wasting a single minute of time day by day? "Wasting!" It depended on your point of view to define that: he was just living for the first time: not wasting life. It was better to love a woman than to be a graduate, or a parson; ay, or a pope!

When he got back to the house, his aunt had gone to bed, and a general consciousness of his neglect seemed written on the face of all things confronting him. He went upstairs without a light, and the dim interior of his room accosted him with sad inquiry. There lay his book open, just as he had left it, and the capital letters on the title page regarded him with fixed reproach in the grey starlight, like the unclosed eyes of a dead man:

Η ΚΑΙΝΗ ΔΙΑΘΗΚΗ.

.   .   .   .   .   .

Jude had to leave early next morning for his usual week of absence at lodgings; and it was with a sense of futility that he threw into his basket upon his tools and other necessaries the unread book he had brought with him.

He kept his impassioned doings a secret almost from himself. Arabella, on the contrary, made them public among all her friends and acquaintance.

Retracing by the light of dawn the road he had followed a few hours earlier, under cover of darkness, with his sweetheart by his side, he reached the bottom of the hill, where he walked slowly, and stood still. He was on the spot where he had given her the first kiss. As the sun had only just risen it was possible that nobody had passed there since. Jude looked on the ground and sighed. He looked closely, and could just discern in the damp dust the imprints of their feet as they had stood locked in each other's arms. She was not there now, and "the embroidery of imagination upon the stuff of nature"[1] so depicted her past presence that a void was in his heart which nothing could fill. A pollard willow[2] stood close to the place, and that willow was different from all other willows in the world. Utter annihilation of the six days which must elapse before he could see her again as he had promised would have been his intensest wish if he had had only the week to live.

An hour and half later Arabella came along the same way with her two companions of the Saturday. She passed unheedingly the scene of the kiss, and the willow that marked it, though chattering freely on the subject to the other two.

"And what did he tell 'ee next?"

"Then he said –" And she related almost word for word some of his tenderest speeches. If Jude had been behind the fence he would have felt not a little surprised at learning how very few of his sayings and doings on the previous evening were private.

"You've got him to care for 'ee a bit, 'nation[3] if you ha'n't!" murmured Anny judicially. "It's well to be[4] you!"

In a few moments Arabella replied in a curiously low, fierce tone of latent sensuousness: "I've got him to care for me: yes! But I want him to more than care for me; I want him to have me – to marry me! I must have him. I can't do without him. He's the sort of man I long for. I shall go mad if I can't give myself to him altogether! I felt I should when I first saw him!"

"As he is a romancing,[5] straightfor'ard, honest chap, he's to be had, and as a husband, if you set about catching him in the right way."

Arabella remained thinking awhile. "What med be the right way?" she asked.

"O you don't know – you don't!" said Sarah, the third girl.

"On my word I don't! – No further, that is, than by plain courting, and taking care he don't go too far!"

---

1 "the embroidery.....nature"] Timothy Hands, editor of the Everyman edition of this novel, says that the quotation is "probably of Hardy's own invention."
2 pollard willow] willow with the crown lopped off so that new branches sprout from the top of the stem.
3 'nation] (coll.:) damnation.
4 well to be] (dl.:) likely to be.
5 romancing] inclined to courting.

The third girl looked at the second. "She *don't* know!"

"'Tis clear she don't!" said Anny.

"And having lived in a town, too, as one may say! Well, we can teach 'ee som'at then, as well as you us."

"Yes. And how do you mean – a sure way to gain a man? Take me for a' innocent, and have done wi' it!"

"As a husband."

"As a husband."

"A countryman that's honourable and serious-minded such as he; God forbid that I should say a sojer, or sailor, or commercial gent from the towns, or any of them that be slippery with poor women! I'd do no friend that harm!"

"Well, such as he, of course!"

Arabella's companions looked at each other, and turning up their eyes in drollery began smirking. Then one went up close to Arabella, and, although nobody was near, imparted some information in a low tone, the other observing curiously the effect upon Arabella.

"Ah!" said the last-named slowly. "I own I didn't think of that way! … But suppose he *isn't* honourable? A woman had better not have tried it!"

"Nothing venture nothing have! Besides, you make sure that he's honourable before you begin. You'd be safe enough with yours. I wish I had the chance! Lots of girls do it; or do you think they'd get married at all?"

Arabella pursued her way in silent thought. "I'll try it!" she whispered; but not to them.

I.-VIII.

AT the week's end Jude was again walking out to his aunt's at Marygreen from his lodging in Alfredston, a walk which now had large attractions for him quite other than his desire to see his aged and morose relative. He diverged to the right before ascending the hill with the single purpose of gaining, on his way, a glimpse of Arabella that should not come into the reckoning of regular appointments. Before quite reaching the homestead his alert eye perceived the top of her head moving quickly hither and thither over the garden hedge.

Entering the gate he found that three young unfattened pigs had escaped from their sty by leaping clean over the top, and that she was endeavouring unassisted to drive them in through the door which she had set open. The lines of her countenance changed from the rigidity of business to the softness of love when she saw Jude, and she bent her eyes languishingly upon him. The animals took advantage of the pause by doubling and bolting out of the way.

"They were only put in this morning!" she cried, stimulated to pursue in spite of her lover's presence. "They were drove from Spaddleholt Farm only yesterday, where father bought 'em at a stiff price enough. They are wanting to get home again, the stupid toads! Will you shut the garden gate, dear, and help me to get 'em in? There be no men-folk at home, only mother, and they'll be lost if we don't mind."

He set himself to assist, and dodged this way and that over the potato rows and the cabbages. Every now and then they ran together, when he caught her for a moment and kissed her. The first pig was got back promptly; the second with some difficulty; the third, a long-legged creature, was more obstinate and agile. He plunged through a hole in the garden hedge, and into the lane.

"He'll be lost if I don't follow 'n!" said she. "Come along with me!"

She rushed in full pursuit out of the garden, Jude alongside her, barely contriving to keep the fugitive in sight. Occasionally they would shout to some boy to stop the animal, but he always wriggled past and ran on as before.

"Let me take your hand, darling," said Jude. "You are getting out of breath." She gave him her now hot hand with apparent willingness, and they trotted along together.

"This comes of driving 'em home," she remarked. "They always know the way back if you do that. They ought to have been carted over."

By this time the pig had reached an unfastened gate admitting to the open down, across which he sped with all the agility his little legs afforded. As soon as the pursuers had entered and ascended to the top of the high ground it became apparent that they would have to run all the way to the farmer's if they wished to get at him. From this summit he could be seen as a minute speck, following an unerring line towards the farm.

"It is no good!" cried Arabella. "He'll be there long before we get there. It don't matter now we know he's not lost or stolen on the way. They'll see it is ours, and send un back. O dear, how hot I be!"

Without relinquishing her hold of Jude's hand she swerved aside and flung herself down on the sod under a stunted thorn, precipitately pulling Jude on to his knees at the same time.

"O, I ask pardon – I nearly threw you down, didn't I! But I am so tired!"

She lay supine, and straight as an arrow, on the sloping sod of this hill-top, gazing up into the blue miles of sky, and still retaining her warm hold of Jude's hand. He reclined on his elbow near her.

"We've run all this way for nothing," she went on, her form heaving and falling in quick pants, her face flushed, her full red lips parted, and a fine dew of perspiration on her skin. "Well – why don't you speak, deary?"

"I'm blown too. It was all up hill."

They were in absolute solitude – the most apparent of all solitudes, that of empty surrounding space. Nobody could be nearer than a mile to them without their seeing him. They were, in fact, on one of the summits of the county, and the distant landscape around Christminster could be discerned from where they lay. But Jude did not think of that then.

"O, I can see such a pretty thing up this tree," said Arabella. "A sort of a – caterpillar, of the most loveliest green and yellow you ever came across!"

"Where?" said Jude, sitting up.

"You can't see him there – you must come here," said she.

He bent nearer and put his head by hers. "No – I can't see it," he said.

"Why, on the limb there where it branches off – close to the moving leaf – there!" She gently pressed his face towards the position.

"I don't see it," he repeated, the back of his head against her cheek. "But I can, perhaps, standing up." He stood accordingly, placing himself in the direct line of her gaze.

"How stupid you are!" she said, crossly, turning away her face.

"I don't care to see it, dear: why should I?" he replied, looking down upon her. "Get up, Abby."

"Why?"

"I want you to let me kiss you. I've been waiting to ever so long!"

She rolled round her face, remained a moment looking deedily aslant at him; then with a slight curl of the lip sprang to her feet, and exclaiming abruptly "I must mizzel!" walked off quickly homeward. Jude followed and rejoined her.

"Just one!" he coaxed.

"Shan't!" she said.

He, surprised: "What's the matter?"

She kept her two lips resentfully together, and Jude followed her like a pet lamb till she slackened her pace and walked beside him, talking calmly on indifferent subjects, and always checking him if he tried to take her hand or clasp her waist. Thus they descended to the precincts of her father's homestead, and Arabella went in, nodding good-bye to him with a supercilious, affronted air.

"I expect I took too much liberty with her, somehow," Jude said to himself, as he withdrew with a sigh and went on to Marygreen.

On Sunday morning the interior of Arabella's home was, as usual, the scene of a grand weekly cooking, the preparation of the special Sunday dinner. Her father was shaving before a little glass hung on the mullion[1] of the window, and her mother and Arabella herself were shelling beans hard by. A neighbour passed on her way home from morning service at the nearest church, and seeing Donn engaged at the window with a razor, nodded and came in.

She at once spoke playfully to Arabella: "I zeed 'ee[2] running with 'un – hee-hee! I hope 'tis coming to something?"

Arabella merely threw a look of consciousness into her face without raising her eyes.

"He's for Christminster, I hear, as soon as he can get there."

"Have you heard that lately – quite lately?" asked Arabella with a jealous, tigerish indrawing of breath.

"O no! But it has been known a long time that it is his plan. He's on'y waiting here for an opening. Ah well: he must walk about with

---

1   mullion] vertical division.
2   I zeed 'ee] (dl.:) I saw you.

somebody I s'pose. Young men don't mean much now-a-days. 'Tis a sip here and a sip there with 'em. 'Twas different in my time."

When the gossip had departed Arabella said suddenly to her mother: "I want you and father to go and inquire how the Edlins be, this evening after tea. Or no – there's evening service at Fensworth – you can walk to that."

"Oh? What's up to-night, then?"

"Nothing. Only I want the house to myself. He's shy; and I can't get un to come in when you are here. I shall let him slip through my fingers if I don't mind, much as I care for 'n!"

"If it is fine we med as well go, since you wish."

In the afternoon Arabella met and walked with Jude, who had now for weeks ceased to look into a book of Greek, Latin, or any other tongue. They wandered up the slopes till they reached the green track along the ridge, which they followed to the circular British earth-bank[1] adjoining, Jude thinking of the great age of the trackway, and of the drovers who had frequented it, probably before the Romans knew the country. Up from the level lands below them floated the chime of church bells. Presently they were reduced to one note, which quickened, and stopped.

"Now we'll go back," said Arabella, who had attended to the sounds.

Jude assented. So long as he was near her he minded little where he was. When they arrived at her house he said lingeringly: "I won't come in. Why are you in such a hurry to go in to-night? It is not near dark."

"Wait a moment," said she. She tried the handle of the door and found it locked.

"Ah – they are gone to church," she added. And searching behind the scraper she found the key and unlocked the door. "Now, you'll come in a moment?" she asked lightly. "We shall be all alone."

"Certainly," said Jude with alacrity, the case being unexpectedly altered.

Indoors they went. Did he want any tea? No, it was too late: he would rather sit and talk to her. She took off her jacket and hat, and they sat down – naturally enough close together.

---

1   earth-bank] corresponds to Segsbury.

"Don't touch me, please," she said softly. "I am part egg-shell. Or perhaps I had better put it in a safe place." She began unfastening the collar of her gown.

"What is it?" said her lover.

"An egg – a bantam's egg. I am hatching a very rare sort. I carry it about everywhere with me, and it will get hatched in less than three weeks."

"Where do you carry it?"

"Just here." She put her hand into her bosom and drew out the egg, which was wrapped in wool, outside it being a piece of pig's bladder, in case of accidents. Having exhibited it to him she put it back, "Now mind you don't come near me. I don't want to get it broke, and have to begin another."

"Why do you do such a strange thing?"

"Just for a fancy. I suppose it is natural for a woman to want to bring live things into the world."

"It is very awkward for me just now," he said, laughing.

"It serves you right. There – that's all you can have of me."

She had turned round her chair, and, reaching over the back of it, presented her cheek to him gingerly.

"That's very shabby of you!"

"You should have catched me a minute ago when I had put the egg down! There!" she said defiantly, "I am without it now!" She had quickly withdrawn the egg a second time; but before he could quite reach her she had put it back as quickly, laughing with the excitement of her strategy. Then there was a little struggle, Jude making a plunge for it and capturing it triumphantly. Her faced flushed; and becoming suddenly conscious he flushed also.

They looked at each other, panting; till he rose and said: "One kiss, now I can do it without damage to property; and I'll go!"

But she had jumped up too. "You must find me first!" she cried.

Her lover followed her as she withdrew. It was now dark inside the room, and the window being small he could not discover for a long time what had become of her, till a laugh revealed her to have rushed up the stairs, whither Jude rushed at her heels.

I.-IX.

It was some two months later in the year, and the pair had met constantly during the interval. Arabella seemed dissatisfied; she was always imagining, and waiting, and wondering.

One day she met the itinerant Vilbert. She, like all the cottagers thereabout, knew the quack well, and they began talking about her experiences. Arabella had been gloomy, but before he left her she had grown brighter. That evening she kept an appointment with Jude, who seemed sad.

"I am going away," he said to her. "I think I ought to go. I think it will be better both for you and for me. I wish some things had never begun! I was much to blame, I know. But it is never too late to mend."

Arabella began to cry. "How do you know it is not too late?" she said. "That's all very well to say! I haven't told you yet!" and she looked into his face with streaming eyes.

"What?" he asked, turning pale. "Not ... ?"

"Yes! And what shall I do if you desert me!"

"O Arabella – how can you say that, my dear! You *know* I wouldn't desert you!"

"Well then ——"

"I have next to no wages as yet, you know; or perhaps I should have thought of this before.... But, of course, if that's the case, we must marry! What other thing do you think I could dream of doing?"

"I thought – I thought, deary, perhaps you would go away all the more for that, and leave me to face it alone!"

"You knew better! Of course I never dreamt six months ago, or even three, of marrying. It is a complete smashing up of my plans – I mean my plans before I knew you, my dear. But what are they, after all! Dreams about books, and degrees, and impossible scholarships, and all that. Certainly we'll marry: we must!"

That night he went out alone, and walked in the dark, self-communing. He knew well, too well, in the secret centre of his brain, that Arabella was not worth a great deal as a specimen of womankind. Yet, such being the custom of rural districts, among honourable young men who had drifted so far into intimacy with a woman as he unfortunately had done, he was ready to abide by what he had said, and take the consequences. For his own soothing he kept up a factitious belief in her. His idea of her was the thing of most consequence, not Arabella herself, he sometimes said laconically.

The banns[1] were put in and published the very next Sunday. The people of the parish all said what a simple fool young Fawley was. All his reading had only come to this, that he would have to sell his books to buy saucepans. Those who guessed the probable state of affairs, Arabella's parents being among them, declared that it was the sort of conduct they would have expected of such an honest young man as Jude in reparation of the wrong he had done his innocent sweetheart. The parson who married them seemed to think it satisfactory too.

And so, standing before the aforesaid officiator, the two swore that at every other time of their lives they would assuredly believe, feel, and desire precisely as they had believed, felt, and desired during the few preceding weeks. What was as remarkable as the undertaking itself was the fact that nobody seemed at all surprised at what they swore.

Fawley's aunt being a baker she made him a bridecake, saying bitterly that it was the last thing she could do for him, poor silly fellow; and that it would have been far better if, instead of his living to trouble her, he had gone underground years before with his father and mother. Of this cake Arabella took some slices, wrapped them up in white note-paper, and sent them to her companions in the pork-dressing business, Anny and Sarah, labelling each packet "*In remembrance of good advice.*"

The prospects of the newly married couple were certainly not very brilliant even to the most sanguine mind. He, a stone-cutter's apprentice, nineteen years of age, was working for half wages till he should be out of his time. His wife was absolutely useless in a town-lodging, where he at first had considered it would be necessary for them to live. But the urgent need of adding to income in ever so little a degree caused him to take a lonely roadside cottage between the Brown House and Marygreen, that he might have the profits of a vegetable garden, and utilize her past experiences by letting her keep a pig. But it was not the sort of life he had bargained for, and it was a long way to walk to and from Alfredston every day. Arabella, however,

---

1   banns] public declaration of intent to marry.

felt that all these makeshifts were temporary; she had gained a husband; that was the thing – a husband with a lot of earning power in him for buying her frocks and hats when he should begin to get frightened a bit, and stick to his trade, and throw aside those stupid books for practical undertakings.

So to the cottage he took her on the evening of the marriage, giving up his old room at his aunt's – where so much of the hard labour at Greek and Latin had been carried on.

A little chill overspread him at her first unrobing. A long tail of hair, which Arabella wore twisted up in an enormous knob at the back of her head, was deliberately unfastened, stroked out, and hung upon the looking-glass which he had bought her.

"What – it wasn't your own?" he said, with a sudden distaste for her.

"O no – it never is nowadays with the better class."

"Nonsense! Perhaps not in towns. But in the country it is supposed to be different. Besides, you've enough of your own, surely? Why, it's a lot!"

"Yes, enough as country notions go. But in towns the men expect more, and when I was a barmaid at Aldbrickham ——"[1]

"Barmaid at Aldbrickham?"

"Well, not exactly barmaid – I used to draw the drink at a public-house there – just for a little time; that was all. Some people put me up to getting this, and I bought it just for a fancy. The more you have the better in Aldbrickham, which is a finer town than all your Christminsters. Every lady of position wears false hair – the barber's assistant told me so."

Jude thought with a feeling of sickness that though this might be true to some extent, for all that he knew, many unsophisticated girls would and did go to towns and remain there for years without losing their simplicity of life and embellishments. Others, alas, had an instinct towards artificiality in their very blood, and became adepts in counterfeiting at the first glimpse of it. However, perhaps there was no great sin in a woman adding to her hair, and he resolved to think no more of it.

A new-made wife can usually manage to look interesting for a few

---

1 Aldbrickham] corresponds to Reading, a large town in Berkshire.

weeks, even though the prospects of the household ways and means are cloudy. There is a certain piquancy about her situation, and her manner to her acquaintance at the sense of it, which carries off the gloom of facts, and renders even the humblest bride independent awhile of the real. Mrs. Jude Fawley was walking in the streets of Alfredston one market-day with this quality in her carriage when she met Anny her former friend, whom she had not seen since the wedding.

As usual they laughed before talking; the world seemed funny to them without saying it.

"So it turned out a good plan you see!" remarked the girl to the wife. "I knew it would with such as him. He's a dear good fellow, and you ought to be proud of un."

"I am," said Mrs. Fawley quietly.

"And when do you expect ——?"

"Ssh! Not at all."

"What!"

"I was mistaken."

"O Arabella, Arabella; you be a deep one! Mistaken! well, that's clever — it's a rale stroke of genius! It is a thing I never thought o', wi' all my experience! I never thought beyond the rale thing — not that one could sham it!"

"Don't you be too quick to cry sham! 'Twasn't sham. I didn't know."

"My word — won't he be in a taking![1] He'll give it to 'ee o' Saturday nights! Whatever it was, he'll say it was a trick — a double one, by the Lord!"

"I'll own to the first, but not to the second.... Pooh — he won't care! He'll be glad I was wrong in what I said. He'll shake down, bless 'ee — men always do. What can 'em do otherwise? Married is married."

Nevertheless it was with a little uneasiness that Arabella approached the time when in the natural course of things she would have to reveal that the alarm she had raised had been without foundation. The occasion was one evening at bed-time, and they were in their chamber in the lonely cottage by the wayside, to which Jude

---

1 in a taking] (dl.:) in a fit of anger.

walked home from his work every day. He had worked hard the whole twelve hours, and had retired to rest before his wife. When she came into the room he was between sleeping and waking, and was barely unconscious of her undressing before the little looking-glass as he lay.

One action of hers, however, brought him to full cognition. Her face being reflected towards him as she sat, he could perceive that she was amusing herself by artificially producing in each cheek the dimple before alluded to, a curious accomplishment of which she was mistress, effecting it by momentary suction. It seemed to him for the first time that the dimples were far oftener absent from her face during his intercourse with her nowadays than they had been in the earlier weeks of their acquaintance.

"Don't do that, Arabella!" he said suddenly. "There is no harm in it, but – I don't like to see you."

She turned and laughed. "Lord, I didn't know you was awake!" she said. "How countrified you are! That's nothing."

"Where did you learn it?"

"Nowhere that I know of. They used to stay without any trouble when I was at the public-house; but now they won't. My face was fatter then."

"I don't care about dimples. I don't think they improve a woman – particularly a married woman, and of full-sized figure like you."

"Most men think otherwise."

"I don't care what most men think, if they do. How do you know?"

"I used to be told so when I was serving in the tap-room."

"Ah – that public-house experience accounts for your knowing about the adulteration of the ale when we went and had some that Sunday evening. I thought when I married you that you had always lived in your father's house."

"You ought to have known better than that, and seen I was a little more finished than I could have been by staying where I was born. There was not much to do at home, and I was eating my head off, so I went away for three months."

"You'll soon have plenty to do now, dear, won't you?"

"How do you mean?"

"Why, of course – little things to make."

"Oh."

"When will it be? Can't you tell me exactly, instead of in such general terms as you have used?"

"Tell you?"

"Yes – the date."

"There's nothing to tell. I made a mistake."

"What?"

"It was a mistake."

He sat bolt upright in bed and looked at her. "How can that be?"

"People fancy wrong things sometimes."

"But —— ! Why, of course, so unprepared as I was, without a stick of furniture, and hardly a shilling, I shouldn't have hurried on our affair, and brought you to a half-furnished hut before I was ready, if it had not been for the news you gave me, which made it necessary to save you, ready or no.... Good God!"

"Don't take on, dear. What's done can't be undone."

"I have no more to say!"

He gave the answer simply, and lay down; and there was silence between them.

When Jude awoke the next morning he seemed to see the world with a different eye. As to the point in question he was compelled to accept her word; in the circumstances he could not have acted otherwise while ordinary notions prevailed. But how came they to prevail?

There seemed to him, vaguely and dimly, something wrong in a social ritual which made necessary a cancelling of well-formed schemes involving years of thought and labour, of foregoing a man's one opportunity of showing himself superior to the lower animals, and of contributing his units of work to the general progress of his generation, because of a momentary surprise by a new and transitory instinct which had nothing in it of the nature of vice, and could be only at the most called weakness. He was inclined to inquire what he had done, or she lost, for that matter, that he deserved to be caught in a gin[1] which would cripple him, if not her also, for the rest of a lifetime? There was perhaps something fortunate in the fact that the immediate reason of his marriage had proved to be non-existent. But the marriage remained.

---

1   gin] trap.

I.-X.

THE time arrived for killing the pig which Jude and his wife had fattened in their sty during the autumn months, and the butchering was timed to take place as soon as it was light in the morning, so that Jude might get to Alfredston without losing more than a quarter of a day.

The night had seemed strangely silent. Jude looked out of the window long before dawn, and perceived that the ground was covered with snow – snow rather deep for the season, it seemed, a few flakes still falling.

"I'm afraid the pig-killer won't be able to come," he said to Arabella.

"O, he'll come. You must wake up and make the water hot, if you want Challow to scald him. Though I like singeing best."

"I'll get up," said Jude. "I like the way of my own county."

He went downstairs, lit the fire under the copper, and began feeding it with bean-stalks, all the time without a candle, the blaze flinging a cheerful shine into the room; though for him the sense of cheerfulness was lessened by thoughts on the reason of that blaze – to heat water to scald an animal that as yet lived, and whose voice could be continually heard from a corner of the garden. At half-past six, the time of appointment with the butcher, the water boiled, and Jude's wife came downstairs.

"Is Challow come?" she asked.

"No."

They waited, and it grew lighter, with the dreary light of a snowy dawn. She went out, gazed along the road, and returning said, "He's not coming. Drunk last night, I expect. The snow is not enough to hinder him, surely!"

"Then we must put it off. It is only the water boiled for nothing. The snow may be deep in the valley."

"Can't be put off. There's no more victuals for the pig. He ate the last mixing o' barleymeal yesterday morning."

"Yesterday morning? What has he lived on since?"

"Nothing."

"What – he has been starving?"

"Yes. We always do it the last day or two, to save bother with the innerds. What ignorance, not to know that!"

"That accounts for his crying so. Poor creature!"

"Well – you must do the sticking – there's no help for it. I'll show you how. Or I'll do it myself – I think I could. Though as it is such a big pig I had rather Challow had done it. However, his basket o' knives and things have already been sent on here, and we can use 'em."

"Of course you shan't do it," said Jude. "I'll do it, since it must be done."

He went out to the sty, shovelled away the snow for the space of a couple of yards or more, and placed the stool in front, with the knives and ropes at hand. A robin peered down at the preparations from the nearest tree, and, not liking the sinister look of the scene, flew away, though hungry. By this time Arabella had joined her husband, and Jude, rope in hand, got into the sty, and noosed the affrighted animal, who, beginning with a squeak of surprise, rose to repeated cries of rage. Arabella opened the sty-door, and together they hoisted the victim on to the stool, legs upward, and while Jude held him Arabella bound him down, looping the cord over his legs to keep him from struggling.

The animal's note changed its quality. It was not now rage, but the cry of despair; long-drawn, slow and hopeless.

"Upon my soul I would sooner have gone without the pig than have had this to do!" said Jude. "A creature I have fed with my own hands."

"Don't be such a tender-hearted fool! There's the sticking-knife – the one with the point. Now whatever you do, don't stick un too deep."

"I'll stick un effectually, so as to make short work of it. That's the chief thing."

"You must not!" she cried. "The meat must be well bled, and to do that he must die slow. We shall lose a shilling a score if the meat is red and bloody! Just touch the vein, that's all. I was brought up to it, and I know. Every good butcher keeps un bleeding long. He ought to be eight or ten minutes dying, at least."

"He shall not be half a minute if I can help it, however the meat may look," said Jude determinedly. Scraping the bristles from the pig's upturned throat, as he had seen the butchers do, he slit the fat; then plunged in the knife with all his might.

"'Od damn it all!" she cried, "that ever I should say it! You've over-stuck un! And I telling you all the time ——"

"Do be quiet, Arabella, and have a little pity on the creature!"

However unworkmanlike the deed, it had been mercifully done. The blood flowed out in a torrent instead of in the trickling stream she had desired. The dying animal's cry assumed its third and final tone, the shriek of agony; his glazing eyes rivetting themselves on Arabella with the eloquently keen reproach of a creature recognizing at last the treachery of those who had seemed his only friends.

"Make un stop that!" said Arabella. "Such a noise will bring somebody or other up here, and I don't want people to know we are doing it ourselves." Picking up the knife from the ground whereon Jude had flung it, she slipped it into the gash, and slit the wind-pipe. The pig was instantly silent, his dying breath coming through the hole.

"That's better," she said.

"It is a hateful business!" said he.

"Pigs must be killed."

The animal heaved in a final convulsion, and, despite the rope, kicked out with all his last strength. A tablespoonful of black clot came forth, the trickling of red blood having ceased for some seconds.

"That's it; now he'll go," said she. "Artful creatures – they always keep back a drop like that as long as they can!"

The last plunge had come so unexpectedly as to make Jude stagger, and in recovering himself he kicked over the vessel in which the blood had been caught.

"There!" she cried, thoroughly in a passion. "Now I can't make any blackpot.[1] There's a waste, all through you!"

Jude put the pan upright, but only about a third of the whole steaming liquid was left in it, the main part being splashed over the snow, and forming a dismal, sordid, ugly spectacle – to those who saw it as other than an ordinary obtaining of meat. The lips and nostrils of the animal turned livid, then white, and the muscles of his limbs relaxed.

"Thank God!" Jude said. "He's dead."

---

1   blackpot] filling for black puddings.

"What's God got to do with such a messy job as a pig-killing, I should like to know!" she said scornfully. "Poor folks must live."

"I know, I know," said he. "I don't scold you."

Suddenly they became aware of a voice at hand.

"Well done, young married volk! I couldn't have carried it out much better myself, cuss me if I could!" The voice, which was husky, came from the garden-gate, and looking up from the scene of slaughter they saw the burly form of Mr. Challow leaning over the gate, critically surveying their performance.

"'Tis well for 'ee to stand there and glane!"[1] said Arabella. "Owing to your being late the meat is blooded and half spoiled! 'Twon't fetch so much by a shilling a score!"[2]

Challow expressed his contrition. "You should have waited a bit," he said, shaking his head, "and not have done this – in the delicate state, too, that you be in at present, ma'am. 'Tis risking yourself too much."

"You needn't be concerned about that," said Arabella, laughing. Jude too laughed, but there was a strong flavour of bitterness in his amusement.

Challow made up for his neglect of the killing by zeal in the scalding and scraping. Jude felt dissatisfied with himself as a man at what he had done, though aware of his lack of common sense, and that the deed would have amounted to the same thing if carried out by deputy. The white snow, stained with the blood of his fellow-mortal, wore an illogical look to him as a lover of justice, not to say a Christian; but he could not see how the matter was to be mended. No doubt he was, as his wife had called him, a tender-hearted fool.

He did not like the road to Alfredston now. It stared him cynically in the face. The wayside objects reminded him so much of his courtship of his wife that, to keep them out of his eyes, he read whenever he could as he walked to and from his work. Yet he sometimes felt that by caring for books he was not escaping commonplace nor gaining rare ideas, every working-man being of that taste now. When passing near the spot by the stream on which he had first made her acquaintance he one day heard voices just as he had done at that

---

1 glane] (dl.:) sneer.
2 shilling a score] shilling on each twenty pounds of weight.

earlier time. One of the girls who had been Arabella's companions was talking to a friend in a shed, himself being the subject of discourse, possibly because they had seen him in the distance. They were quite unaware that the shed-walls were so thin that he could hear their words as he passed.

"Howsomever, 'twas I put her up to it! 'Nothing venture nothing have,' I said. If I hadn't she'd no more have been his mis'ess than I."

"'Tis my belief she knew before...."

What had Arabella been put up to by this woman, so that he should make her his 'mis'ess', otherwise wife? The suggestion was horridly unpleasant, and it rankled in his mind so much that instead of entering his own cottage when he reached it he flung his basket inside the garden-gate and passed on, determined to go and see his old aunt and get some supper there.

This made his arrival home rather late. Arabella, however, was busy melting down lard from fat of the deceased pig, for she had been out on a jaunt all day, and so delayed her work. Dreading lest what he had heard should lead him to say something regrettable to her he spoke little. But Arabella was very talkative, and said among other things that she wanted some money. Seeing the book sticking out of his pocket she added that he ought to earn more.

"An apprentice's wages are not meant to be enough to keep a wife on, as a rule, my dear."

"Then you shouldn't have had one."

"Come, Arabella! That's too bad, when you know how it came about."

"I'll declare afore Heaven that I thought what I told you was true. Doctor Vilbert thought so. It was a good job for you that it wasn't so!"

"I don't mean that," he said hastily. "I mean before that time. I know it was not your fault; but those women friends of yours gave you bad advice. If they hadn't, or you hadn't taken it, we should at this moment have been free from a bond which, not to mince matters, galls both of us devilishly. It may be very sad, but it is true."

"Who's been telling you about my friends? What advice? I insist upon your telling me."

"Pooh – I'd rather not."

"But you shall – you ought to. It is mean of 'ee not to!"

"Very well." And he hinted gently what had been revealed to him. "But I don't wish to dwell upon it. Let us say no more about it."

Her defensive manner collapsed. "That was nothing," she said, laughing coldly. "Every woman has a right to do such as that. The risk is hers."

"I quite deny it, Bella. She might if no life-long penalty attached to it for the man, or, in his default, for herself; if the weakness of the moment could end with the moment, or even with the year. But when effects stretch so far she should not go and do that which entraps a man if he is honest, or herself if he is otherwise."

"What ought I to have done?"

"Given me time.... Why do you fuss yourself about melting down that pig's fat to-night? Please put it away!"

"Then I must do it to-morrow morning. It won't keep."

"Very well – do."

I.-XI.

NEXT morning, which was Sunday, she resumed operations about ten o'clock; and the renewed work recalled the conversation which had accompanied it the night before, and put her back into the same intractable temper.

"That's the story about me in Marygreen, is it – that I entrapped 'ee? Much of a catch you was, Lord send!"[1] As she warmed she saw some of Jude's dear ancient classics on a table where they ought not to have been laid. "I won't have them books here in the way!" she cried petulantly; and seizing them one by one she began throwing them upon the floor.

"Leave my books alone!" he said. "You might have thrown them aside if you had liked, but as to soiling them like that, it is disgusting!" In the operation of making lard Arabella's hands had become smeared with the hot grease, and her fingers consequently left very perceptible imprints on the book-covers. She continued deliberately to toss the books severally upon the floor, till Jude, incensed beyond bearing,

---

1 Lord send] (coll.:) "May the Lord send mercy!"

caught her by the arms to make her leave off. Somehow, in doing so, he loosened the fastening of her hair, and it rolled about her ears.

"Let me go!" she said.

"Promise to leave the books alone."

She hesitated. "Let me go!" she repeated.

"Promise!"

After a pause: "I do."

Jude relinquished his hold, and she crossed the room to the door, out of which she went with a set face, and into the highway. Here she began to saunter up and down, perversely pulling her hair into a worse disorder then he had caused, and unfastening several buttons of her gown. It was a fine Sunday morning, dry, clear and frosty, and the bells of Alfredston Church could be heard on the breeze from the north. People were going along the road, dressed in their holiday clothes; they were mainly lovers – such pairs as Jude and Arabella had been when they sported along the same track some months earlier. These pedestrians turned to stare at the extraordinary spectacle she now presented, bonnetless, her dishevelled hair blowing in the wind, her bodice apart, her sleeves rolled above her elbows for her work, and her hands reeking with melted fat. One of the passers said in mock terror: "Good Lord deliver us!"

"See how he's served me!" she cried. "Making me work Sunday mornings when I ought to be going to my church, and tearing my hair off my head, and my gown off my back!"

Jude was exasperated, and went out to drag her in by main force. Then he suddenly lost his heat. Illuminated with the sense that all was over between them, and that it mattered not what she did, or he, her husband stood still, regarding her. Their lives were ruined, he thought; ruined by the fundamental error of their matrimonial union: that of having based a permanent contract on a temporary feeling which had no necessary connection with affinities that alone render a life-long comradeship tolerable.

"Going to ill-use me on principle, as your father ill-used your mother, and your father's sister ill-used her husband?" she asked. "All you be a queer lot as husbands and wives!"

Jude fixed an arrested, surprised look on her. But she said no more, and continued her saunter till she was tired. He left the spot, and after wandering vaguely a little while, walked in the direction of Mary-green. Here he called upon his great-aunt, whose infirmities daily increased.

"Aunt – did my father ill-use my mother, and my aunt her husband?" said Jude abruptly, sitting down by the fire.

She raised her ancient eyes under the rim of the bygone bonnet that she always wore. "Who's been telling you that?" she said.

"I have heard it spoken of, and want to know all."

"You med so well, I s'pose; though your wife – I reckon 'twas she – must have been a fool to open up that! There isn't much to know after all. Your father and mother couldn't get on together, and they parted. It was coming home from Alfredston market, when you were a baby – on the hill by the Brown House barn – that they had their last difference, and took leave of one another for the last time. Your mother soon afterwards died – she drowned herself, in short, and your father went away with you to South Wessex, and never came here any more."

Jude recalled his father's silence about North Wessex and Jude's mother, never speaking of either till his dying day.

"It was the same with your father's sister. Her husband offended her, and she so disliked living with him afterwards that she went away to London with her little maid.[1] The Fawleys were not made for wedlock: it never seemed to sit well upon us. There's sommat[2] in our blood that won't take kindly to the notion of being bound to do what we do readily enough if not bound. That's why you ought to have hearkened to me, and not ha' married."

"Where did father and mother part – by the Brown House, did you say?"

"A little further on – where the road to Fenworth branches off, and the handpost stands. A gibbet[3] once stood there."

In the dusk of that evening Jude walked away from his old aunt's as if to go home. But as soon as he reached the open down he struck out

---

1 maid] female child. (Here we are told that Sue went to London with her mother; yet later it is implied that Sue went to London with her father.)

2 sommat] (dl.:) something.

3 gibbet] gallows, or a similar structure from which a criminal's corpse might be suspended for display.

upon it till he came to a large round pond. The frost continued, though it was not particularly sharp, and the larger stars overhead came out slow and flickering. Jude put one foot on the edge of the ice, and then the other: it cracked under his weight; but this did not deter him. He ploughed his way inward to the centre, the ice making sharp noises as he went. When just about the middle he looked around him and gave a jump. The cracking repeated itself; but he did not go down. He jumped again, but the cracking had ceased. Jude went back to the edge, and stepped upon the ground.

It was curious, he thought. What was he reserved for? He supposed he was not a sufficiently dignified person for suicide. Peaceful death abhorred him as a subject, and would not take him.

What could he do of a lower kind than self-extermination; what was there less noble, more in keeping with his present degraded position? He could get drunk. Of course that was it; he had forgotten. Drinking was the regular, stereotyped resource of the despairing worthless. He began to see now why some men boozed at inns. He struck down the hill northwards and came to an obscure public-house. On entering and sitting down the sight of the picture of Samson and Delilah on the wall caused him to recognize the place as that he had visited with Arabella on that first Sunday evening of their courtship. He called for liquor and drank briskly for an hour or more.

Staggering homeward late that night, with all his sense of depression gone, and his head fairly clear still, he began to laugh boisterously, and to wonder how Arabella would receive him in his new aspect. The house was in darkness when he entered, and in his stumbling state it was some time before he could get a light. Then he found that, though the marks of pig-dressing, of fats and scallops,[1] were visible, the materials themselves had been taken away. A line written by his wife on the inside of an old envelope was pinned to the cotton blower[2] of the fireplace:

"*Have gone to my friends. Shall not return.*"

All the next day he remained at home, and sent off the carcase of the pig to Alfredston. He then cleaned up the premises, locked the

---

1 scallops] stringy part of the fat, remaining after the rest has been melted out for lard.
2 blower] curtain over the fireplace to induce a draught for the fire.

door, put the key in a place she would know if she came back, and returned to his masonry at Alfredston.

At night when he again plodded home he found she had not visited the house. The next day went in the same way, and the next. Then there came a letter from her.

That she had grown tired of him she frankly admitted. He was such a slow old coach, and she did not care for the sort of life he led. There was no prospect of his ever bettering himself or her. She further went on to say that her parents had, as he knew, for some time considered the question of emigrating to Australia, the pig-jobbing business being a poor one nowadays. They had at last decided to go, and she proposed to go with them, if he had no objection. A woman of her sort would have more chance over there than in this stupid country.

Jude replied that he had not the least objection to her going. He thought it a wise course, since she wished to go, and one that might be to the advantage of both. He enclosed in the packet containing the letter the money that had been realized by the sale of the pig, with all he had besides, which was not much.

From that day he heard no more of her except indirectly, though her father and his household did not immediately leave, but waited till his goods and other effects had been sold off. When Jude learnt that there was to be an auction at the house of the Donns he packed his own household goods into a waggon, and sent them to her at the aforesaid homestead, that she might sell them with the rest, or as many of them as she should choose.

He then went into lodgings at Alfredston, and saw in a shop-window the little handbill announcing the sale of his father-in-law's furniture. He noted its date, which came and passed without Jude's going near the place, or perceiving that the traffic out of Alfredston by the southern road was materially increased by the auction. A few days later he entered a little broker's shop in the main street of the town, and amid a heterogeneous collection of saucepans, a clothes-horse, rolling pin, brass candlestick, swing looking-glass, and other things at the back of the shop, evidently just brought in from a sale, he perceived a little framed photograph, which turned out to be his own portrait.

It was one which he had had specially taken and framed by a local man in bird's-eye maple,[1] as a present for Arabella, and had duly given her on their wedding-day. On the back was still to be read, "*Jude to Arabella,*" with the date. She must have thrown it in with the rest of her property at the auction.

"Oh," said the broker, seeing him look at this and the other articles in the heap, and not perceiving that the portrait was of himself: "It is a small lot of stuff that was knocked down to me at a cottage sale out on the road to Marygreen. The frame is a very useful one, if you take out the likeness. You shall have it for a shilling."

The utter death of every tender sentiment in his wife, as brought home to him by this mute and undesigned evidence of her sale of his portrait and gift, was the conclusive little stroke required to demolish all sentiment in him. He paid the shilling, took the photograph away with him, and burnt it, frame and all, when he reached his lodging.

Two or three days later he heard that Arabella and her parents had departed. He had a sent a message offering to see her for a formal leave-taking, but she had said that it would be better otherwise, since she was bent on going, which perhaps was true. On the evening following their emigration, when his day's work was done, he came out of doors after supper, and strolled in the starlight along the too familiar road towards the upland whereon had been experienced the chief emotions of his life. It seemed to be his own again.

He could not realize himself. On the old track he seemed to be a boy still, hardly a day older than when he had stood dreaming at the top of that hill, inwardly fired for the first time with ardours for Christminster and scholarship. "Yet I am a man," he said. "I have a wife. More, I have arrived at the still riper stage of having disagreed with her, disliked her, had a scuffle with her, and parted from her."

He remembered then that he was standing not far from the spot at which the parting between his father and his mother was said to have occurred.

A little further on was the summit, whence Christminster, or what he had taken for that city, had seemed to be visible. A milestone, now, as always, stood at the roadside hard by. Jude drew near it, and felt

---

1   bird's eye maple] wood of the sugar-maple tree.

rather than read the mileage to the city. He remembered that once on his way home he had proudly cut with his keen new chisel an inscription on the back of that milestone, embodying his aspirations. It had been done in the first week of his apprenticeship, before he had been diverted from his purposes by an unsuitable woman. He wondered if the inscription were legible still, and going to the back of the milestone brushed away the nettles. By the light of a match he could still discern what he had cut so enthusiastically so long ago:

THITHER
J.F. ☞

The sight of it, unimpaired, within its screen of grass and nettles, lit in his soul a spark of the old fire. Surely his plan should be to move onward through good and ill – to avoid morbid sorrow even though he did see ugliness in the world? *Bene agere et lætari* – to do good cheerfully – which he had heard to be the philosophy of one Spinoza,[1] might be his own even now.

He might battle with his evil star, and follow out his original intention.

By moving to a spot a little way off he uncovered the horizon in a north-easterly direction. There actually rose the faint halo, a small dim nebulousness, hardly recognizable save by the eye of faith. It was enough for him. He would go to Christminster as soon as the term of his apprenticeship expired.

He returned to his lodgings in a better mood, and said his prayers.

---

1 *Bene.....*Spinoza] "the man of firm character.....strives his utmost.....to act well and to rejoice (*bene agere et lætari*)": Spinoza (1632–77): *Ethics*, Pt. IV.

PART SECOND

AT CHRISTMINSTER

"Save his own soul he hath no star." – SWINBURNE.[1]

"Notitiam primosque gradus vicinia fecit;
Tempore crevit amor." – OVID.[2]

AT CHRISTMINSTER

II.-I.

THE next noteworthy move in Jude's life was that in which he appeared gliding steadily onward through a dusky landscape of some three years' later leafage than had graced his courtship of Arabella, and the disruption of his coarse conjugal life with her. He was walking towards Christminster City, at a point a mile or two to the southwest.

He had at last found himself clear of Marygreen and Alfredston: he was out of his apprenticeship, and with his tools at his back seemed to be in the way of making a new start – the start to which, barring the interruption involved in his intimacy and married experience with Arabella, he had been looking forward for about ten years.

Jude would now have been described as a young man with a forcible, meditative, and earnest rather than handsome cast of countenance. He was of dark complexion, with dark harmonizing eyes, and he wore a closely trimmed black beard of more advanced growth than is usual at his age; this, with his great mass of black curly hair, was some trouble to him in combing and washing out the stone-dust that

---

1   *"Save.....*SWINBURNE.] The quotation is from the "Prelude" to Algernon Swinburne's *Songs before Sunrise* (1871).
2   *"Notitiam.....*OVID.] "Living so near, they came to know one another, and a friendship was begun; in time, love grew up between them." (Ovid: *Metamophoses*, Bk.4, lines 59-60, describing Pyramus and Thisbe, tragic lovers.)

settled on it in the pursuit of his trade. His capabilities in the latter, having been acquired in the country, were of an all-round sort, including monumental stone-cutting, gothic free-stone work for the restoration of churches, and carving of a general kind. In London he would probably have become specialized and have made himself a moulding mason, a "foliage sculptor" – perhaps a "statuary." [1]

He had that afternoon driven in a cart from Alfredston to the village nearest the city in this direction, and was now walking the remaining four miles rather from choice than from necessity, having always fancied himself arriving thus.

The ultimate impulse to come had had a curious origin – one more nearly related to the emotional side of him than to the intellectual, as is often the case with young men. One day while in lodgings at Alfredston he had gone to Marygreen to see his old aunt, and had observed between the brass candlesticks on her mantelpiece the photograph of a pretty girlish face, in a broad hat, with radiating folds under the brim like the rays of a halo. He had asked who she was. His grand-aunt had gruffly replied that she was his cousin Sue Bridehead, of the inimical branch of the family; and on further questioning the old woman had replied that the girl lived in Christminster, though she did not know where, or what she was doing.

His aunt would not give him the photograph. But it haunted him; and ultimately formed a quickening ingredient in his latent intent of following his friend the schoolmaster thither.

He now paused at the top of a crooked and gentle declivity, and obtained his first near view of the city. Grey stoned and dun-roofed, it stood within hail of the Wessex border, and almost with the tip of one small toe within it, at the northernmost point of the crinkled line along which the leisurely Thames strokes the fields of that ancient kingdom. The buildings now lay quiet in the sunset, a vane here and there on their many spires and domes giving sparkle to a picture of sober secondary and tertiary hues.

Reaching the bottom he moved along the level way between pollard willows growing indistinct in the twilight, and soon confronted the outmost lamps of the town – some of those lamps which had sent into the sky the gleam and glory that caught his strained gaze in his

---

1   a "statuary"] restorer or sculptor of statues.

days of dreaming, so many years ago. They winked their yellow eyes at him dubiously, and as if, though they had been awaiting him all these years, in disappointment at his tarrying, they did not much want him now.

He was a species of Dick Whittington, whose spirit was touched to finer issues than a mere material gain.[1] He went along the outlying streets with the cautious tread of an explorer. He saw nothing of the real city in the suburbs on this side. His first want being a lodging he scrutinized carefully such localities as seemed to offer on inexpensive terms the modest type of accommodation he demanded; and after inquiry took a room in a suburb nick-named "Beersheba,"[2] though he did not know this at the time. Here he installed himself, and having had some tea sallied forth.

It was a windy, whispering, moonless night. To guide himself he opened under a lamp a map he had brought. The breeze ruffled and fluttered it, but he could see enough to decide on the direction he should take to reach the heart of the place.

After many turnings he came up to the first ancient mediæval pile that he had encountered. It was a college, as he could see by the gateway. He entered it, walked round, and penetrated to dark corners which no lamplight reached. Close to this college was another; and a little further on another; and then he began to be encircled as it were with the breath and sentiment of the venerable city. When he passed objects out of harmony with its general expression he allowed his eyes to slip over them as if he did not see them.

A bell began clanging, and he listened till a hundred and one strokes had sounded. He must have made a mistake, he thought: it was meant for a hundred.[3]

When the gates were shut, and he could no longer get into the

---

1 Dick Whittington.....gain] Whittington (1358-1423) walked to London from Gloucestershire, reputedly believing that the streets of London were paved with gold. Returning disappointed, he was recalled (the legend says) by the city's bells. He became wealthy in commerce, was thrice made Lord Mayor, and was knighted.

2 Beersheba] corresponds to the district of Oxford called Jericho, between the Oxford Canal and Walton Street. (Beersheba is a town in Galilee mentioned variously in the Bible.)

3 hundred] "Great Tom", the bell of Christ Church College, regularly tolled (and still tolls) one hundred and one times between five minutes and ten minutes past nine o'clock each evening.

quadrangles, he rambled under the walls and doorways, feeling with his fingers the contours of their mouldings and carving. The minutes passed, fewer and fewer people were visible, and still he serpentined among the shadows, for had he not imagined these scenes through ten bygone years, and what mattered a night's rest for once? High against the black sky the flash of a lamp would show crocketed[1] pinnacles and indented battlements. Down obscure alleys, apparently never trodden now by the foot of man, and whose very existence seemed to be forgotten, there would jut into the path porticoes, oriels,[2] doorways of enriched and florid middle-age design, their extinct air being accentuated by the rottenness of the stones. It seemed impossible that modern thought could house itself in such decrepit and superseded chambers.

Knowing not a human being here, Jude began to be impressed with the isolation of his own personality, as with a self-spectre, the sensation being that of one who walked, but could not make himself seen or heard. He drew his breath pensively, and, seeming thus almost his own ghost, gave his thoughts to the other ghostly presences with which the nooks were haunted.

During the interval of preparation for this venture, since his wife and furniture's uncompromising disappearance into space, he had read and learnt almost all that could be read and learnt by one in his position, of the worthies who had spent their youth within these reverend walls, and whose souls had haunted them in their maturer age. Some of them, by the accidents of his reading, loomed out in his fancy disproportionately large by comparison with the rest. The brushing of the wind against the angles, buttresses, and door-jambs were as the passing of these only other inhabitants, the tappings of each ivy leaf on its neighbour were as the mutterings of their mournful souls, the shadows as their thin shapes in nervous movement, making him comrades in his solitude. In the gloom it was as if he ran against them without feeling their bodily frames.

The streets were now deserted, but on account of these things he could not go in. There were poets abroad, of early date and of late,

---

1   crocketed] ornamented (usually in the form of buds or curled leaves).
2   porticoes, oriels] covered entrances (often with pillars), bay windows (often supported by corbels).

from the friend and eulogist of Shakespeare down to him who has recently passed into silence, and that musical one of the tribe who is still among us.[1] Speculative philosophers passed along, not always with wrinkled foreheads and hoary hair as in framed portraits, but pink-faced, slim, and active as in youth; modern divines sheeted in their surplices, among whom the most real to Jude Fawley were the founders of the religious school called Tractarian; the well-known three, the enthusiast, the poet, and the formularist, the echoes of whose teachings had influenced him even in his obscure home.[2] A start of aversion appeared in his fancy to move them at sight of those other sons of the place, the form in the full-bottomed wig, statesman, rake, reasoner, and sceptic;[3] the smoothly shaven historian so ironically civil to Christianity;[4] with others of the same incredulous temper, who knew each quad as well as the faithful, and took equal freedom in haunting its cloisters.

He regarded the statesmen in their various types, men of firmer movement and less dreamy air; the scholar, the speaker, the plodder; the man whose mind grew with his growth in years, and the man whose mind contracted with the same.

The scientists and philologists followed on in his mind-sight in an odd impossible combination, men of meditative faces, lined foreheads, and weak-eyed as bats with constant research; then official characters – such men as Governor-Generals and Lord-Lieutenants, in whom he took little interest; Chief-Justices and Lord Chancellors, silent thin-lipped figures of whom he knew barely the names. A keener regard attached to the prelates, by reason of his own former hopes. Of them he had an ample band – some men of heart, others rather men of head; he who apologized for the Church in Latin; the

---

1   eulogist.....silenced..... among us] The "friend and eulogist" is Ben Jonson; the poet who has recently "passed into silence" is Robert Browning; and the poet "still among us" is Algernon Swinburne. (Browning was awarded an honorary fellowship by Balliol College and an honorary degree by Oxford University.)

2   three.....home] The three leaders of the Tractarian (or Oxford) Movement were J. H. Newman, John Keble, and Edward Pusey. In *Tracts for the Times*, they advocated a revival of "High Church" modes of Anglican worship.

3   sceptic] Lord Bolingbroke (1678-1751), who, in essays published in 1754, expressed his scepticism about revealed religion.

4   historian.....Christianity] Edward Gibbon (1737-94), author of *The History of the Decline and Fall of the Roman Empire*.

saintly author of the Evening Hymn; and near them the great itinerant preacher, hymn-writer, and zealot, shadowed like Jude by his matrimonial difficulties.[1]

Jude found himself speaking out loud, holding conversations with them, as it were, like an actor in a melodrama who apostrophizes the audience on the other side of the footlights; till he suddenly ceased with a start at his absurdity. Perhaps those incoherent words of the wanderer were heard within the walls by some student or thinker over his lamp; and he may have raised his head, and wondered what voice it was, and what it betokened. Jude now perceived that, so far as solid flesh went, he had the whole aged city to himself with the exception of a belated townsman here and there, and that he seemed to be catching a cold.

A voice reached him out of the shade; a real and local voice:

"You've been a-settin' a long time on that plinth-stone, young man. What med you be up to?"

It came from a policeman who had been observing Jude without the latter observing him.

Jude went home and to bed, after reading up a little about these men and their several messages to the world from a book or two that he had brought with him concerning the sons of the University. As he drew towards sleep various memorable words of theirs that he had just been conning seemed spoken by them in muttering utterances; some audible, some unintelligible to him. One of the spectres (who afterwards railed at Christminster as "the home of lost causes," though Jude did not remember this) was now apostrophizing her thus:

"Beautiful city! So valuable, so lovely, so unravaged by the fierce intellectual life of our century, so serene!... Her ineffable charm keeps ever calling us to the true goal of all of us, to the ideal, to perfection."[2]

Another voice was that of the Corn Law convert, whose phantom he had just seen in the quadrangle with the great bell. Jude thought his soul might have been shaping the historic words of his master-speech:

---

1   he who.....difficulties] Hardy said that he could not remember the identity of him "who apologized for the Church in Latin". The "saintly author" is Bishop Thomas Ken (1637-1711), whose evening hymn, "Glory to Thee, My God, This Night", will soon be quoted by Jude. The "great itinerant preacher" is John Wesley (1703-91).

2   "Beautiful.....perfection"] quoted (with small inaccuracies) from the preface to Matthew Arnold's *Essays in Criticism* (1865).

"Sir, I may be wrong, but my impression is that my duty towards a country threatened with famine requires that that which has been the ordinary remedy under all similar circumstances should be resorted to now, namely, that there should be free access to the food of man from whatever quarter it may come.... Deprive me of office to-morrow, you can never deprive me of the consciousness that I have exercised the powers committed to me from no corrupt or interested motives, from no desire to gratify ambition, for no personal gain."[1]

Then the sly author of the immortal Chapter on Christianity: "How shall we excuse the supine inattention of the Pagan and philosophic world, to those evidences [miracles] which were presented by Omnipotence? ... The sages of Greece and Rome turned aside from the awful spectacle, and appeared unconscious of any alterations in the moral or physical government of the world."[2]

Then the shade of the poet, the last of the optimists:

"How the world is made for each of us!

.   .   .   .   .

And each of the Many helps to recruit
The life of the race by a general plan."[3]

Then one of the three enthusiasts he had seen just now, the author of the *Apologia*:

"My argument was ... that absolute certitude as to the truths of natural theology was the result of an assemblage of concurring and converging probabilities...that probabilities which did not reach to logical certainty might create a mental certitude."[4]

The second of them, no polemic, murmured quieter things:

"Why should we faint, and fear to live alone,

1   "Sir.....gain"] from a speech delivered by Sir Robert Peel, then Prime Minister, on 15 May, 1846. (The wording differs slightly from that in *The Times*, 16 May 1846, p. 5.)

2   "How.....world"] quoted (inaccurately) from Chap. 15 of Gibbon's *Decline and Fall of the Roman Empire*.

3   "How.....plan"] from Robert Browning's "By the Fire-side."

4   "My.....certitude"] quoted (with variants) from Part 3 of Newman's *Apologia pro Vita Sua*.

Since all alone, so Heaven has will'd, we die?"[1]

He likewise heard some phrases spoken by the phantom with the short face, the genial Spectator:

"When I look upon the tombs of the great, every motion of envy dies in me; when I read the epitaphs of the beautiful, every inordinate desire goes out; when I meet with the grief of parents upon a tombstone, my heart melts with compassion; when I see the tombs of the parents themselves, I consider the vanity of grieving for those whom we must quickly follow."[2]

And lastly a gentle-voiced prelate spoke, during whose meek, familiar rhyme, endeared to him from earliest childhood, Jude fell asleep:

> "Teach me to live, that I may dread
> The grave as little as my bed.
> Teach me to die ..."[3]

He did not wake till morning. The ghostly past seemed to have gone, and everything spoke of to-day. He started up in bed, thinking he had overslept himself, and then said:

"By Jove – I had quite forgotten my sweet-faced cousin, and that she's here all the time!...and my old schoolmaster, too." His words about his schoolmaster had, perhaps, less zest in them than his words concerning his cousin.

II.-II.

Necessary meditations on the actual, including the mean bread-and-cheese question, dissipated the phantasmal for a while, and compelled Jude to smother high thinkings under immediate needs. He had to get up, and seek for work, manual work; the only kind deemed

---

1 "Why......die?"] from "Twenty-fourth Sunday after Trinity" in John Keble's popular collection of religious poetry, *The Christian Year* (1827).

2 "When.....follow"] quoted (with minor inaccuracies) from Joseph Addison's *Spectator* 26 (30 March 1711).

3 "Teach.....die ..."] from the "Evening Hymn" of Bishop Ken.

by many of its professors to be work at all.

Passing out into the streets on this errand he found that the colleges had treacherously changed their sympathetic countenances: some were stern; some had put on the look of family vaults above ground; something barbaric loomed in the masonries of all. The spirits of the great men had disappeared.

The numberless architectural pages around him he read, naturally, less as an artist-critic of their forms than as an artizan and comrade of the dead handicraftsmen whose muscles had actually executed those forms. He examined the mouldings, stroked them as one who knew their beginning, said they were difficult or easy in the working, had taken little or much time, were trying to the arm, or convenient to the tool.

What at night had been perfect and ideal was by day the more or less defective real. Cruelties, insults, had, he perceived, been inflicted on the aged erections. The condition of several moved him as he would have been moved by maimed sentient beings. They were wounded, broken, sloughing off their outer shape in the deadly struggle against years, weather, and man.

The rottenness of these historical documents reminded him that he was not, after all, hastening on to begin the morning practically as he had intended. He had come to work, and to live by work, and the morning had nearly gone. It was, in one sense, encouraging to think that in a place of crumbling stones there must be plenty for one of his trade to do in the business of renovation. He asked his way to the work-yard of the stone-cutter whose name had been given him at Alfredston; and soon heard the familiar sound of the rubbers[1] and chisels.

The yard was a little centre of regeneration. Here, with keen edges and smooth curves, were forms in the exact likeness of those he had seen abraded and time-eaten on the walls. These were the ideas in modern prose which the lichened colleges presented in old poetry. Even some of those antiques might have been called prose when they were new. They had done nothing but wait, and had become poetical. How easy to the smallest building; how impossible to most men.

---

1 rubbers] grit-stone implements used to smooth a surface.

He asked for the foreman, and looked round among the new traceries, mullions, transoms,[1] shafts, pinnacles, and battlements standing on the bankers[2] half worked, or waiting to be removed. They were marked by precision, mathematical straightness, smoothness, exactitude: there in the old walls were the broken lines of the original idea; jagged curves, disdain of precision, irregularity, disarray.

For a moment there fell on Jude a true illumination; that here in the stone yard was a centre of effort as worthy as that dignified by the name of scholarly study within the noblest of the colleges. But he lost it under stress of his old idea. He would accept any employment which might be offered him on the strength of his late employer's recommendation; but he would accept it as a provisional thing only. This was his form of the modern vice of unrest.

Moreover he perceived that at best only copying, patching and imitating went on here; which he fancied to be owing to some temporary and local cause. He did not at that time see that mediævalism was as dead as a fern-leaf in a lump of coal; that other developments were shaping in the world around him, in which Gothic architecture and its associations had no place. The deadly animosity of contemporary logic and vision towards so much of what he held in reverence was not yet revealed.

Having failed to obtain work here as yet he went away, and thought again of his cousin, whose presence somewhere at hand he seemed to feel in wavelets of interest, if not of emotion. How he wished he had that pretty portrait of her! At last he wrote to his aunt to send it. She did so, with a request, however, that he was not to bring disturbance into the family by going to see the girl or her relations. Jude, a ridiculously affectionate fellow, promised nothing, put the photograph on the mantelpiece, kissed it – he did not know why – and felt more at home. She seemed to look down and preside over his tea. It was cheering – the one thing uniting him to the emotions of the living city.

There remained the schoolmaster – probably now a reverend parson. But he could not possibly hunt up such a respectable man just

---

1 traceries, mullions, transoms] traceries: lengths of decorative stonework; mullions: upright divisions between the lights of windows; transoms: crosspieces dividing windows horizontally.
2 bankers] stone benches.

yet; so raw and unpolished was his condition, so precarious were his fortunes. Thus he still remained in loneliness. Although people moved round him he virtually saw none. Not as yet having mingled with the active life of the place it was largely non-existent to him. But the saints and prophets in the window-tracery, the paintings in the galleries, the statues, the busts, the gurgoyles, the corbel-heads[1] – these seemed to breathe his atmosphere. Like all new comers to a spot on which the past is deeply graven he heard that past announcing itself with an emphasis altogether unsuspected by, and even incredible to, the habitual residents.

For many days he haunted the cloisters and quadrangles of the colleges at odd minutes in passing them, surprised by impish echoes of his own footsteps, smart as the blows of a mallet. The Christminster "sentiment," as it had been called, ate further and further into him; till he probably knew more about those buildings materially, artistically, and historically, than any one of their inmates.

It was not till now, when he found himself actually on the spot of his enthusiasm, that Jude perceived how far away from the object of that enthusiasm he really was. Only a wall divided him from those happy young contemporaries of his with whom he shared a common mental life; men who had nothing to do from morning till night but to read, mark, learn, and inwardly digest.[2] Only a wall – but what a wall!

Every day, every hour, as he went in search of labour, he saw them going and coming also, rubbed shoulders with them, heard their voices, marked their movements. The conversation of some of the more thoughtful among them seemed oftentimes, owing to his long and persistent preparation for this place, to be peculiarly akin to his own thoughts. Yet he was as far from them as if he had been at the antipodes. Of course he was. He was a young workman in a white blouse, and with stone-dust in the creases of his clothes; and in passing him they did not even see him, or hear him, rather saw through him as through a pane of glass at their familiars beyond. Whatever they

---

1   the gurgoyles, the corbel-heads] gurgoyles or gargoyles are projecting spouts, often
     sculpted to resemble faces; corbels are weight-bearing projections from a wall,
     sometimes sculpted to resemble heads.
2   read.....digest] from the Collect for the second Sunday in Advent (in the *Book of
     Common Prayer*).

were to him, he to them was not on the spot at all; and yet he had fancied he would be close to their lives by coming there.

But the future lay ahead after all; and if he could only be so fortunate as to get into good employment he would put up with the inevitable. So he thanked God for his health and strength, and took courage. For the present he was outside the gates of everything, colleges included: perhaps some day he would be inside those palaces of light and leading; he might some day look down on the world through their panes.

At length he did receive a message from the stone-mason's yard – that a job was waiting for him. It was his first encouragement, and he closed with the offer promptly.

He was young and strong, or he never could have executed with such zest the undertakings to which he now applied himself, since they involved reading most of the night after working all the day. First he bought a shaded lamp for four and sixpence, and obtained a good light. Then he got pens, paper, and such other necessary books as he had been unable to obtain elsewhere. Then, to the consternation of his landlady, he shifted all the furniture of his room – a single one for living and sleeping – rigged up a curtain on a rope across the middle, to make a double chamber out of one, hung up a thick blind that nobody should know how he was curtailing the hours of sleep, laid out his books, and sat down.

Having been deeply encumbered by marrying, getting a cottage, and buying the furniture which had disappeared in the wake of his wife, he had never been able to save any money since the time of those disastrous ventures, and till his wages began to come in he was obliged to live in the narrowest way. After buying a book or two he could not even afford himself a fire; and when the nights reeked with the raw and cold air from the Meadows he sat over his lamp in a great-coat, hat, and woollen gloves.

From his window he could perceive the spire of the Cathedral, and the ogee dome under which resounded the great bell of the city.[1] The tall tower, tall belfry windows, and tall pinnacles of the college by the bridge[2] he could also get a glimpse of by going to the staircase.

---

1 Cathedral.....ogee dome.....city] The Cathedral corresponds to Christ Church Cathedral; "ogee" means "with an S-shaped double curve"; the bell is "Great Tom".
2 the college by the bridge] Magdalen (pronounced "Maudlin").

These objects he used as stimulants when his faith in the future was dim.

Like enthusiasts in general he made no inquiries into details of procedure. Picking up general notions from casual acquaintance, he never dwelt upon them. For the present, he said to himself, the one thing necessary was to get ready by accumulating money and knowledge, and await whatever chances were afforded to such an one of becoming a son of the University. "For wisdom is a defence, and money is a defence; but the excellency of knowledge is, that wisdom giveth life to them that have it."[1] His desire absorbed him, and left no part of him to weigh its practicability.

At this time he received a nervously anxious letter from his poor old aunt, on the subject which had previously distressed her – a fear that Jude would not be strong-minded enough to keep away from his cousin Sue Bridehead and her relations. Sue's parents, his aunt believed, had gone to London, but the girl remained at Christminster. To make her still more objectionable she was an artist or designer of some sort in what was called an ecclesiastical warehouse, which was a perfect seed-bed of idolatry, and she was no doubt abandoned to mummeries[2] on that account – if not quite a Papist.[3] (Miss Drusilla Fawley was of her date, Evangelical.)[4]

As Jude was rather on an intellectual track than a theological, this news of Sue's probable opinions did not much influence him one way or the other, but the clue to her whereabouts was decidedly interesting. With an altogether singular pleasure he walked at his earliest spare minutes past the shops answering to his great-aunt's description; and beheld in one of them a young girl sitting behind a desk, who was suspiciously like the original of the portrait. He ventured to enter on a trivial errand, and having made his purchase lingered on the scene. The shop seemed to be kept entirely by women. It contained Anglican books, stationery, texts, and fancy goods: little plaster angels on brackets, Gothic-framed pictures of saints, ebony crosses that were

---

1 "For wisdom.....it"] Ecclesiastes 7:12.
2 mummeries] foolish performances.
3 Papist] (derogatory term for:) Roman Catholic.
4 Evangelical] The Evangelical movement, very influential in the period 1800-1870, emphasised the importance of intensely personal Christian commitment, particularly an ardent faith in Christ as Redeemer.

almost crucifixes, prayer-books that were almost missals.[1] He felt very shy of looking at the girl in the desk; she was so pretty that he could not believe it possible that she should belong to him. Then she spoke to one of the two older women behind the counter; and he recognized in the accents certain qualities of his own voice; softened and sweetened, but his own. What was she doing? He stole a glance round. Before her lay a piece of zinc, cut to the shape of a scroll three or four feet long, and coated with a dead-surface paint on one side. Hereon she was designing or illuminating, in characters of Church text, the single word

𝕬𝕷𝕷𝕰𝕷𝖀𝕵𝕬[2]

"A sweet, saintly, Christian business, hers!" thought he.

Her presence here was now fairly enough explained, her skill in work of this sort having no doubt been acquired from her father's occupation as an ecclesiastical worker in metal. The lettering on which she was engaged was clearly intended to be fixed up in some chancel to assist devotion.

He came out. It would have been easy to speak to her there and then, but it seemed scarcely honourable towards his aunt to disregard her request so incontinently. She had used him roughly, but she had brought him up: and the fact of her being powerless to control him lent a pathetic force to a wish that would have been inoperative as an argument.

So Jude gave no sign. He would not call upon Sue just yet. He had other reasons against doing so when he had walked away. She seemed so dainty beside himself in his rough working-jacket and dusty trousers that he felt he was as yet unready to encounter her, as he had felt about Mr. Phillotson. And how possible it was that she had inherited the antipathies of her family, and would scorn him, as far as a Christian could, particularly when he had told her that unpleasant part of his history which had resulted in his becoming enchained to one of her own sex whom she would certainly not admire.

---

1 missals] books containing the prayers and rites for the Roman Catholic Masses throughout the year.
2 𝕬𝕷𝕷𝕰𝕷𝖀𝕵𝕬] (Hebrew:) "Praise Yah" (Praise God).

Thus he kept watch over her, and liked to feel she was there. The consciousness of her living presence stimulated him. But she remained more or less an ideal character, about whose form he began to weave curious and fantastic day-dreams.

Between two and three weeks afterwards Jude was engaged with some more men, outside Crozier College in Old-time Street,[1] in getting a block of worked freestone from a waggon across the pavement, before hoisting it to the parapet which they were repairing. Standing in position the head man said, "Spaik[2] when ye heave! He-ho!" And they heaved.

All of a sudden, as he lifted, his cousin stood close to his elbow, pausing a moment on the bend of her foot till the obstructing object should have been removed. She looked right into his face with liquid, untranslatable eyes, that combined, or seemed to him to combine, keenness with tenderness, and mystery with both, their expression, as well as that of her lips, taking its life from some words just spoken to a companion, and being carried on into his face quite unconsciously. She no more observed his presence than that of the dust-motes which his manipulations raised into the sunbeams.

His closeness to her was so suggestive that he trembled, and turned his face away with a shy instinct to prevent her recognizing him, though as she had never once seen him she could not possibly do so; and might very well never have heard even his name. He could perceive that though she was a country-girl at bottom, a latter girlhood of some years in London, and a womanhood here, had taken all rawness out of her.

When she was gone he continued his work, reflecting on her. He had been so caught by her influence that he had taken no count of her general mould and build. He remembered now that she was not a large figure, that she was light and slight, of the type dubbed elegant. That was about all he had seen. There was nothing statuesque in her; all was nervous motion. She was mobile, living, yet a painter might not have called her handsome or beautiful. But the much that she was surprised him. She was quite a long way removed from the rusticity that was his. How could one of his cross-grained, unfortunate,

---

1 Crozier College in Old-time Street] probably Oriel College in Oriel Lane.
2 spaik] (dl.:) speak, yell.

almost accursed stock, have contrived to reach this pitch of niceness? London had done it, he supposed.

From this moment the emotion which had been accumulating in his breast as the bottled-up effect of solitude and the poetized locality he dwelt in, insensibly began to precipitate itself on this half-visionary form; and he perceived that, whatever his obedient wish in a contrary direction, he would soon be unable to resist the desire to make himself known to her.

He affected to think of her quite in a family way, since there were crushing reasons why he should not and could not think of her in any other.

The first reason was that he was married, and it would be wrong. The second was that they were cousins. It was not well for cousins to fall in love, even when circumstances seemed to favour the passion. The third: even were he free, in a family like his own where marriage usually meant a tragic sadness, marriage with a blood-relation would duplicate the adverse conditions, and a tragic sadness might be intensified to a tragic horror.

Therefore, again, he would have to think of Sue with only a relation's mutual interest in one belonging to him; regard her in a practical way as some one to be proud of; to talk and nod to; later on, to be invited to tea by, the emotion spent on her being rigorously that of a kinsman and well-wisher. So would she be to him a kindly star, an elevating power, a companion in Anglican worship, a tender friend.

II.-III.

BUT under the various deterrent influences Jude's instinct was to approach her timidly, and the next Sunday he went to the morning service in the Cathedral-church of Cardinal College to gain a further view of her, for he had found that she frequently attended there.

She did not come, and he awaited her in the afternoon, which was finer. He knew that if she came at all she would approach the building along the eastern side of the great green quadrangle from which it was accessible, and he stood in a corner while the bell was going. A few minutes before the hour for service she appeared as one of the figures walking along under the College walls, and at sight of her he advanced up the side opposite, and followed her into the building, more than ever glad that he had not as yet revealed himself. To see her, and to be himself unseen and unknown, was enough for him at present.

He lingered awhile in the vestibule, and the service was some way advanced when he was put into a seat. It was a louring, mournful, still afternoon, when a religion of some sort seems a necessity to ordinary practical men, and not only a luxury of the emotional and leisured classes. In the dim light and the baffling glare of the clerestory[1] windows, he could discern the opposite worshippers indistinctly only, but he saw that Sue was among them. He had not long discovered the exact seat that she occupied when the chanting of the 119th Psalm in which the choir was engaged reached its second part, *In quo corriget*,[2] the organ changing to a pathetic Gregorian[3] tune as the singers gave forth:

"Wherewithal shall a young man cleanse his way?"

It was the very question that was engaging Jude's attention at this moment. What a wicked worthless fellow he had been to give vent as he had done to an animal passion for a woman, and allow it to lead to such disastrous consequences; then to think of putting an end to himself; then to go recklessly and get drunk. The great waves of pedal music tumbled round the choir, and, nursed on the supernatural as he had been, it is not wonderful that he could hardly believe that the psalm was not specially set by some regardful Providence for this moment of his first entry into the solemn building. And yet it was the ordinary psalm for the twenty-fourth evening of the month.

The girl for whom he was beginning to nourish an extraordinary tenderness, was at this time ensphered by the same harmonies as those which floated into his ears; and the thought was a delight to him. She was probably a frequenter of this place, and, steeped body and soul in church sentiment as she must be by occupation and habit, had, no doubt, much in common with him. To an impressionable and lonely

---

1   clerestory] long wall with windows, above the level of the aisle roof.
2   *In quo corriget*] opening phrase of the Latin version of Psalm 119:9.
3   Gregorian] mediæval style of religious singing.

young man the consciousness of having at last found anchorage for his thoughts, which promised to supply both social and spiritual possibilities, was like the dew of Hermon,[1] and he remained throughout the service in a sustaining atmosphere of ecstasy.

Though he was loth to suspect it, some people might have said to him that the atmosphere blew as distinctly from Cyprus as from Galilee.[2]

Jude waited till she had left her seat and passed under the screen before he himself moved. She did not look towards him, and by the time he reached the door she was half way down the broad path. Being dressed up in his Sunday suit he was inclined to follow her and reveal himself. But he was not quite ready; and, alas, ought he to do so with the kind of feeling that was awakening in him?

For though it had seemed to have an ecclesiastical basis during the service, and he had persuaded himself that such was the case, he could not altogether be blind to the real nature of the magnetism. She was such a stranger that the kinship was affectation, and he said, "It can't be! I, a man with a wife, must not know her!" Still Sue *was* his own kin, and the fact of his having a wife, even though she was not in evidence in this hemisphere, might be a help in one sense. It would put all thought of a tender wish on his part out of Sue's mind, and make her intercourse with him free and fearless. It was with some heartache that he saw how little he cared for the freedom and fearlessness that would result in her from such knowledge.

Some little time before the date of this service in the cathedral the pretty, liquid-eyed, light-footed young woman Sue Bridehead had an afternoon's holiday, and leaving the ecclesiastical establishment in which she not only assisted but lodged, took a walk into the country with a book in her hand. It was one of those cloudless days which sometimes occur in Wessex and elsewhere between days of cold and wet, as if intercalated[3] by caprice of the weather-god. She went along for a mile or two until she came to much higher ground than that of the city she had left behind her. The road passed between green fields,

---

1   dew of Hermon] mountain-dew representing God's blessing (Psalm 133:3).
2   Cyprus.....Galilee] Aphrodite, the Greek goddess of love, emerged from the sea on the coast of Cyprus; the Sea of Galilee was the early location of Jesus's activities.
3   intercalated] inserted in the calendar.

and coming to a stile Sue paused there, to finish the page she was reading, and then looked back at the towers and domes and pinnacles new and old.

On the other side of the stile, in the footpath, she beheld a foreigner with black hair and a sallow face, sitting on the grass beside a large square board whereon were fixed, as closely as they could stand, a number of plaster statuettes, some of them bronzed, which he was re-arranging before proceeding with them on his way. They were in the main reduced copies of ancient marbles, and comprised divinities of a very different character from those the girl was accustomed to see portrayed, among them being a Venus of standard pattern, a Diana, and, of the other sex, Apollo, Bacchus, and Mars. Though the figures were many yards away from her the south-west sun brought them out so brilliantly against the green herbage that she could discern their contours with luminous distinctness; and being almost in a line between herself and the church towers of the city they awoke in her an oddly foreign and contrasting set of ideas by comparison. The man rose, and, seeing her, politely took off his cap, and cried "I-i-i-mages!" in an accent that agreed with his appearance. In a moment he dexterously lifted upon his knee the great board with its assembled notabilities divine and human, and raised it to the top of his head, bringing them on to her and resting the board on the stile. First he offered her his smaller wares – the busts of kings and queens, then a minstrel, then a winged Cupid. She shook her head.

"How much are these two?" she said, touching with her finger the Venus and the Apollo – the largest figures on the tray.

He said she should have them for ten shillings.

"I cannot afford that," said Sue. She offered considerably less, and to her surprise the image-man drew them from their wire stay and handed them over the stile. She clasped them as treasures.

When they were paid for, and the man had gone, she began to be concerned as to what she should do with them. They seemed so very large now that they were in her possession, and so very naked. Being of a nervous temperament she trembled at her enterprise. When she handled them the white pipeclay came off on her gloves and jacket. After carrying them along a little way openly an idea came to her, and, pulling some huge burdock leaves, parsley, and other rank growths from the hedge, she wrapped up her burden as well as she could in these, so that what she carried appeared to be an enormous armful of green stuff, gathered by a zealous lover of nature.

"Well, anything is better than those everlasting church fal-lals!"[1] she said. But she was still in a trembling state, and seemed almost to wish she had not bought the figures.

Occasionally peeping inside the leaves to see that Venus's arm was not broken, she entered with her heathen load into the most Christian city in the country by an obscure street running parallel to the main one, and round a corner to the side door of the establishment to which she was attached. Her purchases were taken straight up to her own chamber, and she at once attempted to lock them in a box that was her very own property; but finding them too cumbersome she wrapped them in large sheets of brown paper, and stood them on the floor in a corner.

The mistress of the house, Miss Fontover, was an elderly lady in spectacles, dressed almost like an abbess; a dab at Ritual,[2] as became one of her business, and a worshipper at the ceremonial church of St. Silas,[3] in the suburb of Beersheba before-mentioned, which Jude also had begun to attend. She was the daughter of a clergyman in reduced circumstances, and at his death, which had occurred several years before this date, she boldly avoided penury by taking over a little shop of church requisites and developing it to its present creditable proportions. She wore a cross and beads round her neck as her only ornament, and knew the Christian Year[4] by heart.

She now came to call Sue to tea, and, finding that the girl did not respond for a moment, entered the room just as the other was hastily putting a string round each parcel.

"Something you have been buying, Miss Bridehead?" she asked, regarding the enwrapped objects.

"Yes – just something to ornament my room," said Sue.

"Well, I should have thought I had put enough here already," said Miss Fontover, looking round at the Gothic-framed prints of saints,

---

1 fal-lals] showy but trivial ornaments.
2 dab at Ritual] (coll.:) expert in High Church modes of worship.
3 church of St. Silas] St Barnabas' Church, off Canal Street, in the Jericho district, was consecrated in 1869 and was soon noted for its High Church rituals (which were elaborately ceremonial). The architect was Sir Arthur Blomfield, who had employed Hardy between 1862 and 1867.
4 Christian Year] Keble's volume.

the Church-text scrolls, and other articles which, having become too stale to sell, had been used to furnish this obscure chamber. "What is it? How bulky!" She tore a little hole, about as big as a wafer, in the brown paper, and tried to peep in. "Why, statuary? Two figures? Where did you get them?"

"O – I bought them of a travelling man who sells casts ——"

"Two saints?"

"Yes."

"What ones?"

"St. Peter and St. – St. Mary Magdalen."

"Well – now come down to tea, and go and finish that organ-text, if there's light enough afterwards."

These little obstacles to the indulgence of what had been the merest passing fancy, created in Sue a great zest for unpacking her objects and looking at them; and at bedtime, when she was sure of being undisturbed, she unrobed the divinities in comfort. Placing the pair of figures on the chest of drawers, a candle on each side of them, she withdrew to the bed, flung herself down thereon, and began reading a book she had taken from her box, which Miss Fontover knew nothing of. It was a volume of Gibbon, and she read the chapter dealing with the reign of Julian the Apostate.[1] Occasionally she looked up at the statuettes, which appeared strange and out of place amid the other objects and pictures in the room, and, as if the scene suggested the action, she at length jumped up and withdrew another book from her box – a volume of verse – and turned to the familiar poem –

"Thou has conquered, O pale Galilean:
The world has grown grey from thy breath!"[2]

which she read to the end. Presently she put out the candles, undressed, and finally extinguished her own light.

---

1   chapter.....Apostate] Chap. 23 of Gibbon's *Decline and Fall of the Roman Empire* tells how the Roman emperor Flavius Claudius Julianus renounced Christianity in 361 A.D. and reinstated worship of the classical deities.

2   "Thou..... breath!"] from Swinburne's scandalous "Hymn to Proserpine" (see Appendix E). The "pale Galilean" is Jesus. On his deathbed, Julian the Apostate is supposed to have said: "Vicisti Galilæe" ("Thou hast conquered, O Galilean").

She was of an age which usually sleeps soundly, yet to-night she kept waking up, and every time she opened her eyes there was enough diffused light from the window to show her the white plaster figures, standing on the chest of drawers in odd contrast to their environment of text and martyr, and the Gothic-framed symbol-picture of what was only discernible now as a Latin cross, the figure thereon being obscured by the shades.

On one of these occasions the church clocks struck some small hour. It fell upon the ears of another person who sat bending over his books at a not very distant spot in the same city. Being Saturday night the morrow was one on which Jude had not set his alarm-clock to call him at his usually early time, and hence he had stayed up, as was his custom, two or three hours later than he could afford to do on any other day of the week. Just then he was earnestly reading from his Griesbach's text. At the very time that Sue was reading, the policeman and belated citizens passing along under his window might have heard, if they had stood still, strange syllables mumbled with fervour within – words that had for Jude an indescribable enchantment: inexplicable sounds something like these: –

"All hemin eis Theos ho Pater, ex ou ta panta, kai hemeis eis auton:"

Till the sounds rolled with reverent loudness, as a book was heard to close: –

"Kai eis Kurios Iesous Christos, di ou ta panta kai hemeis di autou!"[1]

II.-IV.

HE was a handy man at his trade, an all-round man, as artizans in country-towns are apt to be. In London the man who carves the boss[2] or knob of leafage declines to cut the fragment of moulding which

---

1 "All hemin....di autou!"] from the Greek New Testament. "But to us *there is but one* God, the Father, of whom *are* all things, and we in him; and one Lord Jesus Christ, by whom *are* all things, and we by him." (I Corinthians 8: 6.) For the 1903 edition, Hardy corrected his transliteration of the Greek, so that "eis Theos," "ex ou," "eis Kurios," and "di ou" became "heis Theos," "ex hou," "heis Kurios," and "di hou."

2 boss] knob.

merges in that leafage, as if it were a degradation to do the second half of one whole. When there was not much Gothic moulding for Jude to run,[1] or much window-tracery on the bankers, he would go out lettering monuments or tombstones, and take a pleasure in the change of handiwork.

The next time that he saw her was when he was on a ladder executing a job of this sort inside one of the churches. There was a short morning service, and when the parson entered Jude came down from his ladder, and sat with the half-dozen people forming the congregation, till the prayers should be ended, and he could resume his tapping. He did not observe till the service was half over that one of the women was Sue, who had accompanied the elderly Miss Fontover thither.

Jude sat watching her pretty shoulders, her easy, curiously nonchalant, risings and sittings, and her perfunctory genuflexions,[2] and thought what a help such an Anglican would have been to him in happier circumstances. It was not so much his anxiety to get on with his work that made him go up to it immediately the worshippers began to take their leave: it was that he dared not, in this holy spot, confront the woman who was beginning to influence him in such an indescribable manner. Those three enormous reasons why he must not attempt intimate acquaintance with Sue Bridehead now that his interest in her had shown itself to be unmistakably of a sexual kind, - loomed as stubbornly as ever. But it was also obvious that man could not live by work alone; that the particular man Jude, at any rate, wanted something to love. Some men would have rushed incontinently to her, snatched the pleasure of easy friendship which she could hardly refuse, and have left the rest to chance. Not so Jude – at first.

But as the days, and still more particularly the lonely evenings, dragged along, he found himself, to his moral consternation, to be thinking more of her instead of thinking less of her, and experiencing a fearful bliss in doing what was erratic, informal, and unexpected. Surrounded by her influence all day, walking past the spots she frequented, he was always thinking of her, and was obliged to own to himself that his conscience was likely to be the loser in this battle.

---

1 run] mark out and carve.
2 genuflexions] ritualistic knee-bendings.

To be sure she was almost an ideality to him still. Perhaps to know her would be to cure himself of this unexpected and unauthorized passion. A voice whispered that, though he desired to know her, he did not desire to be cured.

There was not the least doubt that from his own orthodox point of view the situation was growing immoral. For Sue to be the loved one of a man who was licensed by the laws of his country to love Arabella and none other unto his life's end, was a pretty bad second beginning, when the man was bent on such a course as Jude purposed. This conviction was so real with him that one day when, as was frequent, he was at work in a neighbouring village church alone, he felt it to be his duty to pray against his weakness. But much as he wished to be an exemplar in these things he could not get on. It was quite impossible, he found, to ask to be delivered from temptation when your heart's desire was to be tempted unto seventy times seven.[1] So he excused himself. "After all," he said, "it is not altogether an *erotolepsy*[2] that is the matter with me, as at that first time. I can see that she is exceptionally bright; and it is partly a wish for intellectual sympathy, and a craving for loving-kindness in my solitude." Thus he went on adoring her, fearing to realize that it was human perversity. For whatever Sue's virtues, talents, or ecclesiastical saturation, it was certain that those items were not at all the cause of his affection for her.

On an afternoon at this time a young girl entered the stone-mason's yard with some hesitation, and, lifting her skirts to avoid draggling them in the white dust, crossed towards the office.

"That's a nice girl," said one of the men known as Uncle Joe.

"Who is she?" asked another.

"I don't know — I've seen her about here and there. Why, yes, she's the daughter of that clever chap Bridehead who did all the wrought ironwork at St. Luke's ten years ago, and went away to London afterwards. I don't know what he's doing now — not much I fancy — as she's come back here."

Meanwhile the young woman had knocked at the office door and asked if Mr. Jude Fawley was at work in the yard. It so happened that

---

1   seventy times seven] Matthew 18:22.
2   *erotolepsy*] seizure by sexual desire.

Jude had gone out somewhere or other that afternoon, which information she received with a look of disappointment, and went away immediately. When Jude returned they told him, and described her, whereupon he exclaimed, "Why – that's my cousin Sue!"

He looked along the street after her, but she was out of sight. He had no longer any thought of a conscientious avoidance of her, and resolved to call upon her that very evening. And when he reached his lodging he found a note from her – a first note – one of those documents which, simple and commonplace in themselves, are seen retrospectively to have been pregnant with impassioned consequences. The very unconsciousness of a looming drama which is shown in such innocent first epistles from women to men, or *vice versâ,* makes them, when such a drama follows, and they are read over by the purple or lurid light of it, all the more impressive, solemn, and in cases, terrible.

Sue's was of the most artless and natural kind. She addressed him as her dear cousin Jude; said she had only just learnt by the merest accident that he was living in Christminster, and reproached him with not letting her know. They might have had such nice times together, she said, for she was thrown much upon herself, and had hardly any congenial friend. But now there was every probability of her soon going away, so that the chance of companionship would be lost perhaps for ever.

A cold sweat overspread Jude at the news that she was going away. That was a contingency he had never thought of, and it spurred him to write all the more quickly to her. He would meet her that very evening, he said, one hour from the time of writing, at the cross in the pavement which marked the spot of the martyrdoms.[1]

When he had despatched the note by a boy he regretted that in his hurry he should have suggested to her to meet him out of doors, when he might have said he would call upon her. It was, in fact, the country custom to meet thus, and nothing else had occurred to him. Arabella had been met in the same way, unfortunately, and it might not seem respectable to a dear girl like Sue. However, it could not be

---

1 cross.....martyrdoms] The horizontal cross-pattern can still be seen in the middle of Broad Street outside Balliol College. The martyrdoms were those of the Protestant Bishops Ridley and Latimer (burnt in 1555) and Archbishop Cranmer (burnt in 1556).

helped now, and he moved towards the point a few minutes before the hour, under the glimmer of the newly lighted lamps.

The broad street was silent, and almost deserted, although it was not late. He saw a figure on the other side, which turned out to be hers, and they both converged towards the cross-mark at the same moment. Before either had reached it she called out to him:

"I am not going to meet you just there, for the first time in my life! Come further on."

The voice, though positive and silvery, had been tremulous. They walked on in parallel lines, and, waiting her pleasure, Jude watched till she showed signs of closing in, when he did likewise, the place being where the carriers' carts stood in the daytime, though there were none on the spot then.

"I am sorry that I asked you to meet me, and didn't call," began Jude with the bashfulness of a lover. "But I thought it would save time if we were going to walk."

"O – I don't mind that," she said with the freedom of a friend. "I have really no place to ask anybody in to. What I meant was that the place you chose was so horrid – I suppose I ought not to say horrid, – I mean gloomy and inauspicious.... But isn't it funny to begin like this, when I don't know you yet?" She looked him up and down curiously, though Jude did not look much at her.

"You seem to know me more than I know you," she added.

"Yes – I have seen you now and then."

"And you knew who I was, and didn't speak? And now I am going away!"

"Yes. That's unfortunate. I have hardly any other friend. I have, indeed, one very old friend here somewhere, but I don't quite like to call on him just yet. I wonder if you know anything of him – Mr. Phillotson? A parson somewhere about the county I think he is."

"No – I only know of one Mr. Phillotson. He lives a little way out in the country, at Lumsdon. He's a village schoolmaster."

"Ah! I wonder if he's the same. Surely it is impossible! Only a schoolmaster still! Do you know his Christian name – is it Richard?"

"Yes – it is; I've directed books to him, though I've never seen him."

"Then he couldn't do it!"

Jude's countenance fell, for how could he succeed in an enterprise wherein the great Phillotson had failed? He would have had a day of despair if the news had not arrived during his sweet Sue's presence, but even at this moment he had visions of how Phillotson's failure in the grand University scheme would depress him when she had gone.

"As we are going to take a walk, suppose we go and call upon him?" said Jude suddenly. "It is not late."

She agreed, and they went along up a hill, and through some prettily wooded country. Presently the embattled tower and square turret of the church rose into the sky, and then the schoolhouse. They inquired of a person in the street if Mr. Phillotson was likely to be at home, and were informed that he was always at home. A knock brought him to the schoolhouse door, with a candle in his hand, and a look of inquiry on his face, which had grown thin and careworn since Jude last set eyes on him.

That after all these years the meeting with Mr. Phillotson should be of this homely complexion destroyed at one stoke the halo which had surrounded the schoolmaster's figure in Jude's imagination ever since their parting. It created in him at the same time a sympathy with Phillotson as an obviously much chastened and disappointed man. Jude told him his name, and said he had come to see him as an old friend who had been kind to him in his youthful days.

"I don't remember you in the least," said the schoolmaster thoughtfully. "You were one of my pupils you say? Yes, no doubt; but they number so many thousands at this time of my life, and have naturally changed so much, that I remember very few except the quite recent ones."

"It was out at Marygreen," said Jude, wishing he had not come.

"Yes. I was there a short time. And is this an old pupil, too?"

"No – that's my cousin.... I wrote to you for some grammars, if you recollect, and you sent them?"

"Ah – yes! – I do dimly recall that incident."

"It was very kind of you to do it. And it was you who first started me on that course. On the morning you left Marygreen, when your goods were on the waggon, you wished me good-bye, and said your scheme was to be a University man and enter the church – that a degree was the necessary hall-mark of one who wanted to do anything as a theologian or teacher."

"I remember I thought all that privately; but I wonder I did not keep my own counsel. The idea was given up years ago."

"I have never forgotten it. It was that which brought me to this part of the country, and out here to see you to-night."

"Come in," said Phillotson. "And your cousin, too."

They entered the parlour of the schoolhouse, where there was a lamp with a paper shade, which threw the light down on three or four books. Phillotson took it off, so that they could see each other better, and the rays fell on the nervous little face and vivacious dark eyes and hair of Sue, on the earnest features of her cousin, and on the schoolmaster's own maturer face and figure, showing him to be a spare and thoughtful personage of five-and-forty, with a thin-lipped, somewhat refined mouth, a lightly stooping habit, and a black frock coat, which from continued frictions shone a little at the shoulder-blades, the middle of the back, and the elbows.

The old friendship was imperceptibly renewed, the schoolmaster speaking of his experiences, and the cousins of theirs. He told them that he still thought of the church sometimes, and that though he could not enter it as he had intended to do in former years he might enter it as a licentiate.[1] Meanwhile, he said, he was comfortable in his present position, though he was in want of a pupil-teacher.

They did not stay to supper, Sue having to be indoors before it grew late, and the road was retraced to Christminster. Though they had talked of nothing more than general subjects Jude was surprised to find what a revelation of woman his cousin was to him. She was so vibrant that everything she did seemed to have its source in feeling. An exciting thought would make her walk ahead so fast that he could hardly keep up with her; and her sensitiveness on some points was such that it might have been misread as vanity. It was with heart-sickness he perceived that, while her sentiments towards him were those of the frankest friendliness only, he loved her more than before becoming acquainted with her; and the gloom of the walk home lay not in the night overhead, but in the thought of her departure.

"Why must you leave Christminster?" he said regretfully. "How can you do otherwise than cling to a city in whose history such men as Newman, Pusey, Ward,[2] Keble, loom so large!"

---

1 licentiate] person licensed to preach, though not ordained as a priest.
2 Ward] W.G. Ward (1812–82), author of *The Ideal of a Christian Church*.

"Yes – they do. Though how large do they loom in the history of the world?...What a funny reason for caring to stay! I should never have thought of it!" She laughed.

"Well – I must go," she continued. "Miss Fontover, one of the partners whom I serve, is offended with me, and I with her; and it is best to go."

"How did that happen?"

"She broke some statuary of mine."

"Oh? Wilfully?"

"Yes. She found it in my room, and though it was my property she threw it on the floor and stamped on it, because it was not according to her taste, and ground the arms and the head of one of the figures all to bits with her heel – a horrid thing!"

"Too Catholic-Apostolic for her, I suppose? No doubt she called them Popish images and talked of the invocation of saints."[1]

"No.... No, she didn't do that. She saw the matter quite differently."

"Ah! Then I am surprised!"

"Yes. It was for quite some other reason that she didn't like my patron-saints. So I was led to retort upon her; and the end of it was that I resolved not to stay, but to get into an occupation in which I shall be more independent."

"Why don't you try teaching again? You once did, I heard."

"I never thought of resuming it; for I was getting on as an art-designer."

"*Do* let me ask Mr. Phillotson to let you try your hand in his school? If you like it, and go to a Training College, and become a first-class certificated mistress, you get twice as large an income as any designer or church artist, and twice as much freedom."

"Well – ask him. Now I must go in. Good-bye, dear Jude! I am so glad we have met at last. We needn't quarrel because our parents did, need we?"

Jude did not like to let her quite see how much he agreed with her, and went his way to the remote street in which he had his lodging.

---

1   invocation of saints] a practice of Catholics which was criticised by many Protestants (including J.H. Newman before his conversion).

To keep Sue Bridehead near him was now a desire which operated without regard of consequences, and the next evening he again set out for Lumsdon, fearing to trust to the persuasive effects of a note only. The schoolmaster was unprepared for such a proposal.

"What I rather wanted was a second year's transfer, as it is called," he said. "Of course your cousin would do, personally; but she has had no experience. O – she has, has she? Does she really think of adopting teaching as a profession?"

Jude said she was disposed to do so, he thought, and his ingenious arguments on her natural fitness for assisting Mr. Phillotson, of which Jude knew nothing whatever, so influenced the schoolmaster that he said he would engage her, assuring Jude as a friend that unless his cousin really meant to follow on in the same course, and regarded this step as the first stage of an apprenticeship, of which her training in a normal school[1] would be the second stage, her time would be wasted quite, the salary being merely nominal.

The day after this visit Phillotson received a letter from Jude, containing the information that he had again consulted his cousin, who took more and more warmly to the idea of tuition; and that she had agreed to come. It did not occur for a moment to the schoolmaster and recluse that Jude's ardour in promoting the arrangement arose from any other feelings towards Sue than the instinct of co-operation common among members of the same family.

II.-V.

THE schoolmaster sat in his homely dwelling attached to the school, both being modern erections; and he looked across the way at the old house in which his teacher Sue had a lodging. The arrangement had been concluded very quickly. A pupil-teacher who was to have been transferred to Mr. Phillotson's school had failed him, and Sue had been taken as stop-gap. All such provisional arrangements as these could only last till the next annual visit of H.M. Inspector,[2] whose approval was necessary to make them permanent. Having taught for

---

1 normal school] school in which teachers are trained.
2 H.M. Inspector] one of Her Majesty's Inspectors of Schools.

some two years in London, though she had abandoned that vocation of late, Miss Bridehead was not exactly an outsider, and Phillotson thought there would be no difficulty in retaining her services, which he already wished to do, though she had only been with him three or four weeks. He had found her quite as bright as Jude had described her; and what master-tradesman does not wish to keep an apprentice who saves him half his labour?

It was a little over half-past eight o'clock in the morning, and he was waiting to see her cross the road to the school, when he would follow. At twenty minutes to nine she did cross, a light hat tossed on her head; and he watched her as a curiosity. A new emanation, which had nothing to do with her skill as a teacher, seemed to surround her this morning. He went to the school also, and Sue remained governing her class at the other end of the room, all day under his eye. She certainly was an excellent teacher.

It was part of his duty to give her private lessons in the evening, and some article in the Code made it necessary that a respectable, elderly woman should be present at these lessons when the teacher and the taught were of different sexes. Richard Phillotson thought of the absurdity of the regulation in this case, when he was old enough to be the girl's father; but he faithfully acted up to it; and sat down with her in a room where Mrs. Hawes, the widow at whose house Sue lodged, occupied herself with sewing. The regulation was, indeed, not easy to evade, for there was no other sitting room in the dwelling.

Sometimes as she figured – it was arithmetic that they were working at – she would involuntarily glance up with a little inquiring smile at him, as if she assumed that, being the master, he must perceive all that was passing in her brain, as right or wrong. Phillotson was not really thinking of the arithmetic at all, but of her, in a novel way which somehow seemed strange to him as preceptor. Perhaps she knew that he was thinking of her thus.

For a few weeks their work had gone on with a monotony which in itself was a delight to him. Then it happened that the children were to be taken to Christminster to see an itinerant exhibition, in the shape of a model of Jerusalem, to which schools were admitted at a penny a head in the interests of education. They marched along the road two and two, she beside her class with her simple cotton sunshade, her little thumb cocked up against its stem; and Phillotson behind in his long dangling coat, handling his walking-stick genteelly, in the musing mood which had come over him since her arrival. The afternoon was one of sun and dust, and when they entered the exhibition room few people were present but themselves.

The model of the ancient city stood in the middle of the apartment, and the proprietor, with a fine religious philanthropy written on his features, walked round it with a pointer in his hand, showing the young people the various quarters and places known to them by name from reading their Bibles; Mount Moriah, the Valley of Jehoshaphat, The City of Zion,[1] the walls and the gates, outside one of which there was a large mound like a tumulus, and on the mound a little white cross. The spot, he said, was Calvary.[2]

"I think," said Sue to the schoolmaster, as she stood with him a little in the background, "that this model, elaborate as it is, is a very imaginary production. How does anybody know that Jerusalem was like this in the time of Christ? I am sure this man doesn't."

"It is made after the best conjectural maps, based on actual visits to the city as it now exists."

"I fancy we have had enough of Jerusalem," she said, "considering we are not descended from the Jews. There was nothing first-rate about the place, or people, after all – as there was about Athens, Rome, Alexandria, and other old cities."

"But my dear girl, consider what it is to us!"

She was silent, for she was easily repressed; and then perceived behind the group of children clustered round the model a young man in a white flannel jacket, his form being bent so low in his intent inspection of the Valley of Jehoshaphat that he was almost hidden from view by the Mount of Olives. "Look at your cousin Jude," continued the schoolmaster. "He doesn't think we have had enough of Jerusalem!"

"Ah – I didn't see him!" she cried in her quick light voice. "Jude – how seriously you are going into it!"

Jude started up from his reverie, and saw her. "O – Sue!" he said,

---

1   Mount.....Zion] Solomon built a temple on Mount Moriah, in eastern Jerusalem; Jehoshaphat is a valley to the east; and Zion is the western part of the city, the site of a citadel, standing on a hill.

2   Calvary] the place where Christ was crucified.

with a glad flush of embarrassment. "These are your school-children, of course! I saw that schools were admitted in the afternoons, and thought you might come; but I got so deeply interested that I didn't remember where I was. How it carries one back, doesn't it! I could examine it for hours, but I have only a few minutes, unfortunately; for I am in the middle of a job out here."

"Your cousin is so terribly clever that she criticizes it unmercifully," said Phillotson, with good-humoured satire. "She is quite sceptical as to its correctness."

"No, Mr. Phillotson, I am not — altogether! I hate to be what is called a clever girl — there are too many of that sort now!" answered Sue sensitively. "I only meant — I don't know what I meant — except that it was what you don't understand!"

"*I* know your meaning," said Jude ardently (although he did not). "And I think you are quite right."

"That's a good Jude — I know *you* believe in me!" She impulsively seized his hand, and leaving a reproachful look on the schoolmaster turned away to Jude, her voice revealing a tremor which she herself felt to be absurdly uncalled for by sarcasm so gentle. She had not the least conception how the hearts of the twain went out to her at this momentary revelation of feeling, and what a complication she was building up thereby in the futures of both.

The model wore too much of an educational aspect for the children not to tire of it soon, and a little later in the afternoon they were all marched back to Lumsdon, Jude returning to his work. He watched the juvenile flock in their clean frocks and pinafores, filing down the street towards the country beside Phillotson and Sue, and a sad, dissatisfied sense of being out of the scheme of the latters' lives had possession of him. Phillotson had invited him to walk out and see them on Friday evening, when there would be no lessons to give to Sue, and Jude had eagerly promised to avail himself of the opportunity.

Meanwhile the scholars and teachers moved homewards, and the next day, on looking on the black-board in Sue's class, Phillotson was surprised to find upon it, skilfully drawn in chalk, a perspective view of Jerusalem, with every building shown in its place.

"I thought you took no interest in the model, and hardly looked at it?" he said.

"I hardly did," said she, "but I remembered that much of it."

"It is more than I had remembered myself."

Her Majesty's school-inspector was at that time paying "surprise-visits" in this neighbourhood to test the teaching unawares; and two days later, in the middle of the morning lessons, the latch of the door was softly lifted, and in walked my gentleman, the king of terrors[1] – to pupil-teachers.

To Mr. Phillotson the surprise was not great; like the lady in the story, he had been played that trick too many times to be unprepared. But Sue's class was at the further end of the room, and her back was towards the entrance; the inspector therefore came and stood behind her and watched her teaching some half-minute before she became aware of his presence. She turned, and realized that an oft-dreaded moment had come. The effect upon her timidity was such that she uttered a cry of fright. Phillotson, with a strange instinct of solicitude quite beyond his control, was at her side just in time to prevent her falling from faintness. She soon recovered herself, and laughed; but when the inspector had gone there was a reaction, and she was so white that Phillotson took her into his room, and gave her some brandy to bring her round. She found him holding her hand.

"You ought to have told me," she gasped petulantly, "that one of the Inspector's surprise-visits was imminent! O what shall I do! Now he'll write and tell the managers that I am no good, and I shall be disgraced for ever!"

"He won't do that, my dear little girl. You are the best teacher ever I had!"

He looked so gently at her that she was moved, and regretted that she had upbraided him. When she was better she went home.

Jude in the meantime had been waiting impatiently for Friday. On both Wednesday and Thursday he had been so much under the influence of his desire to see her that he walked after dark some distance along the road in the direction of the village, and, on returning to his room to read, found himself quite unable to concentrate his mind on the page. On Friday, as soon as he had got himself up as he thought Sue would like to see him, and made a hasty tea, he set out, notwithstanding that the evening was wet. The trees overhead deepened the

---

1   king of terrors] Job 18:14.

gloom of the hour, and they dripped sadly upon him, impressing him with forebodings – illogical forebodings; for though he knew that he loved her he also knew that he could not be more to her than he was.

On turning the corner and entering the village the first sight that greeted his eyes was that of two figures under one umbrella coming out of the vicarage gate. He was too far back for them to notice him, but he knew in a moment that they were Sue and Phillotson. The latter was holding the umbrella over her head, and they had evidently been paying a visit to the vicar – probably on some business connected with the school work. And as they walked along the wet and deserted lane Jude saw Phillotson place his arm round the girl's waist; whereupon she gently removed it; but he replaced it; and she let it remain, looking quickly round her with an air of misgiving. She did not look absolutely behind her, and therefore did not see Jude, who sank into the hedge like one struck with a blight. There he remained hidden till they had reached Sue's cottage and she had passed in, Phillotson going on to the school hard by.

"O, he's too old for her – too old!" cried Jude in all the terrible sickness of hopeless, handicapped love.

He could not interfere. Was he not Arabella's? He was unable to go on further, and retraced his steps towards Christminster. Every tread of his feet seemed to say to him that he must on no account stand in the schoolmaster's way with Sue. Phillotson was perhaps twenty years her senior, but many a happy marriage had been made in such conditions of age. The ironical clinch to his sorrow was given by the thought that the intimacy between his cousin and the schoolmaster had been brought about entirely by himself.

II.-VI.

JUDE's old and embittered aunt lay unwell at Marygreen, and on the following Sunday he went to see her – a visit which was the result of a victorious struggle against his inclination to turn aside to the village of Lumsdon and obtain a miserable interview with his cousin, in which the word nearest his heart could not be spoken, and the sight which had tortured him could not be revealed.

His aunt was now unable to leave her bed, and a great part of

Jude's short day was occupied in making arrangements for her comfort. The little bakery business had been sold to a neighbour, and with the proceeds of this and her savings she was comfortably supplied with necessaries, and more, a widow of the same village living with her and ministering to her wants. It was not till the time had nearly come for him to leave that he obtained a quiet talk with her, and his words tended insensibly towards his cousin.

"Was Sue born here?"

"She was – in this room. They were living here at that time. What made 'ee ask that?"

"O – I wanted to know."

"Now you've been seeing her!" said the harsh old woman. "And what did I tell 'ee?"

"Well – that I was not to see her."

"Have you gossiped with her?"

"Yes."

"Then don't keep it up. She was brought up by her father to hate her mother's family; and she'll look with no favour upon a working chap like you – a townish girl as she's become by now. I never cared much about her. A pert little thing, that's what she was too often, with her tight-strained nerves. Many's the time I've smacked her for her impertinence. Why, one day when she was walking into the pond with her shoes and stockings off, and her petticoats pulled above her knees, afore I could cry out for shame, she said: "Move on, aunty! This is no sight for modest eyes!""

"She was a little child then."

"She was twelve if a day."

"Well – of course. But now she's older she's of a thoughtful, quivering, tender nature, and as sensitive as ——"

"Jude!" cried his aunt, springing up in bed. "Don't you be a fool about her!"

"No, no, of course not."

"Your marrying that woman Arabella was about as bad a thing as a man could possibly do for himself by trying hard. But she's gone to the other side of the world, and med never trouble you again. And there'll be a worse thing if you, tied and bound as you be, should have a fancy for Sue. If your cousin is civil to you, take her civility for what it is worth. But anything more than a relation's good wishes it is stark

madness for ye to give her. If she's townish and wanton it med bring
'ee to ruin."

"Don't say anything against her, aunt! Don't, please!"

A relief was afforded to him by the entry of the companion and
nurse of his aunt, who must have been listening to the conversation,
for she began a commentary on past years, introducing Sue Bridehead as a character in her recollections. She described what an odd
little maid Sue had been when a pupil at the village school across the
green opposite, before her father went to London – how, when the
vicar arranged readings and recitations, she appeared on the platform,
the smallest of them all, "in her little white frock, and shoes, and pink
sash;" how she recited "Excelsior," "There was a sound of revelry by
night," and "Poe's Raven";[1] how during the delivery she would knit
her little brows and glare round tragically, and say to the empty air, as
if some real creature stood there –

> "Ghastly, grim, and ancient Raven,
> Tell me what thy lordly name is,
> On the night's Plutonian shore!"

"She'd bring up the nasty carrion bird that clear," corroborated the
sick woman reluctantly, "as she stood there in her little sash and
things, that you could see un a'most before your very eyes. You too,
Jude, had the same trick as a child of seeming to see things in the air."

The neighbour told also of Sue's accomplishments in other kinds:

"She was not exactly a tomboy, you know; but she could do things
that only boys do, as a rule. I've seen her hit in and steer down the
long slide on yonder pond, with her little curls blowing, one of a file
of twenty moving along against the sky like shapes painted on glass,
and up the back slide without stopping. All boys except herself; and
then they'd cheer her, and then she'd say, "Don't be saucy, boys," and
suddenly run indoors. They'd try to coax her out again. But 'a
wouldn't come."

These retrospective visions of Sue only made Jude the more miserable that he was unable to woo her, and he left the cottage of his

---

1   "Excelsior,".....''Raven''] "Excelsior" is by Henry Longfellow; "There was a sound
     of revelry by night" opens Canto III, verse 21, of Lord Byron's *Childe Harold's Pil-
     grimage*; "The Raven" is by Edgar Allan Poe.

aunt that day with a heavy heart. He would fain have glanced into the school to see the room in which Sue's little figure had so glorified itself; but he checked his desire and went on.

It being Sunday evening, some villagers who had known him during his residence here were standing in a group in their best clothes. Jude was startled by a salute from one of them:

"Ye've got there right enough, then!"

Jude showed that he did not understand.

"Why, to the seat of l'arning – the 'City of Light' you used to talk to us about as a little boy! Is it all you expected of it?"

"Yes; more!" cried Jude.

"When I was there once for an hour I didn't see much in it for my part; auld crumbling buildings, half church, half almshouse, and not much going on at that."

"You are wrong, John; there is more going on than meets the eye of a man walking through the streets. It is a unique centre of thought and religion – the intellectual and spiritual granary of this country. All that silence and absence of goings-on is the stillness of infinite motion – the sleep of the spinning-top, to borrow the simile of a writer."[1]

"O, well, it med be all that, or it med not. As I say, I didn't see nothing of it the hour or two I was there; so I went in and had a pot o' beer, and a penny loaf, and a ha'porth o' cheese, and waited till it was time to come along home. You've j'ined a College by this time, I suppose?"

"Ah, no!" said Jude. "I am almost as far off that as ever."

"How so?"

Jude slapped his pocket.

"Just what we thought! Such places be not for such as you—only for them with plenty o' money."

"There you are wrong," said Jude, with some bitterness. "They are for such ones!"

Still, the remark was sufficient to withdraw Jude's attention from the imaginative world he had lately inhabited, in which an abstract figure, more or less himself, was steeping his mind in a sublimation of the arts and sciences, and making his calling and election sure to a seat in the paradise of the learned. He was set regarding his prospects in a

---

1 the stillness.....writer] "their stillness was but the rest of infinite motion, the *sleep* of a spinning-top" (Carlyle: *Sartor Resartus,* Bk. 1, Chap.3).

cold northern light. He had lately felt that he could not quite satisfy himself in his Greek – in the Greek of the dramatists particularly. So fatigued was he sometimes after his day's work that he could not maintain the critical attention necessary for thorough application. He felt that he wanted a coach – a friend at his elbow to tell him in a moment what sometimes would occupy him a weary month in extracting from unanticipative, clumsy books.

It was decidedly necessary to consider facts a little more closely than he had done of late. What was the good, after all, of using up his spare hours in a vague labour called "private study" without giving an outlook on practicabilities?

"I ought to have thought of this before," he said, as he journeyed back. "It would have been better never to have embarked in the scheme at all than to do it without seeing clearly where I am going, or what I am aiming at.... This hovering outside the walls of the colleges, as if expecting some arm to be stretched out from them to lift me inside, won't do! I must get special information."

The next week accordingly he sought it. What at first seemed an opportunity occurred one afternoon when he saw an elderly gentleman, who had been pointed out as the Head of a particular College, walking in the public path of a parklike enclosure near the spot at which Jude chanced to be sitting. The gentleman came nearer, and Jude looked anxiously at his face. It seemed benign, considerate, yet rather reserved. On second thoughts Jude felt that he could not go up and address him; but he was sufficiently influenced by the incident to think what a wise thing it would be for him to state his difficulties by letter to some of the best and most judicious of these old masters, and obtain their advice.

During the next week or two he accordingly placed himself in such positions about the city as would afford him glimpses of several of the most distinguished among the Provosts, Wardens, and other Heads of Houses; and from those he saw he ultimately selected five whose physiognomies seemed to say to him that they were appreciative and far-seeing men. To these five he addressed letters, briefly stating his difficulties, and asking their opinion on his stranded situation.

When the letters were posted Jude mentally began to criticize them; he wished they had not been sent. "It is just one of those intrusive, vulgar, pushing applications which are so common in these days," he thought. "Why couldn't I know better than address utter strangers in such a way? I may be an impostor, an idle scamp, a man with a bad character, for all that they know to the contrary.... Perhaps that's what I am!"

Nevertheless, he found himself clinging to the hope of some reply as to his one last chance of redemption. He waited day after day, saying that it was perfectly absurd to expect, yet expecting. While he waited he was suddenly stirred by news about Phillotson. Phillotson was giving up the school near Christminster, for a larger one further south, in Mid-Wessex. What this meant; how it would affect his cousin; whether, as seemed possible, it was a practical move of the schoolmaster's towards a larger income, in view of a provision for two instead of one, he would not allow himself to say. And the tender relations between Phillotson and the young girl of whom Jude was passionately enamoured effectually made it repugnant to Jude's tastes to apply to Phillotson for advice on his own scheme.

Meanwhile the academic dignitaries to whom Jude had written vouchsafed no answer, and the young man was thus thrown back entirely on himself, as formerly, with the added gloom of a weakened hope. By indirect inquiries he soon perceived clearly, what he had long uneasily suspected, that to qualify himself for certain open scholarships and exhibitions[1] was the only brilliant course. But to do this a good deal of coaching would be necessary, and much natural ability. It was next to impossible that a man reading on his own system, however widely and thoroughly, even over the prolonged period of ten years, should be able to compete with those who had passed their lives under trained teachers and had worked to ordained lines.

The other course, that of buying himself in, so to speak, seemed the only one really open to men like him, the difficulty being simply of a material kind. With the help of his information he began to reckon the extent of this material obstacle, and ascertained, to his dismay, that, at the rate at which, with the best of fortune, he would be able to save money, fifteen years must elapse before he could be in a position to forward testimonials to the Head of a College and advance to a matriculation examination.[2] The undertaking was hopeless.

---

1 exhibitions] an exhibition is a financial award by a college (of lower value than a scholarship).
2 matriculation examination] examination for admission to a university.

He saw what a curious and cunning glamour the neighbourhood of the place had exercised over him. To get there and live there, to move among the churches and halls and become imbued with the *genius loci*,[1] had seemed to his dreaming youth, as the spot shaped its charms to him from its halo on the horizon, the obvious and ideal thing to do. "Let me only get there," he had said with the fatuousness of Crusoe over his big boat,[2] "and the rest is but a matter of time and energy." It would have been far better for him in every way if he had never come within sight and sound of the delusive precincts, had gone to some busy commercial town with the sole object of making money by his wits, and thence surveyed his plan in true perspective. Well, all that was clear to him amounted to this, that the whole scheme had burst up, like an iridescent soap-bubble, under the touch of a reasoned inquiry. He looked back at himself along the vista of his past years, and his thought was akin to Heine's:

> "Above the youth's inspired and flashing eyes
> I see the motley mocking fool's-cap rise."[3]

Fortunately he had not been allowed to bring his disappointment into his dear Sue's life by involving her in this collapse. And the painful details of his awakening to a sense of his limitations should now be spared her as far as possible. After all, she had only known a little part of the miserable struggle in which he had been engaged thus unequipped, poor, and unforeseeing.

He always remembered the appearance of the afternoon on which he awoke from his dream. Not quite knowing what to do with himself, he went up to an octagonal chamber in the lantern of a singularly built theatre[4] that was set amidst this quaint and singular city. It had windows all round, from which an outlook over the whole town and its edifices could be gained. Jude's eyes swept all the views in succession, meditatively, mournfully, yet sturdily. Those buildings and their

---

1   *genius loci*] (Latin:) spirit of the place.
2   Crusoe.....boat] Defoe's Robinson Crusoe built a large boat in the hope of escaping from his island, but found that it was too heavy to be dragged to the sea.
3   "Above.....rise."] from "Götterdämmerung" in the poetic sequence *Die Heimkehr* by Heinrich Heine (1797-1856).
4   theatre] the Sheldonian, in which ceremonies of the University take place.

associations and privileges were not for him. From the roof of the great library, into which he hardly ever had time to enter, his gaze travelled on to the varied spires, halls, gables, streets, chapels, gardens, quadrangles, which composed the *ensemble*[1] of this unrivalled panorama. He saw that his destiny lay not with these, but among the manual toilers in the shabby purlieu which he himself occupied, unrecognized as part of the city at all by its visitors and panegyrists, yet without whose denizens the hard readers could not read nor the high thinkers live.

He looked over the town into the country beyond, to the trees which screened her whose presence had at first been the support of his heart, and whose loss was now a maddening torture. But for this blow he might have borne with his fate. With Sue as companion he could have renounced his ambitions with a smile. Without her it was inevitable that the reaction from the long strain to which he had subjected himself should affect him disastrously. Phillotson had no doubt passed through a similar intellectual disappointment to that which now enveloped him. the schoolmaster had been since blest with the consolation of sweet Sue, while for him there was no consoler.

Descending to the streets, he went listlessly along till he arrived at an inn, and entered it. Here he drank several glasses of beer in rapid succession, and when he came out it was night. By the light of the flickering lamps he rambled home to supper, and had not long been sitting at table when his landlady brought up a letter that had just arrived for him. She laid it down as if impressed with a sense of its possible importance, and on looking at it Jude perceived that it bore the embossed stamp of one of the Colleges whose heads he had addressed. "*One* – at last!" cried Jude.

The communication was brief, and not exactly what he had expected; though it really was from the Master in person. It ran thus:

"BIBLIOLL COLLEGE.[2]

"SIR, – I have read your letter with interest; and, judging from your description of yourself as a working-man, I venture to think that you will have a much better chance of success in life by remaining in

---

1   *ensemble*] (French:) totality.
2   BIBLIOLL COLLEGE] Balliol College. ("Biblioll" suggests "bibliolatry": excessive devotion to books or to the Bible.)

your own sphere and sticking to your trade than by adopting any other course. That, therefore, is what I advise you to do. Yours faithfully,

T. Tetuphenay.[1]

"To Mr. J. Fawley, Stone-cutter."

This terribly sensible advice exasperated Jude. He had known all that before. He knew it was true. Yet it seemed a hard slap after ten years of labour, and its effect upon him just now was to make him rise recklessly from the table, and, instead of reading as usual, to go downstairs and into the street. He stood at a bar and tossed off two or three glasses, then unconsciously sauntered along till he came to a spot called The Fourways[2] in the middle of the city, gazing abstractedly at the groups of people like one in a trance, till, coming to himself, he began talking to the policeman fixed there.

That officer yawned, stretched out his elbows, elevated himself an inch and a half on the balls of his toes, smiled, and looking humorously at Jude, said, "You've had a wet, young man."

"No; I've only begun," he replied cynically.

Whatever his wetness, his brains were dry enough. He only heard in part the policeman's further remarks, having fallen into thought on what struggling people like himself had stood at that Crossway, whom nobody ever thought of now. It had more history than the oldest college in the city. It was literally teeming, stratified, with the shades of human groups, who had met there for tragedy, comedy, farce; real enactments of the intensest kind. At Fourways men had stood and talked of Napoleon, the loss of America, the execution of King Charles, the burning of the Martyrs, the Crusades, the Norman Conquest, possibly of the arrival of Cæsar. Here the two sexes had met for loving, hating, coupling, parting; had waited, had suffered, for each other; had triumphed over each other; cursed each other in jealousy, blessed each other in forgiveness.

He began to see that the town life was a book of humanity infinitely more palpitating, varied, and compendious than the gown

---

1 Tetuphenay] (Greek:) "to have beaten or struck"; perhaps Hardy intended the name to mean "beater."
2 Fourways] Carfax, a central crossroads in Oxford.

life. These struggling men and women before him were the reality of Christminster, though they knew little of Christ or Minster. That was one of the humours of things. The floating population of students and teachers, who did know both in a way, were not Christminster in a local sense at all.

He looked at his watch, and, in pursuit of this idea, he went on till he came to a public hall, where a promenade concert was in progress. Jude entered, and found the room full of shop youths and girls, soldiers, apprentices, boys of eleven smoking cigarettes, and light women of the more respectable and amateur class. He had tapped the real Christminster life. A band was playing, and the crowd walked about and jostled each other, and every now and then a man got upon a platform and sang a comic song.

The spirit of Sue seemed to hover round him and prevent his flirting and drinking with the frolicsome girls who made advances – wistful to gain a little joy. At ten o'clock he came away, choosing a circuitous route homeward to pass the gates of the College whose Head had just sent him the note.

The gates were shut, and, by an impulse, he took from his pocket the lump of chalk which as a workman he usually carried there, and wrote along the wall:

"*I have understanding as well as you; I am not inferior to you: yea, who knoweth not such things as these?*" – Job xii.3.

II.-VII.

THE stroke of scorn relieved his mind, and the next morning he laughed at his self-conceit. But the laugh was not a healthy one. He re-read the letter from the Master, and the wisdom in its lines, which had at first exasperated him, chilled and depressed him now. He saw himself as a fool indeed.

Deprived of the objects of both intellect and emotion, he could not proceed to his work. Whenever he felt reconciled to his fate as a student, there came to disturb his calm his hopeless relations with Sue. That the one affined soul he had ever met was lost to him through his marriage returned upon him with cruel persistency, till, unable to bear it longer, he again rushed for distraction to the real

Christminster life. He now sought it out in an obscure and low-ceiled tavern up a court which was well known to certain worthies of the place, and in brighter times would have interested him simply by its quaintness. Here he sat more or less all the day, convinced that he was at bottom a vicious character, of whom it was hopeless to expect anything.

In the evening the frequenters of the house dropped in one by one, Jude still retaining his seat in the corner, though his money was all spent, and he had not eaten anything the whole day except a biscuit. He surveyed his gathering companions with all the equanimity and philosophy of a man who has been drinking long and slowly, and made friends with several: to wit, Tinker Taylor, a decayed church-ironmonger who appeared to have been of a religious turn in earlier years, but was somewhat blasphemous now; also a red-nosed auctioneer; also two Gothic masons like himself, called Uncle Jim and Uncle Joe. There were present, too, some clerks, and a gown- and surplice-maker's assistant; two ladies who sported moral characters of various depths of shade, according to their company, nicknamed "Bower o' Bliss" and "Freckles;" some horsey men "in the know" of betting circles; a travelling actor from the theatre, and two devil-may-care young men who proved to be gownless undergraduates; they had slipped in by stealth to meet a man about bull-pups, and stayed to drink and smoke short pipes with the racing gents aforesaid, looking at their watches every now and then.

The conversation waxed general. Christminster society was criticized, the Dons, magistrates, and other people in authority being sincerely pitied for their shortcomings, while opinions on how they ought to conduct themselves and their affairs to be properly respected, were exchanged in a large-minded and disinterested manner.

Jude Fawley, with the self-conceit, effrontery, and *aplomb* of a strong-brained fellow in liquor, threw in his remarks somewhat peremptorily; and his aims having been what they were for so many years, everything the others said turned upon his tongue, by a sort of mechanical craze, to the subject of scholarship and study, the extent of his own learning being dwelt upon with an insistence that would have appeared pitiable to himself in his sane hours.

"I don't care a damn," he was saying, "for any Provost, Warden, Principal, Fellow, or cursed Master of Arts in the University! What I know is that I'd lick 'em on their own ground if they'd give me a chance, and show 'em a few things they are not up to yet!"

"Hear, hear!" said the undergraduates from the corner, where they were talking privately about the pups.

"You always was fond o' books, I've heard," said Tinker Taylor, "and I don't doubt what you state. Now with me 'twas different. I always saw there was more to be learnt outside a book than in; and I took my steps accordingly, or I shouldn't have been the man I am."

"You aim at the Church, I believe?" said Uncle Joe. "If you are such a scholar as to pitch yer hopes so high as that, why not give us a specimen of your scholarship? Canst say the Creed in Latin, man? That was how they once put it to a chap down in my country."

"I should think so!" said Jude haughtily.

"Not he! Like his conceit!" screamed one of the ladies.

"Just you shut up, Bower o' Bliss!" said one of the undergraduates. "Silence!" He drank off the spirits in his tumbler, rapped with it on the counter, and announced, "The gentleman in the corner is going to rehearse the Articles of the Creed, in the Latin tongue, for the edification of the company."

"I won't!" said Jude.

"Yes – have a try!" said the surplice-maker.

"You can't!" said Uncle Joe.

"Yes, he can!" said Tinker Taylor.

"I'll swear I can!" said Jude. "Well, come now, stand me a small Scotch cold, and I'll do it straight off."

"That's a fair offer," said the undergraduate, throwing down the money for the whisky.

The barmaid concocted the mixture with the bearing of a person compelled to live amongst animals of an inferior species, and the glass was handed across to Jude, who, having drunk the contents, stood up and began rhetorically, without hesitation:

"Credo in unum Deum, Patrem omnipotentem, Factorem cœli et terræ, visibilium omnium et invisibilium."[1]

"Good! Excellent Latin!" cried one of the undergraduates, who, however, had not the slightest conception of a single word.

---

1 "Credo.....invisibilium"] "I believe in one God the Father Almighty, Maker of heaven and earth, And of all things visible and invisible....." (Translation in *Book of Common Prayer*.)

A silence reigned among the rest in the bar, and the maid stood still, Jude's voice echoing sonorously into the inner parlour, where the landlord was dozing, and bringing him out to see what was going on. Jude had declaimed steadily ahead, and was continuing:

"Crucifixus etiam pro nobis: sub Pontio Pilato passus, et sepultus est. Et resurrexit tertia die, secundum Scripturas."[1]

"That's the Nicene," sneered the second undergraduate. "And we wanted the Apostles'!"[2]

"You didn't say so! And every fool knows, except you, that the Nicene is the only historic creed!"

"Let un go on, let un go on!" said the auctioneer.

But Jude's mind seemed to grow confused soon, and he could not get on. He put his hand to his forehead, and his face assumed an expression of pain.

"Give him another glass – then he'll fetch up and get through it," said Tinker Taylor.

Somebody threw down threepence, the glass was handed, Jude stretched out his arm for it without looking, and having swallowed the liquor, went on in a moment in a revived voice, continuing to the end with the manner of a priest leading a congregation:

"Et unam Catholicam et Apostolicam Ecclesiam. Confiteor unum Baptisma in remissionem peccatorum. Et expecto Resurrectionem mortuorum. Et vitam venturi saeculi. Amen."[3]

"Well done!" said several, enjoying the last word, as being the first and only one they had recognized.

Then Jude seemed to shake the fumes from his brain, as he stared round upon them.

"You pack of fools!" he cried. "Which one of you knows whether I have said it or no? It might have been the Ratcatcher's Daughter[4] in

---

1 "Crucifixus.....Scripturas"] "[C]rucified also for us under Pontious Pilate. He suffered and was buried, And the third day he rose again according to the Scriptures."

2 Nicene.....Apostles'] The Nicene creed, formulated at Nicaea in A.D. 325, is recited during the Catholic Mass and the Anglican Holy Communion. The Apostles' creed dates from about A.D. 500 and is thus "less historic."

3 "Et unam.....Amen"] "And [I believe] one Catholick and Apostolick Church. I acknowledge one Baptism for the remission of sins. And I look for the Resurrection of the dead, And the life of the world to come. Amen."

4 Ratcatcher's Daughter] an anonymous popular ballad of tragic love: when the daughter accidentally drowns, her lover cuts his throat and dies.

double Dutch for all that your besotted heads can tell! See what I have brought myself to – the crew I have come among!"

The landlord, who had already had his license endorsed for harbouring queer characters, feared a riot, and came outside the counter; but Jude, in his sudden flash of reason, had turned in disgust and left the scene, the door slamming with a dull thud behind him.

He hastened down the lane and round into the straight broad street, which he followed till it merged in the highway, and all sound of his late companions had been left behind. Onward he still went, under the influence of a childlike yearning for the one being in the world to whom it seemed possible to fly – an unreasoning desire, whose ill judgment was not apparent to him now. In the course of an hour, when it was between ten and eleven o'clock, he entered the village of Lumsdon, and reaching the cottage, saw that a light was burning in a downstairs room, which he assumed, rightly as it happened, to be hers.

Jude stepped close to the wall, and tapped with his finger on the pane, saying impatiently, "Sue, Sue!"

She must have recognized his voice, for the light disappeared from the apartment, and in a second or two the door was unlocked and opened, and Sue appeared with a candle in her hand.

"Is it Jude? Yes, it is! My dear, dear cousin, what's the matter?"

"O, I am – I couldn't help coming, Sue!" said he, sinking down upon the doorstep. "I am so wicked, Sue – my heart is nearly broken, and I could not bear my life as it was! So I have been drinking, and blaspheming, or next door to it, and saying holy things in disreputable quarters – repeating in idle bravado words which ought never to be uttered but reverently! O, do anything with me, Sue – kill me – I don't care! Only don't hate me and despise me like all the rest of the world!"

"You are ill, poor dear! No, I won't despise you; of course I won't! Come in and rest, and let me see what I can do for you. Now lean on me, and don't mind." With one hand holding the candle and the other supporting him, she led him indoors, and placed him in the only easy-chair the meagrely furnished house afforded, stretching his feet upon another, and pulling off his boots. Jude, now getting towards his sober senses, could only say, "Dear, dear Sue!" in a voice broken by grief and contrition.

She asked him if he wanted anything to eat, but he shook his head. Then telling him to go to sleep, and that she would come down early in the morning and get him some breakfast, she bade him good-night, and ascended the stairs.

Almost immediately he fell into a heavy slumber, and did not wake till dawn. At first he did not know where he was, but by degrees his situation cleared to him, and he beheld it in all the ghastliness of a right mind. She knew the worst of him – the very worst. How could he face her now? She would soon be coming down to see about breakfast, as she had said, and there would he be in all his shame confronting her. He could not bear the thought, and softly drawing on his boots, and taking his hat from the nail on which she had hung it, he slipped noiselessly out of the house.

His fixed idea was to get away to some obscure spot and hide, and perhaps pray; and the only spot which occurred to him was Marygreen. He called at his lodging in Christminster, where he found awaiting him a note of dismissal from his employer; and having packed up, he turned his back upon the city that had been such a thorn in his side and struck southward into Wessex. He had no money left in his pocket, his small savings, deposited at one of the banks in Christminster, having fortunately been left untouched. To get to Marygreen, therefore, his only course was walking; and the distance being nearly twenty miles, he had ample time to complete on the way the sobering process begun in him.

At some hour of the evening he reached Alfredston. Here he pawned his waistcoat, and having gone out of the town a mile or two, slept under a rick that night. At dawn he rose, shook off the hayseeds and stems from his clothes, and started again, breasting the long white road up the hill to the downs, which had been visible to him a long way off, and passing the milestone at the top, whereon he had carved his hopes years ago.

He reached the ancient hamlet while the people were at breakfast. Weary and mud-bespattered, but quite possessed of his ordinary clearness of brain, he sat down by the well, thinking as he did so what a poor Christ he made.[1] Seeing a trough of water near, he bathed his

---

1   well.....made] "Now Jacob's well was there. Jesus therefore, being wearied with *his* journey, sat thus on the well: *and* it was about the sixth hour." (John 4:6.)

face, and went on to the cottage of his great-aunt, whom he found breakfasting in bed, attended by the woman who lived with her.

"What – out o'work?" asked his relative, regarding him through eyes sunken deep, under lids heavy as pot-covers, no other cause for his tumbled appearance suggesting itself to one whose whole life had been a struggle with material things.

"Yes," said Jude heavily. "I think I must have a little rest."

Refreshed by some breakfast, he went up to his old room and lay down in his shirt-sleeves, after the manner of the artizan. He fell asleep for a short while, and when he awoke it was as if he had awakened in hell. It *was* hell – "the hell of conscious failure,"[1] both in ambition and in love. He thought of that previous abyss into which he had fallen before leaving this part of the country; the deepest deep he had supposed it then; but it was not so deep as this. That had been the breaking in of the outer bulwarks of his hope: this was of his second line.

If he had been a woman he must have screamed under the nervous tension which he was now undergoing. But that relief being denied to his virility, he clenched his teeth in misery, bringing lines about his mouth like those in the Laocoon,[2] and corrugations between his brows.

A mournful wind blew through the trees, and sounded in the chimney like the pedal notes[3] of an organ. Each ivy leaf overgrowing the wall of the churchless churchyard hard by, now abandoned, pecked its neighbour smartly, and the vane on the new German-Gothic church in the new spot had already begun to creak. Yet apparently it was not always the outdoor wind that made the deep murmurs; it was a voice. He guessed its origin in a moment or two; the curate was praying with his aunt in the adjoining room. He remembered her speaking of him. Presently the sounds ceased, and a step seemed to cross the landing. Jude sat up, and shouted "Hoi!"

The step made for his door, which was open, and a man looked in. It was a young clergyman.

---

1   "hell.....failure"] cf. "There is not a fiercer hell than the failure in a great object" (Keats: Preface to *Endymion*).

2   Laocoon] classical sculpture depicting the agony of Laocoön (a Trojan priest) and his two sons as they are mortally entwined by serpents as a punishment for offending Apollo.

3   pedal notes] bass notes played by foot-operated keys of an organ.

"I think you are Mr. Highridge," said Jude. "My aunt has mentioned you more than once. Well, here I am, just come home; a fellow gone to the bad; though I had the best intentions in the world at one time. Now I am melancholy mad, what with drinking and one thing and another."

Slowly Jude unfolded to the curate his late plans and movements, by an unconscious bias dwelling less upon the intellectual and ambitious side of his dream, and more upon the theological, though this had, up till now, been merely a portion of the general plan of advancement.

"Now I know I have been a fool, and that folly is with me,"[1] added Jude in conclusion. "And I don't regret the collapse of my University hopes one jot. I wouldn't begin again if I were sure to succeed. I don't care for social success any more at all. But I do feel I should like to do some good thing; and I bitterly regret the Church, and the loss of my chance of being her ordained minister."

The curate, who was a new man to this neighbourhood, had grown deeply interested, and at last he said: "If you feel a real call to the ministry, and I won't say from your conversation that you do not, for it is that of a thoughtful and educated man, you might enter the Church as a licentiate. Only you must make up your mind to avoid strong drink."

"I could avoid that easily enough, if I had any kind of hope to support me!"

---

1 fool.....folly] cf. "Nabal [Fool] *is* his name, and folly *is* with him" (1 Samuel 25:25).

PART THIRD

AT MELCHESTER

"For there was no other girl, O bridegroom, like her!"[1]
— SAPPHO (H.T.Wharton).

III.-I.

IT was a new idea – the ecclesiastical and altruistic life as distinct from the intellectual and emulative life. A man could preach and do good to his fellow-creatures without taking double-firsts[2] in the schools of Christminster, or having anything but ordinary knowledge. The old fancy which had led on to the culminating vision of the bishopric had not been an ethical or theological enthusiasm at all, but a mundane ambition masquerading in a surplice. He feared that his whole scheme had degenerated to, even though it might not have originated in, a social unrest which had no foundation in the nobler instincts; which was purely an artificial product of civilization. There were thousands of young men on the same self-seeking track at the present moment. The sensual hind[3] who ate, drank, and lived carelessly with his wife through the days of his vanity[4] was a more likable being than he.

But to enter the Church in such an unscholarly way that he could not in any probability rise to a higher grade through all his career than that of the humble curate wearing his life out in an obscure village or city slum – that might have a touch of goodness and great-

---

1   "*For.....her!*"] the translation of a fragment (cited as item 106) In H.T.Wharton's *Sappho* (1885).

2   double-firsts] degrees in which certain candidates have gained first class results in the examinations of (usually) both the penultimate year and the final year of study.

3   hind] farm-servant.

4   days.....vanity] "Live joyfully with the wife whom thou lovest all the days of the life of thy vanity" (Ecclesiastes 9:9).

ness in it; that might be true religion, and a purgatorial course worthy of being followed by a remorseful man.

The favourable light in which this new thought showed itself by contrast with his foregone intentions cheered Jude, as he sat there, shabby and lonely; and it may be said to have given, during the next few days, the *coup de grâce*[1] to his intellectual career – a career which had extended over the greater part of a dozen years. He did nothing, however, for some long stagnant time to advance his new desire, occupying himself with little local jobs in putting up and lettering headstones about the neighbouring villages, and submitting to be regarded as a social failure, a returned purchase, by the half-dozen or so of farmers and other country-people who condescended to nod to him.

The human interest of the new intention – and a human interest is indispensable to the most spiritual and self-sacrificing – was created by a letter from Sue, bearing a fresh postmark. She evidently wrote with anxiety, and told very little about her own doings, more than that she had passed some sort of examination for a Queen's Scholarship, and was going to enter a Training College at Melchester[2] to complete herself for the vocation she had chosen, partly by his influence. There was a Theological College at Melchester; Melchester was a quiet and soothing place, almost entirely ecclesiastical in its tone; a spot where worldly learning and intellectual smartness had no establishment; where the altruistic feeling that he did possess would perhaps be more highly estimated than a brilliancy which he did not.

As it would be necessary that he should continue for a time to work at his trade while reading up Divinity, which he had neglected at Christminster for the ordinary classical grind, what better course for him than to get employment at the further city, and pursue this plan of reading? That his excessive human interest in the new place was entirely of Sue's making, while at the same time Sue was to be regarded even less than formerly as proper to create it, had an ethical contradictoriness to which he was not blind. But that much he conceded to human frailty, and hoped to learn to love her only as a friend and kinswoman.

---

1   *coup de grâce*] (French:) lethal blow.
2   Melchester] based on Salisbury.

He considered that he might so mark out his coming years as to begin his ministry at the age of thirty – an age which much attracted him as being that of his exemplar when he first began to teach in Galilee.[1] This would allow him plenty of time for deliberate study, and for acquiring capital by his trade to help his after-course of keeping the necessary terms at a Theological College.

Christmas had come and passed, and Sue had gone to the Melchester Normal School. The time was just the worst in the year for Jude to get into new employment, and he had written suggesting to her that he should postpone his arrival for a month or so, till the days had lengthened. She had acquiesced so readily that he wished he had not proposed it – she evidently did not much care about him, though she had never once reproached him for his strange conduct in coming to her that night, and his silent disappearance. Neither had she ever said a word about her relations with Mr. Phillotson.

Suddenly, however, quite a passionate letter arrived from Sue. She was quite lonely and miserable, she told him. She hated the place she was in; it was worse than the ecclesiastical designer's; worse than anywhere. She felt utterly friendless; could he come immediately? – though when he did come she would only be able to see him at limited times, the rules of the establishment she found herself in being strict to a degree. It was Mr. Phillotson who had advised her to come there, and she wished she had never listened to him.

Phillotson's suit was not exactly prospering, evidently; and Jude felt unreasonably glad. He packed up his things and went to Melchester with a lighter heart than he had known for months.

This being the turning over a new leaf he duly looked about for a temperance hotel,[2] and found a little establishment of that description in the street leading from the station. When he had had something to eat he walked out into the dull winter light over the town bridge, and turned the corner towards the Close. The day was foggy, and standing under the walls of the most graceful architectural pile in England[3] he paused and looked up. The lofty building was visible as far as the roof-ridge; above, the dwindling spire rose more and more remotely, till its

---

1 Galilee] Jesus was thirty when he began his public ministry in the region of Galilee.
2 temperance hotel] hotel which does not serve alcoholic drinks.
3 most.....England] Salisbury Cathedral, built 1220–1340, has a 404-foot spire, the highest in England.

apex was quite lost in the mist drifting across it.

The lamps now began to be lighted, and turning to the west front he walked round. He took it as a good omen that numerous blocks of stone were lying about, which signified that the cathedral was undergoing restoration or repair to a considerable extent. It seemed to him, full of the superstitions of his beliefs, that this was an exercise of forethought on the part of a ruling Power, that he might find plenty to do in the art he practised while waiting for a call to higher labours.

Then a wave of warmth came over him as he thought how near he now stood to the bright-eyed vivacious girl with the broad forehead and pile of dark hair above it; the girl with the kindling glance, daringly soft at times – something like that of the girls he had seen in engravings from paintings of the Spanish school. She was here – actually in this Close – in one of the houses confronting this very west façade.

He went down the broad gravel path towards the building. It was an ancient edifice of the fifteenth century, once a palace, now a training-school, with mullioned and transomed windows, and a courtyard in front shut in from the road by a wall. Jude opened the gate and went up to the door through which, on inquiring for his cousin, he was gingerly admitted to a waiting-room, and in a few minutes she came.

Though she had been here such a short while, she was not as he had seen her last. All her bounding manner was gone; her curves of motion had become subdued lines. The screens and subtleties of convention had likewise disappeared. Yet neither was she quite the woman who had written the letter that summoned him. That had plainly been dashed off in an impulse which second thoughts had somewhat regretted; thoughts that were possibly of his recent self-disgrace. Jude was quite overcome with emotion.

"You don't – think me a demoralized wretch – for coming to you as I was – and going so shamefully, Sue?"

"O, I have tried not to! You said enough to let me know what had caused it. I hope I shall never have any doubt of your worthiness, my poor Jude! And I am glad you have come!"

She wore a murrey-coloured[1] gown with a little lace collar. It was

---

1 murrey-coloured] mulberry-coloured, dark purple.

made quite plain, and hung about her slight figure with clinging gracefulness. Her hair, which formerly she had worn according to the custom of the day, was now twisted up tightly, and she had altogether the air of a woman clipped and pruned by severe discipline, an under-brightness shining through from the depths which that discipline had not yet been able to reach.

She had come forward prettily; but Jude felt that she had hardly expected him to kiss her, as he was burning to do, under other colours than those of cousinship. He could not perceive the least sign that Sue regarded him as a lover, or ever would do so, now that she knew the worst of him, even if he had the right to behave as one; and this helped on his growing resolve to tell her of his matrimonial entanglement, which he had put off doing from time to time in sheer dread of losing the bliss of her company.

Sue came out into the town with him, and they walked and talked with tongues centred only on the passing moments. Jude said he would like to buy her a little present of some sort, and then she confessed, with something of shame, that she was dreadfully hungry. They were kept on very short allowances in the College, and a dinner, tea, and supper all in one was the present she most desired in the world. Jude thereupon took her to an inn and ordered whatever the house afforded, which was not much. The place, however, gave them a delightful opportunity for a *tête-à-tête*,[1] nobody else being in the room, and they talked freely.

She told him about the school as it was at that date, and the rough living, and the mixed character of her fellow-students, gathered together from all parts of the diocese, and how she had to get up and work by gaslight in the early morning, with all the bitterness of a young person to whom restraint was new. To all this he listened; but it was not what he wanted especially to know – her relations with Phillotson. That was what she did not tell. When they had sat and eaten, Jude impulsively placed his hand upon hers; she looked up and smiled, and took his quite freely into her own little soft one, dividing his fingers and coolly examining them, as if they were the fingers of a glove she was purchasing.

"Your hands are rather rough, Jude, aren't they?" she said.

---

1   *tête-à-tête*] (Fr.:) private conversation.

"Yes. So would yours be if they held a mallet and chisel all day."

"I don't dislike it, you know. I think it is noble to see a man's hands subdued to what he works in....[1] Well, I'm rather glad I came to this Training School, after all. See how independent I shall be after the two years' training! I shall pass pretty high, I expect, and Mr. Phillotson will use his influence to get me a big school."

She had touched the subject at last. "I had a suspicion, a fear," said Jude, "that he – cared about you rather warmly, and perhaps wanted to marry you."

"Now don't be such a silly boy!"

"He has said something about it, I expect."

"If he had, what would it matter? An old man like him!"

"O, come, Sue; he's not so very old. And I know what I saw him doing ——"

"Not kissing me – that I'm certain!"

"No. But putting his arm round your waist."

"Ah – I remember. But I didn't know he was going to."

"You are wriggling out of it, Sue, and it isn't quite kind!"

Her ever-sensitive lip began to quiver, and her eye to blink, at something this reproof was deciding her to say.

"I know you'll be angry if I tell you everything, and that's why I don't want to!"

"Very well, then, dear," he said soothingly. "I have no real right to ask you, and I don't wish to know."

"I shall tell you!" said she, with the perverseness that was part of her. "This is what I have done: I have promised – I have promised – that I will marry him when I come out of the Training-School two years hence, and have got my Certificate; his plan being that we shall then take a large double school in a great town – he the boys' and I the girls' – as married school-teachers often do, and make a good income between us."

"O, Sue!....But of course it is right – you couldn't have done better!"

He glanced at her and their eyes met, the reproach in his own belying his words. Then he drew his hand quite away from hers, and

---

1 subdued.....in] "And almost thence my nature is subdued / To what it works in, like the dyer's hand" (Shakespeare: Sonnet 111).

turned his face in estrangement from her to the window. Sue regarded him passively without moving.

"I knew you would be angry!" she said with an air of no emotion whatever. "Very well – I am wrong, I suppose! I ought not to have let you come to see me! We had better not meet again; and we'll only correspond at long intervals, on purely business matters!"

This was just the one thing he would not be able to bear, as she probably knew, and it brought him round at once. "O yes, we will," he said quickly. "Your being engaged can make no difference to me whatever. I have a perfect right to see you when I want to; and I shall!"

"Then don't let us talk of it any more. It is quite spoiling our evening together. What does it matter about what one is going to do two years hence!"

She was something of a riddle to him, and he let the subject drift away. "Shall we go and sit in the Cathedral?" he asked, when their meal was finished.

"Cathedral? Yes. Though I think I'd rather sit in the railway station," she answered, a remnant of vexation still in her voice. "That's the centre of the town life now. The Cathedral has had its day!"

"How modern you are!"

"So would you be if you had lived so much in the Middle Ages as I have done these last few years! The Cathedral was a very good place four or five centuries ago; but it is played out now ... I am not modern, either. I am more ancient than mediævalism, if you only knew."

Jude looked distressed.

"There – I won't say any more of that!" she cried. "Only you don't know how bad I am, from your point of view, or you wouldn't think so much of me, or care whether I was engaged or not. Now there's just time for us to walk round the Close, and then I must go in, or I shall be locked out for the night."

He took her to the gate and they parted. Jude had a conviction that his unhappy visit to her on that sad night had precipitated this marriage engagement, and it did anything but add to his happiness. Her reproach had taken that shape, then, and not the shape of words. However, next day he set about seeking employment, which it was not so easy to get as at Christminster, there being, as a rule, less stone-cutting in progress in this quiet city, and hands being mostly permanent. But he edged himself in by degrees. His first work was some carving at the cemetery on the hill; and ultimately he became engaged on the labour he most desired – the Cathedral repairs, which were very extensive, the whole interior fittings having been swept away, to be replaced by new.

It might be a labour of years to get it all done, and he had confidence enough in his own skill with the mallet and chisel to feel that it would be a matter of choice with himself how long he would stay.

The lodgings he took near the Close Gate would not have disgraced a curate, the rent representing a higher percentage on his wages than mechanics of any sort usually care to pay. His combined bed and sitting room was furnished with framed photographs of the rectories and deaneries at which his landlady had lived as trusted servant in her time, and the parlour downstairs bore a clock on the mantelpiece inscribed to the effect that it was presented to the same serious-minded woman by her fellow-servants on the occasion of her marriage. Jude added to the furniture of his room by unpacking photographs of the ecclesiastical carvings and monuments that he had executed with his own hands; and he was deemed a satisfactory acquisition as tenant of the vacant apartment.

He found an ample supply of theological books in the city bookshops, and with these his studies were recommenced in a different spirit and direction from his former course. As a relaxation from the Fathers, and such stock works as Paley and Butler,[1] he read Newman, Pusey, and many other modern lights. He hired a harmonium,[2] set it up in his lodging, and practised chants thereon, single and double.

---

1   Paley and Butler] William Paley's *A View of the Evidences of Christianity* (1794) and *Natural Theology* (1802) were influential defences of the faith, as was Joseph Butler's *The Analogy of Religion* (1736).
2   harmonium] portable organ with a keyboard and air-impelling foot-pedals.

III.-II.

"To-morrow is our grand day, you know. Where shall we go?"

"I have leave from three till nine. Wherever we can get to and come back from in that time. Not ruins, Jude — I don't care for them."

"Well — Wardour Castle.[1] And then we can do Fonthill[2] if we like — all in the same afternoon."

"Wardour is Gothic ruins[3] — and I hate Gothic!"

"No, Quite otherwise. It is a classic building — Corinthian,[4] I think; with a lot of pictures."

"Ah — that will do. I like the sound of Corinthian. We'll go."

Their conversation had run thus some few weeks later, and next morning they prepared to start. Every detail of the outing was a facet reflecting a sparkle to Jude, and he did not venture to meditate on the life of inconsistency he was leading. His Sue's conduct was one lovely conundrum to him; he could say no more.

There duly came the charm of calling at the College door for her; her emergence in a nunlike simplicity of costume that was rather enforced than desired; the traipsing[5] along to the station, the porter's "B'your leave!" the screaming of the trains — everything formed the basis of a beautiful crystallization. Nobody stared at Sue, because she was so plainly dressed, which comforted Jude in the thought that only himself knew the charms those habiliments subdued. A matter of ten pounds spent in a drapery-shop, which had no connection with her real life or her real self, would have set all Melchester staring. The guard of the train thought they were lovers, and put them into a compartment all by themselves.

"That's a good intention wasted!" said she.

Jude did not respond. He thought the remark unnecessarily cruel, and partly untrue.

They reached the Park and Castle and wandered through the picture-galleries, Jude stopping by preference in front of the devotional

---

1 Wardour Castle] in Wiltshire, built 1770-76 in classical style.
2 Fonthill] Fonthill Abbey in Wiltshire, built 1796-1807 in Gothic (late Mediæval) style.
3 Gothic ruins] Sue is confusing Wardour Castle with Wardour Old Castle, the latter (built in the late fourteenth century) having fallen into ruins.
4 Corinthian] having elaborate capitals with acanthus-leaf designs.
5 traipsing] walking (usually trudging).

pictures by Del Sarto, Guido Reni, Spagnoletto, Sassoferrato, Carlo Dolci,[1] and others. Sue paused patiently beside him, and stole critical looks into his face as, regarding the Virgins, Holy Families, and Saints, it grew reverent and abstracted. When she had thoroughly estimated him at this, she would move on and wait for him before a Lely or Reynolds.[2] It was evident that her cousin deeply interested her, as one might be interested in a man puzzling out his way along a labyrinth from which one had one's self escaped.

When they came out a long time still remained to them, and Jude proposed that as soon as they had had something to eat they should walk across the high country to the north of their present position, and intercept the train of another railway leading back to Melchester, at a station about seven miles off. Sue, who was inclined for any adventure that would intensify the sense of her day's freedom, readily agreed; and away they went, leaving the adjoining station behind them.

It was indeed open country, wide and high. They talked and bounded on, Jude cutting from a little covert a long walking-stick for Sue as tall as herself, with a great crook which made her look like a shepherdess. About half-way on their journey they crossed a main road running due east and west – the old road from London to Land's End. They paused, and looked up and down it for a moment, and remarked upon the desolation which had come over this once lively thoroughfare, while the wind dipped to earth and scooped straws and hay-stems from the ground.

They crossed the road and passed on, but during the next half-mile Sue seemed to grow tired, and Jude began to be distressed for her. They had walked a good distance altogether, and if they could not reach the other station it would be rather awkward. For a long time there was no cottage visible on the wide expanse of down and turnip-land; but presently they came to a sheepfold, and next to the shepherd, pitching hurdles. He told them that the only house near was his mother's and his, pointing to a little dip ahead from which a faint blue smoke arose, and recommended them to go on and rest there.

---

1 Del Sarto.....Dolci] religious painters of the sixteenth and seventeenth centuries.
2 Sir Peter Lely (1618-80) and Sir Joshua Reynolds (1723-92), secular portrait-painters.

This they did, and entered the house, admitted by an old woman without a single tooth, to whom they were as civil as strangers can be when their only chance of rest and shelter lies in the favour of the householder.

"A nice little cottage," said Jude.

"O, I don't know about the niceness. I shall have to thatch it soon, and where the thatch is to come from I can't tell, for straw do get that dear, that 'twill soon be cheaper to cover your house wi' chainey plates[1] than thatch."

They sat there resting, and the shepherd came in. "Don't 'ee mind I," he said, with a deprecating wave of the hand; "bide here as long as ye will. But mid[2] you be thinking o' getting back to Melchester to-night by train? Because you'll never do it in this world, since you don't know the lie of the country. I don't mind going with ye some o' the ways, but even then the train mid be gone."

They started up.

"You can bide here, you know, over the night – can't 'em, mother? The place is welcome to ye. 'Tis hard lying, rather, but volk may do worse." He turned to Jude and asked privately: "Be you a married couple?"

"Hsh – no!" said Jude.

"O – I meant nothing ba'dy[3] – not I! Well, then, she can go into mother's room, and you and I can lie in the outer chimmer[4] after they've gone through. I can call ye soon enough to catch the first train back. You've lost this one now."

On consideration they decided to close with this offer, and drew up and shared with the shepherd and his mother the boiled bacon and greens for supper.

"I rather like this," said Sue, while their entertainers were clearing away the dishes. "Outside all laws except gravitation and germination."

"You only think you like it; you don't: you are quite a product of civilization," said Jude, a recollection of her engagement reviving his soreness a little.

---

1 chainey plates] (dl.:) china plates.
2 mid] (dl.:) may, might.
3 ba'dy] (dl.:) bawdy, indecent.
4 chimmer] (dl.:) chamber, room.

"Indeed I am not, Jude. I like reading and all that, but I crave to get back to the life of my infancy and its freedom."

"Do you remember it so well? You seem to me to have nothing unconventional at all about you."

"O, haven't I! You don't know what's inside me."

"What?"

"The Ishmaelite."[1]

"An urban miss is what you are."

She looked severe disagreement, and turned away.

The shepherd aroused them the next morning, as he had said. It was bright and clear, and the four miles to the train were accomplished pleasantly. When they had reached Melchester, and walked to the Close, and the gables of the old building in which she was again to be immured rose before Sue's eyes, she looked a little scared. "I expect I shall catch it!" she murmured.

They rang the great bell and waited.

"O, I bought something for you, which I had nearly forgotten," she said quickly, searching her pocket. "It is a new little photograph of me. Would you like it?"

"*Would* I!" He took it gladly, and the porter came. There seemed to be an ominous glance on his face when he opened the gate. She passed in, looking back at Jude, and waving her hand.

III.-III.

THE seventy young women, of ages varying in the main from nineteen to one-and-twenty, though several were older, who at this date filled the species of nunnery known as the Training-School at Melchester, formed a very mixed community, which included the daughters of mechanics, curates, surgeons, shopkeepers, farmers, dairymen, soldiers, sailors, and villagers. They sat in the large school-room of the establishment on the evening previously described, and word was passed round that Sue Bridehead had not come in at closing-time.

"She went out with her young man," said a second-year's student,

---

1 Ishmaelite] rebel. "Ishmael.....will be a wild man; his hand *will be* against every man, and every man's hand against him" (Genesis 16:11-12).

who knew about young men. "And Miss Traceley saw her at the station with him. She'll have it hot when she does come."

"She said it was her cousin," observed a youthful new girl.

"That excuse has been made a little too often in this school to be effectual in saving our souls," said the head girl of the year, drily.

The fact was that, only twelve months before, there had occurred a lamentable seduction of one of the pupils, who had made the same statement in order to gain meetings with her lover. The affair had created a scandal, and the management had consequently been rough on cousins ever since.

At nine o'clock the names were called, Sue's being pronounced three times sonorously by Miss Traceley without eliciting an answer.

At a quarter past nine the seventy stood up to sing the "Evening Hymn," and then knelt down to prayers. After prayers they went in to supper, and every girl's thought was, Where is Sue Bridehead? Some of the students, who had seen Jude from the window, felt that they would not mind risking her punishment for the pleasure of being kissed by such a kindly-faced young man. Hardly one among them believed in the cousinship.

Half-an-hour later they all lay in their cubicles, their tender feminine faces upturned to the flaring gas-jets which at intervals stretched down the long dormitories, every face bearing the legend "The Weaker" upon it, as the penalty of the sex wherein they were moulded, which by no possible exertion of their willing hearts and abilities could be made strong while the inexorable laws of nature remain what they are. They formed a pretty, suggestive, pathetic sight, of whose pathos and beauty they were themselves unconscious, and would not discover till, amid the storms and strains of after-years, with their injustice, loneliness, child-bearing, and bereavement, their minds would revert to this experience as to something which had been allowed to slip past them insufficiently regarded.

One of the mistresses came in to turn out the lights, and before doing so gave a final glance at Sue's cot, which remained empty, and at her little dressing-table at the foot, which, like all the rest, was ornamented with various girlish trifles, framed photographs being not the least conspicuous among them. Sue's table had a moderate show, two men in their filigree and velvet frames standing together beside her looking-glass.

"Who are these men – did she ever say?" asked the mistress. "Strictly speaking, relations' portraits only are allowed on these tables, you know."

"One – the middle-aged man," said a student in the next bed – "is the schoolmaster she served under – Mr. Phillotson."

"And the other – this undergraduate in cap and gown – who is he?"

"He is a friend, or was. She has never told his name."

"Was it either of these two who came for her?"

"No."

"You are sure 'twas not the undergraduate?"

"Quite. He was a young man with a black beard."

The lights were promptly extinguished, and till they fell asleep the girls indulged in conjectures about Sue, and wondered what games she had carried on in London and at Christminster before she came here, some of the more restless ones getting out of bed and looking from the mullioned windows at the vast west front of the Cathedral opposite, and the spire rising behind it.

When they awoke the next morning they glanced into Sue's nook, to find it still without a tenant. After the early lessons by gas-light, in half-toilet,[1] and when they had come up to dress for break-fast, the bell of the entrance gate was heard to ring loudly. The mistress of the dormitory went away, and presently came back to say that the Principal's orders were that nobody was to speak to Bride-head without permission.

When, accordingly, Sue came into the dormitory to hastily tidy herself, looking flushed and tired, she went to her cubicle in silence, none of them coming out to greet her or to make inquiry. When they had gone downstairs they found that she did not follow them into the dining-hall to breakfast, and they then learnt that she had been severely reprimanded, and ordered to a solitary room for a week, there to be confined, and take her meals, and do all her reading.

At this the seventy murmured, the sentence being, they thought, too severe. A round robin[2] was prepared and sent in to the Principal, asking for a remission of Sue's punishment. No notice was taken.

1   in half-toilet] half-dressed.
2   round robin] letter or petition signed by numerous people (originally with signatures prudently arranged in a circle).

Towards evening, when the geography mistress began dictating her subject, the girls in the class sat with folded arms.

"You mean that you are not going to work?" said the mistress at last. "I may as well tell you that it has been ascertained that the young man Bridehead stayed out with was not her cousin, for the very good reason that she has no such relative. We have written to Christminster to ascertain."

"We are willing to take her word," said the head girl.

"This young man was discharged from his work at Christminster for drunkenness and blasphemy in public-houses, and he has come here to live, entirely to be near her."

However, they remained stolid and motionless, and the mistress left the room to inquire from her superiors what was to be done.

Presently, towards dusk, the pupils, as they sat, heard exclamations from the first-year's girls in an adjoining class-room, and one rushed in to say that Sue Bridehead had got out of the back window of the room in which she had been confined, escaped in the dark across the lawn, and disappeared. How she had managed to get out of the garden nobody could tell, as it was bounded by the river at the bottom, and the side door was locked.

They went and looked at the empty room, the casement[1] between the middle mullions of which stood open. The lawn was again searched with a lantern, every bush and shrub being examined, but she was nowhere hidden. Then the porter of the front gate was interrogated, and on reflection he said that he remembered hearing a sort of splashing in the stream at the back, but he had taken no notice, thinking some ducks had come down the river from above.

"She must have walked through the river!" said a mistress.

"Or drounded herself," said the porter.

The mind of the matron was horrified – not so much at the possible death of Sue as at the possible half-column detailing that event in all the newspapers, which, added to the scandal of the year before, would give the College an unenviable notoriety for many months to come.

More lanterns were procured, and the river examined; and then, at last, on the opposite shore, which was open to the fields, some little

---

1 casement] hinged part of a window, opening outwards.

boot-tracks were discerned in the mud, which left no doubt that the too excitable girl had waded through a depth of water reaching nearly to her shoulders – for this was the chief river of the county, and was mentioned in all the geography books with respect. As Sue had not brought disgrace upon the school by drowning herself, the matron began to speak superciliously of her, and to express gladness that she was gone.

On the self-same evening Jude sat in his lodgings by the Close Gate. Often at this hour after dusk he would enter the silent Close, and stand opposite the house that contained Sue, and watch the shadows of the girl's heads passing to and fro upon the blinds, and wish he had nothing else to do but to sit reading and learning all day what many of the thoughtless inmates despised. But to-night, having finished tea and brushed himself up, he was deep in the perusal of the Twenty-ninth Volume of Pusey's Library of the Fathers,[1] a set of books which he had purchased of a second-hand dealer at a price that seemed to him one of miraculous cheapness for that invaluable work. He fancied he heard something rattle lightly against his window; then he heard it again. Certainly somebody had thrown gravel. He rose and gently lifted the sash.

"Jude!" (from below).

"Sue!"

"Yes – it is! Can I come up without being seen?"

"O yes!"

"Then don't come down. Shut the window."

Jude waited, knowing that she could enter easily enough, the front door being opened merely by a knob which anybody could turn, as in most old country towns. He palpitated at the thought that she had fled to him in her trouble as he had fled to her in his. What counterparts they were! He unlatched the door of his room, heard a stealthy rustle on the dark stairs, and in a moment she appeared in the light of his lamp. He went up to seize her hand, and found she was clammy as a marine deity, and that her clothes clung to her like the robes upon the figures in the Parthenon frieze.[2]

---

1 Pusey's.....Fathers] Edward B. Pusey was the general editor of the 51 volumes of *A Library of the Fathers of the Holy Catholic Church* (Oxford, 1838–85).

2 robes.....frieze] Hardy had seen such sculpted figures, removed from the Athenian Parthenon, at the British Museum.

"I'm so cold!" she said through her chattering teeth. "Can I come by your fire, Jude?"

She crossed to his little grate and very little fire, but as the water dripped from her as she moved, the idea of drying herself was absurd. "Whatever have you done, darling?" he asked, with alarm, the tender epithet slipping out unawares.

"Walked through the largest river in the county – that's what I've done! They locked me up for being out with you; and it seemed so unjust that I couldn't bear it, so I got out of the window and escaped across the stream!" She had begun the explanation in her usual slightly independent tones, but before she had finished the thin pink lips trembled, and she could hardly refrain from crying.

"Dear Sue!" he said. "You must take off all your things! And let me see – you must borrow some from the landlady. I'll ask her."

"No, no! Don't let her know, for God's sake! We are so near the school that they'll come after me!"

"Then you must put on mine. You don't mind?"

"O no."

"My Sunday suit, you know. It is close here." In fact, everything was close and handy in Jude's single chamber, because there was not room for it to be otherwise. He opened a drawer, took out his best dark suit, and giving the garments a shake, said, "Now, how long shall I give you?"

"Ten minutes."

Jude left the room and went into the street, where he walked up and down. A clock struck half-past seven, and he returned. Sitting in his only arm-chair he saw a slim and fragile being masquerading as himself on a Sunday, so pathetic in her defencelessness that his heart felt big with the sense of it. On two other chairs before the fire were her wet garments. She blushed as he sat down beside her, but only for a moment.

"I suppose, Jude, it is odd that you should see me like this and all my things hanging there? Yet what nonsense! They are only a woman's clothes – sexless cloth and linen.... I wish I didn't feel so ill and sick! Will you dry my clothes now? Please do, Jude, and I'll get a lodging by-and-by. It is not late yet."

"No, you shan't, if you are ill. You must stay here. Dear, dear Sue, what can I get for you?"

"I don't know! I can't help shivering. I wish I could get warm."
Jude put on her his great-coat in addition, and then ran out to the
nearest public-house, whence he returned with a little bottle in his
hand. "Here's six[1] of best brandy," he said. "Now you drink it, dear; all
of it."

"I can't out of the bottle, can I?" Jude fetched the glass from the
dressing-table, and administered the spirit in some water. She gasped a
little, but gulped it down, and lay back in the arm-chair.

She then began to relate circumstantially her experiences since
they had parted; but in the middle of her story her voice faltered, her
head nodded, and she ceased. She was in a sound sleep. Jude, dying of
anxiety lest she should have caught a chill which might permanently
injure her, was glad to hear the regular breathing. He softly went
nearer to her, and observed that a warm flush now rosed her hitherto
blue cheeks, and felt that her hanging hand was no longer cold. Then
he stood with his back to the fire regarding her, and saw in her almost
a divinity.

III.-IV.

JUDE'S reverie was interrupted by the creak of footsteps ascending
the stairs.

He whisked Sue's clothing from the chair where it was drying,
thrust it under the bed, and sat down to his book. Somebody
knocked and opened the door immediately. It was the landlady.

"O, I didn't know whether you was in or not, Mr. Fawley. I wanted to know if you would require supper. I see you've a young gentleman ——"

"Yes, ma'am. But I think I won't come down to-night. Will you
bring supper up on a tray, and I'll have a cup of tea as well."

It was Jude's custom to go downstairs to the kitchen, and eat his
meals with the family, to save trouble. His landlady brought up the
supper, however, on this occasion, and he took it from her at the
door.

When she had descended he set the teapot on the hob, and drew

---

1   six] sixpennyworth.

out Sue's clothes anew; but they were far from dry. A thick woollen gown, he found, held a deal of water. So he hung them up again, and kept up his fire and mused as the steam from the garments went up the chimney.

Suddenly she said, "Jude!"

"Yes. All right. How do you feel now?"

"Better. Quite well. Why, I fell asleep, didn't I? What time is it? Not late surely?"

"It is past ten."

"Is it really? What *shall* I do!" she said, starting up.

"Stay where you are."

"Yes; that's what I want to do. But I don't know what they would say! And what will you do?"

"I am going to sit here by the fire all night, and read. To-morrow is Sunday, and I haven't to go out anywhere. Perhaps you will be saved a severe illness by resting there. Don't be frightened. I'm all right. Look here, what I have got for you. Some supper."

When she had sat upright she breathed plaintively and said, "I do feel rather weak still. I thought I was well; and I ought not to be here, ought I?" But the supper fortified her somewhat, and when she had had some tea and had lain back again she was bright and cheerful.

The tea must have been green, or too long drawn, for she seemed preternaturally wakeful afterwards, though Jude, who had not taken any, began to feel heavy; till her conversation fixed his attention.

"You called me a creature of civilization, or something, didn't you?" she said, breaking a silence. "It was very odd you should have done that."

"Why?"

"Well, because it is provokingly wrong. I am a sort of negation of it."

"You are very philosophical. 'A negation' is profound talking."

"Is it? Do I strike you as being learned?" she asked, with a touch of raillery.

"No – not learned. Only you don't talk quite like a girl – well, a girl who has had no advantages."

"I have had advantages. I don't know Latin and Greek, though I know the grammars of those tongues. But I know most of the Greek and Latin classics through translations, and other books too. I read

Lemprière, Catullus, Martial, Juvenal, Lucian, Beaumont and Fletcher, Boccaccio, Scarron, De Brantôme, Sterne, De Foe, Smollet, Fielding, Shakespeare, the Bible,[1] and other such; and found that all interest in the unwholesome part of those books ended with its mystery."

"You have read more than I," he said with a sigh. "How came you to read some of those queerer ones?"

"Well," she said thoughtfully, "it was by accident. My life has been entirely shaped by what people call a peculiarity in me. I have no fear of men, as such, nor of their books. I have mixed with them – one or two of them particularly – almost as one of their own sex. I mean I have not felt about them as most women are taught to feel – to be on their guard against attacks on their virtue; for no average man – no man short of a sensual savage – will molest a woman by day or night, at home or abroad, unless she invites him. Until she says by a look 'Come on' he is always afraid to, and if you never say it, or look it, he never comes. However, what I was going to say is that when I was eighteen I formed a friendly intimacy with an undergraduate at Christminster, and he taught me a great deal, and lent me books which I should never have got hold of otherwise."

"Is your friendship broken off?"

"O yes. He died, poor fellow, two or three years after he had taken his degree and left Christminster."

"You saw a good deal of him, I suppose?"

"Yes. We used to go about together – on walking tours, reading tours, and things of that sort – like two men almost. He asked me to live with him, and I agreed to by letter. But when I joined him in London I found he meant a different thing from what I meant. He wanted to be my lover, in fact, but I wasn't in love with him – and on my saying I should go away if he didn't agree to my plan, he did so. We shared a sitting-room for fifteen months; and he became a leader-writer for one of the great London dailies; till he was taken ill, and had to go abroad. He said I was breaking his heart by holding out against him so long at such close quarters; he could never have believed it of woman. I might play that game once too often, he said. He came home merely to die. His death caused a terrible remorse in

---

1   Lemprière.....Bible] As does the Bible, the works of the listed authors contain sexu-
    ally frank material which some Victorians would have found shocking.

me for my cruelty – though I hope he died of consumption and not of me entirely. I went down to Sandbourne[1] to his funeral, and was his only mourner. He left me a little money – because I broke his heart, I suppose. That's how men are – so much better than women!"

"Good heavens! – what did you do then?"

"Ah – now you are angry with me!" she said, a contralto note of tragedy coming suddenly into her silvery voice. "I wouldn't have told you if I had known!"

"No, I am not. Tell me all."

"Well, I invested his money, poor fellow, in a bubble scheme,[2] and lost it. I lived about London by myself for some time, and then I returned to Christminster, as my father – who was also in London, and had started as an art metal-worker near Long-Acre – wouldn't have me back; and I got that occupation in the artist-shop where you found me.... I said you didn't know how bad I was!"

Jude looked round upon the arm-chair and its occupant, as if to read more carefully the creature he had given shelter to. His voice trembled as he said: "However you have lived, Sue, I believe you are as innocent as you are unconventional!"

"I am not particularly innocent, as you see, now that I have

'twitched the robe
From that blank lay-figure your fancy draped,'"[3]

said she, with an ostensible sneer, though he could hear that she was brimming with tears. "But I have never yielded myself to any lover, if that's what you mean! I have remained as I began."

"I quite believe you. But some women would not have remained as they began."

"Perhaps not. Better women would not. People say I must be cold-natured, – sexless – on account of it. But I won't have it! Some of the most passionately erotic poets have been the most self-contained in their daily lives."

---

1 Sandbourne] fictional counterpart to Bournemouth.
2 bubble scheme] speculative investment scheme which (like the "South Sea Bubble") is initially profitable but finally disastrous.
3 'twitched.....draped,'] from Browning's poem "Too Late."

"Have you told Mr. Phillotson about this University-scholar-friend?"

"Yes – long ago. I have never made any secret of it to anybody."

"What did he say?"

"He did not pass any criticism – only said I was everything to him, whatever I did; and things like that."

Jude felt much depressed; she seemed to get further and further away from him with her strange ways and curious unconsciousness of gender.

"Aren't you *really* vexed with me, dear Jude?" she suddenly asked, in a voice of such extraordinary tenderness that it hardly seemed to come from the same woman who had just told her story so lightly. "I would rather offend anybody in the world than you, I think!"

"I don't know whether I am vexed or not. I know I care very much about you!"

"I care as much for you as for anybody I ever met."

"You don't care *more*! There, I ought not to say that. Don't answer it!"

There was another long silence. He felt that she was treating him cruelly, though he could not quite say in what way. Her very helplessness seemed to make her so much stronger than he.

"I am awfully ignorant on general matters, although I have worked so hard," he said, to turn the subject. "I am absorbed in Theology, you know. And what do you think I should be doing just about now, if you weren't here? I should be saying my evening prayers. I suppose you wouldn't like ——"

"O no, no," she answered, "I would rather not, if you don't mind. I should seem so – such a hypocrite."

"I thought you wouldn't join, so I didn't propose it. You must remember that I hope to be a useful minister some day."

"To be ordained, I think you said?"

"Yes."

"Then you haven't given up the idea? – I thought that perhaps you had by this time."

"Of course not. I fondly thought at first that you felt as I do about that, as you were so steeped in Christminster. And Mr. Phillotson ——"

"I have no respect for Christminster whatever, except, in a qualified degree, on its intellectual side," said Sue Bridehead earnestly. "My friend I spoke of took that out of me. He was the most irreligious man I ever knew, and the most moral. And intellect at Christminster is new wine in old bottles.[1] The mediævalism of Christminster must go, be sloughed off, or Christminster itself will have to go. To be sure, at times one couldn't help having a sneaking liking for the traditions of the old faith, as preserved by a section of the thinkers there in touching and simple sincerity; but when I was in my saddest, rightest mind I always felt,

'O ghastly glories of saints, dead limbs of gibbeted Gods!'"...[2]

"Sue, you are not a good friend of mine to talk like that!"

"Then I won't, dear Jude!" The emotional throat-note had come back, and she turned her face away.

"I still think Christminster has much that is glorious; though I was resentful because I couldn't get there." He spoke gently, and resisted his impulse to pique her on to tears.

"It is an ignorant place, except as to the townspeople, artizans, drunkards, and paupers," she said, hurt still at his differing from her. "*They* see life as it is, of course; but few of the people in the colleges do. You prove it in your own person. You are one of the very men Christminster was intended for when the colleges were founded;[3] a man with a passion for learning, but no money, or opportunities, or friends. But you were elbowed off the pavement by the millionaires' sons."

"Well, I can do without what it confers. I care for something higher."

"And I for something broader, truer," she insisted.

"At present intellect in Christminster is pushing one way, and

---

1 new wine in old bottles] The original source of the metaphor is the New Testament (e.g.: Matthew 9:17; Mark 2:22), but Hardy is recalling Matthew Arnold's essay "Heine", which says that in modern Europe there is conflict between the "new wine" of modern ideas and the "old bottles" of outmoded forms. (See Appendix E.)

2 'O.....Gods!'"...] from Swinburne's "Hymn to Proserpine." (See Appendix E.)

3 You.....founded] A common object of many of the early endowments of Oxford colleges was indeed the education of the poor.

religion the other; and so they stand stock-still, like two rams butting each other."

"What would Mr. Phillotson ——"

"It is a place full of fetichists and ghost-seers!"

He noticed that whenever he tried to speak of the schoolmaster she turned the conversation to some generalizations about the offending University. Jude was extremely, morbidly, curious about her life as Phillotson's *protégée*[1] and betrothed; yet she would not enlighten him.

"Well, that's just what I am, too," he said. "I am fearful of life, spectre-seeing always."

"But you are good and dear!" she murmured.

His heart bumped, and he made no reply.

"You are in the Tractarian stage just now, are you not?" she added, putting on flippancy to hide real feeling, a common trick with her. "Let me see – when was I there? – In the year eighteen hundred and ——"

"There's a sarcasm in that which is rather unpleasant to me, Sue. Now will you do what I want you to? At this time I read a chapter, and then say prayers, as I told you. Now will you concentrate your attention on any book of these you like, and sit with your back to me, and leave me to my custom? You are sure you won't join me?"

"I'll look at you."

"No. Don't tease, Sue!"

"Very well – I'll do just as you bid me, and I won't vex you, Jude," she replied, in the tone of a child who was going to be good for ever after, turning her back upon him accordingly. A small Bible other than the one he used lay near her, and during his retreat she took it up, and turned over the leaves.

"Jude," she said brightly, when he had finished and come back to her; "will you let me make you a *new* New Testament, like the one I made for myself at Christminster?"

"O yes. How was that made?"

"I altered my old one by cutting up all the Epistles and Gospels into separate *brochures,* and re-arranging them in chronological order

---

1 *protégée*] (Fr.:) female who is subject to the patronage of someone.

as written, beginning the book with Romans, following on with the early Epistles, and putting the Gospels much further on. Then I had the volume rebound. My University friend Mr.—— — but never mind his name, poor boy – said it was an excellent idea. I know that reading it afterwards made it twice as interesting as before, and twice as understandable."

"H'm!" said Jude, with a sense of sacrilege.

"And what a literary enormity this is," she said, as she glanced into the pages of Solomon's Song. "I mean the synopsis at the head of each chapter, explaining away the real nature of that rhapsody. You needn't be alarmed: nobody claims inspiration for the chapter headings. Indeed, many divines treat them with contempt. It seems the drollest thing to think of the four and twenty elders, or bishops, or whatever number they were, sitting with long faces and writing down such misinformation."

Jude looked pained. "You are quite Voltairean!"[1] he murmured.

"Indeed? Then I won't say any more, except that people have no right to falsify the Bible! I *hate* such humbug as could attempt to plaster over with ecclesiastical abstractions such ecstatic, natural, human love as lies in that great and passionate song!" Her speech had grown spirited, and almost petulant at his rebuke, and her eyes moist. "I *wish* I had a friend here to support me; but nobody is ever on my side!"

"But, my dear Sue, my very dear Sue, I am not against you!" he said, taking her hand, and surprised at her introducing personal feeling into mere argument.

"Yes you are, yes you are!" she cried, turning away her face that he might not see her brimming eyes. "You are on the side of the people in the Training School – at least you seem almost to be! What I insist on is, that to explain such verses as this: 'Whither is thy beloved gone, O thou fairest among women?' by the note: '*The Church professeth her faith*'[2] is supremely ridiculous!"

"Well then, let it be! You make such a personal matter of everything! I am – only too inclined just now to apply the words profanely. You know *you* are fairest among women to me, come to that!"

---

1 Voltairean] sceptical and anti-clerical, like the satirist Voltaire.

2 Whither.....*faith*] The heading, "*The church professeth her faith in Christ*", precedes the verse of the Song of Solomon (6:1) quoted by Sue.

"But you are not to say it now!" Sue replied, her voice changing to its softest note of severity. Then their eyes met, and they shook hands like cronies in a tavern, and Jude saw the absurdity of quarrelling on such a hypothetical subject, and she the silliness of crying about what was written in an old book like the Bible.

"I won't disturb your convictions – I really won't!" she went on soothingly, for now he was rather more ruffled than she. "But I did want and long to ennoble some man to high aims; and when I saw you, and knew you wanted to be my comrade, I – shall I confess it? – thought that man might be you. But you take so much tradition on trust that I don't know what to say."

"Well, dear; I suppose one must take some things on trust. Life isn't long enough to work out everything in Euclid problems[1] before you believe it. I take Christianity."

"Well, perhaps you might take something worse."

"Indeed I might. Perhaps I have done so!" He thought of Arabella.

"I won't ask what, because we are going to be *very* nice with each other, aren't we, and never, never, vex each other any more?" She looked up trustfully, and her voice seemed trying to nestle in his breast.

"I shall always care for you!" said Jude.

"And I for you. Because you are single-hearted, and forgiving to your faulty and tiresome little Sue!"

He looked away, for that epicene tenderness of hers was too harrowing. Was it that which had broken the heart of the poor leader-writer; and was he to be the next one? ... But Sue was so dear! ... If he could only get over the sense of her sex, as she seemed to be able to do so easily of his, what a comrade she would make; for their difference of opinion on conjectural subjects only drew them closer together on matters of daily human experience. She was nearer to him than any other woman he had ever met, and he could scarcely believe that time, creed, or absence, would ever divide him from her.

But his grief at her incredulities returned. They sat on till she fell asleep again, and he nodded in his chair likewise. Whenever he aroused himself he turned her things, and made up the fire anew. About six o'clock he awoke completely, and lighting a candle, found

---

1   Euclid problems] basic geometrical exercises and formulæ established by Euclid.

that her clothes were dry. Her chair being a far more comfortable one than his she still slept on, inside his great-coat, looking warm as a new bun and boyish as a Ganymedes.[1] Placing the garments by her and touching her on the shoulder he went downstairs, and washed himself by starlight in the yard.

III.-V.

WHEN he returned she was dressed as usual.

"Now could I get out without anybody seeing me?" she asked.

"The town is not yet astir."

"But you have had no breakfast."

"O, I don't want any! I fear I ought not to have run away from that school! Things seem so different in the cold light of the morning, don't they? What Mr. Phillotson will say I don't know! It was quite by his wish that I went there. He is the only man in the world for whom I have any respect or fear. I hope he'll forgive me; but he'll scold me dreadfully, I expect!"

"I'll go to him and explain –" began Jude.

"O no, you shan't. I don't care for him! He may think what he likes – I shall do just as I choose!"

"But you just this moment said ———"

"Well, if I did, I shall do as I like for all him! I have thought of what I shall do – go to the sister of one of my fellow-students in the Training School, who has asked me to visit her. She has a school near Shaston,[2] about eighteen miles from here – and I shall stay there till this has blown over, and I get back to the Training School again."

At the last moment he persuaded her to let him make her a cup of coffee, in a portable apparatus he kept in his room for use on rising to go to his work every day before the household was astir.

"Now a dew-bit[3] to eat with it," he said; "and off we go. You can have a regular breakfast when you get there."

They went quietly out of the house, Jude accompanying her to the station. As they departed along the street a head was softly thrust out

---

1 Ganymedes] the beautiful youth loved by Zeus.
2 Shaston] Shaftesbury in Dorsetshire.
3 dew-bit] (dl.:) small snack taken before breakfast.

of an upper window, and quicky withdrawn. Sue still seemed sorry for her rashness, and to wish she had not rebelled; telling him at parting that she would let him know as soon as she got re-admitted to the Training School. They stood rather miserably together on the platform; and it was apparent that he wanted to say more.

"I want to tell you something – two things," he said hurriedly as the train came up. "One is a warm one, the other a cold one!"

"Jude," she said. "I know one of them. And you mustn't!"

"What?"

"You mustn't love me. You are to like me – that's all!"

Jude's face became so full of complicated glooms that hers was agitated in sympathy as she bade him adieu through the carriage window. And then the train moved on, and waving her pretty hand to him she vanished away.

Melchester was a dismal place enough for Jude that Sunday of her departure, and the Close so hateful that he did not go once to the Cathedral services. The next morning there came a letter from her, which, with her usual promptitude, she had written directly she had reached her friend's house. She told him of her safe arrival and comfortable quarters, and then added: –

"What I really write about, dear Jude, is something I said to you at parting. You had been so very good and kind to me that when you were out of sight I felt what a cruel and ungrateful woman I was to say it, and it has reproached me ever since. *If you want to love me, Jude, you may:* I don't mind at all; and I'll never say again that you mustn't!

"Now I won't write any more about that. You do forgive your thoughtless friend for her cruelty? and won't make her miserable by saying you don't? – Ever,

SUE."

It would be superfluous to say what his answer was; and how he thought what he would have done had he been free, which should have rendered a long residence with a female friend quite unnecessary for Sue. He felt he might have been pretty sure of his own victory, if it had come to a conflict between Phillotson and himself for the possession of her.

Yet Jude was in danger of attaching more meaning to Sue's impulsive note than it really was intended to bear.

After the lapse of a few days he found himself hoping that she would write again. But he received no further communication; and in the intensity of his solicitude he sent another note, suggesting that he should pay her a visit some Sunday, the distance being under eighteen miles.

He expected a reply on the second morning after despatching his missive; but none came. The third morning arrived; the postman did not stop. This was Saturday, and in a feverish state of anxiety about her he sent off three brief lines stating that he was coming the following day, for he felt sure something had happened.

His first and natural thought had been that she was ill from her immersion; but it soon occurred to him that somebody would have written for her in such a case. Conjectures were put an end to by his arrival at the village school-house near Shaston on the bright morning of Sunday, between eleven and twelve o'clock, when the parish was as vacant as a desert, most of the inhabitants having gathered inside the church, whence their voices could occasionally be heard in unison.

A little girl opened the door. "Miss Bridehead is upstairs," she said. "And will you please walk up to her?"

"Is she ill?" asked Jude hastily.

"Only a little – not very."

Jude entered and ascended. On reaching the landing a voice told him which way to turn – the voice of Sue calling his name. He passed the doorway, and found her lying in a little bed in a room a dozen feet square.

"O Sue!" he cried, sitting down beside her and taking her hand. "How is this! You couldn't write?"

"No – it wasn't that!" she answered. "I did catch a bad cold – but I could have written. Only I wouldn't!"

"Why not? – frightening me like this!"

"Yes – that was what I was afraid of! But I had decided not to write to you any more. They won't have me back at the school – that's why I couldn't write. Not the fact, but the reason!"

"Well?"

"They not only won't have me, but they give me a parting piece of advice ——"

"What?"

She did not answer directly. "I vowed I would never tell you, Jude – it is so vulgar and distressing!"

"Is it about us?"

"Yes."

"But do tell me!"

"Well – somebody has sent them baseless reports about us, and they say you and I ought to marry as soon as possible, for the sake of my reputation! …There – now I have told you, and I wish I hadn't!"

"O poor Sue!"

"I don't think of you like that means! It did just *occur* to me to regard you in the way they think I do, but I hadn't begun to. I *have* recognized that the cousinship was merely nominal, since we met as total strangers. But my marrying you, dear Jude – why, of course, if I had reckoned upon marrying you I shouldn't have come to you so often! And I never supposed you thought of such a thing as marrying me till the other evening; when I began to fancy you did love me a little. Perhaps I ought not to have been so intimate with you. It is all my fault. Everything is my fault always!"

The speech seemed a little forced and unreal, and they regarded each other with a mutual distress.

"I was so blind at first!" she went on. "I didn't see what you felt at all. O you have been unkind to me – you have – to look upon me as a sweetheart without saying a word, and leaving me to discover it myself! Your attitude to me has become known; and naturally they think we've been doing wrong! I'll never trust you again!"

"Yes, Sue," he said simply, "I am to blame – more than you think. I was quite aware that you did not suspect till within the last meeting or two what I was feeling about you. I admit that our meeting as strangers prevented a sense of relationship, and that it was a sort of subterfuge to avail myself of it. But don't you think I deserve a little consideration for concealing my wrong, very wrong, sentiments, since I couldn't help having them?"

She turned her eyes doubtfully towards him, and then looked away as if afraid she might forgive him.

By every law of nature and sex a kiss was the only rejoinder that fitted the mood and the moment, under the suasion of which Sue's undemonstrative regard of him might not inconceivably have changed its temperature. Some men would have cast scruples to the winds, and ventured it, oblivious both of Sue's declaration of her neutral feelings, and of the pair of autographs in the vestry chest of Arabella's parish church. Jude did not. He had, in fact, come in part to tell his own fatal story. It was upon his lips; yet at the hour of this distress he could not disclose it. He preferred to dwell upon the recognized barriers between them.

"Of course – I know you don't – care about me in any particular way," he said huskily. "You ought not, and you are right. You belong to – Mr. Phillotson. I suppose he has been to see you?"

"Yes," she said shortly, her face changing a little. "Though I didn't ask him to come. You are glad, of course, that he has been! But I shouldn't care if he didn't come any more!"

It was very perplexing to her lover that she should be piqued at his honest acquiescence in his rival, if Jude's feelings of love were deprecated by her. He went on to something else.

"This will blow over, dear Sue," he said. "The Training School authorities are not all the world. You can get to be a student in some other, no doubt."

"I'll ask Mr. Phillotson," she said decisively.

Sue's kind hostess now returned from church, and there was no more intimate conversation. Jude left in the afternoon, hopelessly unhappy. But he had seen her, and sat with her. Such intercourse as that would have to content him for the remainder of his life. The lesson of renunciation it was necessary and proper that he, as a parish priest, should learn.

But the next morning when he awoke he felt rather vexed with her, and decided that she was rather unreasonable, not to say capricious. Then, in illustration of what he had begun to discern as one of her redeeming characteristics there came promptly a note, which she must have written almost immediately he had gone from her:

"Forgive me for my petulance yesterday! I was horrid to you; I know it, and I feel perfectly miserable at my horridness. It was so dear of you not to be angry! Jude, please still keep me as your friend and associate, with all my faults. I'll try not to be like it again.

"I am coming to Melchester on Saturday, to get my things away from the T. S., &c. I could walk with you for half-an-hour, if you would like? — Your repentant

SUE."

Jude forgave her straightway, and asked her to call for him at the Cathedral works when she came.

III.-VI.

MEANWHILE a middle-aged man was dreaming a dream of great beauty concerning the writer of the above letter. He was Richard Phillotson, who had recently removed from the mixed village school at Lumsdon near Christminster, to undertake a large boys' school in his native town of Shaston, which stood on a hill sixty miles to the south-west as the crow flies.

A glance at the place and its accessories was almost enough to reveal that the schoolmaster's plans and dreams so long indulged in had been abandoned for some new dream with which neither the Church nor literature had much in common. Essentially an unpractical man, he was now bent on making and saving money for a practical purpose — that of keeping a wife, who, if she chose, might conduct one of the girls' schools adjoining his own; for which purpose he had advised her to go into training, since she would not marry him offhand.[1]

About the time that Jude was removing from Marygreen to Melchester, and entering on adventures at the latter place with Sue, the schoolmaster was settling down in the new schoolhouse at Shaston. All the furniture being fixed, the books shelved, and the nails driven, he had begun to sit in his parlour during the dark winter nights and re-attempt some of his old studies — one branch of which had included Roman-Britannic antiquities — an unremunerative labour for a National schoolmaster,[2] but a subject that, after his abandonment of the University scheme, had interested him as being a

---

1   offhand] without preparation; promptly.
2   National schoolmaster] master at a school established by the National Society for Promoting the Education of the Poor in the Principles of the Established Church.

comparatively unworked mine; practicable to those, who, like himself, had lived in lonely spots where these remains were abundant, and were seen to compel inferences in startling contrast to accepted views on the civilization of that time.[1]

A resumption of this investigation was the outward and apparent hobby of Phillotson at present – his ostensible reason for going alone into fields where causeways, dykes, and tumuli abounded, or shutting himself up in his house with a few urns, tiles, and mosaics he had collected, instead of calling round upon his new neighbours, who for their part had showed themselves willing enough to be friendly with him. But it was not the real, or the whole, reason, after all. Thus on a particular evening in the month, when it had grown quite late – to near midnight, indeed – and the light of his lamp, shining from his window at a salient angle of the hill-top town over infinite miles of valley westward, announced as by words a place and person given over to study, he was not exactly studying.

The interior of the room – the books, the furniture, the schoolmaster's loose coat, his attitude at the table, even the flickering of the fire, bespoke the same dignified tale of undistracted research – more than creditable to a man who had had no advantages beyond those of his own making. And yet the tale, true enough till latterly, was not true now. What he was regarding was not history. They were historic notes, written in a bold womanly hand at his dictation some months before, and it was the clerical rendering of word after word that absorbed him.

He presently took from a drawer a carefully tied bundle of letters, few, very few, as correspondence counts nowadays. Each was in its envelope just as it had arrived, and the handwriting was of the same womanly character as the historic notes. He unfolded them one by one and read them musingly. At first sight there seemed in these small documents to be absolutely nothing to muse over. They were straightforward, frank letters, signed "Sue B—"; just such ones as would be written during short absences, with no other thought than their speedy destruction, and chiefly concerning books in reading and other experiences of a Training School, forgotten doubtless by the

---

1 inferences.....time] as he infers that that civilisation was more advanced and complex than had been supposed.

writer with the passing of the day of their inditing. In one of them – quite a recent note – the young woman said that she had received his considerate letter, and that it was honourable and generous of him to say he would not come to see her oftener than she desired (the school being such an awkward place for callers, and because of her strong wish that her engagement to him should not be known, which it would infallibly be if he visited her often). Over these phrases the schoolmaster pored. What precise shade of satisfaction was to be gathered from a woman's gratitude that the man who loved her had not been often to see her? The problem occupied him, distracted him.

He opened another drawer, and found therein an envelope, from which he drew a photograph of Sue as a child, long before he had known her, standing under trellis-work with a little basket in her hand. There was another of her as a young woman, her dark eyes and hair making a very distinct and attractive picture of her, which just disclosed, too, the thoughtfulness that lay behind her lighter moods. It was a duplicate of the one she had given Jude, and would have given to any man. Phillotson brought it half-way to his lips, but withdrew it in doubt at her perplexing phrases: ultimately kissing the dead paste-board with all the passionateness, and more than all the devotion, of a young man of eighteen.

The schoolmaster's was an unhealthy-looking, old-fashioned[1] face, rendered more old-fashioned by his style of shaving. A certain gentle-manliness had been imparted to it by nature, suggesting an inherent wish to do rightly by all. His speech was a little slow, but his tones were sincere enough to make his hesitation no defect. His greying hair was curly, and radiated from a point in the middle of his crown. There were four lines across his forehead, and he only wore spectacles when reading at night. It was almost certainly a renunciation forced upon him by his academic purpose, rather than a distaste for women, which had hitherto kept him from closing with one of the sex in matrimony.

Such silent proceedings as those of this evening were repeated many and oft times when he was not under the eye of the boys,

---

1   old-fashioned] (a) with a quizzically doubtful or disapproving appearance; (b) out of date, belonging to the past.

whose quick and penetrating regard would frequently become almost intolerable to the self-conscious master in his present anxious care for Sue, making him, in the grey hours of morning, dread to meet anew the gimlet[1] glances, lest they should read what the dream within him was.

He had honourably acquiesced in Sue's announced wish that he was not often to visit her at the Training School; but at length, his patience being sorely tried, he set out one Saturday afternoon to pay her an unexpected call. There the news of her departure – expulsion as it might almost have been considered – was flashed upon him without warning or mitigation as he stood at the door expecting in a few minutes to behold her face; and when he turned away he could hardly see the road before him.

Sue had, in fact, never written a line to her suitor on the subject, although it was fourteen days old. A short reflection told him that this proved nothing, a natural delicacy being as ample a reason for silence as any degree of blameworthiness.

They had informed him at the school where she was living, and having no immediate anxiety about her comfort his thoughts took the direction of a burning indignation against the Training School Committee. In his bewilderment Phillotson entered the adjacent cathedral, just now in a direly dismantled state by reason of the repairs. He sat down on a block of freestone, regardless of the dusty imprint it made on his breeches; and his listless eyes following the movements of the workmen he presently became aware that the reputed culprit, Sue's lover Jude, was one amongst them.

Jude had never spoken to his former hero since the meeting by the model of Jerusalem. Having inadvertently witnessed Phillotson's tentative courtship of Sue in the lane there had grown up in the younger man's mind a curious dislike to think of the elder, to meet him, to communicate in any way with him; and since Phillotson's success in obtaining at least her promise had become known to Jude, he had frankly recognized that he did not wish to see or hear of his senior any more, learn anything of his pursuits, or even imagine again what excellencies might appertain to his character. On this very day of the schoolmaster's visit Jude was expecting Sue, as she had promised, and when therefore he saw the schoolmaster in the nave of the building;

---

1   gimlet] penetrating.

saw, moreover, that he was coming to speak to him, he felt no little embarrassment; which Phillotson's own embarrassment prevented his observing.

Jude joined him, and they both withdrew from the other workmen to the spot where Phillotson had been sitting. Jude offered him a piece of sackcloth for a cushion, and told him it was dangerous to sit on the bare block.

"Yes; yes," said Phillotson abstractedly, as he reseated himself, his eyes resting on the ground as if he were trying to remember where he was. "I won't keep you long. It was merely that I have heard that you have seen my little friend Sue recently. It occurred to me to speak to you on that account. I merely want to ask – about her."

"I think I know what!" Jude hurriedly said. "About her escaping from the Training School, and her coming to me?"

"Yes."

"Well" – Jude for a moment felt an unprincipled and fiendish wish to annihilate his rival at all cost. By the exercise of that treachery which love for the same woman renders possible to men the most honourable in every other relation of life, he could send off Phillotson in agony and defeat by saying that the scandal was true, and that Sue had irretrievably committed herself with him. But his action did not respond for a moment to his animal instinct; and what he said was, "I am glad of your kindness in coming to talk plainly to me about it. You know what they say? – that I ought to marry her."

"What!"

"And I wish with all my soul I could!"

Phillotson trembled, and his naturally pale face acquired a corpselike sharpness in its lines. "I had no idea that it was of this nature! God forbid!"

"No, no!" said Jude aghast. "I thought you understood? I mean that were I in a position to marry her, or some one, and settle down, instead of living in lodgings here and there, I should be glad!"

What he had really meant was simply that he loved her.

"But – since this painful matter has been opened up – what really happened?" asked Phillotson, with the firmness of a man who felt that a sharp smart now was better than a long agony of suspense hereafter. "Cases arise, and this is one, when even ungenerous questions must be put to make false assumptions impossible, and to kill scandal."

Jude explained readily; giving the whole series of adventures, including the night at the shepherd's, her wet arrival at his lodging, her indisposition from her immersion, their vigil of discussion, and his seeing her off next morning.

"Well now," said Phillotson at the conclusion, "I take it as your final word, and I know I can believe you, that the suspicion which led to her rustication is an absolutely baseless one?"

"It is," said Jude solemnly. "Absolutely. So help me God!"

The schoolmaster rose. Each of the twain felt that the interview could not comfortably merge in a friendly discussion of their recent experiences, after the manner of friends; and when Jude had taken him round, and shown him some features of the renovation which the old cathedral was undergoing, Phillotson bade the young man good-day and went away.

This visit took place about eleven o'clock in the morning; but no Sue appeared. When Jude went to his dinner at one he saw his beloved ahead of him in the street leading up from the North Gate, walking as if in no way looking for him. Speedily overtaking her he remarked that he had asked her to come to him at the Cathedral, and she had promised.

"I have been to get my things from the College," she said – an observation which he was expected to take as an answer, though it was not one. Finding her to be in this evasive mood he felt inclined to give her the information so long withheld.

"You have not seen Mr. Phillotson to-day?" he ventured to inquire.

"I have not. But I am not going to be cross-examined about him; and if you ask anything more I won't answer!"

"It is very odd that –" He stopped, regarding her.

"What?"

"That you are never so nice in your real presence as you are in your letters!"

"Does it really seem so to you?" said she, smiling with quick curiosity. "Well, that's strange; but I feel just the same about you, Jude. When you are gone away I seem such a cold-hearted ——"

As she knew his sentiment towards her Jude saw that they were getting upon dangerous ground. It was now, he thought, that he must speak as an honest man.

But he did not speak, and she continued: "It was that which made me write and say – I didn't mind your loving me, – if you wanted to, much!"

The exultation he might have felt at what that implied, or seemed to imply, was nullified by his intention, and he rested rigid till he began: "I have never told you —"

"Yes you have," murmured she.

"I mean, I have never told you my history – all of it."

"But I guess it. I know nearly."

Jude looked up. Could she possibly know of that morning performance of his with Arabella; which in a few months had ceased to be a marriage more completely than by death? He saw that she did not.

"I can't quite tell you here in the street," he went on with a gloomy tongue. "And you had better not come to my lodgings. Let us go in here."

The building by which they stood was the market-house; it was the only place available; and they entered, the market being over, and the stalls and areas empty. He would have preferred a more congenial spot, but, as usually happens, in place of a romantic field or solemn aisle for his tale, it was told while they walked up and down over a floor littered with rotten cabbage-leaves, and amid all the usual squalors of decayed vegetable matter and unsaleable refuse. He began and finished his brief narrative, which merely led up to the information that he had married a wife some years earlier, and that his wife was living still. Almost before her countenance had time to change she hurried out the words,

"Why didn't you tell me before!"

"I couldn't. It seemed so cruel to tell it."

"To yourself, Jude. So it was better to be cruel to me!"

"No, dear darling!" cried Jude passionately. He tried to take her hand, but she withdrew it. Their old relations of confidence seemed suddenly to have ended, and the antagonisms of sex to sex were left without any counterpoising predilections. She was his comrade, friend, unconscious sweetheart no longer; and her eyes regarded him in estranged silence.

"I was ashamed of the episode in my life which brought about the marriage," he continued. "I can't explain it precisely now. I could have done it if you had taken it differently!"

"But how can I?" she burst out. "Here I have been saying, or writing, that – that you might love me, or something of the sort! – just out of charity – and all the time – O it is perfectly damnable how things are!" she said, stamping her foot in a nervous quiver.

"You take me wrong, Sue!" I never thought you cared for me at all, till quite lately; so I felt it did not matter! Do you care for me, Sue? – you know how I mean? – I don't like 'out of charity' at all!"

It was a question which in the circumstances Sue did not choose to answer.

"I suppose she – your wife – is – a very pretty woman, even if she's wicked?" she asked quickly.

"She's pretty enough, as far as that goes."

"Prettier than I am, no doubt!"

"You are not the least alike. And I have never seen her for years.... But she's sure to come back – they always do!"

"How strange of you to stay apart from her like this!" said Sue, her trembling lip and lumpy throat belying her irony. "You, such a religious man. How will the demi-gods in your Pantheon[1] – I mean those legendary persons you call Saints – intercede for you after this? Now if I had done such a thing it would have been different, and not remarkable, for I at least don't regard marriage as a Sacrament. Your theories are not so advanced as your practice!"

"Sue, you are terribly cutting when you like to be – a perfect Voltaire! But you must treat me as you will!"

When she saw how wretched he was she softened, and trying to blink away her sympathetic tears said with all the winning reproachfulness of a heart-hurt woman: "Ah – you should have told me before you gave me that idea that you wanted to be allowed to love me! I had no feeling before that moment at the railway-station, except –" For once Sue was as miserable as he, in her attempts to keep herself free from emotion, and her less than half-success.

"Don't cry, dear!" he implored.

"I am – not crying – because I love you; but because of your want of – confidence!"

They were quite screened from the Market-square without, and he could not help putting out his arm towards her waist. His momentary

---

1 Pantheon] temple dedicated to all the gods.

desire was the means of her rallying. "No, no!" she said, drawing back stringently, and wiping her eyes. "Of course not! It would be hypocrisy to pretend that it would be meant as from my cousin; and it can't be in any other way."

They moved on a dozen paces, and she showed herself recovered. It was distracting to Jude, and his heart would have ached less had she appeared anyhow but as she did appear; essentially large-minded and generous on reflection, despite a previous exercise of those narrow womanly humours on impulse that were necessary to give her sex.

"I don't blame you for what you couldn't help," she said smiling. "How should I be so foolish! I do blame you a little bit for not telling me before. But after all it doesn't matter. We should have had to keep apart, you see, even if this had not been in your life."

"No, we shouldn't Sue! This is the only obstacle!"

"You forget that I must have loved you, and wanted to be your wife, even if there had been no obstacle," said Sue, with a gentle seriousness which did not reveal her mind. "And then we are cousins, and it is bad for cousins to marry. And – I am engaged to somebody else. As to our going on together as we were going, in a sort of friendly way, the people round us would have made it unable to continue. Their views of the relations of man and woman are limited, as is proved by their expelling me from the school. Their philosophy only recognizes relations based on animal desire. The wide field of strong attachment where desire plays, at least, only a secondary part, is ignored by them – the part of – who is it? – Venus Urania."[1]

Her being able to talk learnedly showed that she was mistress of herself again; and before they parted she had almost regained her vivacious glance, her reciprocity of tone, her gay manner, and her second-thought attitude of critical largeness towards others of her age and sex.

He could speak more freely now. "There were several reasons against my telling you rashly. One was what I have said; another, that it was always impressed upon me that I ought not to marry – that I belonged to an odd and peculiar family – the wrong breed for marriage."

"Ah – who used to say that to you?"

---

1 Venus Urania] Venus as deity of spiritual love.

"My great-aunt. She said it always ended badly with us Fawleys."

"That's strange. My father used to say the same to me!"

They stood possessed by the same thought, ugly enough, even as an assumption: that a union between them, had such been possible, would have meant a terrible intensification of unfitness – two bitters in one dish.

"O but there can't be anything in it!" she said with nervous lightness. "Our family have been unlucky of late years in choosing mates – that's all."

And then they tried to persuade themselves that all that had happened was of no consequence, and that they could still be cousins and friends and warm correspondents, and have happy genial times when they met, even if they met less frequently than before. Their parting was in good friendship, and yet Jude's last look into her eyes was tinged with inquiry, for he felt that he did not even now quite know her mind.

III.-VII.

TIDINGS from Sue a day or two after passed across Jude like a withering blast.

Before reading the letter he was led to suspect that its contents were of a somewhat serious kind by catching sight of the signature – which was in her full name, never used in her correspondence with him since her first note:

"MY DEAR JUDE, – I have something to tell you which perhaps you will not be surprised to hear, though certainly it may strike you as being accelerated (as the railway companies say of their trains). Mr. Phillotson and I are to be married quite soon – in three or four weeks. We had intended, as you know, to wait till I had gone through my course of training and obtained my certificate, so as to assist him, if necessary, in the teaching. But he generously says he does not see any object in waiting, now I am not at the Training School. It is so good of him, because the awkwardness of my situation has really come about by my fault in getting expelled.

"Wish me joy. Remember I say you are to, and you mustn't refuse!
–Your affectionate cousin,

"SUSANNA FLORENCE MARY BRIDEHEAD."

Jude staggered under the news; could eat no breakfast; and kept on
drinking tea because his mouth was so dry. Then presently he went
back to his work and laughed the usual bitter laugh of a man so confronted. Everything seemed turning to satire. And yet, what could the
poor girl do? he asked himself: and felt worse than shedding tears.

"O Susanna Florence Mary!" he said as he worked. "You don't
know what marriage means!"

Could it be possible that his announcement of his own marriage
had pricked her on to this, just as his visit to her when in liquor may
have pricked her on to her engagement? To be sure, there seemed to
exist these other and sufficient reasons, practical and social, for her
decision; but Sue was not a very practical or calculating person; and
he was compelled to think that a pique at having his secret sprung
upon her had moved her to give way to Phillotson's probable repre-
sentations, that the best course to prove how unfounded were the suspicions of the school authorities would be to marry him off-hand, as
in fulfilment of an ordinary engagement. Sue had, in fact, been placed
in an awkward corner. Poor Sue!

He determined to play the Spartan;[1] to make the best of it, and
support her; but he could not write the requested good wishes for a
day or two. Meanwhile there came another note from his impatient
little dear:

"Jude, will you give me away? I have nobody else who could do it
so conveniently as you, being the only married relation I have here
on the spot, even if my father were friendly enough to be willing,
which he isn't. I hope you won't think it a trouble? I have been looking at the marriage service in the Prayer-book, and it seems to me
very humiliating that a giver-away should be required at all. According to the ceremony as there printed, my bridegroom chooses me of
his own will and pleasure; but I don't choose him. Somebody *gives* me

---

1   play the Spartan] be stoical (as the ancient Spartans were brave and self-denying).

to him, like a she-ass or she-goat, or any other domestic animal.[1] Bless your exalted views of woman, O Churchman! But I forget: I am no longer privileged to tease you. – Ever,

"SUSANNA FLORENCE MARY BRIDEHEAD."

Jude screwed himself up to heroic key; and replied:

"MY DEAR SUE, – Of course I wish you joy! And also of course I will give you away. What I suggest is that, as you have no house of your own, you do not marry from your school friend's, but from mine. It would be more proper, I think, since I am, as you say, the person nearest related to you in this part of the world.

"I don't see why you sign your letter in such a new and terribly formal way? Surely you care a bit about me still! – Ever your affectionate,

JUDE."

What had jarred on him even more than the signature was a little sting he had been silent on – the phrase "married relation" – What an idiot it made him seem as her lover! If Sue had written that in satire, he could hardly forgive her; if in suffering – ah, that was another thing!

His offer of his lodging must have commended itself to Phillotson at any rate, for the schoolmaster sent him a line of warm thanks, accepting the convenience. Sue also thanked him. Jude immediately moved into more commodious quarters, as much to escape the espionage of the suspicious landlady who had been one cause of Sue's unpleasant experience as for the sake of room.

Then Sue wrote to tell him the day fixed for the wedding; and Jude decided, after inquiry, that she should come into residence on the following Saturday, which would allow of a ten days' stay in the city prior to the ceremony, sufficiently representing a nominal residence of fifteen.

She arrived by the ten o'clock train on the day aforesaid, Jude not going to meet her at the station, by her special request, that he should

---

1 Somebody *gives*.....animal] "Who giveth this woman to be married to this man?" ("The Form of Solemnization of Matrimony" in *The Book of Common Prayer*.)

not lose a morning's work and pay, she said (if this were her true reason). But so well by this time did he know Sue that the remembrance of their mutual sensitiveness at emotional crises might, he thought, have weighed with her in this. When he came home to dinner she had taken possession of her apartment.

She lived in the same house with him, but on a different floor, and they saw each other little, an occasional supper being the only meal they took together, when Sue's manner was something that of a scared child. What she felt he did not know; their conversation was mechanical, though she did not look pale or ill. Phillotson came frequently, but mostly when Jude was absent. On the morning of the wedding, when Jude had given himself a holiday, Sue and her cousin had breakfast together, for the first and last time during this curious interval; in his room – the parlour – which he had hired for the period of Sue's residence. Seeing, as women do, how helpless he was in making the place comfortable, she bustled about.

"What's the matter, Jude?" she said suddenly.

He was leaning with his elbows on the table and his chin on his hands, looking into a futurity which seemed to be sketched out on the tablecloth.

"O – nothing!"

"You are 'father,' you know. That's what they call the man who gives you away."

Jude could have said "Phillotson's age entitles him to be called that!" But he would not annoy her by such a cheap retort.

She talked incessantly, as if she dreaded his indulgence in reflection, and before the meal was over both he and she wished they had not put such confidence in their new view of things, and had taken breakfast apart. What oppressed Jude was the thought that, having done a wrong thing of this sort himself, he was aiding and abetting the woman he loved in doing a like wrong thing, instead of imploring and warning her against it. It was on his tongue to say, "You have quite made up your mind?"

After breakfast they went out on an errand together, moved by a mutual thought that it was the last opportunity they would have of indulging in unceremonious companionship. By the irony of fate, and the curious trick in Sue's nature of tempting Providence at critical times, she took his arm as they walked through the muddy street – a thing she had never done before in her life – and on turning the corner they found themselves close to a grey Perpendicular church with a low-pitched roof – the church of St. Thomas.[1]

"That's the church," said Jude.

"Where I am going to be married?"

"Yes."

"Indeed!" she exclaimed with curiosity. "How I should like to go in and see what the spot is like where I am so soon to kneel and do it."

Again he said to himself, "She does not realize what marriage means!"

He passively acquiesced in her wish to go in, and they entered by the western door. The only person inside the gloomy building was a charwoman cleaning. Sue still held Jude's arm, almost as if she loved him. Cruelly sweet, indeed, she had been to him that morning; but his thoughts of a penance in store for her were tempered by an ache:

> "... I can find no way
> How a blow should fall, such as falls on men,
> Nor prove too much for your womanhood!"[2]

They strolled undemonstratively up the nave towards the altar railing, which they stood against in silence, turning then and walking down the nave again, her hand still on his arm, precisely like a couple just married. The too suggestive incident, entirely of her making, nearly broke down Jude.

"I like to do things like this," she said in the delicate voice of an epicure in emotions, which left no doubt that she spoke the truth.

"I know you do!" said Jude.

"They are interesting, because they have probably never been done before. I shall walk down the church like this with my husband in about two hours, shan't I!"

"No doubt you will!"

---

1 Perpendicular.....St. Thomas] In Salisbury, the parish church of St. Thomas, in St. Thomas's Square, is largely in authentic Perpendicular (late English Gothic) style, and has a distinctively low-pitched roof.

2 "I.....womanhood!"] from Browning's poem "The Worst of It."

"Was it like this when you were married?"

"Good God, Sue – don't be so awfully merciless!...There, dear one, I didn't mean it!"

"Ah – you are vexed!" she said regretfully, as she blinked away an access of eye moisture. "And I promised never to vex you! ... I suppose I ought not to have asked you to bring me in here. O I oughtn't! I see it now. My curiosity to hunt up a new sensation always leads me into these scrapes. Forgive me! ...You will, won't you Jude?"

The appeal was so remorseful that Jude's eyes were even wetter than hers as he pressed her hand for Yes.

"Now we'll hurry away, and I won't do it any more!" she continued humbly; and they came out of the building, Sue intending to go on to the station to meet Phillotson. But the first person they encountered on entering the main street was the schoolmaster himself, whose train had arrived sooner than Sue expected. There was nothing really to demur to in her leaning on Jude's arm; but she withdrew her hand; and Jude thought that Phillotson had looked surprised.

"We have been doing such a funny thing!" said she, smiling candidly. "We've been to the church, rehearsing as it were. Haven't we, Jude?"

"How?" said Phillotson curiously.

Jude inwardly deplored what he thought to be unnecessary frankness; but she had gone too far not to explain all, which she accordingly did, telling him how they had marched up to the altar.

Seeing how puzzled Phillotson seemed, Jude said as cheerfully as he could, "I am going to buy her another little present. Will you both come to the shop with me?"

"No," said Sue, "I'll go on to the house with him;" and requesting her lover not to be a long time she departed with the schoolmaster.

Jude soon joined them at his rooms, and shortly after they prepared for the ceremony. Phillotson's hair was brushed to a painful extent, and his shirt collar appeared stiffer than it had been for the previous twenty years. Beyond this he looked dignified and thoughtful, and altogether a man of whom it was not unsafe to predicate that he would make a kind and considerate husband. That he adored Sue was obvious; and she could almost be seen to feel that she was undeserving his adoration.

Although the distance was so short he had hired a fly[1] from the Red Lion,[2] and six or seven women and children had gathered by the door when they came out. The schoolmaster and Sue were unknown, though Jude was getting to be recognized as a citizen; and the couple were judged to be some relations of his from a distance, nobody supposing Sue to have been a recent pupil at the Training School.

In the carriage Jude took from his pocket his extra little wedding-present, which turned out to be two or three yards of white tulle, which he threw over her, bonnet and all, as a veil.

"It looks so odd over a bonnet," she said. "I'll take the bonnet off."

"O no – let it stay," said Phillotson. And she obeyed.

When they had passed up the church and were standing in their places Jude found that the antecedent visit had certainly taken off the edge of this performance, but by the time they were half way on with the service he wished from his heart that he had not undertaken the business of giving her away. How could Sue have had the temerity to ask him to do it – a cruelty possibly to herself as well as to him? Women were different from men in such matters. Was it that they were, instead of more sensitive, as reputed, more callous, and less romantic; or were they more heroic? Or was Sue simply so perverse that she wilfully gave herself and him pain for the odd and mournful luxury of practising long-suffering in her own person, and of being touched with tender pity for him at having made him practise it? He could perceive that her face was nervously set, and when they reached the trying ordeal of Jude giving her to Phillotson she could hardly command herself; rather, however, as it seemed, from her knowledge of what her cousin must feel, whom she need not have had there at all, than from self-consideration. Possibly she would go on inflicting such pains again and again, and grieving for the sufferer again and again, in all her colossal inconsistency.

Phillotson seemed not to notice, to be surrounded by a mist which prevented his seeing the emotions of others. As soon as they had signed their names and come away, and the suspense was over, Jude felt relieved.

---

1 fly] light one-horse carriage.
2 Red Lion] a coaching inn on Milford Street, from which St. Thomas's Church is a five minutes' walk.

The meal at his lodging was a very simple affair, and at two o'clock they went off. In crossing the pavement to the fly she looked back; and there was a frightened light in her eyes. Could it be that Sue had acted with such unusual foolishness as to plunge into she knew not what for the sake of asserting her independence of him, of retaliating on him for his secrecy? Perhaps Sue was thus venturesome with men because she was childishly ignorant of that side of their natures which wore out women's hearts and lives.

When her foot was on the carriage-step she turned round, saying that she had forgotten something. Jude and the landlady offered to get it.

"No," she said, running back. "It is my handkerchief. I know where I left it."

Jude followed her back. She had found it, and came holding it in her hand. She looked into his eyes with her own tearful ones, and her lips suddenly parted as if she were going to say something. But she went on; and whatever she had meant to say remained unspoken.

III.-VIII.

JUDE wondered if she had really left her handkerchief behind; or whether it were that she had miserably wished to tell him of a love that at the last moment she could not bring herself to express.

He could not stay in his silent lodging when they were gone, and fearing that he might be tempted to drown his misery in alcohol he went upstairs, changed his dark clothes for his white, his thin boots for his thick, and proceeded to his customary work for the afternoon.

But in the cathedral he seemed to hear a voice behind him, and to be possessed with an idea that she would come back. She could not possibly go home with Phillotson, he fancied. The feeling grew and stirred. The moment that the clock struck the last of his working hours he threw down his tools and rushed homeward. "Has anybody been for me?" he asked.

Nobody had been there.

As he could claim the downstairs sitting-room till twelve o'clock that night he sat in it all the evening; and even when the clock had struck eleven, and the family had retired, he could not shake off the feeling that she would come back and sleep in the little room adjoining his own, in which she had slept so many previous days. Her actions were always unpredictable: why should she not come? Gladly would he have compounded for the denial of her as a sweetheart and wife by having her live thus as a fellow-lodger and friend, even on the most distant terms. His supper still remained spread; and going to the front door, and softly setting it open, he returned to the room and sat as watchers sit on Old-Midsummer eves, expecting the phantom of the Beloved.[1] But she did not come.

Having indulged in this wild hope he went upstairs, and looked out of the window, and pictured her through the evening journey to London, whither she and Phillotson had gone for their holiday; their rattling along through the damp night to their hotel, under the same sky of ribbed cloud as that he beheld, through which the moon showed its position rather than its shape, and one or two of the larger stars made themselves visible as faint nebulæ only. It was a new beginning of Sue's history. He projected his mind into the future, and saw her with children more or less in her own likeness around her. But the consolation of regarding them as a continuation of her identity was denied to him, as to all such dreamers, by the wilfulness of Nature in not allowing issue from one parent alone. Every desired renewal of an existence is debased by being half alloy. "If at the estrangement or death of my lost love, I could go and see her child – hers solely – there would be comfort in it!" said Jude. And then he again uneasily saw, as he had latterly seen with more and more frequency, the scorn of Nature for man's finer emotions, and her lack of interest in his aspirations.

The oppressive strength of his affection for Sue showed itself on the morrow and following days yet more clearly. He could no longer endure the light of the Melchester lamps; the sunshine was as drab paint; and the blue sky as zinc. Then he received news that his old aunt was dangerously ill at Marygreen, which intelligence almost coincided with a letter from his former employer at Christminster,

---

1 watchers.....Beloved] referring to the rural superstition that on the eve of the old Midsummer Day (June 24), apparitions of lovers (and others) may be seen. Hardy's notebook entry for June 1871 includes: "Old Midsummer custom: on old Midsr. eve, at going to bed: 'I put my shoes in the form of a T, / And trust my true love for to see.'"

who offered him permanent work of a good class if he would come back. The letters were almost a relief to him. He started to visit Aunt Drusilla, and resolved to go onward to Christminster to see what worth there might be in the builder's offer.

Jude found his aunt even worse than the communication from the Widow Edlin had led him to expect. There was every possibility of her lingering on for weeks or months, though little likelihood. He wrote to Sue informing her of the state of her aunt, and suggesting that she might like to see her aged relative alive. He would meet her at Alfredston Road, the following evening, Monday, on his way back from Christminster, if she could come by the up-train which crossed his down-train at that station. Next morning, accordingly, he went on to Christminster, intending to return to Alfredston soon enough to keep the suggested appointment with Sue.

The city of learning wore an estranged look, and he had lost all feeling for its associations. Yet as the sun made vivid lights and shades of the mullioned architecture of the façades, and drew patterns of the crinkled battlements on the young turf of the quadrangles, Jude thought he had never seen the place look more beautiful. He came to the street in which he had first beheld Sue. The chair she had occupied when, leaning over her ecclesiastical scrolls, a hog-hair brush in her hand, her girlish figure had arrested the gaze of his inquiring eyes, stood precisely in its former spot, empty. It was as if she were dead, and nobody had been found capable of succeeding her in that artistic pursuit. Hers was now the City phantom, while those of the intellectual and devotional worthies who had once moved him to emotion were no longer able to assert their presence there.

However, here he was; and in fulfilment of his intention he went on to his former lodging in "Beersheba," near the ceremonial church of St. Silas. The old landlady who opened the door seemed glad to see him again, and bringing some lunch informed him that the builder who had employed him had called to inquire his address.

Jude went on to the stone-yard where he had worked. But the old sheds and bankers were distasteful to him; he felt it impossible to engage himself to return and stay in this place of vanished dreams. He longed for the hour of the homeward train to Alfredston, where he might probably meet Sue.

Then, for one ghastly half-hour of depression caused by these scenes, there returned upon him that feeling which had been his undoing more than once – that he was not worth the trouble of being taken care of either by himself or others; and during this half-hour he met Tinker Taylor, the bankrupt ecclesiastical ironmonger, at Fourways, who proposed that they should adjourn to a bar and drink together. They walked along the street till they stood before one of the great palpitating centres of Christminster life, the inn wherein he formerly had responded to the challenge to rehearse the Creed in Latin – now a popular tavern[1] with a spacious and inviting entrance, which gave admittance to a bar that had been entirely renovated and refitted in modern style since Jude's residence here.

Tinker Taylor drank off his glass and departed, saying it was too stylish a place now for him to feel at home in, unless he was drunker than he had money to be just then. Jude was longer finishing his, and stood abstractedly silent in the almost empty place. The bar had been gutted and newly arranged throughout, mahogany fixtures having taken the place of the old painted ones, while at the back of the standing-space there were stuffed sofa-benches. The room was divided into compartments in the approved manner, between which were screens of ground glass in mahogany framing, to prevent topers in one compartment being put to the blush by the recognitions of those in the next. On the inside of the counter two barmaids leant over the white-handled beer-engines, and the row of little silvered taps inside, dripping into a pewter trough.

Feeling tired, and having nothing more to do till the train left, Jude sat down on one of the sofas. At the back of the barmaids rose bevelled mirrors, with glass shelves running along their front, on which stood precious liquids that Jude did not know the name of, in bottles of topaz, sapphire, ruby and amethyst. The moment was enlivened by the entrance of some customers into the next compartment, and the starting of the mechanical tell-tale of monies received, which emitted a ting-ting every time a coin was put in.

The barmaid attending to this compartment was invisible to Jude's direct glance, though a reflection of her back in the glass behind her was occasionally caught by his eyes. He had only observed this

---

1 popular tavern] the Lamb and Flag, a tavern since about 1695, to the north of St. John's College.

listlessly, when she turned her face for a moment to the glass to set her hair tidy. Then he was amazed to discover that the face was Arabella's.

If she had come on to his compartment she would have seen him. But she did not, this being presided over by the maiden on the other side. Abby was in a black gown, with white linen cuffs and a broad white collar,[1] and her figure, more developed than formerly, was accentuated by a bunch of daffodils that she wore on her left bosom. In the compartment she served stood an electro-plated fountain of water over a spirit-lamp, whose blue flame sent a steam from the top, all this being visible to him only in the mirror behind her; which also reflected the faces of the men she was attending to – one of them a handsome, dissipated young fellow, possibly an undergraduate, who had been relating to her an experience of some humorous sort.

"O, Mr. Cockman, now! How can you tell such a tale to me in my innocence!" she cried gaily. "Mr. Cockman, what do you use to make your moustache curl so beautiful?" As the young man was clean shaven the retort provoked a laugh at his expense.

"Come!" said he, "I'll have a Curaçoa;[2] and a light, please."

She served the liqueur from one of the lovely bottles, and striking a match held it to his cigarette while he whiffed.

"Well, have you heard from your husband lately, my dear?" he asked.

"Not a sound," said she.

"Where is he?"

"I left him in Australia; and I suppose he's there still."

Jude's eyes grew rounder.

"What made you part from him?"

"Don't you ask questions, and you won't hear lies."

"Come then, give me my change, which you've been keeping from me for the last quarter of an hour; and I'll romantically vanish up the street of this picturesque city."

She handed the change over the counter, in taking which he caught her fingers and held them. There was a slight struggle and titter, and he bade her good-bye and left.

---

1   Abby.....white collar] The description brings to mind the barmaid and her setting in Manet's painting, "Un bar aux Folies-Bergère" (1881-2).
2   Curaçoa (English mis-spelling of the Spanish *Curaçao*:) orange-flavoured liqueur.

Jude had looked on with the eye of a dazed philosopher.[1] It was extraordinary how far removed from his life Arabella now seemed to be. He could not realize their nominal closeness. And, this being the case, in his present frame of mind he was indifferent to the fact that Arabella was his wife indeed.

The compartment that she served emptied itself of visitors, and after a brief thought he entered it, and went forward to the counter. Arabella did not recognize him for a moment. Then their glances met. She started; till a humorous impudence sparkled in her eyes, and she spoke.

"Well, I'm blest! I thought you were underground years ago!"

"Oh!"

"I never heard anything of you, or I don't know that I should have come here. But never mind! What shall I treat you to this afternoon? A Scotch and soda? Come, anything that the house will afford, for old acquaintance' sake!"

"Thanks, Arabella," said Jude without a smile. "But I don't want anything more than I've had." The fact was that her unexpected presence there had destroyed at a stroke his momentary taste for strong liquor as completely as if it had whisked him back to his milk-fed infancy.

"That's a pity, now you could get it for nothing."

"How long have you been here?"

"About six weeks. I returned from Sydney three months ago. I always liked this business, you know."

"I wonder you came to this place!"

"Well, as I say, I thought you were gone to glory, and being in London I saw the situation in an advertisement. Nobody was likely to know me here, even if I had minded, for I was never in Christminster in my growing up."

"Why did you return from Australia?"

"Oh, I had my reasons.... Then you are not a Don yet?"

"No."

"Not even a Reverend?"

"No."

"Nor so much as a Rather Reverend dissenting gentleman?"[2]

---

1 philosopher] i.e. stoically.
2 Rather.....gentleman?] nonconformist minister.

"I am as I was."

"True – you look so." She idly allowed her fingers to rest on the pull of the beer-engine as she inspected him critically. He observed that her hands were smaller and whiter than when he had lived with her, and that on the hand which pulled the engine she wore an ornamental ring set with what seemed to be a real sapphire – which it was, indeed, and was much admired as such by the young men who frequented the bar.

"So you pass as married," he continued.

"Yes. I thought it might be awkward if I called myself a widow, as I should have liked."

"True. I am known here a little."

"I didn't mean on that account – for as I said I didn't expect you. It was for other reasons."

"What were they?"

"I don't care to go into them," she replied evasively. "I make a very good living, and I don't know that I want your company."

Here a chappie with no chin, and a moustache like a lady's eyebrow, came and asked for a curiously compounded drink, and Arabella was obliged to go and attend to him. "We can't talk here," she said, stepping back a moment. "Can't you wait till nine? Say yes, and don't be a fool. I can get off duty two hours sooner than usual, if I ask. I am not living in the house at present."

He reflected and said gloomily, "I'll come back. I suppose we'd better arrange something!"

"O bother arranging! I'm not going to arrange anything!"

"But I must know a thing or two; and, as you say, we can't talk here. Very well; I'll call for you."

Depositing his unemptied glass he went out and walked up and down the street. Here was a rude flounce[1] into the pellucid sentimentality of his sad attachment to Sue. Though Arabella's word was absolutely untrustworthy, he thought there might be some truth in her implication that she had not wished to disturb him, and had really supposed him dead. However, there was only one thing now to be done, and that was to play a straightforward part, the law being the law, and the woman between whom and himself there was no more

---

1 flounce] plunging intrusion.

unity than between east and west being in the eye of the Church one person with him.

Having to meet Arabella here, it was impossible to meet Sue at Alfredston as he had promised. At every thought of this a pang had gone through him; but the conjuncture could not be helped. Arabella was perhaps an intended intervention to punish him for his unauthorized love. Passing the evening, therefore, in a desultory waiting about the town wherein he avoided the precincts of every Cloister and Hall, because he could not bear to behold them, he repaired to the tavern bar while the hundred and one strokes were resounding from the Great Bell of Cardinal College, a coincidence which seemed to him gratuitous irony. The inn was now brilliantly lighted up, and the scene was altogether more brisk and gay. The faces of the bar-maidens had risen in colour, each having a pink flush on her cheek; their manners were still more vivacious than before – more abandoned, more excited, more sensuous, and they expressed their sentiments and desires less euphemistically, laughing in a lackadaisical tone, without reserve.

The bar had been crowded with men of all sorts during the previous hour, and he had heard from without the hubbub of their voices; but the customers were fewer just now. He nodded to Arabella, and told her that she would find him outside the door when she came away.

"But you must have something with me first," she said with great good-humour. "Just an early nightcap: I always do. Then you can go out and wait a minute, as it is best we should not be seen going together." She drew a couple of liqueur glasses of brandy; and though she had evidently, from her countenance, already taken in enough alcohol either by drinking or, more probably, from the atmosphere she had breathed for so many hours, she finished hers quickly. He also drank his, and went outside the house.

In a few minutes she came, in a thick jacket and a hat with a black feather. "I live quite near," she said, taking his arm, "and can let myself in by a latch-key at any time. What arrangement do you want to come to?"

"O – none in particular," he answered, thoroughly sick and tired, his thoughts again reverting to Alfredston, and the train he did not go by; the probable disappointment of Sue that he was not there when she arrived, and the missed pleasure of her company on the long and lonely climb by starlight up the hills to Marygreen. "I ought to have gone back really! My aunt is on her deathbed, I fear."

"I'll go over with you to-morrow morning. I think I could get a day off."

There was something particularly uncongenial in the idea of Arabella, who had no more sympathy than a tigress with his relations or him, coming to the bedside of his dying aunt, and meeting Sue. Yet he said, "Of course, if you'd like to, you can."

"Well, that we'll consider.... Now, until we have come to some agreement it is awkward our being together here – where you are known, and I am getting known, though without any suspicion that I have anything to do with you. As we are going towards the station suppose we take the nine-forty train to Aldbrickham?[1] We shall be there in little more than half-an-hour, and nobody will know us for one night, and we shall be quite free to act as we choose till we have made up our minds whether we'll make anything public or not."

"As you like."

"Then wait till I get two or three things. This is my lodging. Sometimes when late I sleep at the hotel where I am engaged, so nobody will think anything of my staying out."

She speedily returned, and they went on to the railway, and made the half-hour's journey to Aldbrickham, where they entered a third-rate inn near the station in time for a late supper.

III.-IX.

ON the morrow between nine and half-past they were journeying back to Christminster, the only two occupants of a compartment in a third-class railway-carriage. Having, like Jude, made rather a hasty toilet to catch the train, Arabella looked a little frowsy, and her face was very far from possessing the animation which had characterized it at the bar the night before. When they came out of the station she found

---

1 Aldbrickham] Reading in Berkshire.

that she still had half-an-hour to spare before she was due at the bar. They walked in silence a little way out of the town in the direction of Alfredston. Jude looked up the far highway.

"Ah ... poor feeble me!" he murmured at last.

"What?" said she.

"This is the very road by which I came into Christminster years ago full of plans!"

"Well, whatever the road is I think my time is nearly up, as I have to be in the bar by eleven o'clock. And as I said, I shan't ask for the day to go with you to see your aunt. So perhaps we had better part here. I'd sooner not walk up Chief Street[1] with you, since we've come to no conclusion at all."

"Very well. But you said when we were getting up this morning that you had something you wished to tell me before I left?"

"So I had – two things – one in particular. But you wouldn't promise to keep it a secret. I'll tell you now if you promise? As an honest woman I wish you to know it.... It was what I began telling you in the night – about that gentleman who managed the Sydney hotel." Arabella spoke somewhat hurriedly for her. "You'll keep it close?"

"Yes – yes – I promise!" said Jude impatiently. "Of course I don't want to reveal your secrets."

"Whenever I met him out for a walk, he used to say that he was much taken with my looks, and he kept pressing me to marry him. I never thought of coming back to England again; and being out there in Australia, with no home of my own after leaving my father, I at last agreed, and did."

"What – marry him?"

"Yes."

"Regularly – legally – in church?"

"Yes. And lived with him till shortly before I left. It was stupid, I know; but I did! There, now I've told you. Don't round upon me! He's never coming back to England, poor old chap. And if he does, he won't be likely to find me."

Jude stood pale and fixed.

"Why the devil didn't you tell me last night!" he said.

---

1 Chief Street] High Street ("The High").

"Well – I didn't.... Won't you make it up with me, then?"

"I have nothing more to say!" replied Jude with sternness. "I have nothing more to say about the – crime – you've confessed to!"

"Crime! Pooh. They don't think much of such as that over there! Lots of 'em do it.... Well, if you take it like that I shall go back to him! He was very fond of me, and we lived honourable enough, and as respectable as any married couple in the Colony! How did I know where you were?"

"I won't go blaming you. I could say a good deal; but perhaps it would be misplaced. What do you wish me to do?"

"Nothing. There was one thing more I wanted to tell you; but I fancy we've seen enough of one another for the present! I shall think over what you said about your circumstances, and let you know."

Thus they parted. Jude watched her disappear in the direction of the hotel, and entered the railway station close by. Finding that it wanted three-quarters of an hour of the time at which he could get a train back to Alfredston, he strolled mechanically into the city as far as to the Fourways, where he stood as he had so often stood before, and surveyed Chief Street stretching ahead, with its college after college, in picturesqueness unrivalled except by such Continental vistas as the Street of Palaces in Genoa; the lines of the buildings being as distinct in the morning air as in an architectural drawing. But Jude was far from seeing or criticizing these things; they were hidden by an indescribable consciousness of Arabella's midnight contiguity, a sense of degradation at his revived experiences with her, of her appearance as she lay asleep at dawn, which set upon his motionless face a look as of one accurst. If he could only have felt resentment towards her he would have been less unhappy; but he pitied while he contemned her.

Jude turned and retraced his steps. Drawing again towards the station he started at hearing his name pronounced – less at the name than at the voice. To his great surprise no other than Sue stood like a vision before him – her look bodeful and anxious as in a dream, her little mouth nervous, and her strained eyes speaking reproachful inquiry.

"O Jude – I am so glad – to meet you like this!" she said in quick, uneven accents not far from a sob. Then she flushed as she observed his thought that they had not met since her marriage.

They looked away from each other to hide their emotion, took each other's hand without further speech, and went on together awhile, till she glanced at him with furtive solicitude. "I arrived at Alfredston station last night, as you asked me to, and there was nobody to meet me! But I reached Marygreen alone, and they told me aunt was a trifle better. I sat up with her, and as you did not come all night I was frightened about you – I thought that perhaps, when you found yourself back in the old city, you were upset at – at thinking I was – married and not there as I used to be; and that you had nobody to speak to; so you had tried to drown your gloom! – as you did at that former time when you were disappointed about entering as a student, and had forgotten your promise to me that you never would again. And this, I thought, was why you hadn't come to meet me!"

"And you came to hunt me up, and deliver me, like a good angel!"

"I thought I would come by the morning train and try to find you – in case – in case ———"

"I did think of my promise to you, dear, continually! I shall never break out again as I did, I am sure. I may have been doing nothing better, but I was not doing that – I loathe the thought of it."

"I am glad your staying had nothing to do with that. But," she said, the faintest pout entering into her tone, "you didn't come back last night and meet me, as you engaged to!"

"I didn't – I am sorry to say. I had an appointment at nine o'clock – too late for me to catch the train that would have met yours, or to get home at all."

Looking at his loved one as she appeared to him now, in his tender thought the sweetest and most disinterested comrade that he had ever had, living largely in vivid imaginings, so ethereal a creature that her spirit could be seen trembling through her limbs, he felt heartily ashamed of his earthliness in spending the hours he had spent in Arabella's company. There was something rude and immoral in thrusting these recent facts of his life upon the mind of one who, to him, was so uncarnate as to seem at times impossible as a human wife to any average man. And yet she was Phillotson's. How she had become such, how she lived as such, passed his comprehension as he regarded her to-day.

"You'll go back with me?" he said. "There's a train just now. I wonder how my aunt is by this time.... And so, Sue, you really came on my account all this way! At what an early time you must have started, poor thing!"

"Yes. Sitting up watching alone made me all nerves for you, and instead of going to bed when it got light I started. And now you won't frighten me like this again about your morals for nothing?"

He was not so sure that she had been frightened about his morals for nothing. He released her hand till they had entered the train, – it seemed the same carriage he had lately got out of with another – where they sat down side by side, Sue between him and the window. He regarded the delicate lines of her profile and the small, tight, apple-like curves of her bodice, so different from Arabella's amplitudes. Though she knew he was looking at her she did not turn to him, but kept her eyes forward, as if afraid that by meeting his own some troublous discussion would be initiated.

"Sue – you are married now, you know, like me; and yet we have been in such a hurry that we have not said a word about it!"

"There's no necessity," she quickly returned.

"O well – perhaps not.... But I wish ——"

"Jude – don't talk about *me* – I wish you wouldn't!" she entreated. "It distresses me, rather. Forgive my saying it! ... Where did you stay last night?"

She had asked the question in perfect innocence, to change the topic. He knew that, and said merely, "At an inn," though it would have been a relief to tell her of his meeting with an unexpected one. But the latter's final announcement of her marriage in Australia bewildered him lest what he might say should do his ignorant wife an injury.

Their talk proceeded but awkwardly till they reached Alfredston. That Sue was not as she had been, but was labelled "Phillotson," paralyzed Jude whenever he wanted to commune with her as an individual. Yet she seemed unaltered – he could not say why. There remained the five-mile extra journey into the country, which it was just as easy to walk as to drive, the greater part of it being uphill. Jude had never before in his life gone that road with Sue, though he had with another. It was now as if he carried a bright light which temporarily banished the shady associations of the earlier time.

Sue talked; but Jude noticed that she still kept the conversation from herself. At length he inquired if her husband were well.

"O yes," she said. "He is obliged to be in the school all the day, or he would have come with me. He is so good and kind that to accompany me he would have dismissed the school for a day, even against his principles – for he is strongly opposed to giving casual holidays – only I wouldn't let him. I felt it would be better to come alone. Aunt Drusilla, I knew, was so very eccentric; and his being almost a stranger to her now would have made it irksome to both. Since it turns out that she is hardly conscious I am glad I did not ask him."

Jude had walked moodily while this praise of Phillotson was being expressed. "Mr. Phillotson obliges you in everything, as he ought," he said.

"Of course."

"You ought to be a happy wife."

"And of course I am."

"Bride, I might almost have said, as yet. It is not so many weeks since I gave you to him, and ——"

"Yes, I know! I know!" There was something in her face which belied her late assuring words, so strictly proper and so lifelessly spoken that they might have been taken from a list of model speeches in "The Wife's Guide to Conduct." Jude knew the quality of every vibration in Sue's voice, could read every symptom of her mental condition; and he was convinced that she was unhappy, although she had not been a month married. But her rushing away thus from home, to see the last of a relative whom she had hardly known in her life, proved nothing; for Sue naturally did such things as those.

"Well, you have my good wishes now as always, Mrs. Phillotson."

She reproached him by a glance.

"No, you are not Mrs. Phillotson," murmured Jude. "You are dear, free Sue Bridehead, only you don't know it! Wifedom has not yet annihilated and digested you in its vast maw as an atom which has no further individuality."

Sue put on a look of being offended, till she answered, "Nor has husbandom you, so far as I can see!"

"But it has!" he said, shaking his head sadly.

When they reached the lone cottage under the firs, between the Brown House and Marygreen, in which Jude and Arabella had lived and quarrelled, he turned to look at it. A squalid family lived there now. He could not help saying to Sue: "That's the house my wife and I occupied the whole of the time we lived together. I brought her home to that house."

She looked at it. "That to you was what the school-house at Shaston is to me."

"Yes; but I was not very happy there, as you are in yours."

She closed her lips in retortive silence, and they walked some way till she glanced at him to see how he was taking it. "Of course I may have exaggerated your happiness – one never knows," he continued blandly.

"Don't think that, Jude, for a moment, even though you may have said it to sting me! He's as good to me as a man can be, and gives me perfect liberty – which elderly husbands don't do in general.... If you think I am not happy because he's too old for me, you are wrong."

"I don't think anything against him – to you, dear."

"And you won't say things to distress me, will you?"

"I will not."

He said no more, but he knew that, from some cause or other, in taking Phillotson as a husband, Sue felt that she had done what she ought not to have done.

They plunged into the concave field on the other side of which rose the village – the field wherein Jude had received a thrashing from the farmer many years earlier. On ascending to the village and approaching the house they found Mrs. Edlin standing at the door, who at sight of them lifted her hands deprecatingly. "She's downstairs, if you'll believe me!" cried the widow. "Out o' bed she got, and nothing could turn her. What will come o't I do not know!"

On entering, there indeed by the fireplace sat the old woman, wrapped in blankets, and turning upon them a countenance like that of Sebastiano's Lazarus.[1] They must have looked their amazement, for she said in a hollow voice:

"Ah – sceered ye, have I! I wasn't going to bide up there no longer, to please nobody! 'Tis more than flesh and blood can bear, to

---

1   Lazarus] who looks gaunt and grim in "The Raising of Lazarus", a painting by Sebastiano del Piombo (c. 1485-1547).

be ordered to do this and that by a feller that don't know half as well as you do yourself! ...Ah – you'll rue this marrying as well as he!" she added, turning to Sue. "All our family do, – and nearly all everybody else's. You should have done as I did, you simpleton! And Phillotson the schoolmaster, of all men! What made 'ee marry him?"

"What makes most women marry, aunt?"

"Ah! You mean to say you loved the man!"

"I don't mean to say anything definite."

"Do ye love un?"

"Don't ask me, aunt."

"I can mind the man very well. A very civil, honourable liver; but Lord! – I don't want to wownd your feelings, but – there be certain men here and there that no woman of any niceness can stomach. I should have said he was one. I don't say so *now*, since you must ha' known better than I, – but that's what I *should* have said!"

Sue jumped up and went out. Jude followed her, and found her in the outhouse, crying.

"Don't cry, dear!" said Jude in distress. "She means well, but is very crusty and queer now, you know."

"O no – it isn't that!" said Sue, trying to dry her eyes. "I don't mind her roughness one bit."

"What is it, then?"

"It is that what she says is – is true!"

"God – what – you don't like him?" asked Jude.

"I don't mean that!" she said hastily. "That I ought – perhaps I ought not to have married!"

He wondered if she had really been going to say that at first. They went back, and the subject was smoothed over, and her aunt took rather kindly to Sue, telling her that not many young women newly married would have come so far to see a sick old crone like her. In the afternoon Sue prepared to depart, Jude hiring a neighbour to drive her to Alfredston.

"I'll go with you to the station, if you'd like?" he said.

She would not let him. The man came round with the trap, and Jude helped her into it, perhaps with unnecessary attention, for she looked at him prohibitively.

"I suppose – I may come to see you some day, when I am back again at Melchester?" he half-crossly observed.

She bent down and said softly: "No, dear – you are not to come yet. I don't think you are in a good mood."

"Very well," said Jude. "Good-bye!"

"Good-bye!" She waved her hand and was gone.

"She's right! I won't go!" he murmured.

He passed the evening and following days in mortifying by every possible means his wish to see her, nearly starving himself in attempts to extinguish by fasting his passionate tendency to love her. He read sermons on discipline; and hunted up passages in Church history that treated of the Ascetics[1] of the second century. Before he had returned from Marygreen to Melchester there arrived a letter from Arabella. The sight of it revived a stronger feeling of self-condemnation for his brief return to her society than for his attachment to Sue.

The letter, he perceived, bore a London postmark instead of the Christminster one. Arabella informed him that a few days after their parting in the morning at Christminster, she had been surprised by an affectionate letter from her Australian husband, formerly manager of the hotel in Sydney. He had come to England on purpose to find her; and had taken a free, fully-licensed public,[2] in Lambeth, where he wished her to join him in conducting the business, which was likely to be a very thriving one, the house being situated in an excellent, densely populated, gin-drinking neighbourhood, and already doing a trade of £200 a month, which could be easily doubled.

As he had said that he loved her very much still, and implored her to tell him where she was, and as they had only parted in a slight tiff, and as her engagement in Christminster was only temporary, she had just gone to join him as he urged. She could not help feeling that she belonged to him more than to Jude, since she had properly married him, and had lived with him much longer than with her first husband. In thus wishing Jude good-bye she bore him no ill-will, and trusted he would not turn upon her, a weak woman, and inform against her, and bring her to ruin now that she had a chance of improving her circumstances and leading a genteel life.

---

1 Ascetics] early Christians who practised self-denial.
2 public] public house; tavern.

JUDE returned to Melchester, which had the questionable recommendation of being only a dozen and a half miles from his Sue's now
permanent residence. At first he felt that this nearness was a distinct
reason for not going southward at all; but Christminster was too sad a
place to bear, while the proximity of Shaston to Melchester might
afford him the glory of worsting the Enemy in a close engagement,
such as was deliberately sought by the priests and virgins of the early
Church, who, disdaining an ignominious flight from temptation,
became even chamber-partners with impunity. Jude did not pause to
remember that, in the laconic words of the historian, "insulted Nature
sometimes vindicated her rights"[1] in such circumstances.

He now returned with feverish desperation to his study for the
priesthood – in the recognition that the single-mindedness of his
aims, and his fidelity to the cause, had been more than questionable of
late. His passion for Sue troubled his soul; yet his abandonment to the
society of Arabella for twelve hours seemed instinctively a worse
thing – even though she had not told him of her Sydney husband till
afterwards. He had, he verily believed, overcome all tendency to fly to
liquor – which, indeed, he had never done from taste, but merely as
an escape from intolerable misery of mind. Yet he perceived with
despondency that, taken all round, he was a man of too many passions
to make a good clergyman; the utmost he could hope for was that in
a life of constant internal warfare between flesh and spirit the former
might not always be victorious.

As a hobby, auxiliary to his readings in Divinity, he developed his
slight skill in church-music and thorough-bass,[2] till he could join in
part-singing[3] from notation with some accuracy. A mile or two from
Melchester there was a restored village church, to which Jude had
originally gone to fix the new columns and capitals. By this means he
had become acquainted with the organist, and the ultimate result was
that he joined the choir as a bass voice.

---

1 the priests....."insulted.....rights"] as reported by Gibbon, *Decline and Fall*, Chap. 15.
   See Appendix E.
2 thorough-bass] a bass part underlying a tune.
3 part-singing] singing in harmonised parts.

He walked out to this parish twice every Sunday, and sometimes in the week. One evening about Easter the choir met for practice, and a new hymn which Jude had heard of as being by a Wessex composer was to be tried and prepared for the following week. It turned out to be a strangely emotional composition. As they all sang it over and over again its harmonies grew upon Jude, and moved him exceedingly.

When they had finished he went round to the organist to make inquiries. The score was in manuscript, the name of the composer being at the head, together with the title of the hymn: – "The Foot of the Cross."

"Yes," said the organist. "He is a local man. He is a professional musician at Kennetbridge[1] – between here and Christminster. The vicar knows him. He was brought up and educated in Christminster traditions, which accounts for the quality of the piece. I think he plays in the large church there, and has a surpliced choir. He comes to Melchester sometimes, and once tried to get the Cathedral organ when the post was vacant. The hymn is getting about everywhere this Easter."

As he walked, humming the air, on his way home, Jude fell to musing on its composer, and the reasons why he composed it. What a man of sympathies he must be! Perplexed and harassed as he himself was about Sue, and Arabella, and troubled as was his conscience by the complication of his position, how he would like to know that man! "He of all men would understand my difficulties," said the impulsive Jude. If there were any person in the world to choose as a confidant, this composer would be the one, for he must have suffered, and throbbed, and yearned.

In brief, ill as he could afford the time and money for the journey, Fawley resolved, like the child that he was, to go to Kennetbridge the very next Sunday. He duly started, early in the morning, for it was only by a series of crooked railways that he could get to the town. About mid-day he reached it, and crossing the bridge into the quaint old borough he inquired for the house of the composer.

They told him it was a red brick building some little way further

---

1 Kennetbridge] Newbury in Berkshire.

on. Also that the gentleman himself had just passed along the street not five minutes before.

"Which way?" asked Jude with alacrity.

"Straight along homeward from church."

Jude hastened on, and soon had the pleasure of observing a man in a black coat and a black slouched felt hat no considerable distance ahead. Stretching out his legs yet more widely he stalked after. "A hungry soul in pursuit of a full soul!" he said. "I must speak to that man!"

He could not, however, overtake the musician before he had entered his own house, and then arose the question if this were an expedient time to call. Whether or not he decided to do so there and then, now that he had got here, the distance home being too great for him to wait till late in the afternoon. This man of soul would understand scant ceremony, and might be quite a perfect adviser in a case in which an earthly and illegitimate passion had cunningly obtained entrance into his heart through the opening afforded for religion.

Jude accordingly rang the bell, and was admitted.

The musician came to him in a moment, and being respectably dressed, good-looking, and frank in manner, Jude obtained a favourable reception. He was nevertheless conscious that there would be a certain awkwardness in explaining his errand.

"I have been singing in the choir of a little church near Melchester," he said. "And we have this week practised 'The Foot of the Cross,' which I understand, sir, that you composed?"

"I did – a year or so ago."

"I – like it. I think it supremely beautiful!"

"Ah well – other people have said so too. Yes, there's money in it, if I could only see about getting it published. I have other compositions to go with it, too; I wish I could bring them out; for I haven't made a five-pound note out of any of them yet. These publishing people – they want the copyright of an obscure composer's work, such as mine is, for almost less than I should have to pay a person for making a fair manuscript copy of the score. The one you speak of I have lent to various friends about here and Melchester, and so it has got to be sung a little. But music is a poor staff to lean on – I am giving it up entirely. You must go into trade if you want to make money nowadays. The

wine business is what I am thinking of. This is my forthcoming list –
it is not issued yet – but you can take one."

He handed Jude an advertisement list of several pages in booklet
shape, ornamentally margined with a red line, in which were set forth
the various clarets, champagnes, ports, sherries, and other wines with
which he purposed to initiate his new venture. It took Jude rather by
surprise that the man with the soul was thus and thus; and he felt that
he could not open up his confidences.

They talked a little longer, but constrainedly, for when the
musician found that Jude was a poor man his manner changed from
what it had been while Jude's appearance and address deceived him as
to his position and pursuits. Jude stammered out something about his
feelings in wishing to congratulate the author on such an exalted
composition, and took an embarrassed leave.

All the way home by the slow Sunday train, sitting in the fireless
waiting-rooms on this cold spring day, he was depressed enough at his
simplicity in taking such a journey. But no sooner did he reach his
Melchester lodging than he found awaiting him a letter which had
arrived that morning a few minutes after he had left the house. It was
a contrite little note from Sue, in which she said, with sweet humility,
that she felt she had been horrid in telling him he was not to come to
see her; that she despised herself for having been so conventional; and
that he was to be sure to come by the eleven-forty-five train that very
Sunday, and have dinner with them at half-past one.

Jude almost tore his hair at having missed this letter till it was too
late to act upon its contents; but he had chastened himself considerably of late, and at last his chimerical expedition to Kennetbridge
really did seem to have been another special intervention of Providence to keep him away from temptation. But a growing impatience
of faith, which he had noticed in himself more than once of late,
made him pass over in ridicule the idea that God sent people on
fools' errands. He longed to see her; he was angry at having missed
her: and he wrote instantly, telling her what had happened, and saying
he had not enough patience to wait till the following Sunday, but
would come any day in the week that she liked to name.

Since he wrote a little over-ardently, Sue, as her manner was,
delayed her reply till Thursday before Good Friday, when she said he

might come that afternoon if he wished, this being the earliest day on which she could welcome him, for she was now assistant-teacher in her husband's school. Jude therefore got leave from the Cathedral works at the trifling expense of a stoppage of pay, and went.

PART FOURTH

AT SHASTON

"Whoso prefers either Matrimony or other Ordinance before the Good of Man and the plain Exigence of Charity, let him profess Papist, or Protestant, or what he will, he is no better than a Pharisee." — J. MILTON.[1]

IV. - I.

SHASTON,[2] the ancient British Palladour,

"From whose foundation first such strange reports arise,"[3]

(as Drayton sang it), was, and is, in itself the city of a dream. Vague imaginings of its castle, its three mints, its magnificent apsidal[4] Abbey, the chief glory of South Wessex, its twelve churches, its shrines, chantries,[5] hospitals, its gabled freestone mansions – all now ruthlessly swept away – throw the visitor, even against his will, into a pensive melancholy, which the stimulating atmosphere and limitless landscape around him can scarcely dispel. The spot was the burial-place of a king and a queen, of abbots and abbesses, saints and bishops, knights and squires. The bones of King Edward "the Martyr,"[6] carefully

---

1 "*Whoso.....*MILTON] The quotation is from the introductory epistle of John Milton's pamphlet, *The Doctrine and Discipline of Divorce* (1643).
2 SHASTON] Shaftesbury in Dorsetshire. Much of the following description was taken by Hardy from John Hutchins' *The History and Antiquities of the County of Dorset*, vol. 3 (3rd edn., 1868), which says that "Shaston" is the modern abbreviation of "Shaftesbury" (p. 1).
3 "*From.....arise,*"] Michael Drayton's *Poly-Olbion* (1622), II, line 151.
4 apsidal] with an apse (a semi-circular or polygonal recess, often at the eastern end of an ecclesiastical building).
5 chantries] chapels in which masses are sung.
6 Martyr] King of England 975-78; assassinated.

removed hither for holy preservation, brought Shaston a renown which made it the resort of pilgrims from every part of Europe, and enabled it to maintain a reputation extending far beyond English shores. To this fair creation of the great Middle-Age the Dissolution was, as historians tell us, the death-knell.[1] With the destruction of the enormous abbey the whole place collapsed in a general ruin: the Martyr's bones met with the fate of the sacred pile that held them, and not a stone is now left to tell where they lie.

The natural picturesqueness and singularity of the town still remain; but strange to say these qualities, which were noted by many writers in ages when scenic beauty is said to have been unappreciated, are passed over in this, and one of the queerest and quaintest spots in England stands virtually unvisited to-day.

It has a unique position on the summit of an almost perpendicular scarp, rising on the north, south, and west sides of the borough out of the deep alluvial Vale of Blackmoor,[2] the view from the Castle Green over three counties of verdant pasture – South, Mid and Nether Wessex – being as sudden a surprise to the unexpectant traveller's eyes as the medicinal air is to his lungs. Impossible to a railway, it can best be reached on foot, next best by light vehicles; and it is hardly accessible to these but by a sort of isthmus on the north-east, that connects it with the high chalk table-land on that side.

Such is, and such was, the now world-forgotten Shaston or Palladour. Its situation rendered water the great want of the town; and within living memory, horses, donkeys and men may have been seen toiling up the winding ways to the top of the steep, laden with tubs and barrels filled from the wells beneath the mountain, and hawkers retailing their contents at the price of a halfpenny a bucketful.

This difficulty in the water supply, together with two other odd facts, namely, that the chief graveyard slopes up as steeply as a roof behind the church, and that in former times the town passed through a curious period of corruption, conventual and domestic, gave rise to the saying that Shaston was remarkable for three consolations to man, such as the world afforded not elsewhere. It was a place where the

---

1   Dissolution.....death-knell] Henry VIII dissolved many Catholic religious establishments between 1536 and 1540. Hutchins (p. 32) says that the Abbey "seems to have been ruined immediately upon the Dissolution."

2   Vale of Blackmoor] to the south and south-west of Shaftesbury in Dorsetshire.

churchyard lay nearer heaven than the church steeple, where beer was more plentiful than water, and where there were more wanton women than honest wives and maids. It is also said that after the middle ages the inhabitants were too poor to pay their priests, and hence were compelled to pull down their churches, and refrain altogether from the public worship of God; a necessity which they bemoaned over their cups in the settles of their inns on Sunday afternoons. In those days the Shastonians were apparently not without a sense of humour.

There was another peculiarity – this a modern one – which Shaston appeared to owe to its site. It was the resting-place and headquarters of the proprietors of wandering vans, shows, shooting-galleries, and other itinerant concerns, whose business lay largely at fairs and markets. As strange wild birds are seen assembled on some lofty promontory, meditatively pausing for longer flights, or to return by the course they followed thither, so here, in this cliff-town, stood in stultified silence the yellow and green caravans bearing names not local, as if surprised by a change in the landscape so violent as to hinder their further progress; and here they usually remained all the winter till they turned to seek again their old tracks in the following spring.

It was to this breezy and whimsical spot that Jude ascended from the nearest station for the first time in his life about four o'clock one afternoon, and entering on the summit of the peak after a toilsome climb, passed the first houses of the aërial town; and drew towards the school-house. The hour was too early; the pupils were still in school, humming small, like a swarm of gnats; and he withdrew a few steps along Abbey Walk, whence he regarded the spot which fate had made the home of all he loved best in the world. In front of the schools, which were extensive and stone-built, grew two enormous beeches with smooth mouse-coloured trunks, as such trees will only[1] grow on chalk uplands. Within the mullioned and transomed windows he could see the black, brown, and flaxen crowns of the scholars over the sills, and to pass the time away he walked down to the level terrace where the Abbey gardens once had spread, his heart throbbing in spite of him.

---

1   will only] the manuscript has "only will", which seems more accurate.

Unwilling to enter till the children were dismissed he remained here till young voices could be heard in the open air, and girls in white pinafores over red and blue frocks appeared dancing along the paths which the abbess, prioress, sub-prioress, and fifty nuns had demurely paced three centuries earlier. Retracing his steps he found that he had waited too long, and that Sue had gone out into the town at the heels of the last scholar, Mr. Phillotson having been absent all the afternoon at a teachers' meeting at Shottsford.

Jude went into the empty schoolroom and sat down, the girl who was sweeping the floor having informed him that Mrs. Phillotson would be back again in a few minutes. A piano stood near – actually the old piano that Phillotson had possessed at Marygreen – and though the dark afternoon almost prevented him seeing the notes Jude touched them in his humble way, and could not help modulating into the hymn which had so affected him in the previous week.

A figure moved behind him, and thinking it was still the girl with the broom Jude took no notice, till the person came close and laid her fingers lightly upon his bass hand. The imposed hand was a little one he seemed to know, and he turned.

"Don't stop," said Sue. "I like it. I learnt it before I left Melchester. They used to play it in the Training School."

"I can't strum before you! Play it for me."

"O well – I don't mind."

Sue sat down, and her rendering of the piece, though not remarkable, seemed divine as compared with his own. She, like him, was evidently touched – to her own surprise – by the recalled air; and when she had finished, and he moved his hand towards hers, it met his own half-way. Jude grasped it – just as he had done before her marriage.

"It is odd," she said, in a voice quite changed, "that I should care about that air; because ——"

"Because what?"

"I am not that sort – quite."

"Not easily moved?"

"I didn't quite mean that."

"O, but you *are* one of that sort, for you are just like me at heart!"

"But not at head."

She played on, and suddenly turned round; and by an unpremeditated instinct each clasped the other's hand again.

She uttered a forced little laugh as she relinquished his quickly. "How funny!" she said. "I wonder what we both did that for?"

"I suppose because we are both alike, as I said before."

"Not in our thoughts! Perhaps a little in our feelings."

"And they rule thoughts.... Isn't it enough to make one blaspheme that the composer of that hymn is one of the most commonplace men I ever met!"

"What – you know him?"

"I went to see him."

"O you goose – to do just what I should have done! Why did you?"

"Because we are not alike," he said drily.

"Now we'll have some tea," said Sue. "Shall we have it here instead of in my house? It is no trouble to get the kettle and things brought in. We don't live at the school, you now, but in that ancient dwelling across the way called Old-Grove's Place. It is so antique and dismal that it depresses me dreadfully. Such houses are very well to visit, but not to live in – I feel crushed into the earth by the weight of so many previous lives there spent. In a new place like these schools there is only your own life to support. Sit down, and I'll tell Ada to bring the tea-things across."

He waited in the light of the stove, the door of which she flung open before going out, and when she returned, followed by the maiden with tea, they sat down by the same light, assisted by the blue rays of a spirit-lamp under the brass kettle on the stand.

"This is one of your wedding-presents to me," she said, signifying the latter.

"Yes," said Jude.

The kettle of his gift sang with some satire in its note, to his mind; and to change the subject he said, "Do you know of any good readable edition of the uncanonical books of the New Testament? You don't read them in the school, I suppose?"

"O dear no! – 'twould alarm the neighbourhood.... Yes, there is one. I am not familiar with it now, though I was interested in it when my former friend was alive. Cowper's *Apocryphal Gospels*."[1]

---

1 Cowper's *Apocryphal Gospels*] *The Apocryphal Gospels and Other Documents relating to the History of Christ*, tr. and ed. B.H. Cowper (1867).

"That sounds like what I want." His thoughts, however, reverted with a twinge to the "former friend" – by whom she meant, as he knew, the University comrade of her earlier days. He wondered if she talked of him to Phillotson.

"The Gospel of Nicodemus is very nice," she went on, to keep him from his jealous thoughts, which she read clearly, as she always did. Indeed when they talked on an indifferent subject, as now, there was ever a second silent conversation passing between their emotions, so perfect was the reciprocity between them. "It is quite like the genuine article. All cut up into verses, too;[1] so that it is like one of the other evangelists read in a dream, when things are the same, yet not the same. But Jude, do you take an interest in those questions still? Are you getting up *Apologetica*?"[2]

"Yes. I am reading Divinity harder than ever."

She regarded him curiously.

"Why do you look at me like that?" said Jude.

"Oh – why do you want to know?"

"I am sure you can tell me anything I may be ignorant of in that subject. You must have learnt a lot of everything from your dear dead friend!"

"We won't get on to that now!" she coaxed. "Will you be carving out at that church again next week, where you learnt the pretty hymn?"

"Yes, perhaps."

"That will be very nice. Shall I come and see you there? It is in this direction, and I could come any afternoon by train for half-an-hour?"

"No. Don't come!"

"What – aren't we going to be friends, then, any longer, as we used to be?"

"No."

"I didn't know that. I thought you were always going to be kind to me!"

"No, I am not."

---

1   verses, too] Cowper's edition contains (pp. 227-388) "The Gospel of Nicodemus", but divided only into numbered chapters, not numbered verses.
2   *Apologetica*] (Latin, from Greek:) writings in defence of Christianity.

"What have I done, then? I am sure I thought we two ——" The *tremolo* in her voice caused her to break off.

"Sue, I sometimes think you are a flirt," said he abruptly.

There was a momentary pause, till she suddenly jumped up; and to his surprise he saw by the kettle-flame that her face was flushed.

"I can't talk to you any longer, Jude!" she said, the tragic contralto note having come back as of old. "It is getting too dark to stay together like this, after playing morbid Good Friday tunes[1] that make one feel what one shouldn't! ... We mustn't sit and talk in this way any more. Yes – you must go away, for you mistake me! I am very much the reverse of what you say so cruelly – O Jude, it *was* cruel to say that! Yet I can't tell you the truth – I should shock you by letting you know how I give way to my impulses, and how much I feel that I shouldn't have been provided with attractiveness unless it were meant to be exercised! Some women's love of being loved is insatiable; and so, often, is their love of loving; and in the last case they may find that they can't give it continuously to the chamber-officer appointed by the bishop's licence to receive it. But you are so straightforward, Jude, that you can't understand me! ... Now you must go. I am sorry my husband is not at home."

"Are you?"

"I perceive I have said that in mere convention! Honestly I don't think I am sorry. It does not matter, either way, sad to say!"

As they had overdone the grasp of hands some time sooner, she touched his fingers but lightly when he went out now. He had hardly gone from the door when, with a dissatisfied look, she jumped on a form and opened the iron casement of a window beneath which he was passing in the path without. "When do you leave here to catch your train, Jude?" she asked.

He looked up in some surprise. "The coach that runs to meet it goes in three-quarters of an hour or so."

"What will you do with yourself for the time?"

"O – wander about, I suppose. Perhaps I shall go and sit in the old church."

"It does seem hard of me to pack you off so! You have thought

---

1   Good Friday tunes] hymns about Christ's crucifixion.

enough of churches, Heaven knows, without going into one in the dark. Stay there."

"Where?"

"Where you are. I can talk to you better like this than when you were inside.... It was so kind and tender of you to give up half a day's work to come to see me! ...You are Joseph the dreamer of dreams,[1] dear Jude. And a tragic Don Quixote.[2] And sometimes you are St. Stephen, who, while they were stoning him, could see Heaven opened.[3] O my poor friend and comrade, you'll suffer yet!"

Now that the high window-sill was between them, so that he could not get at her, she seemed not to mind indulging in a frankness she had feared at close quarters. "I have been thinking," she continued, still in the tone of one brimful of feeling, "that the social moulds civilization fits us into have no more relation to our actual shapes than the conventional shapes of the constellations have to the real star-patterns. I am called Mrs. Richard Phillotson, living a calm wedded life with my counterpart of that name. But I am not really Mrs. Richard Phillotson, but a woman tossed about, all alone, with aberrant passions, and unaccountable antipathies.... Now you mustn't wait longer, or you will lose the coach. Come and see me again. You must come to the house then."

"Yes!" said Jude. "When shall it be?"

"To-morrow week. Good-bye – good-bye!" She stretched out her hand and stroked his forehead pitifully – just once. Jude said good-bye, and went away into the darkness.

Passing along Bimport Street he thought he heard the wheels of the coach departing, and, truly enough, when he reached the Duke's Arms in the Market Place the coach had gone. It was impossible for him to get to the station on foot in time for this train, and he settled himself perforce to wait for the next – the last to Melchester that night.

He wandered about awhile, obtained something to eat; and then, having another half-hour on his hands, his feet involuntarily took him through the venerable graveyard of Trinity Church, with its avenues

---

1   Joseph.....dreams] Genesis 37:5-10.

2   Quixote] Cervantes's Don Quixote is a deluded idealist.

3   Stephen.....opened] "And [he] said, Behold, I see the heavens opened.....Then they .....cast *him* out of the city, and stoned *him*" (Acts 7:56-8).

of limes, in the direction of the schools again. They were entirely in darkness. She had said she lived over the way at Old-Grove's Place, a house which he soon discovered from her description of its antiquity.

A glimmering candle-light shone from a front window, the shutters being yet unclosed. He could see the interior clearly – the floor sinking a couple of steps below the road without, which had become raised during the centuries since the house was built. Sue, evidently just come in, was standing with her hat on in this front parlour or sitting-room, whose walls were lined with wainscoting of panelled oak reaching from floor to ceiling, the latter being crossed by huge moulded beams only a little way above her head. The mantel-piece was of the same heavy description, carved with Jacobean pilasters[1] and scroll-work. The centuries did, indeed, ponderously overhang a young wife who passed her time here.

She had opened a rosewood work-box, and was looking at a photograph. Having contemplated it a little while she pressed it against her bosom, and put it again it its place.

Then becoming aware that she had not obscured the windows she came forward to do so, candle in hand. It was too dark for her to see Jude without, but he could see her face distinctly, and there was an unmistakable tearfulness about the dark, long-lashed eyes.

She closed the shutters, and Jude turned away to pursue his solitary journey home. "Whose photograph was she looking at?" he said. He had once given her his; but she had others, he knew. Yet it was his, surely?

He knew he should go to see her again, according to her invitation. Those earnest men he read of, the saints, whom Sue, with gentle irreverence, called his demi-gods, would have shunned such encounters, if they doubted their own strength. But he could not. He might fast and pray during the whole interval, but the human was more powerful in him than the Divine.

---

1   Jacobean pilasters] Jacobean: in the style fashionable in or around the reign of James
    I (1603-25). Pilasters: here, rectangular columns set into the wooden surround.

IV.-II.

HOWEVER, if God disposed not, woman did.[1] The next morning but one brought him this note from her:

"Don't come next week. On your own account don't! We were too free, under the influence of that morbid hymn and the twilight. Think no more than you can help of

"SUSANNA FLORENCE MARY."

The disappointment was keen. He knew her mood, the look of her face, when she subscribed herself at length thus. But whatever her mood he could not say she was wrong in her view. He replied:

"I acquiesce. You are right. It is a lesson in renunciation which I suppose I ought to learn at this season.[2]

JUDE."

He despatched the note on Easter Eve, and there seemed a finality in their decisions. But other forces and laws than theirs were in operation. On Easter Monday morning he received a message from the Widow Edlin, whom he had directed to telegraph if anything serious happened:

"Your aunt is sinking. Come at once."

He threw down his tools and went. Three and a half hours later he was crossing the downs about Marygreen, and presently plunged into the concave field across which the short cut was made to the village. As he ascended on the other side a labouring man, who had been watching his approach from a gate across the path, moved uneasily, and prepared to speak. "I can see in his face that she is dead," said Jude. "Poor Aunt Drusilla!"

---

1 if.....did] cf. "Man proposes, but God disposes" (Thomas à Kempis: *The Imitation of Christ*, Bk. I, Chap. 19).

2 this season] Lent, the season of renunciations, extending from Ash Wednesday to Easter Sunday.

It was as he had supposed, and Mrs. Edlin had sent out the man to break the news to him.

"She wouldn't have knowed 'ee. She lay like a doll wi' glass eyes; so it didn't matter that you wasn't here," said he.

Jude went on to the house, and in the afternoon, when everything was done, and the layers-out had finished their beer, and gone, he sat down alone in the silent place. It was absolutely necessary to communicate with Sue, though two or three days earlier they had agreed to mutual severance. He wrote in the briefest terms:

"Aunt Drusilla is dead, having been taken almost suddenly. The funeral is on Friday afternoon."

He remained in and about Marygreen through the intervening days, went out on Friday morning to see that the grave was finished, and wondered if Sue would come. She had not written, and that seemed to signify rather that she would come than that she would not. Having timed her by her only possible train, he locked the door about mid-day, and crossed the hollow field to the verge of the upland by the Brown House, where he stood and looked over the vast prospect northwards, and over the nearer landscape in which Alfredston stood. Two miles behind it a jet of white steam was travelling from the left to the right of the picture.

There was a long time to wait, even now, till he would know if she had arrived. He did wait, however, and at last a small hired vehicle pulled up at the bottom of the hill, and a person alighted, the conveyance going back, while the passenger began ascending the hill. He knew her; and she looked so slender to-day that it seemed as if she might be crushed in the intensity of a too passionate embrace – such as it was not for him to give. Two-thirds of the way up her head suddenly took a solicitous poise, and he knew that she had at that moment recognized him. Her face soon began a pensive smile, which lasted till, having descended a little way, he met her.

"I thought," she began with nervous quickness, "that it would be so sad to let you attend the funeral alone! And so – at the last moment – I came."

"Dear faithful Sue!" murmured Jude.

With the elusiveness of her curious double nature, however, Sue did not stand still for any further greeting, though it wanted some time to the burial. A pathos so unusually compounded as that which attached to this hour was unlikely to repeat itself for years, if ever, and Jude would have paused, and meditated, and conversed. But Sue either saw it not at all, or, seeing it more than he, would not allow herself to feel it.

The sad and simple ceremony was soon over, their progress to the church being almost at a trot, the bustling undertaker having a more important funeral an hour later, three miles off. Drusilla was put into the new ground, quite away from her ancestors. Sue and Jude had gone side by side to the grave, and now sat down to tea in the familiar house; their lives united at least in this last attention to the dead.

"She was opposed to marriage, from first to last, you say?" murmured Sue.

"Yes. Particularly for members of our family."

Her eyes met his, and remained on him awhile.

"We are rather a sad family, don't you think, Jude?"

"She said we made bad husbands and wives. Certainly we make unhappy ones. At all events, I do, for one!"

Sue was silent. "Is it wrong, Jude," she said with a tentative tremor, "for a husband or wife to tell a third person that they are unhappy in their marriage? If a marriage ceremony is a religious thing, it is possibly wrong; but if it is only a sordid contract, based on material convenience in householding, rating, and taxing, and the inheritance of land and money by children, making it necessary that the male parent should be known – which it seems to be – why surely a person may say, even proclaim upon the housetops, that it hurts and grieves him or her?"

"I have said so, anyhow, to you."

Presently she went on: "Are there many couples, do you think, where one dislikes the other for no definite fault?"

"Yes, I suppose. If either cares for another person, for instance."

"But even apart from that? Wouldn't the woman, for example, be very bad-natured if she didn't like to live with her husband; merely" – her voice undulated, and he guessed things – "merely because she had a personal feeling against it – a physical objection – a fastidiousness, or whatever it may be called – although she might respect and be grateful to him? I am merely putting a case. Ought she to try to over-come her pruderies?"

Jude threw a troubled look at her. He said, looking away: "It would be just one of those cases in which my experiences go contrary to my dogmas. Speaking as an order-loving man – which I hope I am, though I fear I am not – I should say, yes. Speaking from experience and unbiassed nature, I should say, no ... Sue, I believe you are not happy!"

"Yes I am!" said she excitedly. "How can a woman be unhappy who has only been married eight weeks to a man she chose freely?"

"'Chose freely!'"

"Why do you repeat it? ... But I have to go back by the six o'clock train. You will be staying on here, I suppose?"

"For a few days to wind up aunt's affairs. This house is gone now. Shall I go to the train with you?"

A little laugh of objection came from Sue. "I think not. You may come part of the way."

"But stop – you can't go to-night! That train won't take you to Shaston. You must stay and go back to-morrow. Mrs. Edlin has plenty of room, if you don't like to stay here?"

"Very well," she said dubiously. "I didn't tell him I would come for certain."

Jude went to the widow's house adjoining, to let her know; and returning in a few minutes sat down again.

"It is horrible how we are circumstanced, Sue – horrible!" he said abruptly, with his eyes bent to the floor.

"No! Why?"

"I can't tell you all my part of the gloom. Your part is that you ought not to have married him. I saw it before you had done it, but I thought I mustn't interfere. I was wrong. I ought to have!"

"But what makes you assume all this, dear?"

"Because – I can see you through your feathers, my poor little bird!"

Her hand lay on the table, and Jude put his upon it. Sue drew hers away.

"That's absurd, Sue," cried he, "after what we've been talking about! I am more strict and formal than you, if it comes to that; and that you should object to such an innocent action shows that you are ridiculously inconsistent!"

"Perhaps it was too prudish," she said repentantly. "Only I have fancied it was a sort of trick of ours – too frequent perhaps. There, you may hold it as much as you like. Is that good of me?"

"Yes; very."

"But I must tell him."

"Who?"

"Richard."

"O – of course, if you think it necessary. But as it means nothing it may be bothering him needlessly."

"Well – are you sure you mean it only as my cousin?"

"Absolutely sure. I have no feelings of love left in me."

"That's news. How has it come to be?"

"I've seen Arabella."

She winced at the hit; then said curiously, "When did you see her?"

"When I was at Christminster."

"So she's come back; and you never told me! I suppose you will live with her now?"

"Of course – just as you live with your husband."

She looked at the window pots with the geraniums and cactuses, withered for want of attention, and through them at the outer distance, till her eyes began to grow moist. "What is it?" said Jude, in a softened tone.

"Why should you be so glad to go back to her if – if – what you used to say to me is still true – I mean if it were true then! Of course it is not now! How could your heart go back to Arabella so soon?"

"A special Providence, I suppose, helped it on its way."

"Ah – it isn't true!" she said with gentle resentment. "You are testing me – that's all – because you think I am not happy!"

"I don't know. I don't wish to know."

"If I were unhappy it would be my fault, my wickedness; not that I should have a right to dislike him! He is considerate to me in everything; and he is very interesting, from the amount of general knowledge he has acquired by reading everything that comes in his way.... Do you think, Jude, that a man ought to marry a woman his own age, or one younger than himself – eighteen years – as I am than he?"

"It depends upon what they feel for each other."

He gave her no opportunity of self-satisfaction, and she had to go on unaided, which she did in a vanquished tone, verging on tears:

"I – I think I must be equally honest with you as you have been with me. Perhaps you have seen what it is I want to say? – that though I like Mr. Phillotson as a friend, I don't like him – it is a torture to me to – live with him as a husband! – There, now I have let it out – I couldn't help it, although I have been – pretending I am happy. – Now you'll have a contempt for me for ever, I suppose!" She bent down her face upon her hands as they lay upon the cloth, and silently sobbed in little jerks that made the fragile three-legged table quiver.

"I have only been married a month or two!" she went on, still remaining bent upon the table, and talking into her hands. "And it is said that what a woman shrinks from – in the early days of her marriage – she shakes down to with comfortable indifference in half-a-dozen years. But that is much like saying that the amputation of a limb is no affliction, since a person gets comfortably accustomed to the use of a wooden leg or arm in the course of time!"

Jude could hardly speak, but he said, "I thought there was something wrong, Sue! O, I thought there was!"

"But it is not as you think! – there is nothing wrong except my own wickedness, I suppose you'd call it – a repugnance on my part, for a reason I cannot disclose, and what would not be admitted as one by the world in general! ... What tortures me so much is the necessity of being responsive to this man whenever he wishes, good as he is morally! – the dreadful contract to feel in a particular way, in a matter whose essence is its voluntariness![1] ... I wish he would beat me, or be faithless to me, or do some open thing that I could talk about as a justification for feeling as I do! But he does nothing, except that he has grown a little cold since he has found out how I feel. That's why he didn't come to the funeral.... O, I am very miserable – I don't know what to do! ... Don't come near me, Jude, because you mustn't."

But he had jumped up and put his face against hers – or rather against her ear, her face being inaccessible.

---

1 essence.....voluntariness] cf. "Love withers under constraint: its very essence is liberty" (Shelley's notes to *Queen Mab*, quoted in Walter Bagehot's *Estimates*, 1858, a
work read by Hardy).

"I told you not to, Jude!"

"I know you did – I only wish to – console you! It all arose through my being married before we met, didn't it? You would have been my wife, Sue, wouldn't you, if it hadn't been for that?"

Instead of replying she rose quickly, and saying she was going to walk to her aunt's grave in the churchyard to recover herself, went out of the house. Jude did not follow her. Twenty minutes later he saw her cross the village green towards Mrs. Edlin's, and soon she sent a little girl to fetch her bag, and tell him she was too tired to see him again that night.

In the lonely room of his aunt's house, Jude sat watching the cottage of the Widow Edlin as it disappeared behind the night shade. He knew that Sue was sitting within its walls equally lonely and disheartened; and again questioned his devotional motto that all was for the best.

He retired to rest early, but his sleep was fitful from the sense that Sue was so near at hand. At some time near two o'clock, when he was beginning to sleep more soundly, he was aroused by a shrill squeak that had been familiar to him when he lived regularly at Marygreen. It was the cry of a rabbit caught in a gin. As was the little creature's habit, it did not soon repeat its cry; and probably would not do so more than once or twice; but would remain bearing its torture till the morrow, when the trapper would come and knock it on the head.

He who in his childhood had saved the lives of the earthworms now began to picture the agonies of the rabbit from its lacerated leg. If it were a "bad catch" by the hind-leg, the animal would tug during the ensuing six hours till the iron teeth of the trap had stripped the leg-bone of its flesh, when, should a weak-springed instrument enable it to escape, it would die in the fields from the mortification of the limb. If it were a "good catch," namely, by the fore-leg, the bone would be broken, and the limb nearly torn in two in attempts at an impossible escape.

Almost half-an-hour passed, and the rabbit repeated its cry. Jude could rest no longer till he had put it out of its pain, so dressing himself quickly he descended, and by the light of the moon went across the green in the direction of the sound. He reached the hedge bordering the widow's garden, when he stood still. The faint click of the trap as dragged about by the writhing animal guided him now, and reaching the spot he struck the rabbit on the back of the neck with the side of his palm, and it stretched itself out dead.

He was turning away when he saw a woman looking out of the open casement at a window on the ground floor of the adjacent cottage. "Jude!" said a voice timidly – Sue's voice. "It is you – is it not?"

"Yes, dear!"

"I haven't been able to sleep at all, and then I heard the rabbit, and couldn't help thinking of what it suffered, till I felt I must come down and kill it! But I am so glad you got there first.... They ought not to be allowed to set these steel traps, ought they!"

Jude had reached the window, which was quite a low one, so that she was visible down to her waist. She let go the casement-stay and put her hand upon his, her moonlit face regarding him wistfully.

"Did it keep you awake?" he said.

"No – I was awake."

"How was that?"

"O, you know – now! I know you, with your religious doctrines, think that a married woman in trouble of a kind like mine commits a mortal sin in making a man the confidant of it, as I did you. I wish I hadn't, now!"

"Don't wish it, dear," he said. "That may have *been* my view; but my doctrines and I begin to part company."

"I knew it – I knew it! And that's why I vowed I wouldn't disturb your beliefs. But – I am *so glad* to see you! – and, O, I didn't mean to see you again, now the last tie between us, Aunt Drusilla, is dead!"

Jude seized her hand and kissed it. "There is a stronger one left!" he said. "I'll never care about my doctrines or my religion any more! Let them go! Let me help you, even if I do love you, and even if you ... "

"Don't say it! – I know what you mean; but I can't admit so much as that. There! Guess what you like but don't press me to answer questions!"

"I wish you were happy, whatever I may be!"

"I *can't* be! So few could enter into my feeling – they would say 'twas my fanciful fastidiousness, or something of that sort, and condemn me.... It is none of the natural tragedies of love that's love's usual tragedy in civilized life, but a tragedy artificially manufactured for people who in a natural state would find relief in parting! ... It would have been wrong, perhaps, for me to tell my distress to you, if I had been able to tell it to anybody else. But I have nobody. And I *must* tell somebody! Jude, before I married him I had never thought out fully what marriage meant, even though I knew. It was idiotic of me – there is no excuse. I was old enough, and I thought I was very experienced. So I rushed on, when I had got into that Training School scrape, with all the cocksureness of the fool that I was! ... I am certain one ought to be allowed to undo what one has done so ignorantly! I daresay it happens to lots of women; only they submit, and I kick.... When people of a later age look back upon the barbarous customs and superstitions of the times that we have the unhappiness to live in, what *will* they say!"

"You are very bitter, darling Sue! How I wish – I wish ——"

"You must go in now!"

In a moment of impulse she bent over the sill, and laid her face upon his hair, weeping, and then imprinting a scarcely perceptible little kiss upon the top of his head, withdrawing quickly, so that he could not put his arms round her, as he unquestionably would have otherwise done. She shut the casement, and he returned to his cottage.

IV.–III.

SUE's distressful confession recurred to Jude's mind all the night as being a sorrow indeed.

The morning after, when it was time for her to go, the neighbours saw her companion and herself disappearing on foot down the hill path which led into the lonely road to Alfredston. An hour passed before he returned along the same route, and in his face there was a look of exaltation not unmixed with recklessness. An incident had occurred.

They had stood parting in the silent highway, and their tense and passionate moods had led to bewildered inquiries of each other on how far their intimacy ought to go; till they had almost quarrelled, and she had said tearfully that it was hardly proper of him as a parson in embryo to think of such a thing as kissing her even in farewell, as he now wished to do. Then she had conceded that the fact of the kiss would be nothing: all would depend upon the spirit of it. If given in the spirit of a cousin and a friend she saw no objection: if in the spirit of a lover she could not permit it. "Will you swear that it will not be in that spirit?" she had said.

No: he would not. And then they had turned from each other in estrangement, and gone their several ways, till at a distance of twenty or thirty yards both had looked round simultaneously. That look behind was fatal to the reserve hitherto more or less maintained. They had quickly run back, and met, and embracing most unpremeditatedly, kissed each other. When they parted for good it was with flushed cheeks on her side, and a beating heart on his.

The kiss was a turning-point in Jude's career. Back again in the cottage, and left to reflection, he saw one thing: that though his kiss of that aërial being had seemed the purest moment of his faultful life, as long as he nourished this unlicensed tenderness it was glaringly inconsistent for him to pursue the idea of becoming the soldier and servant of a religion in which sexual love was regarded as at its best a frailty, and at its worst damnation. What Sue had said in warmth was really the cold truth. When to defend his affection tooth and nail, to persist with headlong force in impassioned attentions to her, was all he thought of, he was condemned *ipso facto*[1] as a professor of the accepted school of morals. He was as unfit, obviously, by nature, as he had been by social position, to fill the part of a propounder of accredited dogma.

Strange that his first aspiration — towards academical proficiency — had been checked by a woman, and that his second aspiration — towards apostleship — had also been checked by a woman. "Is it," he said, "that the women are to blame; or is it the artificial system of things, under which the normal sex-impulses are turned into devilish domestic gins and springes[2] to noose and hold back those who want to progress?"

It had been his standing desire to become a prophet, however humble, to his struggling fellow-creatures, without any thought of personal gain. Yet with a wife living away from him with another husband, and himself in love erratically, the loved one's revolt against

---

1 *ipso facto*] (Latin:) by that very fact.
2 gins and springes] a gin is a powerful spring-trap with metal teeth; a springe is a snare with noose and spring.

her state being possibly on his account, he had sunk to be barely respectable according to regulation views.

It was not for him to consider further: he had only to confront the obvious, which was that he had made himself quite an impostor as a law-abiding religious teacher.

At dusk that evening he went into the garden and dug a shallow hole, to which he brought out all the theological and ethical works that he possessed. He knew that, in this country of true believers, most of them were not saleable at a much higher price than waste-paper value, and preferred to get rid of them in his own way, even if he should sacrifice a little money to the sentiment of thus destroying them. Lighting some loose pamphlets to begin with, he cut the volumes into pieces as well as he could, and with a three-pronged fork shook them over the flames. They kindled, and lighted up the back of the house, the pigsty, and his own face, till they were more or less consumed.

Though he was almost a stranger here now, passing cottagers talked to him over the garden hedge.

"Burning up your awld aunt's rubbidge I suppose? Ay; a lot gets heaped up in nooks and corners when you've lived eighty years in one house."

It was nearly one o'clock in the morning before the leaves, covers, and binding of Jeremy Taylor, Butler, Doddridge, Paley, Pusey, Newman[1] and the rest had gone to ashes; but the night was quiet, and as he turned and turned the paper shreds with the fork, the sense of being no longer a hypocrite to himself afforded a relief to his mind which gave him calm. He might go on believing as before, but he professed nothing, and no longer owned and exhibited engines of faith which, as their proprietor, he might naturally be supposed to exercise on himself first of all. In his passion for Sue he could now stand as an ordinary sinner, and not as a whited sepulchre.[2]

Meanwhile Sue, after parting from him earlier in the day, had gone along to the station, with tears in her eyes for having run back and let him kiss her. Jude ought not to have pretended that he was not a lover, and made her give way to an impulse to act unconventionally, if not wrongly. She was inclined to call it the latter; for Sue's logic was

---

1 Jeremy Taylor.....Newman] influential theological writers.
2 whited sepulchre] hypocrite (Matthew 23: 27).

extraordinarily compounded, and seemed to maintain that before a thing was done it might be right to do, but that being done it became wrong; or, in other words, that things which were right in theory were wrong in practice.

"I have been too weak I think!" she jerked out as she pranced on, shaking down tear-drops now and then. "It was burning, like a lover's – O it was! And I won't write to him any more, or at least for a long time, to impress him with my dignity! And I hope it will hurt him very much – expecting a letter to-morrow morning, and the next, and the next, and no letter coming. He'll suffer then with suspense – won't he, that's all! – and I am very glad of it!" – Tears of pity for Jude's approaching sufferings at her hands mingled with those which had surged up in pity for herself.

Then the slim little wife of a husband whose person was disagreeable to her, the ethereal, fine-nerved, sensitive girl, quite unfitted by temperament and instinct to fulfil the conditions of the matrimonial relation with Phillotson, possibly with any man, walked fitfully along, and panted, and brought weariness into her eyes by gazing and worrying hopelessly.

Phillotson met her at the arrival station, and, seeing that she was troubled, thought it must be owing to the depressing effect of her aunt's death and funeral. He began telling her of his day's doings, and how his friend Gillingham, a neighbouring schoolmaster whom he had not seen for years, had called upon him. While ascending to the town, seated on the top of the omnibus beside him, she said suddenly and with an air of self-chastisement, regarding the white road and its bordering bushes of hazel:

"Richard – I let Mr. Fawley hold my hand. I don't know whether you think it wrong?"

He, waking apparently from thoughts of far different mould, said vaguely, "O, did you? What did you do that for?"

"I don't know. He wanted to, and I let him."

"I hope it pleased him. I should think it was hardly a novelty."

They lapsed into silence. Had this been a case in the court of an omniscient judge he might have entered on his notes the curious fact that Sue had placed the minor for the major indiscretion, and had not said a word about the kiss.

After tea that evening Phillotson sat balancing the school registers.

She remained in an unusually silent, tense, and restless condition, and at last, saying she was tired, went to bed early. When Phillotson arrived upstairs, weary with the drudgery of the attendance-numbers, it was a quarter to twelve o'clock. Entering their chamber, which by day commanded a view of some thirty or forty miles over the Vale of Blackmoor, and even into Outer Wessex, he went to the window, and, pressing his face against the pane, gazed with hard-breathing fixity into the mysterious darkness which now covered the far-reaching scene. He was musing. "I think," he said at last, without turning his head, "that I must get the Committee to change the school-stationer. All the copy books are sent wrong this time."

There was no reply. Thinking Sue was dozing he went on:

"And there must be a re-arrangement of that ventilator in the class-room. The wind blows down upon my head unmercifully, and gives me the earache."

As the silence seemed more absolute than ordinarily he turned round. The heavy, gloomy oak wainscot, which extended over the walls upstairs and down in the dilapidated "Old-Grove's House," and the massive chimney-piece reaching to the ceiling, stood in odd contrast to the new and shining brass bedstead, and the new suite of birch furniture that he had bought for her, the two styles seeming to nod to each other across three centuries upon the shaking floor.

"Soo!" he said (this being the way in which he pronounced her name). [1]

She was not in the bed, though she had apparently been there – the clothes on her side being flung back. Thinking she might have forgotten some kitchen detail and gone downstairs for a moment to see to it, he pulled off his coat and idled quietly enough for a few minutes, when, finding she did not come, he went out upon the landing, candle in hand, and said again "Soo!"

"Yes!" came back to him in her voice, from the distant kitchen quarter.

"What are you doing down there at midnight – tiring yourself out for nothing!"

"I am not sleepy; I am reading; and there is a larger fire here."

He went to bed. Some time in the night he awoke. She was not

---

1   "Soo!".....name] Evidently Hardy assumes the normal pronunciation to be "S-yoo".

there, even now. Lighting a candle he hastily stepped out upon the landing, and again called her name.

She answered "Yes!" as before; but the tones were small and confined, and whence they came he could not at first understand. Under the staircase was a large clothes-closet, without a window; they seemed to come from it. The door was shut, but there was no lock or other fastening. Phillotson, alarmed, went towards it, wondering if she had suddenly become deranged.

"What are you doing in there?" he asked.

"Not to disturb you I came here, as it was so late."

"But there's no bed, is there? And no ventilation! Why, you'll be suffocated if you stay all night!"

"O no, I think not. Don't trouble about me."

"But –" Phillotson seized the knob and pulled at the door. She had fastened it inside with a piece of string, which broke at his pull. There being no bedstead she had flung down some rugs and made a little nest for herself in the very cramped quarters the closet afforded.

When he looked in upon her she sprang out of her lair, trembling.

"You ought not to have pulled open the door!" she cried excitedly. "It is not becoming in you! O, will you go away; please will you!"

She looked so pitiful and pleading in her white night-gown against the shadowy lumber-hole that he was quite worried. She continued to beseech him not to disturb her.

He said: "I've been kind to you, and given you every liberty; and it is monstrous that you should feel in this way!"

"Yes," said she, weeping. "I know that! It is wrong and wicked of me, I suppose! I am very sorry. But it is not I altogether that am to blame!"

"Who is then? Am I?"

"No – I don't know! The universe, I suppose – things in general, because they are so horrid and cruel!"

"Well, it is no use talking like that. Making a man's house so unseemly at this time o'night! Eliza will hear, if we don't mind." (He meant the servant.) "Just think if either of the parsons in this town was to see us now! I hate such eccentricities, Sue. There's no order or regularity in your sentiments! ... But I won't intrude on you further; only I would advise you not to shut the door too tight, or I shall find you stifled to-morrow."

On rising the next morning he immediately looked into the closet, but Sue had already gone downstairs. There was a little nest where she had lain, and spiders' webs hung overhead. "What must a woman's aversion be when it is stronger than her fear of spiders!" he said bitterly.

He found her sitting at the breakfast-table, and the meal began almost in silence, the burghers walking past upon the pavement – or rather roadway, pavements being scarce here – which was two or three feet above the level of the parlour floor. They nodded down to the happy couple their morning greetings, as they went on.

"Richard," she said all at once; "would you mind my living away from you?"

"Away from me? Why, that's what you were doing when I married you. What then was the meaning of marrying at all?"

"You wouldn't like me any the better for telling you."

"I don't object to know."

"Because I thought I could do nothing else. You had got my promise a long time before that, remember. Then, as time went on, I regretted I had promised you, and was trying to see an honourable way to break it off. But as I couldn't I became rather reckless and careless about the conventions. Then you know what was said, and how I was turned out of the Training School you had taken such time and trouble to prepare me for and get me into; and this frightened me, and it seemed then that the one thing I could do would be to let the engagement stand. Of course I, of all people, ought not to have cared what was said, for it was just what I fancied I never did care for. But I was a coward – as so many women are – and my theoretic unconventionality broke down. If that had not entered into the case it would have been better to have hurt your feelings once for all then, than to marry you and hurt them all my life after.... And you were so generous in never giving credit for a moment to the rumour."

"I am bound in honesty to tell you that I weighed its probability, and inquired of your cousin about it."

"Ah!" she said with pained surprise.

"I didn't doubt you."

"But you inquired!"

"I took his word."

Her eyes had filled. "*He* wouldn't have inquired!" she said. "But you haven't answered me. Will you let me go away? I know how irregular it is of me to ask it ——"

"It is irregular."

"But I do ask it! Domestic laws should be made according to temperaments, which should be classified. If people are at all peculiar in character they have to suffer from the very rules that produce comfort in others! ... Will you let me?"

"But we married ——"

"What is the use of thinking of laws and ordinances," she burst out, "if they make you miserable when you know you are committing no sin?"

"But you are committing a sin in not liking me."

"I *do* like you! But I didn't reflect it would be – that it would be so much more than that.... For a man and woman to live on intimate terms when one feels as I do is adultery, in any circumstances, however legal. There – I've said it! ... Will you let me, Richard?"

"You distress me, Susanna, by such importunity!"

"Why can't we agree to free each other? We made the compact, and surely we can cancel it – not legally, of course; but we can morally, especially as no new interests, in the shape of children, have arisen to be looked after. Then we might be friends, and meet without pain to either. O Richard, be my friend and have pity! We shall both be dead in a few years, and then what will it matter to anybody that you relieved me from constraint for a little while? I daresay you think me eccentric, or super-sensitive, or something absurd. Well – why should I suffer for what I was born to be, if it doesn't hurt other people?"

"But it does – it hurts *me!* And you vowed to love me."

"Yes – that's it! I am in the wrong. I always am! It is as culpable to bind yourself to love always as to believe a creed always, and as silly as to vow always to like a particular food or drink!"

"And do you mean, by living away from me, living by yourself?"

"Well, if you insisted, yes. But I meant living with Jude."

"As his wife?"

"As I choose."

Phillotson writhed.

Sue continued: "She, or he, 'who lets the world, or his own portion of it, choose his plan of life for him, has no need of any other faculty than the ape-like one of imitation.'[1] J.S. Mill's words, those are. Why can't you act upon them? I wish to, always."

"What do I care about J. S. Mill!" moaned he. "I only want to lead a quiet life! Do you mind my saying that I have guessed what never once occurred to me before our marriage – that you were in love, and are in love, with Jude Fawley!"

"You may go on guessing that I am, since you have begun. But do you suppose that if I had been I should have asked you to let me go and live with him?"

The ringing of the school bell saved Phillotson from the necessity of replying at present to what apparently did not strike him as being such a convincing *argumentum ad verecundiam*[2] as she, in her loss of courage at the last moment, meant it to appear. She was beginning to be so puzzling and unpredicable[3] that he was ready to throw in with her other little peculiarities the extremest request which a wife could make.

They proceeded to the schools that morning as usual, Sue entering the class-room, where he could see the back of her head through the glass partition whenever he turned his eyes that way. As he went on giving and hearing lessons his forehead and eyebrows twitched from concentrated agitation of thought; till at length he tore a scrap from a sheet of scribbling paper and wrote:

"Your request prevents my attending to work at all. I don't know what I am doing! Was it seriously made?"

He folded the piece of paper very small, and give it to a little boy to take to Sue. The child toddled off into the class-room. Phillotson saw his wife turn and take the note, and the bend of her pretty head as she read it, her lips slightly crisped, to prevent undue expression under fire of so many young eyes. He could not see her hands, but she changed her position, and soon the child returned, bringing nothing

---

1 'who.....imitation'] from J.S. Mill's *On Liberty* (1859), Chap. 3. See Appendix E.
2 *argumentum ad verecundiam*] (Latin:) argument based on an appeal to reverence for an authority.
3 unpredicable] indefinable. (It may, as on p. 210, be an error for "unpredictable," but here Hardy later changed it to "unstateable".)

in reply. In a few minutes, however, one of Sue's class appeared, with a little note similar to his own. These words only were pencilled therein:

"I am sincerely sorry to say that it was seriously made."

Phillotson looked more disturbed than before, and the meeting-place of his brows twitched again. In ten minutes he called up the child he had just sent to her, and despatched another missive:

"God knows I don't want to thwart you in any reasonable way. My whole thought is to make you comfortable and happy. But I cannot agree to such a preposterous notion as your going to live with your lover. You would lose everybody's respect and regard; and so should I!"

After an interval a similar part was enacted in the class-room, and an answer came:

"I know you mean my good. But I don't want to be respectable! To produce 'Human development in its richest diversity' (to quote Humboldt)[1] is to my mind far above respectability. No doubt my tastes are low – in your view – hopelessly low! If you won't let me go to him, will you grant me this one request – allow me to live in your house in a separate way?"

To this he returned no answer.
She wrote again:

"I know what you think. But cannot you have pity on me? I beg you to; I implore you to be merciful! I would not ask if I were not almost compelled by what I can't bear! No poor woman has ever wished more than I that Eve had not fallen, so that (as the primitive Christians believed) some harmless mode of vegetation might have

---

1   To produce.....Humboldt] The phrase "human development in its richest diversity" is part of the epigraph of J.S. Mill's *On Liberty*, that epigraph being a quotation from Baron Wilhelm von Humboldt's *The Sphere and Duties of Government*.

peopled Paradise.[1] But I won't trifle! Be kind to me – even though I have not been kind to you! I will go away, go abroad, anywhere, and never trouble you."

Nearly an hour passed, and then he returned an answer:

"I do not wish to pain you. How well you *know* I don't! Give me a little time. I am disposed to agree to your last request."

One line from her:

"Thank you from my heart, Richard. I do not deserve your kindness."

All day Phillotson bent a dazed regard upon her through the glazed partition; and he felt as lonely as when he had not known her.

But he was as good as his word, and consented to her living apart in the house. At first, when they met at meals, she had seemed more composed under the new arrangement; but the irksomeness of their position worked on her temperament, and the fibres of her nature seemed strained like harp-strings. She talked vaguely and indiscriminately to prevent his talking pertinently.

IV.-IV.

PHILLOTSON was sitting up late, as was often his custom, trying to get together the materials for his long neglected hobby of Roman antiquities. For the first time since reviving the subject he felt a return of his old interest in it. He forgot time and place, and when he remembered himself and ascended to rest it was nearly two o'clock.

His preoccupation was such that, though he now slept on the other side of the house, he mechanically went to the room that he and his wife had occupied when he first became a tenant of Old-Grove's Place, which since his differences with Sue had been hers exclusively. He entered, and unconsciously began to undress.

---

1   some.....Paradise] Sue is here quoting Gibbon's *Decline and Fall,* Chap. 15. See Appendix E.

There was a cry from the bed, and a quick movement. Before the schoolmaster had realized where he was he perceived Sue starting up half-awake, staring wildly, and springing out upon the floor on the side away from him, which was towards the window. This was somewhat hidden by the canopy of the bedstead, and in a moment he heard her flinging up the sash. Before he had thought that she meant to do more than get air she had mounted upon the sill and leapt out. She disappeared in the darkness, and he heard her fall below.

Phillotson, horrified, ran downstairs, striking himself sharply against the newel[1] in his haste. Opening the heavy door he ascended the two or three steps to the level of the ground, and there on the gravel before him lay a white heap. Phillotson seized it in his arms, and bringing Sue into the hall seated her on a chair, where he gazed at her by the flapping light of the candle which he had set down in the draught on the bottom stair.

She had certainly not broken her neck. She looked at him with eyes that seemed not to take him in; and though not particularly large in general they appeared so now. She pressed her side and rubbed her arm, as if conscious of pain: then stood up, averting her face, in evident distress at his gaze.

"Thank God – you are not killed! Though it's not for want of trying – nor much hurt I hope?"

Her fall, in fact, had not been a serious one, probably owing to the lowness of the old rooms and to the high level of the ground outside. Beyond a scraped elbow and a blow in the side she had apparently incurred little harm.

"I was asleep, I think!" she began, her pale face still turned away from him. "And something frightened me – a terrible dream – I thought I saw you –" The actual circumstances seemed to come back to her, and she was silent.

Her cloak was hanging at the back of the door, and the wretched Phillotson flung it round her. "Shall I help you upstairs?" he asked drearily; for the significance of all this sickened him of himself and of everything.

"No thank you, Richard, I am very little hurt. I can walk."

"You ought to lock your door," he mechanically said, as if

I   newel] post supporting a hand-rail.

lecturing in school. "Then no one could intrude even by accident."

"I have tried – it won't lock. All the doors are out of order."

The aspect of things was not improved by her admission. She ascended the staircase slowly, the waving light of the candle shining on her. Phillotson did not approach her, or attempt to ascend himself till he heard her enter her room. Then he fastened up the front door, and returning sat down on the lower stairs, holding the newel with one hand, and bowing his face into the other. Thus he remained for a long long time – a pitiable object enough to one who had seen him; till, raising his head and sighing a sigh which seemed to say that the business of his life must be carried on, whether he had a wife or no, he took the candle and went upstairs to his lonely room on the other side of the landing.

No further incident touching the matter between them occurred till the following evening, when, immediately school was over, Phillotson walked out of Shaston, saying he required no tea, and not informing Sue where he was going. He descended from the town level by a steep road in a north-westerly direction, and continued to move downwards till the soil changed from its white dryness to a tough brown clay. He was now on the low alluvial beds

> "Where Duncliffe is the traveller's mark,
> And cloty Stour's a-rolling."

More than once he looked back in the increasing obscurity of evening. Against the sky was Shaston, dimly visible

> "On the grey-topp'd height
> Of Paladore, as pale day wore
> Away ... "[1]

The new-lit lights from its windows burnt with a steady shine as if watching him, one of which windows was his own. Above it he could just discern the pinnacled tower of Trinity Church. The air down here, tempered by the thick damp bed of tenacious clay, was not as it had been above, but soft and relaxing, so that when he had

---

1   William Barnes. [Hardy's note.] (Both quotations are from Barnes's poem in Dorsetshire dialect, "Shaftesbury Feäir.")

walked a mile or two he was obliged to wipe his face with his hand-kerchief.

Leaving Duncliffe Hill on the left he proceeded without hesitation through the shade, as a man goes on, night or day, in a district over which he has played as a boy. He had walked altogether about four and a half miles[1] when he crossed a tributary of the Stour, and reached Leddenton[2] – a little town of three or four thousand inhabitants – where he went on to the boys' school, and knocked at the door of the master's residence.

A boy pupil-teacher opened it, and to Phillotson's inquiry if Mr. Gillingham was at home replied that he was, going at once off to his own house, and leaving Phillotson to find his way in as he could. He discovered his friend putting away some books from which he had been giving evening lessons. The light of the paraffin lamp fell on Phillotson's face – pale and wretched by contrast with his friend's, who had a cool, practical look. They had been schoolmates in boyhood, and fellow-students at Wintoncester[3] Training College, many years before this time.

"Glad to see you, Dick! But you don't look well? Nothing the matter?"

Phillotson advanced without replying, and Gillingham closed the cupboard and pulled up beside his visitor.

"Why you haven't been here – let me see – since you were married? I called, you know, but you were out; and upon my word it is such a climb after dark that I have been waiting till the days are longer before lumpering[4] up again. I am glad you didn't wait, however."

Though well-trained and even proficient masters, they occasionally used a dialect-word of their boyhood to each other in private.

"I've come, George, to explain to you my reasons for taking a step that I am about to take, so that you, at least, will understand my motives if other people question them anywhen – as they may, indeed certainly will.... But anything is better than the present condition of

---

1   miles] In the 1912 text, Hardy added here a quotation from Drayton's *Poly-Olbion*: "Where Stour receives her strength, / From six cleere fountains fed,".
2   Leddenton] Gillingham, a Dorsetshire market-town on the River Stour.
3   Wintoncester] Winchester, county-town of Hampshire.
4   lumpering] (dl.:) plodding.

things. God forbid that you should ever have such an experience as mine!"

"Sit down. You don't mean – anything wrong between you and Mrs. Phillotson?"

"I do.... My wretched state is that I've a wife I love, who not only does not love me, but – but —— Well, I won't say. I know her feeling! I should prefer hatred from her!"

"Ssh!"

"And the sad part of it is that she is not so much to blame as I. She was a pupil-teacher under me, as you know, and I took advantage of her inexperience, and toled[1] her out for walks, and got her to agree to a long engagement before she well knew her own mind. Afterwards she saw somebody else, but she blindly fulfilled her engagement."

"Loving the other?"

"Yes, with a curious tender solicitude seemingly; though her exact feeling for him is a riddle to me – and to him too, I think – possibly to herself. She is one of the oddest creatures I ever met. However, I have been struck with these two facts; the extraordinary sympathy, or similarity, between the pair. (He is her cousin, which perhaps accounts for some of it. They seem to be one person split in two!) And with her unconquerable aversion to myself as a husband, even though she may like me as a friend, 'tis too much to bear longer. She has conscientiously struggled against it, but to no purpose. I cannot bear it – I cannot! I can't answer her arguments – she has read ten times as much as I. Her intellect sparkles like diamonds, while mine smoulders like brown paper....She's one too many for me!"

"She'll get over it, good-now?"[2]

"Never! It is – but I won't go into it – there are reasons why she never will. At last she calmly and firmly asked if she might leave me and go to him. The climax came last night, when, owing to my entering her room by accident, she jumped out of window – so strong was her dread of me! She pretended it was a dream, but that was to soothe me. Now when a woman jumps out of window without caring whether she breaks her neck or no, she's not to be mistaken; and this being the case I have come to a conclusion: that it

---

1   toled] (dl.:) enticed.
2   good-now] Hardy said that this Wessex idiom meant "You may be sure."

is wrong to so torture a fellow-creature any longer; and I won't be the inhuman wretch to do it, cost what it may!"

"What – you'll let her go? And with her lover?"

"Whom with is her matter. I shall let her go; with him certainly, if she wishes. I know I may be wrong – I know I can't logically, or religiously, defend my concession to such a wish of hers; or harmonize it with the doctrines I was brought up in. Only I know one thing: something within me tells me I am doing wrong in refusing her. I, like other men, profess to hold that if a husband gets such a so-called preposterous request from his wife, the only course that can possibly be regarded as right and proper and honourable in him is to refuse it, and put her virtuously under lock and key, and murder her lover perhaps. But is that essentially right, and proper, and honourable, or is it contemptibly mean and selfish? I don't profess to decide. I simply am going to act by instinct, and let principles take care of themselves. If a person who has blindly walked into a quagmire cries for help, I am inclined to give it, if possible."

"But – you see, there's the question of neighbours and society – what will happen if everybody —"

"O, I am not going to be a philosopher any longer! I only see what's under my eyes."

"Well – I don't agree with your instinct, Dick!" said Gillingham gravely. "I am quite amazed, to tell the truth, that such a sedate, plodding fellow as you should have entertained such a craze for a moment. You said when I called that she was puzzling and peculiar: I think you are!"

"Have you ever stood before a woman whom you know to be intrinsically a good woman, while she has pleaded for release – been the man she has knelt to and implored indulgence of?"

"I am thankful to say I haven't."

"Then I don't think you are in a position to give an opinion. I have been that man, and it makes all the difference in the world, if one has any manliness or chivalry in him. I had not the remotest idea – living apart from women as I have done for so many years – that merely taking a woman to church and putting a ring upon her finger could by any possibility involve one in such a daily, continuous tragedy as that now shared by her and me!"

"Well, I could admit some excuse for letting her leave you, provided she kept to herself. But to go attended by a cavalier – that makes a difference."

"Not a bit. Suppose, as I believe, she would rather endure her present misery than be made to promise to keep apart from him? All that is a question for herself. It is not the same thing at all as the treachery of living on with a husband and playing him false.... However, she has not distinctly implied living with him as wife, though I think she means to.... And to the best of my understanding it is not an ignoble, merely animal, feeling between the two: that is the worst of it; because it makes me think their affection will be enduring. I did not mean to confess to you that in the first jealous weeks of my marriage, before I had come to my right mind, I hid myself in the school one evening when they were together there, and I heard what they said. I am ashamed of it now, though I suppose I was only exercising a legal right. I found from their manner that an extraordinary affinity, or sympathy, entered into their attachment, which somehow took away all flavour of grossness. Their supreme desire is to be together – to share each other's emotions, and fancies, and dreams."

"Platonic!"[1]

"Well no. Shelleyan would be nearer to it. They remind me of Laon and Cythna.[2] Also of Paul and Virginia[3] a little. The more I reflect, the more *entirely* I am on their side!"

"But if people did as you want to do, there'd be a general domestic disintegration. The family would no longer be the social unit."

"Yes – I am all abroad,[4] I suppose!" said Phillotson sadly. "I was never a very bright reasoner, you remember.... And yet, I don't see why the woman and the children should not be the unit without the man."

"By the Lord Harry! – Matriarchy! ... Does *she* say all this too?"

"O no. She little thinks I have out-Sued Sue in this – all in the last twelve hours!"

---

1   Platonic] idealistic and not physical.

2   Laon and Cythna] siblings and lovers in Shelley's poem *Laon and Cythna* (later retitled *The Revolt of Islam*), 1818.

3   Paul and Virginia] lovers (who grew up as though brother and sister) in J.-H. Bernardin de Saint-Pierre's *Paul et Virginie* (1788).

4   all abroad] (coll.:) illogical.

"It will upset all received opinion hereabout. Good God – what will Shaston say!"

"I don't say that it won't. I don't know – I don't know! ...As I say, I am only a feeler, not a reasoner."

"Now," said Gillingham, "let us take it quietly, and have something to drink over it." He went under the stairs, and produced a bottle of cider-wine,[1] of which they drank a rummer[2] each. "I think you are rafted,[3] and not yourself," he continued. "Do go back and make up your mind to put up with a few whims. But keep her. I hear on all sides that she's a charming young thing."

"Ah yes! That's the bitterness of it! Well, I won't stay. I have a long walk before me."

Gillingham accompanied his friend a mile on his way, and at parting expressed his hope that this consultation, singular as its subject was, would be the renewal of their old comradeship. "Stick to her!" were his last words, flung into the darkness after Phillotson; from which his friend answered "Ay, ay!"

But when Phillotson was alone under the clouds of night, and no sound was audible but that of the purling tributaries of the Stour, he said, "So Gillingham, my friend, you had no stronger arguments against it than those!"

"I think she ought to be smacked, and brought to her senses – that's what I think!" murmured Gillingham, as he walked back alone.

The next morning came, and at breakfast Phillotson told Sue:

"You may go – with whom you will. I absolutely and unconditionally agree."

Having once come to this conclusion it seemed to Phillotson more and more indubitably the true one. He mild serenity at the sense that he was doing his duty by a woman who was at his mercy almost overpowered his grief at relinquishing her.

Some days passed, and the evening of their last meal together was come – a cloudy evening with wind – which indeed was very seldom absent in this elevated place. How permanently it was imprinted upon his vision; that look of her as she glided into the parlour to tea; a slim flexible figure; a face, strained from its roundness, and marked

---

1   cider-wine] beverage made from cider flavoured with sugar and spices.
2   rummer] large drinking-glass.
3   rafted] (dl.:) upset.

by the pallors of restless days and nights, suggesting tragic possibilities quite at variance with her times of buoyancy; a trying of this morsel and that, and an inability to eat either. Her nervous manner, begotten of a fear lest he should be injured by her course, might have been interpreted by a stranger as displeasure that Phillotson intruded his presence on her for the few brief minutes that remained.

"You had better have a slice of ham, or an egg, or something with your tea? You can't travel on a mouthful of bread and butter."

She took the slice he helped her to; and they discussed as they sat trivial questions of housekeeping, such as where he would find the key of this or that cupboard, what little bills were paid, and what not.

"I am a bachelor by nature, as you know, Sue," he said, in a heroic attempt to put her at her ease. "So that being without a wife will not really be irksome to me, as it might be to other men who have had one a little while. I have, too, this grand hobby in my head of writing 'The Roman Antiquities of Wessex,' which will much will occupy all my spare hours."

"If you will send me some of the manuscript to copy at any time, as you used to, I will do it with so much pleasure!" she said with amenable gentleness. "I should much like to be some help to you still – as a f-f-friend."

Phillotson mused, and said: "No, I think we ought to be really separate, if we are to be at all. And for this reason, that I don't wish to ask you any questions, and particularly wish you not to give me information as to your movements, or even your address.... Now, what money do you want? You must have some, you know."

"O, of course, Richard, I couldn't think of having any of *your* money to go away from you with! I don't want any either. I have enough of my own to last me for a long while, and Jude will let me have ——"

"I would rather not know anything about him, if you don't mind. You are free, absolutely; and your course is your own."

"Very well. But I'll just say that I have packed only a change or two of my own personal clothing, and one or two little things besides that are my very own. I wish you would look into my trunk before it is closed. Besides that I have only a small parcel that will go into Jude's portmanteau."[1]

---

1 portmanteau] large travelling-bag that folds back flat from the middle.

"Of course I shall do no such thing as examine your luggage! I wish you would take three-quarters of the household furniture. I don't want to be bothered with it. I have a sort of affection for a little of it that belonged to my poor mother and father. But the rest you are welcome to whenever you like to send for it."

"That I shall never do."

"You go by the six-thirty train, don't you? It is now a quarter to six."

"You ... you don't seem very sorry I am going, Richard!"

"O no – perhaps not."

"I like you much for how you have behaved. It is a curious thing that directly I have begun to regard you as not my husband, but as my old teacher, I like you. I won't be so affected as to say I love you, because you know I don't, except as a friend. But you do seem that to me!"

Sue was for a few moments a little tearful at these reflections, and then the station omnibus came round to take her up. Phillotson saw her things put on the top, handed her in, and was obliged to make an appearance of kissing her as he wished her good-bye, though she shrank even from that. From the cheerful manner in which they parted the omnibus-man had no other idea than that she was going for a short visit.

When Phillotson got back into the house he went upstairs and opened the window in the direction the omnibus had taken. Soon the noise of its wheels died away. He came down then, his face compressed like that of one bearing pain; he put on his hat and went out, following by the same route for nearly a mile. Suddenly turning round he came home.

He had no sooner entered than the voice of his friend Gillingham greeted him from the front room.

"I could make nobody hear; so finding your door open I walked in, and made myself comfortable. I said I would call, you remember."

"Yes. I am much obliged to you, Gillingham, particularly for coming to-night."

"How is Mrs. ——"

"She is quite well. She is gone – just gone. That's her tea-cup, that she drank out of only an hour ago. And that's the plate she –" Phillotson's throat got choked up, and he could not go on. He turned and pushed the tea-things aside.

"Have you had any tea, by-the-bye?" he asked presently in a renewed voice.

"No – yes – never mind," said Gillingham, preoccupied. "Gone, you say she is?"

"Yes.... I would have died for her; but I wouldn't be cruel to her in the name of the law. She is, as I understand, gone to join her lover. What they are going to do I cannot say. Whatever it may be she has my full consent to."

There was a stability, a ballast, in Phillotson's pronouncement which restrained his friend's comment. "Shall I – leave you?" he asked.

"No, no. It is a mercy to me that you have come. I have some articles to arrange and clear away. Would you help me?"

Gillingham assented; and having gone to the upper rooms the schoolmaster opened drawers, and began taking out all Sue's things that she had left behind, and laying them in a large box. "She wouldn't take all I wanted her to," he continued. "But when I made up my mind to her going to live in her own way I did make up my mind."

"Some men would have stopped at an agreement to separate."

"I've gone into all that, and don't wish to argue it. I was, and am, the most old-fashioned man in the world on the question of marriage – in fact I had never thought critically about its ethics at all. But certain facts stared me in the face, and I couldn't go against them."

They went on with the packing silently. When it was done Phillotson closed the box and turned the key.

"There," he said. "To adorn her in somebody's eyes; never again in mine!"

IV. - V.

Four and twenty hours before this time Sue had written the following note to Jude:

"It is as I told you; and I am leaving to-morrow evening. Richard and I thought it could be done with less obtrusiveness after dark. I feel rather frightened, and therefore ask you to be sure you are on the platform to meet me by the train arriving at a quarter to nine. I know you will, of course, dear Jude; but I feel so timid that I can't help begging you to be punctual. He has been so *very* kind to me through it all!

"Now to our meeting!

S."

As she was carried by the omnibus further and further down from the mountain town – the single passenger that evening – she regarded the receding road with a sad face. But no hesitation was apparent therein.

The up-train by which she was departing stopped by signal only. To Sue it seemed strange that such a powerful organization as a railway-train should be brought to a standstill on purpose for her – a fugitive from her lawful home.

The twenty minutes' journey drew towards its close, and Sue began gathering her things together to alight. At the moment that the train came to a standstill by the Melchester platform a hand was laid on the door, and she beheld Jude. He entered the compartment promptly. He had a black bag in his hand, and was dressed in the dark suit he wore on Sundays and in the evening after work. Altogether he looked a very handsome young fellow, his ardent affection for her burning in his eyes.

"O Jude!" She clasped his hand with both hers, and her tense state caused her to simmer over in a little succession of dry sobs. "I – I am so glad! I get out here?"

"No. I get in, dear one! I've packed. Besides this bag I've only a big box which is labelled."

"But don't I get out? Aren't we going to stay here?"

"We couldn't possibly, don't you see. We are known here – I, at any rate, am well known. I've booked for Aldbrickham; and here's your ticket for the same place, as you have only one to here."

"I thought we should have stayed here," she repeated.

"It wouldn't have done at all."

"Ah! – Perhaps not."

"There wasn't time for me to write and say the place I had decided on. Aldbrickham is a much bigger town – sixty or seventy thousand inhabitants – and nobody knows anything about us there."

"And you have given up your Cathedral work here?"

"Yes. It was rather sudden – your message coming unexpectedly. Strictly, I might have been made to finish out the week. But I pleaded urgency and I was let off. I would have deserted any day at your command, dear Sue. I have deserted more than that for you!"

"I fear I am doing you a lot of harm. Ruining your prospects of the Church; ruining your progress in your trade; everything!"

"The Church is no more to me. Let it lie! *I* am not to be one of

> 'The soldier-saints who, row on row,
> Burn upward each to his point of bliss,'[1]

if any such there be! My point of bliss is not upward, but here."

"O I seem so bad – upsetting men's courses like this!" said she, taking up in her voice the emotion that had begun in his. But she recovered her equanimity by the time they had travelled a dozen miles.

"He has been so good in letting me go," she resumed. "And here's a note I found on my dressing-table, addressed to you."

"Yes. He's not an unworthy fellow," said Jude, glancing at the note. "And I am ashamed of myself for hating him because he married you."

"According to the rule of women's whims I suppose I ought to suddenly love him, because he has let me go so generously and unexpectedly," she answered smiling. "But I am so cold, or devoid of gratitude, or so something, that even this generosity hasn't made me love him, or repent, or want to stay with him as his wife; although I do feel I like his large-mindedness, and respect him more than ever."

"It may not work so well for us as if he had been less kind, and you had run away against his will," murmured Jude.

"That I *never* would have done."

Jude's eyes rested musingly on her face. Then he suddenly kissed her; and was going to kiss her again. "No – only once now – please, Jude!"

"That's rather cruel," he answered; but acquiesced. "Such a strange thing has happened to me," Jude continued after a silence. "Arabella has actually written to ask me to get a divorce from her – in kindness to her, she says. She wants to honestly and legally marry that

---

1 bliss] from Browning's poem, "The Statue and the Bust."

man she has already married virtually; and begs me to enable her to do it."

"What have you done?"

"I have agreed. I thought at first I couldn't do it without getting her into trouble about that second marriage, and I don't want to injure her in any way. Perhaps she's no worse than I am, after all! But nobody knows about it over here, and I find it will not be a difficult proceeding at all. If she wants to start afresh I have only too obvious reasons for not hindering her."

"Then you'll be free?"

"Yes, I shall be free."

"Where are we booked for?" she asked, with the discontinuity that marked her to-night.

"Aldbrickham, as I said."

"But it will be very late when we get there?"

"Yes. I thought of that, and I wired for a room for us at the Temperance Hotel there."

"One?"

"Yes – one."

She looked at him. "O Jude!" Sue bent her forehead against the corner of the compartment. "I thought you might do it; and that I was deceiving you. But I didn't mean that!"

In the pause which followed, Jude's eyes fixed themselves with a stultified expression on the opposite seat. "Well!" he said.... "Well!"

He remained in silence; and seeing how discomfited he was she put her face against his cheek, murmuring, "Don't be vexed, dear!"

"Oh – there's no harm done," he said. "But – I understood it like that.... Is this a sudden change of mind?"

"You have no right to ask me such a question; and I shan't answer!" she said, smiling.

"My dear one, your happiness is more to me than anything – although we seem to verge on quarrelling so often! – and your will is law to me. I am something more than a mere – selfish fellow, I hope. Have it as you wish!" On reflection his brow showed perplexity. "But perhaps it is that you don't love me – not that you have become con-ventional! Much as, under your teaching, I hate convention, I hope it *is* that, not the other terrible alternative!"

Even at this obvious moment for candour Sue could not be quite candid as to the state of that mystery, her heart. "Put it down to my timidity," she said with hurried evasiveness; "to a woman's natural timidity when the crisis comes. I *may* feel as well as you that I have a perfect right to live with you as you thought – from this moment. I *may* hold the opinion that, in a proper state of society, the father of a woman's child will be as much a private matter of hers as the cut of her under-linen, on whom nobody will have any right to conjecture. But partly, perhaps, because it is by his generosity that I am now free, I would rather not be other than a little rigid. If there had been a rope-ladder, and he had run after us with pistols, it would have seemed different, and I may have acted otherwise. But don't press me and criticize me, Jude! Assume that I haven't the courage of my opinions. I know I am a poor miserable creature. My nature is not so passionate as yours!"

He repeated simply: "I thought – what I naturally thought. But if we are not lovers, we are not. Phillotson thought so, I am sure. See, here is what he has written to me." He opened the letter she had brought, and read:

"I make only one condition – that you are tender and kind to her. I know you love her. But even love may be cruel at times. You are made for each other: it is obvious, palpable, to any unbiassed third person. You were all along 'the shadowy third'[1] in my short life with her. I repeat, take care of Sue."

"He's a good fellow, isn't he!" she said with latent tears. On reconsideration she added, "He was very resigned to letting me go – too resigned almost! I never was so near being in love with him as when he made such thoughtful arrangements for my being comfortable on my journey, and offering to provide money. Yet I was not. If I loved him ever so little as a wife, I'd go back to him even now."

"But you don't, do you?"

"It is true – O so terribly true! – I don't."

"Nor me neither, I half fear!" he said pettishly. "Nor anybody perhaps! – Sue, sometimes, when I am vexed with you, I think you are incapable of real love."

"That's not good and loyal of you!" she said, and drawing away from him as far as she could, looked severely out into the darkness.

---

1   shadowy third] from stanza 46 of Browning's poem, "By the Fire-side."

She presently added, in hurt tones, turning round: "My liking for you is not as some women's perhaps. But it is a delight in being with you, of a supremely delicate kind, and I don't want to go further and risk it by – an attempt to intensify it! I quite realized that, as woman with man, it was a risk to come. But as *me* with *you*, I resolved to trust you to set my wishes above your gratification. Don't discuss it further, dear Jude!"

"Of course, if it would make you reproach yourself ... but you do like me very much, Sue? say you do! Say that you do a quarter, a tenth, as much as I do you; and I'll be content!"

"I've let you kiss me, and that tells enough."

"Just once or so!"

"Well – don't be a greedy boy."

He leant back, and did not look at her for a long time. That episode in her past history of which she had told him – of the poor Christminster graduate whom she had handled thus, returned to Jude's mind; and he saw himself as a possible second in such a torturing destiny.

"This is a queer elopement!" he murmured. "Perhaps you are making a cat's-paw[1] of me with Phillotson all this time. Upon my word it almost seems so – to see you sitting up there so prim!"

"Now you mustn't be angry – I won't let you!" she coaxed, turning and moving nearer to him. "You did kiss me just now, you know; and I didn't dislike you to, very much, Jude.[2] Only I don't want to let you do it again, just yet – considering how we are circumstanced, don't you see!"

He could never resist her when she pleaded (as she well knew). And they sat side by side with joined hands, till she aroused herself at some thought.

"I can't possibly go to that Temperance Inn, after your telegraphing that message!"

"Why not?"

"You can see well enough!"

"Very well; there'll be some other one open, no doubt. I have sometimes thought, since your marrying Phillotson because of a

---

1   cat's-paw] person who is made the tool of another.
2   very much, Jude] In 1912, Hardy changed the phrase to "I own it, Jude."

stupid scandal, that under the affectation of independent views you are as enslaved to the social code as any woman I know!"

"Not mentally. But I haven't the courage of my views, as I said before. I didn't marry him altogether because of the scandal. But sometimes a woman's *love of being loved* gets the better of her conscience, and though she is agonized at the thought of treating a man cruelly, she encourages him to love her while she doesn't love him at all. Then, when she sees him suffering, her remorse sets in, and she does what she can to repair the wrong."

"You simply mean that you flirted outrageously with him, poor old chap, and then repented, and to make reparation, married him, though you tortured yourself to death by doing it."

"Well – if you will put it brutally! – it was a little like that – that and the scandal together – and your concealing from me what you ought to have told me before!"

He could see that she was distressed and tearful at his criticisms, and soothed her, saying: "There, dear; don't mind! Crucify me, if you will! You know you are all the world to me, whatever you do!"

"I am very bad and unprincipled – I know you think that!" she said, trying to blink away her tears.

"I think and know you are my dear Sue, from whom neither length nor breadth, nor things present nor things to come, can divide me!"[1]

Though so sophisticated in many things she was such a child in others that this satisfied her, and they reached the end of their journey on the best of terms. It was about ten o'clock when they arrived at Aldbrickham, the county town of North Wessex. As she would not go to the Temperance Hotel because of the form of his telegram, Jude inquired for another; and a youth who volunteered to find one wheeled their luggage to a place near at hand, which proved to be the inn at which Jude had stayed with Arabella on that one occasion of their meeting after their division for years.

Owing, however, to their now entering it by another door, and to his preoccupation, he did not at first recognize the place. When they had engaged their respective rooms they went down to a late supper.

---

1   from whom.....divide me] cf. "nor things present, nor things to come, Nor height, nor depth, nor any other creature, shall be able to separate us from the love of God" (Romans 8:38-9).

During Jude's temporary absence the waiting-maid spoke to Sue.

"I think, ma'am, I remember your relation, or friend, or whatever he is, coming here once before – late, just like this, with his wife – a lady, at any rate, that wasn't you by no manner of means – just as med be with you now."

"O do you?" said Sue, with a certain sickness of heart. "Though I think you must be mistaken! How long ago was it?"

"About a month or two. A handsome, full-figured woman."[1]

When Jude came back and sat down to supper Sue seemed moping and miserable. "Jude," she said to him plaintively, at their parting that night upon the landing, "it is not so nice and pleasant as it used to be with us! I don't like it here – I can't bear the place! And I don't like you so well as I did!"

"How fidgeted[2] you seem, dear! Why do you change like this?"

"Because it was cruel to bring me here!"

"Why?"

"You were lately here with Arabella. There, now I have said it!"

"Dear me, why –" said Jude, looking round him. "Yes – it is the same! I really didn't know it, Sue. Well – it is not cruel, since we have come as we have – two relations staying together."

"How long ago was it you were here? Tell me, tell me!"

"The day before I met you in Christminster, when we went back to Marygreen together. I told you I had met her."

"Yes, you said you had met her, but you didn't tell me all. Your story was that you had met as estranged people, who were not husband and wife at all in Heaven's sight – not that you had made it up with her."

"We didn't make it up," he said sadly. "I can't explain, Sue."

"You've been false to me; you, my last hope! And I shall never forget it, never!"

"But by your own wish, dear Sue, we are only to be friends, not lovers! It is so very inconsistent of you to ——"

"Friends can be jealous!"

"I don't see that. You concede nothing to me and I have to

---

1   woman] in 1912 "full-figured woman." became "full-figured woman. They had this room."
2   fidgeted] nervously restless.

concede everything to you. After all, you were on good terms with your husband at that time."

"No, I wasn't, Jude. O how can you think so! And you have taken me in, even if you didn't intend to." She was so mortified that he was obliged to take her into her room and close the door lest the people should hear. "Was it this room? Yes it was – I see by your look it was! I won't have it for mine! O it was treacherous of you to have her again! *I* jumped out of the window!"

"But Sue, she was, after all, my legal wife, if not ———"

Slipping down on her knees Sue buried her face in the bed and wept.

"I never knew such an unreasonable – such a dog-in-the-manger feeling," said Jude. "I am not to approach you, nor anybody else!"

"O don't you *understand* my feeling! *Why* don't you! Why are you so gross! *I* jumped out of the window!"

"Jumped out of window?"

"I can't explain!"

It was true that he did not understand her feeling very well. But he did a little; and began to love her none the less.

"I – I thought you cared for nobody – desired nobody in the world but me at that time – and ever since!" continued Sue.

"It is true. I did not, and don't now!" said Jude, as distressed as she.

"But you must have thought much of her! Or ———"

"No – I need not – you don't understand me either – women never do! Why should you get into such a tantrum about nothing?"

Looking up from the quilt she replied provokingly: "If it hadn't been for that, perhaps I would have gone on to the Temperance Hotel, after all, as you proposed; for I was beginning to think I did belong to you!"

"O, it is of no consequence!" said Jude distantly.

"I thought, of course, that she had never been really your wife since she left you of her own accord years and years ago! My sense of it was, that a parting such as yours from her, and mine from him, ended the marriage."

"I can't say more without speaking against her, and I don't want to do that," said he. "Yet I must tell you one thing, which would settle the matter in any case. She has married another man – really married him! I knew nothing about it till after the visit we made here."

"Married another? ... It is a crime – as the world treats it, but does not believe."

"There – now you are yourself again. Yes, it is a crime – as you don't hold, but would fearfully concede. But I shall never inform against her! and it is evidently a prick of conscience in her that has led her to urge me to get a divorce, that she may re-marry this man legally. So you perceive I shall not be likely to see her again."

"And you didn't really know anything of this when you saw her?" said Sue more gently, as she rose.

"I did not. Considering all things, I don't think you ought to be angry, darling!"

"I am not. But I shan't go to the Temperance Hotel!"

He laughed. "Never mind!" he said. "So that I am near you, I am comparatively happy. It is more than this earthly wretch called Me deserves – you spirit, you disembodied creature, you dear, sweet, tantalizing phantom – hardly flesh at all; so that when I put my arms round you I almost expect them to pass through you as through air! Forgive me for being gross, as you call it! Remember that our calling cousins when really strangers was a snare. The enmity of our parents gave a piquancy to you in my eyes that was intenser even than the novelty of ordinary new acquaintance."

"Say those pretty lines, then, from Shelley's 'Epipsychidion' as if they meant me!" she solicited, slanting up closer to him as they stood. "Don't you know them?"

"I know hardly any poetry," he replied mournfully.

"Don't you? These are some of them:

> 'There was a Being whom my spirit oft
> Met on its visioned wanderings far aloft.
>
> .   .   .   .   .
>
> A seraph of Heaven, too gentle to be human,
> Veiling beneath that radiant form of woman...'[1]

O it is too flattering, so I won't go on! But say it's me! – say it's me!"

"It *is* you, dear; exactly like you!"

---

1   There.....woman] lines 190-91 and 21-2 of Shelley's "Epipsychidion."

"Now I forgive you! And you shall kiss me just once there – not very long." She put the tip of her finger gingerly to her cheek; and he did as commanded. "You do care for me very much, don't you, in spite of my not – you know?"

"Yes, sweet!" he said with a sigh; and bade her good-night.

IV.-VI.

In returning to his native town of Shaston as schoolmaster Phillotson had won the interest and awakened the memories of the inhabitants, who, though they did not honour him for his miscellaneous acquirements as he would have been honoured elsewhere, retained for him a sincere regard. When, shortly after his arrival, he brought home a pretty wife – awkwardly pretty for him, if he did not take care, they said – they were glad to have her settle among them.

For some time after her flight from that home Sue's absence did not excite comment. Her place as monitor[1] in the school was taken by another young woman within a few days of her vacating it, which substitution also passed without remark, Sue's services having been of a provisional nature only. When, however, a month had passed, and Phillotson casually admitted to acquaintance that he didn't know where his wife was staying, curiosity began to be aroused; till, jumping to conclusions, people ventured to affirm that Sue had played him false and run away from him. The schoolmaster's growing languor and listlessness over his work gave countenance to the idea.

Though Phillotson had held his tongue as long as he could, except to his friend Gillingham, his honesty and directness would not allow him to do so when misapprehensions as to Sue's conduct spread abroad. On a Monday morning the chairman of the School Committee called, and after attending to the business of the school drew Phillotson aside out of earshot of the children.

"You'll excuse my asking, Phillotson, since everybody is talking of it: is this true as to your domestic affairs – that your wife's going away was on no visit, but a secret elopement with a lover? If so, I condole with you."

---

1 monitor] teacher's assistant.

"Don't," said Phillotson. "There was no secret about it."

"She has gone to visit friends?"

"No."

"Then what has happened?"

"She has gone away under circumstances that usually call for condolence with the husband. But I gave my consent."

The chairman looked as if he had not apprehended the remark.

"What I say is quite true," Phillotson continued testily. "She asked leave to go away with her lover, and I let her. Why shouldn't I? A woman of full age, it was a question for her own conscience – not for me. I was not her gaoler. I can't explain any further. I don't wish to be questioned."

The children observed that much seriousness marked the faces of the two men, and went home and told their parents that something new had happened about Mrs. Phillotson. Then Phillotson's little maidservant, who was a schoolgirl just out of her standards,[1] said that Mr. Phillotson had helped in his wife's packing, had offered her what money she required, and had written a friendly letter to her young man, telling him to take care of her. The chairman of committee thought the matter over, and talked to the other managers of the school, till a request came to Phillotson to meet them privately. The meeting lasted a long time, and at the end the schoolmaster came home, looking as usual pale and worn. Gillingham was sitting in his house awaiting him.

"Well; it is as you said," observed Phillotson, flinging himself down wearily in a chair. "They have requested me to send in my resignation on account of my scandalous conduct in giving my tortured wife her liberty – or, as they call it, condoning her adultery. But I shan't resign!"

"I think I would."

"I won't. It is no business of theirs. It doesn't affect me in my public capacity at all. They may expel me if they like."

"If you make a fuss it will get into the papers, and you'll never get appointed to another school. You see, they have to consider what you did as done by a teacher of youth – and its effects as such upon the morals of the town; and, to ordinary opinion, your position is

---

1 out of her standards] having passed the proficiency-tests.

indefensible. You must let me say that."

To this good advice, however, Phillotson would not listen.

"I don't care," he said. "I don't go unless I am turned out. And for this reason; that by resigning I acknowledge I have acted wrongly by her; when I am more and more convinced every day that in the sight of Heaven and by all natural, straightforward humanity, I have acted rightly."

Gillingham saw that his rather headstrong friend would not be able to maintain such a position as this; but he said nothing further, and in due time – indeed, in a quarter of an hour – the formal letter of dismissal arrived, the managers having remained behind to write it after Phillotson's withdrawal. The latter replied that he should not accept dismissal; and called a public meeting, which he attended, although he looked so weak and ill that his friend implored him to stay at home. When he stood up to give his reasons for contesting the decision of the managers he advanced them firmly, as he had done to his friend, and contended, moreover, that the matter was a domestic theory which did not concern them. This they over-ruled, insisting that the private eccentricities of a teacher came quite within their sphere of control, as it touched the morals of those he taught. Phillotson replied that he did not see how an act of natural charity could injure morals.

All the respectable inhabitants and well-to-do fellow-natives of the town were against Phillotson to a man. But, somewhat to his surprise, some dozen or more champions rose up in his defence as from the ground.

It has been stated that Shaston was the anchorage of a curious and interesting group of itinerants, who frequented the numerous fairs and markets held up and down Wessex during the summer and autumn months. Although Phillotson had never spoken to one of these gentlemen they now nobly led the forlorn hope[1] in his defence. The body included two cheap-jacks,[2] a shooting-gallery proprietor and the ladies who loaded the guns, a pair of boxing-masters, a steam-roundabout manager, two travelling broom-makers, who called them-

---

1 the forlorn hope] the name given to a unit of British troops which, during the Napoleonic Wars, stormed Ciudad Rodrigo, Spain, in January 1812.
2 cheap-jacks] people selling cheap and shoddy goods.

selves widows, a gingerbread-stall keeper, a swing-boat owner, and a "test-your-strength" man.

This generous phalanx[1] of supporters, and a few others of independent judgement, whose own domestic experiences had been not without vicissitude, came up and warmly shook hands with Phillotson; after which they expressed their thoughts so strongly to the meeting that issue was joined, the result being a general scuffle, wherein a blackboard was split, three panes of the school-windows were broken, an inkbottle spilled over a town-councillor's shirt-front,[2] and some black eyes and bleeding noses given, one of which, to everybody's horror, was the venerable incumbent's, owing to the zeal of an emancipated chimney-sweep, who took the side of Phillotson's party. When Phillotson saw the blood running down the rector's face he deplored almost in groans the untoward and degrading circumstances, regretted that he had not resigned when called upon, and went home so ill that next morning he could not leave his bed.

The farcical yet melancholy event was the beginning of a serious illness for him; and he lay in his lonely bed in the pathetic state of mind of a middle-aged man who perceives at length that his life, intellectual and domestic, is tending to failure and gloom. Gillingham came to see him in the evenings, and on one occasion mentioned Sue's name.

"She doesn't care anything about me!" said Phillotson. "Why should she?"

"She doesn't know you are ill."

"So much the better for both of us."

"Where are her lover and she living?"

"At Melchester – I suppose; at least he was living there some time ago."

When Gillingham reached home he sat and reflected, and at last wrote an anonymous line to Sue, on the bare chance of its reaching her, the letter being enclosed in an envelope addressed to Jude at the diocesan capital. Arriving at that place it was forwarded to Marygreen in North Wessex, and thence to Aldbrickham by the only

---

1   phalanx] strong array (usually of soldiers).
2   shirt-front,] In 1912 Hardy added: "a church-warden was dealt such a topper with the map of Palestine that his head went right through Samaria,".

person who knew his present address – the widow who had nursed his aunt.

Three days later, in the evening, when the sun was going down in splendour over the lowlands of Blackmoor, and making the Shaston windows like tongues of fire to the eyes of the rustics in that Vale, the sick man fancied that he heard somebody come to the house, and a few minutes after there was a tap at the bedroom door. Phillotson did not speak; the door was hesitatingly opened, and there entered – Sue.

She was in light spring clothing, and her advent seemed ghostly – like the flitting in of a moth. He turned his eyes upon her, and flushed; but appeared to check his primary impulse to speak.

"I have no business here," she said, bending her frightened face to him. "But I heard you were ill – very ill; and – and as I know that you recognize other feelings between man and woman than physical love, I have come."

"I am not very ill, my dear friend. Only unwell."

"I didn't know that; and I am afraid that only a severe illness would have justified my coming!"

"Yes ... yes. And I almost wish you had not come! It is a little too soon – that's all I mean. Still, let us make the best of it. You haven't heard about the school, I suppose?"

"No – what about it?"

"Only that I am going away from here to another place. The managers and I don't agree, and we are going to part – that's all."

Sue did not for a moment, either now or later, suspect what troubles had resulted to him from letting her go; it never once seemed to cross her mind, and she had received no news whatever from Shaston. They talked on slight and ephemeral subjects, and when his tea was brought up he told the amazed little servant that a cup was to be set for Sue. That young person was much more interested in their history than they supposed, and as she descended the stairs she lifted her eyes and hands in grotesque amazement. While they sipped Sue went to the window and thoughtfully said, "It is such a beautiful sunset, Richard."

"They are mostly beautiful from here, owing to the rays crossing the mist of the Vale. But I lose them all, as they don't shine into this gloomy corner where I lie."

"Wouldn't you like to see this particular one? It is like heaven opened."

"Ah yes! But I can't."

"I'll help you to."

"No – the bedstead can't be shifted."

"But see how I mean."

She went to where a swing-glass¹ stood, and taking it in her hands carried it to a spot by the window where it could catch the sunshine, moving the glass till the beams were reflected into Phillotson's face.

"There – you can see the great red sun now!" she said. "And I am sure it will cheer you – I do so hope it will!" She spoke with a child-like, repentant kindness, as if she could not do too much for him.

Phillotson smiled sadly. "You are an odd creature!" he murmured as the sun glowed in his eyes. "The idea of your coming to see me after what has passed!"

"Don't let us go back upon that!" she said quickly. "I have to catch the omnibus for the train, as Jude doesn't know I have come; he was out when I started; so I must return home almost directly. Richard, I am so very glad you are better. You don't hate me, do you? You have been such a kind friend to me!"

"I am glad to know you think so," said Phillotson huskily. "No. I don't hate you!"

It grew dusk quickly in the gloomy room during their intermittent chat, and when candles were brought and it was time to leave she put her hand in his – or rather allowed it to flit through his; for she was significantly light in touch. She had nearly closed the door when he said, "Sue!" He had noticed that, in turning away from him, tears were on her face and a quiver in her lip.

It was bad policy to recall her – he knew it while he pursued it. But he could not help it. She came back.

"Sue," he murmured, "do you wish to make it up, and stay? I'll forgive you and condone everything!"

"O you can't, you can't!" she said hastily. "You can't condone it now!"

---

1   swing-glass] swivelling mirror. In his journal for 22 March 1881, when he was ill in bed, Hardy noted that Margaret Macmillan arranged to set a mirror so that he could see a gorgeous sunset.

"*He* is your husband now, in effect, you mean, of course?"

"You may assume it. He is obtaining a divorce from his wife Arabella."

"His wife! It is altogether news to me that he has a wife."

"It was a bad marriage."

"Like yours."

"Like mine. He is not doing it so much on his own account as on hers. She wrote and told him it would be a kindness to her, since then she could marry and live respectably. And Jude has agreed."

"A wife.... A kindness to her. Ah, yes; a kindness to her to release her altogether.... But I don't like the sound of it. *I* can forgive, Sue."

"No, no! You can't have me back now I have been so wicked – as to do what I have done!"

There had arisen in Sue's face that incipient fright which showed itself whenever he changed from friend to husband, and which made her adopt any line of defence against marital feeling in him. " I *must* go now. I'll come again – may I?"

"I don't ask you to go, even now. I ask you to stay."

"I thank you, Richard; but I must. As you are not so ill as I thought, I *cannot* stay!"

"She's his – his from lips to heel!" said Phillotson; but so faintly that in closing the door she did not hear it. The dread of a reactionary change in the schoolmaster's sentiments, coupled, perhaps, with a faint shamefacedness at letting even him know what a slipshod lack of thoroughness, from a man's point of view, characterized her transferred allegiance, prevented her telling him of her, thus far, incomplete relations with Jude; and Phillotson lay writhing like a man in hell as he pictured the prettily dressed, maddening compound of sympathy and averseness who bore his name, returning impatiently to the home of her lover.

Gillingham was so interested in Phillotson's affairs, and so seriously concerned about him, that he walked up the hillside to Shaston two or three times a week, although, there and back, it was a journey of nine miles, which had to be performed between tea and supper, after a hard day's work in school. When he called on the next occasion after Sue's visit, his friend was downstairs, and Gillingham noticed that his restless mood had been supplanted by a more fixed and composed one.

"She's been here since you called last," said Phillotson.

"Not Mrs. Phillotson?"

"Yes."

"Ah! You have made it up?"

"No.... She just came, patted my pillow with her little white hand, played the thoughtful nurse for half-an-hour, and went away."

"Well – I'm hanged! A little hussy!"

"What do you say?"

"O – nothing!"

"What do you mean?"

"I mean, what a tantalizing, capricious little woman! If she were not your wife ———"

"She is not; she's another man's except in name and law. And I have been thinking – it was suggested to me by a conversation I had with her – that, in kindness to her, I ought to dissolve the legal tie altogether; which, singularly enough, I think I can do, now she has been back, and refused my request to stay after I said I had forgiven her. I believe that fact would afford me opportunity of doing it, though I did not see it at the moment. What's the use of keeping her chained on to me if she doesn't belong to me? I know – I feel absolutely certain – that she would welcome my taking such a step as the greatest charity to her. For though as a fellow-creature she sympa-thizes with, and pities me, and even weeps for me, as a husband she cannot endure me – she loathes me – there's no use in mincing words – she loathes me, and my only manly, and dignified, and merciful course is to complete what I have begun.... And for worldly reasons, too, it will be better for her to be independent. I have hopelessly ruined my prospects because of my decision as to what was best for us, though she does not know it; I see only dire poverty ahead from my feet to the grave; for I can be accepted as teacher no more. I shall probably have enough to do to make both ends meet during the remainder of my life, now my occupation's gone; and I shall be better able to bear it alone. I may as well tell you that what has suggested my letting her go is some news she brought me – the news that Fawley is doing the same."

"O – he had a spouse, too? A queer couple, these lovers!"

"Well – I don't want your opinion on that. What I was going to say is that my liberating her can do her no possible harm, and will open up a chance of happiness for her which she has never dreamt of hitherto. For then they'll be able to marry, as they ought to have done at first."

Gillingham did not hurry to reply. "I may disagree with your motive," he said gently, for he respected views he could not share. "But I think you are right in your determination – if you can carry it out. I doubt, however, if you can."

PART FIFTH

AT ALDBRICKHAM AND ELSEWHERE

"Thy aërial part, and all the fiery parts which are mingled in thee, though by nature they have an upward tendency, still in obedience to the disposition of the universe they are over-powered here in the compound mass the body."[1]

M. ANTONINUS (Long).

AT ALDBRICKHAM AND ELSEWHERE

V. - I .

How Gillingham's doubts were disposed of will most quickly appear by passing over the series of dreary months and incidents that followed the events of the last chapter, and coming on to a Sunday in the February of the year following.

Sue and Jude were living in Aldbrickham, in precisely the same relations that they had established between themselves when she left Shaston to join him the year before. The proceedings in the Law-Courts had reached their consciousness but as a distant sound, and an occasional missive which they hardly understood.

They had met, as usual, to breakfast together in the little house with Jude's name on it, that he had taken at fifteen pounds a year, with three-pounds-ten extra for rates and taxes, and furnished with his aunt's ancient and lumbering goods, which had cost him about their full value to bring all the way from Marygreen. Sue kept house, and managed everything.

As he entered the room this morning Sue held up a letter she had just received.

"Well; and what is it about?" he said after kissing her.

---

[1] "*Thy.....body*"] from George Long's translation, *The Thoughts of the Emperor M. Aurelius Antoninus* (London, 1862), p. 197 (with small variants by Hardy).

"That the decree *nisi* in the case of Phillotson *versus* Phillotson and Fawley, pronounced six months ago, has just been made absolute."[1]

"Ah," said Jude, as he sat down.

The same concluding incident in Jude's suit against Arabella had occurred about a month or two earlier. Both cases had been too insignificant to be reported in the papers, further than by name in a long list of other undefended cases.

"Now then, Sue, at any rate, you can do what you like!" He looked at his sweetheart curiously.

"Are we – you and I – just as free now as if we had never married at all?"

"Just as free – except, I believe, that a clergyman may object personally to re-marry you, and hand the job on to somebody else."

"But I wonder – do you think it is really so with us? I know it is generally. But I have an uncomfortable feeling that my freedom has been obtained under false pretences!"

"How?"

"Well – if the truth about us had been known, the decree wouldn't have been pronounced.[2] It is only, is it, because we have made no defence, and have led them into a false supposition? Therefore is my freedom lawful, however proper it may be?"

"Well – why did you let it be under false pretences? You have only yourself to blame," he said mischievously.

"Jude – don't! You ought not to be touchy about that still. You must take me as I am."

"Very well, darling: so I will. Perhaps you were right. As to your question, we were not obliged to prove anything. That was their business. Anyhow we are living together."

"Yes. Though not in their sense."

"One thing is certain, that however brought about, a marriage is dissolved when it is dissolved. There is this advantage in being poor obscure people like us – that these things are done for us in a rough and ready fashion. It was the same with me and Arabella. I was afraid her criminal second marriage would have been discovered, and she

---

1   decree *nisi*.....absolute] A "decree *nisi*" is a conditional state of divorce; if no legal obstacles occur, the divorce becomes "absolute" or final after six months.

2   wouldn't have been pronounced] if it had been known that adultery had not taken place.

punished; but nobody took any interest in her – nobody inquired, nobody suspected it. If we'd been patented nobilities we should have had infinite trouble, and days and weeks would have been spent in investigations."

By degrees Sue acquired her lover's cheerfulness at the sense of freedom, and proposed that they should take a walk in the fields, even if they had to put up with a cold dinner on account of it. Jude agreed, and Sue went upstairs and prepared to start, putting on a joyful coloured gown in observance of her liberty; seeing which Jude put on a lighter tie.

"Now we'll strut arm in arm," he said, "like any other engaged couple. We've a legal right to."

They rambled out of the town, and along a path over the low-lying lands that bordered it, though these were frosty now, and the extensive seed-fields were bare of colour and produce. The pair, however, were so absorbed in their own situation that their surroundings were little in their consciousness.

"Well, my dearest, the result of all this is that we can marry after a decent interval."

"Yes; I suppose we can," said Sue, without enthusiasm.

"And aren't we going to?"

"I don't like to say no, dear Jude; but I feel just the same about it now as I have done all along. I have just the same dread lest an iron contract should extinguish your tenderness for me, and mine for you, as it did between our unfortunate parents."

"Still, what can we do? I do love you, as you know, Sue."

"I know it abundantly. But I think I would much rather go on living always as lovers, as we are living now, and only meeting by day. It is so much sweeter – for the woman at least, and when she is sure of the man. And henceforward we needn't be so particular as we have been about appearances."

"Our experiences of matrimony with others have not been encouraging, I own," said he with some gloom; "either owing to our own dissatisfied, unpractical natures, or by our misfortune. But we two ——"

"Should be two dissatisfied ones linked together, which would be twice as bad as before.... I think I should begin to be afraid of you, Jude, the moment you had contracted to cherish me under a Government stamp, and I was licensed to be loved on the premises[1] by you – Ugh, how horrible and sordid! Although, as you are, free, I trust you more than any other man in the world."

"No, no – don't say I should change!" he expostulated; yet there was misgiving in his own voice also.

"Apart from ourselves, and our unhappy peculiarities, it is foreign to a man's nature to go on loving a person when he is told that he must and shall be that person's lover. There would be a much likelier chance of his doing it if he were not told to love. If the marriage ceremony consisted in an oath and signed contract between the parties to cease loving from that day forward, in consideration of personal possession being given, and to avoid each other's society as much as possible in public, there would be more loving couples than there are now. Fancy the secret meetings between the perjuring husband and wife, the denials of having seen each other, the clambering in at bedroom windows, and the hiding in closets! There'd be little cooling then."

"Yes; but admitting this, or something like it, to be true, you are not the only one in the world to see it, dear little Sue. People go on marrying because they can't resist natural forces, although many of them may know perfectly well that they are possibly buying a month's pleasure with a life's discomfort. No doubt my father and mother, and your father and mother, saw it, if they at all resembled us in habits of observation. But then they went and married just the same, because they had ordinary passions. But you, Sue, are such a phantasmal, bodiless creature, one who – if you'll allow me to say it – has so little animal passion in you, that you can act upon reason in the matter, when we poor unfortunate wretches of grosser substance can't."

"Well," she sighed, "You've owned that it would probably end in misery for us. And I am not so exceptional a woman as you think. Fewer woman like marriage than you suppose, only they enter into it for the dignity it is assumed to confer, and the social advantages it gains them sometimes – a dignity and an advantage that I am quite willing to do without."

---

1 licensed to be loved on the premises] echoing the notice, inscribed above the door of a tavern, stating that the publican is licensed to sell beers, wines, and spirits for consumption "on the premises".

Jude fell back upon his old complaint – that, intimate as they were, he had never once had from her an honest, candid declaration that she loved or could love him. "I really fear sometimes that you cannot," he said, with a dubiousness approaching anger. "And you are so reticent. I know that women are taught by other women that they must never admit the full truth to a man. But the highest form of affection is based on full sincerity on both sides. Not being men, these women don't know that in looking back on those he has had tender relations with, a man's heart returns closest to her who was the soul of truth in her conduct. The better class of man, even if caught by airy affectations of dodging and parrying, is not retained by them. A Nemesis[1] attends the woman who plays the game of elusiveness too often, in the utter contempt for her that, sooner or later, her old admirers feel; under which they allow her to go unlamented to her grave."

Sue, who was regarding the distance, had acquired a guilty look; and she suddenly replied in a tragic voice: "I don't think I like you today so well as I did, Jude!"

"Don't you? Why?"

"O, well – you are not nice – too sermony. Though I suppose I am so bad and worthless that I deserve the utmost rigour of lecturing!"

"No, you are not bad. You are a dear. But as slippery as an eel when I want to get a confession from you."

"O yes I am bad, and obstinate, and all sorts! It is no use your pretending I am not! People who are good don't want scolding as I do .... But now that I have nobody but you, and nobody to defend me, it is *very* hard that I mustn't have my own way in deciding how I'll live with you, and whether I'll be married or no!"

"Sue, my own comrade and sweetheart, I don't want to force you either to marry or to do the other thing – of course I don't! It is too wicked of you to be so pettish! Now we won't say any more about it, and go on just the same as we have done; and during the rest of our walk we'll talk of the meadows only, and the floods, and the prospects of the farmers this coming year."

After this the subject of marriage was not mentioned by them for several days, though living as they were with only a landing between

---

1 Nemesis] Greek goddess of retribution.

them it was constantly in their minds. Sue was assisting Jude very materially now: he had laterally occupied himself on his own account in working and lettering headstones, which he kept in a little yard at the back of his little house, where in the intervals of domestic duties she marked out the letters full size for him, and blacked them in after he had cut them. It was a lower class of handicraft than were his former performances as a cathedral mason, and his only patrons were the poor people who lived in his own neighbourhood, and knew what a cheap man this "Jude Fawley: Monumental Mason" (as he called himself on his front door) was to employ for the simple memorials they required for their dead. But he seemed more independent than before, and it was the only arrangement under which Sue, who particularly wished to be no burden on him, could render any assistance.

V.-II.

IT was an evening at the end of the month, and Jude had just returned home from hearing a lecture on ancient history in the public hall not far off. When he entered Sue, who had been keeping indoors during his absence, laid out supper for him. Contrary to custom she did not speak. Jude had taken up some illustrated paper, which he perused till, raising his eyes, he saw that her face was troubled.

"Are you depressed, Sue?" he said.

She paused a moment. "I have a message for you," she answered.

"Somebody has called?"

"Yes. A woman." Sue's voice quavered as she spoke, and she suddenly sat down from her preparations, laid her hands in her lap, and looked into the fire. "I don't know whether I did right or not!" she continued. "I said you were not at home, and when she said she would wait, I said I thought you might not be able to see her."

"Why did you say that, dear? I suppose she wanted a headstone. Was she in mourning?"

"No. She wasn't in mourning and she didn't want a headstone; and I thought you wouldn't see her." Sue looked critically and imploringly at him.

"But who was she? Didn't she say?"

"No. She wouldn't give her name. But I know who she was — I think I do! It was Arabella!"

"Heaven save us! What should Arabella come for? What made you think it was she?"

"O, I can hardly tell. But I know it was! I feel perfectly certain it was — by the light in her eyes as she looked at me. She was a fleshy, coarse woman."

"Well — I should not have called Arabella coarse exactly, except in speech, though she may be getting so by this time under the duties of the public-house. She was rather handsome when I knew her."

"Handsome! But yes! — so she is!"

"I think I heard a quiver in your little mouth. Well, waiving that, as she is nothing to me, and virtuously married to another man, why should she come troubling us?"

"Are you sure she's married? Have you definite news of it?"

"No — not definite news. But that was why she asked me to release her. She and the man both wanted to lead a proper life, as I understood."

"O Jude — it was, it *was* Arabella!" cried Sue, covering her eyes with her hand. "And I am so miserable! It seems such an ill-omen, whatever she may have come for. You could not possibly see her, could you?"

"I don't really think I could. It would be so very painful to talk to her now — for her as much as for me. However, she's gone. Did she say she would come again?"

"No. But she went away very reluctantly."

Sue, whom the least thing upset, could not eat any supper, and when Jude had finished his he prepared to go to bed. He had no sooner raked out the fire, fastened the doors, and got to the top of the stairs than there came a knock. Sue instantly emerged from her room, which she had but just entered.

"There she is again!" Sue whispered in appalled accents.

"How do you know?"

"She knocked like that last time."

They listened, and the knocking came again. No servant was kept in the house, and if the summons were to be responded to one of them would have to do it in person. "I'll open a window," said Jude. "Whoever it is cannot be expected to be let in at this time."

He accordingly went into his bedroom and lifted the sash. The obscure street of early retiring work-people was empty from end to end save of one figure – that of a woman walking up and down by the lamp a few yards off.

"Who's there?" he asked.

"Is that Mr. Fawley?" came up from the woman, in a voice which was unmistakably Arabella's.

Jude replied that it was.

"Is it she?" asked Sue from the door, with lips apart.

"Yes, dear," said Jude. "What do you want, Arabella?" he inquired.

"I beg your pardon, Jude, for disturbing you," said Arabella humbly. "But I called earlier – I wanted particularly to see you to-night, if I could. I am in trouble, and have nobody to help me!"

"In trouble, are you?"

"Yes."

There was a silence. An inconvenient sympathy seemed to be rising in Jude's breast at the appeal. "But aren't you married?" he said.

Arabella hesitated. "No, Jude, I am not," she returned. "He wouldn't, after all. And I am in great difficulty. I hope to get another situation as barmaid soon. But it takes time, and I really am in great distress, because of a sudden responsibility that's been sprung upon me from Australia; or I wouldn't trouble you – believe me I wouldn't. I want to tell you about it."

Sue remained at gaze, in painful tension, hearing every word, but speaking none.

"You are not really in want of money, Arabella?" He asked, in a distinctly softened tone.

"I have enough to pay for the night's lodging I have obtained, but barely enough to take me back again."

"Where are you living?"

"In London still." She was about to give the address, but she said, "I am afraid somebody may hear, so I don't like to call out particulars of myself so loud. If you could come down and walk a little way with me towards the Prince Inn, where I am staying to-night, I would explain all. You may as well, for old time's sake!"

"Poor thing! – I must do her the kindness of hearing what's the matter, I suppose," said Jude in much perplexity. "As she's going back to-morrow it can't make much difference."

"But you can go and see her to-morrow, Jude! Don't go now, Jude!" came in plaintive accents from the doorway. "O, it is only to entrap you, I know it is, as she did before! Don't, don't go, dear! She is such a low-passioned woman – I can see it in her shape, and hear it in her voice!"

"But I shall go," said Jude. "Don't attempt to detain me, Sue. God knows I love her little enough now, but I don't want to be cruel to her." He turned to the stairs.

"But she's not your wife!" cried Sue distractedly. "And I ——"

"And you are not either, dear, yet," said Jude.

"O, but are you going to her? Don't! Stay at home! Please, please stay at home, Jude, and not go to her, now she's not your wife any more than I!"

"Well, she is, rather more than you, come to that," he said, taking his hat determinedly. "I've wanted you to be, and I've waited with the patience of Job, and I don't see that I've got anything by my self-denial. I shall certainly give her something, and hear what it is she is so anxious to tell me; no man could do less!"

There was that in his manner which she knew it would be futile to oppose. She said no more, but, turning to her room as meekly as a martyr, heard him go downstairs, unbolt the door, and close it behind him. With a woman's disregard of her dignity when in the presence of nobody but herself, she also trotted down, sobbing articulately as she went. She listened. She knew exactly how far it was to the inn that Arabella had named as her lodging. It would occupy about seven minutes to get there at an ordinary walking pace; seven to come back again. If he did not return in fourteen minutes he would have lingered. She looked at the clock. It was twenty-five minutes to eleven. He *might* enter the inn with Arabella, as they would reach it before closing time; she might get him to drink with her; and Heaven only knew what disasters would befall him then.

In a still suspense she waited on. It seemed as if the whole time had nearly elapsed when the door was opened again, and Jude appeared.

Sue gave a little ecstatic cry. "O, I knew I could trust you! – how good you are!" – she began.

"I can't find her anywhere in this street, and I went out in my slippers only. She has walked on, thinking I've been so hard-hearted as to refuse her requests entirely, poor woman. I've come back for my boots, as it is beginning to rain."

"O, but why should you take such trouble for a woman who has served you so badly!" said Sue in a jealous burst of disappointment.

"But, Sue, she's a woman, and I once cared for her; and one can't be a brute in such circumstances."

"She isn't your wife any longer!" exclaimed Sue, passionately excited. "You *mustn't* go out to find her! It isn't right! You *can't* join her, now she's a stranger to you. How can you forget such a thing, my dear, dear one!"

"She seems much the same as ever – an erring, careless, unreflecting fellow-creature," he said, continuing to pull on his boots. "What those legal fellows have been playing at in London makes no difference in my real relations to her. If she was my wife while she was away in Australia with another husband she's my wife now."

"But she wasn't! That's just what I hold! There's the absurdity! – Well – you'll come straight back, after a few minutes, won't you, dear? She is too low, too coarse for you to talk to long, Jude, and was always!"

"Perhaps I am coarse too, worse luck! I have the germs of every human infirmity in me, I verily believe – that was why I saw it was so preposterous of me to think of being a curate. I have cured myself of drunkenness I think; but I never know in what new form a suppressed vice will break out in me! I do love you, Sue, though I have danced attendance on you so long for such poor returns! All that's best and noblest in me loves you, and your freedom from everything that's gross has elevated me, and enabled me to do what I should never have dreamt myself capable of, or any man, a year or two ago. It is all very well to preach about self-control, and the wickedness of coercing a woman. But I should just like a few virtuous people who have condemned me in the past, about Arabella and other things, to have been in my tantalizing position with you through these late weeks! – they'd believe, I think, that I have exercised some little restraint in always giving in to your wishes – living here in one house, and not a soul between us."

"Yes, you have been good to me, Jude; I know you have, my dear protector."

"Well – Arabella appeals to me.[1] I must go out and speak to her, Sue, at least!"

"I can't say any more! – O, if you must, you must!" she said, bursting out into sobs that seemed to tear her heart. "I have nobody but you, Jude, and you are deserting me! I didn't know you were like this – I can't bear it, I can't! If she were yours it would be different!"

"Or if you were."

"Very well then – if I must I must. Since you will have it so, I agree! I will be. Only I didn't mean to! And I didn't want to marry again, either! ... But, yes – I agree, I agree![2] I ought to have known that you would conquer in the long run, living like this!"

She ran across and flung her arms round his neck. "I am not a cold-natured, sexless creature, am I, for keeping you at such a distance? I am sure you don't think so! Wait and see! I do belong to you, don't I? I give in!"

"And I'll arrange for our marriage to-morrow, or as soon as ever you wish."

"Yes, Jude."

"Then I'll let her go," said he, embracing Sue softly. "I do feel that it would be unfair to you to see her, and perhaps unfair to her. She is not like you, my darling, and never was: it is only bare justice to say that. Don't cry any more. There; and there; and there!" He kissed her on one side, and on the other, and in the middle, and rebolted the front door.

The next morning it was wet.

"Now, dear," said Jude gaily at breakfast; "as this is Saturday I mean to call about the banns at once, so as to get the first publishing done to-morrow, or we shall lose a week. Banns will do? We shall save a pound or two."[3]

1   appeals to me] In the 1912 text this became "has appealed to me for help."
2   agree!] For the 1912 text Hardy added "I do love you."
3   banns.....pound or two] banns: a notice (of intent to marry) read out in church on three successive Sundays. Jude presumably thinks that he and Sue will "save a pound or two" by not also publishing a notice in a newspaper.

Sue absently agreed to banns. But her mind for the moment was running on something else. A glow had passed away from her, and depression sat upon her features.

"I feel I was wickedly selfish last night!" she murmured. "It was sheer unkindness in me – or worse – to treat Arabella as I did. I didn't care about her being in trouble, and what she wished to tell you! Perhaps it was really something she was justified in telling you. That's some more of my badness, I suppose! Love has its own dark morality when rivalry enters in – at least, mine has, if other people's hasn't.... I wonder how she got on? I hope she reached the inn all right, poor woman."

"O yes: she got on all right," said Jude placidly.

"I hope she wasn't shut out, and that she hadn't to walk the streets in the rain. Do you mind my putting on my waterproof and going to see if she got in? I've been thinking of her all the morning."

"Well – is it necessary? You haven't the least idea how Arabella is able to shift for herself. Still, darling, if you want to go and inquire you can."

There was no limit to the strange and unnecessary penances which Sue would meekly undertake when in a contrite mood; and this going to see all sorts of extraordinary persons whose relation to her was precisely of a kind that would have made other people shun them, was her instinct ever, so that the request did not surprise him.

"And when you come back," he added, "I'll be ready to go about the banns. You'll come with me?"

Sue agreed, and went off under cloak and umbrella, letting Jude kiss her freely, and returning his kisses in a way she had never done before. Times had decidedly changed. "The little bird is caught at last!" she said, a sadness showing in her smile.

"No – only nested," he assured her.

She walked along the muddy street till she reached the public-house mentioned by Arabella, which was not so very far off. She was informed that Arabella had not yet left, and in doubt how to announce herself so that her predecessor in Jude's affections would recognize her, she sent up word that a friend from Spring Street had called, naming the place of Jude's residence. She was asked to step upstairs, and on being shown into a room found that it was Arabella's bedroom, and that the latter had not risen. She halted on the turn of her toe till Arabella cried from the bed, "Come in and shut the door," which Sue accordingly did.

Arabella lay facing the window, and did not at once turn her head: and Sue was wicked enough, despite her penitence, to wish for a moment that Jude could behold her forerunner now, with the daylight full upon her. She may have seemed handsome enough in profile under the lamps, but a frowsiness was apparent this morning; and the sight of her own fresh charms in the looking-glass made Sue's manner bright, till she reflected what a meanly sexual emotion this was in her, and hated herself for it.

"I've just looked in to see if you got back comfortably last night, that's all," she said gently. "I was afraid afterwards that you might have met with any mishap?"

"O – how stupid this is! I thought my visitor was – your friend – your husband – Mrs. Fawley, as I suppose you call yourself?" said Arabella, flinging her head back upon the pillows with a disappointed toss, and ceasing to retain the dimple she had just taken the trouble to produce.

"Indeed I don't," said Sue.

"O, I thought you might have, even if he's not legally yours. Decency is decency, any hour of the twenty-four."

"I don't know what you mean," said Sue stiffly. "He is mine, if you come to that!"

"He wasn't yesterday."

Sue coloured roseate, and said "How do you know?"

"From your manner when you talked to me at the door. Well, my dear, you've been quick about it, and I expect my visit last night helped it on – ha-ha! But I don't want to get him away from you."

Sue looked out at the rain, and at the dirty toilet-cover, and at the detached tail of Arabella's hair hanging on the looking-glass, just as it had done in Jude's time; and wished she had not come. In the pause there was a knock at the door, and the chambermaid brought in a telegram for "Mrs. Cartlett."

Arabella opened it as she lay, and her ruffled look disappeared.

"I am much obliged to you for your anxiety about me," she said blandly when the maid had gone; "but it is not necessary you should feel it. My man finds he can't do without me after all, and agrees to stand by the promise to marry again over here that he has made me all along. See here! This is in answer to one from me." She held out the telegram for Sue to read, but Sue did not take it. "He asks me to come back. His little corner public in Lambeth would go to pieces without me, he says. But he isn't going to knock me about when he has had a drop, any more after we are spliced[1] by English law than before! ... As for you, I should coax Jude to take me before the parson straight off, and have done with it, if I were in your place. I say it as a friend, my dear."

"He's waiting to, any day," returned Sue with frigid pride.

"Then let him, in Heaven's name. Life with a man is more business-like after it, and money matters work better. And then, you see, if you have rows, and he turns you out of doors, you can get the law to protect you,[2] which you can't otherwise, unless he half runs you through with a knife, or cracks your noddle[3] with a poker. And if he bolts away from you – I say it friendly, as woman to woman, for there's never any knowing what a man med do – you'll have the sticks o' furniture, and won't be looked upon as a thief. I shall marry my man over again, now he's willing, as there was a little flaw in the first ceremony. In my telegram last night which this is an answer to, I told him I had almost made it up with Jude; and that frightened him, I expect! Perhaps I should quite have done it if it hadn't been for you," she said laughing; "and then how different our histories might have been from to-day! Never such a tender fool as Jude is if a woman seems in trouble, and coaxes him a bit! Just as he used to be about birds and things. However, as it happens, it is just as well as if I had made it up, and I forgive you. And, as I say, I'd advise you to get the business legally done as soon as possible. You'll find it an awful bother later on if you don't."

"I have told you he is asking me to marry him – to make our natural marriage a legal one," said Sue, with yet more dignity. "It was quite by my wish that he didn't the moment I was free."

"Ah, yes – you are a oneyer[4] too, like myself," said Arabella, eyeing

---

1 spliced] (coll.:) married.
2 law to protect you] the lot of wives had been improved by the Married Women's Property Acts (1870, 1874, and 1882) and the Maintenance of Wives Acts (1878 and 1886).
3 noddle] (coll.:) head.
4 oneyer] (coll.:) individualist; singular person.

her visitor with humorous criticism. "Bolted from your first, didn't you, like me?"

"Good morning! – I must go," said Sue hastily.

"And I, too, must up and off!" replied the other, springing out of bed so suddenly that the soft parts of her person shook. Sue jumped aside in trepidation. "Lord, I am only a woman – not a six-foot sojer! ... Just a moment, dear," she continued, putting her hand on Sue's arm. "I really did want to consult Jude on a little matter of business, as I told him. I came about that more than anything else. Would he run up to speak to me at the station as I am going? You think not. Well, I'll write to him about it. I didn't want to write it, but never mind – I will."

V.-III.

WHEN Sue reached home Jude was awaiting her at the door to take the initial step towards their marriage. She clasped his arm, and they went along silently together, as true comrades ofttimes do. He saw that she was preoccupied, and forbore to question her.

"O Jude – I've been talking to her," she said at last. "I wish I hadn't! And yet it is best to be reminded of things."

"I hope she was civil."

"Yes. I – I can't help liking her – just a little bit! She's not an ungenerous nature; and I am so glad her difficulties have all suddenly ended." She explained how Arabella had been summoned back, and would be enabled to retrieve her position. "I was referring to our old question. What Arabella has been saying to me has made me feel more than ever how hopelessly vulgar an institution legal marriage is – a sort of trap to catch a man – I can't bear to think of it. I wish I hadn't promised to let you put up the banns this morning!"

"O, don't mind me. Any time will do for me. I thought you might like to get it over quickly, now."

"Indeed, I don't feel any more anxious now than I did before. Perhaps with any other man I might be a little anxious; but among the very few virtues possessed by your family and mine, dear, I think I may set staunchness. So I am not a bit frightened about losing you, now I really am yours and you really are mine. In fact, I am easier in my mind than I was, for my conscience is clear about Richard, who now has a right to his freedom. I felt we were deceiving him before."

"Sue, you seem when you are like this to be one of the women of some grand old civilization, whom I used to read about in my bygone, wasted, classical days, rather than a denizen of a mere Christian country. I almost expect you to say at these times that you have just been talking to some friend whom you met in the Via Sacra,[1] about the latest news of Octavia[2] or Livia;[3] or have been listening to Aspasia's eloquence,[4] or have been watching Praxiteles[5] chiselling away at his latest Venus, while Phryne[6] made complaint that she was tired of posing."

They had now reached the house of the parish-clerk. Sue stood back, while her lover went up to the door. His hand was raised to knock when she said: "Jude!"

He looked round.

"Wait a minute, would you mind?"

He came back to her.

"Just let us think," she said timidly. "I had such a horrid dream one night! ... And Arabella ——"

"What did Arabella say to you?" he asked.

"O, she said that when people were tied up you could get the law of a man better if he beat you – and how when couples quarrelled.... Jude, do you think that when you *must* have me with you by law, we shall be so happy as we are now? The men and women of our family are very generous when everything depends upon their good-will, but they always kick against compulsion. Don't you dread the attitude that insensibly arises out of legal obligation? Don't you think it is destructive to a passion whose essence is it gratuitousness?"

"Upon my word, love, you are beginning to frighten me, too, with all this foreboding! Well, let's go back and think it over."

Her face brightened. "Yes – so we will!" said she. And they turned

---

1   Via Sacra] "Sacred Way": road in ancient Rome.
2   Octavia] sister of Emperor Octavianus Augustus.
3   Livia] wife of Emperor Octavianus Augustus.
4   Aspasia's eloquence] Aspasia was a courtesan, hostess to intellectuals, and lover of Pericles, the celebrated orator of ancient Athens.
5   Praxiteles] celebrated Greek sculptor.
6   Phryne] beautiful courtesan and model for the "Aphrodite" of Praxiteles.

from the clerk's door, Sue taking his arm and murmuring as they walked homeward:

"Can you keep the bee from ranging,
 Or the ring-dove's neck from changing?
 No! Nor fetter'd love ..."[1]

They thought it over, or postponed thinking. Certainly they postponed action, and seemed to live on in a dreamy paradise. At the end of a fortnight or three weeks matters remained unadvanced, and no banns were announced to the ears of any Aldbrickham congregation.

Whilst they were postponing and postponing thus a letter and a newspaper arrived before breakfast one morning from Arabella. Seeing the handwriting Jude went up to Sue's room and told her, and as soon as she was dressed she hastened down. Sue opened the newspaper; Jude the letter. After glancing at the paper she held across the first page to him with her finger on a paragraph; but he was so absorbed in his letter that he did not turn awhile.

"Look!" said she.

He looked and read. The paper was one that circulated in South London only, and the marked advertisement was simply the announcement of a marriage at St. John's Church, Waterloo Road, under the names, "CARTLETT–DONN"; the united pair being Arabella and the innkeeper.

"Well, it is satisfactory," said Sue complacently. "Though, after this, it seems rather low to do likewise, and I am glad – However, she is provided for now in a way, I suppose, whatever her faults, poor thing. It is nicer that we are able to think that, than to be uneasy about her. I ought, too, to write to Richard and ask him how he is getting on, perhaps?"

But Jude's attention was still absorbed. Having merely glanced at the announcement he said in a disturbed voice: "Listen to this letter. What shall I say or do?

'THE THREE HORNS, LAMBETH.

'DEAR JUDE (I won't be so distant as to call you Mr. Fawley), – I send

---

1 "Can.....love"] from "Song" ("How delicious is the winning") by Thomas Campbell (1777-1844). See Appendix E.

to-day a newspaper, from which useful document you will learn that I was married over again to Cartlett last Tuesday. So that business is settled right and tight at last. But what I write about more particular is that private affair I wanted to speak to you on when I came down to Aldbrickham. I couldn't very well tell it to your lady friend, and should much have liked to let you know it by word of mouth, as I could have explained better than by letter. The fact is, Jude, that, though I have never informed you before, there was a boy born of our marriage, eight months after I left you, when I was at Sydney, living with my father and mother. All that is easily provable. As I had separated from you before I thought such a thing was going to happen, and I was over there, and our quarrel had been sharp, I did not think it convenient to write about the birth. I was then looking out for a good situation, so my parents took the child, and he has been with them ever since. That was why I did not mention it when I met you in Christminster, nor at the law proceedings. He is now of an intelligent age, of course, and my mother and father have lately written to say that, as they have rather a hard struggle over there, and I am settled comfortably here, they don't see why they should be encumbered with the child any longer, his parents being alive. I would have him with me here in a moment, but he is not old enough to be of any use in the bar, nor will be for years and years, and naturally Cartlett might think him in the way. They have, however, packed him off to me in charge of some friends who happened to be coming home, and I must ask you to take him when he arrives, for I don't know what to do with him. He is lawfully yours, that I solemnly swear. If anybody says he isn't, call them brimstone liars, for my sake. Whatever I may have done before or afterwards, I was honest to you from the time we were married till I went away, and I remain, yours, &c.,

ARABELLA CARTLETT.'"

Sue's look was one of dismay. "What will you do, dear?" she asked faintly.

Jude did not reply, and Sue watched him anxiously, with heavy breaths.

"It hits me hard!" said he in an under-voice. "It *may* be true! I can't make it out. Certainly, if his age is exactly what it ought to be.... I cannot think why she didn't tell me when I met her at Christminster, and came on here that evening with her! ... Ah – I do remember now that she said something about having a thing on her mind that she would like me to know, if ever we lived together again."

"The poor child seems to be wanted by nobody!" Sue replied, and her eyes filled.

Jude had by this time come to himself. "What a view of life he must have, mine or not mine!" he said. "I must say that, if I were better off, I should not stop for a moment to think whose he might be. I would take him and bring him up. The beggarly question of parentage – what is it, after all? What does it matter, when you come to think of it, whether a child is yours by blood or not? All the little ones of our time are collectively the children of us adults of the time, and entitled to our general care. That excessive regard of parents for their own children, and their dislike of other people's, is, like class-feeling, patriotism, save-your-own-soul-ism, and other virtues, a mean exclusiveness at bottom."

Sue jumped up and kissed Jude with passionate devotion. "Yes – so it is, dearest! And we'll have him here! And if he isn't yours it makes it all the better. I do hope he isn't – though perhaps I ought not to feel quite that! If he isn't, I should like so much for us to have him as an adopted child!"

"Well, you must assume about him what is most pleasing to you, my curious little comrade!" he said. "I feel that, anyhow, I don't like to leave the unfortunate little fellow to neglect. Just think of his life in a Lambeth pothouse,[1] and all its evil influences, with a parent who doesn't want him, and has, indeed, hardly seen him, and a stepfather who doesn't know him. 'Let the day perish wherein I was born, and the night in which it was said, There is a man child conceived!'[2] That's what the boy – *my* boy, perhaps, will find himself saying before long!"

"O no!"

"As I was the petitioner, I am really entitled to his custody, I suppose."

"Whether or no, we must have him. I see that. I'll do the best I can to be a mother to him, and we can afford to keep him somehow. I'll work harder. I wonder when he'll arrive?"

---

1 Lambeth pothouse] low tavern in this working-class district of London.
2 "Let.....conceived!"] Job 3:3.

"In the course of a few weeks, I suppose."

"I wish – When shall we have courage to marry, Jude?"

"Whenever you have it, I think I shall. It remains with you entirely, dear. Only say the word, and it's done."

"Before the boy comes?"

"Certainly."

"It would make a more natural home for him, perhaps," she murmured.

Jude thereupon wrote in purely formal terms to request that the boy should be sent on to them as soon as he arrived, making no remark whatever on the surprising nature of Arabella's information, nor vouchsafing a single word of opinion on the boy's paternity, nor on whether, had he known all this, his conduct towards her would have been quite the same.

In the down train that was timed to reach Aldbrickham station about ten o'clock the next evening, a small, pale child's face could be seen in the gloom of a third-class carriage. He had large, frightened eyes, and wore a white woollen cravat, over which a key was suspended round his neck by a piece of common string: the key attracting attention by its occasional shine in the lamp-light. In the band of his hat his half-ticket was stuck. His eyes remained mostly fixed on the back of the seat opposite, and never turned to the window even when a station was reached and called. On the other seat were two or three passengers, one of them a working woman who held a basket on her lap, in which was a tabby kitten. The woman opened the cover now and then, whereupon the kitten would put out its head, and indulge in playful antics. At these the fellow-passengers laughed, except the solitary boy bearing the key and ticket, who, regarding the kitten with his saucer eyes, seemed mutely to say: "All laughing comes from misapprehension. Rightly looked at there is no laughable thing under the sun."

Occasionally at a stoppage the guard would look into the compartment and say to the boy, "All right, my man. Your box is safe in the van." The boy would say, "Yes," without animation, would try to smile, and fail.

He was Age masquerading as Juvenility, and doing it so badly that his real self showed through crevices. A ground swell from ancient years of night seemed now and then to lift the child in this his morning-life, when his face took a back view over some great Atlantic of time, and appeared not to care about what it saw.

When the other travellers closed their eyes, which they did one by one – even the kitten curling itself up in the basket, weary of its too circumscribed play – the boy remained just as before. He then seemed to be doubly awake, like an enslaved and dwarfed Divinity, sitting passive and regarding his companions as if he saw their whole rounded lives rather than their immediate figures.

This was Arabella's boy. With her usual carelessness she had postponed writing to Jude about him till the eve of his landing, when she could absolutely postpone no longer, though she had known for weeks of his approaching arrival, and had, as she truly said, visited Aldbrickham mainly to reveal the boy's existence and his near home-coming to Jude. This very day on which she had received her former husband's answer at some time in the afternoon, the child reached the London Docks, and the family in whose charge he had come, having put him into a cab for Lambeth, and directed the cabman to his mother's house, bade him good-bye, and went their way.

On his arrival at the Three Horns, Arabella had looked him over with an expression that was as good as saying, "You are very much what I expected you to be," had given him a good meal, a little money, and, late as it was getting, despatched him to Jude by the next train, wishing her husband Cartlett, who was out, not to see him.

The train reached Aldbrickham, and the boy was deposited on the lonely platform beside his box. The collector took his ticket and, with a meditative sense of the unfitness of things, asked him where he was going by himself at that time of the night?

"Going to Spring Street," said the little one impassively.

"Why, that's a long way from here; a'most out in the country; and the folks will be gone to bed."

"I've got to go there."

"You must have a fly for your box."

"No. I must walk."

"O well: you'd better leave your box here and send for it. There's a 'bus goes half-way, but you'll have to walk the rest."

"I am not afraid."

"Why didn't your friends come to meet 'ee?"

"I suppose they didn't know I was coming."

"Who is your friends?"

"Mother didn't wish me to say."

"All I can do, then, is to take charge of this. Now walk as fast as you can."

Saying nothing further the boy came out into the street, looking round to see that nobody followed or observed him. When he had walked some little distance he asked for the street of his destination. He was told to go straight on quite into the outskirts of the place.

The child fell into a steady mechanical creep which had in it an impersonal quality – the movement of the wave, or of the breeze, or of the cloud. He followed his directions literally, without an inquiring gaze at anything. It could have been seen that the boy's ideas of life were different from those of the local boys. Children begin with detail, and learn up to the general; they begin with the contiguous, and gradually comprehend the universal. The boy seemed to have begun with the generals of life, and never to have concerned himself with the particulars. To him the houses, the willows, the obscure fields beyond, were apparently regarded not as brick residences, pollards, meadows; but as human dwellings in the abstract, vegetation, and the wide dark world.

He found the way to the little lane, and knocked at the door of Jude's house. Jude had just retired to bed, and Sue was about to enter her chamber adjoining when she heard the knock and came down.

"Is this where father lives?" asked the child.

"Who?"

"Mr. Fawley, that's his name."

Sue ran up to Jude's room and told him, and he hurried down as soon as he could, though to her impatience he seemed long.

"What – is it he – so soon?" she asked as Jude came.

She scrutinized the child's features, and suddenly went away into the little sitting-room adjoining. Jude lifted the boy to a level with himself, keenly regarded him with gloomy tenderness, and telling him he would have been met if they had known of his coming so soon, set him provisionally in a chair whilst he went to look for Sue, whose super-sensitiveness was disturbed, as he knew. He found her in the dark, bending over an arm-chair. He enclosed her with his arm, and putting his face by hers, whispered "What's the matter?"

"What Arabella says is true – true! I see you in him!"

"Well: that's one thing in my life as it should be, at any rate."

"But the other half of him is – *she!* And that's what I can't bear! But I ought to – I'll try to get used to it; yes, I ought!"

"Jealous little Sue! I withdraw all remarks about your sexlessness. Never mind! Time may right things.... And Sue, darling; I have an idea! We'll educate and train him with a view to the University. What I couldn't accomplish in my own person perhaps I can carry out through him? They are making it easier for poor students[1] now, you know."

"O you dreamer!" said she, and holding his hand returned to the child with him. The boy looked at her as she had looked at him. "Is it you who's my *real* mother at last?" he inquired.

"Why? Do I look like your father's wife?"

"Well, yes; 'cept he seems fond of you, and you of him. Can I call you mother?"

Then a yearning look came over the child, and he began to cry. Sue thereupon could not refrain from instantly doing likewise, being a harp which the least wind of emotion from another's heart could make to vibrate as readily as a radical stir in her own.

"You may call me mother, if you wish to, you poor dear!" she said, bending her cheek against his to hide her tears.

"What's this round your neck?" asked Jude with affected calmness.

"The key of my box that's at the station."

They bustled about and got him some supper, and made him up a temporary bed, where he soon fell asleep. Both went and looked at him as he lay.

"He called you mother two or three times before he dropped off," murmured Jude. "Wasn't it odd that he should have wanted to!"

"Well – it was significant," said Sue. "There's more for us to think about in that one little hungry heart than in all the stars of the sky.... I suppose, dear, we *must* pluck up courage, and get that ceremony over? It is no use struggling against the current, and I feel myself getting intertwined with my kind. O Jude, you'll love me dearly, won't you, afterwards! I do want to be kind to this child, and to be a mother to him; and our adding the legal form to our marriage might make it easier for me."

---

1   easier.....students] See Appendix F.

THEIR next and second attempt thereat was more deliberately made, though it was begun on the morning following the singular child's arrival at their home.

Him they found to be in the habit of sitting silent, his quaint and weird face set, and his eyes resting on things they did not see in the substantial world.

"His face is like the tragic mark of Melpomene,"[1] said Sue. "What is your name, dear? Did you tell us?"

"Little Father Time is what they always called me. It is a nickname; because I look so aged, they say."

"And you talk so, too," said Sue tenderly. "It is strange, Jude, that these preternaturally old boys almost always come from new countries? But what were you christened?"

"I never was."

"Why was that?"

"Because, if I died in damnation, 'twould save the expense of a Christian funeral."

"O — your name is not Jude, then?" said his father with some disappointment.

The boy shook his head. "Never heerd on it."

"Of course not," said Sue quickly; "since she was hating you all the time!"

"We'll have him christened," said Jude; and privately to Sue: "The day we are married." Yet the advent of the child disturbed him.

Their position lent them shyness, and having an impression that a marriage at a Superintendent Registrar's office was more private than an ecclesiastical one, they decided to avoid a church this time. Both Sue and Jude together went to the office of the district to give notice: they had become such companions that they could hardly do anything of importance except in each other's company.

Jude Fawley signed the form of notice, Sue looking over his shoulder and watching his hand as it traced the words. As she read the four-square undertaking, never before seen by her, into which her own and Jude's names were inserted, and by which that very volatile essence, their love for each other, was supposed to be made perma-

---

1   Melpomene] Greek muse of Tragedy.

nent, her face seemed to grow painfully apprehensive. "Names and Surnames of the Parties" – (they were to be parties now, not lovers, she thought). "Condition" – (a horrid idea) – "Rank or Occupation" – "Age" – "Dwelling at" – "Length of Residence" – "Church or Building in which the marriage is to be solemnized" – "District and County in which the Parties respectively dwell."

"It spoils the sentiment, doesn't it!" she said on their way home. "It seems making a more sordid business of it even than signing the contract in a vestry. There is a little poetry in a church. But we'll try to get through with it, dearest, now."

"We will. 'For what man is he that hath betrothed a wife and hath not taken her? Let him go and return unto his house, lest he die in the battle, and another man take her.'[1] So said the Jewish law-giver."

"How you know the Scriptures, Jude! You really ought to have been a parson. I can only quote profane writers!"

During the interval before the issuing of the certificate Sue, in her housekeeping errands, sometimes walked past the office, and furtively glancing in saw affixed to the wall the notice of the purposed clinch to their union. She could not bear its aspect. Coming after her previous experience of matrimony, all the romance of their attachment seemed to be starved away by placing her present case in the same category. She was usually leading little Father Time by the hand, and fancied that people thought him hers, and regarded the intended ceremony as the patching up of an old error.

Meanwhile Jude decided to link his present with his past in some slight degree by inviting to the wedding the only person remaining on earth who was associated with his early life at Marygreen – the aged widow Mrs. Edlin, who had been his great-aunt's friend and nurse in her last illness. He hardly expected that she would come; but she did, bringing singular presents, in the form of apples, jam, brass snuffers,[2] an ancient pewter dish, a warming-pan, and an enormous bag of goose feathers towards a bed. She was allotted the spare room in Jude's house, whither she retired early, and where they could hear her through the ceiling below, honestly saying the Lord's Prayer in a loud voice, as the Rubric directed.[3]

---

1   'For what.....take her'] Deuteronomy 20:7 (slightly misquoted).
2   snuffers] for trimming the wick of a candle.
3   as the Rubric directed] "Then the Minister, Clerks, and people shall say the Lord's Prayer with a loud voice" (*Book of Common Prayer*).

As, however, she could not sleep, and discovered that Sue and Jude were still sitting up – it being in fact only ten o'clock – she dressed herself again, and came down; and they all sat by the fire till a late hour – Father Time included; though, as he never spoke, they were hardly conscious of him.

"Well, I bain't set against marrying as your great-aunt was," said the widow. "And I hope 'twill be a jocund wedding for ye in all respects this time. Nobody can hope it more, knowing what I do of your families, which is more, I suppose, than anybody else now living. For they have been unlucky that way, God knows."

Sue breathed uneasily.

"They was always good-hearted people, too – wouldn't kill a fly if they knowed it," continued the wedding guest. "But things happened to thwart 'em, and if everything wasn't vitty¹ they were upset. No doubt that's how he that the tale is told of came to do what 'a did – if he *were* one of your family."

"What was that?" said Jude.

"Well – that tale, ye know; he that was gibbeted² just on the brow of the hill by the Brown House – not far from the milestone between Marygreen and Alfredston, where the other road branches off. But Lord, 'twas in my grandfather's time; and it medn' have been one of your folk at all."

"I know where the gibbet is said to have stood, very well," murmured Jude. "But I never heard of this. What – did this man – my ancestor and Sue's – kill his wife?"

"'Twer not that exactly. She ran away from him, with their child, to her friends; and while she was there the child died. He wanted the body, to bury it where his people lay, but she wouldn't give it up. Her husband then came in the night with a cart, and broke into the house to steal the coffin away; but he was catched, and being obstinate, wouldn't tell what he broke in for. They brought it in burglary, and that's why he was hanged and gibbeted on Brown House Hill. His wife went mad after he was dead. But it medn' be true that he belonged to ye more than to me."

A small slow voice rose from the shade of the fireside, as if out of

---

1 vitty] (dl.:) pleasant, fitting.
2 gibbeted] displayed (possibly in a cage) hanging from a gallows.

the earth: "If I was you, mother, I wouldn't marry father!" It came from little Time, and they started, for they had forgotten him.

"O, it is only a tale," said Sue cheeringly.

After this exhilarating tradition from the widow on the eve of the solemnization they rose, and, wishing their guest good-night, retired.

The next morning Sue, whose nervousness intensified with the hours, took Jude privately into the sitting-room before starting. "Jude, I want you to kiss me, as a lover, incorporeally," she said, tremulously nestling up to him, with damp lashes. "It won't be ever like this any more, will it! I wish we hadn't begun the business. But I suppose we must go on. How horrid that story was last night! It spoilt my thoughts of to-day. It makes me feel as if a tragic doom overhung our family, as it did the house of Atreus."[1]

"Or the house of Jeroboam,"[2] said the quondam[3] theologian.

"Yes. And it seems awful temerity in us two to go marrying! I am going to vow to you in the same words I vowed in to my other husband, and you to me in the same as you used to your other wife; regardless of the deterrent lesson we were taught by those experiments!"

"If you are uneasy I am made unhappy," said he. "I had hoped you would feel quite joyful. But if you don't, you don't. It is no use pretending. It is a dismal business to you, and that makes it so to me!"

"It is unpleasantly like that other morning – that's all," she murmured. "Let us go on now."

They started arm and arm for the office aforesaid, no witness accompanying them except the Widow Edlin. The day was chilly and dull, and a clammy fog blew through the town from "Royal-tower'd Thame."[4] On the steps of the office there were the muddy footmarks of people who had entered, and in the entry were damp umbrellas. Within the office several persons were gathered, and our couple perceived that a marriage between a soldier and a young woman was just in progress. Sue, Jude, and the widow stood in the background while this was going on, Sue reading the notices of marriage on the wall.

---

1   house of Atreus] in ancient Greek legends, an accursed dynasty; the subject of Æschylus's tragic trilogy, *The Oresteia*.

2   house of Jeroboam] King Jeroboam's family was cursed by God (1 Kings 13–14).

3   quondam] former.

4   "Royal-tower'd Thame"] from John Milton's poem "At a Vacation Exercise."

The room was a dreary place to two of their temperament, though to its usual frequenters it doubtless seemed ordinary enough. Law-books in musty calf covered one wall, and elsewhere were Post-Office Directories, and other books of reference. Papers in packets tied with red tape were pigeon-holed around, and some iron safes filled a recess; while the bare wood floor was, like the doorstep, stained by previous visitors.

The soldier was sullen and reluctant: the bride sad and timid; she was soon, obviously, to become a mother, and she had a black eye. Their little business was soon done, and the twain and their friends straggled out, one of the witnesses saying casually to Jude and Sue in passing, as if he had known them before: "See the couple just come in? Ha, ha! That fellow is just out of gaol this morning. She met him at the gaol gates, and brought him straight here. She's paying for everything."

She turned her head and saw an ill-favoured man, closely cropped, with a broad-faced, pock-marked woman on his arm, ruddy with liquor and the satisfaction of being on the brink of a gratified desire.[1] They jocosely saluted the outgoing couple, and went forward in front of Jude and Sue, whose diffidence was increasing. The latter drew back and turned to her lover, her mouth shaping itself like that of a child about to give way to grief:

"Jude – I don't like it here! I wish we hadn't come! The place gives me the horrors: it seems so unnatural as the climax of our love! I wish it had been at church, if it had to be at all. It is not so vulgar there!"

"Dear little girl," said Jude. "How troubled and pale you look!"

"It must be performed here now, I suppose?"

"No – perhaps not necessarily."

He spoke to the clerk, and came back, "No – we need not marry here or anywhere, unless we like, even now," he said. "We can be married in a church, if not with the same certificate with another he'll give us, I think. Anyhow, let us go out till you are calmer, dear, and I too, and talk it over."

They went out stealthily and guiltily, as if they had committed a misdemeanour, closing the door without noise, and telling the widow, who had remained in the entry, to go home and await them;

---

1 gratified desire] cf. "The lineaments of Gratified Desire" (Blake: "The Question Answer'd").

that they would call in any casual passers as witnesses, if necessary. When in the street they turned into an unfrequented side alley, where they walked up and down as they had done long ago in the Market-house at Melchester.

"Now darling, what shall we do? We are making a mess of it, it strikes me. Still, *anything* that pleases you will please me."

"But Jude, dearest, I am worrying you! You wanted it to be there, didn't you?"

"Well, to tell the truth, when I got inside I felt as if I didn't care much about it. The place depressed me almost as much as it did you – it was ugly. And then I thought of what you had said this morning as to whether we ought."

They walked on vaguely, till she paused, and her little voice began anew: "It seems so weak, too, to vacillate this! And yet how much better than to act rashly a second time.... How terrible that scene was to me! The expression in that flabby woman's face, leading her on to give herself to that gaol-bird, not for a few hours, as she would, but for a lifetime, as she must. And the other poor soul – to escape a nominal shame which was owing to the weakness of her character, degrading herself to the real shame of bondage to a tyrant who scorned her – a man whom to avoid for ever was her only chance of salvation.... This is our parish church, isn't it? This is where it would have to be, if we did it in the usual way? A service or something seems to be going on."

Jude went up and looked in at the door. "Why – it is a wedding here too," he said. "Everybody seems to be on our tack[1] to-day."

Sue said she supposed it was because Lent[2] was just over, when there was always a crowd of marriages. "Let us listen," she said, "and find how it feels to us when performed in a church."

They stepped in, and entered a back seat, and watched the proceedings at the altar. The contracting couple appeared to belong to the well-to-do middle class, and the wedding altogether was of ordinary prettiness and interest. They could see the flowers tremble in the bride's hand, even at that distance, and could hear her mechanical

---

1 on our tack] going in our direction.
2 Lent] During Lent (from Ash Wednesday to Holy Saturday) marriages were not solemnised.

murmur of words whose meaning her brain seemed to gather not at all under the pressure of her self-consciousness. Sue and Jude listened, and severally saw themselves in time past going through the same form of self-committal.

"It is not the same to her, poor thing, as it would be to me doing it over again with my present knowledge," Sue whispered. "You see, they are fresh to it, and take the proceedings as a matter of course. But having been awakened to its awful solemnity as we have, or at least as I have, by experience, and to my own too squeamish feelings perhaps sometimes, it really does seem immoral in me to go and undertake the same thing again with open eyes. Coming in here and seeing this has frightened me from a church wedding as much as the other did from a registry one.... We are a weak, tremulous pair, Jude, and what others may feel confident in I feel doubts of – my being proof against the sordid conditions of a business contract again!"

Then they tried to laugh, and went on debating in whispers the object-lesson before them. And Jude said he also thought they were both too thin-skinned – that they ought never to have been born – much less have come together for the most preposterous of all joint-ventures for *them* – matrimony.

His betrothed shuddered; and asked him earnestly if he indeed felt that they ought not to go in cold blood and sign that life-undertaking again? "It is awful if you think we have found ourselves not strong enough for it, and knowing this, are proposing to perjure ourselves," she said.

"I fancy I do think it – since you ask me," said Jude. "Remember I'll do it if you wish, own darling." While she hesitated he went on to confess that, though he thought they ought to be able to do it, he felt checked by the dread of incompetency just as she did – from their peculiarities, perhaps, because they were unlike other people. "We are horribly sensitive; that's really what's the matter with us, Sue!" he declared.

"I fancy more are like us than we think!"

"Well, I don't know. The intention of the contract is good, and right for many, no doubt; but in our case it may defeat its own ends because we are the queer sort of people we are – folk in whom domestic ties of a forced kind snuff out cordiality and spontaneous-ness."

Sue still held that there was nothing queer or exceptional in it: that all were so. "Everybody is getting to feel as we do. We are a little beforehand, that's all. In fifty, ay, twenty years, the descendants of these two will act and feel worse than we. They will see weltering humanity still more vividly than we do now, as

'Shapes like our own selves hideously multiplied,'[1]

and will be afraid to reproduce them."

"What a terrible line of poetry! ... Though I have felt it myself about my fellow-creatures, at morbid times."

Thus they murmured on, till Sue said more brightly:

"Well — the general question is not our business, and why should we plague ourselves about it? However different our reasons are we come to the same conclusion; that for us particular two, an irrevocable oath is risky. Then, Jude, let us go home without killing our dream! Yes? How good you are, my friend: you give way to all my whims!"

"They accord very much with my own."

He gave her a little kiss behind a pillar while the attention of everybody present was taken up in observing the bridal procession entering the vestry; and then they came outside the building. By the door they waited till two or three carriages, which had gone away for a while, returned, and the new husband and wife came into the open daylight. Sue sighed.

"The flowers in the bride's hand are sadly like the garland which decked the heifers of sacrifice in old times!"

"Still, Sue, it is no worse for the woman than for the man. That's what some women fail to see, and instead of protesting against the conditions they protest against the man, the other victim; just as a woman in a crowd will abuse the man who crushes against her, when he is only the helpless transmitter of the pressure put upon him."

"Yes — some are like that, instead of uniting with the man against the common enemy, coercion." The bride and bridegroom had by this time driven off, and the two moved away with the rest of the

---

1   'Shapes......multiplied'] a version of Shelley's line "All shapes like mine own self, hideously multiplied" (*Revolt of Islam*, Canto III, stanza 23).

idlers. "No – don't let's do it," she continued. "At least just now."

They reached home, and passing the window arm in arm saw the widow looking out at them. "Well," cried their guest when they entered, "I said to myself when I zeed ye coming so loving up to the door, 'They made up their minds at last, then!'"

They briefly hinted that they had not.

"What – and ha'n't ye really done it? Chok' it all; that I should have lived to see a good old saying like 'marry in haste and repent at leisure' spoiled like this by you two! 'Tis time I got back again to Marygreen – sakes if tidden¹– if this is what the new notions be leading us to ! Nobody thought o' being afeard o' matrimony in my time, nor of much else but a cannonball or empty cupboard! Why when I and my poor man were married we thought no more o't than of a game o' dibs!"²

"Don't tell the child when he comes in," whispered Sue nervously. "He'll think it has all gone on right, and it will be better that he should not be surprised and puzzled. Of course it is only put off for reconsideration. If we are happy as we are, what does it matter to anybody?"

V. - V.

THE purpose of a chronicler of moods and deeds does not require him to express his personal views upon the grave controversy above given. That the twain were happy – between their times of sadness – was indubitable. And when the unexpected apparition of Jude's child in the house had shown itself to be no such disturbing event as it had looked, but one that brought into their lives a new and tender interest of an ennobling and unselfish kind, it rather helped than injured their happiness.

To be sure, with such pleasing anxious beings³ as they were, the boy's coming also brought with it much thought for the future,

---

1 sakes if tidden] (dl.:) bless me if it isn't.
2 dibs] children's game in which small objects are thrown from the palm and caught on the back of the hand.
3 pleasing anxious beings] adaptation of "This pleasing anxious being," a phrase in Gray's "Elegy Written in a Country Church-Yard." See Appendix E.

particularly as he seemed at present to be singularly deficient in all the usual hopes of childhood. But the pair tried to dismiss, for a while at least, a too strenuously forward view.

There is in Upper Wessex an old town of nine or ten thousand souls; the town may be called Stoke-Barehills.¹ It stands with its gaunt, unattractive, ancient church, and its new red brick suburb, amid the open, chalk-soiled cornlands, near the middle of an imaginary triangle which has for its three corners the towns of Aldbrickham and Wintoncester, and the important military station of Quartershot.² The great western highway from London passes through it, near a point where the road branches into two, merely to unite again some twenty miles further westward. Out of this bifurcation and reunion there used to arise among wheeled travellers, before railway days, endless questions of choice between the respective ways. But the question is now as dead as the scot-and-lot freeholder,³ the road waggoner, and the mail coachman who disputed it; and probably not a single inhabitant of Stoke-Barehills is now even aware that the two roads which part in his town ever meet again; for nobody now drives up and down the great western highway daily.

The most familiar object in Stoke-Barehills nowadays is its cemetery, standing among some picturesque mediæval ruins beside the railway; the modern chapels, modern tombs, and modern shrubs, having a look of intrusiveness amid the crumbling and ivy-covered decay of the ancient walls.

On a certain day, however, in the particular year which has now been reached by this narrative – the month being early June – the features of the town excite little interest, though many visitors arrive by the trains; some down trains, in especial, nearly emptying themselves here. It is the week of the Great Wessex Agricultural Show, whose vast encampment spreads over the open outskirts of the town like the tents of an investing army. Rows of marquees, huts, booths, pavilions, arcades, porticoes – every kind of structure short of a permanent one – cover the green field for the space of a square half-

---

1   Stoke-Barehills] Basingstoke, market town in Hampshire.
2   Quartershot] Aldershot (in Hampshire), established in 1855 as an army base.
3   scot-and-lot freeholder] a municipal ratepayer who was thereby entitled to vote in elections, in the days before electoral reforms (notably in 1832 and 1867) extended the franchise.

mile, and the crowds of arrivals walk through the town in a mass, and make straight for the exhibition ground. The way thereto is lined with shows, stalls, and hawkers[1] on foot, who make a market-place of the whole roadway to the show proper, and lead some of the improvident to lighten their pockets appreciably before they reach the gates of the exhibition they came expressly to see.

It is the popular day, the shilling day, and of the fast arriving excursion trains two from different directions enter the two contiguous railway-stations at almost the same minute. One, like several which have preceded it, comes from London: the other by a cross-line from Aldbrickham; and from the London train alights a couple; a short, rather bloated man, with a globular stomach and small legs, resembling a top on two pegs, accompanied by a woman of rather fine figure and rather red face, dressed in black material, and covered with beads from bonnet to skirt, that made her glisten as if clad in chain-mail.

They cast their eyes around. The man was about to hire a fly as some others had done, when the woman said, "Don't be in such a hurry, Cartlett. It isn't so very far to the show-yard. Let us walk down the street into the place. Perhaps I can pick up a cheap bit of furniture or old china. It is years since I was here – never since I lived as a girl at Aldbrickham, and used to come across for a trip sometimes with my young man."

"You can't carry home furniture by excursion train," said, in a thick voice, her husband, the landlord of The Three Horns, Lambeth; for they had both come down from the tavern in that "excellent, densely populated, gin-drinking neighbourhood," which they had occupied ever since the advertisement in those words had attracted them thither. The configuration of the landlord showed that he, too, like his customers, was becoming affected by the liquors he retailed.

"Then I'll get it sent, if I see any worth having," said his wife.

They sauntered on, but had barely entered the town when her attention was attracted by a young couple leading a child, who had come out from the second platform, into which the train from Aldbrickham had steamed. They were walking just in front of the innkeepers.

---

1   hawkers] travelling vendors.

"Sakes alive!" said Arabella.

"What's that?" said Cartlett.

"Who do you think that couple is? Don't you recognize the man?"

"No."

"Not from the photos I have showed you?"

"Is it Fawley?"

"Yes – of course."

"Oh, well. I suppose he was inclined for a little sight-seeing like the rest of us." Cartlett's interest in Jude, whatever it might have been when Arabella was new to him, had plainly flagged since her charms and her idiosyncrasies, her supernumerary hair-coils, and her optional dimples, were becoming as a tale that is told.[1]

Arabella so regulated her pace and her husband's as to keep just in the rear of the other three, which it was easy to do without notice in such a stream of pedestrians. Her answers to Cartlett's remarks were vague and slight, for the group in front interested her more than all the rest of the spectacle.

"They are rather fond of one another and of their child, seemingly," continued the publican.

"*Their* child! 'Tisn't their child," said Arabella with a curious, sudden fierceness. "They haven't been married long enough for it to be theirs!"

But although the smouldering maternal instinct was strong enough in her to lead her to quash her husband's conjecture, she was not disposed on second thoughts to be more candid than necessary. Mr. Cartlett had no other idea than that his wife's child by her first husband was with his grandparents at the Antipodes.

"O I suppose not. She looks quite a girl."

"They are only lovers, or lately married, and have the child in charge, as anybody can see."

All continued to move ahead. The unwitting Sue and Jude, the couple in question, had determined to make this Agricultural Exhibition within twenty miles of their own town the occasion of a day's excursion which should combine exercise and amusement with instruction, at small expense. Not regardful of themselves alone, they

---

1   as a tale that is told] cf. "we spend our years as a tale that is told" (Psalm 90:9).

had taken care to bring Father Time, to try every means of making him kindle and laugh like other boys, though he was to some extent a hindrance to the delightfully unreserved intercourse in their pilgrimages which they so much enjoyed. But they soon ceased to consider him an observer, and went along with that tender attention to each other which the shyest can scarcely disguise, and which these, among entire strangers as they imagined, took less trouble to disguise than they might have done at home. Sue, in her new summer clothes, flexible and light as a bird, her little thumb stuck up by the stem of her white cotton sunshade, went along as if she hardly touched ground, and as if a moderately strong puff of wind would float her over the hedge in to the next field. Jude, in his light grey holiday-suit, was really proud of her companionship, not more for her external attractiveness than for her sympathetic words and ways. That complete mutual understanding, in which every glance and movement was as effectual as speech for conveying intelligence between them, made them almost the two parts of a singe whole.

The pair with their charge passed through the turnstiles, Arabella and her husband not far behind them. When inside the enclosure the publican's wife could see that the two ahead began to take trouble with the youngster, pointing out and explaining the many objects of interest, alive and dead; and a passing sadness would touch their faces at their every failure to disturb his indifference.

"How she sticks to him!" said Arabella. "O no – I fancy they are not married, or they wouldn't be so much to one another as that.... I wonder!"

"But I thought you said he did marry her?"

"I heard he was going to – that's all, going to make another attempt, after putting it off once or twice.... As far as they themselves are concerned they are the only two in the show. I should be ashamed of making myself so silly if I were he!"

"I don't see as how there's anything remarkable in their behaviour. I should never have noticed their being in love, if you hadn't said so."

"You never see anything," she rejoined. Nevertheless Cartlett's view of the lovers' or married pair's conduct was undoubtedly that of the general crowd, whose attention seemed to be in no way attracted by what Arabella's sharpened vision discerned.

"He's charmed by her as if she were some fairy!" continued Arabella. "See how he looks round at her, and lets his eyes rest on her. I am inclined to think that she don't care for him quite so much as he does for her. She's not a particular warm-hearted creature to my thinking, though she cares for him pretty middling much – as much as she's able to; and he could make her heart ache a bit if he liked to try – which he's too simple to do. There – now they are going across to the cart-horse sheds. Come along."

"I don't want to see the cart-horses. It is no business of ours to follow these two. If we have come to see the show let us see it in our own way, as they do in theirs."

"Well – suppose we agree to meet somewhere in an hour's time – say at that refreshment tent over there, and go about independent? Then you can look at what you choose to, and so can I."

Cartlett was not loth to agree to this, and they parted – he proceeding to the shed where malting processes were being exhibited, and Arabella in the direction taken by Jude and Sue. Before, however, she had regained their wake a laughing face met her own, and she was confronted by Anny, the friend of her girlhood.

Anny had burst out in hearty laughter at the mere fact of the chance rencounter. "I be still living down there," she said, as soon as she was composed. "I am soon going to be married, but my intended couldn't come up here to-day. But there's lots of us come by excursion, though I've lost the rest of 'em for the present."

"Have you met Jude and his young woman, or wife, or whatever she is? I saw 'em by now."

"No. Not a glimpse of un for years!"

"Well, they are close by here somewhere. Yes – there they are – by that grey horse!"

"O, that's his present young woman – wife did you say? Has he married again?"

"I don't know."

"She's pretty, isn't she!"

"Yes – nothing to complain of; or jump at. Not much to depend on, though; a slim, fidgety little thing like that."

"He's a nice-looking chap, too! You ought to ha' stuck to un, Arabella."

"I don't know but I ought," murmured she.

Anny laughed. "That's you, Arabella! Always wanting another man than your own."

"Well, and what woman don't I should like to know? As for that body with him – she don't know what love is – at least what I call love! I can see in her face she don't."

"And perhaps, Abby dear, you don't know what she calls love."

"I'm sure I don't wish to! ... Ah – they are making for the Art Department. I should like to see some pictures myself. Suppose we go that way? – Why, if all Wessex isn't here, I verily believe! There's Dr. Vilbert. Haven't seen him for years and he's not looking a day older than when I used to know him. How do you do, Physician? I was just saying that you don't look a day older than when you knew me as a girl."

"Simply the result of taking my own pills regular, ma'am. Only two and threepence[1] a box – warranted efficacious by the Government stamp. Now let me advise you to purchase the same immunity from the ravages of Time by following my example? Only two-and-three."

The physician had produced a box from his waistcoat pocket, and Arabella was induced to make the purchase.

"At the same time," continued he, when the pills were paid for, "you have the advantage of me, Mrs. – Surely not Mrs. Fawley, once Miss Donn, of the vicinity of Marygreen?"

"Yes. But Mrs. Cartlett now."

"Ah – you lost him, then? Promising young fellow! A pupil of mine, you know. I taught him the dead languages. And believe me, he soon knew nearly as much as I."

"I lost him; but not as you think," said Arabella drily. "The lawyers untied us. There he is, look, alive and lusty; along with that young woman, entering the Art exhibition."

"Ah – dear me! Fond of her, apparently."

"They *say* they are cousins."

"Cousinship is a great convenience to their feelings, I should say?"

"Yes. So her husband thought, no doubt, when he divorced her.... Shall we look at the pictures, too?"

---

1 two and threepence] two shillings and three pence, a sum nominally equivalent to about eleven pence in current British coinage, but then worth considerably more.

The trio followed across the green and entered. Jude and Sue, with the child, unaware of the interest they were exciting, had gone up to a model at one end of the building, which they regarded with considerable attention for a long while before they went on. Arabella and her friends came to it in due course, and the inscription it bore was: "Model of Cardinal College, Christminster; by J. Fawley and S. F. M. Bridehead."

"Admiring their own work," said Arabella. "How like Jude – always thinking of Colleges and Christminster, instead of attending to his business!"

They glanced cursorily at the pictures, and proceeded to the bandstand. When they had stood a little while listening to the music of the military performers, Jude, Sue, and the child came up on the other side. Arabella did not care if they should recognize her; but they were too deeply absorbed in their own lives, as translated into emotion by the military band, to perceive her under her beaded veil. She walked round the outside of the listening throng, passing behind the lovers, whose movements had an unexpected fascination for her to-day. Scrutinizing them narrowly from the rear she noticed that Jude's hand sought Sue's as they stood, the two standing close together so as to conceal, as they supposed, this tacit expression of their mutual responsiveness.

"Silly fools – like two children!" Arabella whispered to herself morosely, as she rejoined her companions, with whom she preserved a preoccupied silence.

Anny meanwhile had jokingly remarked to Vilbert on Arabella's hankering interest in her first husband.

"Now," said the physician to Arabella, apart; "do you want anything such as this, Mrs. Cartlett? It is not compounded out of my regular pharmacopœia,[1] but I am sometimes asked for such a thing." He produced a small phial of clear liquid. "A love-philter, such as was used by the Ancients with great effect. I found it out by study of their writings, and have never known it to fail."

"What is it made of?" asked Arabella curiously.

"Well – a distillation of the juices of doves' hearts – otherwise pigeons' – is one of the ingredients. It took nearly a hundred hearts to produce that small bottle full."

---

1 pharmacopœia] stock of drugs.

"How do you get pigeons enough?"

"To tell a secret, I get a piece of rock-salt, of which pigeons are inordinately fond, and place it in a dovecote on my roof. In a few hours the birds come to it from all points of the compass – east, west, north and south – and thus I secure as many as I require. You use the liquid by contriving that the desired man shall take about ten drops of it in his drink. But remember, all this is told you because I gather from your questions that you mean to be a purchaser. You must keep faith with me?"

"Very well – I don't mind a bottle – to give some friend or other to try it on her young man." She produced five shillings, the price asked, and slipped the phial in her capacious bosom. Saying presently that she was due at an appointment with her husband she sauntered away towards the refreshment bar, Jude, his companion, and the child having gone on to the horticultural tent, where Arabella caught a glimpse of them standing before a group of roses in bloom.

She waited a few minutes observing them, and then proceeded to join her spouse with no very amiable sentiments. She found him seated on a stool by the bar, talking to one of the gaily dressed maids who had served him with spirits.

"I should think you had enough of this business at home!" Arabella remarked gloomily. "Surely you didn't come fifty miles from your own bar to go into another? Come, take me round the show, as other men do their wives! Dammy, one would think you were a young bachelor, with nobody to look after but yourself!"

"But we agreed to meet here; and what could I do but wait?"

"Well, now we have met, come along," she returned, ready to quarrel with the sun for shining on her. And they left the tent together, this pot-bellied man and florid woman, in the antipathetic, recriminatory mood of the average husband and wife of Christendom.

In the meantime the more exceptional couple and the boy still lingered in the pavilion of flowers – an enchanted palace to their appreciative taste – Sue's usually pale cheeks reflecting the pink of the tinted roses at which she gazed; for the gay sights, the air, the music, and the excitement of a day's outing with Jude, had quickened her blood and made her eyes sparkle with vivacity. She adored roses, and what Arabella had witnessed was Sue detaining Jude almost against his will while she learnt the names of this variety and that, and put her face within an inch of their blooms to smell them.

"I should like to push my face quite into them – the dears!" she had said. "But I suppose it is against the rules to touch them – isn't it, Jude?"

"Yes, you baby," said he: and then playfully gave her a little push, so that her nose went among the petals.

"The policemen will be down on us, and I shall say it was my husband's fault!"

Then she looked up at him, and smiled in a way that told so much to Arabella.

"Happy?" he murmured.

She nodded.

"Why? Because you have come to the great Wessex Agricultural Show – or because *we* have come?"

"You are always trying to make me confess to all sorts of absurdities. Because I am improving my mind, of course, by seeing all these steam-ploughs, and threshing-machines, and chaff-cutters, and cows, and pigs, and sheep."

Jude was quite content with a baffle[1] from his ever evasive companion. But when he had forgotten that he had put the question, and because he no longer wished for an answer, she went on: "I feel that we have returned to Greek joyousness, and have blinded ourselves to sickness and sorrow, and have forgotten what twenty-five centuries have taught the race since their time, as one of your Christminster luminaries says....[2] There is one immediate shadow, however,– only one." And she looked at the aged child, whom, though they had taken him to everything likely to attract a young intelligence, they had utterly failed to interest.

He knew what they were saying and thinking. "I am very, very sorry, father and mother," he said. "But please don't mind! – I can't help it. I should like the flowers very very much, if I didn't keep on thinking they'd be all withered in a few days!"

---

1 baffle] evasive or perplexing reply.
2 one.....luminaries] Hardy noted Matthew Arnold's essay, "Pagan and Mediæval Religious Sentiment", which says: "The ideal, cheerful, sensuous pagan life is not sick or sorry."

V.-VI.

THE unnoticed lives that the pair had hitherto led began, from the day of the suspended wedding onwards, to be observed and discussed by other persons than Arabella. The society of Spring Street and the neighbourhood generally did not understand, and probably could not have been made to understand, Sue and Jude's private minds, emotions, positions, and fears. The curious facts of a child coming to them unexpectedly, who called Jude father, and Sue mother, and a hitch in a marriage ceremony intended for quietness to be performed at a registrar's office, together with rumours of the undefended cases in the law-courts, bore only one translation to plain minds.

Little Time – for though he was formally turned into "Jude," the apt nickname stuck to him – would come home from school in the evening, and repeat inquiries and remarks that had been made to him by the other boys; and cause Sue, and Jude when he heard them, a great deal of pain and sadness.

The result was that shortly after the attempt at the registrar's the pair went off – to London it was believed – for several days, hiring somebody to look to the boy. When they came back they let it be understood indirectly, and with total indifference and weariness of mien, that they were legally married at last. Sue, who had previously been called Mrs. Bridehead, now openly adopted the name of Mrs. Fawley. Her dull, cowed, and listless manner for days seemed to substantiate all this.

But the mistake (as it was called) of their going away so secretly to do the business, kept up much of the mystery of their lives; and they found that they made not such advances with their neighbours as they had expected to do thereby. A living mystery was not much less interesting than a dead scandal.

The baker's lad and the grocer's boy, who at first had used to lift their hats gallantly to Sue, when they came to execute their errands, in these days no longer took the trouble to render her that homage, and the neighbouring artizans' wives looked straight along the pavement when they encountered her.

Nobody molested them, it is true; but an oppressive atmosphere began to encircle their souls, particularly after their excursion to the Show, as if that visit had brought some evil influence to bear on them.

And their temperaments were precisely of a kind to suffer from this atmosphere, and to be indisposed to lighten it by vigorous and open statements. Their apparent attempt at reparation had come too late to be effective.

The headstone and epitaph orders fell off: and two or three months later, when autumn came, Jude perceived that he would have to return to journey-work again, a course all the more unfortunate just now, in that he had not as yet cleared off the debt he had unavoidably incurred in the payment of the law-costs of the previous year.

One evening he sat down to share the common meal with Sue and the child as usual. "I am thinking," he said to her, "that I'll hold on here no longer. The life suits us, certainly; but if we could get away to a place where we are unknown, we should be lighter hearted, and have a better chance. And so I am afraid we must break it up here, however awkward for you, poor dear!"

Sue was always much affected at a picture of herself as an object of pity, and a tear came at this.

"Well – I am not sorry," said she presently. "I am much depressed at the way they look at me here. And you have been keeping on this house and furniture entirely for me and the boy! You don't want it yourself, and the expense is unnecessary. But whatever we do, wherever we go, you won't take him away from me, Jude dear? I could not let him go now! The cloud upon his young mind makes him so pathetic to me; I do hope to lift it some day! And he loves me so. You won't take him away from me?"

"Certainly I won't, dear little girl! We'll get nice lodgings, wherever we go. I shall be moving about probably – getting a job here and a job there."

"I shall do something too, of course, till – till —— Well, now I can't be useful in the lettering it behoves me to turn my hand to something else."

"Don't hurry about getting employment," he said regretfully. "I don't want you to do that. I wish you wouldn't, Sue. The boy and yourself are enough for you to attend to."

There was a knock at the door, and Jude answered it. Sue could hear the conversation:

"Is Mr. Fawley at home?.... Biles and Willis the building contractors sent me to know if you'll undertake the relettering of the Ten Commandments in a little church they've been restoring lately in the country near here."

Jude reflected, and said he could undertake it.

"It is not a very artistic job," continued the messenger. "The clergyman is a very old-fashioned chap, and he has refused to let anything more be done to the church than cleaning and repairing."

"Excellent old man!" said Sue to herself, who was sentimentally opposed to the horrors of over-restoration.

"The Ten Commandments are fixed to the east end," the messenger went on, "and they want doing up with the rest of the wall there, since he won't have them carted off as old materials belonging to the contractor, in the usual way of the trade."

A bargain as to terms was struck, and Jude came indoors. "There, you see," he said cheerfully. "One more job yet, at any rate, and you can help in it – at least you can try. We shall have all the church to ourselves, as the rest of the work is finished."

Next day Jude went out to the church, which was only two miles off. He found that what the contractor's clerk had said was true. The tables of the Jewish law[1] towered sternly over the utensils of Christian grace,[2] as the chief ornament of the chancel end, in the fine dry style of the last century. And as their framework was constructed of ornamental plaster they could not be taken down for repair. A portion, crumbled by damp, required renewal; and when this had been done, and the whole cleansed, he began to renew the lettering. On the second morning Sue came to see what assistance she could render, and also because they liked to be together.

The silence and emptiness of the building gave her confidence, and standing on a safe low platform erected by Jude, which she was nevertheless timid at mounting, she began painting in the letters of the first Table while he set about mending a portion of the second. She was quite pleased at her powers; she had acquired them in the days she painted illumined texts for the church-fitting shop at Christminster. Nobody seemed likely to disturb them; and the pleasant

---

1 table.....law] two boards inscribed with the Ten Commandments issued by God to Moses (Exodus 20:1-17).

2 utensils.....grace] utensils (e.g., dish and chalice) for Holy Communion.

twitter of birds, and rustle of October leafage, came in through an open window, and mingled with their talk.

They were not, however, to be left thus snug and peaceful for long. About half-past twelve there came footsteps on the gravel without. The old vicar and his churchwarden entered, and, coming up to see what was being done, seemed surprised to discover that a young woman was assisting. They passed on into an aisle, at which time the door again opened, and another figure entered – a small one, that of little Time, who was crying. Sue had told him where he might find her between school-hours, if he wished. She came down from her perch, and said, "What's the matter, my dear?"

"I couldn't stay to eat my dinner in school, because they said –" He described how some boys had taunted him about his nominal mother, and Sue, grieved, expressed her indignation to Jude aloft. The child went into the churchyard, and Sue returned to her work. Meanwhile the door had opened again, and there shuffled in with a business-like air the white-aproned woman who cleaned the church. Sue recognized her as one who had friends in Spring Street, whom she visited. The church-cleaner looked at Sue, gaped, and lifted her hands; she had evidently recognized Jude's companion as the latter had recognized her. Next came two ladies, and after talking to the charwoman they also moved forward, and as Sue stood reaching upward, watched her hand tracing the letters, and critically regarded her person in relief against the white wall, till she grew so nervous that she trembled visibly.

They went back to where the others were standing, talking in undertones: and one said – Sue could not hear which – "She's his wife, I suppose?"

"Some say Yes: some say No," was the reply from the charwoman.

"Not? Then she ought to be, or somebody's – that's very clear!"

"They've only been married a very few weeks, whether or no."

"A strange pair to be painting the Two Tables! I wonder Biles and Willis could think of such a thing as hiring those!"

The churchwarden supposed that Biles and Willis knew of nothing wrong, and then the other, who had been talking to the old woman, explained what she meant by calling them strange people.

The probable drift of the subdued conversation which followed was made plain by the churchwarden breaking into an anecdote, in a voice that everybody in the church could hear, though obviously suggested by the present situation:

"Well, now, it is a curious thing, but my grandfather told me a strange tale of a most immoral case that happened at the painting of the Commandments in a church out by Gaymead – which is quite within a walk of this one. In them days Commandments were mostly done in gilt letters on a black ground, and that's how they were out where I say, before the owld church was rebuilded. It must have been somewhere about a hundred years ago that them Commandments wanted doing up, just as ours do here, and they had to get men from Aldbrickham to do 'em. Now they wished to get the job finished by a particular Sunday, so the men had to work late Saturday night, against their will, for over-time was not paid then as 'tis now. There was no true religion in the country at that date, neither among pa'sons, clerks, nor people, and to keep the men up to their work the vicar had to let 'em have plenty of drink during the afternoon. As evening drawed on they sent for some more themselves; rum, by all account. It got later and later, and they got more and more fuddled, till at last they went a putting their rum-bottle and rummers upon the Communion table, and drawed up a trestle or two, and sate round comfortable, and poured out again right hearty bumpers.[1] No sooner had they tossed off their glasses than, so the story goes, they fell down senseless, one and all. How long they bode so they didn't know, but when they came to themselves there was a terrible thunderstorm a-raging, and they seemed to see in the gloom a dark figure with very thin legs and a curious voot,[2] a-standing on the ladder, and finishing their work. When it got daylight they could see that the work was really finished, and couldn't at all mind finishing it themselves. They went home, and the next thing they heard was that a great scandal had been caused in the church that Sunday morning, for when the people came and service began, all saw that the Ten Commandments wez painted with the 'Nots' left out. Decent people wouldn't attend service there for a long time, and the Bishop had to be sent for to re-consecrate the church. That's the tradition as I used to hear it as a child. You must take it for what it is wo'th, but this case to-day has reminded me o't, as I say."

---

1 bumpers] glasses filled to the brim.
2 voot] (dl.:) foot (the Devil's foot being cloven).

The visitors gave one more glance, as if to see whether Jude and Sue had left the Nots out likewise, and then severally left the church, even the old woman at last. Sue and Jude who had not stopped working, sent back the child to school, and remained without speaking; till, looking at her narrowly, he found she had been crying silently.

"Never mind, comrade!" he said. "I know what it is!"

"I can't *bear* that they, and everybody, should think people wicked because they may have chosen to live their own way! It is really these opinions that make the best intentioned people reckless, and actually become immoral!"

"Never be cast down! It was only a funny story."

"Ah, but we suggested it! I am afraid I have done you mischief, Jude, instead of helping you by coming!"

To have suggested such a story was certainly not very exhilarating, in a serious view of their position. However, in a few minutes Sue seemed to see that their position this morning had a ludicrous side, and wiping her eyes she laughed.

"It is droll, after all," she said, "that we two, of all people, with our queer history, should happen to be here doing this! You a reprobate, and I – in my condition.... O dear!" ... And with her hand over her eyes she laughed again silently and intermittently, till she was quite weak.

"That's better," said Jude gaily. "Now we are right again, aren't we, little girl!"

"O but it is serious, all the same!" she sighed as she took up the brush and righted herself. "But do you see they don't think we are married? They *won't* believe it! It is extraordinary!"

"I don't care whether they think so or not," said Jude. "I shan't take any more trouble to make them."

They sat down to lunch – which they had brought with them not to hinder time – and having eaten it were about to set to work anew when a man entered the church, and Jude recognized in him the contractor Willis. He beckoned to Jude, and spoke to him apart.

"Here – I've just had a complaint about this," he said, with rather breathless awkwardness. "I don't wish to go into the matter – as of course I didn't know what was going on – but I am afraid I must ask you and her to leave off, and let somebody else finish this! It is best, to avoid all unpleasantness. I'll pay you for the week, all the same."

Jude was too independent to make any fuss; and the contractor paid him, and left. Jude picked up his tools, and Sue cleansed her brush. Then their eyes met.

"How could we – be so simple – as to suppose we might do this!" said she, dropping to her tragic note. "Of course we ought not – I ought not – to have come!"

"I had no idea that anybody was going to intrude into such a lonely place and see us!" Jude returned. "Well, it can't be helped, dear; and of course I wouldn't wish to injure Willis's trade-connection by staying." They sat down passively for a few minutes, proceeded out of the church, and overtaking the boy pursued their thoughtful way to Aldbrickham.

Fawley had still a pretty zeal in the cause of education, and, as was natural with his experiences, he was active in furthering "equality of opportunity" by any humble means open to him. He had joined an Artizans' Mutual Improvement Society established in the town about the time of his arrival there; its members being young men of all creeds and denominations, including Churchmen, Congregationalists, Baptists, Unitarians, Positivists, and others – Agnostics[1] had scarcely been heard of at this time – their one common wish to enlarge their minds forming a sufficiently close bond of union. The subscription was small, and the room homely; and Jude's activity, uncustomary acquirements, and above all, singular intuition on what to read and how to set about it – begotten of his years of struggle against malignant stars – had led to his being placed on the committee.

A few evenings after his dismissal from the church repairs, and before he had obtained any more work to do, he went to attend a meeting of the aforesaid committee. It was late when he arrived: all the others had come, and as he entered they looked dubiously at him, and hardly uttered a word of greeting. He guessed that something bearing on himself had been either discussed or mooted. Some

---

1   Congregationalists.....Agnostics] Congregationalists: Protestants whose congrega-
tions are largely autonomous. Baptists: Protestants believing in adult baptism, usually by total immersion. Unitarians: members of a religious organisation believing in
God but denying the doctrine of the Holy Trinity (by denying the divinity of Jesus
and the Holy Ghost). Positivists: followers of the system of Auguste Comte, which,
denying metaphysics and theism, advocates empirical science and a "religion of
Humanity." Agnostics: then a recent term, coined by Thomas Huxley, to denote
people who do not know whether God exists.

ordinary business was transacted, and it was disclosed that the number of subscriptions had shown a sudden falling off for that quarter. One member – a really well-meaning and upright man – began speaking in enigmas about certain possible causes: that it behoved them to look well into their constitution; for if the committee were not respected, and had not at least, in their differences, a common standard of *conduct*, they would bring the institution to the ground. Nothing further was said in Jude's presence, but he knew what this meant; and turning to the table wrote a note resigning his office there and then.

Thus the supersensitive couple were more and more impelled to go away. And then bills were sent in, and the question arose, what could Jude do with his great-aunt's heavy old furniture, if he left the town to travel he knew not whither? This, and the necessity of ready money, compelled him to decide on an auction, much as he would have preferred to keep the venerable goods.

The day of the sale came on; and Sue for the last time cooked her own, the child's, and Jude's breakfast in the little house he had furnished. It chanced to be a wet day; moreover Sue was unwell, and not wishing to desert her poor Jude in such gloomy circumstances, for he was compelled to stay awhile, she acted on the suggestion of the auctioneer's man, and ensconced herself in an upper room, which could be emptied of its effects, and so kept closed to the bidders. Here Jude discovered her; and with the child, and their few trunks, baskets, and bundles, and two chairs and a table that were not in the sale, the two sat in meditative talk.

Footsteps began stamping up and down the bare stairs, the comers inspecting the goods, some of which were of so quaint and ancient a make as to acquire an adventitious value as art. Their door was tried once or twice, and to guard themselves against intrusion Jude wrote "Private" on a scrap of paper, and stuck it upon the panel.

They soon found that, instead of the furniture, their own personal histories and past conduct began to be discussed to an unexpected and intolerable extent by the intending bidders. It was not till now that they really discovered what a fools' paradise of supposed unrecognition they had been living in of late. Sue silently took her companion's hand, and with eyes on each other they heard these passing remarks – the quaint and mysterious personality of Father Time being a subject which formed a large ingredient in the hints and innuendoes. At length the auction began in the room below, whence they could hear each familiar article knocked down, the highly prized ones cheaply, the unconsidered at an unexpected price.

"People don't understand us," he sighed heavily. "I am glad we have decided to go."

"The question is, where to go."

"It ought to be to London. There one can live as one chooses."

"No – not London, dear! I know it well. We should be unhappy there."

"Why?"

"Can't you think?"

"Because Arabella is there?"

"That's the chief reason."

"But in the country I shall always be uneasy lest there should be some more of our late experience. And I don't care to lessen it by explaining, for one thing, all about the boy's history. To cut him off from his past I have determined to keep silence. I am sickened of ecclesiastical work now; and I shouldn't like to accept it, if offered me!"

"You ought to have learnt Classic. Gothic is barbaric art, after all. Pugin was wrong, and Wren was right.[1] Remember the interior of Christminster Cathedral – almost the first place in which we looked in each other's faces. Under the picturesqueness of those Norman details one can see the grotesque childishness of uncouth people trying to imitate the vanished Roman forms, remembered by dim tradition only."

"Yes – you have half converted me to that view by what you have said before. But one can work, and despise what one does. I must do something, if not church-gothic."

"I wish we could both follow an occupation in which personal circumstances don't count," she said, smiling up wistfully. "I am as disqualified for teaching as you are for ecclesiastical art. You must fall back upon railway stations, bridges, theatres, music-halls, hotels – everything that has no connection with conduct."

"I am not skilled in those.... I ought to take to bread-baking.

---

1   Pugin.....Wren.....] Augustus Pugin (1812-52), architect and advocate of the Gothic Revival. Sir Christopher Wren (1631-1723), architect of buildings in classical style.

I grew up in the baking business with aunt, you know. But even a baker must be conventional, to get customers."

"Unless he keeps a cake and gingerbread stall at markets and fairs, where people are gloriously indifferent to everything except the quality of the goods."

Their thoughts were diverted by the voice of the auctioneer: "Now this antique oak settle – a unique example of old English furniture, worthy the attention of all collectors!"

"That was my great-grandfather's," said Jude. "I wish we could have kept the poor old thing!"

One by one the articles went, and the afternoon passed away. Jude and the other two were getting tired and hungry, but after the conversation they had heard they were shy of going out while the purchasers were in their line of retreat. However, the later lots drew on, and it became necessary to emerge into the rain soon, to take on Sue's things to their temporary lodging.

"Now the next lot: two pairs of pigeons, all alive and plump – a nice pie for somebody for next Sunday's dinner!"

The impending sale of these birds had been the most trying suspense of the whole afternoon. They were Sue's pets, and when it was found that they could not possibly be kept, more sadness was caused than by parting from all the furniture. Sue tried to think away her tears as she heard the trifling sum that her dears were deemed to be worth advanced by small stages to the price at which they were finally knocked down. The purchaser was a neighbouring poulterer, and they were unquestionably doomed to die before the next market day.

Seeing her dissembled distress Jude kissed her, and said it was time to go and see if the lodgings were ready. He would go on with the boy, and fetch her soon.

When she was left alone she waited patiently, but Jude did not come back. At last she started, the coast being clear, and on passing the poulterer's shop, not far off, she saw her pigeons in a hamper by the door. An emotion at sight of them, assisted by the growing dusk of evening, caused her to act on impulse, and first looking around her quickly, she pulled out the peg which fastened down the cover, and went on. The cover was lifted from within, and the pigeons flew away with a clatter that brought the chagrined poulterer cursing and swearing to the door.

Sue reached the lodging trembling, and found Jude and the boy making it comfortable for her. "Do the buyers pay before they bring away the things?" she asked breathlessly.

"Yes, I think. Why?"

"Because, then, I've done such a wicked thing!" And she explained, in bitter contrition.

"I shall have to pay the poulterer for them if he doesn't catch them," said Jude. "But never mind. Don't fret about it, dear."

"It was so foolish of me! O why should Nature's law be mutual butchery!"

"Is it so, mother?" asked the boy intently.

"Yes!" said Sue vehemently.

"Well, they must take their chance, now, poor things," said Jude. "As soon as the sale-account is wound up, and our bills paid, we go."

"Where do we go to?" asked Time, in suspense.

"We must sail under sealed orders, that nobody may trace us.... We mustn't go to Alfredston, or to Melchester, or to Shaston, or to Christminster. Apart from those we may go anywhere."

"Why mustn't we go there, father?"

"Because of a cloud that has gathered over us; though 'we have wronged no man, corrupted no man, defrauded no man!' Though perhaps we have 'done that which was right in our own eyes.'"[1]

V.-VII.

FROM that week Jude Fawley and Sue walked no more in the town of Aldbrickham.

Whither they had gone nobody knew, chiefly because nobody cared to know. Any one sufficiently curious to trace the steps of such an obscure pair might have discovered without great trouble that they had taken advantage of his adaptive craftsmanship to enter on a shifting, almost nomadic, life, which was not without its pleasantness for a time.

Wherever Jude heard of freestone work to be done, thither he went, choosing by preference places remote from his old haunts and

---

1   'we have wronged.....eyes'] adapted from 2 Corinthians 7:2 and Judges 17:6.

Sue's. He laboured at a job, long or briefly, till it was finished; and then moved on.

Two whole years and a half passed thus. Sometimes he might have been found shaping the mullions of a country mansion, sometimes setting the parapet of a town-hall, sometimes ashlaring[1] an hotel at Sandbourne, sometimes a museum at Casterbridge, sometimes as far down as Exonbury, sometimes at Stoke-Barehills. Later still he was at Kennetbridge,[2] a thriving town not more than a dozen miles south of Marygreen, this being his nearest approach to the village where he was known; for he had a sensitive dread of being questioned as to his life and fortunes by those who had been acquainted with him during his ardent young manhood of study and promise, and his brief and unhappy married life at that time.

At some of these places he would be detained for months, at others only a few weeks. His curious and sudden antipathy to ecclesiastical work, both episcopal and nonconformist, which had risen in him when suffering under a smarting sense of misconception, remained with him in cold blood, less from any fear of renewed censure than from an ultra-conscientiousness which would not allow him to seek a living out of those who would disapprove of his ways; also, too, from a sense of inconsistency between his former dogmas and his present practice, hardly a shred of the beliefs with which he had first gone up to Christminster now remaining with him. He was mentally approaching the position which Sue had occupied when he first met her.

On a Saturday evening in May, nearly three years after Arabella's recognition of Sue and himself at the Agricultural Show, some of those who there encountered each other met again.

It was the spring fair at Kennetbridge, and, though this ancient trade-meeting had much dwindled from its dimensions of former times, the long straight street of the borough presented a lively scene about midday. At this hour a light trap, among other vehicles, was driven into the town by the north road, and up to the door of a temperance inn. There alighted two women, one the driver, an ordinary country person, the other a finely built figure in the deep mourning

---

1 ashlaring] adding a stone façade (usually to a brick wall).
2 Kennetbridge] Newbury, a market-town (on the River Kennet) in Berkshire.

of a widow. Her sombre suit, of pronounced cut, caused her to appear a little out of place in the medley and bustle of a provincial fair.

"I will just find out where it is, Anny," said the widow-lady to her companion, when the horse and cart had been taken by a man who came forward: "and then I'll come back, and meet you here: and we'll go in and have something to eat and drink. I begin to feel quite a sinking."

"With all my heart," said the other. "Though I would sooner have put up at the Chequers or The Jack. You can't get much at these temperance houses."

"Now, don't you give way to gluttonous desires, my child," said the woman in weeds[1] reprovingly. "This is the proper place. Very well: we'll meet in half-an-hour, unless you come with me to find out where the site of the new chapel is?"

"I don't care to. You can tell me."

The companions then went their several ways, the one in crape walking firmly along with a mien of disconnection from her miscellaneous surroundings. Making inquiries, she came to a hoarding, within which were excavations denoting the foundations of a building; and on the boards without one or two large posters announcing that the foundation-stone of the chapel about to be erected would be laid that afternoon at three o'clock by a London preacher of great popularity among his body.

Having ascertained thus much the immensely weeded widow retraced her steps, and gave herself leisure to observe the movements of the fair. By and by her attention was arrested by a little stall of cakes and gingerbreads, standing between the more pretentious erections of trestles and canvas. It was covered with an immaculate cloth, and tended by a young woman apparently unused to the business, she being accompanied by a boy with an octogenarian face, who assisted her.

"Upon my – senses!" murmured the widow to herself. "His wife Sue – if she is so!" She drew nearer to the stall. "How do you do, Mrs. Fawley?" she said blandly.

Sue changed colour and recognized Arabella through the crape veil.

---

1   weeds] "widow's weeds": mourning dress.

"How are you, Mrs. Cartlett?" she said stiffly. And then perceiving Arabella's garb her voice grew sympathetic in spite of herself. "What? – you have lost ——"

"My poor husband. Yes. He died suddenly, six weeks ago, leaving me none too well off, though he was a kind husband to me. But whatever profit there is in public-house keeping goes to them that brew the liquors, and not to them that retail 'em.... And you, my little old man! You don't know me, I expect?"

"Yes, I do. You be the woman I thought wer my mother for a bit, till I found you wasn't," replied Father Time, who had learned to use the Wessex tongue quite naturally by now.

"All right. Never mind. I am a friend."

"Juey," said Sue suddenly, "go down to the station platform with this tray – there's another train coming in, I think."

When he was gone Arabella continued: "He'll never be a beauty, will he, poor chap! Does he know I am his mother really?"

"No. He thinks there is some mystery about his parentage – that's all. Jude is going to tell him when he is a little older."

"But how do you come to be doing this? I am surprised."

"It is only a temporary occupation – a fancy of our while we are in a difficulty."

"Then you are living with him still?"

"Yes."

"Married?"

"Of course."

"Any children?"

"Two."

"And another coming soon, I see."

Sue writhed under the hard and direct questioning, and her tender little mouth began to quiver.

"Lord – I mean goodness gracious – what is there to cry about? Some folks would be proud enough!"

"It is not that I am ashamed – not as you think! But it seems such a terribly tragic thing to bring beings into the world – so presumptuous – that I question my right to do it sometimes!"

"Take it easy, my dear.... But you don't tell me why you do such a thing as this? Jude used to be a proud sort of chap – above any business almost, leave alone keeping a standing."[1]

"Perhaps my husband has altered a little since then. I am sure he is not proud now!" And Sue's lips quivered again. "I am doing this because he caught a chill early in the year while putting up some stonework of a music-hall, at Quartershot, which he had to do in the rain, the work having to be executed by a fixed day. He is better than he was; but it has been a long, weary time! We have had an old widow friend with us to help us through it; but she's leaving soon."

"Well, I am respectable too, thank God, and of a serious way of thinking since my loss. Why did you choose to sell gingerbreads?"

"That's a pure accident. He was brought up to the baking business, and it occurred to him to try his hand at these, which he can make without coming out of doors. We call them Christminster cakes. They are a great success."

"I never saw any like 'em. Why, they are windows and towers, and pinnacles! And upon my word they are very nice." She had helped herself, and was unceremoniously munching one of the cakes.

"Yes. They are reminiscences of the Christminster Colleges. Traceried windows, and cloisters, you see. It was a whim of his to do them in pastry."

"Still harping on Christminster – even in his cakes!" laughed Arabella. "Just like Jude. A ruling passion. What a queer fellow he is, and always will be!"

Sue sighed, and she looked her distress at hearing him criticized.

"Don't you think he is? Come now; you do, though you are so fond of him!"

"Of course Christminster is a sort of fixed vision with him, which I suppose he'll never be cured of believing in. He still thinks it a great centre of high and fearless thought, instead of what it is, a nest of commonplace schoolmasters, whose characteristic is timid obsequiousness to tradition."

Arabella was quizzing[2] Sue with more regard of how she was speaking than of what she was saying. "How odd to hear a woman selling cakes talk like that!" she said. "Why don't you go back to school-keeping?"

---

1 standing] stall.
2 quizzing] looking inquisitively and superciliously.

Sue shook her head. "They won't have me."

"Because of the divorce, I suppose?"

"That and other things. And there is no reason to wish it. We gave up all ambition, and were never so happy in our lives till his illness came."

"Where are you living?"

"I don't care to say."

"Here in Kennetbridge?"

Sue's manner showed Arabella that her random guess was right.

"Here comes the boy back again," continued Arabella. "My boy and Jude's!"

Sue's eyes darted a spark. "You needn't throw that in my face!" she cried.

"Very well – though I half feel as if I should like to have him with me! ... But Lord, I don't want to take him from 'ee – ever I should sin to speak so profane – though I should think you must have enough of your own! He's in very good hands, that I know; and I am not the woman to find fault with what the Lord has ordained. I've reached a more resigned frame of mind."

"Indeed! I wish I had been able to do so."

"You should try," replied the widow, from the serene heights of a mind conscious not only of spiritual but of social superiority. "I make no boast of my awakening, but I'm not what I was. After Cartlett's death I was passing the chapel in the street next ours, and went into it for shelter from a shower of rain. I felt a need of some sort of support under my loss, and, as 'twas righter than gin, I took to going there regular, and found it a great comfort. But I've left London now, you know, and at present I am living at Alfredston, with my friend Anny, to be near my own old country. I'm not come here to the fair to-day. There's to be the foundation-stone of a new chapel laid this afternoon by a popular London preacher, and I drove over with Anny. Now I must go back to meet her."

Then Arabella wished Sue good-bye, and went on.

V.-VIII.

In the afternoon Sue and the other people bustling about Kennetbridge fair could hear singing inside the placarded hoarding further
down the street. Those who peeped through the opening saw a crowd
of persons in broadcloth, with hymn-books in their hands, standing
round the excavations for the new chapel-walls. Arabella Cartlett and
her weeds stood among them. She had a clear, powerful voice, which
could be distinctly heard with the rest, rising and falling to the tune,
her inflated bosom being also seen doing likewise.

It was two hours later on the same day that Anny and Mrs.
Cartlett, having had tea at the Temperance hotel, started on their
return journey across the high and open country which stretches
between Kennetbridge and Alfredston. Arabella was in a thoughtful
mood; but her thoughts were not of the new chapel, as Anny at first
surmised.

"No – it is something else," at last said Arabella sullenly. "I came
here to-day never thinking of anybody but poor Cartlett, or of anything but spreading the Gospel by means of this new tabernacle
they've begun this afternoon. But something has happened to turn
my mind another way quite. Anny, I've heard of un again, and I've
seen *her!*"

"Who?"

"I've heard of Jude, and I've seen his wife. And ever since, do what
I will, and though I sung the hymns wi' all my strength, I have not
been able to help thinking about 'n; which I've no right to do as a
chapel member."

"Can't ye fix your mind upon what was said by the London
preacher to-day, and try to get rid of your wandering fancies that
way?"

"I do. But my wicked heart will ramble off in spite of myself!"

"Well – I know what it is to have a wanton mind o' my own, too!
If you on'y knew what I do dream sometimes o' nights quite against
my wishes, you'd say I had my struggles!" (Anny too, had grown
rather serious of late, her lover having jilted her.)

"What shall I do about it?" urged Arabella morbidly.

"You could take a lock of your late-lost husband's hair, and have it
made into a mourning brooch, and look at it every hour of the day."

"I haven't a morsel! – and if I had 'twould be no good.... After all that's said about the comforts of this religion, I wish I had Jude back again!"

"You must fight valiant against the feeling, since he's another's. And I've heard that another good thing for it, when it afflicts volupshious widows, is to go to your husband's grave in the dusk of evening, and stand a long while a-bowed down."

"Pooh! I know as well as you what I must do; only I don't do it!"

They drove in silence along the straight road till they were within the horizon of Marygreen, which lay not far to the left of their route. They came to the junction of the highway and the cross-lane leading to that village, whose church-tower could be seen athwart the hollow. When they got yet further on, and were passing the lonely house in which Arabella and Jude had lived during the first months of their marriage, and where the pig-killing had taken place, she could control herself no longer.

"He's more mine than hers!" she burst out. "What right has she to him, I should like to know! I'd take him from her if I could!"

"Fie, Abby! And your husband only a month gone! Pray against it!"

"Be damned if I do! Feelings are feelings! I won't be a creeping hypocrite any longer – so there!"

Arabella had hastily drawn from her pocket a bundle of tracts which she had brought with her to distribute at the fair, and of which she had given away several. As she spoke she flung the whole remainder of the packet into the hedge. "I've tried that sort o' physic and have failed wi' it. I must be as I was born!"

"Hush! You be excited, dear! Now you come along home quiet, and have a cup of tea, and don't let us talk about un no more. We won't come out this road again, as it leads to where he is, because it inflames 'ee so. You'll be all right again soon."

Arabella did calm herself down by degrees; and they crossed the Ridge-way. When they began to descend the long, straight hill, they saw plodding along in front of them an elderly man of spare stature and thoughtful gait. In his hand he carried a basket; and there was a touch of slovenliness in his attire, together with that indefinable something in his whole appearance which suggested one who was his own housekeeper, purveyor, confidant, and friend, through possessing nobody else at all in the world to act in those capacities for him. The remainder of the journey was down-hill, and guessing him to be going to Alfredston, they offered him a lift, which he accepted.

Arabella looked at him, and looked again, till at length she spoke. "If I don't mistake I am talking to Mr. Phillotson?"

The wayfarer faced round and regarded her in turn. "Yes; my name is Phillotson," he said. "But I don't recognize you, ma'am."

"I remember you well enough when you used to be schoolmaster out at Marygreen, and I one of your scholars. I used to walk up there from Cresscombe every day, because we had only a mistress down at our place, and you taught better. But you wouldn't remember me as I should you? – Arabella Donn."

He shook his head. "No," he said politely, "I don't recall the name. And I should hardly recognize in your present portly self the slim school child no doubt you were then."

"Well, I always had plenty of flesh on my bones. However, I am staying down here with some friends at present. You know, I suppose, who I married?"

"No."

"Jude Fawley – also a scholar of yours – at least a night scholar – for some little time I think? And known to you afterwards, if I am not mistaken."

"Dear me, dear me," said Phillotson, starting out of his stiffness. "*You* Fawley's wife? To be sure – he had a wife! And he – I understood ——"

"Divorced her – as you did yours – perhaps for better reasons."

"Indeed?"

"Well – he med have been right in doing it – right for both; for I soon married again, and all went pretty straight till my husband died lately. But you – you were decidedly wrong!"

"No," said Phillotson, with sudden testiness. "I would rather not talk of this, but – I am convinced I did only what was right, and just, and moral. I have suffered for my act and opinions, but I hold to them; though her loss was a loss to me in more ways than one!"

"You lost your school and good income through her, did you not?"

"I don't care to talk of it. I have recently come back here – to Marygreen, I mean."

"You are keeping the school there again, just as formerly?"

The pressure of a sadness that would out unsealed him. "I am there," he replied. "Just as formerly, no. Merely on sufferance. It was a last resource – a small thing to return to after my move upwards, and my long indulged hopes – a returning to zero, with all its humiliations. But it is a refuge. I like the seclusion of the place, and the vicar having known me before my so-called eccentric conduct towards my wife had ruined my reputation as a schoolmaster, he accepted my services when all other schools were closed against me. However, although I take fifty pounds a year here after taking above two hundred elsewhere, I prefer it to running the risk of having my old domestic experiences raked up against me, as I should do if I tried to make a move."

"Right you are. A contented mind is a continual feast.[1] She has done no better."

"She is not doing well, you mean?"

"I met her by accident at Kennetbridge this very day, and she is anything but thriving. Her husband is ill, and she anxious. You made a fool of a mistake about her, I tell 'ee again, and the harm you did yourself by dirting your own nest serves you right, excusing the liberty."

"How?"

"She was innocent."

"But nonsense! They did not even defend the case!"

"That was because they didn't care to. She was quite innocent of what obtained you your freedom, at the time you obtained it. I saw her just afterwards, and proved it to myself completely by talking to her."

Phillotson grasped the edge of the spring-cart, and appeared to be much stressed and worried by the information. "Still – she wanted to go," he said.

"Yes. But you shouldn't have let her. That's the only way with these fanciful women that chaw high[2] – innocent or guilty. She'd have come round in time. We all do! Custom does it! it's all the same in the

---

1   a contented.....feast] "he that is of a merry heart *hath* a continual feast" (Proverbs 15:15).

2   chaw high] (dl.:) seem fastidious, have exalted notions.

end! However, I think she's fond of her man still – whatever he med be of her. You were too quick about her. *I* shouldn't have let her go! I should have kept her chained on – her spirit for kicking would have been broke soon enough! There's nothing like bondage and a stone-deaf taskmaster for taming us women. Besides, you've got the laws on your side. Moses knew. Don't you call to mind what he says?"

"Not for the moment, ma'am, I regret to say."

"Call yourself a schoolmaster! I used to think o't when they read it in church, and I was carrying on a bit. 'Then shall the man be guiltless; but the woman shall bear her iniquity.'[1] Damn rough on us women; but we must grin and put up wi' it! – Haw haw! – Well; she's got her deserts now."

"Yes," said Phillotson, with biting sadness. "Cruelty is the law pervading all nature and society; and we can't get out of it if we would!"

"Well – don't you forget to try it next time, old man."

"I cannot answer you, madam. I have never known much of womankind."

They had now reached the low levels bordering Alfredston, and passing through the outskirts approached a mill, to which Phillotson said his errand led him; whereupon they drew up, and he alighted, bidding them good-night in a preoccupied mood.

In the meantime Sue, though remarkably successful in her provisional business at Kennetbridge fair, had lost the temporary brightness which had begun to sit upon her sadness on account of that success. When all her "Christminster" cakes had been disposed of she took upon her arm the empty basket, and the cloth which had covered the standing she had hired, and giving the other things to the boy left the street with him. They followed a lane to a distance of half a mile, till they met an old woman carrying a child in short clothes, and leading a toddler in the other hand.

Sue kissed the children, and said, "How is he now?"

"Still better!" returned Mrs. Edlin cheerfully. "Before you are ill your husband will be well enough – don't 'ee trouble."

They turned, and came to some old, dun-tiled[2] cottages with gardens and fruit-trees. Into one of these they entered by lifting the latch

---

1 "Then.....iniquity"] adapted from Numbers 5:31.

2 dun-tiled] with tiles of greyish-brown colour.

without knocking, and were at once in the general living-room. Here they greeted Jude, who was sitting in an arm-chair, the increased delicacy of his normally delicate features, and the childishly expectant look in his eyes, being alone sufficient to show that he had been passing through a severe illness.

"What – you have sold them all?" he said, a gleam of interest lighting up his face.

"Yes. Arcades, gables, east windows and all." She told him the pecuniary results, and then hesitated. At last, when they were left alone, she informed him of the unexpected meeting with Arabella, and the latter's widowhood.

Jude was discomposed. "What – is she living here?" he said.

"No; at Alfredston," said Sue.

Jude's countenance remained clouded. "I thought I had better tell you?" she continued, kissing him anxiously.

"Yes.... Dear me! Arabella not in the depths of London, but down here! It is only a little over a dozen miles across the country to Alfredston. What is she doing there?"

She told him all she knew. "She has taken to chapel-going," Sue added; "and talks accordingly."

"Well," said Jude, "perhaps it is for the best that we have almost decided to move on. I feel much better to-day, and shall be well enough to leave in a week or two. Then Mrs. Edlin can go home again – dear faithful old soul – the only friend we have in the world!"

"Where do you think to go to?" Sue asked, a tearfulness in her tones.

Then Jude confessed what was in his mind. He said it would surprise her, perhaps, after his having resolutely avoided all the old places for so long. But one thing and another had made him think a great deal of Christminster lately, and, if she didn't mind, he would like to go back there. Why should they care if they were known? It was oversensitive of them to mind so much. They could go on selling cakes there, for that matter, if he couldn't work. He had no sense of shame at mere poverty; and perhaps he would be as strong as ever soon, and able to set up stone-cutting for himself there.

"Why should you care so much for Christminster?" she said pensively. "Christminster cares nothing for you, poor dear!"

"Well, I do, I can't help it. I love the place – although I know how it hates all men like me – the so-called Self-taught, – how it scorns our laboured acquisitions, when it should be the first to respect them; how it sneers at our false quantities[1] and mispronunciations, when it should say, I see you want help, my poor friend! ... Nevertheless, it is the centre of the universe to me, because of my early dream: and nothing can alter it. Perhaps it will soon wake up, and be generous. I pray so! ... I should like to go back to live there – perhaps to die there! In two or three weeks I might, I think. It will then be June, and I should like to be there by a particular day."

His hope that he was recovering proved so far well grounded that in three weeks they had arrived in the city of many memories; were actually treading its pavements, receiving the reflection of the sunshine from its wasting walls.

---

1   false quantities] with incorrect rendering of long and short syllables or vowels.

PART SIXTH

AT CHRISTMINSTER AGAIN

"…*And she humbled her body greatly, and all the places of her joy she filled with her torn hair.*"[1] — ESTHER (Apoc.).

"*There are two who decline, a woman and I,*
And enjoy our death in the darkness here."[2]
— R. BROWNING.

AT CHRISTMINSTER AGAIN

VI.-I.

ON their arrival the station was lively with straw-hatted young men, welcoming young girls who bore a remarkable family likeness to their welcomers, and who were dressed up in the brightest and lightest of raiment.

"The place seems gay," said Sue. "Why – it is Remembrance Day![3] – Jude – how sly of you – you came to-day on purpose!"

"Yes," said Jude quietly, as he took charge of the small child, and told Arabella's boy to keep close to them, Sue attending to their own eldest. "I thought we might as well come to-day as on any other."

"But I am afraid it will depress you!" she said looking anxiously at him, up and down.

"O, I mustn't let it interfere with our business; and we have a good deal to do before we shall be settled here. The first thing is lodgings."

Having left their luggage and his tools at the station they proceed-

---

1 "*And.....hair*"] Apocrypha: Esther 14:2.
2 "*There are.....here*"] from stanza 10 of Browning's poem "Too Late."
3 Remembrance Day] Encaenia, Oxford University's annual commemoration-day at the end of the academic year, when founders and benefactors are remembered, and famous people are given honorary degrees.

ed on foot up the familiar street, the holiday people all drifting in the same direction. Reaching the Fourways they were about to turn off to where accommodation was likely to be found when, looking at the clock and the hurrying crowd, Jude said: "Let us go and see the procession, and never mind the lodgings just now? We can get them afterwards."

"Oughtn't we to get a house over heads first?" she asked.

But his soul seemed full of the anniversary, and together they went down Chief Street, their smallest child in Jude's arms, Sue leading her little girl, and Arabella's boy walking thoughtfully and silently beside them. Crowds of pretty sisters in airy costumes, and meekly ignorant parents, who had known no College in their youth, were under convoy in the same direction by brothers and sons bearing the opinion written large on them, that no properly qualified human beings had lived on earth till they came to grace it here and now.

"My failure is reflected on me by every one of those young fellows," said Jude. "A lesson on presumption is awaiting me to-day! – Humiliation Day for me! ... If you, my dear darling, hadn't come to my rescue, I should have gone to the dogs with despair!"

She saw from his face that he was getting into one of his tempestuous, self-harrowing moods. "It would have been better if we had gone at once about our own affairs, dear," she answered. "I am sure this sight will awaken old sorrows in you, and do no good!"

"Well – we are near; we will see it now," said he.

They turned in on the left by the church with the Italian porch, whose helical columns[1] were heavily draped with creepers, and pursued the lane till there arose on Jude's sight the circular theatre[2] with that well-known lantern above it, which stood in his mind as the sad symbol of his abandoned hopes; for it was from that outlook that he had finally surveyed the City of Colleges on the afternoon of his great meditation, which convinced him at last of the futility of his attempt to be a son of the University.

To-day, in the open space stretching between this building and the nearest college, stood a crowd of expectant people. A passage was kept clear through their midst by two barriers of timber, extending from

---

1 church.....helical columns] St Mary's, the University church, which has distinctive spiral (helical) columns.
2 circular theatre] the Sheldonian.

the door of the college to the door of the large building[1] between it and the theatre.

"Here is the place – they are just going to pass!" cried Jude in sudden excitement. And pushing his way to the front he took up a position close to the barrier, still hugging the youngest child in his arms, while Sue and the others kept immediately behind him. The crowd filled in at their back, and fell to talking, joking, and laughing as carriage after carriage drew up at the lower door of the college, and solemn stately figures in blood-red robes[2] began to alight. The sky had grown overcast and livid, and thunder rumbled now and then.

Father Time shuddered. "It do seem like the Judgment Day!"[3] he whispered.

"They are only learned Doctors," said Sue.

While they waited big drops of rain fell on their heads and shoulders, and the delay grew tedious. Sue again wished not to stay.

"They won't be long now," said Jude, without turning his head.

But the procession did not come forth, and somebody in the crowd, to pass the time, looked at the façade of the nearest college, and said he wondered what was meant by the Latin inscription[4] in its midst. Jude, who stood near the inquirer, explained it, and finding that the people all round him were listening with interest, went on to describe the carving of the frieze (which he had studied years before), and to criticize some details of masonry in other college fronts about the city.

The idle crowd, including the two policemen at the doors, stared like the Lycaonians at Paul,[5] for Jude was apt to get too enthusiastic over any subject in hand, and they seemed to wonder how the stranger should know more about the buildings of their town than they themselves did; till one of them said: "Why, I know that man; he used to work here years ago – Jude Fawley, that's his name! Don't you

---

1   large building] the Bodleian Library.
2   blood-red robes] of people who hold doctorates.
3   Judgment Day] the time of God's final judgment of all people (Revelation 20:12).
4   inscription] Above the main doorway of Hertford College is a sculpted medallion depicting a hart drinking, encircled by the Latin inscription, "Ad fontes aquarum sicut cervus anhelat": "As the hart panteth after the water brooks" (Psalms 42:1).
5   Lycaonians at Paul] The people of Lycaonia, being amazed when St Paul healed a cripple, said: "The gods are come down to us in the likeness of men" (Acts 14:11).

mind[1] he used to be nicknamed Tutor of St. Slums, d'ye mind? –
because he aimed at that line o' business? He's married, I suppose,
then, and that's his child he's carrying. Taylor would know him, as he
knows everybody."

The speaker was a man named Jack Stagg, with whom Jude had
formerly worked in repairing the college masonries; Tinker Taylor
was seen to be standing near. Having his attention called the latter
cried across the barriers to Jude: "You've honoured us by coming
back again, my friend!"

Jude nodded.

"An' you don't seem to have done any great things for yourself by
going away?"

Jude assented to this also.

"Except found more months to fill!" This came in a new voice,
and Jude recognized its owner to be Uncle Joe, another mason whom
he had known.

Jude replied good-humouredly that he could not dispute it; and
from remark to remark something like a general conversation arose
between him and the crowd of idlers, during which Tinker Taylor
asked Jude if he remembered the Apostles' Creed in Latin still, and the
night of the challenge in the public-house.

"But Fortune didn't lie that way?" threw in Joe. "Yer powers wasn't
enough to carry 'ee through?"

"Don't answer them any more!" entreated Sue.

"I don't think I like Christminster!" murmured little Time mournfully, as he stood submerged and invisible in the crowd.

But finding himself the centre of curiosity, quizzing, and comment, Jude was not inclined to shrink from open declarations of what
he had no great reason to be ashamed of; and in a little while was
stimulated to say in a loud voice to the listening throng generally:

"It is a difficult question, my friends, for any young man – that
question I had to grapple with, and which thousands are weighing at
the present moment in these uprising times – whether to follow
uncritically the track he finds himself in, without considering his aptness for it, or to consider what his aptness or bent may be, and re-
shape his course accordingly. I tried to do the latter, and I failed. But I

---

1   mind] (dl.:) remember.

don't admit that my failure proved my view to be a wrong one, or that my success would have made it a right one; though that's how we appraise such attempts nowadays – I mean, not by their essential soundness, but by their accidental outcomes. If I had ended by becoming like one of these gentlemen in red and black that we saw dropping in here by now, everybody would have said: 'See how wise that young man was, to follow the bent of his nature!' But having ended no better than I began they say: 'See what a fool that fellow was in following a freak of his fancy!'

"However it was my poverty and not my will that consented to be beaten.[1] It takes two or three generations to do what I tried to do in one; and my impulses – affections – vices perhaps they should be called – were too strong not to hamper a man without advantages; who should be as cold-blooded as a fish and as selfish as a pig to have a really good chance of being one of his country's worthies. You may ridicule me – I am quite willing that you should – I am a fit subject, no doubt. But I think if you knew what I have gone through these last few years you would rather pity me. And if they knew" – he nodded towards the college at which the Dons were severally arriving – "it is just possible they would do the same."

"He do look ill and worn-out, it is true!" said a woman.

Sue's face grew more emotional; but though she stood close to Jude she was screened.

"I may do some good before I am dead – be a sort of success as a frightful example of what not to do; and so illustrate a moral story," continued Jude, beginning to grow bitter, though he had opened serenely enough. "I was, perhaps, after all, a paltry victim to the spirit of mental and social restlessness, that makes so many unhappy in these days!"

"Don't tell them that!" whispered Sue with tears, at perceiving Jude's state of mind. "You weren't that. You struggled nobly to acquire knowledge, and only the meanest souls in the world would blame you!"

Jude shifted the child into a more easy position on his arm, and concluded: "And what I appear, a sick and poor man, is not the worst

---

1 my poverty.....consented.....] "My poverty, but not my will consents" (Shakespeare: *Romeo and Juliet*, V.i.75).

of me. I am in a chaos of principles – groping in the dark – acting by instinct and not after example. Eight or nine years ago when I came here first, I had a neat stock of fixed opinions, but they dropped away one by one; and the further I get the less sure I am. I doubt if I have anything more for my present rule of life than following inclinations which do me and nobody else any harm, and actually give pleasure to those I love best. There, gentlemen, since you wanted to know how I was getting on, I have told you. Much good may it do you! I cannot explain further here. I perceive there is something wrong somewhere in our social formulas: what it is can only be discovered by men or women with greater insight than mine, – if, indeed, they ever discover it – at least in our time. 'For who knoweth what is good for man in this life? – and who can tell a man what shall be after him under the sun?'"[1]

"Hear, hear," said the populace.

"Well preached!" said Tinker Taylor. And privately to his neighbours: "Why, one of them jobbing pa'sons swarming about here, that takes the services when our head Reverends want a holiday, wouldn't ha' discoursed such doctrine for less than a guinea[2] down? Hey? I'll take my oath not one o' em would! And then he must have had it wrote down for 'n. And this only a working man!"

As a sort of objective commentary on Jude's remarks there drove up at this moment with a belated Doctor, robed and panting, a cab whose horse failed to stop at the exact point required for setting down the hirer, who jumped out and entered the door. The driver, alighting, began to kick the animal in the belly.

"If that can be done," said Jude, "at college gates in the most religious and educational city in the world, what shall we say as to how far we've got?"

"Order!" said one of the policemen, who had been engaged with a comrade in opening the large doors opposite the college. "Keep yer tongue quiet, my man, while the procession passes." The rain came on more heavily, and all who had umbrellas opened them. Jude was not one of these, and Sue only possessed a small one, half sunshade. She had grown pale, though Jude did not notice it then.

---

1 'For who.....sun?'] adapted from Ecclesiastes 6:12.

2 guinea] coin or amount to the value of one pound and one shilling (now one pound and five pence).

"Let us go on, dear," she whispered, endeavouring to shelter him. "We haven't any lodgings yet, remember, and all our things are at the station; and you are by no means well yet. I am afraid this wet will hurt you!"

"They are coming now. Just a moment, and I'll go!" said he.

A peal of six bells struck out, human faces began to crowd the windows around, and the procession of Heads of Houses and new Doctors emerged, their red and black gowned forms passing across the field of Jude's vision like inaccessible planets across an object glass.[1]

As they went their names were called by knowing informants; and when they reached the old round theatre of Wren a cheer rose high.

"Let's go that way!" cried Jude, and though it now rained steadily he seemed not to know it, and took them round to the Theatre. Here they stood upon the straw that was laid to drown the discordant noise of wheels, where the quaint and frost-eaten stone busts encircling the building looked with pallid grimness on the proceedings, and in particular at the bedraggled Jude, Sue, and their children, as at ludicrous persons who had no business there.

"I wish I could get in!" he said to her fervidly. "Listen – I may catch a few words of the Latin speech by staying here; the windows are open."

However, beyond the peals of the organ, and the shouts and hurrahs between each piece of oratory, Jude's standing in the wet did not bring much Latin to his intelligence more than, now and then, a sonorous word in *um* or *ibus*.

"Well – I'm an outsider to the end of my days!" he sighed after a while. "Now I'll go, my patient Sue. How good of you to wait in the rain all this time – to gratify my infatuation! I'll never care any more about the infernal cursed place, upon my soul I won't! But what made you tremble so when we were at the barrier? And how pale you are, Sue!"

"I saw Richard amongst the people on the other side."

"Ah – did you!"

"He is evidently come up to Jerusalem to see the festival[2] like the rest of us: and on that account is probably living not so very far away.

---

1 object glass] magnifying lens in telescope.
2 He.....festival] Jesus went to Jerusalem for the Feast of the Passover (Luke 2:41-2).

He had the same hankering for the University that you had, in a milder form. I don't think he saw me, though he must have heard you speaking to the crowd. But he seemed not to notice."

"Well – suppose he did. Your mind is free from worries about him now, my Sue?"

"Yes, I suppose so. But I am weak. Although I know it is all right with our plans, I felt a curious dread of him; an awe, or terror, of conventions I don't believe in. It comes over me at times like a sort of creeping paralysis, and makes me so sad!"

"You are getting tired, Sue. O – I forgot,[1] darling! Yes, we'll go on at once."

They started in quest of the lodging, and at last found something that seemed to promise well, in Mildew Lane – a spot which to Jude was irresistible – though to Sue it was not so fascinating – a narrow lane close to the back of a college, but having no communication with it. The little houses were darkened to gloom by the high collegiate buildings, within which life was so far removed from that of the people in the lane as if it had been on the opposite sides of the globe; yet only a thickness of wall divided them. Two or three of the houses had notices of rooms to let, and the newcomers knocked at the door of one, which a woman opened.

"Ah – listen!" said Jude suddenly, instead of addressing her.

"What?"

"Why the bells – what church can that be? The tones are familiar."

Another peal of bells had begun to sound out at some distance off.

"I don't know!" said the landlady tartly. "Did you knock to ask that?"

"No; for lodgings," said Jude, coming to himself.

The householder scrutinized Sue a moment. "We haven't any to let," said she, shutting the door.

Jude looked discomfited, and the boy distressed. "Now, Jude," said Sue, "let me try. You don't know the way."

They found a second place hard by; but here the occupier, observing not only Sue, but the boy and the small children, said civilly, "I am sorry to say we don't let where there are children;" and also closed the door.

---

1   forgot] forgot her pregnant state.

The small child squared its mouth and cried silently, with an instinct that trouble loomed. The boy sighed. "I don't like Christminster!" he said. "Are the great old houses gaols?"

"No, colleges," said Jude; "which perhaps you'll study in some day."

"I'd rather not!" the boy rejoined.

"Now we'll try again," said Sue. "I'll pull my cloak more round me .... Leaving Kennetbridge for this place is like coming from Caiaphas to Pilate![1] ... How do I look now, dear?"

"Nobody would notice it now," said Jude.

There was one other house, and they tried a third time. The woman was more amiable; but she had little room to spare, and could only agree to take in Sue and the children if her husband could go elsewhere. This arrangement they perforce adopted, in the stress from delaying their search till so late. They came to terms with her, though her price was rather high for their pockets. But they could not afford to be critical, till Jude had time to get a more permanent abode; and in this house Sue took possession of a back room on the second floor with an inner closet-room for the children. Jude stayed and had a cup of tea; and was pleased to find that the window commanded the back of one of the colleges. Kissing all four he went to get a few necessaries and look for lodgings for himself.

When he was gone the landlady came up to talk a little with Sue, and gather something of the circumstances of the family she had taken in. Sue had not the art of prevarication, and, after admitting several facts as to their late difficulties and wanderings, she was startled by the landlady saying suddenly:

"Are you really a married woman?"

Sue hesitated; and then impulsively told the woman that her husband and herself had each been unhappy in their first marriages, after which, terrified at the thought of a second irrevocable union, and lest the conditions of the contract should kill their love, yet wishing to be together, they had literally not found the courage to repeat it, though they had attempted it two or three times. Therefore, though in her own sense of the words she was a married woman, in the landlady's sense she was not.

---

1 from Caiaphas to Pilate] from bad to worse. Jesus was first tried by Caiaphas, the Jewish High Priest; then he was tried by Pontious Pilate, the Roman Procurator, who sentenced him to death (Matthew 26-7).

The housewife looked embarrassed, and went downstairs. Sue sat by the window in a reverie, watching the rain. Her quiet was broken by the noise of some one entering the house, and then the voices of a man and woman in conversation in the passage below. The landlady's husband had arrived, and she was explaining to him the incoming of the lodgers during his absence.

His voice rose in sudden anger. "Now who wants such a woman here? And perhaps a confinement! ... Besides, didn't I say I wouldn't have children? The hall and stairs fresh painted, to be kicked about by them! You must have known all was not straight with 'em – coming like that. Taking in a family when I said a single man."

The wife expostulated, but, as it seemed, the husband insisted on his point; for presently a tap came to Sue's door, and the woman appeared.

"I am sorry to tell you, ma'am," she said, "that I can't let you have the room for the week after all. My husband objects: and therefore I must ask you to go. I don't mind your staying over to-night, as it is getting late in the afternoon; but I shall be glad if you can leave early in the morning."

Though she knew that she was entitled to the lodging for a week, Sue did not wish to create a disturbance between the wife and husband, and she said she would leave as requested. When the landlady had gone Sue looked out of the window again. Finding that the rain had ceased she proposed to the boy that, after putting the little ones to bed, they should go out and search about for another place, and bespeak it for the morrow, so as not to be so hard driven then as they had been that day.

Therefore, instead of unpacking her boxes, which had just been sent on from the station by Jude, they sallied out into the damp, though not unpleasant, streets, Sue resolving not to disturb her husband with the news of her notice to quit while he was perhaps worried in obtaining a lodging for himself. In the company of the boy she wandered into this street and into that; but though she tried a dozen different houses she fared far worse alone than she had fared in Jude's company, and could get nobody to promise her a room for the following day. Every householder looked askance at such a woman and child inquiring for accommodation in the gloom.

"I ought not to be born, ought I?" said the boy with misgiving.

Thoroughly tired at last Sue returned to the place where she was not welcome, but where at least she had temporary shelter. In her absence Jude had left his address; but knowing how weak he still was she adhered to her determination not to disturb him till the next day.

VI.-II.

Sue sat looking at the bare floor of the room, the house being little more than an old intramural[1] cottage, and then she regarded the scene outside the uncurtained window. At some distance opposite, the outer walls of Sarcophagus College – silent, black and windowless – threw their four centuries of gloom, bigotry, and decay into the little room she occupied, shutting out the moonlight by night and the sun by day. The outlines of Rubric College[2] also were discernible beyond the other, and the tower of a third further off still. She thought of the strange operation of a simple-minded man's ruling passion, that it should have led Jude, who loved her and the children so tenderly, to place them here in this depressing purlieu,[3] because he was still haunted by his dream. Even now he did not distinctly hear the freezing negative that those scholared walls had echoed to his desire.

The failure to find another lodging, and the lack of room in this house for his father, had made a deep impression on the boy; – a brooding undemonstrative horror seemed to have seized him. The silence was broken by his saying: "Mother, *what* shall we do tomorrow!"

"I don't know!" said Sue despondently. "I am afraid this will trouble your father."

"I wish father was quite well, and there had been room for him! Then it wouldn't matter so much! Poor father!"

"It wouldn't!"

"Can I do anything?"

"No! All is trouble, adversity and suffering!"

"Father went away to give us children room, didn't he?"

---

1 intramural] within the old city walls.
2 Sarcophagus.....Rubric] Lincoln College (possibly) and Brasenose.
3 purlieu] area.

"Partly."

"It would be better to be out o' the world than in it, wouldn't it?"

"It would almost, dear."

"'Tis because of us children, too, isn't it, that you can't get a good lodging?"

"Well – people do object to children sometimes."

"Then if children make so much trouble, who do people have 'em?"

"O — because it is a law of nature."

"But we don't ask to be born?"

"No indeed."

"And what makes it worse with me is that you are not my real mother, and you needn't have had me unless you liked. I oughtn't to have come to 'ee – that's the real truth! I troubled 'em in Australia, and I trouble folk here. I wish I hadn't been born!"

"You couldn't help it, my dear."

"I think that whenever children be born that are not wanted they should be killed directly, before their souls come to 'em, and not allowed to grow big and walk about!"

Sue did not reply. She was doubtfully pondering how to treat this too reflective child.

She at last concluded that, so far as circumstances permitted, she would be honest and candid with one who entered into her difficulties like an aged friend.

"There is going to be another in our family soon," she hesitatingly remarked.

"How?"

"There is going to be another baby."

"What!" The boy jumped up wildly. "O God, mother, you've never a-sent for another; and such trouble with what you've got!"

"Yes, I have, I am sorry to say!" murmured Sue, her eyes glistening with suspended tears.

The boy burst out weeping. "O you don't care, you don't care!" he cried in bitter reproach. "How *ever* could you, mother, be so wicked and cruel as this, when you needn't have done it till we was better off, and father well! – To bring us all into *more* trouble! No room for us, and father a-forced to go away, and we turned out to-morrow; and yet you be going to have another of us soon! ... 'Tis done o' purpose!

– 'tis – 'tis!" He walked up and down sobbing.

"Y-you must forgive me, little Jude!" she pleaded, her bosom heaving now as much as the boy's. "I can't explain – I will when you are older. It does seem – as if I had done it on purpose, now we are in these difficulties! I can't explain, dear! But it – is not quite on purpose – I can't help it!"[1]

"Yes it is – it must be! For nobody would interfere with us, like that, unless you agreed! I won't forgive you, ever, ever! I'll never believe you care for me, or father, or any of us any more!"

He got up, and went away into the closet adjoining her room, in which a bed had been spread on the floor. There she heard him say: "If we children was gone there'd be no trouble at all!"

"Don't think that, dear," she cried, rather peremptorily. "But go to sleep!"

The following morning she awoke at a little past six, and decided to get up and run across before breakfast to the inn which Jude had informed her to be his quarters, to tell him what had happened before he went out. She arose softly, to avoid disturbing the children, who, as she knew, must be fatigued by their exertions of yesterday.

She found Jude at breakfast in the obscure tavern he had chosen as a counterpoise to the expense of her lodging: and she explained to him her homelessness. He had been so anxious about her all night, he said. Somehow, now it was morning, the request to leave the lodgings did not seem such a depressing incident as it had seemed the night before, nor did even her failure to find another place affect her so deeply as at first. Jude agreed with her that it would not be worth while to insist upon her right to stay a week, but to take immediate steps for removal.

"You must all come to this inn for a day or two," he said. "It is a rough place, and it will not be so nice for the children, but we shall have more time to look round. There are plenty of lodgings in the suburbs – in my old quarter of Beersheba. Have breakfast with me now you are here, my bird. You are sure you are well? There will be plenty of time to get back and prepare the children's meal before they wake. In fact, I'll go with you."

---

1   I can't help it!] Remarkably, Sue appears to be unaware of the contraceptive sponge, which had been quite widely publicised.

She joined Jude in a hasty meal, and in a quarter of an hour they started together, resolving to clear out from Sue's too respectable lodging immediately. On reaching the place and going upstairs she found that all was quiet in the children's room, and called to the landlady in timorous tones to please bring up the tea-kettle and something for their breakfast. This was perfunctorily done, and producing a couple of eggs which she had brought with her she put them into the boiling kettle, and summoned Jude to watch them for the youngsters, while she went to call them, it being now about half-past eight o'clock.

Jude stood bending over the kettle, with his watch in his hand, timing the eggs, so that his back was turned to the little inner chamber where the children lay. A shriek from Sue suddenly caused him to start round. He saw that the door of the room, or rather closet – which had seemed to go heavily upon its hinges as she pushed it back – was open, and that Sue had sunk to the floor just within it. Hastening forward to pick her up he turned his eyes to the little bed spread on the boards; no children were there. He looked in bewilderment round the room. At the back of the door were fixed two hooks for hanging garments, and from these the forms of the two youngest children were suspended, by a piece of box-cord round each of their necks, while from a nail a few yards off the body of little Jude was hanging in a similar manner. An overturned chair was near the elder boy, and his glazed eyes were staring into the room; but those of the girl and baby boy were closed.

Half paralyzed by the grotesque and hideous horror of the scene he let Sue lie, cut the cords with his pocket-knife and threw the three children on the bed; but the feel of their bodies in the momentary handling seemed to say that they were dead. He caught up Sue, who was in fainting fits, and put her on the bed in the other room, after which he breathlessly summoned the landlady and ran out for a doctor.

When he got back Sue had come to herself, and the two helpless women, bending over the children in wild efforts to restore them, and the triplet of little corpses, formed a scene which overthrew his self-command. The nearest surgeon came in, but, as Jude had inferred, his presence was superfluous. The children were past saving, for though their bodies were still barely cold it was conjectured that they had been hanging more than an hour. The probability held by the parents later on, when they were able to reason on the case, was that the elder boy, on waking, looked into the outer room for Sue, and, finding her absent, was thrown into a fit of aggravated despondency that the events and information of the evening before had induced in his morbid temperament. Moreover a piece of paper was found upon the floor, on which was written, in the boy's hand, with the bit of lead pencil that he carried:

"Done because we are too menny."

At sight of this Sue's nerves utterly gave way, an awful conviction that her discourse with the boy had been the main cause of the tragedy, throwing her into a convulsive agony which knew no abatement. They carried her away against her wish to a room on the lower floor; and there she lay, her slight figure shaken with her gasps, and her eyes staring at the ceiling, the woman of the house vainly trying to soothe her.

They could hear from this chamber the people moving about above, and she implored to be allowed to go back, and was only kept from doing so by the assurance that, if there were any hope, her presence might do harm, and the reminder that it was necessary to take care of herself lest she should endanger a coming life. Her inquiries were incessant, and at last Jude came down and told here there was no hope. As soon as she could speak she informed him what she had said to the boy, and how she thought herself the cause of this.

"No," said Jude. "It was in his nature to do it. The doctor says there are such boys springing up amongst us – boys of a sort unknown in the last generation – the outcome of new views of life. They seem to see all its terrors before they are old enough to have staying power to resist them. He says it is the beginning of the coming universal wish not to live. He's an advanced man, the doctor: but he can give no consolation to ——"

Jude had kept back his own grief on account of her; but he now broke down; and this stimulated Sue to efforts of sympathy which in some degree distracted her from her poignant self-reproach. When everybody was gone, she was allowed to see the children.

The boy's face expressed the whole tale of their situation. On that little shape had converged all the inauspiciousness and shadow which had darkened the first union of Jude, and all the accidents, mistakes, fears, errors of the last. He was their nodal point, their focus, their expression in a single term. For the rashness of those parents he had groaned, for their ill-assortment he had quaked, and for the misfortunes of these he had died.

When the house was silent, and they could do nothing but await the coroner's inquest, a subdued, large, low voice spread into the air of the room from behind the heavy walls at the back.

"What is it?" said Sue, her spasmodic breathing suspended.

"The organ of the College chapel. The organist practising I suppose. It's the anthem from the seventy-third Psalm; 'Truly God is loving unto Israel.'"

She sobbed again. "O my babies! They had done no harm! Why should they have been taken away, and not I!"

There was another stillness – broken at last by two persons in conversation somewhere without.

"They are talking about us, no doubt!" moaned Sue. "'We are made a spectacle unto the world, and to angels, and to men!'"[1]

Jude listened – "No – they are not talking of us," he said. "They are two clergymen of different views, arguing about the eastward position."[2]

Then another silence, till she was seized with another uncontrollable fit of grief. "There is something external to us which says, 'You shan't!' First it said, 'You shan't learn!' Then it said, 'You shan't labour!' Now it says, 'You shan't love!'"

He tried to soothe her by saying, "That's bitter of you, darling."

"But it's true!"

Thus they waited, and she went back again to her room. The baby's frock, shoes, and socks, which had been lying on a chair at the time of his death, she would not now have removed, though Jude would fain have got them out of her sight. But whenever he touched

---

1 'We are made....men!'] St Paul says this of the apostles: 1 Corinthians 4:9.

2 eastward position] Some clergymen thought that in Holy Communion the priest should face east (as the Tractarians held), others that the priest should face west. (For the 1912 edition, Hardy augmented the text at this point. After "eastward position.", Jude exclaims: "Good God – the eastward position, and all creation groaning!")

them she implored him to let them lie, and burst out almost savagely at the woman of the house when she also attempted to put them away.

Jude dreaded her dull apathetic silences almost more than her paroxysms. "Why don't you speak to me, Jude?" she said after one of these. "Don't turn away from me! I can't bear the loneliness of being out of your looks!"

"There, dear; here I am," he said, putting his face close to hers.

"Yes.... O my comrade, our perfect union – our two-in-oneness – is now stained with blood!"

"Shadowed by death – that's all."

"Ah; but it was I who incited him really, though I didn't know I was doing it! I talked to the child as one should only talk to people of mature age. I said the world was against us, that it was better to be out of life than in it at this price; and he took it literally. And I told him I was going to have another child. It upset him. O how bitterly he upbraided me!"

"Why did you do it, Sue?"

"I can't tell. It was that I wanted to be truthful. I couldn't bear deceiving him as to the facts of life. And yet I wasn't truthful, for with a false delicacy I told him too obscurely. – Why was I half wiser than my fellow-women? and not entirely wiser! Why didn't I tell him pleasant untruths, instead of half realities? It was my want of self-control, so that I could neither conceal things nor reveal them!"

"Your plan might have been a good one for the majority of cases; only in our peculiar case it chanced to work badly perhaps. He must have known sooner or later."

"And I was just making my baby darling a new frock; and now I shall never see him in it, and never talk to him any more! ... My eyes are so swollen that I can scarcely see; and yet little more than a year ago I called myself happy! We went about loving each other too much – indulging ourselves to utter selfishness with each other! We said – do you remember? – that we would make a virtue of joy. I said it was Nature's intention, Nature's law and *raison d'être*[1] that we should be joyful in what instincts she afforded us – instincts which civilization and taken upon itself to thwart. What dreadful things I said! And

---

1   *raison d'être*] (Fr.:) reason for being; justification.

now Fate has given us this stab in the back for being such fools as to take Nature at her word!"

She sank into a quiet contemplation, till she said, "It is best, perhaps, that they should be gone. – Yes – I see it is! Better that they should be plucked fresh than stay to wither away miserably!"

"Yes," replied Jude. "Some say that the elders should rejoice when their children die in infancy."

"But they don't know! ... O my babies, my babies, could you be alive now! You may say the boy wished to be out of life, or he wouldn't have done it. It was not unreasonable for him to die: it was part of his incurably sad nature, poor little fellow! But then the others – my *own* children and yours!"

Again Sue looked at the hanging little frock, and at the socks and shoes; and her figure quivered like a string. "I am a pitiable creature," she said, "good neither for earth nor heaven any more! I am driven out of my mind by things! What ought to be done?" She stared at Jude, and tightly held his hand.

"Nothing can be done," he replied. "Things are as they are, and will be brought to their destined issue."

She paused. "Yes! Who said that?" she asked heavily.

"It comes in the chorus of the *Agamemnon*.[1] It has been in my mind continually since this happened."

"My poor Jude – how you've missed everything! – you more than I, for I did get you! To think you should know that by your unassisted reading, and yet be in poverty and despair!"

After such momentary diversions her grief would return in a wave.

The jury duly came and viewed the bodies, the inquest was held; and next arrived the melancholy morning of the funeral. Accounts in the newspapers had brought to the spot curious idlers, who stood apparently counting the window-panes and the stones of the walls. Doubt of the real relations of the couple added zest to their curiosity. Sue had declared that she would follow the two little ones to the grave, but at the last moment she gave way, and the coffins were quietly carried out of the house while she was lying down. Jude got into the vehicle, and it drove away, much to the relief of the landlord,

---

1 *Agamemnon*] in lines 67-8 of Æschylus's tragic drama about the accursed house of Atreus.

who now had only Sue and her luggage remaining on his hands, which he hoped to be also clear of later on in the day, and so to have freed his house from the exasperating notoriety it had acquired during the week through his wife's unlucky admission of these strangers. In the afternoon he privately consulted with the owner of the house, and they agreed that if any objection to it arose from the tragedy which had occurred there they would try to get its number changed.

When Jude had seen the two little boxes – one containing little Jude, and the other the two smallest – deposited in the earth he hastened back to Sue, who was still in her room, and he therefore did not disturb her just then. Feeling anxious, however, he went again about four o'clock. The woman thought she was still lying down, but returned to him to say that she was not in her bedroom after all. Her hat and jacket, too, were missing: she had gone out. Jude hurried off to the public-house where he was sleeping. She had not been there. Then bethinking himself of possibilities he went along the road to the cemetery, which he entered, and crossed to where the interments had recently taken place. The idlers who had followed to the spot by reason of the tragedy were all gone now. A man with a shovel in his hands was attempting to earth in the common grave of the three children, but his arm was held back by an expostulating woman who stood in the half-filled hole. It was Sue, whose coloured clothing, which she had never thought of changing for the mourning he had bought, suggested to the eye a deeper grief than the conventional garb of bereavement could express.

"He's filling them in, and he shan't till I've seen my little ones again!" she cried wildly when she saw Jude. "I want to see them once more. O Jude – please Jude – I want to see them! I didn't know you would let them be taken away while I was asleep! You said perhaps I should see them once more before they were screwed down; and then you didn't, but took them away! O Jude, you are cruel to me too!"

"She's been wanting me to dig out the grave again, and let her get to the coffins," said the man with the spade. "She ought to be took home, by the look o' her. She is hardly responsible, poor thing, seemingly. Can't dig 'em up again now, ma'am. Do ye go home with your husband, and take it quiet, and thank God that there'll be another soon to swage[1] yer grief."

---

1 swage] assuage; reduce.

But Sue kept asking: "Can't I see them once more – just once! Can't I ? Only just one little minute, Jude? It would not take long! And I should be so glad, Jude! I will be so good, and not disobey you ever any more, Jude, if you will let me? I would go home quietly afterwards, and not want to see them any more! Can't I? Why can't I?"

Thus she went on. Jude was thrown into such acute sorrow that he almost felt he would try to get the man to accede. But it could do no good, and might make her still worse; and he saw that it was imperative to get her home at once. So he coaxed her, and whispered tenderly, and put his arm round her to support her; till she helplessly gave in, and was induced to leave the cemetery.

He wished to obtain a fly to take her back in, but economy being so imperative she deprecated his doing so, and they walked along slowly, Jude in black crape, she in brown and red clothing. They were to have gone to a new lodging that afternoon, but Jude saw that it was not practicable, and in course of time they entered the now hated house. Sue was at once got to bed, and the doctor sent for.

Jude waited all the evening downstairs. At a very late hour the intelligence was brought to him that a child had been prematurely born, and that it, like the others, was a corpse.

VI.-III.

SUE was convalescent, though she had hoped for death, and Jude had again obtained work at his old trade. They were in other lodgings now, in the direction of Beersheba, and not far from the ceremonial Church of Saint Silas.

They would sit silent, more bodeful of the direct antagonism of things than of their insensate and stolid obstructiveness. Vague and quaint imaginings had haunted Sue, in the days when her intellect scintillated like a star, that the world resembled a stanza or melody composed in a dream; it was wonderfully excellent to the half-aroused intelligence, but hopelessly absurd at the full waking; that the First Cause worked automatically like a somnambulist, and not reflectively like a sage; that at the framing of the terrestrial conditions there seemed never to have been contemplated such a development of emotional perceptiveness among the creatures subject to those conditions as that reached by thinking and educated humanity.[1] But affliction makes opposing forces loom anthropomorphous; and those ideas were now exchanged for a sense of Jude and herself fleeing from a persecutor.

"We must conform!" she said mournfully. "All the ancient wrath of the Power above us has been vented upon us, His poor creatures, and we must submit. There is no choice. We must. It is no use fighting against God!"

"It is only against man and senseless circumstance," said Jude.

"True!" she murmured. "What have I been thinking of! I am getting as superstitious as a savage! ... But whoever or whatever our foe may be, I am cowed into submission. I have no more fighting strength left; no more enterprize. I am beaten, beaten! ... 'We are made a spectacle unto the world, and to angels, and to men!'[2] I am always saying that now."

"I feel the same!"

"What shall we do? You are in work now; but remember, it may only be because our history and relations are not absolutely known .... Possibly, if they knew our marriage had not been formalized they would turn you out of your job as they did at Aldbrickham!"

"I hardly know. Perhaps they would hardly do that. However, I think that we ought to make it legal now – as soon as you are able to go out."

"You think we ought?"

"Certainly."

And Jude fell into thought. "I have seemed to myself lately," he said, "to belong to that vast band of men shunned by the virtuous – the men called seducers. It amazes me when I think of it! I have not been conscious of it, or of any wrong-doing towards you, whom I love more than myself. Yet I *am* one of those men! I wonder if any other of them are the same purblind, simple creatures as I? ... Yes, Sue – that's what I am. I seduced you.... You were a distinct type – a refined creature, intended by Nature to be left intact. But I couldn't leave you alone!"

---

1 that the First Cause.....humanity] Hardy, too, held these ideas; they receive fullest expression in *The Dynasts*.

2 'We.....men!'] again, 1 Corinthians 4:9.

"No, no, Jude!" she said quickly. "Don't reproach yourself with being what you are not. If anybody is to blame it is I."

"I supported you in your resolve to leave Phillotson; and without me perhaps you wouldn't have urged him to let you go."

"I should have, just the same. As to ourselves, the fact of our not having entered into a legal contract is the saving feature in our union. We have thereby avoided insulting, as it were, the solemnity of our first marriages."

"Solemnity?" Jude looked at her with some surprise, and grew conscious that she was not the Sue of their earlier time.

"Yes," she said, with a little quiver in her words, "I have had dreadful fears, a dreadful sense of my own insolence of action. I have thought – that I am still his wife!"

"Whose?"

"Richard's."

"Good God, dearest! – why?"

"O I can't explain! Only the thought comes to me."

"It is your weakness – a sick fancy, without reason or meaning! Don't let it trouble you."

Sue sighed uneasily.

As a set-off against such discussions as these there had come an improvement in their pecuniary position, which earlier in their experience would have made them cheerful. Jude had quite unexpectedly found good employment at his old trade almost directly he arrived, the summer weather suiting his fragile constitution; and outwardly his days went on with that monotonous uniformity which is in itself so grateful after vicissitude. People seemed to have forgotten that he had ever shown any awkward aberrancies: and he daily mounted to the parapets and copings[1] of colleges he could never enter, and renewed the crumbling freestones[2] of mullioned windows he would never look from, as if he had known no wish to do otherwise.

There was this change in him; that he did not often go to any service at the churches now. One thing troubled him more than any other; that Sue and himself had mentally travelled in opposite directions since the tragedy: events which had enlarged his own views of

---

1 copings] topmost masonry or brickwork in walls.
2 freestones] sections of easily-wrought stone.

life, laws, customs, and dogmas, had not operated in the same manner on Sue's. She was no longer the same as in the independent days, when her intellect played like lambent lightning over conventions and formalities which he at that time respected, though he did not now.

On a particular Sunday evening he came in rather late. She was not at home, but she soon returned, when he found her silent and meditative.

"What are you thinking of, little woman?" he asked curiously.

"O I can't tell clearly! I have thought that we have been selfish, careless, even impious, in our courses, you and I. Our life has been a vain attempt at self-delight. But self-abnegation is the higher road. We should mortify the flesh – the terrible flesh – the curse of Adam!"

"Sue!" he murmured. "What has come over you?"

"We ought to be continually sacrificing ourselves on the altar of duty! But I have always striven to do what has pleased me. I well deserved the scourging I have got! I wish something would take the evil right out of me, and all my monstrous errors, and all my sinful ways!"

"Sue – my own too suffering dear! – there's no evil woman in you. Your natural instincts are perfectly healthy; not quite so impassioned, perhaps, as I could wish; but good, and dear, and pure. And as I have often said, you are absolutely the most ethereal, least sensual woman I ever knew to exist without inhuman sexlessness. Why do you talk in such a changed way? We have not been selfish, except when no one could profit by our being otherwise. You used to say that human nature was noble and long-suffering, not vile and corrupt, and at last I thought you spoke truly. And now you seem to take such a much lower view!"

"I want a humble heart; and a chastened mind; and I have never had them yet!"

"You have been fearless, both as a thinker and as a feeler, and you deserved more admiration than I gave. I was too full of narrow dogmas at that time to see it."

"Don't say that, Jude! I wish my every fearless word and thought could be rooted out of my history. Self-renunciation – that's everything! I cannot humiliate myself too much. I should like to prick myself all over with pins and bleed out the badness that's in me!"

"Hush!" he said, pressing her little face against his breast as if she were an infant. "It is bereavement that has brought you to this! Such remorse is not for you, my sensitive plant,[1] but for the wicked ones of the earth – who never feel it!"

"I ought not to stay like this," she murmured, when she had remained in the position a long while.

"Why not?"

"It is indulgence."

"Still on the same tack! But is there anything better on earth than that we should love one another?"

"Yes. It depends on the sort of love; and yours – ours – is the wrong."

"I won't have it, Sue! Come, when do you wish our marriage to be signed in a vestry?"

She paused, and looked up uneasily. "Never," she whispered.

Not knowing the whole of her meaning he took the objection serenely, and said nothing. Several minutes elapsed, and he thought she had fallen asleep; but he spoke softly, and found that she was wide awake all the time. She sat upright and sighed.

"There is a strange, indescribable perfume or atmosphere about you to-night, Sue," he said. "I mean not only mentally, but about your clothes, also. A sort of vegetable scent, which I seem to know, yet cannot remember."

"It is incense."

"Incense?"

"I have been to the service of St. Silas', and I was in the fumes of it."

"Oh – St. Silas'."

"Yes. I go there sometimes."

"Indeed. You go there!"

"You see, Jude, it is lonely here in the week-day mornings, when you are at work, and I think and think of – of my –" She stopped till she could control the lumpiness of her throat. "And I have taken to go in there, as it is so near."

"O well – of course, I say nothing against it. Only it is odd, for

---

1   sensitive plant] plant (e.g. *Mimosa pudica*) that closes or declines its leaves when touched; a subject of Shelley's poem "The Sensitive Plant."

you. They little think what sort of chiel is amang them!"[1]

"What do you mean, Jude?"

"Well – a sceptic, to be plain."

"How can you pain me so, dear Jude, in my trouble! Yet I know you didn't mean it. But you ought not to say that."

"I won't. But I am much surprised!"

"Well – I want to tell you something else, Jude. You won't be angry, will you? I have thought of it a good deal since my babies died. I don't think I ought to be your wife – or as your wife – any longer."

"What? ... But you *are!*"

"From your point of view; but ——"

"Of course we were afraid of the ceremony, and a good many others would have been in our places, with such strong reasons for fears. But experience has proved how we misjudged ourselves, and overrated our infirmities; and if you are beginning to respect rites and ceremonies, as you seem to be, I wonder you don't say it shall be carried out instantly? You certainly *are* my wife, Sue, in all but law. What do you mean by what you said?"

"I don't think I am!"

"Not? But suppose we *had* gone through the ceremony? Would you feel that you were than?"

"No. I should not feel even then that I was. I should feel worse than I do now."

"Why so – in the name of all that's perverse, my dear?"

"Because I am Richard's."

"Ah – you hinted that absurd fancy to me before!"

"It was only an impression with me then; I feel more and more convinced as time goes on that – I belong to him, or to nobody."

"My good heavens – how we are changing places!"

"Yes. Perhaps so."

Some few days later, in the dusk of the summer evening, they were sitting in the same small room downstairs, when a knock came to the front door of the carpenter's house where they were lodging, and in a few moments there was a tap at the door of their room. Before they

---

1 chiel is amang them] "A chiel's amang you takin' notes" (from Robert Burns's poem, "On the Late Captain Grose's Peregrinations thro' Scotland"). A "chiel" is a fellow.

could open it the comer did so, and a woman's form appeared.

"Is Mr. Fawley here?"

Jude and Sue started as he mechanically replied in the affirmative, for the voice was Arabella's.

He formally requested her to come in, and she sat down in the window bench, where they could distinctly see her outline against the light; but no characteristic that enabled them to estimate her general aspect and air. Yet something seemed to denote that she was not quite so comfortably circumstanced, nor so bouncingly attired, as she had been during Cartlett's lifetime.

The three attempted an awkward conversation about the tragedy, of which Jude had felt it to be his duty to inform her immediately, though she had never replied to his letter.

"I have just come from the cemetery," she said. "I inquired and found the child's grave. I couldn't come to the funeral – thank you for inviting me all the same. I read all about it in the papers, and I felt I wasn't wanted.... No – I couldn't come to the funeral," repeated Arabella, who, seeming utterly unable to reach the ideal of a catastrophic manner, fumbled with reiterations. "But I am glad I found the grave. As 'tis your trade, Jude, you'll be able to put up a handsome stone to 'em."

"I shall put up a headstone," said Jude drearily.

"He was my child, and naturally I feel for him."

"I hope so. We all did."

"The others that weren't mine I didn't feel so much for, as was natural."

"Of course."

A sigh came from the dark corner where Sue sat.

"I had often wished I had mine with me," continued Mrs. Cartlett. "Perhaps 'twouldn't have happened then! But of course I didn't wish to take him away from your wife."

"I am not his wife," came from Sue.

The unexpectedness of her words struck Jude silent.

"O I beg your pardon, I'm sure," said Arabella. "I thought you were!"

Jude had known from the quality of Sue's tone that her new and transcendental views lurked in her words; but all except their obvious meaning was, naturally, missed by Arabella. The latter, after evincing that she was struck by Sue's avowal, recovered herself, and went on to talk with placid bluntness about "her" boy, for whom, though in his lifetime she had shown no care at all, she now exhibited a ceremonial mournfulness that was apparently sustaining to the conscience. She alluded to the past, and in making some remark appealed again to Sue. There was no answer: Sue had invisibly left the room.

"She said she was not your wife?" resumed Arabella in another voice. "Why should she do that?"

"I cannot inform you," said Jude shortly.

"She is, isn't she? She once told me so."

"I don't criticize what she says."

"Ah – I see! Well, my time is up. I am staying here to-night, and thought I could do no less than call, after our mutual affliction. I am sleeping at the place where I used to be barmaid, and to-morrow I go back to Alfredston. Father is come home again, and I am living with him."

"He has returned from Australia?" said Jude with languid curiosity.

"Yes. Couldn't get on there. Had a rough time of it. Mother died of dys – what do you call it – in the hot weather, and father and two of the young ones have just got back. He has got a cottage near the old place, and for the present I am keeping house for him."

Jude's former wife had maintained a stereotyped manner of strict good breeding even now that Sue was gone, and limited her stay to a number of minutes that should accord with the highest respectability. When she had departed Jude, much relieved, went to the stairs and called Sue – feeling anxious as to what had become of her.

There was no answer, and the carpenter who kept the lodgings said she had not come in. Jude was puzzled, and became quite alarmed at her absence, for the hour was growing late. The carpenter called his wife, who conjectured that Sue might have gone to St. Silas' church, as she often went there.

"Surely not at this time o' night?" said Jude. "It is shut."

"She knows somebody who keeps the key, and she has it whenever she wants it."

"How long has she been going on with this?"

"Oh, some few weeks, I think."

Jude went vaguely in the direction of the church, which he had never once approached since he lived out that way years before, when his young opinions were more mystical than they were now. The spot was deserted, but the door was certainly unfastened; he lifted the latch without notice, and pushing the door to behind him, stood absolutely still inside. The prevalent silence seemed to contain a faint sound, explicable as a breathing, or a sobbing, which came from the other end of the building. The floor-cloth deadened his footsteps as he moved in that direction through the obscurity, which was broken only by the faintest reflected night-light from without.

High overhead, above the chancel steps, Jude could discern a huge, solidly constructed Latin cross[1] – as large, probably, as the original it was designed to commemorate. It seemed to be suspended in the air by invisible wires; it was set with large jewels, which faintly glimmered in some weak ray caught from outside, as the cross swayed to and fro in a silent and scarcely perceptible motion. Underneath, upon the floor, lay what appeared to be a heap of black clothes, and from this was repeated the sobbing that he had heard before. It was his Sue's form, prostrate on the paving.

"Sue!" he whispered.

Something white disclosed itself; she had turned up her face.

"What – do you want with me here, Jude?" she said. "You shouldn't come! I wanted to be alone! Why did you intrude here?"

"How can you ask!" he retorted in quick reproach, for his full heart was wounded to its centre at this attitude of hers towards him. "Why do I come? Who has a right to come, I should like to know, if I have not! I, who love you better than my own self – better – O far better – than you have loved me! What made you leave me to come here alone?"

"Don't criticize me, Jude – I can't bear it! – I have often told you so. You must take me as I am. I am a wretch – broken by my distractions! I couldn't *bear* it when Arabella came – I felt so utterly miserable I had to come away. She seems to be your wife still, and Richard to be my husband!"

"But they are nothing to us!"

"Yes, dear friend, they are. I see marriage differently now. My babies have been taken from me to show me this! Arabella's child killing mine was a judgement – the right slaying the wrong. What,

1   cross] More than a century later, this ornate cross still hung over the chancel steps of St Barnabas' Church.

what shall I do! I am such a vile creature – too worthless to mix with ordinary human beings!"

"This is terrible!" said Jude, almost in tears. "It is monstrous and unnatural for you to be so remorseful when you have done no wrong!"

"Ah – you don't know my badness!"

He returned vehemently: "I do! Every atom and dreg of it! You make me hate Christianity, or mysticism, or Sacerdotalism,[1] or whatever it may be called, if it's that which has caused this deterioration in you. That a woman-poet, a woman-seer, a woman whose soul shone like a diamond – whom all the wise of the world would have been proud of, if they could have known you – should degrade herself like this! I am glad I had nothing to do with Divinity – damn glad – if it's going to ruin you in this way!"

"You are angry, Jude, and unkind to me, and don't see how things are."

"Then come along home with me, dearest, and perhaps I shall. I am over-burdened – and you, too, are unhinged just now." He put his arm round her and lifted her; but though she came, she preferred to walk without his support.

"I don't dislike you, Jude," she said in a sweet and imploring voice. "I love you as much as ever! Only – I ought not to love you – any more. O I must not any more!"

"I can't own it."

"But I have made up my mind that I am not your wife! I belong to him – I sacramentally joined myself to him for life. Nothing can alter it!"

"But surely we are man and wife, if ever two people were in this world? Nature's own marriage it is, unquestionably!"

"But not Heaven's. Another was made for me there, and ratified eternally in the church at Melchester."

"Sue, Sue – affliction has brought you to this unreasonable state! After converting me to your views on so many things, to find you suddenly turn to the right-about like this – for no reason whatever, confounding all you have formerly said through sentiment merely! You root out of me what little affection and reverence I had left in

---

1 Sacerdotalism] the doctrine that priests, when ordained, gain supernatural powers.

me for the Church as an old acquaintance.... What I can't understand in you is your extraordinary blindness now to your old logic. Is it peculiar to you, or is it common to woman? Is a woman a thinking unit at all, or a fraction always wanting its integer?[1] How you argued that marriage was only a clumsy contract – which it is – how you showed all the objections to it – all the absurdities! If two and two made four when we were happy together, surely they make four now? I can't understand it, I repeat!"

"Ah, dear Jude; that's because you are like a totally deaf man observing people listening to music. You say 'What are they regarding? Nothing is there.' But something is."

"That is a hard saying from you; and not a true parallel! You threw off old husks of prejudices, and taught me to do it; and now you go back upon yourself. I confess I am utterly stultified in my estimate of you."

"Dear friend, my only friend, don't be hard with me! I can't help being as I am, and I am convinced I am right – that I see the light at last. But O, how to profit by it!"

They walked along a few more steps till they were outside the building, and she had returned the key. "Can this be the girl," said Jude when she came back, feeling a slight renewal of elasticity now that he was in the open street; "can this be the girl who brought the Pagan deities into this most Christian city? – Who mimicked Miss Fontover when she crushed them with her heel? – quoted Gibbon, and Shelley, and Mill? Where are dear Apollo, and dear Venus now!"

"O don't, don't be so cruel to me, Jude, and I so unhappy!" she sobbed. "I can't bear it! I was in error – I cannot reason with you. I was wrong – proud in my own conceit! Arabella's coming was the finish. Don't satirize me: it cuts like a knife!"

He flung his arms round her and kissed her passionately there in the silent street, before she could hinder him. They went on till they came to a little coffee-house. "Jude," she said with suppressed tears, "would you mind getting a lodging here?"

"I will – if, if you really wish? But do you? Let me go to our door and understand you."

He went and conducted her in. She said she wanted no supper,

---

1 integer] whole number.

and went in the dark upstairs and struck a light. Turning she found that Jude had followed her, and was standing at the chamber door. She went to him, put her hand in his, and said "Good-night."

"But Sue! Don't we live here?"

"You said you would do as I wished!"

"Yes. Very well! ... Perhaps it was wrong of me to argue distastefully as I have done! Perhaps as we couldn't conscientiously marry at first in the old-fashioned way, we ought to have parted. Perhaps the world is not illuminated enough for such experiments as ours! Who were we, to think we could act as pioneers!"

"I am so glad you see that much, at any rate. I never deliberately meant to do as I did. I slipped into my false position through jealousy and agitation!"

"But surely through love – you loved me?"

"Yes. But I wanted to let it stop there, and go on always as mere lovers; until ——"

"But people in love couldn't live for ever like that!"

"Women could: men can't, because they – won't. An average woman is in this superior to an average man – that she never instigates, only responds. We ought to have lived in mental communion, and no more."

"I was the unhappy cause of the change, as I have said before! ... Well, as you will! ... But human nature can't help being itself."

"O yes – that's just what it has to learn – self-mastery."

"I repeat – if either were to blame it was not you, but I."

"No – it was I. Your wickedness was only the natural man's desire to possess the woman. Mine was not the reciprocal wish till envy stimulated me to oust Arabella. I had thought I ought in charity to let you approach me – that it was damnably selfish to torture you as I did my other friend. But I shouldn't have given way if you hadn't broken me down by making me fear you would go back to her.... But don't let us say any more about it! Jude, will you leave me to myself now?"

"Yes.... But Sue – my wife, as you are!" he burst out; "my old reproach to you was, after all, a true one. You have never loved me as I love you – never – never! Yours is not a passionate heart – your heart does not burn in a flame! You are, upon the whole, cold, – a sort of fay, or sprite – not a woman!"

"At first I did not love you, Jude; that I own. When I first knew you I merely wanted you to love me. I did not exactly flirt with you; but that inborn craving which undermines some women's morals almost more than unbridled passion – the craving to attract and captivate, regardless of the injury it may do the man – was in me; and when I found I had caught you, I was frightened. And then – I don't know how it was – I couldn't bear to let you go – possibly to Arabella again – and so I got to love you, Jude. But you see, however it ended, it began in the selfish and cruel wish to make your heart ache for me without letting mine ache for you."

"And now you add to your cruelty by leaving me!"

"Ah – yes! The further I flounder, the more harm I do!"

"O Sue!" said he with a sudden sense of his own danger. "Do not do an immoral thing for moral reasons! You have been my social salvation. Stay with me for humanity's sake! You know what a weak fellow I am. My two Arch Enemies you know – my weakness for women, and my impulse to strong liquor. Don't abandon me to them, Sue, to save your own soul only! They have been kept entirely at a distance since you became my guardian-angel! Since I have had you I have been able to go into any temptations of the sort, without risk. Isn't my safety worth a little sacrifice of dogmatic principle? I am in terror lest, if you leave me, it will be with me another case of the pig that was washed turning back to his wallowing in the mire!"[1]

Sue burst out weeping. "O but you must not, Jude! You won't! I'll pray for you night and day!"

"Well – never mind; don't grieve," said Jude generously. "I did suffer, God knows, about you at that time; and now I suffer again. But perhaps not so much as you. The woman mostly gets the worst of it in the long run!"

"She does."

"Unless she is absolutely worthless and contemptible. And this one is not that, anyhow!"

Sue drew a nervous breath or two. "She is – I fear! ... Now Jude – good-night, – please!"

"I mustn't stay? – Not just once more? As it has been so many times – O Sue, my wife, why not!"

---

1   pig.....mire] "the sow that was washed [turned] to her wallowing in the mire" (2 Peter 2:22).

"No – no – not wife! ... I am in your hands, Jude – don't tempt me back now I have advanced so far!"

"Very well. I do your bidding. I owe that to you, darling, in penance for how I over-ruled it at the first time. My God, how selfish I was! Perhaps – perhaps I spoilt one of the highest and purest loves that ever existed between man and woman! ... Then let the veil of our temple be rent in two from this hour!"[1]

He went to the bed, removed one of the pair of pillows thereon, and flung it to the floor.

Sue looked at him, and bending over the bed-rail wept silently. "You don't see that it is a matter of conscience with me, and not of dislike to you!" she brokenly murmured. "Dislike to you! But I can't say any more – it breaks my heart – it will be undoing all I have begun! Jude – good-night!"

"Good-night," he said, and turned to go.

"O but you shall kiss me!" said she, starting up. "I can't–bear——!"

He clasped her, and kissed her weeping face as he had scarcely ever done before, and they remained in silence till she said, "Good-bye, good-bye!" And then gently pressing him away she got free, trying to mitigate the sadness by saying: "We'll be dear friends just the same, Jude, won't we? And we'll see each other sometimes – Yes! – and forget all this, and try to be as we were long ago?"

Jude did not permit himself to speak, but turned and descended the stairs.

VI.–IV.

THE man whom Sue, in her mental volte-face,[2] was now regarding as her inseparable husband, lived still at Marygreen.

On the day before the tragedy of the children, Phillotson had seen both her and Jude as they stood in the rain at Christminster watching the procession to the Theatre. But he had said nothing of it at the moment to his companion Gillingham, who, being an old friend, was

---

1   veil.....hour] When Jesus died, "the veil of the temple was rent in twain" (Matthew 27:51).
2   volte-face] (Fr.:) reversal.

staying with him at the village aforesaid, and had, indeed, suggested the day's trip to Christminster.

"What are you thinking of?" said Gillingham, as they went home. "The University degree you never obtained?"

"No, no," said Phillotson gruffly. "Of somebody I saw to-day." In a moment he added, "Susanna."

"I saw her, too."

"You said nothing."

"I didn't wish to draw your attention to her. But, as you did see her, you should have said: 'How d'ye do, my dear-that-was?'"

"Ah, well. I might have. But what do you think of this: I have good reason for supposing that she was innocent when I divorced her – that I was all wrong. Yes, indeed! Awkward, isn't it?"

"She has taken care to set you right since, anyhow, apparently."

"H'm. That's a cheap sneer. I ought to have waited, unquestionably."

At the end of the week, when Gillingham had gone back to his school near Shaston, Phillotson, as was his custom, went to Alfredston market; ruminating again on Arabella's intelligence as he walked down the long hill which he had known before Jude knew it, though his history had not beaten so intensely upon its incline. Arrived in the town he bought his usual weekly local paper; and when he had sat down in an inn to refresh himself for the five miles' walk back, he pulled the paper from his pocket and read awhile. The account of the "Strange suicide of a stone-cutter's children" met his eye.

Unimpassioned as he was, it impressed him painfully, and puzzled him not a little, for he could not understand the age of the elder child being what it was stated to be. However, there was no doubt that the newspaper report was in some way true.

"Their cup of sorrow is now full!" he said: and thought and thought of Sue, and what she had gained by leaving him.

Arabella having made her home at Alfredston, and the schoolmaster coming to market there every Saturday, it was not wonderful that in a few weeks they met again – the precise time being just after her return from Christminster, where she had stayed much longer than she had at first intended, keeping an interested eye on Jude, though Jude had seen no more of her. Phillotson was on his way homeward when he encountered Arabella, and she was approaching the town.

"You like walking out this way, Mrs. Cartlett?" he said.

"I've just begun to again," she replied. "It is where I lived as maid and wife, and all the past things of my life that are interesting to my feelings are mixed up with this road. And they have been stirred up in me too, lately; for I've been visiting at Christminster. Yes; I've seen Jude."

"Ah! How do they bear their terrible affliction?"

"In a ve-ry strange way – ve-ry strange! She don't live with him any longer. I only heard of it as a certainty just before I left; though I had thought things were drifting that way from their manner when I called on them."

"Not live with her husband? Why, I should have thought 'twould have united them more."

"He's not her husband, afer all. She has never really married him although they have passed as man and wife so long. And now, instead of this sad event making 'em hurry up, and get the thing done legally, she's took in a queer religious way, just as I was in my affliction at losing Cartlett, only hers is of a more 'sterical sort than mine. And she says, so I was told, that she's your wife in the eye of Heaven and the Church – yours only; and can't be anybody else's by any act of man."

"Ah – indeed? ... Separated, have they!"

"You see, the eldest boy was mine —"

"O – yours!"

"Yes, poor little fellow – born in lawful wedlock, thank God. And perhaps she feels, over and above other things, that I ought to have been in her place. I can't say. However, as for me, I am soon off from here. I've got father to look after now, and we can't live in such a humdrum place as this. I hope soon to be in a bar again at Christminster, or some other big town."

They parted. When Phillotson had ascended the hill a few steps he stopped, hastened back, and called her.

"What is, or was, their address?"

Arabella gave it.

"Thank you. Good afternoon."

Arabella smiled grimly as she resumed her way, and practised dimple-making all along the road, from where the pollard willows begin to the old almshouses in the first street of the town.

Meanwhile Phillotson ascended to Marygreen, and for the first time during a lengthened period he lived with a forward eye. On crossing under the large trees of the green to the humble schoolhouse to which he had been reduced he stood a moment, and pictured Sue coming out of the door to meet him. No man had ever suffered more inconvenience from his own charity, Christian or heathen, than Phillotson had done in letting Sue go. He had been knocked about from pillar to post at the hands of the virtuous almost beyond endurance; he had been nearly starved, and was now dependent entirely upon the very small stipend from the school of this village (where the parson had got ill-spoken of for befriending him). He had often thought of Arabella's remarks that he should have been more severe with Sue, that her recalcitrant spirit would soon have been broken. Yet such was his obstinate and illogical disregard of opinion, and of the principles in which he had been trained, that his convictions on the rightness of his course with his wife had not been disturbed.

Principles which could be subverted by feeling in one direction were liable to the same catastrophe in another. The instincts which had allowed him to give Sue her liberty now enabled him to regard her as none the worse for her life with Jude. He wished for her still, in his curious way, if he did not love her, and, apart from policy, soon felt that he would be gratified to have her again as his, always provided that she came willingly.

But artifice was necessary, he had found, for stemming the cold and inhumane blast of the world's contempt. And here were the materials ready made. By getting Sue back and re-marrying her on the respectable plea of having entertained erroneous views of her, and gained his divorce wrongfully, he might acquire some comfort, resume his old courses, perhaps return to the Shaston school, if not even to the Church itself as a licentiate.

He thought he would write to Gillingham to inquire his views, and what he thought of his, Phillotson's, sending a letter to her. Gillingham replied, naturally, that now she was gone it were best to let her be; and considered that if she were anybody's wife she was the wife of the man to whom she had borne three children and owed such tragical adventures. Probably, as his attachment to her seemed unusually strong, the singular pair would make their union legal in course of time, and all would be well, and decent, and in order.

"But they won't – Sue won't!" exclaimed Phillotson to himself. "Gillingham is so old-fashioned. She's affected by Christminster sentiment and teaching. I can see her views on the indissolubility of marriage well enough, and I know where she got them. They are not mine; but I shall make use of them to further mine."

He wrote a brief reply to Gillingham. "I know I am entirely wrong, but I don't agree with you. As to her having lived with and had three children by him, my feeling is (though I can advance no logical or moral defence of it, on the old lines) that it has done little more than finish her education. I shall write to her, and learn whether what that woman said is true or no."

As he had made up his mind to do this before he had written to his friend, there had not been much reason for writing to the latter at all. However, it was Phillotson's way to act thus.

He accordingly addressed a carefully considered epistle to Sue, and, knowing her emotional temperament, threw a Rhadamanthine strictness[1] into it here and there, carefully hiding his heterodox feelings, not to frighten her. He stated that, it having come to his knowledge that her views had considerably changed, he felt compelled to say that his own, too, were largely modified by events subsequent to their parting. He would not conceal from her that passionate love had little to do with his communication. It arose from a wish to make their lives, if not a success, at least no such disastrous failure as they threatened to become, through his acting on what he had considered at the time a principle of justice, charity, and reason.

To indulge one's instinctive and uncontrolled sense of justice and right, was not, he had found, permitted with impunity in an old civilization like ours. It was necessary to act under an acquired and artificial sense of the same, if you wished to enjoy an average share of comfort and honour; and to let loving-kindness take care of itself.

He suggested that she should come to him there at Marygreen.

On second thoughts he took out the last paragraph but one; and having re-written the letter he despatched it immediately, and in some excitement awaited the issue.

---

1 Rhadamanthine strictness] In Greek mythology, Rhadamanthus was a severe judge of souls in the underworld.

A few days after a figure moved through the white fog which enveloped the Beersheba suburb of Christminster, towards the quarter in which Jude Fawley had taken up his lodging since his division from Sue. A timid knock sounded upon the door of his abode.

It was evening – so he was at home; and by a species of divination he jumped up and rushed to the door himself.

"Will you come out with me? I would rather not come in. I want to – to talk with you – and to go with you to the cemetery."

It had been in the trembling accents of Sue that these words came. Jude put on his hat. "It is dreary for you to be out," he said. "But if you prefer not to come in, I don't mind."

"Yes – I do. I shall not keep you long."

Jude was too much affected to go on talking at first; she, too, was now such a mere cluster of nerves that all initiatory power seemed to have left her, and they proceeded through the fog like Acherontic shades[1] for a long while, without sound or gesture.

"I want to tell you," she presently said, her voice now quick, now slow, "so that you may not hear of it by chance. I am going back to Richard. He has – so magnanimously – agreed to forgive all."

"Going back? How can you go ——"

"He is going to marry me again. That is for form's sake, and to satisfy the world, which does not see things as they are. But of course I *am* his wife already. Nothing has changed that."

He turned upon her with an anguish that was well-nigh fierce.

"But you are *my* wife! Yes, you are. You know it. I have always regretted that feint of ours in going away and pretending to come back legally married, to save appearances. I loved you, and you loved me; and we closed with each other; and that made the marriage. We still love – you as well as I – I *know* it, Sue! Therefore our marriage is not cancelled."

"Yes; I know how you see it," she answered with despairing self-suppression. "But I am going to marry him again, as it would be called by you. Strictly speaking you, too, – don't mind my saying it, Jude! – you should take back – Arabella."

"I should? Good God – what next! But how if you and I had married legally, as we were on the point of doing?"

"I should have felt just the same – that ours was not a marriage.

---

1   Acherontic shades] souls of the dead that cross the murky underworld river Acheron ("River of Grief").

And I would go back to Richard without repeating the sacrament, if he asked me. But 'the world and its ways have a certain worth'[1] (I suppose): therefore I concede a repetition of the ceremony.... Don't crush all the life out of me by satire and argument, I implore you! I was strongest once, I know, and perhaps I treated you cruelly. But Jude, return good for evil! I am the weaker now. Don't retaliate upon me, but be kind. O be kind to me – a poor wicked woman who is trying to mend!"

He shook his head hopelessly, his eyes wet. The blow of her bereavement seemed to have destroyed her reasoning faculty. The once keen vision was dimmed. "All wrong, all wrong!" he said huskily. "Error – perversity! It drives me out of my senses. Do you care for him? Do you love him? You know you don't! It will be a fanatic prostitution – God forgive me, yes – that's what it will be!"

"I don't love him – I must, must, own it, in deepest remorse! But I shall try to learn to love him by obeying him."

Jude argued, urged, implored; but her conviction was proof against all. It seemed to be the one thing on earth on which she was firm, and that her firmness in this had left her tottering in every other impulse and wish she possessed.

"I have been considerate enough to let you know the whole truth, and to tell it you myself," she said in cut tones; "that you might not consider yourself slighted by hearing of it at second-hand. I have even owned the extreme fact that I do not love him. I did not think you would be so rough with me for doing so! I was going to ask you ..."

"To give you away?"

"No. To send – my boxes to me – if you would. But I suppose you won't."

"Why, of course I will. What – isn't he coming to fetch you – to marry you from here? He won't condescend to do that?"

"No – I won't let him. I go to him voluntarily, just as I went away from him. We are to be married at his little church at Marygreen."

She was so sadly sweet in what he called her wrong-headedness that Jude could not help being moved to tears more than once for pity of her. "I never knew such a woman for doing impulsive penances as you, Sue! No sooner does one expect you to go straight on, as the one rational proceeding, than you double round the corner!"

---

1 'the world.....worth'] from Browning's poem "The Statue and the Bust."

"Ah, well; let that go! ... Jude, I must say good-bye! But I wanted you to go to the cemetery with me. Let our farewell be there – beside the graves of those who died to bring home to me the error of my views."

They turned in the direction of the place, and the gate was opened to them on application. Sue had been there often, and she knew the way to the spot in the dark. They reached it, and stood still.

"It is here – I should like to part," said she.

"So be it!"

"Don't think me hard because I have acted on conviction. Your generous devotion to me is unparalleled, Jude! Your worldly failure, if you have failed, is to your credit rather than to your blame. Remember that the best and greatest among mankind are those who do themselves no worldly good. Every successful man is more or less a selfish man. The devoted fail.... 'Charity seeketh not her own.'"[1]

"In that chapter we are at one, ever beloved darling, and on it we'll part friends. Its verses will stand fast when all the rest that you call religion has passed away!"

"Well – don't discuss it. Good-bye, Jude; my fellow-sinner, and kindest friend!"

"Good-bye, my mistaken wife. Good-bye!"

VI.-V.

THE next afternoon the familiar Christminster fog still hung over all things. Sue's slim shape was only just discernible going towards the station.

Jude had no heart to go to his work that day. Neither could he go anywhere in the direction by which she would be likely to pass. He went in an opposite one, to a dreary, strange, flat scene, where boughs dripped, and coughs and consumption lurked, and where he had never been before.

"Sue's gone from me – gone!" he murmured miserably.

She in the meantime had left by the train, and reached Alfredston

---

1 'Charity.....own'] 1 Corinthians 13:4-5.

Road, where she entered the steam-tram[1] and was conveyed into the town. It had been her request to Phillotson that he should not meet her. She wished, she said, to come to him voluntarily, to his very house and hearthstone.

It was Friday evening, which had been chosen because the schoolmaster was disengaged at four o'clock that day till the Monday morning following. The little car[2] she hired at The Bear[3] to drive her to Marygreen set her down at the end of the lane, half-a-mile from the village, by her desire, and preceded her to the schoolhouse with such portion of her luggage as she had brought. On its return she encountered it, and asked the driver if he had found the master's house open. The man informed her that he had, and that her things had been taken in by the schoolmaster himself.

She could now enter Marygreen without exciting much observation. She crossed by the well and under the trees to the pretty new school on the other side, and lifted the latch of the dwelling without knocking. Phillotson stood in the middle of the room, awaiting her, as requested.

"I've come, Richard," said she, looking pale and shaken, and sinking into a chair. "I cannot believe – you forgive your – wife!"

"Everything, darling Susanna," said Phillotson.

She started at the endearment, though it had been spoken advisedly without fervour. Then she nerved herself again.

"My children – are dead – and it is right that they should be! I am glad – almost. They were sin-begotten. They were sacrificed to teach me how to live! – their death was the first stage of my purification. That's why they have not died in vain! ...You will take me back?"

He was so stirred by her pitiful words and tone that he did more than he had meant to do. He bent and kissed her cheek.

Sue imperceptibly shrank away, her flesh quivering under the touch of his lips.

Phillotson's heart sank, for desire was renascent in him. "You still have an aversion to me!"

"O no, dear – I – have been driving through the damp, and I was

---

1 steam-tram] known as the Grantham Car. During the late nineteenth century, some horse-drawn trams were replaced by these steam-engined vehicles.
2 car] horse-drawn cab.
3 Bear] corresponds to the Bear Hotel, Market Place, Wantage.

chilly!" she said, with a hurried smile of apprehension. "When are we going to have the marriage? Soon?"

"To-morrow morning, early, I thought – if you really wish. I am sending round to the vicar to let him know you are come. I have told him all, and he highly approves – he says it will bring our lives to a triumphant and satisfactory issue. But – are you sure of yourself? It is not too late to refuse now if – you think you can't bring yourself to it, you know?"

"Yes, yes, I can! I want it done quick. Tell him, tell him at once! My strength is tried by the undertaking – I can't wait long!"

"Have something to eat and drink then, and go over to your room at Mrs. Edlin's. I'll tell the vicar half-past eight to-morrow, before anybody is about – if that's not too soon for you? My friend Gillingham is here to help us in the ceremony. He's been good enough to come all the way from Shaston at great inconvenience to himself."

Unlike a woman in ordinary, whose eye is so keen for material things, Sue seemed to see nothing of the room they were in, or any detail of her environment. But on moving across the parlour to put down her muff she uttered a little "O!" and grew paler than before. Her look was that of the condemned criminal who catches sight of his coffin.

"What?" said Phillotson.

The flap of the bureau chanced to be open, and in placing her muff upon it her eye had caught a document which lay there. "O – only a – funny surprise!" she said, trying to laugh away her cry as she came back to the table.

"Ah! Yes," said Phillotson. "The license.... It has just come."

Gillingham now joined them from his room above, and Sue nervously made herself agreeable to him by talking on whatever she thought likely to interest him, except herself, though that interested him most of all. She obediently eat[1] some supper, and prepared to leave for her lodging hard by. Phillotson crossed the green with her, bidding her good-night at Mrs. Edlin's door.

The old woman accompanied Sue to her temporary quarters, and helped her to unpack. Among other things she laid out a nightgown tastefully embroidered.

---

1   eat] archaic variant of "ate."

"O – I didn't know *that* was put in!" said Sue quickly. "I didn't mean it to be. Here is a different one." She handed a new and absolutely plain garment, of coarse and unbleached calico.

"But this is the prettiest," said Mrs. Edlin. "That one is no better than very sackcloth o' Scripture!"[1]

"Yes – I meant it to be. Give me the other."

She took it, and began rending it with all her might, the tears resounding through the house like a screech-owl.

"But my dear, dear! – whatever ... "

"It is adulterous! It signifies what I don't feel – I bought it long ago – to please Jude. It must be destroyed!"

Mrs. Edlin lifted her hands, and Sue excitedly continued to tear the linen into strips, laying the pieces in the fire.

"You med ha' give it to me!" said the widow. "It do make my heart ache to see such pretty open-work[2] as that a-burned by the flames – not that ornamental night-rails[3] can be much use to a' ould 'ooman like I. My days for such be all past and gone!"

"It is an accursed thing – it reminds me of what I want to forget!" Sue repeated. "It is only fit for the fire."

"Lord, you be too strict! What do ye use such words for, and condemn to hell your dear little innocent children that's lost to 'ee! Upon my life I don't call that religion!"

Sue flung her face upon the bed, sobbing. 'O, don't, don't! That kills me!" She remained shaken with her grief, and slipped down upon her knees.

"I'll tell 'ee what – you ought not to marry this man again!" said Mrs. Edlin indignantly. "You are in love wi' t' other still!"

"Yes I must – I am his already!"

"Pshoo! You be t'other man's. If you didn't like to commit yourselves to the binding vow again, just at first, 'twas all the more credit to your consciences, considering your reasons, and you med ha' lived on, and made it all right at last. After all, it concerned nobody but your own two selves."

"Richard says he'll have me back, and I'm bound to go! If he had

---

1 sackcloth o'Scripture] coarse cloth worn in penitence or mourning (as in Esther 4:1-3).
2 open-work] embroidery with a pattern of holes.
3 night-rails] (dl.:) night-gowns.

refused, it might not have been so much my duty to – give up Jude. But –" She remained with her face in the bedclothes, and Mrs. Edlin left the room.

Phillotson in the interval had gone back to his friend Gillingham, who still sat over the supper-table. They soon rose, and walked out on the green to smoke awhile. A light was burning in Sue's room, a shadow moving now and then across the blind.

Gillingham had evidently been impressed with the indefinable charm of Sue, and after a silence he said, "Well: you've all but got her again at last. She can't very well go a second time. The pear has dropped into your hand."

"Yes! ... I suppose I am right in taking her at her word. I confess there seems a touch of selfishness in it. Apart from her being what she is, of course, a luxury for a fogey[1] like me, it will set me right in the eyes of the clergy and orthodox laity, who have never forgiven me for letting her go. So I may get back in some degree into my old track."

"Well – if you've got any sound reason for marrying her again, do it now in God's name! I was always against your opening the cage-door and letting the bird go in such an obviously suicidal way. You might have been a school inspector by this time, or a reverend, if you hadn't been so weak about her."

"I did myself irreparable damage – I know it."

"Once you've got her housed again, stick to her."

Phillotson was more evasive to-night. He did not care to admit clearly that his taking Sue to him again had at bottom nothing to do with repentance of letting her go, but was, primarily, a human instinct flying in the face of custom and profession. He said, "Yes – I shall do that. I know woman better now. Whatever justice there was in releasing her, there was little logic, for one holding my views on other subjects."

Gillingham looked at him, and wondered whether it would ever happen that the reactionary spirit induced by the world's sneers and his own physical wishes would make Phillotson more orthodoxly cruel to her than he had erstwhile been informally and perversely kind.

"I perceive it won't do to give way to impulse," Phillotson

---

1 fogey] (coll.:) person with old-fashioned ideas.

resumed, feeling more and more every minute the necessity of acting up to his position. "I flew in the face of the Church's teaching; but I did it without malice prepense.[1] Women are so strange in their influence, that they tempt you to misplaced kindness. However, I know myself better now. A little judicious severity, perhaps.... "

"Yes; but you must tighten the reins by degrees only. Don't be too strenuous at first. She'll come to any terms in time."

The caution was unnecessary, though Phillotson did not say so. "I remember what my vicar at Shaston said, when I left after the row that was made about my agreeing to her elopement. 'The only thing you can do to retrieve your position and hers is to admit your error in not restraining her with a wise and strong hand, and to get her back again if she'll come, and be firm in the future.' But I was so headstrong at that time that I paid no heed. And that after the divorce she should have thought of doing so I did not dream."

The gate of Mrs. Edlin's cottage clicked, and somebody began crossing in the direction of the school. Phillotson said "Good-night."

"O, is that Mr. Phillotson," said Mrs. Edlin. "I was going over to see 'ee. I've been upstairs with her, helping her to unpack her things; and upon my word, sir, I don't think this ought to be!"

"What — the wedding?"

"Yes. She's forcing herself to it, poor dear little thing; and you've no notion what she's suffering. I was never much for religion nor against it, but it can't be right to let her do this, and you ought to persuade her out of it. Of course everybody will say it was very good and forgiving of 'ee to take her to 'ee again. But for my part I don't."

"It's her wish, and I am willing," said Phillotson with grave reserve, opposition making him illogically tenacious now. "A great piece of laxity will be rectified."

"I don't believe it. She's his wife if anybody's. She's had three children by him, and he loves her dearly; and it's a wicked shame to egg her on to this, poor little quivering thing! She's got nobody on her side. The one man who'd be her friend the obstinate creature won't allow to come near her. What first put her into this mood o' mind, I wonder!"

"I can't tell. Not I certainly. It is all voluntary on her part. Now

---

1 malice prepense] premeditated malice.

that's all I have to say." Phillotson spoke stiffly. "You've turned round, Mrs. Edlin. It is unseemly of you!"

"Well, I knowed you'd be affronted at what I had to say; but I don't mind that. The truth's the truth."

"I'm not affronted, Mrs. Edlin. You've been too kind a neighbour for that. But I must be allowed to know what's best for myself and Susanna. I suppose you won't go to church with us, then?"

"No. Be hanged if I can... I don't know what the times be coming to! Matrimony have growed to be that serious in these days that one really do feel afeard to move in it at all. In my time we took it more careless; and I don't know that we was any the worse for it! When I and my poor man were jined in it we kept up the junketing[1] all the week, and drunk the parish dry, and had to borrow half-a-crown to begin housekeeping!"

When Mrs. Edlin had gone back to her cottage Phillotson spoke moodily. "I don't know whether I ought to do it – at any rate quite so rapidly."

"Why?"

"If she is really compelling herself to this against her instincts – merely from this new sense of duty or religion – I ought perhaps to let her wait a bit."

"Now you've got so far you ought not to back out of it. That's my opinion."

"I can't very well put it off now; that's true. But I had a qualm when she gave the little cry at sight of the license."

"Now, never you have qualms, old boy. I mean to give her away to-morrow morning, and you mean to take her. It has always been on my conscience that I didn't urge more objections to your letting her go, and now we've got to this stage I shan't be content if I don't help you to set the matter right."

Phillotson nodded, and seeing how staunch his friend was, became more frank. "No doubt when it gets known what I've done I shall be thought a soft fool by many. But they don't know Sue as I do. Hers is such a straight and open nature[2] that I don't think she has ever done anything against her conscience. The fact of her having lived with

---

1 junketing] feasting and carousing.
2 Hers is.....nature] In 1912 this became: "Though so elusive, hers is such an honest nature at bottom".

Fawley goes for nothing. At the time she left me for him she thought she was quite within her right. Now she thinks otherwise."

The next morning came, and the self-sacrifice of the woman on the altar of what she was pleased to call her principles was acquiesced in by these two friends, each from his own point of view. Phillotson went across to the Widow Edlin's to fetch Sue a few minutes after eight o'clock. The fog of the previous day or two on the lowlands had travelled up here by now, and the trees on the green caught armfuls, and turned them into showers of big drops. The bride was waiting, ready; bonnet and all on. She had never in her life looked so much like the lily her name connoted[1] as she did in that pallid morning light. Chastened, world-weary, remorseful, the strain on her nerves had preyed upon her flesh and bones, and she appeared smaller in outline than she had formerly done, though Sue had not been a large woman in her days of rudest health.

"Prompt," said the schoolmaster, magnanimously taking her hand. But he checked his impulse to kiss her, remembering her start of yesterday, which unpleasantly lingered in his mind.

Gillingham joined them, and they left the house, Widow Edlin continuing steadfast in her refusal to assist in the ceremony.

"Where is the church?" said Sue. She had not lived there for any length of time since the old church was pulled down, and in her preoccupation forgot the new one.

"Up here," said Phillotson; and presently the tower loomed large and solemn in the fog. The vicar had already crossed to the building, and when they entered he said pleasantly: "We almost want candles."

"You do – wish me to be yours, Richard?" gasped Sue in a whisper.

"Certainly, dear: above all things in the world."

Sue said no more; and for the second or third time he felt he was not quite following out the humane instinct which had induced him to let her go.

There they stood, five altogether: the parson, the clerk, the couple and Gillingham; and the holy ordinance was re-solemnized forthwith. In the nave of the edifice were two or three villagers, and when the clergyman came to the words, "What God hath joined," a

---

1   lily.....connoted] "Susanna" derives from the Hebrew for "lily."

woman's voice from among these was heard to utter audibly:

"God hath jined indeed!"

It was like a re-enactment by the ghosts of their former selves of the similar scene which had taken place at Melchester years before. When the books were signed the vicar congratulated the husband and wife on having performed a noble, and righteous, and mutually forgiving act. "All's well that ends well,"[1] he said smiling. "May you long be happy together, after thus having been 'saved as by fire.'"[2]

They came down the nearly empty building, and crossed to the schoolhouse. Gillingham wanted to get home that night, and left early. He, too, congratulated the couple. "Now," he said in parting from Phillotson, who walked out a little way, "I shall be able to tell the people in your native place a good round tale; and they'll all say 'Well done,' depend on it."

When the schoolmaster got back Sue was making a pretence of doing some housewifery as if she lived there. But she seemed timid at his approach.

"Of course, my dear, I shan't expect to intrude upon your personal privacy any more than I did before," he said gravely. "It is for our good socially to do this, and that's its justification, if it was not my reason."

Sue brightened a little.

VI.-VI.

THE place was the door of Jude's lodging in the outskirts of Christminster — far from the precincts of St. Silas' where he had formerly lived, which saddened him to sickness. The rain was coming down. A woman in shabby black stood on the doorstep talking to Jude, who held the door in his hand.

"I am lonely, destitute, and houseless — that's what I am! Father has turned me out of doors after borrowing every penny I'd got, to put it into his business, and then accusing me of laziness when I was only waiting for a situation. I am at the mercy of the world! If you can't

---

1 All's well that ends well] proverbial (in *Gesta Romanorum* and John Heywood's *Proverbes*) before Shakespeare wrote his comedy with that title.

2 'saved as by fire'] from 1 Corinthians 3:15.

take me and help me, Jude, I must go to the workhouse,[1] or to something worse. Only just now two undergraduates winked at me as I came along. 'Tis hard for a woman to keep virtuous where there's so many young men!"

The woman in the rain who spoke thus was Arabella, the evening being that of the day after Sue's re-marriage with Phillotson.

"I am sorry for you, but I am only in lodgings," said Jude coldly.

"Then you turn me away?"

"I'll give you enough to get food and lodging for a few days."

"O, but can't you have the kindness to take me in? I cannot endure going to a public-house to lodge; and I am so lonely. Please, Jude, for old times' sake!"

"No, no," said Jude hastily. "I don't want to be reminded of those things; and if you talk about them I shall not help you."

"Then I suppose I must go!" said Arabella. She bent her head against the doorpost and began sobbing.

"The house is full," said Jude. "And I have only a little extra room – not much more than a closet – where I keep my tools, and templates,[2] and the few books I have left!"

"That would be a palace for me!"

"There is no bedstead in it."

"A bit of a bed could be made on the floor. It would be good enough for me."

Unable to be harsh with her, and not knowing what to do, Jude called the man who let the lodgings, and said this was an acquaintance of his in great distress for want of temporary shelter.

"You may remember me as barmaid at the Lamb and Flag[3] formerly?" spoke up Arabella. "My father has insulted me this afternoon, and I've left him, though without a penny!"

The householder said he could not recall her features. "But still, if you are a friend of Mr. Fawley's we'll do what we can for a day or two – if he'll make himself answerable?"

"Yes, yes," said Jude. "She has really taken me quite unawares; but I should wish to help her out of her difficulty." And an arrangement

---

1 workhouse] hostel and workshop for the destitute.
2 templates] patterns used to guide stone-cutting.
3 Lamb and Flag] the Oxford tavern (named after the emblem of John the Baptist) described in Part Second, Chap. VII, and Part Third, Chap. VIII.

was ultimately come to under which a bed was to be thrown down in Jude's lumber-room, to make it comfortable for Arabella till she could get out of the strait she was in – not by her own fault, as she declared – and return to her father's again.

While they were waiting for this to be done Arabella said: "You know the news, I suppose?"

"I guess what you mean; but I know nothing."

"I had a letter from Anny at Alfredston to-day. She had just heard that the wedding was to be yesterday: but she didn't know if it had come off."

"I don't wish to talk of it."

"No, no: of course you don't. Only it shows what kind of woman——"

"Don't speak of her I say! She's a fool! – And she's an angel, too, poor dear!"

"If it's done, he'll have a chance of getting back to his old position, by everybody's account, so Anny says. All his well-wishers will be pleased, including the bishop himself."

"Do spare me, Arabella."

Arabella was duly installed in the little attic, and at first she did not come near Jude at all. She went to and fro, about her own business, which, when they met for a moment on the stairs or in the passage, she informed him was that of obtaining another place in the occupation she understood best. When Jude suggested London as affording the most likely opening in the liquor trade, she shook her head. "No – the temptations are too many," she said. "Any humble tavern in the country before that for me."

On the Sunday morning following, when he breakfasted later than on other days, she meekly asked him if she might come in to breakfast with him, as she had broken her teapot, and could not replace it immediately, the shops being shut.

"Yes, if you like," he said indifferently.

While they sat without speaking she suddenly observed: "You seem all in a brood, old man. I"m sorry for you."

"I am all in a brood."

"It is about her, I know. It's no business of mine, but I could find out all about the wedding – if it really did take place – if you wanted to know."

"How could you?"

"I wanted to go to Alfredston to get a few things I left there. And I could see Anny, who'll be sure to have heard all about it, as she has friends at Marygreen."

Jude could not bear to acquiesce in this proposal; but his suspense pitted itself against his discretion, and won in the struggle. "You can ask about it if you like," he said. "I've not heard a sound from there. It must have been very private, if – they have married."

"I am afraid I haven't enough cash to take me there and back, or I should have gone before. I must wait till I have earned some."

"O – I can pay the journey for you," he said impatiently. And thus his suspense as to Sue's welfare, and the possible marriage, moved him to despatch for intelligence the last emissary he would have thought of choosing deliberately.

Arabella went, Jude requesting her to be home not later than by the seven o'clock train. When she had gone he said: "Why should I have charged her to be back by a particular time! She's nothing to me: – nor the other neither!"

But having finished work he could not help going to the station to meet Arabella, dragged thither by feverish haste to get the news she might bring, and know the worst. Arabella had made dimples most successfully all the way home, and when she stepped out of the railway carriage she smiled. He merely said "Well?" with the very reverse of a smile.

"They are married."

"Yes – of course they are!" he returned. She observed, however, the hard strain upon his lip as he spoke.

"Anny says she has heard form Belinda, her relation out at Marygreen, that it was very sad, and curious!"

"How do you mean sad? She wanted to marry him again, didn't she? – and he her!"

"Yes – that was it. She wanted to in one sense, but not in the other. Mrs. Edlin was much upset by it all, and spoke out her mind at Phillotson. But Sue was that excited about it that she burnt her best embroidery, that she'd worn with you, to blot you out entirely. Well – if a woman feels like it, she ought to do it. I commend her for it, though others don't." Arabella sighed. "She felt he was her only husband, and that she belonged to nobody else in the sight of God

A'mighty while he lived. Perhaps another woman feels the same about herself, too!" Arabella sighed again.

"I don't want any cant!" exclaimed Jude.

"It isn't cant," said Arabella. "I feel exactly the same as she!"

He closed that issue by remarking abruptly: "Well – now I know all I wanted to know. Many thanks for your information. I am not going back to my lodgings just yet." And he left her straightway.

In his misery and depression Jude walked to well-nigh every spot in the city that he had visited with Sue; thence he did not know whither, and then thought of going home to his usual evening meal. But having all the vices of his virtues, and some to spare, he turned into a public-house, for the first time during many months. Among the possible consequences of her marriage Sue had not dwelt on this.

Arabella, meanwhile, had gone back. The evening passed, and Jude did not return. At half-past nine Arabella herself went out, first proceeding to an outlying district near the river where her father lived, and had opened a small and precarious pork-shop lately.

"Well," she said to him, "for all your rowing me[1] that night, I've come back, for I have something to tell you. I think I shall get married and settled again. Only you must help me: and you can do no less, after what I've stood 'ee."

"I'll do anything to get thee off my hands!"

"Very well. I am now going to look for my young man. He's on the loose I'm afraid, and I must get him home. All I want you to do to-night is not to fasten the door, in case I should want to sleep here, and should be late."

"I thought you'd soon get tired of giving yourself airs and keeping away!"

"Well – don't do the door. That's all I say."

She then sallied out again, and first hastening back to Jude's to make sure that he had not returned, began her search for him. A shrewd guess as to his probable course took her straight to the tavern which Jude had formerly frequented, and where she had been barmaid for a brief term. She had no sooner opened the door of the "Private Bar" than her eyes fell upon him – siting in the shade at the back of the compartment, with his eyes fixed on the floor in a blank

---

1 rowing me] (coll.:) shouting at me.

stare. He was drinking nothing stronger than ale just then. He did not observe her, and she entered and sat beside him.

Jude looked up, and said without surprise: "You've come to have something, Arabella? .... I'm trying to forget her: that's all! But I can't; and I am going home." She saw that he was a little way on in liquor, but only a little as yet.

"I've come entirely to look for you, dear boy. You are not well. Now you must have something better than that." Arabella held up her finger to the barmaid. "You shall have a liqueur – that's better fit for a man of education than beer. You shall have maraschino,[1] or curaçoa dry or sweet, or cherry brandy. I'll treat you, poor chap!"

"I don't care which! Say cherry brandy.... Sue has served me badly, very badly. I didn't expect it of Sue! I stuck to her, and she ought to have stuck to me. I'd have sold my soul for her sake, but she wouldn't risk hers a jot for me. To save her own soul she lets mine go damn! ... But it isn't her fault, poor little girl – I am sure it isn't!"

How Arabella had obtained money did not appear, but she ordered a liqueur each, and paid for them. When they had drunk these Arabella suggested another; and Jude had the pleasure of being, as it were, personally conducted through the varieties of spirituous delectation by one who knew the landmarks well. Arabella kept very considerably in the rear of Jude; but though she only sipped where he drank, she took as much as she could safely take without losing her head – which was not a little, as the crimson upon her countenance showed.

Her tone towards him to-night was uniformly soothing and cajoling; and whenever he said, "I don't care what happens to me," a thing he did continually, she replied, "But I do very much!" The closing hour came, and they were compelled to turn out; whereupon Arabella put her arm round his waist, and guided his unsteady footsteps.

When they were in the streets she said: "I don't know what our landlord will say to my bringing you home in this state. I expect we are fastened out, so that he'll have to come down and let us in."

"I don't know – I don't know."

"That's the worst of not having a home of your own. I tell you, Jude, what we had best do. Come round to my father's – I made it up

---

1   maraschino] liqueur made from black cherries.

with him a bit to-day. I can let you in, and nobody will see you at all; and by to-morrow morning you'll be all right."

"Anything – anywhere," replied Jude. "What the devil does it matter to me?"

They went along together, like any other fuddling couple, her arm still round his waist, and his, at last, round hers; though with no amatory intent; but merely because he was weary, unstable, and in need of support.

"This – is th' Martyrs' – burning-place," he stammered, as they dragged across a broad street. "I remember – in old Fuller's 'Holy State'¹ – and I am reminded of it – by our passing by here – old Fuller in his 'Holy State' says, that at the burning of Ridley, Doctor Smith – preached sermon, and took as his text '*Though I give my body to be burned, and have not charity, it profiteth me nothing.*'² – Often think of it as I pass here. Ridley was a ———"

"Yes. Exactly. Very thoughtful of you, deary, even though it hasn't much to do with our present business."

"Why, yes it has! I'm giving my body to be burned! But – ah – you don't understand! – it wants Sue to understand such things! And I was her seducer – poor little girl! And she's gone – and I don't care about myself! Do what you like with me! ... and yet she did it for conscience' sake, poor little Sue!"

"Hang her! – I mean, I think she was right," hiccuped Arabella. "I've my feelings too, like her; and I feel I belong to you in Heaven's eye, and to nobody else, till death us do part!³ It is – hic – never too late – hic – to mend!"

They had reached her father's house, and she softly unfastened the door, groping about for a light within.

The circumstances were not altogether unlike those of their entry into the cottage at Cresscombe, such a long time before. Nor were perhaps Arabella's motives. But Jude did not think of that, though she did.

"I can't find the matches, dear," she said when she had fastened up

---

1 Fuller's 'Holy State'] Thomas Fuller's *The Holy State and the Profane State* (1642).
2 '*Though.....nothing*'] 1 Corinthians 13:3. Thomas Fuller reports that Dr. Smith of Oxford scornfully cited this text when Nicholas Ridley, the Protestant martyr, was burnt to death in 1555.
3 till.....part] from the Anglican Service, the Solemnization of Matrimony.

the door. "But never mind – this way. As quiet as you can, please."

"It is as dark as pitch," said Jude.

"Give me your hand, and I'll lead you. That's it. Just sit down here, and I'll pull off your boots. I don't want to wake him."

"Who?"

"Father. He'd make a row, perhaps."

She pulled off his boots. "Now," she whispered, "take hold of me – never mind your weight. Now – first stair, second stair ———"

"But, – are we out in our old house by Marygreen?" asked the stupefied Jude. "I haven't been inside it for years till now! Hey? And where are my books? That's what I want to know?"

"We are at my house, dear, where there's nobody to spy out how ill you are. Now – third stair, fourth stair – that's it. Now we shall get on."

VI.-VII.

ARABELLA was preparing breakfast in the downstairs room of this small, recently hired tenement of her father's. She put her head into the little pork-shop in front, and told Mr. Donn it was ready. Donn, endeavouring to look like a master pork-butcher, in a greasy blue blouse, and with a strap round his waist from which a steel[1] dangled, came in promptly.

"You must mind the shop this morning," he said casually. "I've to go and get some inwards and half a pig from Lumsdon, and to call elsewhere. If you live here you must put your shoulder to the wheel, at least till I get the business started!"

"Well, for to-day I can't say." She looked deedily into his face. "I've got a prize upstairs."

"Oh? – What's that?"

"A husband – almost."

"No!"

"Yes. It's Jude. He's come back to me."

"Your old original one? Well, I'm damned!"

"Well, I always did like him, that I will say."

---

1 steel] steel rod for sharpening knives.

"But how does he come to be up there?" said Donn, humour-struck, and nodding to the ceiling.

"Don't ask inconvenient questions, father. What we've to do is to keep him here till he and I are – as we were."

"How was that?"

"Married."

"Ah.... Well it is the rummest[1] thing I ever heard of – marrying an old husband again, and so much new blood in the world! He's no catch, to my thinking. I'd have had a new one while I was about it."

"It isn't rum for a woman to want her old husband back, for respectability, though for a man to want his old wife back – well, per-haps it is funny, rather!" And Arabella was suddenly seized with a fit of loud laughter, in which her father joined more moderately.

"Be civil to him, and I'll do the rest," she said when she had recov-ered seriousness. "He told me this morning that his head ached fit to burst, and he hardly seemed to know where he was. And no wonder, considering how he mixed his drink last night. We must keep him jolly and cheerful here for a day or two, and not let him go back to his lodging. Whatever you advance I'll pay back to you again. But I must go up and see how he is now, poor deary."

Arabella ascended the stairs, softly opened the door of the first bedroom, and peeped in. Finding that her shorn Samson[2] was asleep she entered to the bedside and stood regarding him. The fevered flush on his face from the debauch of the previous evening lessened the fragility of his ordinary appearance, and his long lashes, dark brows, and curly black hair and beard against the white pillow, completed the physiognomy of one whom Arabella, as a woman of rank passions, still felt it worth while to recapture, highly important to recapture as a woman straitened both in means and in reputation. Her ardent gaze seemed to affect him; his quick breathing became suspended, and he opened his eyes.

"How are you now, dear?" said she. "It is I – Arabella."

"Ah – where – O yes, I remember! You gave me shelter.... I am stranded – ill – demoralized – damn bad! That's what I am!"

---

1   rummest] (coll.:) strangest.

2   shorn Samson] The treacherous Delilah found that the secret of Samson's strength was his hair; shorn while asleep, he was captured by the Philistines (Judges 16:17-21).

"Then do stay there. There's nobody in the house but father and me, and you can rest till you are thoroughly well. I'll tell them at the stone-works that you are knocked up."[1]

"I wonder what they are thinking at the lodgings!"

"I'll go round and explain. Perhaps you had better let me pay up, or they'll think we've run away?"

"Yes. You'll find enough money in my pocket there."

Quite indifferent, and shutting his eyes because he could not bear the daylight in his throbbing eyeballs, Jude seemed to doze again. Arabella took his purse, softly left the room, and putting on her out-door things went off to the lodgings she and he had quitted the evening before.

Scarcely half-an-hour had elapsed ere she reappeared round the corner, walking beside a lad wheeling a truck on which were piled all Jude's household possessions, and also the few of Arabella's things which she had taken to the lodging for her short sojourn there. Jude was in such physical pain from his unfortunate breakdown of the previous night, and in such mental pain from the loss of Sue and from having yielded in his half-somnolent state to Arabella, that when he saw his few chattels unpacked and standing before his eyes in this strange bedroom, intermixed with woman's apparel, he scarcely considered how they had come there, or what their coming signalized.

"Now," said Arabella to her father downstairs, "we must keep plenty of good liquor going in the house these next few days. I know his nature, and if he once gets into that fearfully low state that he does get into sometimes, he'll never do the honourable thing by me in this world, and I shall be left in the lurch. He must be kept cheerful. He has a little money in the savings bank, and he has given me his purse to pay for anything necessary. Well, that will be the license; for I must have that ready at hand, to catch him the moment he's in the humour. You must pay for the liquor. A few friends, and a quiet convivial party would be the thing, if we could get it up. It would advertise the shop, and help me too."

"That can be got up easy enough by anybody who'll afford victuals and drink.... Well yes – it would advertise the shop – that's true."

---

1   knocked up] (coll.:) ill.

Three days later, when Jude had recovered somewhat from the fearful throbbing of his eyes and brain, but was still considerably confused in his mind by what had been supplied to him by Arabella during the interval – to keep him jolly, as she expressed it – the little convivial gathering suggested by her, to wind Jude up to the striking point, took place.

Donn had only just opened his miserable little pork and sausage shop, which had as yet scarce any customers; nevertheless that party advertised it well, and the Donns acquired a real notoriety among a certain class in Christminster who knew not the colleges, not their works, nor their ways. Jude was asked if he could suggest any guest in addition to those named by Arabella and her father, and in a saturnine humour of perfect recklessness mentioned Uncle Joe, and Stagg, and the decayed auctioneer, and others whom he remembered as having been frequenters of the well-known tavern during his bout therein years before. He also suggested Freckles and Bower o' Bliss. Arabella took him at his word so far as the men went, but drew the line at the ladies.

Another man they knew, Tinker Taylor, though he lived in the same street, was not invited; but as he went homeward from a late job on the evening of the party, he had occasion to call at the shop for trotters. There were none in, but he was promised some the next morning. While making his inquiry Taylor glanced into the back room, and saw the guests sitting round, card-playing, and drinking, and otherwise enjoying themselves at Donn's expense. He went home to bed, and on his way out next morning wondered how the party went off. He thought it hardly worth while to call at the shop for his provisions at that hour, Donn and his daughter being probably not up, if they caroused late the night before. However, he found in passing that the door was open, and he could hear voices within, though the shutters of the meat-stall were not down. He went and tapped at the sitting-room door, and opened it.

"Well – to be sure!" he said, astonished.

Hosts and guests were sitting card-playing, smoking, and talking, precisely as he had left them eleven hours earlier; the gas was burning and the curtains drawn, though it had been broad daylight for two hours out of doors.

"Yes!" cried Arabella, laughing. "Here we are, just the same. We ought to be ashamed of ourselves, oughtn't we! But it is a sort of housewarming, you see; and our friends are in no hurry. Come in, Mr. Taylor, and sit down."

The tinker, or rather reduced ironmonger, was nothing loth, and entered and took a seat. "I shall lose a quarter, but never mind," he said. "Well, really, I could hardly believe my eyes when I looked in! It seemed as if I was flung back again into last night, all of a sudden."

"So you are. Pour out for Mr. Taylor."

He now perceived that she was sitting beside Jude, her arm being round his waist. Jude, like the rest of the company, bore on his face the signs of how deeply he had been indulging.

"Well, we've been waiting for certain legal hours to arrive, to tell the truth," she continued bashfully, and making her spirituous crimson look as much like a maiden blush as possible. "Jude and I have decided to make up matters between us by tying the knot again, as we find we can't do without one another after all. So, as a bright notion, we agreed to sit on till it was late enough, and go and do it off-hand."

Jude seemed to pay no great heed to what she was announcing, or indeed to anything whatever. The entrance of Taylor infused fresh spirit into the company, and they remained sitting, till Arabella whispered to her father: "Now we may as well go."

"But the parson don't know?"

"Yes, I told him last night that we might come between eight and nine, as there were reasons of decency for doing it as early and quiet as possible, on account of it being our second marriage, which might make people curious to look on if they knew. He highly approved."

"O very well: I'm ready," said her father, getting up and shaking himself.

"Now, old darling," she said to Jude. "Come along, as you promised."

"When did I promise anything?" asked he, whom she had made so tipsy by her special knowledge of that line of business as almost to have made him sober again – or to seem so to those who did not know him.

"Why!" said Arabella, affecting dismay. "You've promised to marry me several times as we've sat here to-night. These gentlemen have heard you."

"I don't remember it," said Jude doggedly. "There's only one woman – but I won't mention her in this Capharnaum!"[1]

Arabella looked towards her father. "Now, Mr. Fawley, be honourable," said Donn. "You and my daughter have been living here together these three or four days, quite on the understanding that you were going to marry her. Of course I shouldn't have had such goings on in my house if I hadn't understood that. As a point of honour you must do it now."

"Don't say anything against my honour!" enjoined Jude hotly, standing up. "I'd marry the W—— of Babylon[2] rather than do anything dishonourable! No reflection on you, my dear. It is a mere rhetorical figure – what they call in the books, hyperbole."

"Keep your figures for your debts to friends who shelter you," said Donn.

"If I am bound in honour to marry her – as I suppose I am – though how I came to be here with her I know no more than a dead man – marry her I will, so help me God! I have never behaved dishonourably to a woman or to any living thing. I am not a man who wants to save himself at the expense of the weaker among us!"

"There – never mind him, deary," said she, putting her cheek against Jude's. "Come up and wash your face, and just put yourself tidy, and off we'll go. Make it up with father."

They shook hands. Jude went upstairs with her, and soon came down looking tidy and calm. Arabella, too, had hastily arranged herself, and accompanied by Donn away they went.

"Don't go," she said to the guests at parting. "I've told the little maid to get the breakfast while we are gone; and when we come back we'll all have some. A good strong cup of tea will set everybody right for going home."

When Arabella, Jude and Donn had disappeared on their matrimonial errand the assembled guests yawned themselves wider awake, and discussed the situation with great interest. Tinker Taylor, being the

---

1   Capharnaum] place of sinners: "And thou, Capernaum,…..shalt be brought down to hell" (Matthew 11:23).

2   W— of Babylon] The Whore of Babylon is a monstrous figure of evil described in Revelation 17-19 ("the inhabitants of the earth have been made drunk with the wine of her fornication").

most sober, reasoned the most lucidly.

"I don't wish to speak against friends," he said. "But it do seem a rare curiosity for a couple to marry over again! If they couldn't get on the first time when their minds were limp,[1] they won't the second, by my reckoning."

"Do you think he'll do it?"

"He's been put upon his honour by the woman, so he med."

"He'd hardly do it straight off like this. He's got no license nor anything."

"She's got that, bless you. Didn't you hear her say so to her father?"

"Well," said Tinker Taylor, re-lighting his pipe at the gas-jet. "Take her all together, limb by limb, she's not such a bad-looking piece – particular by candlelight. To be sure, halfpence that have been in circulation can't be expected to look like new ones from the Mint. But for a woman that's been knocking about the four hemispheres for some time, she's passable enough. A little bit thick in the flitch[2] perhaps: but I like woman that a puff o' wind won't blow down."

Their eyes followed the movements of the little girl as she spread the breakfast-cloth on the table they had been using, without wiping up the slops of the liquor. The curtains were undrawn, and the expression of the house made to look like morning. Some of the guests, however, fell asleep in their chairs. One or two went to the door, and gazed along the street more than once. Tinker Taylor was the chief of these, and after a time he came in with a leer on his face.

"By Gad, they are coming! I think the deed's done!"

"No," said Uncle Joe, following him in. "Take my word, he turned rusty[3] at the last minute. They are walking in a very unusual way; and that's the meaning of it!"

They waited in silence till the wedding party could be heard entering the house. First into the room came Arabella boisterously; and her face was enough to show that her strategy had succeeded.

"Mrs. Fawley, I presume?" said Tinker Taylor with mock courtesy.

"Certainly. Mrs Fawley again," replied Arabella blandly, pulling off her glove and holding out her left hand. "There's the padlock, see...."

---

1 limp] (dl.:) limber, flexible.
2 thick in the flitch] plump in figure (a flitch being a side of pork).
3 rusty] surly.

Well, he was a very, nice, gentlemanly man indeed. I mean the clergyman. He said to me as gentle as a babe when all was done: 'Mrs. Fawley, I congratulate you heartily,' he says. 'For having heard your history, and that of your husband, I think you have both done the right and proper thing. And for your past errors as a wife, and his as a husband, I think you ought now to be forgiven by the world, as you have forgiven each other,' says he. Yes: he was a very, nice, gentlemanly man. 'The Church don't recognize divorce in her dogma, strictly speaking,' he says: 'and bear in mind the words of the Service in your goings out and your comings in: What God hath joined together let no man put asunder.' Yes: he was a very, nice, gentlemanly man.... But Jude, my dear, you were enough to make a cat laugh! You walked that straight, and held yourself that steady, that one would have thought you were going 'prentice to a judge; though I knew you were seeing double all the time, from the way you fumbled with my finger."

"I said I'd do anything to − save a woman's honour," muttered Jude. "And I've done it!"

"Well now, old deary, come along and have some breakfast."

"I want − some − more whisky," said Jude stolidly.

"Nonsense, dear. Not now! There's no more left. The tea will take the muddle out of our heads, and we shall be as fresh as larks."

"All right. I've − married you. She said I ought to marry you again, and I have straightway. It is true religion! Ha − ha − ha!"

VI.-VIII.

MICHAELMAS[1] came and passed, and Jude and his wife, who had lived but a short time in her father's house after their marriage, were in lodgings on the top floor of a house nearer to the centre of the city.

He had done a few days' work during the two or three months since the event, but his health had been indifferent, and it was now precarious. He was sitting in an arm-chair before the fire, and coughed a good deal.

"I've got a bargain for my trouble in marrying thee over again!"

---

1 MICHAELMAS] 29 September.

Arabella was saying to him. "I shall have to keep 'ee entirely, – that's what 'twill come to! I shall have to make black-pot and sausages, and hawk 'em about the street, all to support an invalid husband I'd no business to be saddled with at all. Why didn't you keep your health, deceiving one like this? You were well enough when I married you!"

"Ah, yes!" said he, laughing acridly. "I have been thinking of my foolish feeling about the pig you and I killed during our first marriage. I feel now that the greatest mercy that could be vouchsafed to me would be that something should serve me as I served that animal."

This was the sort of discourse that went on between them every day now. The landlord of the lodging, who had heard that they were a queer couple, had doubted if they were married at all, especially as he had seen Arabella kiss Jude one evening when she had taken a little cordial; and he was about to give them notice to quit, till by chance overhearing her one night haranguing Jude in rattling terms, and ultimately flinging a shoe at his head, he recognized the note of ordinary wedlock; and concluding that they must be respectable, said no more.

Jude did not get any better, and one day he requested Arabella, with considerable hesitation, to execute a commission for him. She asked him indifferently what it was.

"To write to Sue."

"What in the name – do you want me to write to her for?"

"To ask how she is, and if she'll come to see me, because I'm ill, and should like to see her – once again."

"It is like you to insult a lawful wife by asking such a thing!"

"It is just in order not to insult you that I ask you to do it. You know I love Sue. I don't wish to mince the matter – there stands the fact: I love her. I could find a dozen ways of sending a letter to her without your knowledge. But I wish to be quite above-board with you, and with her husband. A message through you asking her to come is at least free from any odour of intrigue. If she retains any of her old nature at all, she'll come."

"You've no respect for marriage whatever, or its rights and duties!"

"What *does* it matter what my opinions are – a wretch like me! Can it matter to anybody in the world who comes to see me for half-an-hour – here with one foot in the grave! ... Come, please write, Arabella!" he pleaded. "Repay my candour by a little generosity!"

"I should think *not!*"

"Not just once? – O do!" He felt that his physical weakness had taken away all his dignity.

"What do you want *her* to know how you are for? She don't want to see 'ee. She's the rat that forsook the sinking ship!"

"Don't, don't!"

"And I stuck to un – the more fool I! Have that strumpet in the house indeed!"

Almost as soon as the words were spoken Jude sprang from the chair, and before Arabella knew where she was he had her on her back upon a little couch which stood there, he kneeling above her.

"Say another word of that sort," he whispered, "and I'll kill you – here and now! I've everything to gain by it – my own death not being the least part. So don't think there's no meaning in what I say!"

"What do you want me to do?" gasped Arabella.

"Promise never to speak of her."

"Very well. I do."

"I take your word," he said scornfully as he loosened her. "But what it is worth I can't say."

"You couldn't kill the pig, but you could kill me!"

"Ah – there you have me! No – I couldn't kill you – even in a passion. Taunt away!"

He then began coughing very much, and she estimated his life with an appraiser's eye as he sank back ghastly pale. "I'll send for her," Arabella murmured, "if you'll agree to my being in the room with you all the time she's here."

The softer side of his nature, the desire to see Sue, made him unable to resist the offer even now, provoked as he had been; and he replied breathlessly: "Yes, I agree. Only send for her!"

In the evening he inquired if she had written.

"Yes," she said; "I wrote a note telling her you were ill, and asking her to come to-morrow or the day after. I haven't posted it yet."

The next day Jude wondered if she really did post it, but would not ask her; and foolish Hope, that lives on a drop and a crumb, made him restless with expectation. He knew the times of the possible trains, and listened on each occasion for sounds of her.

She did not come; but Jude would not address Arabella again

thereon. He hoped and expected all the next day; but no Sue appeared; neither was there any note of reply. Then Jude decided in the privacy of his mind that Arabella had never posted hers, although she had written it. There was something in her manner which told it. His physical weakness was such that he shed tears at the disappointment when she was not there to see. His suspicions were, in fact, well founded. Arabella, like other nurses, thought that your duty towards your invalid was to pacify him by any means short of really acting upon his fancies.

He never said another word to her about his wish or his conjecture. A silent, undiscerned resolve grew up in him, which gave him, if not strength, stability and calm. One midday when, after an absence of two hours, she came into the room, she beheld the chair empty.

Down she flopped on the bed, and sitting, meditated. "Now where the devil is my man gone to!" she said.

A driving rain from the north-east had been falling with more or less intermission all the morning, and looking from the window at the dripping spouts it seemed impossible to believe that any sick man would have ventured out to almost certain death. Yet a conviction possessed Arabella that he had gone out, and it became a certainty when she had searched the house. "If he's such a fool, let him be!" she said. "I can do no more."

Jude was at the moment in a railway train that was drawing near to Alfredston, oddly swathed, pale as a monumental figure in alabaster, and much stared at by other passengers. An hour later his thin form, in the long great-coat and blanket he had come with, but without an umbrella, could have been seen walking along the five-mile road to Marygreen. On his face showed the determined purpose that alone sustained him, but to which his weakness afforded a sorry foundation. By the uphill walk he was quite blown, but he pressed on; and at half-past three o'clock stood by the familiar well at Marygreen. The rain was keeping everybody indoors; Jude crossed the green to the church without observation, and found the building open. Here he stood, looking forth at the school, whence he could hear the usual sing-song tones of the little voices that had not learnt Creation's groan.

He waited till a small boy came from the school – one evidently allowed out before hours for some reason or other. Jude held up his hand, and the child came.

"Please call at the schoolhouse and ask Mrs. Phillotson if she will be kind enough to come to the church for a few minutes."

The child departed, and Jude heard him knock at the door of the dwelling. He himself went further into the church. Everything was new, except a few pieces of carving preserved from the wrecked old fabric, now fixed against the new walls. He stood by these: they seemed akin to the perished people of that place who were his ancestors and Sue's.

A light footstep, which might have been accounted no more than an added drip to the rainfall, sounded in the porch, and he looked round.

"O – I didn't think it was you! I didn't – O Jude!" A hysterical catch in her breath ended in a succession of them. He advanced, but she quickly recovered and went back.

"Don't go – don't go!" he implored. "This is my last time! I thought it would be less intrusive than to enter your house. And I shall never come again. Don't then be unmerciful. Sue, Sue! We are acting by the letter; and 'the letter killeth!'"[1]

"I'll stay – I won't be unkind!" she said, her mouth quivering and her tears flowing as she allowed him to come closer. "But why did you come, and do this wrong thing, after doing such a right thing as you have done?"

"What right thing?"

"Marrying Arabella again. It was in the Alfredston paper. She has never been other than yours, Jude – in a proper sense. And therefore you did so well – O so well! – in recognizing it – and taking her to you again."

"God above – and is that all I've come to hear? If there is anything more degrading, immoral, unnatural, than another in my life, it is this meretricious contract with Arabella which has been called doing the right thing! And you too – you call yourself Phillotson's wife! *His* wife! You are mine."

"Don't make me rush away from you – I can't bear much! But on this point I am decided."

"I cannot understand how you did it – how you think it – I cannot!"

---

1 'The letter killeth'] 2 Corinthians 3:6 (again).

"Never mind that. He is a kind husband to me – And I – I've wrestled and struggled, and fasted, and prayed. I have nearly brought my body into complete subjection. And you mustn't – will you – wake ——"

"O you darling little fool; where is your reason? You seem to have suffered the loss of your faculties! I would argue with you if I didn't know that a woman in your state of feeling is quite beyond all appeals to her brains. Or is it that you are humbugging yourself, as so many women do about these things; and don't actually believe what you pretend to, and only are indulging in the luxury of the emotion raised by an affected belief?"

"Luxury! How can you be so cruel!"

"You dear, sad, soft, most melancholy wreck of a promising human intellect that it has ever been my lot to behold! Where is your scorn of convention gone? I *would* have died game!"

"You crush, almost insult me, Jude! Go away from me!" She turned off quickly.

"I will. I would never come to see you again, even if I had the strength to come, which I shall not have any more. Sue, Sue, you are not worth a man's love!"

Her bosom began to go up and down. "I can't endure you to say that!" she burst out, and her eye resting on him a moment, she turned back impulsively. "Don't, don't scorn me! Kiss me, O kiss me lots of times, and say I am not a coward and a contemptible humbug – I can't bear it!" She rushed up to him and, with her mouth on his, continued: "I must tell you – O I must – my darling Love! It has been – only a church marriage – an apparent marriage I mean! He suggested it at the very first!"

"How?"

"I mean it is a nominal marriage only. It hasn't been more than that at all since I came back to him!"

"Sue!" he said. Pressing her to him in his arms he bruised her lips with kisses: "If misery can know happiness, I have a moment's happiness now! Now, in the name of all you hold holy, tell me the truth, and no lie. You do love me still?"

"I do! You know it too well! ... But I *mustn't* do this! – I mustn't kiss you back as I would!"

"But do!"

"And yet you are so dear! – and you look so ill ——"

"And so do you! There's one more, in memory of our dead little children – yours and mine!"

The words struck her like a blow, and she bent her head. "I *mustn't* – I *can't* go on with this!" she gasped presently. "But there, there, darling; I give you back your kisses; I do, I do! ...And now I'll *hate* myself for ever for my sin!"

"No – let me make my last appeal. Listen to this! We've both re-married out of our senses. I was made drunk to do it. You were the same. I was gin-drunk; you were creed-drunk. Either form of intoxication takes away the nobler vision.... Let us then shake off our mistakes, and run away together!"

"No; again no! ...Why do you tempt me so far, Jude! It is too merciless! ... But I've got over myself now. Don't follow me – don't look at me. Leave me, for pity's sake!"

She ran up the church to the east end, and Jude did as she requested. He did not turn his head, but took up his blanket, which she had not seen, and went straight out. As he passed the end of the church she heard his coughs mingling with the rain on the windows, and in a last instinct of human affection, even now unsubdued by her fetters, she sprang up as if to go and succour him. But she knelt down again, and stopped her ears with her hands till all possible sound of him had passed away.

He was by this time at the corner of the green, from which the path ran across the fields in which he had scared rooks as a boy. He turned and looked back, once, at the building which still contained Sue; and then went on, knowing that his eyes would light on that scene no more.

There are cold spots up and down Wessex in autumn and winter weather; but the coldest of all when a north or east wind is blowing is the crest of the down by the Brown House, where the road to Alfredston crosses the old Ridgeway. Here the first winter sleets and snows fall and lie, and here the spring frost lingers last unthawed. Here in the teeth of the north-east wind and rain Jude now pursued his way, wet through, the necessary slowness of his walk from lack of his former strength being insufficient to maintain his heat. He came to the milestone, and, raining as it was, spread his blanket and lay down there to rest. Before moving on he went and felt at the back of the stone for his own carving. It was still there; but nearly obliterated by moss. He passed the spot where the gibbet of his ancestor and Sue's had stood, and descended the hill.

It was dark when he reached Alfredston, where he had a cup of tea, the deadly chill that began to creep into his bones being too much for him to endure fasting. To get home he had to travel by a steam tramcar, and two branches of railway, with much waiting at a junction. He did not reach Christminster till ten o'clock.

VI.-IX.

ON the platform stood Arabella. She looked him up and down.

"You've been to see her?"she asked.

"I have," said Jude, literally tottering with cold and lassitude.

"Well, now you'd best march along home."

The water ran out of him as he went, and he was compelled to lean against the wall to support himself while coughing.

"You've done for yourself by this, young man," said she. "I don't know whether you know it."

"Of course I do. I meant to do for myself."

"What − to commit suicide?"

"Certainly."

"Well, I'm blest! Kill yourself for a woman."

"Listen to me, Arabella. You think you are the stronger; and so you are, in a physical sense, now. You could push me over like a ninepin. You did not send that letter the other day, and I could not resent your conduct. But I am not so weak in another way as you think. I made up my mind that a man confined to his room by inflammation of the lungs, a fellow who had only two wishes left in the world, to see a particular woman, and then to die, could neatly accomplish those two wishes at one stroke by taking this journey in the rain. That I've done. I have seen her for the last time, and I've finished myself − put an end to a feverish life which ought never to have been begun!"

"Lord − you do talk lofty! Won't you have something warm to drink?"

"No thank you. Let's get home."

They went along by the silent colleges, and Jude kept stopping.

"What are you looking at?"

"Stupid fancies. I see, in a way, those spirits of the dead again, on this my last walk, that I saw when I first came here!"

"What a curious chap you are!"

"I seem to see them, and almost hear them rustling. But I don't revere all of them as I did then. I don't believe in half of them. The theologians, the apologists, and their kin the metaphysicians, the high-handed statesmen, and others, no longer interest me. All that has been spoilt for me by the grind of stern reality!"

The expression of Jude's corpse-like face in the watery lamplight was indeed as if he saw people where there was nobody. At moments he stood still by an archway, like one watching a figure walk out; then he would look at a window like one discerning a familiar face behind it. He seemed to hear voices, whose words he repeated as if to gather their meaning.

"They seem laughing at me!"

"Who?"

"O – I was talking to myself! The phantoms all about here, in the college archways, and windows. They used to look friendly in the old days, particularly Addison, and Gibbon, and Johnson, and Dr. Browne,[1] and Bishop Ken ——"

"Come along do! Phantoms! There's neither living nor dead hereabouts except a damn policeman! I never saw the streets emptier."

"Fancy! The Poet of Liberty[2] used to walk here, and the great Dissector of Melancholy[3] there!"

"I don't want to hear about 'em! They bore me."

"Walter Raleigh[4] is beckoning to me from that lane – Wycliffe – Harvey – Hooker[5] - Arnold – and a whole crowd of Tractarian Shades ——"

"I *don't want* to know their names, I tell you! What do I care about

1   Johnson.....Browne] Samuel Johnson (1709-84), the critic, editor, and lexicographer awarded an honorary doctorate by Oxford University; Sir Thomas Browne (1605-82), author of *Religio Medici*.
2   Poet of Liberty] P.B. Shelley (1792-1822).
3   Dissector of Melancholy] Robert Burton (1577-1640), author of *The Anatomy of Melancholy*.
4   Raleigh] Sir Walter Raleigh (1552?-1618), poet, scholar, explorer, adventurer.
5   Wycliffe – Harvey – Hooker] John Wycliffe (1330?-84), religious reformer and Master of Balliol; William Harvey (1578-1657), discoverer of the process of the circulation of the blood; Richard Hooker (1554-1600), theological writer.

folk dead and gone? Upon my soul you are more sober when you've been drinking than when you have not!"

"I must rest a moment," he said; and as he paused, holding to the railings, he measured with his eye the height of a college front. "This is old Rubric. And this Sarcophagus; and up that lane Crozier and Tudor: and all down there is Cardinal with its long front, and its windows with lifted eyebrows, representing the polite surprise of the University at the efforts of such as I."

"Come along, and I'll treat you!"

"Very well. It will help me home, for I feel the chilly fog from the meadows of Cardinal as if death-claws were grabbing me through and through. As Antigone said, I am neither a dweller among men nor ghosts.[1] But, Arabella, when I am dead, you'll see my spirit flitting up and down here among these!"

"Pooh! You won't die. You are tough enough yet, old man."

It was night at Marygreen, and the rain of the afternoon showed no sign of abatement. About the time at which Jude and Arabella were walking the streets of Christminster homeward, the Widow Edlin crossed the green, and opened the back door of the schoolmaster's dwelling, which she often did now before bedtime, to assist Sue in putting things away.

Sue was muddling helplessly in the kitchen, for she was not a good housewife, though she tried to be, and grew impatient of domestic details.

"Lord love 'ee, what do ye do that yourself for, when I've come o' purpose! You knew I should come."

"O – I don't know – I forgot! No, I didn't forget. I did it to discipline myself. I have scrubbed the stairs since eight o'clock. I *must* practise myself in my household duties. I've shamefully neglected them!"

"Why should ye? He'll get a better school, perhaps be a parson, in time, and you'll keep two servants. 'Tis a pity to spoil them pretty hands."

"Don't talk of my pretty hands, Mrs. Edlin. This pretty body of mine has been the ruin of me already!"

---

1   I.....ghosts] Near the end of Sophocles' tragedy *Antigone*, the heroine speaks to this effect as she is about to be walled up in a cave to die.

"Pshoo – you've got no body to speak of! You put me more in mind of a sperrit. But there seems something wrong to-night, my dear. Husband cross?"

"No. He never is. He's gone to bed early."

"Then what is it?"

"I cannot tell you. I have done wrong to-day. And I want to eradicate it.... Well – I will tell you this – Jude has been here this afternoon, and I find I still love him – O, grossly! I cannot tell you more."

"Ah!" said the widow. "I told 'ee how 'twould be!"

"But it shan't be! I have not told my husband of his visit; it is not necessary to trouble him about it, as I never mean to see Jude any more. But I am going to make my conscience right on my duty to Richard – by doing a penance – the ultimate thing. I must!"

"I wouldn't – since he agrees to it being otherwise, and it has gone on three months very well as it is."

"Yes – he agrees to my living as I choose; but I feel it is an indulgence I ought not to exact from him. It ought not to have been accepted by me. To reverse it will be terrible – but I must be more just to him. O why was I so unheroic!"

"What is it you don't like in him?" asked Mrs. Edlin curiously.

"I cannot tell you. It is something ... I cannot say. The mournful thing is, that nobody would admit it as a reason for feeling as I do; so that no excuse is left me."

"Did you ever tell Jude what it was?"

"Never."

"I've heard strange tales o' husbands in my time," observed the widow in a lowered voice. "They say that when the saints were upon the earth devils used to take husbands' forms o' nights, and get poor women into all sorts of trouble. But I don't know why that should come into my head, for it is only a tale.... What a wind and rain it is to-night! Well – don't be in a hurry to alter things, my dear. Think it over."

"No, no! I've screwed my weak soul up to treating him more courteously – and it must be now – at once – before I break down!"

"I don't think you ought to force your nature. No woman ought to be expected to."

"It is my duty. I will drink my cup to the dregs!"

Half-an-hour later when Mrs. Edlin put on her bonnet and shawl to leave, Sue seemed to be seized with vague terror.

"No, no – don't go, Mrs. Edlin," she implored, her eyes enlarged, and with a quick nervous look over her shoulder.

"But it is bed-time, child."

"Yes, but – there's the little spare room – my room that was. It is quite ready. Please stay, Mrs. Edlin! – I shall want you in the morning."

"O well – I don't mind, if you wish. Nothing will happen to my four old walls, whether I be there or no."

She then fastened up the doors, and they ascended the stairs together.

"Wait here, Mrs. Edlin," said Sue. "I'll go into my old room a moment by myself."

Leaving the widow on the landing Sue turned to the chamber which had been hers exclusively since her arrival at Marygreen, and pushing to the door knelt down by the bed for a minute or two. She then arose, and taking her nightgown from the pillow undressed and came out to Mrs. Edlin. A man could be heard snoring in the room opposite. She wished Mrs. Edlin good-night, and the widow entered the room that Sue had just vacated.

Sue unlatched the other chamber door, and, as if seized with faintness, sank down outside it. Getting up again she half opened the door, and said "Richard." As the word came out of her mouth she visibly shuddered.

The snoring had quite ceased for some time, but he did not reply. Sue seemed relieved, and hurried back to Mrs. Edlin's chamber. "Are you in bed, Mrs. Edlin?" she asked.

"No, dear," said the widow, opening the door. "I be old and slow, and it takes me a long while to un-ray.[1] I ha'n't unlaced my jumps[2] yet."

"I – don't hear him! And perhaps – perhaps ——"

"What, child?"

"Perhaps he's dead!" she gasped. "And then – I should be *free*, and I could go to Jude! .... Ah – no – I forgot *her* – and God!"

---

1   un-ray] (dl.:) undress.
2   jumps] (dl.:) stays.

"Let's go and hearken. No – he's snoring again. But the rain and the wind is so loud that you can hardly hear anything but between whiles."

Sue had dragged herself back. "Mrs. Edlin, good night again! I am sorry I called you out." The widow retreated a second time.

The strained, resigned look returned to Sue's face when she was alone. "I must do it – I must! I must drink to the dregs!" she whispered. "Richard!" she said again.

"Hey – what? Is that you, Susanna?"

"Yes."

"What do you want? Anything the matter? Wait a moment." He pulled on some articles of clothing, and came to the door. "Yes?"

"When we were at Shaston I jumped out of the window rather than that you should come near me. I have never reversed that treatment till now – when I have come to beg your pardon for it, and ask you to let me in."

"Perhaps you only think you ought to do this? I don't wish you to come against your impulses, as I have said."

"But I beg to be admitted." She waited a moment, and repeated, "I beg to be admitted! I have been in error – even to-day. I have exceeded my rights. I did not mean to tell you, but perhaps I ought. I sinned against you this afternoon."

"How?"

"I met Jude! I didn't know he was coming. And ——"

"Well?"

"I kissed him, and let him kiss me."

"O – the old story!"

"Richard, I didn't know we were going to kiss each other till we did!"

"How many times?"

"A good many. I don't know. I am horrified to look back on it, and the least I can do after it is to come to you like this."

"Come – this is pretty bad, after what I've done! ... Anything else to confess?"

"No." She had been intending to say: "I called him my darling Love." But, as a contrite woman always keeps back a little, that portion of the scene remained untold. She went on: "I am never going to see him any more. He spoke of some things of the past: and it overcame me. He spoke of – the children. – But, as I have said, I am glad – almost glad I mean – that they are dead, Richard. It blots out all that life of mine!"

"Well – about not seeing him again any more. Come – you really mean this?" There was something in Phillotson's tone now which seemed to show that his three months of re-marriage with Sue had somehow not been so satisfactory as his magnanimity or amative patience had anticipated.

"Yes, yes!"

"Perhaps you'll swear it on the New Testament?"

"I will."

He went back to the room and brought out a little brown Testament. "Now then: So help you God!"

She swore.

"Very good!"

"Now I supplicate you, Richard, to whom I belong, and whom I wish to honour and obey, as I vowed, to let me in."

"Think it over well. You know what it means. Having you back was one thing – this another. So think again."

"I have thought – I wish this!"

"That's a complaisant spirit – and perhaps you are right. With a lover hanging about, a half-marriage should be completed. But I repeat my reminder this third and last time."

"It is my wish! ... O God!"

"What did you say O God for?"

"I don't know!"

"Yes you do! But ... " He gloomily considered her thin and fragile form a moment longer as she crouched before him in her night-clothes. "Well, I thought it might end like this," he said presently. "I owe you nothing, after these signs; but I'll take you in at your word, and forgive you."

He put his arm round her to lift her up. Sue started back.

"What's the matter?" he asked, speaking for the first time sternly. "You shrink from me again? – just as formerly!"

"No, Richard – I – I – was not thinking ——."

"You wish to come in here?"

"Yes."

"You still bear in mind what it means?"

"Yes. It is my duty!"

Placing the candlestick on the chest of drawers he led her through the doorway, and lifting her bodily, kissed her. A wild look of aversion passed over her face, but clenching her teeth she uttered no cry.

Mrs. Edlin had by this time undressed, and was about to get into bed when she said to herself: "Ah – perhaps I'd better go and see if the little thing is all right. How it do blow and rain!"

The widow went out on the landing, and saw that Sue had disappeared. "Ah! Poor soul! Weddings be funerals 'a b'lieve nowadays. Fifty-five years ago, come Fall, since my man and I married! Times have changed since then!"

VI.-X.

DESPITE himself, Jude recovered somewhat, and worked at his trade for several weeks. After Christmas, however, he broke down again.

With the money he had earned he shifted his lodgings to a yet more central part of the town. But Arabella saw that he was not likely to do much work for a long while, and was cross enough at the turn affairs had taken since her re-marriage to him. "I'm hanged if you haven't been clever in this last stroke!" she would say, "to get a nurse for nothing by marrying me!"

Jude was absolutely indifferent to what she said, and, indeed, often regarded her abuse in a humorous light. Sometimes his mood was more earnest, and as he lay he often rambled on upon the defeat of his early aims.

"Every man has some little power in some one direction," he would say. "I was never really stout enough for the stone trade, particularly the fixing. Moving the blocks always used to strain me, and standing the trying draughts in buildings before the windows are in, always gave me colds, and I think that began the mischief inside. But I felt I could do one thing if I had the opportunity. I could accumulate ideas, and impart them to others. I wonder if the Founders had such as I in their minds – a fellow good for nothing else but that particular thing? ... I hear that soon there is going to be a better chance for such helpless students as I was.[1] There are schemes afoot for making the University less exclusive, and extending its influence. I don't know much about it. And it is too late, too late for me! Ah – and for how many worthier ones before me!"

"How you keep a-mumbling!" said Arabella. "I should have thought you'd have got over all that craze about books by this time. And so you would, if you'd had any sense to begin with. You are as bad now as when we were first married."

On one occasion while soliloquizing thus he called her "Sue" unconsciously.

"I wish you'd mind who you are talking to!" said Arabella indignantly. "Calling a respectable married woman by the name of that –" She remembered herself and he did not catch the word.

But in the course of time, when she saw how things were going, and how very little she had to fear from Sue's rivalry, she had a fit of generosity. "I suppose you want to see your – Sue?" she said. "Well, I don't mind her coming. You can have her here if you like."

"I don't wish to see her again."

"O – that's a change!"

"And don't tell her anything about me – that I'm ill, or anything. She has chosen her course. Let her go!"

One day he received a surprise. Mrs. Edlin came to see him, quite on her own account. Jude's wife, whose feelings as to where his affections were centred had reached absolute indifference by this time, went out, leaving the old woman alone with Jude. He impulsively asked how Sue was, and then said bluntly, remembering what Sue had told him: "I suppose they are still only husband and wife in name?"

Mrs. Edlin hesitated. "Well, no – it's different now. She's begun it quite lately – all of her own free will."

"When did she begin?" he asked quickly.

"The night after you came. But as a punishment to her poor self. He didn't wish it, but she insisted."

"Sue, my Sue – you darling fool – this is almost more than I can endure! ... Mrs. Edlin – don't be frightened at my rambling – I've got to talk to myself lying here so many hours alone – she was once a

---

1 better.....was] See Appendix F.

woman whose intellect was to mine like a star to a benzoline lamp:[1] who saw all *my* superstitions as cobwebs that she could brush away with a word. Then bitter affliction came to us, and her intellect broke, and she veered round to darkness. Strange difference of sex, that time and circumstance, which enlarge the views of most men, narrow the views of women almost invariably. And now the ultimate horror has come – her giving herself like this to what she loathes, in her enslavement to forms! – she, so sensitive, so shrinking, that the very wind seemed to blow on her with a touch of deference.[2] ... As for Sue and me when we were at our own best, long ago – when our minds were clear, and our love of truth fearless – the time was not ripe for us! Our ideas were fifty years too soon to be any good to us. And so the resistance they met with brought reaction in her, and recklessness and ruin on me! ... There – this, Mrs. Edlin, is how I go on to myself continually, as I lie here. I must be boring you awfully."

"Not at all, my dear boy. I could hearken to 'ee all day."

As Jude reflected more and more on her news, and grew more restless, he began in his mental agony to use terribly profane language about social conventions, which started a fit of coughing. Presently there came a knock at the door downstairs. As nobody answered it Mrs. Edlin herself went down.

The visitor said blandly: "The doctor." The lanky form was that of Physician Vilbert, who had been called in by Arabella.

"How is my patient at present?" asked the physician.

"O bad – very bad! Poor chap, he got excited, and do blaspeam terribly, since I let out some gossip by accident – the more to my blame. But there – you must excuse a man in suffering for what he says, and I hope God will forgive him."

"Ah. I'll go up and see him. Mrs. Fawley at home?"

"She's not in at present, but she'll be here soon."

Vilbert went; but though Jude had hitherto taken the medicines of that skilful practitioner with the greatest indifference, whenever poured down his throat by Arabella, he was now so brought to bay by events that he vented his opinion of Vilbert in the physician's face, and so forcibly, and with such striking epithets, that Vilbert soon scurried downstairs again. At the door he met Arabella, Mrs. Edlin having

---

1   benzoline lamp] lamp fuelled by impure benzene oil.
2   wind.....deference] perhaps an echo of *Hamlet*, I.ii.141-2.

left. Arabella inquired how he thought her husband was now, and seeing that the doctor looked ruffled, asked him to take something. He assented.

"I'll bring it to you here in the passage," she said. "There's nobody but me about the house to-day."

She brought him a bottle and a glass, and he drank. Arabella began shaking with suppressed laughter. "What is this, my dear?" he asked, smacking his lips.

"O – a drop of wine – and something in it." Laughing again she said: "I poured your own love-philter into it, that you sold me at the Agricultural Show, don't you remember?"

"I do, I do! Clever woman! But you must be prepared for the consequences." Putting his arm round her shoulders he kissed her there and then.

"Don't, don't," she whispered, laughing good-humouredly. "My man will hear."

She let him out of the house, and as she went back she said to herself: "Well! Weak women must provide for a rainy day. And if my poor fellow upstairs do go off – as I suppose he will soon – it's well to keep chances open. And I can't pick and choose now as I could when I was younger. And one must take the old if one can't get the young."

VI.-XI.

THE last pages to which the chronicler of these lives would ask the reader's attention are concerned with the scene in and out of Jude's bedroom when leafy summer came round again.

His face was now so thin that his old friends would hardly have known him. It was afternoon, and Arabella was at the looking-glass curling her hair, which operation she performed by heating an umbrella-stay in the flame of a candle she had lighted, and using it upon the flowing lock. When she had finished this, practised a dimple, and put on her things, she cast her eyes round upon Jude. He seemed to be sleeping, though his position was an elevated one, his malady preventing him lying down.

Arabella, hatted, gloved, and ready, sat down and waited, as if expecting some one to come and take her place as nurse.

Certain sounds from without revealed that the town was in festivity, though little of the festival, whatever it might have been, could be seen here. Bells began to ring, and the notes came into the room through the open window, and travelled round Jude's head in a hum. They made her restless, and at last she said to herself: "Why ever doesn't father come!"

She looked again at Jude, critically gauged his ebbing life, as she had done so many times during the late months, and glancing at his watch, which was hung up by way of timepiece, rose impatiently. Still he slept, and coming to a resolution she slipped from the room, closed the door noiselessly, and descended the stairs. The house was empty. The attraction which moved Arabella to go abroad had evidently drawn away the other inmates long before.

It was a warm, cloudless, enticing day. She shut the front door, and hastened round into Chief Street, and when near the Theatre could hear the notes of the organ, a rehearsal for a coming concert being in progress. She entered under the archway of Oldgate College,[1] where men were putting up awnings round the quadrangle for a ball in the Hall that evening. People who had come up from the country for the day were picnicking on the grass, and Arabella walked along the gravel paths and under the aged limes. But finding this place rather dull she returned to the streets, and watched the carriages drawing up for the concert, numerous Dons and their wives, and undergraduates with gay female companions, crowding up likewise. When the doors were closed, and the concert began, she moved on.

The powerful notes of that concert rolled forth through the swinging yellow blinds of the open windows, over the house-tops, and into the still air of the lanes. They reached so far as to the room in which Jude lay; and it was about this time that his cough began again and awakened him.

As soon as he could speak he murmured, his eyes still closed: "A little water, please."[2]

Nothing but the deserted room received his appeal, and he coughed to exhaustion again – saying still more feebly: "Water – some water – Sue – Arabella!"

---

1 Oldgate College] New College.
2 "A little water, please."] cf. "Jesus.....saith, I thirst" (John 19:28), and the "terrible thirst" of the dying Tenor in Sarah Grand's *The Heavenly Twins*.

The room remained still as before. Presently he gasped again: "Throat – water – Sue – darling – drop of water – please – O please!"

No water came, and the organ notes, faint as a bee's hum, rolled in as before.

While he remained, his face changing, shouts and hurrahs came from somewhere in the direction of the river.

"Ah – yes! The Remembrance games," he murmured. "And I here. And Sue defiled!"

The hurrahs were repeated, drowning the faint organ notes. Jude's face changed more: he whispered slowly, his lips scarcely moving:

"*Let the day perish wherein I was born, and the night in which it was said, There is a man child conceived.*"

("Hurrah!")

"*Let that day be darkness; let not God regard it from above, neither let the light shine upon it. Lo, let that night be solitary, let no joyful voice come therein.*"

("Hurrah!")

"*Why died I not from the womb? Why did I not give up the ghost when I came out of the belly? … For now should I have lain still and been quiet. I should have slept: then had I been at rest!*"

("Hurrah!")

"*There the prisoners rest together; they hear not the voice of the oppressor …. The small and the great are there; and the servant is free from his master. Wherefore is light given to him that is in misery, and life unto the bitter in soul?*"[1]

Meanwhile Arabella, on her journey to discover what was going on, took a short cut down a narrow street and through an obscure nook into the quad of Cardinal. It was full of bustle, and brilliant in the sunlight with flowers and other preparations for a ball here also. A carpenter nodded to her, one who had formerly been a fellow-workman of Jude's. A corridor was in course of erection from the entrance to the Hall staircase, of gay red and buff bunting. Waggon-loads of boxes containing bright plants in full bloom were being placed about, and the great staircase was covered with red cloth. She nodded to one workman and another, and ascended to the Hall on the strength of

---

1   "*Let……soul?*"] Job 3:3, 4, 7, 11, 13, 18, 19, 20.

their acquaintance, where they were putting down a new floor and decorating for the dance. The cathedral bell close at hand was sounding for five o'clock service.

"I should not mind having a spin there with a fellow's arm round my waist," she said to one of the men. "But Lord, I must be getting home again – there's a lot to do. No dancing for me!"

When she reached home she was met at the door by Stagg, and one or two other of Jude's fellow stoneworkers. "We are just going down to the river," said the former, "to see the boat-bumping. But we've called round on our way to ask how your husband is."

"He's sleeping nicely, thank you," said Arabella.

"That's right. Well now, can't you give yourself half-an-hour's relaxation, Mrs. Fawley, and come along with us? 'Twould do you good."

"I should like to go," said she. "I've never seen the boat-racing, and I hear it is good fun."

"Come along!"

"How I *wish* I could!" She looked longingly down the street. "Wait a minute, then. I'll just run up and see how he is now. Father is with him, I believe; so I can most likely come."

They waited, and she entered. Downstairs the inmates were absent as before, having, in fact, gone in a body to the river where the procession of boats was to pass. When she reached the bedroom she found that her father had not even now come.

"Why couldn't he have been here!" she said impatiently. "He wants to see the boats himself – that's what it is!"

However, on looking round to the bed, she brightened, for she saw that Jude was apparently sleeping, though he was not in the usual half-elevated posture necessitated by his cough. He had slipped down, and lay flat. A second glance caused her to start, and she went to the bed. His face was quite white, and gradually becoming rigid. She touched his fingers; they were cold, though his body was still warm. She listened at his chest. All was still within. The bumping of near thirty years had ceased.

After her first appalled sense of what had happened the faint notes of a military or other brass band from the river reached her ears; and in a provoked tone she exclaimed, "To think he should die just now! Why did he die just now!" Then meditating another moment or two

432 THOMAS HARDY

she went to the door, softly closed it as before, and again descended the stairs.

"Here she is!" said one of the workmen. "We wondered if you were coming after all. Come along; we must be quick to get a good place... Well, how is he? Sleeping well still? Of course, we don't want to drag 'ee away if –"

"O yes – sleeping quite sound. He won't wake yet," she said hurriedly.

They went with the crowd down Cardinal Street, where they presently reached the bridge,[1] and the gay barges burst upon their view. Thence they passed by a narrow slit down to the riverside path – now dusty, hot, and thronged. Almost as soon as they had arrived the grand procession of boats began; the oars smacking with a loud kiss on the face of the stream, as they were lowered from the perpendicular.

"O, I say – how jolly! I'm glad I've come," said Arabella. "And – it can't hurt my husband – my being away."

On the opposite side of the river, on the crowded barges, were gorgeous nosegays of feminine beauty, fashionably arrayed in green, pink, blue, and white. The blue flag of the Boat Club denoted the centre of interest, beneath which a band in red uniform gave out the notes she had already heard in the death-chamber. Collegians of all sorts, in canoes with ladies, watching keenly for "our" boat, darted up and down. While she regarded the lively scene somebody touched Arabella in the ribs, and looking round she saw Vilbert.

"That philter is operating, you know!" he said with a leer. "Shame on 'ee to wreck a heart so!"

"I shan't talk of love to-day."

"Why not? It is a general holiday."

She did not reply. Vilbert's arm stole round her waist, which act could be performed unobserved in the crowd. An arch expression overspread Arabella's face at the feel of the arm, but she kept her eyes on the river as if she did not know the embrace.

The crowd surged, pushing Arabella and her friends sometimes nearly into the river, and she would have laughed heartily at the horse-play that succeeded, if the imprint on her mind's eye of a pale,

---

1 Cardinal Street.....bridge] St Aldate's Street and Folly Bridge.

statuesque countenance she had lately gazed upon, had not sobered her a little.

The fun on the water reached the acme of excitement; there were immersions, there were shouts: the race was lost and won, the pink and blue and yellow ladies retired from the barges, and the people who had watched began to move.

"Well – it's been awfully good," cried Arabella. "But I think I must get back to my poor man. Father is there, so far as I know; but I had better get back."

"What's your hurry?"

"Well, I must go.... Dear, dear, this is awkward!"

At the narrow gangway where the people ascended from the river-side path to the bridge the crowd was literally jammed into one hot mass – Arabella and Vilbert with the rest; and here they remained motionless, Arabella exclaiming, "Dear, dear!" more and more impatiently; for it had just occurred to her mind that if Jude were discovered to have died alone an inquest might be deemed necessary.

"What a fidget you are, my love," said the physician, who, being pressed close against her by the throng, had no need of personal effort for contact. "Just as well have patience: there's no getting away yet!"

It was nearly ten minutes before the wedged multitude moved sufficiently to let them pass through. As soon as she got up into the street Arabella hastened on, forbidding the physician to accompany her further that day. She did not go straight to her house; but to the abode of a woman who performed the last necessary offices for the poorer dead; where she knocked.

"My husband has just gone, poor soul," she said. "Can you come and lay him out?"

Arabella waited a few minutes; and the two women went along, elbowing their way through the stream of fashionable people pouring out of Cardinal meadow, and being nearly knocked down by the carriages.

"I must call at the sexton's about the bell, too," said Arabella. "It is just round here, isn't it? I'll meet you at my door."

By ten o'clock that night Jude was lying on the bedstead at his lodging covered with a sheet, and straight as an arrow. Through the partly opened window the joyous throb of a waltz entered from the ball-room at Cardinal.

Two days later, when the sky was equally cloudless, and the air equally still, two persons stood beside Jude's open coffin in the same little bedroom. On one side was Arabella, on the other the Widow Edlin. They were both looking at Jude's face, the worn old eyelids of Mrs. Edlin being red.

"How beautiful he is!" said she.

"Yes. He's a 'andsome corpse," said Arabella.

The window was still open to ventilate the room, and it being about noontide the clear air was motionless and quiet without. From a distance came voices; and an apparent noise of persons stamping.

"What's that?" murmured the old woman.

"Oh, that's the doctors in the Theatre, conferring Honorary degrees on the Duke of Hamptonshire and a lot more illustrious gents of that sort. It's Remembrance Week, you know. The cheers come from the young men."

"Ay; young and strong-lunged! Not like our poor boy here."

An occasional word, as from some one making a speech, floated from the open windows of the Theatre across to this quite corner, at which there seemed to be a smile of some sort upon the marble features of Jude; while the old, superseded, Delphin editions of Virgil and Homer, and the dog-eared Greek Testament on the neighbouring shelf, and the few other volumes of the sort that he had not parted with, roughened with stone-dust where he had been in the habit of catching them up for a few minutes between his labours, seemed to pale to a sickly cast[1] at the sounds. The bells struck out joyously; and their reverberations travelled round the bedroom.

Arabella's eyes removed from Jude to Mrs. Edlin. "D'ye think she will come?" she asked.

"I could not say. She swore not to see him again."

"How is she looking?"

"Tired and miserable, poor heart. Years and years older than when you saw her last. Quite a staid, worn woman now. 'Tis the man; – she can't stomach un, even now!"

"If Jude had been alive to see her, he would hardly have cared for her any more, perhaps."

---

1 pale.....cast] cf. "sicklied o'er with the pale cast of thought" (*Hamlet*, III.i.85).

"That's what we don't know.... Didn't he ever ask you to send for her, since he came to see her in that strange way?"

"No. Quite the contrary. I offered to send, and he said I was not to let her know how ill he was."

"Did he forgive her?"

"Not as I know."

"Well – poor little thing, 'tis to be believed she's found forgiveness somewhere! She said she had found peace!"

"She may swear that on her knees to the holy cross upon her necklace till she's hoarse, but it won't be true!" said Arabella. "She's never found peace since she left his arms, and never will again till she's as he is now!"

THE END

Appendix A: Major Textual Changes

Jude the Obscure is a more protean work than we may at first appreciate. Initially it was conceived as a short story. Hardy's journal for 28 April 1888 says: "A short story of a young man – 'who could not go to Oxford' – His struggles and ultimate failure. Suicide." The writing extended between 1890 and 1895. A manuscript of the resultant novel has survived, having been presented by the author to the Fitzwilliam Museum, Cambridge, in October 1911. (Sir Sydney Cockerell, the Fitzwilliam's Director, acted as intermediary.) This manuscript is incomplete and bears temporary alterations made solely for the first published version, the serial text. The serial differs significantly from the first book edition. Subsequently Hardy made various revisions for the book editions of 1903 and 1912.

The manuscript, which bears the title *Jude the Obscure* above a sequence of cancelled titles (*The Simpletons* / *Part First* / *Hearts Insurgent* / *The Dreamer*), lacks a number of pages dealing with sexual encounters. These had to be deleted for the purposes of serialisation. Although otherwise the manuscript corresponds in the main to the first book text, it bears some alterations to adapt the narrative to the serial's bowdlerisations. Hardy's notes on pp. 1 and 52 of the MS emphasise that those alterations made for serial publication "have no authority beyond". In the early pages, various cancelled passages show that the author, who initially names the hero "Jack" rather than "Jude", intended his hero's interest in Christminster to be aroused by the knowledge that his cousin Sue was there, she having been adopted by the Provost of "Cloister College"; and originally it was she, not Phillotson, who sent to the young lad the package of Latin grammarbooks. For example, Jack's great-aunt originally said to him: "Jack, Jack, why dont you go & get the Head of a College to adopt ee, as your cousin has done." Hardy later substituted the following words: "Jude, Jude, why didsn't go off with that schoolmaster of thine to Christminster or somewhere!" Other changes indicate that Hardy went back over the pages to make insertions which initiate ironic sequences: thus Phillotson's early advice to Jude to "be kind to animals and birds" was an insertion apparently generated in retrospect from the farmer's chastisement of the kindly rook-scarer. Other changes refine the ironies: Hardy crossed out a reference to the old Marygreen church as "the ancient temple of God" and substituted "the ancient temple to the Christian divinities". There were also retrospective thematic refinements. Originally the picture which, at the rural inn, looked down on Arabella and Jude showed "Susannah & the Elders" (incidentally revealing one reason for naming the book's heroine Susanna), but Hardy substituted "Samson & Delilah", so as to make a sardonic commentary on Arabella's seduction of the young hero. In short, the manuscript is a fine illustration of the evolutionary nature of the process of literary composition; its absent leaves mutely condemn Victorian bowdlerisation; and its very presence in the manuscript department of the Fitzwilliam makes an irony that Hardy had foreseen and invited by his donation, for now scholars enter this academic citadel to study these hallowed pages which tell the story of a studious man who failed to enter a university.

Serialisation took place between December 1894 and November 1895. In the first instalment, the title was *The Simpletons*; in the second, it became *Hearts Insurgent*, because, as Hardy explained, the original choice was too close to the title of a previously-published novel (Charles Reade's *A Simpleton*). Hardy even asked for the serial to be re-titled *The Recalcitrants*, but his request came too late, after the heading *Hearts Insurgent* had been set in type.

The international publication certainly helped to swell Hardy's fame or notoriety. *Harper's New Monthly Magazine*, based in New York, reached a wide American public. *Harper's Monthly Magazine* (without the *New* and with different volume-numbers in its otherwise-matching European edition), issued in London under the ægis of Osgood, McIlvaine and Company, distributed the text to British and continental readers.

Harper's New Monthly Magazine had commissioned a novel which should be "in every respect suitable for a family magazine", and Hardy had promised that "it would be a tale that could not offend the most fastidious maiden." As he worked on it, however, he felt obliged to warn the editor that it "was carrying him into unexpected fields" and therefore asked to be allowed to cancel the agreement. No cancellation occurred, but, in response to requests from the editor, Hardy agreed to bowdlerise the text, drastically reducing its sexual frankness. For example: in the serial version, Jude marries Arabella not because she has seduced him and claims to be pregnant but because she falsely declares that she has received a postal offer of marriage from a rival suitor. When, after their separation, he encounters her again, at Christminster, he does not spend the night with her. At Aldbrickham Jude and Sue live in separate houses; Sue never copulates with Jude; and instead of bearing two children, she merely adopts another child in addition to "Father Time". The scene of Sue's eventual sexual submission to Phillotson was omitted. As in subsequent versions, nevertheless, Arabella does initially attract Jude's attention by throwing a pig's penis at him.

By means of careful work both before and at the proof stage, Hardy restored the novel's originally-envisaged boldness and frankness for the first book edition. This was the London edition, wrongly dated "1896", published by Osgood, McIlvaine and Co. on 1 November 1895 in one volume at six shillings. (The American first edition, issued by Harper, New York, on 9 November, had many petty differences in "house style" – in publishing-house editorial conventions of spelling and punctuation – but no substantive authorial differences from the London volume.) The proofs, preserved in the Signet Library at Edinburgh, show that Hardy made numerous significant last-minute changes. For example: when Sue is begging Phillotson to release her from their marriage, she quotes J. S. Mill; and, at the proof stage, Hardy added the following words to Phillotson's response: "'What do I care about J. S. Mill!' moaned he. 'I only want to lead a quiet life!'" Simon Gatrell (in *Hardy the Creator*, 162) comments:

> This gives, in a way that nothing else in the whole debate does, the sense of a nondescript, average, unheroic man driven into a corner by an extraordinary, impossible woman.

In 1903 a new edition was published in Great Britain by Macmillan as Vol. VIII of "The Wessex Novels". This contained numerous revisions by Hardy, and it is clear that, for all his indignation at the critical attacks on the 1895 edition, he was prepared to modify the novel in the light of those attacks. For instance, the references to the pig's penis were toned down so that the missile became less conspicuous and its exact nature rather less evident. In the 1895 version, the pizzle draws the reluctant yet fascinated attention of Jude and Arabella, as here:

She, too, looked in another direction, and took the piece as though ignorant of what her hand was doing. She hung it temporarily on the rail of the bridge, and then, by a species of mutual curiosity, they both turned, and regarded it.....

They talked a little more and a little more, as they stood regarding the limp object dangling across the hand-rail of the bridge.

In the 1903 version, their attention is directed rather towards each other:

But she, slily looking in another direction, swayed herself backwards and forwards on her hand as it clutched the rail of the bridge; till, moved by amatory curiosity, she turned her eyes critically upon him.....

They talked a little more and a little more, as they stood regarding each other and leaning against the hand-rail of the bridge.

Arabella herself, who, in the manuscript, the serial and the 1895 book, was termed a "substantial female human", became (in a change to annoy latter-day feminist readers) a "substantial female animal". Jude's Greek New Testament, which in 1895 was inconsistently described as closed and open on the same occasion, was now consistently left open. Numerous smaller changes were made.

In 1912 *Jude the Obscure* appeared as Vol. III of the Macmillan "Wessex Edition", an extensive collected edition of prose and verse; and for this Hardy made considerable further revisions. The brawl occasioned by Phillotson's forced resignation was made somewhat more farcical, and some sexual details were made more explicit. For instance, when Sue and Jude are denied accommodation because a householder observes that Sue is pregnant, the 1903 edition said, "The householder scrutinized Sue a moment" (415), whereas the 1912 edition says, "The householder scrutinized Sue's figure a moment" (397) – a change which makes clear that her pregnancy is conspicuous. A sequence of other modifications made Sue rather more sympathetic. Whereas the 1903 text said at one point that Jude and Sue "kissed each other" (272), the 1912 version says that they "kissed close and

long" (260-61). Her consoling words, previously "You did kiss me just
now, you know; and I didn't dislike you to, very much, Jude" (302),
became "You did kiss me just now, you know; and I didn't dislike you
to, I own it, Jude" (289). Her declaration to him, "I agree! I ought to
have known that you would conquer....." (334), became "I agree! I do
love you. I ought to have known that you would conquer....." (321).

Given that the 1912 edition represented Hardy's considered reap-
praisal of the material, it is understandable that this was the text
which tended to be reprinted by subsequent British editors. In the
United States, in contrast, the 1895 version dominated reprints until
1957, when the Harper's Modern Classics edition issued the text of
1912. By 1990, the editions published by Harper, Penguin Books,
Macmillan, Oxford University Press and Norton all maintained the
"New Wessex" text. This editorial consensus did, however, have certain unfortunate consequences. It meant, for example, that readers
were then consulting a text which differed quite significantly from
the historically important edition of 1895. It was that first edition
which attracted widespread attention from the reviewers and which
provoked the furore that largely contributed to Hardy's decision to
cease novel-writing. Thus, readers of the reprints of the 1912 text
were not seeing the text which had been so important in Hardy's
development; and, crucially, the 1912 version was out of phase with
that notorious critical furore of the 1890s. In order to judge the fair-
ness or otherwise of those critical comments, it is proper that readers
should see the text that provoked them. Furthermore, though the
revisions of 1903 and 1912 represent the fruits of Hardy's later reflections, there is no guarantee that the older Hardy (who, after all, was in
his sixties and seventies at those times) was a wiser author than the
younger man who had completed the 1895 version. Sometimes the
revisions mitigate (and thereby make more conventional) certain bold
features of characterisation and situation which were appropriate to
the general thematic radicalism of the novel. Even where the text is
unchanged, criticisms of, say, the sanctity of marriage were bolder
when uttered in the context of 1895 than were identical criticisms
made in the somewhat less inhibited context of 1912.

In the light of these considerations, it is the 1895 text that is represented in this volume. While the first edition had various small flaws,
the revisions published in 1903 and 1912 sometimes reduced the

impact of the original. There can, of course, be no "definitive" text of *Jude the Obscure*; indeed, it is salutary to notice that the purportedly "authoritative" version published by Norton in 1978 contained various errors, notably mis-spellings and the omission of a line of dialogue. Current conditions of publication arguably make it more likely than was the case a century ago that printed works will be blemished by petty errors.

When we look back over the history of the modifications of *Jude the Obscure*, we see that Hardy was prepared to adulterate his novel to secure the very large payments from *Harper's New Monthly*; that the mode of censorship operated far more forcefully in the case of such a "family magazine" than in the case of more specialised periodicals like the *New Review*, *Cosmopolis* or *Savoy*; and that he and Osgood, McIlvaine and Company (and Harper's in the United States) showed considerable courage in releasing the relatively unexpurgated text of the first book edition. As has been noted earlier, the critical controversy aroused by the book proved lucrative: within three months of *Jude's* appearance, an advertisement in the *Saturday Review* declared that the British print-run already totalled 20,000 copies. (Joseph Conrad's "best seller", *Chance*, would take two years to sell 13,000 British copies after its appearance in 1914.) Throughout the remaining years of Hardy's life, *Jude the Obscure* was frequently reprinted in various editions, notably Macmillan's Collected Edition in the "Three-and-Sixpenny Library of Books by Popular Authors". After his death, the flow of reprints continued, paperbacks enabling them to reach a wider readership; and the temporary expiry of his copyright in 1978 ensured a new burgeoning of hardback and paperback reprints. (In the 1990s, however, European laws extended the British copyright period from fifty years after the death of the author to seventy years.) Film versions of *Jude* for television (1971) and cinema (1996) boosted sales of the books. Hardy, who was never an undergraduate, would have been delighted not only to find that his novel had become a "set text" in numerous literature courses at universities, but also to see that it had reached audiences of millions.

Appendix B: Comments by Hardy

[From Hardy's diary: an entry for 28 April 1888, as quoted in *The Early Life of Thomas Hardy*, 272-3. In this passage alone, the square-bracketed phrases are Hardy's.]

A short story of a young man – "who could not go to Oxford" – His struggles and ultimate failure. Suicide. [Probably the germ of *Jude the Obscure*.] There is something [in this] the world ought to be shown, and I am the one to show it them – although I was not altogether hindered going, at least to Cambridge, and could have gone up easily at five-and-twenty.

[From a letter to Edmund Gosse, 10 November 1895 (in *The Collected Letters of Thomas Hardy*, vol. 2, 93):]

It required an artist to see that the plot is almost geometrically constructed – I ought not to say *constructed*, for, beyond a certain point, the characters necessitated it, & I simply let it come. As to the story itself, it is really sent out to those into whose souls the iron has entered, & has entered deeply, at some time of their lives.....

It is curious that some of the papers should look upon the novel as a manifesto on "the marriage question" (although, of course, it involves it) – seeing that it is concerned first with the labours of a poor student to get a University degree, & secondly with the tragic issues of two bad marriages, owing in the main to a doom or curse of hereditary temperament peculiar to the family of the parties.

.....The "grimy" features of the story go to show the contrast between the ideal life a man wished to lead, & the squalid real life he was fated to lead.....

[From a letter to W. Hatherell, 10 November 1895 (*Collected Letters of Thomas Hardy*, vol. 2, 94). William Hatherell (1855-1928) illustrated the twelve instalments of *Jude* in *Harper's*. "Jude at the Mile-Stone" accompanied the final instalment, November 1895.]

Allow me to express my sincere admiration for the illustration of "Jude at the Milestone." The picture is a tragedy in itself: & I do not remember ever before having an artist who grasped a situation so thoroughly.

[From a letter to Florence Henniker, 10 November 1895 (*Collected Letters of Thomas Hardy*, vol. 2, 94):]

I suppose I have missed the mark in the pig-killing scene the papers are making such a fuss about: I fully expected that, though described in that particular place for the purely artistic reason of bringing out A.'s character, it might serve a humane end in showing people the cruelty that goes on unheeded under the barbarous *régime* we call civilization.

[From a letter to Edmund Gosse, 20 November 1895 (*Collected Letters of Thomas Hardy*, vol. 2, 99):]

[Sue's] sexual instinct [is] healthy so far as it goes, but unusually weak & fastidious...., and one of her reasons for fearing the marriage ceremony is that she fears it wd be breaking faith with Jude to withhold herself at pleasure, or altogether, after it; though while uncontracted she feels at liberty to yield herself as seldom as she chooses. This has tended to keep his passion as hot at the end as at the beginning, & helps to break his heart. He has never really possessed her as freely as he desired.... As to the "coarse" scenes with Arabella, the battle in the school room, &c., the newspaper critics might, I thought, have sneered at them for their Fielding-ism rather than for their Zolaism. I am in read in Zola very little, but have felt akin locally to Fielding, so many of his scenes having been laid down this way, & his home near.

[From another letter to Gosse, 4 January 1896 (*Collected Letters of Thomas Hardy*, vol. 2, 105):]

The "rectangular" lines of the story were not premeditated, but came by chance; except, of course, that the involutions of four lives must necessarily be a sort of quadrille. The only point in the novel on which I feel sure is that it makes for morality; & that delicacy or indelicacy in a writer is according to his object. If I say to a lady "I met a naked woman", it is indelicate. But if I go on to say "I found she was mad with sorrow", it ceases to be indelicate. And in writing Jude my mind was fixed on the ending.

[From a letter to Florence Henniker, 1 June 1896 (*Collected Letters of Thomas Hardy*, vol. 2, 122):]

The unexpected result of *Jude* is that I am overwhelmed with requests for stories.....By the way, I have been offended with you for some time, though I have forgotten to say so, for what you said – that I was an advocate for "free love". I hold no theory whatever on the subject, except by way of experimental remarks at tea parties, & seriously I don't see any possible scheme for the union of the sexes that wd be satisfactory.

[From *The Later Years of Thomas Hardy*, 65:]

The misrepresentations of the last two or three years [i.e. since the appearance of *Jude*] affected but little, if at all, the informed appreciation of Hardy's writings, being heeded almost entirely by those who had not read him; and turned out ultimately to be the best thing that could have happened; for they wellnigh compelled him, in his own judgement at any rate, if he wished to retain any shadow of self-respect, to abandon at once a form of literary art he had long intended to abandon at some indefinite time, and resume openly that form of it [poetry] which had always been more intuitive with him, and which he had just been able to keep alive from his early years, half in secrecy, under the pressure of magazine writing.....

The change, after all, was not so great as it seemed.....He had mostly aimed at keeping his narratives close to natural life and as near to poetry in their subject as the conditions would allow.....

[From *The Later Years of Thomas Hardy*, 196:]

[A reply to an enquirer:] "To your inquiry if *Jude the Obscure* is autobiographical, I have to answer that there is not a scrap of personal detail in it, it having the least to do with his own life of all his books."

Appendix C: Contemporaneous Reviews and a Parody.

[The earliest reviews of *Jude the Obscure* were numerous and often lengthy, and the range of judgement was remarkable. At one extreme were reviewers who damned the book for its immorality and coarseness; at the opposite extreme were reviewers who acclaimed it as a great and truthful work; and between them were those who offered a mixed, qualified account.

The *Guardian's* anonymous critic likened the novel to "a shameful nightmare, which one only wishes to forget as quickly and as completely as possible". Mrs Oliphant, in *Blackwood's Magazine*, found the book full of "grossness, indecency, and horror"; it contained depraved passages, and the death of Jude's children was "pure farce". (A long extract from her appraisal is presented below.) An unsigned review in *The Athenæum* declared, "here we have a titanically bad book", and argued (shrewdly) that Hardy was tempted to envisage fate not as a blind force but as a spiteful one:

> The way it is done is extremely simple: you take a man with good aspirations – a weak man he must be, of course – and put down to his credit all his aspirations and the feeble attempts he makes to realize them, while all the mistakes he makes, which render his life a failure, you put down to the savage deity who lies in wait to trip him up.

Jude and Sue asked for trouble by living together unmarried; having chosen to defy society, "it is absurd of them to repine". The plot, in the contrivance of the double re-marriage, "makes the whole book appear dangerously near to farce"; the dialogue is sometimes implausibly didactic; and Jude is made to suffer so that "Mr. Hardy may rage furiously". Nevertheless, even this reviewer found time to praise the depiction of the rural background and of the minor characters.

The *Pall Mall Gazette* referred to the novel as "Jude the Obscene", summarised it facetiously (see below), and asked the author to supply a "cleaner" book, "to take the bad taste out of our mouths". This reviewer, like several others, was clearly offended by the scene of the children's deaths. The *Spectator* found the book too offensive to be reviewed, declaring that Hardy and Grant Allen were propagandists for an immoral "New Morality": "*Jude the Obscure* is too deplorable a falling-off from Mr. Hardy's former achievements to be reckoned with at all." The *Fortnightly Review* declared it "a dismal treatise" in which Hardy "is depressing because he is himself somewhat depressed", and criticised the implausibly pedantic dialogues of Jude and Sue. On 9 December 1895, however, Hardy remarked to Sir George Douglas: "Yes 'Jude' is going very well. I find that London society is not at all represented by the shocked critics."

The main defences of the novel came, predictably, from relatively radical or "advanced" magazines. The *Saturday Review* (from which an extract is cited below) claimed that the sexual matter which had so annoyed intemperate critics was secondary; what counted mainly was the original and sympathetic treatment of a working-class hero, which made this the "most splendid" of Hardy's works. For the *Westminster Review* (cited below), it was so moving a novel as to confirm that Hardy "is the greatest living English writer of fiction"; and the *Free Review* found it, in its realism and poignancy, "the supreme achievement of a great artist" – an opinion echoed by Richard le Gallienne in *The Idler*. Havelock Ellis (in the *Savoy Magazine*, cited later) offered a lengthy defence of *Jude* against its detractors, praising its realism:

> In *Jude the Obscure* we find for the first time in our literature the reality of marriage clearly recognized as something wholly apart from the mere ceremony with which our novelists have usually identified it.

Edmund Gosse, in another lengthy and measured appraisal (in *Cosmopolis*; extract below) found the story "ghastly" in summary, yet the vigour and vividness of the telling made *Jude the Obscure* "an irresistible book". Since Gosse was a friend and correspondent of Hardy, the predominantly favourable verdict was perhaps foreseeable.

Meanwhile, American reviews displayed much the same range, extending from disgust and revulsion to high praise for the novel's tragic power. In the New York *World*, Jeannette Gilder denounced it as foul – as is shown below – but then wrote to Hardy to request the privilege of an interview. (Shocked by her review, Hardy told his American publishers to withdraw the novel if they judged that step advisable. No interview with Gilder occurred.) The *Critic* said that if the work's characters were true to life, "we may as well accept a cage full of monkeys as a microcosm of humanity". In *Harper's Weekly*, however, W. D. Howells (quoted below) praised it for its unity and tragic intensity.

Undoubtedly, the extent of the controversy increased the book's sales; and, in the subsequent decades, there were few critical verdicts which had not been anticipated in the ample range of those early appraisals.]

Extracts from the review in the *Pall Mall Gazette*, 12 November 1895, 4:

.....And so in due course an unblessed family appears; and soon early and later infants are attracting momentary attention by hanging each other with box-cord on little pegs all round the room. After this come inquests, and remorse, and a new consciousness of sin, ending up in the re-marriage of all the divorcees, making, to the best of our reckoning, a total of six marriages and two obscenities to the count of two couples and a half – a record performance, we should think. And they all lived unhappily ever after, except Jude, who spat blood and died; while Arabella curled her hair with an umbrella stay and looked archly at her old acquaintance the itinerant quack.

.....The "series of seemings" stand forth in naked squalor and ugliness, shaped indeed by the hand of a master, but of a master in a nightmare.

Extracts from W. D. Howells' review in *Harper's Weekly*, 7 December 1895, 1156:

[In] the world where his hapless people have their being, there is not only no Providence, but there is Fate alone; and the environment is such that character itself cannot avail against it. We have back the old conception of an absolutely subject humanity, unguided and unfriended. The gods, careless of mankind, are again over all; only, now, they call themselves conditions.

The story is a tragedy, and tragedy almost unrelieved by the humorous touch which the poet is master of. The grotesque is there abundantly, but not the comic; and at times this ugliness heightens the pathos to almost intolerable effect. But I must say that the figure of Jude himself is, in spite of all his weakness and debasement, one of inviolable dignity. He is the sport of fate, but he is never otherwise than sublime; he suffers more for others than for himself. The wretched Sue who spoils his life and her own, helplessly, inevitably, is the kind of fool who finds the fool in the poet and prophet so often, and brings him to naught.....One may indeed blame the author for presenting such a conception of life; one may say that it is demoralizing if not immoral; but as to his dealing with his creations in the circumstances which he has imagined, one can only praise him for his truth.

The story has to do with some things not hitherto touched in fiction, or Anglo-Saxon fiction at least; and there cannot be any doubt of the duty of criticism to warn the reader that it is not for all readers. But not to affirm the entire purity of the book in these matters would be to fail of another duty of which there can be as little doubt.

.....I suppose it can be called morbid, and I do not deny that it is. But I have not been able to find it untrue, while I know that the world is full of truth that contradicts it.....

I allow that there are many displeasing things in the book, and few pleasing. Arabella's dimple-making, the pig-killing, the boy suicide and homicide; Jude's drunken second marriage; Sue's wilful self-surrender to Phillotson: these and other incidents are revolting. They make us shiver with horror and grovel with shame, but we know that they are deeply founded in the condition, if not in the nature of humanity.....If the experience of Jude with Arabella seems to arraign marriage,.....it is surely not the lesson of the story that any other relation than marriage is tolerable for the man and woman who live together.....

I find myself defending the book on the ethical side when I meant chiefly to praise it for what seems to me its artistic excellence. It has not only the solemn and lofty effect of a great tragedy; a work far faultier might impart this; but it has a unity very uncommon in the novel, and especially the English novel.

Extracts from Jeannette L. Gilder's review in the *World* (New York), 8 December 1895, 33:

What has happened to Thomas Hardy? What has gone wrong with the hand that wrote *Far from the Madding Crowd*? I am shocked, appalled by this story.....It is almost the worst book I have ever read. I only know of one of Balzac's that is as bad. To think that such a story as this should be written by Thomas Hardy, one of the few really great writers of modern fiction! What has twisted this brilliant mind? What caused those clear eyes to see so darkly?

.....I do not believe that there is a newspaper in England or America that would print this story of Thomas Hardy's as it stands in the book. Aside from its immorality, there is its coarseness, which is beyond belief. Unnecessary coarseness.....Brutal, horrible coarseness.....

No one will be the better for having read this book, but many will be the worse for it. When I finished the story I opened the windows and let in the fresh air, and I turned to my book-shelves and I said: "Thank God for Kipling and Stevenson, Barrie and Mrs. Humphry Ward. Here are four great writers who have never trailed their talents in the dirt."

Extracts from Margaret Oliphant's "The Anti-Marriage League" in *Blackwood's Magazine* 159 (January 1896), 135-49 (extracts, 138-42):

The present writer does not pretend to a knowledge of the works of Zola, which perhaps she ought to have before presuming to say that nothing so coarsely indecent as the whole history of Jude in his relations with his wife Arabella has ever been put in English print – that is to say, from the hands of a Master. There may be books more disgusting, more impious as regards human nature, more foul in detail, in those dark corners where the amateurs of filth find garbage to their taste; but not, we repeat, from any Master's hand.....In the history of Jude, the half-educated and by no means uninteresting hero in whose early self-training there is much that is admirable – Mr Hardy has given us a chapter in what used to be called the conflict between vice and virtue.....[Jude] falls into the hands of a woman so completely animal that it is at once too little and too much to call her vicious. She is a human pig.....After the man has been subjugated,.....he is made for the rest of his life into a puppet flung about between them by two women – the fleshly animal Arabella and the fantastic Susan, the one ready to gratify him in whatever circumstances they may meet, the other holding him on the tiptoe of expectation, with a pretended reserve which is almost more indecent still.

.....[T]he author's object must be, having glorified women by the creation of Tess, to show after all what destructive and ruinous creatures they are, in general circumstances and in every development, whether brutal or refined.....Mr Hardy informs us he has taken elaborate precautions to secure the double profit of the serial writer, by subduing his colours and diminishing his effect, in the presence of the less corrupt, so as to keep the perfection of filthiness for those who love it.

.....[*Jude the Obscure*] is intended as an assault on the stronghold of marriage, which is now beleaguered on every side. The motto is, "The letter killeth"; and I presume this must refer to the fact of Jude's early and unwilling union to Arabella, and that the lesson the novelist would have us learn is, that if marriage were not exacted, and people were free to form connections as the spirit moves them, none of these complications would have occurred, and all would have been well.....Had it been made possible for him to have visited Arabella as long as the new and transitory influence lasted, and then to have lived with Susan as long as she was pleased to permit him to do so, which was the best that could happen were marriage abolished, how would that have altered the circumstances? When Susan changed her mind would he have been less unhappy? when Arabella claimed him again would he have been less weak?

Mr Hardy's solution of the great insoluble question of what is to be the fate of the children in such circumstances brings this nauseous tragedy suddenly and at a stroke into the regions of pure farce – which is a surprise of the first quality, one too grotesque to be amusing.....Does Mr Hardy think this is really a good way of disposing of the unfortunate progeny of such connections? does he recommend it for general adoption? It is at least a clean and decisive cut of the knot, leaving no ragged ends; but then there is no natural provision in families of such a wise small child to get its progenitors out of trouble.....

Extracts from Edmund Gosse's review, "Mr. Hardy's New Novel", in *Cosmopolis* 1 (January 1896), 60-69 (extracts, 66-8):

It is a ghastly story.....But it does not appear to me that we have any business to call in question the right of a novelist of Mr. Hardy's extreme distinction to treat what themes he will. We may wish – and I for my part cordially wish – that more pleasing, more charming plots than this could take his fancy. But I do not feel at liberty to challenge his discretion. One thing, however, the critic of comparative literature must note. We have, in such a book as *Jude the Obscure*, traced the full circle of propriety. A hundred and fifty years ago, Fielding and Smollett brought up before us pictures, used expressions, described conduct, which appeared to their immediate successors a little more crude than general reading warranted. In Miss Burney's hands and Miss Austin's [*sic*], the morals were still further hedged about. Scott was even more daintily reserved. We came at last to Dickens, where the clamorous passions of mankind, the coarser accidents of life, were absolutely ignored, and the whole question of population seemed reduced to the theory of the gooseberry bush. This was the *ne plus ultra* of decency; Thackeray and George Eliot relaxed this intensity of prudishness; once on the turn, the tide flowed rapidly, and here is Mr. Hardy ready to say any mortal thing that Fielding said, and a good deal more too.

So much we note, but to censure it, if it calls for censure, is the duty of the moralist and not the critic. Criticism asks how the thing is done, whether the execution is fine and convincing. To tell so squalid and so abnormal a story in an interesting way is in itself a feat, and this, it must be universally admitted, Mr. Hardy has achieved. *Jude the Obscure* is an irresistible book; it is one of those novels into which we descend and are carried on by a steady impetus to the close, when we return, dazzled, to the light of common day. The two women, in particular, are surely created by a master. Every impulse, every speech, which reveals to us the coarse and animal, but not hateful Arabella, adds to the solidity of her portrait. We may dislike her, we may hold her intrusion into our consciousness a disagreeable one, but of her reality there can be no question: Arabella lives.

It is conceivable that not so generally will it be admitted that Sue Bridehead is convincing. Arabella is the excess of vulgar normality;

every public bar and village fair knows Arabella, but Sue is a strange and unwelcome product of exhaustion. The *vita sexualis* [sexual life] of Sue is the central interest of the book, and enough is told about it to fill the specimen tables of a German specialist. Fewer testimonies will be given to her reality than to Arabella's because hers is much the rarer case. But her picture is not less admirably drawn; Mr. Hardy has, perhaps, never devoted so much care to the portrait of a woman. She is a poor, maimed "degenerate," ignorant of herself and of the perversion of her instincts, full of febrile, amiable illusions, ready to dramatize her empty life, and play at loving though she cannot love. Her adventure with the undergraduate has not taught her what she is; she quits Philottson [*sic*] still ignorant of the source of her repulsion; she lives with Jude, after a long, agonizing struggle, in a relation that she accepts with distaste, and when the tragedy comes, and her children are killed, her poor extravagant brain slips one grade further down, and she sees in this calamity the chastisement of God. What has she done to be chastened? She does not know, but supposes it must be her abandonment of Philottson, to whom, in a spasm of self-abasement, and shuddering with repulsion, she returns without a thought for the misery of Jude. It is a terrible study in pathology, but of the splendid success of it, of the contained intellectual force implied in the evolution of it, there cannot, I think, be two opinions.

One word must be added about the speech of the author and of the characters in *Jude the Obscure*. Is it too late to urge Mr. Hardy to struggle against the jarring note of rebellion which seems growing upon him? It sounded in *Tess*, and here it is, more roughly expressed, further acerbated. What has Providence done to Mr. Hardy that he should rise up in the arable land of Wessex and shake his fist at his Creator? He should not force his talent, not give way to these chimerical outbursts of philosophy falsely so called. His early romances were full of calm and lovely pantheism; he seemed in them to feel the deep-hued country landscapes full of rural gods, all homely and benign. We wish he would go back to Egdon Heath and listen to the singing in the heather. And as to the conversations of his semi-educated characters, they are really terrible. Sue and Jude talk a sort of University Extension jargon that breaks the heart. "The mediævalism of Christminster must go, be sloughed off, or Christminster will have to go," says Sue, as she sits in a pair of Jude's trousers, while Jude dries her petticoat at his garret-fire. Hoity-toity, for a minx! the reader cries; or, rather, although he firmly believes in the existence of Sue, and in the truth of the episode, he is convinced that Mr. Hardy is mistaken in what he heard her say. She *could* not have talked like that.

Extracts from D. F. Hannigan's review in the *Westminster Review* 145 (January 1896), 136-9 (extracts, 136, 137-9):

Those who have satisfied themselves by observation and experience of the essentially artificial character of so-called British "morality" will not be surprised to find that certain critics of the didactic school have condemned Mr. Thomas Hardy's latest novel, *Jude the Obscure*, on the grounds of its outspokenness and its flagrant disregard of Mrs. Grundy's tender feelings. *Tess of the D'Urbervilles* offended the susceptibilities of such critics as Mr. Andrew Lang and Mr. James Payn, who worship the venerable Walter Scott, and prefer romance to realism. But *Jude the Obscure* will be *anathema maranatha* [intensely accursed] to hundreds of comparatively liberal-minded people who see no such harm in such works as *Jane Eyre* or *Adam Bede*. Mr. Hardy does not write, like Sir Walter Besant, merely for the edification of "the Young Person." When invited to give his personal views some time since on the subject of "Candour in Fiction", he emphatically claimed for the novelist the right to deal fearlessly with all the facts of life. His sympathies are manifestly with the French naturalistic school of fiction, though I for one cannot regard him as a writer of the same class as M. Zola or the late Guy de Maupassant. Through all that Mr. Hardy has written vibrates a passionate chivalry, to which we find no parallel in French realism. In our generation there has been no novelist capable of exhibiting the mysterious fascination of woman upon the other sex with the same art, with the same force of imagination. All his heroines are ideals, or at least idealised types, rather than portraits drawn from real life. To this extent, therefore, Mr. Hardy is not "realistic" in the vulgar sense of the word. He has shrunk from the portrayal of commonplace women – if we except the case of Arabella in his last novel – and the charming creatures around whom the interest of *Far from the Madding Crowd*, *The Trumpet Major*, and nearly all his other works, including *Tess of the D'Urbervilles*, centres, seem like etherealised beings – fays, sirens, who disguise themselves as farmeresses, parsons' daughters, unconventional heiresses, bishops' wives, schoolmistresses, or agricultural working-girls.

.....The history of Jude's ineffectual efforts to obtain a University education is intensely pathetic. If Samuel Johnson could come back to earth and read this portion of Mr. Hardy's last novel, I venture to think that he would have found it hard to keep back his tears, stern Briton though he was; and, but for the miserable priggery of this tail-end of the nineteenth century, the first part of *Jude the Obscure* would be held up by the critics as one of the most touching records in all literature. This story of crushed aspirations can only be appreciated by those who have the power of true sympathy. Unfortunately, we live in an age when nearly all human beings are concerned only with their material success in life. The word "failure" makes them tremble; and, no doubt Mr. Hardy's apparent pessimism is distasteful to the innumerable throng of vulgar-minded aspirants whose only gospel is to "get on" by hook or by crook. How could we expect the modern young man, whose thoughts are fixed solely on the Woolsack or on the results of a successful experiment on the Turf or the Stock Exchange, to enter into the feelings of a poor rustic stone-cutter who dreamed of taking out his degree and becoming a clergyman! The love-affairs of so obscure an individual may excite the attention of the unambitious middle-aged man, but not of the youthful prig of our day. The relations between Sue and her cousin will necessarily appear impure to those who see nothing but uncleanness in the relations of a married man and a woman who is not his wife. But Mr. Hardy is not to blame for the brutishness of some of his readers' minds any more than Miranda (to borrow a favourite illustration of Mr. Ruskin) is to blame for Caliban's beastly thoughts about her.

The "plot" (hideous word!) of *Jude the Obscure* has been sketched, and, indeed, misrepresented, by so many of the smug journalistic critics of this book, that it is better to let all intelligent and honest readers find out the true history of Jude Fawley for themselves by reading the novel. It is certainly "strong meat," but there is nothing prurient, nothing artificial, in this work; it is *human* in the widest sense of that comprehensive word. The tragic chapter with which the novel closes is perhaps the finest specimen of pure narrative that Mr. Hardy has ever given us.....Some of the language put into the mouth of Phillotson, the husband of Sue, is a little incongruous, for it is scarcely likely

that a village schoolmaster would talk about "the matriarchal system."
But in spite of certain defects of form which are perhaps inevitable, having regard to the intricacies of a story involving matrimonial complications, *Jude the Obscure* is the best English novel which has appeared since *Tess of the D'Urbervilles*. Mr. George Meredith's epigrammatic cleverness cannot atone for his poverty of invention, his lack of incident, his fantastic system of misreading human nature, and, if the word "novelist" means a writer of human history, Mr. Hardy is incomparably superior to his supposed rival. I would class the author of *Tess* with Fielding, Balzac, Flaubert, Turgenev, George Eliot and Dostoievsky; while Mr. Meredith is the literary brother of Bulwer Lytton, Peacock and Mérimée. The mosquito-like criticism of the day need not trouble a novelist who has already won fame. He is the greatest living English writer of fiction. In intensity, in grip of life, and, above all, in the artistic combination of the real and the ideal, he surpasses any of his French contemporaries. *Jude the Obscure* is not his greatest work; but no other living novelist could have written it.

Extracts from H. G. Wells's unsigned review in the *Saturday Review* 81 (8 February 1896), 153-4 (extracts, 153, 154):

It is now the better part of a year ago since the collapse of the "New Woman" fiction began.....And the reviewers.....have changed with the greatest dexterity from a chorus praising "outspoken purity" to a band of public informers against indecorum.....

If the reader has trusted the reviewers for his estimate of this great novel, he may even be surprised to learn that its main theme is not sexual at all.....For the first time in English literature the almost intolerable difficulties that beset an ambitious man of the working class – the snares, the obstacles, the countless rejections and humiliations by which our society eludes the services of these volunteers – receive adequate treatment.....

It is impossible by scrappy quotations to do justice to Mr. Hardy's tremendous indictment of the system which closes our three English teaching universities to what is, and what has always been, the noblest material in the intellectual life of this country – the untaught.....

There is no other novelists alive with the breadth of sympathy, the knowledge, or the power for the creation of Jude. Had Mr. Hardy never written another book, this would still place him at the head of English novelists.

Extracts from A. J. Butler's "Mr. Hardy as a Decadent" in *National Review* 27 (May 1896), 384-90 (extracts, 388, 389, 390):

[E]xtensive as Mr. Hardy's knowledge of human nature is, it is evidently incomplete, or else he has been guilty of what is surely unpardonable in a "realistic" writer, a suppression of a whole side of the truth. Life may not be "all beer and skittles," but neither is it all squalid, unredeemed tragedy; nor is it usually found that out of any dozen persons with whom we may fortuitously be brought into contact, there will not be one to whom can be attributed the possession of any elevated or generous feeling, together with sufficient resolution to act upon it. Yet in his latest story, *Jude the Obscure*, the reading of which has called forth these remarks, it may safely be said that Mr. Hardy has not given a hint showing any knowledge on his part that such people exist.....

It is all very well to talk about writing for men and women; but there are passages in Mr. Hardy's later books which will offend men in direct proportion to their manliness, and which all women, save the utterly abandoned – and it is not among these presumably that Mr. Hardy seeks his readers – will hurry over with shuddering disgust..... Whatever sport may lie in the defiance of "Mrs. Grundy" there can be nothing more certain in literature than that a tendency to dwell on foul details has never been a "note" of any but third-rate work.

Extracts from R. Y. Tyrrell's review in *Fortnightly Review*, n.s. 59 (June 1896), 857-64 (extracts, 863-4):

The book is addressed by the writer expressly "to men and women of full age," and he adds – in a tone which seems to show that he thinks the matter of very little moment – "I am not aware that there is anything in the handling to which exception can be taken." .....It seems that if his readers are of full age they are bound to accept without question his manner of handling his subject, whatever it may be. If it should seem prurient or coarse, being of full age they are bound to suppress all protest against it. This is a new and terrible penalty imposed on the elderly, a harmless though not very interesting class.....[We] should expect that the reader of full age would belong to just that class who would feel that the world presents other and to them more tractable difficulties than sex-problems, or marriage-problems (which, however, they would gladly see treated carefully by the Leckys and Herbert Spencers of the day), and that life is serious enough to dispose them to turn away with some impatience from a work in which there is not a practical suggestion for reform, and (what is worse) in which there is not material for a smile from the first page to the last – a dismal treatise as "chap-fallen" as Yorick's skull in the hands of Hamlet.

Extracts from Havelock Ellis's "Concerning *Jude the Obscure*" in *The Savoy* 6 (October 1896), 35-49 (extracts, 40, 41-2, 43):

In all the great qualities of literature *Jude the Obscure* seems to me the greatest novel written in England for many years.

.....In *Jude the Obscure* there is a fine self-restraint, a complete mastery of all the elements of an exceedingly human story. There is nothing here of the distressing melodrama into which Mr. Hardy was wont to fall in his early novels. Yet in plot *Jude* might be a farce.....

Only at one point, it seems to me, is there a serious lapse in the art of the book, and that is when the door of the bedroom closet is sprung open on us to reveal the row of childish corpses. Up to that one admires the strength and sobriety of the narrative, its complete reliance on the interests that lie in common humanity. We feel that here are real human beings of the sort we all know, engaged in obscure struggles that are latent in the life we all know. But with the opening of that cupboard we are thrust out of the large field of common life into the small field of the police court or the lunatic asylum, among the things which for most of us are comparatively unreal.....

.....[T]his book, it is said, is immoral, and indecent as well.

So are most of our great novels. *Jane Eyre*, we know on the authority of a *Quarterly* reviewer, could not have been written by a respectable woman, while another *Quarterly* (or maybe *Edinburgh*) reviewer declared that certain scenes in *Adam Bede* are indecently suggestive. *Tom Jones* is even yet regarded as unfit to be read in an unabridged form.....It seems, indeed, on a review of all the facts, that the surer a novel is of a certain immortality, the surer it is also to be regarded at first as indecent, as subversive of public morality. So that when, as in the present case, such charges are recklessly flung about in all the most influential quarters, we are simply called upon to accept them placidly as necessary incidents in the career of a great novel.

A parody, "Dude the Diffuse", in *Punch, or The London Charivari*, 109 (14 December 1895), 285:

DUDE THE DIFFUSE
BY TOOMUCH TOO HARDY

DUDE was in a rhapsodically enthusiastic mood. Although the weather was exceedingly foggy, he seemed to see his way along the path leading to his Uncle's, where it was his intention to call and execute a small commission. It being the end of the week, his funds were low; nevertheless, a glow of self-conceit cheered him when he thought of what he had already accomplished. After he had received that memorable, but ignominious, blow from practical Farmer PIKEHAM, he determined to give up the occupation of scaring crows, and apply himself assiduously to learning. And so far he had done satisfactorily. "I am already pretty good at the classics, Latin particularly." This was, indeed, no exaggeration of the truth, DUDE's extraordinary acquirements in that language now enabling him to *think* therein with far greater ease than in his native tongue. "I have translated HOMER's *Odyssey* into the Aztec; I know all the *Iliad* by heart; I have done the *Treaty of Shimonoseki* and *Ruff's Guide* into Greek Iambics; SOCRATES, HESIOD, THUCYDIDES, XENOPHON, ARISTOPHANES, and PLATO are more familiar to me than my own name. No one can teach me much in modern or ancient history; I can repeat from memory any chapter of the *Decline and Fall*. As to mathematics, the intricacies of the differential calculus are plainer to me than the added result of $2 + 2$. I could tell EUCLID a thing or two were he alive. My leisure moments – if I have any – are filled in by researches into Esoteric Buddhism. But all this is nothing – the ignorance of babes and sucklings, the mere shadow of a commencement – in comparison with what I intend to accomplish. My ambition is boundless. I even aspire, some day, to fathom the hidden depths of a Meredithian epigram, and to arrive at a correct reason for the existence of the *cacoethes Hilltopendi*. The first thing, though, is to make money."

Thus musing, he entered his uncle's residence...and upon emerging, after the lapse of a few minutes, re-commenced his reverie. As soon as he made an income of £5000 per annum, what an example he would set! He would live up to £10,000, and would give away the rest! What would he be? An eminent botanist! No, on second thoughts, botany was absurd! It had never struck him in that light before! He would draw the line at distinction as a landscape gardener! – DUDE now entered a building, and, making his way to the second floor, rang the electric bell beside a door which bore the legend "New Athens Club." He was admitted into a room full of sage-looking personages who were watching – apparently with great interest – a curious machine that stood in a corner of the apartment and gave forth sharp clicking sounds (which always reminded DUDE of his days with the "clacker"). He went up to two men, who seemed to be in authority near the odd instrument, and said "A dollar each way *Thuringia*." Presently the machine clicked more loudly; DUDE looked anxious, and someone called out "*Burton*, first; *Shore*, second; *Lyric*, third." DUDE sighed, and murmured, "I'll be a maker of books before I have done!"

Appendix D: Hardy's Outlook.

The items quoted in this Appendix illustrate Hardy's pessimism, his notions of a possibly-evolving creative force, and his warnings to readers who might simplify his outlook. The first item is one of his earliest and most significant poems, "Hap", a sonnet dated 1866. (The text, which differs locally from later versions, is from *Wessex Poems and Other Verses*, London: Harper & Brothers, 1898, 7-8.) The poem denies the existence of a hostile, vengeful god, and says that instead there are only "purblind Doomsters" – "Crass Casualty" (stupid chance) and "dicing Time". It says that these impersonal forces could as readily have given happiness as wretchedness. Nevertheless, the clear drift of the poem is that, in fact, the speaker has known wretchedness rather than happiness. He might even have found consolation (been "Half-eased") in recognizing a hostile god, for that would have made moral sense of the suffering. Instead, there have been merely these impersonal forces at work. Yet, in the very act of describing their actions and providing personifying capitalizations ("Casualty", "Time", "Doomsters"), the speaker makes them sound not unlike that hostile god: they are powerful and, in his case, callous, for they have slain joy and made hope "unbloom". In short, what the poem vigorously suggests (in its contorted, gnarled and forceful phrasing) blurs the logical distinction it purports to be defining. It thus reveals Hardy's own tendency to let his avowed agnosticism be sometimes tainted by antitheism (the sense that there is a hostile supernatural force). The second poem, "Nature's Questioning" (from *Wessex Poems*, 177-8), runs the gamut of Hardy's metaphysical conjectures. The third, "To a Lady" (*Wessex Poems*, 173-4), makes a stoical comment on an offended reader.

I.   Hap

> If but some vengeful god would call to me
> From up the sky, and laugh: "Thou suffering thing,
> Know that thy sorrow is my ecstasy,
> That thy love's loss is my hate's profiting!"

Then would I bear it, and clench myself, and die,
Steeled by the sense of ire unmerited;
Half-eased, too, that a Powerfuller than I
Had willed and meted me the tears I shed.

But not so. How arrives it joy lies slain,
And why unblooms the best hope ever sown?
– Crass Casualty obstructs the sun and rain,
And dicing Time for gladness casts a moan...
These purblind Doomsters had as readily strown
Blisses about my pilgrimage as pain.

2.   **Nature's Questioning**

When I look forth at dawning, pool,
        Field, flock, and lonely tree,
        All seem to look at me
Like chastened children sitting silent in a school;

Their faces dulled, constrained, and worn,
        As though the master's ways
        Through the long teaching days
Their first terrestrial zest had chilled and overborne.

And on them stirs, in lippings mere
        (As if once clear in call,
        But now scarce breathed at all) –
"We wonder, ever wonder, why we find us here!

"Has some Vast Imbecility,
        Mighty to build and blend,
        But impotent to tend,
Framed us in jest, and left us now to hazardry?

"Or come we of an Automaton
        Unconscious of our pains?...
        Or are we live remains
Of Godhead dying downwards, brain and eye now gone?

"Or is it that some high Plan betides,
      As yet not understood,
      Of Evil stormed by Good,
We the Forlorn Hope over which Achievement strides?"

   Thus things around. No answerer I...
      Meanwhile the winds, and rains,
      And Earth's old glooms and pains
Are still the same, and gladdest Life Death neighbours nigh.

3.   **To a Lady Offended by a Book of the Writer's**

   Now that my page upcloses, doomed, maybe,
   Never to press thy cosy cushions more,
   Or wake thy ready Yeas as heretofore,
   Or stir thy gentle vows of faith in me:

   Knowing thy natural receptivity,
   I figure that, as flambeaux banish eve,
   My sombre image, warped by insidious heave
   Of those less forthright, must lose place in thee.

   So be it. I have borne such. Let thy dreams
   Of me and mine diminish day by day,
   And yield their space to shine of smugger things;
   Till I shape to thee but in fitful gleams,
   And then in far and feeble visitings,
   And then surcease. Truth will be truth alway.

4. From *The Later Years of Thomas Hardy*, 91:

Pessimism (or rather what is called such) is, in brief, playing the sure game. You cannot lose at it; you may gain. It is the only view of life in which you can never be disappointed. Having reckoned what to do in the worst possible circumstances, when better arise, as they may, life becomes child's play.

5. From *The Later Years of Thomas Hardy*, 121-2:

We enter church, and we have to say, "We have erred and strayed from thy ways like lost sheep", when what we want to say is, "Why are we made to err and stray like lost sheep?" Then we have to sing, "My soul doth magnify the Lord", when what we want to sing is, "O that my soul could find some Lord that it could magnify! Till it can, let us magnify good works, and develop all means of easing mortals' progress through a world not worthy of them."

6. From *The Later Years of Thomas Hardy*, 124-5:

That the Unconscious Will of the Universe is growing aware of Itself I believe I may claim as my own idea solely – at which I arrived by reflecting that what has already taken place in a fraction of the whole (*i.e.* so much of the world as has become conscious) is likely to take place in the mass; and.....the whole Will becomes conscious thereby: and ultimately, it is to be hoped, sympathetic.

7. From *The Later Years of Thomas Hardy*, 165-6:

[The Great War] destroyed all Hardy's belief in the gradual ennoblement of man.....Moreover, the war gave the *coup de grâce* to any conception he may have nourished of a fundamental ultimate Wisdom at the back of things.....[E]vents seemed to show him that a fancy he had often held and expressed, that the never-ending push of the Universe was an unpurposive and irresponsible groping in the direction of least resistance, might possibly be the real truth.

8. From a letter to Alfred Noyes, 19 December 1920 (*Collected Letters*, vol. 6, 54):

My fancy may have often run away with me; but all the same my sober opinion – so far as I have any definite one – of the Cause of Things, has been defined in scores of places, and is that of a great many ordinary thinkers: – that the said Cause is neither moral nor immoral, but *un*moral.....

9. From the "General Preface" (dated "October 1911") to the Wessex Edition of 1912-14 (vol. 1, *Tess of the d'Urbervilles*, xii-xiii):

Positive views on the Whence and the Wherefore of things have never been advanced by this pen as a consistent philosophy.....[T]he sentiments in the following pages have been stated truly to be mere impressions of the moment, and not convictions or arguments.

That these impressions have been condemned as "pessimistic" – as if that were a very wicked adjective – shows a curious muddle-mindedness. It must be obvious that there is a higher characteristic of philosophy than pessimism, or than meliorism, or even than the optimism of these critics – which is truth.....

And there is another consideration. Differing natures find their tongue in the presence of differing spectacles. Some natures become vocal at tragedy, some are made vocal by comedy, and it seems to me that to whichever of these aspects of life a writer's instinct for expression the more readily responds, to that he should allow it to respond. That before a contrasting side of things he remains undemonstrative need not be assumed to mean that he remains unperceiving.

Appendix E: Influences and Contexts: Cultural Extracts.

1. From the Bible.

[The following extracts are taken from the King James version (with which Hardy was intimately familiar), as are the biblical quotations in *Jude the Obscure*. Extracts 1.1 and 1.2 give passages from the Book of Job, some of which are explicitly cited in the novel, most notably at the time of Jude's death. This Book tells how God permitted Satan to inflict numerous woes on Job; eventually, however, Job (unlike Jude) received ample compensation. Extract 1.3 gives part of the Song of Solomon, which particularly interests Sue in Part Third, Chap. IV. Extract 1.4 gives the entirety of the General Epistle of Jude, which, in its warnings against "*filthy* dreamers [who] defile the flesh" and people who "[have] men's persons in admiration because of advantage", relates to the thematic preoccupations of the novel.]

1.1: The Book of Job, Chap. 3:

1 *Job curses the day and services of his birth.* 13 *The ease of death.* 20 *He complaineth of life, because of his anguish.*
After this opened Job his mouth, and cursed his day.

2 And Job spake, and said,

3 Let the day perish wherein I was born, and the night *in which* it was said, There is a man child conceived.

4 Let that day be darkness; let not God regard it from above, neither let the light shine upon it.

5 Let darkness and the shadow of death stain it; let a cloud dwell upon it; let the blackness of the day terrify it.

6 *As for* that night, let darkness seize upon it; let it not be joined unto the days of the year, let it not come into the number of the months.

7 Lo, let that night be solitary, let no joyful voice come therein.

8 Let them curse it that curse the day, who are ready to raise up their mourning.

9 Let the stars of the twilight thereof be dark; let it look for light, but *have* none; neither let it see the dawning of the day:

10 Because it shut not up the doors of my *mother's* womb, nor hid sorrow from mine eyes.

11 Why died I not from the womb? *why* did I *not* give up the ghost when I came out of the belly?

12 Why did the knees prevent me? or why the breasts that I should suck?

13 For now should I have lain still and been quiet, I should have slept: then had I been at rest,

14 With kings and counsellors of the earth, which built desolate places for themselves;

15 Or with princes that had gold, who filled their houses with silver:

16 Or as an hidden untimely birth I had not been; as infants *which* never saw light.

17 There the wicked cease *from* troubling; and there the weary be at rest.

18 *There* the prisoners rest together; they hear not the voice of the oppressor.

19 The small and great are there; and the servant *is* free from his master.

20 Wherefore is light given to him that is in misery, and life unto the bitter *in* soul;

21 Which long for death, but it *cometh* not; and dig for it more than for hid treasures;

22 Which rejoice exceedingly, *and* are glad, when they can find the grave?

23 *Why is light given* to a man whose way is hid, and whom God hath hedged in?

24 For my sighing cometh before I eat, and my roarings are poured out like the waters.

25 For the thing which I greatly feared is come upon me, and that which I was afraid of is come unto me.

26 I was not in safety, neither had I rest, neither was I quiet; yet trouble came.

1.2: From The Book of Job, Chap. 42:

1 *Job submitteth himself unto God.* 7 *God, preferring Job's cause, maketh his friends submit themselves, and accepteth him.* 10 *He magnifieth and blesseth Job.* 16 *Job's age and death.*

Then Job answered the Lord, and said,

2 I know that thou canst do every *thing*, and *that* no thought can be withholden from thee.

3 Who *is* he that hideth counsel without knowledge? therefore have I uttered that I understood not; things too wonderful for me, which I knew not.

4 Hear, I beseech thee, and I will speak: I will demand of thee, and declare thou unto me.

5 I have heard of thee by the hearing of the ear: but now mine eye seeth thee.

6 Wherefore I abhor *myself*, and repent in dust and ashes.....

10 And the Lord turned the captivity of Job, when he prayed for his friends: also the Lord gave Job twice as much as he had before.

11 Then came there unto him all his brethren, and all his sisters, and all they that had been of his acquaintance before, and did eat bread with him in his house: and they bemoaned him, and comforted him over all the evil that the Lord had brought upon him: every man also gave him a piece of money, and every one an earring of gold.

12 So the Lord blessed the latter end of Job more than his beginning: for he had fourteen thousand sheep, and six thousand camels, and a thousand yoke of oxen, and a thousand she asses.

13 He had also seven sons and three daughters.....

16 After this lived Job an hundred and forty years, and saw his sons, and his sons' sons, *even* four generations.

17 So Job died, *being* old and full of days.

1.3: From the Song of Solomon, Chap. 6:

1 *The church professeth her faith in Christ.* 4 *Christ sheweth the graces of the church,* 10 *and his love towards her.*

Whither is thy beloved gone, O thou fairest among women? whither is thy beloved turned aside? that we may seek him with thee.

2 My beloved is gone down into his garden, to the beds of spices, to feed in the gardens, and to gather lilies.

3 I *am* my beloved's, and my beloved *is* mine: he feedeth among the lilies.

4 Thou *art* beautiful, O my love, as Tirzah, comely as Jerusalem, terrible as *an army* with banners.

5 Turn away thine eyes from me, for they have overcome me: thy hair *is* as a flock of goats that appear from Gilead.

6 Thy teeth *are* as a flock of sheep which go up from the washing, whereof every one beareth twins, and *there is* not one barren among them.

7 As a piece of pomegranate *are* thy temples within thy locks.

8 There are threescore queens, and fourscore concubines, and virgins without number.

9 My dove, my undefiled is *but* one; she *is* the *only* one of her mother, she *is* the choice *one* of her that bare her. The daughters saw her, and blessed her; *yea*, the queens and the concubines, and they praised her.

10 Who *is* she *that* looketh forth as the morning, fair as the moon, clear as the sun, *and* terrible as *an army* with banners?.....

1.4: The General Epistle of Jude:

He exhorteth them to be constant in the profession of the faith. 4 False teachers are crept in to seduce them: for whose damnable doctrine and manners horrible punishment is prepared: 20 whereas the godly, by the assistance of the Holy Spirit, and prayers to God, may persevere, and grow in grace, and keep themselves, and recover others out of the snares of those deceivers.

Jude, the servant of Jesus Christ, and brother of James, to them that are sanctified by God the Father, and preserved in Jesus Christ, *and* called:

2 Mercy unto you, and peace, and love, be multiplied.

3 Beloved, when I gave all diligence to write unto you of the common salvation, it was needful for me to write unto you, and

exhort *you* that ye should earnestly contend for the faith which was once delivered unto the saints.

4 For there are certain men crept in unawares, who were before of old ordained to this condemnation, ungodly men, turning the grace of our God into lasciviousness, and denying the only Lord God, and our Lord Jesus Christ.

5 I will therefore put you in remembrance, though ye once knew this, how that the Lord, having saved the people out of the land of Egypt, afterward destroyed them that believed not.

6 And the angels which kept not their first estate, but left their own habitation, he hath reserved in everlasting chains under darkness unto the judgment of the great day.

7 Even as Sodom and Gomorrha, and the cities about them in like manner, giving themselves over to fornication, and going after strange flesh, are set forth for an example, suffering the vengeance of eternal fire.

8 Likewise also these *filthy* dreamers defile the flesh, despise dominion, and speak evil of dignities.

9 Yet Michael the archangel, when contending with the devil he disputed about the body of Moses, durst not bring against him a railing accusation, but said, The Lord rebuke thee.

10 But these speak evil of those things which they know not: but what they know naturally, as brute beasts, in those things they corrupt themselves.

11 Woe unto them! for they have gone in the way of Cain, and ran greedily after the error of Balaam for reward, and perished in the gainsaying of Core.

12 These are spots in your feasts of charity, when they feast with you, feeding themselves without fear: clouds *they are* without water, carried about of winds; trees whose fruit withereth, without fruit, twice dead, plucked up by the roots;

13 Raging waves of the sea, foaming out their own shame; wandering stars, to whom is reserved the blackness of darkness for ever.

14 And Enoch also, the seventh from Adam, prophesied of these, saying, Behold, the Lord cometh with ten thousands of his saints,

15 To execute judgment upon all, and to convince all that are ungodly among them of all their ungodly deeds which they have ungodly committed, and of their hard *speeches* which ungodly sinners have spoken against him.

16 These are murmurers, complainers, walking after their own lusts; and their mouth speaketh great swelling *words*, having men's persons in admiration because of advantage.

17 But, beloved, remember ye the words which were spoken before of the apostles of our Lord Jesus Christ;

18 How that they told you there should be mockers in the last time, who should walk after their own ungodly lusts.

19 These be they who separate themselves, sensual, having not the Spirit.

20 But ye, beloved, building up yourselves on your most holy faith, praying in the Holy Ghost,

21 Keep yourselves in the love of God, looking for the mercy of our Lord Jesus Christ unto eternal life.

22 And of some have compassion, making a difference:

23 And others save with fear, pulling *them* out of the fire; hating even the garment spotted by the flesh.

24 Now unto him that is able to keep you from falling, and to present *you* faultless before the presence of his glory with exceeding joy,

25 To the only wise God our Saviour, *be* glory and majesty, dominion and power, both now and ever. Amen.

2. From Thomas Gray's "Elegy Written in a Country Church-Yard" (1751).

[This famous poem by Thomas Gray (1716-71) was well known to Hardy; it provided him with the title of one of his most successful novels (*Far from the Madding Crowd*) and is quoted in *Jude the Obscure*. With intensely memorable eloquence, the elegy expresses various themes which are developed in *Jude the Obscure*: one being that poverty repeatedly prevents the fulfilment of human potentialities, another being the general vanity of human wishes. The line "On some fond breast the parting soul relies" may remind us of the sad isolation of the dying Jude. The extract below is taken from the "Aldine" edition used by Hardy: *The Poetical Works of Thomas Gray* (London: Bell and Daldy, n.d.), 98-102, 104-5.]

.....Let not ambition mock their useful toil,
　　Their homely joys, and destiny obscure;

Nor grandeur hear with a disdainful smile
The short and simple annals of the poor.

The boast of heraldry, the pomp of pow'r,
And all that beauty, all that wealth e'er gave,
Await alike th' inevitable hour.
The paths of glory lead but to the grave.

Nor you, ye proud, impute to these the fault,
If memory o'er their tomb no trophies raise,
Where through the long-drawn aile and fretted vault
The pealing anthem swells the note of praise.

Can storied urn, or animated bust,
Back to its mansion call the fleeting breath?
Can honour's voice provoke the silent dust,
Or flatt'ry soothe the dull cold ear of death?

Perhaps in this neglected spot is laid
Some heart once pregnant with celestial fire;
Hands, that the rod of empire might have sway'd,
Or wak'd to extasy the living lyre.

But knowledge to their eyes her ample page
Rich with the spoils of time did ne'er unroll;
Chill penury repress'd their noble rage,
And froze the genial current of the soul.

Full many a gem of purest ray serene
The dark unfathom'd caves of ocean bear:
Full many a flower is born to blush unseen,
And waste its sweetness on the desert air.

Some village Hampden, that, with dauntless breast,
The little tyrant of his fields withstood,
Some mute inglorious Milton here may rest,
Some Cromwell guiltless of his country's blood.....

Far from the madding crowd's ignoble strife,
    Their sober wishes never learn'd to stray;
Along the cool sequester'd vale of life
    They kept the noiseless tenour of their way.

Yet ev'n these bones from insult to protect
    Some frail memorial still erected nigh,
With uncouth rhymes and shapeless sculpture deck'd,
    Implores the passing tribute of a sigh.

Their name, their years, spelt by th' unletter'd Muse,
    The place of fame and elegy supply:
And many a holy text around she strews,
    That teach the rustic moralist to die.

For who, to dumb forgetfulness a prey,
    This pleasing anxious being e'er resign'd,
Left the warm precincts of the cheerful day,
    Nor cast one longing ling'ring look behind?.....

3. From Edward Gibbon's *History of the Decline and Fall of the Roman Empire*, first published between 1776 and 1788.

[In *Jude the Obscure*, Hardy several times cites this work which, in its accounts of religion, is often drily ironic. The extracts below are taken from the 1854 edition used by Hardy (6 vols.; London: Bohn), Vol. II, Chap. 15, 45-6, 84. The passage about lust triumphing over piety ("insulted Nature sometimes vindicated her rights") is quoted in *Jude*, Part Third, Chap. X. The early Christians' wish that "some harmless mode of vegetation might have peopled paradise" is quoted in Part Fourth, Chap. IV; and the sceptical passage on miracles is cited in Part Second, Chap. I. More importantly, Gibbon's discussion of the sexual views, dilemmas and hypocrisies of the early Christians embodies themes which Hardy develops at large in *Jude the Obscure*; and sometimes Hardy seeks, stylistically, to emulate the drily or pedantically ironic tones of Gibbon.]

The virtue of the primitive Christians, like that of the first Romans, was very frequently guarded by poverty and ignorance. The chaste severity of the fathers, in whatever related to the commerce of the two sexes, flowed from the same principle; their abhorrence of every enjoyment which might gratify the sensual, and degrade the spiritual, nature of man. It was their favourite opinion, that if Adam had preserved his obedience to the Creator, he would have lived for ever in a state of virgin purity, and that some harmless mode of vegetation might have peopled paradise with a race of innocent and immortal beings. The use of marriage was permitted only to his fallen posterity, as a necessary expedient to continue the human species, and as a restraint, however imperfect, on the natural licentiousness of desire. The hesitation of the orthodox casuists on this interesting subject betrays the perplexity of men, unwilling to approve an institution which they were compelled to tolerate. The enumeration of the very whimsical laws which they most circumstantially imposed on the marriage bed, would force a smile from the young and a blush from the fair. It was their unanimous sentiment, that a first marriage was adequate to all the purposes of nature and of society. The sensual connexion was refined into a resemblance of the mystic union of Christ with his church, and was pronounced to be indissoluble either by divorce or by death. The practice of second nuptials was branded with the name of a legal adultery; and the persons who were guilty of so scandalous an offence against Christian purity, were soon excluded from the honours, and even from the alms, of the church. Since desire was imputed as a crime, and marriage was tolerated as a defect, it was consistent with the same principles to consider a state of celibacy as the nearest approach to the divine perfection. It was with the utmost difficulty that ancient Rome could support the institution of six vestals, but the primitive church was filled with a great number of persons of either sex, who had devoted themselves to the profession of perpetual chastity. A few of these, among whom we may reckon the learned Origen, judged it the most prudent to disarm the tempter. Some were insensible and some were invincible against the assaults of the flesh. Disdaining an ignominious flight, the virgins of the warm climate of Africa encountered the enemy in the closest engagement; they permitted priests and deacons to share their bed, and gloried amidst the flames in their unsullied purity. But insulted Nature sometimes vindicated her rights, and this new species of martyrdom served only to introduced a new scandal into the church. Among the Christian Ascetics, however (a name which they soon acquired from their painful exercise), many, as they were less presumptuous, were probably more successful. The loss of sensual pleasure was supplied and compensated by spiritual pride.....

But how shall we excuse the supine inattention of the Pagan and philosophic world, to those evidences which were presented by the hand of Omnipotence, not to their reason, but to their senses? During the age of Christ, of his apostles, and of their first disciples, the doctrine which they preached was confirmed by innumerable prodigies. The lame walked, the blind saw, the sick were healed, the dead were raised, demons were expelled, and the laws of nature were frequently suspended for the benefit of the church. But the sages of Greece and Rome turned aside from the awful spectacle, and, pursuing the ordinary occupations of life and study, appeared unconscious of any alterations in the moral or physical government of the world.

4. Thomas Campbell's "Song" ("How delicious is the winning").

[The poet Thomas Campbell (1777-1844) was immensely popular in his own day, but his fame has declined; now he is remembered mainly for a few war-songs and ballads (notably "Ye Mariners of England" and "Lord Ullin's Daughter"). The deftly-imaged poem given below is quoted approvingly by Sue in Part Fifth, Chap. III, of the novel. Its claim that free love is rapturous whereas wedlock kills love is given plenty of support by Hardy. The text is taken from *The Poetical Works of Thomas Campbell* (London: Moxon, 1840), 266-7.]

SONG

How delicious is the winning
Of a kiss at Love's beginning,
When two mutual hearts are sighing
For the knot there's no untying!

Yet, remember, 'midst your wooing,
Love has bliss, but Love has ruing;

Other smiles may make you fickle,
Tears for other charms may trickle.

Love he comes, and Love he tarries,
Just as fate or fancy carries;
Longest stays, when sorest chidden;
Laughs and flies, when press'd and bidden.

Bind the sea to slumber stilly,
Bind its odour to the lily,
Bind the aspen ne'er to quiver,
Then bind Love to last for ever!

Love's a fire that needs renewal
Of fresh beauty for its fuel;
Love's wing moults when caged and captured,
Only free, he soars enraptured.

Can you keep the bee from ranging,
Or the ringdove's neck from changing?
No! nor fetter'd Love from dying
In the knot there's no untying.

5. From the writings of Schopenhauer.

[Arthur Schopenhauer (1788-1860) expressed such extreme pessimism in his philosophical writings that the substantial length of his life seems curiously anomalous. Hardy owned Schopenhauer's *Two Essays* (London: Bell, 1889), annotated *Studies in Pessimism* (London: Swan Sonnenschein, 1891), and included the German in a list of philosophers whom he respected (see *Literary Notebooks*, vol. 1, 374, and vol. 2, 28-31). Schopenhauer claimed that in the universe a life-force generates beings who are doomed to suffer; the wise person seeks detachment from this futile vitality. The "advanced" doctor in *Jude the Obscure* refers to "the beginning of the coming universal wish not to live"; and an early reviewer scornfully attributed to the novel the notion that "baby Schopenhauers.....are coming into the world in shoals". Hardy had noted that an article by Sidney Alexander entitled

"Pessimism and Progress" (*Contemporary Review*, January 1893) claimed: "In philosophy Schopenhauer has given place to Hegel – the hope of cosmic suicide to the thought of a spiritual society, the vision of that City of God to wh[ich] the race of men is slowly climbing nearer." Hardy commented that this view was "comforting, but false" (*Literary Notebooks*, vol. 2, 55). Extract 5.1 shows that Schopenhauer anticipates Hardy's indignation at the ill-treatment of animals, and brings to mind not only the pig-slaughtering episode in Part First, Chap. X, of *Jude* but also the incident in Part Fifth, Chapter VII, in which Sue liberates the pigeons. The material at 5.2 illustrates the philosopher's belief in a pervasive life-force or will, a concept which profoundly influenced Hardy; that at 5.3 illustrates his extreme pessimism and misogyny.]

5.1. From "Religion: A Dialogue" *and Other Essays, tr. T.B. Saunders (London: Swan Sonnenschein, 1889), 112-13:*

I may mention here another fundamental error of Christianity, an error which cannot be explained away, and the mischievous consequences of which are obvious every day: I mean the unnatural distinction Christianity makes between man and the animal world to which he really belongs. It sets up man as all-important, and looks upon animals as merely things. Brahmanism and Buddhism, on the other hand, true to the facts, recognise in a positive way that man is related generally to the whole of nature, and specially and principally to animal nature; and in their systems man is always represented, by the theory of metempsychosis and otherwise, as closely connected with the animal world. The important part played by animals all through Buddhism and Brahmanism, compared with the total disregard of them in Judaism and Christianity, puts an end to any question as to which system is nearer perfection, however much we in Europe may have become accustomed to the absurdity of the claim. Christianity contains, in fact, a great and essential imperfection in limiting its precepts to man, and in refusing rights to the entire animal world.....[When] a Brahman or Buddhist has a slice of good luck, a happy issue in any affair, instead of mumbling a *Te Deum*, he goes to the market-place and buys birds and opens their cages at the city gate.....On the other hand, look at the revolting ruffianism with which our Christian public treats its animals; killing them for no object at all, and laughing over it, or mutilating or torturing them.....One might say with truth, Mankind are the devils of the earth, and the animals the souls they torment.

5.2: From Two Essays, *tr. K. Hillebrand (London: Bell, 1889), 309:*

I am the first who has asserted that a *will* must be attributed to all that is lifeless and inorganic. For, with me, the will is not, as has hitherto been assumed, an accident of cognition and therefore of life; but life itself is manifestation of will. Knowledge, on the contrary, is really an accident of life, and life of Matter. But Matter itself is only the perceptibility of the phenomena of the will. Therefore we are compelled to recognise *volition* in every effort or tendency which proceeds from the nature of a material body, and properly speaking constitutes that nature, or manifests itself as phenomenon by means of that nature; and there can consequently be no Matter without manifestation of will. The lowest and on that account most universal manifestation of will is *gravity*, wherefore it has been called a primary and essential property of Matter.

5.3: From Studies in Pessimism, *tr. T.B. Saunders (London: Swan Sonnenschein, 1891), 11, 12, 13, 13-14, 15, 19, 24, 27, 117, 118, 120, 123:*

Unless *suffering* is the direct and immediate object of life, our existence must entirely fail of its aim.....

We are like lambs in a field, disporting themselves under the eye of the butcher, who chooses out first one and then another for his prey.

.....Could we foresee it, there are times when children might seem like innocent prisoners, condemned, not to death, but to life, and as yet all unconscious of what their sentence means.....

If you try to imagine, as nearly as you can, what an amount of misery, pain and suffering of every kind the sun shines upon in its course, you will admit that it would be much better if on the earth as little as on the moon the sun were able to call forth the phenomena of life.....

Again, you may look upon life as an unprofitable episode, disturbing the blessed calm of non-existence. And, in any case, even though things have gone with you tolerably well, the longer you live the more clearly you will feel that, on the whole, life is *a disappointment, nay, a cheat*.....

He who lives to see two or three generations is like a man who sits some time in the conjurer's booth at a fair, and witnesses the performance twice or thrice in succession. The tricks were meant to be seen only once; and when they are no longer a novelty and cease to deceive, their effect is gone.....

If children were brought into the world by an act of pure reason alone, would the human race continue to exist? Would not a man rather have so much sympathy with the coming generation as to spare it the burden of existence?.....

The brute is much more content with mere existence than man; the plant is wholly so; and man finds satisfaction in it just in proportion as he is dull and obtuse.

.....[M]an.....is a burlesque of what he should be.....

If you want a safe compass to guide you through life,.....you cannot do better than accustom yourself to regard this world as a penitentiary, a sort of penal colony.....

.....In our part of the world where monogamy is the rule, to marry means to halve one's rights and double one's duties.....

.....In London alone there are 80,000 prostitutes. What are they but the women, who, under the institution of monogamy, have come off worst?

.....Where are there, then, any real monogamists? We all live, at any rate, for a time, and most of us, always, in polygamy. And so, since every man needs many women, there is nothing fairer than to allow him, nay, to make it incumbent upon him, to provide for many women. This will reduce woman to her true and natural position as a subordinate being.....

That woman is by nature meant to obey may be seen by the fact that every woman who is placed in the unnatural position of complete independence, immediately attaches herself to some man, by whom she allows herself to be guided and ruled. It is because she needs a lord and master. If she is young, it will be a lover; if she is old, a priest.

6. From Shelley's "Epipsychidion".

[Percy Bysshe Shelley (1792-1822) was one of Hardy's favourite poets. Ardently romantic, Shelley was an advocate of libertarian anarchism and of "free love". In Part Fourth, Chap. V, of *Jude*, Sue takes narcissistic pleasure in likening herself to the image of ideal love in Shelley's poem "Epipsychidion" (written in 1821, prompted by his love-relationship with Emilia Viviani). In its criticism of monogamy, "Epipsychidion" is thematically harmonic with the novel's satiric treatment of "holy wedlock"; but the poem's extreme romanticism contrasts with the novel's sour realism. Below, I quote from the poem lines 21-8, 149-59 and 190-205. The edition used is *The Poetical Works of Percy Bysshe Shelley*, ed. W. M. Rossetti (London: Moxon, n.d. [1870]), 376, 379, 380.]

> Seraph of heaven, too gentle to be human,
> Veiling beneath that radiant form of Woman
> All that is insupportable in thee
> Of light and love and immortality!
> Sweet benediction in the eternal curse!
> Veiled glory of this lampless universe!
> Thou moon beyond the clouds! thou living form
> Among the dead! thou star above the storm!.....
> I never was attached to that great sect
> Whose doctrine is that each one should select
> Out of the crowd a mistress or a friend,
> And all the rest, though fair and wise, commend
> To cold oblivion; though it is in the code
> Of modern morals, and the beaten road
> Which those poor slaves with weary footsteps tread,
> Who travel to their home among the dead
> By the broad highway of the world, and so
> With one chained friend, perhaps a jealous foe,
> The dreariest and the longest journey go.....
> There was a Being whom my spirit oft
> Met on its visioned wanderings, far aloft,
> In the clear golden prime of my youth's dawn,
> Upon the fairy isles of sunny lawn,

Amid the enchanted mountains, and the caves
Of divine sleep, and on the air-like waves
Of wonder-level dream, whose tremulous floor
Paved her light steps. On an imagined shore,
Under the gray beak of some promontory,
She met me, robed in such exceeding glory
That I beheld her not. In solitudes
Her voice came to me through the whispering woods,
And from the fountains, and the odours deep
Of flowers, which, like lips murmuring in their sleep
Of the sweet kisses which had lulled them there,
Breathed but of her to the enamoured air.....

7. From the writings of Auguste Comte.

[Auguste Comte (1798-1857) founded Positivism, a system based on
the notion that human understanding of the world evolves from a
theological to a metaphysical stage, and thence onwards to a "positive" stage which concentrates on scientific observation. Comte also
instituted a "religion of humanity" in which the objects of devotion
are not supernatural entities but renowned human beings. Hardy displayed considerable interest in Comte's ideas. He owned Comte's *A
General View of Positivism* (London: Trübner, 1865) and made notes on
Vol. 3 of Comte's *System of Positive Polity* (London: Longmans, Green,
1876). In 1903 he wrote to Lady Grove: "I am not a Positivist, as you
know, but I agree with Anatole France when he says.....that no person
of serious thought in these times could be said to stand aloof from
Positivist teaching & ideals" (*Collected Letters*, vol. 3, 53). Hardy read
numerous writers who were sympathetic to Comte, among them J. S.
Mill, George Eliot, G. H. Lewes, Harriet Martineau, J. H. Bridges, E.
S. Beesly, John Morley and Frederic Harrison, and he knew the last
three personally. Harrison claimed that *Tess of the d'Urbervilles* "reads
like a Positivist allegory or sermon". In *Jude the Obscure*, one sign that
Sue has been influenced by Comte is her remark in Part Third, Chap.
IV, that Christminster University is "full of fetichists and ghost-seers".
Hardy's *Literary Notebooks* (vol. 1, 66-7, 77) include such annotations
of Comte as these: "*Fetichism* – universal adoration of matter"; "*Astro-
latry* – a celestial fetichism"; "Fetichism (worship of material things)";

"*There is no harm* in Fetichistic hypotheses now – error too easily perceived to be dangerous." (Comte had claimed that fetishism gave way,
historically, to polytheism followed by monotheism.) Comte's evolutionary scope would have appealed to the eventual author of *The
Dynasts.* There is no doubt, however, that Hardy would have repudiat-
ed Comte's idealisation of marriage and his advocacy of the "worship
of Woman".]

7.1: From Comte's A General View of Positivism, *tr. J. H. Bridges
(London: Trübner, 1865), 34-5, 49-50, 98, 250-51, 264, 276, 277:*

[O]ur speculations upon all subjects whatsoever, pass necessarily
through three successive stages: the Theological stage, in which free
play is given to spontaneous fictions admitting of no proof; the Metaphysical stage, characterised by the prevalence of personified abstractions or entities; lastly, the Positive stage, based upon an exact view of
the real facts of the case.....We begin with theological Imagination,
thence we pass through metaphysical Discussion, and we end at last
with positive Demonstration. Thus by means of this one general law
we are enabled to take a comprehensive and simultaneous view of the
past, present, and future of Humanity.

.....The true Positive spirit consists in substituting the study of the
invariable Laws of phenomena, for that of their so-called Causes,
whether proximate or primary; in a word, studying the *How* instead
of the *Why.....* If we insist upon penetrating the unattainable mystery
of the essential Cause that produces phenomena, there is no hypothesis more satisfactory than that they proceed from Wills dwelling in
them or outside them..... The Order of Nature is doubtless very
imperfect in every respect; but its production is far more compatible
with the hypothesis of an intelligent Will than with that of a blind
mechanism.....What is called Atheism is usually a phase of Pantheism,
which is really nothing but a relapse disguised under learned terms,
into a vague and abstract form of Fetichism.....

To the Positivist the object of morals is to make our sympathetic
instincts preponderate as far as possible over the selfish instincts; social
feelings over personal feelings.

.....Marriage is the most elementary and yet the most perfect
mode of social life. It is the only association in which entire identity

of interests is possible. In this union, to the moral completeness of which the language of all civilised nations bears testimony, the noblest aim of human life is realised, as far as it ever can be.....

It is true that sexual instinct, which, in man's case at all events, was the origin of conjugal attachment, is a feeling purely selfish. It is also true that its absence would in the majority of cases, diminish the energy of affection. But woman, with her more loving heart, has usually far less need of this coarse stimulus than man. The influence of her purity reacts on man, and ennobles his affection.

.....If women were to obtain that equality in the affairs of life which their so-called champions are claiming for them without their wish, not only would they suffer morally, but their social position would be endangered. They would be subject in almost every occupation to a degree of competition which they would not be able to sustain. Moreover, by rivalry in the pursuits of life, mutual affection between the sexes would be corrupted at its source.

.....The Positivist will never forget that moral perfection, the primary condition of public and private happiness, is principally due to the influence of Woman over Man, first as mother, then as wife.....

Originating in spontaneous feelings of gratitude, the worship of Woman, when it has assumed a more systematic shape, will be valued for its own sake as a new instrument of happiness and moral growth. Inert as the tender sympathies are in Man, it is most desirable to strengthen them by such exercise as the public and private institution of this worship will afford. And here it is that Positivists will find all the elevating influences which Catholicism derived from Prayer.

7.2: From Comte's System of Positive Polity *(4 vols.; London: Longmans, Green, 1876), vol. 3, tr. J. H. Bridges,* Social Dynamics, or The General Theory of Human Progress, *68-9, 71, 73:*

Not only does history always find Fetichism at the birth of every civilisation, but in the growth of the individual there is ample evidence that this is the necessary starting-point of all intellect, whether human or animal. It is still, and will always be, possible for the best minds to verify by their own experience our involuntary tendency to philosophise like fetichists, when we seek for Causes for want of knowing Laws......

From the logical point of view the Fetichist hypothesis conforms spontaneously to the fundamental rule of Positivism in being the most simple that will account for all the facts, while the Polytheistic hypothesis directly violates it. Consequently the former can be brought to the test of verification, which the latter never can be. To attribute life to the External World is no doubt an error of capital importance. But we can show that it is an error, and then we can get rid of it. This is no longer the case when for direct, you substitute indirect wills, belonging to beings purely imaginary. For the existence of these beings can no more be decisively disproved than it can be demonstrated.....

When we aspire to penetrate to Causes properly so called, we may avoid attributing physical phenomena, whether celestial or terrestrial, to supernatural beings; but to do so without the hypothesis that material objects have affections and wills like those of men is beyond our power. When we subsequently give up the idea of knowing anything beyond Real Laws – that is to say, when we confine ourselves to seeking for general facts – we set aside this hypothetical assimilation of life and death as incompatible with the superior regularity of the Material Order.....

Theologism was necessary to the *Social* evolution of Humanity as a means of passing from the Fetichist regime to the Positivist state, and we must value it accordingly. At the same time we must regret that the original justness of intellect should have been so much impaired during that long transition.

8. From J. S. Mill's *On Liberty*.

[This influential work by John Stuart Mill (1806-73) first appeared in 1859. The extracts below are taken from the 1867 edition (London: Longmans, Green), which was owned and annotated by Hardy. Here, in Chapter 3, pp. 33 and 34, Mill develops those criticisms of conventional conduct which are echoed by Sue in *Jude the Obscure*, Part Fourth, Chap. III.]

Few persons, out of Germany, even comprehend the meaning of the doctrine which Wilhelm von Humboldt, so eminent both as a *savant* and as a politician, made the text of a treatise – that "the end of man, or that which is prescribed by the eternal or immutable dictates of reason, and not suggested by vague and transient desires, is the highest and most harmonious development of his powers to a complete and consistent whole;" that, therefore, the object "towards which every human being must ceaselessly direct his efforts.....is the individuality of power and development;" that for this there are two requisites, "freedom, and variety of situations;" and that from the union of these arise "individual vigour and manifold diversity," which combine themselves in "originality."

.....He who does anything because it is the custom, makes no choice. He gains no practice either in discerning or in desiring what is best. The mental and moral, like the muscular powers, are improved only by being used. The faculties are called into no exercise by doing a thing merely because others do it, no more than by believing a thing only because others believe it.....

He who lets the world, or his own portion of it, choose his plan of life for him, has no need of any other faculty than the ape-like one of imitation. He who chooses his plan for himself, employs all his faculties. He must use observation to see, reasoning and judgment to foresee, activity to gather materials for decision, discrimination to decide, and when he has decided, firmness and self-control to hold to his deliberate decision.....Human nature is not a machine to be built after a model, and set to do exactly the work prescribed for it, but a tree, which requires to grow and develop itself on all sides, according to the tendency of the inward forces which make it a living thing.

9. From Tennyson's *In Memoriam*, 1850.

[Hardy knew personally Alfred, Lord Tennyson (1809-92), and, like so many other Victorians, was familiar with Tennyson's poetry, notably *In Memoriam*. This long meditative poem was written before the publication of Charles Darwin's *Origin of Species* but after Charles Lyell's *Principles of Geology*, and some of its most memorable passages are pessimistic reflections on the implications of evolutionary theory. When Sue, in *Jude the Obscure*, cries, "O why should Nature's law be mutual butchery!," Tennyson's verses below (in sections 55-6) provide an appropriate context. I quote *The Works of Alfred Lord Tennyson* (London: Macmillan, 1884), 261.]

Are God and Nature then at strife,
    That Nature lends such evil dreams?
    So careful of the type she seems,
So careless of the single life.....

"So careful of the type?" but no.
    From scarped cliff and quarried stone
    She cries, "A thousand types are gone:
I care for nothing, all shall go.

"Thou makest thine appeal to me:
    I bring to life, I bring to death:
    The spirit does but mean the breath;
I know no more." And he, shall he,

Man, her last work, who seem'd so fair,
    Such splendid purpose in his eyes,
    Who roll'd the psalm to wintry skies,
Who built him fanes of fruitless prayer,

Who trusted God was love indeed
    And love Creation's final law —
    Tho' Nature, red in tooth and claw
With ravine, shriek'd against his creed —

Who loved, who suffer'd countless ills,
    Who battled for the True, the Just,
    Be blown about the desert dust,
Or seal'd within the iron hills?

10. From the writings of Sir Charles Darwin (1809-82).

[Extract 10.1 below is taken from the conclusion of the first edition of Darwin's epoch-making work, *On the Origin of Species by Means of Natural Selection* (London: Murray, 1859, 488-90). Here Darwin gives an optimistic gloss to his theory by stressing the wondrous diversity that has emerged from simple beginnings. Hardy, however, gained a sense of the cruel wastefulness of the evolutionary process and of the anomalous situation of reflective human beings within an unresponsive cosmos. In *The Dynasts* and elsewhere, Hardy entertained the idea that the creative force might gain awareness and benevolence. Another consequence of Darwin's theory of evolution, Hardy felt, was the recognition that, since human beings and animals formed one family, vivisection was unjustifiable, and cruelty to animals in general was abhorrent. The descent of humans from the higher primates, and ultimately from some "fish-like animal", was discussed in Darwin's *The Descent of Man, and Selection in Relation to Sex* (London: Murray, 1871); sequence 10.2 is taken from pp. 389-90, 394-6 and 404-5 of that first edition. The text differs significantly from that of later editions.]

10.1: From The Origin of Species:

When I view all beings not as special creations, but as the lineal descendants of some few beings which lived long before the first bed of the Silurian system was deposited, they seem to me to become ennobled.....As all the living forms of life are the lineal descendants of those which lived long before the Silurian epoch, we may feel certain that the ordinary succession by generation has never once been broken, and that no cataclysm has desolated the whole world. Hence we may look with some confidence to a secure future of equally inappreciable length. And as natural selection works solely by and for the good of each being, all corporeal and mental endowments will tend to progress towards perfection.

It is interesting to contemplate an entangled bank, clothed with many plants of many kinds, with birds singing on the bushes, with various insects flitting about, and with worms crawling through the damp earth, and to reflect that these elaborately constructed forms, so different from each other, and dependent on each other in so complex a manner, have all been produced by laws acting around us. These laws.....being Growth with Reproduction; Inheritance.....; Variability.....; a Ratio of Increase so high as to lead to a Struggle for Life, and as a consequence to Natural Selection, entailing Divergence of Character and the Extinction of less-improved forms. Thus, from the war of nature, from famine and death, the most exalted object which we are capable of conceiving, namely, the production of the higher animals, directly follows. There is grandeur in this view of life, with its several powers, having been originally breathed into a few forms or one; and that, whilst this planet has gone cycling on according to the fixed law of gravity, from so simple a beginning endless forms most beautiful and most wonderful have been, and are being, evolved.

10.2: From The Descent of Man:

By considering the embryological structure of man, – the homologies which he presents with the lower animals, – the rudiments which he retains, – and the reversions to which he is liable, we can partly recall in imagination the former condition of our early progenitors; and can approximately place them in their proper position in the zoological series. We thus learn that man is descended from a hairy quadruped, furnished with a tail and pointed ears, probably arboreal in its habits, and an inhabitant of the Old World. This creature, if its whole structure had been examined by a naturalist, would have been classed amongst the Quadrumana [simians], as surely as would the common and still more ancient progenitor of the Old and New World monkeys. The Quadrumana and all the higher mammals are probably derived from an ancient marsupial animal, and this through a long line of diversified forms, either from some reptile-like or some amphibian-like creature, and this again from some fish-like animal. In the dim obscurity of the past we can see that the early progenitor of all the Vertebrata must have been an aquatic animal, provided with branchiæ, with the two sexes united in the same individual, and with the most important organs of the body (such as the brain and heart) imperfectly developed. This animal seems to have been more like the larvæ of our existing marine Ascidians than any other known form.....

The belief in God has often been advanced as not only the greatest, but the most complete of all the distinctions between man and the lower animals. It is however impossible, as we have seen, to maintain that this belief is innate or instinctive in man. On the other hand a belief in all-pervading spiritual agencies seems to be universal; and apparently follows from a considerable advance in the reasoning powers of man, and from a still greater advance in his faculties of imagination, curiosity and wonder. I am aware that the assumed instinctive belief in God has been used by many persons as an argument for His existence. But this is a rash argument, as we should thus be compelled to believe in the existence of many cruel and malignant spirits, possessing only a little more power than man; for the belief in them is far more general than of [sic] a beneficent Deity. The idea of a universal and beneficent Creator of the universe does not seem to arise in the mind of man, until he has been elevated by long-continued culture.

He who believes in the advancement of man from some lowly-organised form, will naturally ask how does this bear on the belief in the immortality of the soul. The barbarous races of man, as Sir J. Lubbock has shewn, possess no clear belief of this kind; but arguments derived from the primeval beliefs of savages are, as we have just seen, of little or no avail. Few persons feel any anxiety from the impossibility of determining at what precise period in the development of the individual, from the first trace of the minute germinal vesicle to the child either before or after birth, man becomes an immortal being; and there is no greater cause for anxiety because the period in the gradually ascending organic scale cannot possibly be determined.

I am aware that the conclusions arrived at in this work will be denounced by some as highly irreligious; but he who thus denounces them is bound to shew why it is more irreligious to explain the origin of man as a distinct species by descent from some lower form, through the laws of variation and natural selection, than to explain the birth of the individual through the laws of ordinary reproduction. The birth both of the species and of the individual are equally parts of that grand sequence of events, which our minds refuse to accept as the result of blind chance. The understanding revolts at such a conclusion, whether or not we are able to believe that every slight variation of structure, – the union of each pair in marriage, – the dissemination of each seed, – and other such events, have all been ordained for some special purpose.....

The main conclusion arrived at in this work, namely that man is descended from some lowly-organised form, will, I regret to think, be highly distasteful to many. But there can hardly be a doubt that we are descended from barbarians. The astonishment which I felt on first seeing a party of Fuegians on a wild and broken shore will never be forgotten by me, for the reflection at once rushed into my mind – such were our ancestors. These men were absolutely naked and bedaubed with paint, their long hair was tangled, their mouths frothed with excitement, and their expression was wild, startled, and distrustful. They possessed hardly any arts, and like wild animals lived on what they could catch; they had no government, and were merciless to every one not of their own small tribe. He who has seen a savage in his native land will not feel much shame, if forced to acknowledge that the blood of some more humble creature flows in his veins. For my own part I would as soon be descended from that heroic little monkey, who braved his dreaded enemy in order to save the life of his keeper; or from that old baboon, who, descending from the mountains, carried away in triumph his young comrade from a crowd of astonished dogs – as from a savage who delights to torture his enemies, offers up bloody sacrifices, practises infanticide without remorse, treats his wives like slaves, knows no decency, and is haunted by the grossest superstitions.

Man may be excused for feeling some pride at having risen, though not through his own exertions, to the very summit of the organic scale; and the fact of his having thus risen, instead of having been aboriginally placed there, may give him hope for a still higher destiny in the distant future. But we are not here concerned with hopes or fears, only with the truth as far as our reason allows us to discover it. I have given the evidence to the best of my ability; and we must acknowledge, as it seems to me, that man with all his noble qualities, with sympathy which feels for the most debased, with benevolence which extends not only to other men but to the humblest living creature, with his god-like intellect which has penetrated into the movements and constitution of the solar system – with all these exalted powers – Man still bears in his bodily frame the indelible stamp of his lowly origin.

11. Extracts from *Essays and Reviews*, 1860.

[*Essays and Reviews* was a volume by seven scholars who became known as "The Seven against Christ". Hardy found it impressive. Formally condemned by the Anglican Church in 1864, the book caused controversy because of its keenly critical discussions of a range of religious topics. In particular, it drew attention to the limitations and inconsistencies of biblical narratives. Sue seems to partake of this critical spirit when, in Part Third of *Jude*, she comments on the Bible's lack of chronological order and on the anomalous chapter-headings of the Song of Solomon. The extracts here are taken from Benjamin Jowett's "On the Interpretation of Scripture", the seventh item in *Essays and Reviews* (London: Parker and Son, 1860); I cite pp. 345–6 and 354–5 of this, the first edition.]

There is no appearance in their writings that the Evangelists or Apostles had any inward gift, or were subject to any power external to them different from that of preaching or teaching which they daily exercised; nor do they anywhere lead us to suppose that they were free from error or infirmity.....And the result is in accordance with the simple profession and style in which they describe themselves; there is no appearance, that is to say, of insincerity or want of faith; but neither is there perfect accuracy or agreement. One supposes the original dwelling-place of our Lord's parents to have been Bethlehem (Matthew II. i, 22), another Nazareth (Luke II. 4); they trace his [*sic*] genealogy in different ways; one mentions the thieves blaspheming, another has preserved to after-ages the record of the penitent thief; they appear to differ about the day and hour of the Crucifixion; the narrative of the woman who anointed our Lord's feet with ointment is told in all four, each narrative having more or less considerable variations.

.....Much of the language of the Epistles (passages for example such as Romans I. 2; Philippians II. 6) would lose their meaning if distributed in alternate clauses between our Lord's humanity and divinity. Still greater difficulties would be introduced into the Gospels by the attempt to identify them with the Creeds. We should have to suppose that He was and was not tempted; that when he prayed to his Father he prayed also to Himself; that He knew and did not know "of that hour" of which He as well as the angels were ignorant. How could He have said "My God, my God, why hast thou forsaken me?" or "Father, if it be possible let this cup pass from me." How could He have doubted whether "when the Son cometh he shall find faith upon the earth?" These simple and touching words have to be taken out of their natural meaning and connexion to be made the theme of apologetic discourses if we insist on reconciling them with the distinctions of later ages.

Neither, as has been already remarked, would the substitution of any other precise or definite rule of faith, as for example the Unitarian, be more favourable to the interpretation of Scripture. How could the Evangelist St. John have said "the Word was God," or "God was the Word" (according to either mode of translating), or how would our Lord Himself have said, "I and the Father are one," if either had meant that Christ was a mere man, "a prophet or as one of the prophets?"

12. Extracts from Matthew Arnold's *Essays in Criticism* (London and Cambridge: Macmillan, 1865) and *Culture and Anarchy* (London: Smith, Elder, 1869), followed by Arnold's poem "Dover Beach."

[Matthew Arnold (1822-88) was a leading poet and intellectual of the Victorian Age. The "Preface" of his *Essays on Criticism* is recalled by Jude in Part Second, Chap. I; the essay on Heine is recalled by Sue in Part Third, Chap. IV. In *Culture and Anarchy*, Arnold's discussion of "Hebraism" and "Hellenism" has general thematic relevance to the novel and particularly to the characterisation of Jude and Sue, while his remarks on imprudent parenthood provide an ironic context. "Dover Beach" has long been regarded as a resonant epitome of the loss of religious certainty and the ensuing melancholia which were experienced by many Victorians. The reference in the poem to Sophocles may be to lines 583 ff. of his tragedy *Antigone*. The text of "Dover Beach" here is that of its first publication in book form, in Arnold's *New Poems* (London: Macmillan, 1867), 112-14.]

12.1: From "Preface" (xviii-xix):

No; we are all seekers still: seekers often make mistakes, and I wish mine to redound to my own discredit only, and not to touch Oxford. Beautiful city! so venerable, so lovely, so unravaged by the fierce intellectual life of our century, so serene!

"There are our young barbarians, all at play."

And yet, steeped in sentiment as she lies, spreading her gardens to the moonlight, and whispering from her towers the last enchantments of the Middle Age, who will deny that Oxford, by her ineffable charm, keeps ever calling us near to the true goal of all of us, to the ideal, to perfection, – to beauty, in a word, which is only truth seen from another side? – nearer, perhaps, than all the science of Tübingen. Adorable dreamer, whose heart has been so romantic! who hast given thyself so prodigally, given thyself to sides and to heroes not mine, only never to the Philistines! home of lost causes, and forsaken beliefs, and unpopular names, and impossible loyalties! what example could ever so inspire us to keep down the Philistine in ourselves.....?

12.2: From "Heinrich Heine" (154-5):

Modern times find themselves with an immense system of institutions, established facts, accredited dogmas, customs, rules, which have come to them from times not modern. In this system their life has to be carried forward; yet they have a sense that this system is not of their own creation, that it by no means corresponds exactly with the wants of their actual life, that, for them, it is customary, not rational. The awakening of this sense is the awakening of the modern spirit. The modern spirit is now awake almost everywhere; the sense of want of correspondence between the forms of modern Europe and its spirit, between the new wine of the eighteenth and nineteenth centuries, and the old bottles of the eleventh and twelfth centuries, or even of the sixteenth and seventeenth, almost every one now perceives; it is no longer dangerous to affirm that this want of correspondence exists; people are even beginning to be shy of denying it. To remove this want of correspondence is beginning to be the settled endeavour of most persons of good sense. Dissolvents of the old European system of dominant ideas and facts we must all be, all of us who have any power of working; what we have to study is that we may not be acrid dissolvents of it.

12.3: From Culture and Anarchy, *91, 92, 94, 95, 119, 153:*

The uppermost idea with Hellenism is to see things as they really are; the uppermost idea with Hebraism is conduct and obedience.....The governing idea of Hellenism is *spontaneity of consciousness*; that of Hebraism, *strictness of conscience*.

.....To get rid of one's ignorance, to see things as they are, and by seeing as they are to see them in their beauty, is the simple and attractive ideal which Hellenism holds out before human nature; and from the simplicity and charm of this ideal, Hellenism, and human life in the hands of Hellenism, is invested with a kind of aërial ease, clearness, and radiancy; they are full of what we call sweetness and light.

.....[T]he space which sin fills in Hebraism, as compared with Hellenism, is indeed prodigious. This obstacle to perfection fills the whole scene, and perfection appears remote and rising away from earth, in the background. Under the name of sin, the difficulties of knowing oneself and conquering oneself which impede man's passage to perfection, become, for Hebraism, a positive, active entity hostile to man, a mysterious power which I heard Dr. Pusey the other day, in one of his impressive sermons, compare to a hideous hunchback seated on our shoulders, and which it is the main business of our lives to hate and oppose.

.....[W]e are in a false line in having developed our Hebrew side so exclusively, and our Hellenic side so feebly and at random.....

[T]o bring people into the world, when one cannot afford to keep them and oneself decently and not too precariously, or to bring more of them into the world than one can afford to keep thus, is.....just as wrong, just as contrary to reason and the will of God, as for a man to have horses, or carriages, or pictures, when he cannot afford them.....

12.4:   Dover Beach

          The sea is calm to-night,
          The tide is full, the moon lies fair
          Upon the Straits; – on the French coast, the light
          Gleams, and is gone; the cliffs of England stand,
          Glimmering and vast, out in the tranquil bay.
          Come to the window, sweet is the night air!
          Only, from the long line of spray
          Where the ebb meets the moon-blanch'd sand,
          Listen! you hear the grating roar
          Of pebbles which the waves suck back, and fling,
          At their return, up the high strand,
          Begin, and cease, and then again begin,
          With tremulous cadence slow, and bring

The eternal note of sadness in.

Sophocles long ago
Heard it on the Ægean, and it brought
Into his mind the turbid ebb and flow
Of human misery; we
Find also in the sound a thought,
Hearing it by this distant northern sea.

The sea of faith
Was once, too, at the full, and round earth's shore
Lay like the folds of a bright girdle furl'd;
But now I only hear
Its melancholy, long, withdrawing roar,
Retreating to the breath
Of the night-wind down the vast edges drear
And naked shingles of the world.

Ah, love, let us be true
To one another! for the world, which seems
To lie before us like a land of dreams,
So various, so beautiful, so new,
Hath really neither joy, nor love, nor light,
Nor certitude, nor peace, nor help for pain;
And we are here as on a darkling plain
Swept with confused alarms of struggle and flight,
Where ignorant armies clash by night.

13. From "Hymn to Proserpine" by Algernon Charles Swinburne (1837-1909).

[This anti-Christian poem was one of the more scandalous pieces in Swinburne's volume, *Poems and Ballads* (London: Hotten, 1866). Predictably, it is one of Sue Bridehead's favourites: she cites it twice. After reading *Jude*, Swinburne wrote to Hardy to praise the novel, while remarking "But.....how cruel you are! Only the great and awful father of 'Pierrette' and 'L'Enfant Maudit' [i.e. Balzac] was ever so merciless to his children." He later quoted to Hardy a Scottish paper which said: "Swinburne planteth, Hardy watereth, and Satan giveth the increase." The extract below is taken from the first edition of *Poems and Ballads* (79-80, 84).]

> Thou hast conquered, O pale Galilean; the world has grown grey
>   from thy breath;
> We have drunk of things Lethean, and fed on the fulness of death.
> Laurel is green for a season, and love is sweet for a day;
> But love grows bitter with treason, and laurel outlives not May.
> Sleep, shall we sleep after all? for the world is not sweet in the
>   end;
> For the old faiths loosen and fall, the new years ruin and rend.
> Fate is a sea without shore, and the soul is a rock that abides;
> But her ears are vexed with the roar and her face with the foam
>   of the tides.
> O lips that the live blood faints in, the leavings of racks and rods!
> O ghastly glories of saints, dead limbs of gibbeted Gods!
> Though all men abase them before you in spirit, and all knees
>   bend,
> I kneel not neither adore you, but standing, look to the end.....
> I shall die as my fathers died, and sleep as they sleep; even so.
> For the glass of the years is brittle wherein we gaze for a span;
> A little soul for a little bears up this corpse which is man.
> So long I endure, no longer; and laugh not again, neither weep.
> For there is no God found stronger than death; and death is a
>   sleep.

14. From *Keynotes* (1893) by "George Egerton" (Mary Clairmonte).

[Mary Chavelita Clairmonte (1859-1945) was the Australian-born writer of *Keynotes*, a controversial collection of tales depicting the "New Woman". Hardy read it while writing *Jude the Obscure*; and, in a letter to her (22 December 1895), he remarked: "how much I felt the verisimilitude of the stories, & how you seemed to make us breathe the atmosphere of the scenes". She had written to him on 22 November 1895, describing Sue Bridehead as "a marvellously true psychological study of a temperament less rare than the ordinary male observer supposes". Chavelita Clairmonte later married Reginald

Golding Bright, literary agent for Hardy's dramatisations. The passages quoted below from *Keynotes* (London: Elkin Mathews and John Lane, 1893, 21-2, 28, 40-41) illustrate the way in which Clairmonte gives prominence to the disparity between male and female views of "woman's nature". In January 1894, while writing *Jude*, Hardy copied parts of these passages into his notebooks: see *Literary Notebooks*, vol. 2, 60-61.]

14.1: From the tale "A Cross Line":

And she laughs, laughs softly to herself because the denseness of man, his chivalrous conservative devotion to the female idea he has created blinds him, perhaps happily, to the problems of her complex nature. Ay, she mutters musingly, the wisest of them can only say we are enigmas.....They have all overlooked the eternal wildness, the untamed primitive savage temperament that lurks in the mildest, best woman.....Perhaps many of our seeming contradictions are only the outward evidences of inward chafing.

14.2: From the tale "Now Spring Has Come":

It seems as if all the religions, all the advancement, all the culture of the past, has only been a forging of chains to cripple posterity, a laborious building up of moral and legal prisons based on false conceptions of sin and shame, to cramp men's minds and hearts and souls, not to speak of women's. What half creatures we are, we women! Hermaphrodite by force of circumstances. Deformed results of a fight of centuries between physical suppression and natural impulse to fulfil our destiny. Every social revolution has told hardest on us: when a sacrifice was demanded, let woman make it.....Why it came about? Because men manufactured an artificial morality, made sins of things that were as clean in themselves as the pairing of birds on the wing; crushed nature, robbed it of its beauty and meaning, and established a system that means war, and always war, because it is a struggle between instinctive truths and cultivated lies.

Appendix F: Oxford, Jowett, and Educational Opportunity.

Jude was not the first fictional artisan to complain at the historical injustice of his exclusion from the halls of higher education: he had been anticipated by the eponymous tailor in Charles Kingsley's *Alton Locke* (1850). This is illustrated in passage 1 below. When Jude is seeking advice on admission to the University of Christiminster, he writes to five distinguished academics at various colleges. Four fail to reply; the fifth, the Master of "Biblioll" (a name which obviously echoes "Balliol", a famous college of Oxford University), advises him to stick to his trade. This gives the impression that Oxford is deaf to the claims to higher education which might be made by members of the lower middle class (as is Jude, a skilled craftsman) or of the working class. The impression is not wholly fair. From 1870 until the end of his life, the Master of Balliol was Benjamin Jowett (1817-93), classical scholar and liberal educationalist; and the extracts (item 2 below) from *The Life and Letters of Benjamin Jowett* show that he was active in encouraging the extension of educational opportunity. (The writer Graham Greene, who studied at Balliol in the 1920s, portrays him sympathetically in the play *The Great Jowett*, 1939.) One of the earliest centres of the Oxford University "Extension Movement", which provided lecture-courses for the public, was Reading, the basis of "Aldbrickham" in Hardy's novel. Some senior members of Christ Church College, Oxford, encouraged by Jowett, were instrumental in establishing Reading's University Extension College in 1892; from this developed the eventual University of Reading. The extension movement is briefly described in item 3.

A related innovation was the growth of university "settlements". These were missions, established in urban areas, in which college men could meet and teach people of the working class; sometimes such missions were bases for extension work. In 1884 Toynbee Hall was opened. It had been established partly by the efforts of men of St John's College, Cambridge, and commemorated Arnold Toynbee, a tutor of Balliol College. One of the earliest students at Toynbee Hall was Albert Mansbridge, who concluded that the Co-operative

Society should combine with the trade unions and the universities to form a new educational organisation. Accordingly, he founded the Workers' Educational Association in 1903, and by 1914 it had 179 branches and over 11,000 members. As we have noted previously, Ruskin College was founded at Oxford in 1899 to provide higher education for adults who lacked formal qualifications; there they could take diplomas and possibly proceed to degree courses at other institutions.

Another relevant matter is that in the latter half of the nineteenth century, London University was able to award "external" degrees to students who qualified after attending day or evening classes, or purchasing correspondence courses, or simply toiling on their own. In 1883-4 H. G. Wells, by dint of hard study and the taking of various examinations, won a studentship (provided by the governmental Department of Education) to the Normal School of Science in South Kensington. The studentship paid his fees and provided a maintenance grant. After many vicissitudes (for instance, he failed the geology examination in 1887), Wells eventually gained in 1890 his London University B.Sc.degree. Although large-scale State Scholarships were not initiated until 1919, from 1902 English local authorities could give grants to university students; and by 1911-12 more than 1,300 scholars were thus being maintained at universities. In England and Wales the total population of undergraduates rose from 1,128 in 1800 to 19,458 in 1913-14. (See *The Universities in the Nineteenth Century*, ed. Michael Sanderson. London and Boston: Routledge & Kegan Paul, 1975.)

1. From Charles Kingsley's *Alton Locke, Tailor and Poet. An Autobiography* (London: Chapman and Hall, 1850), vol. 1, 199-201.

[The phrasing of this, the first edition, sometimes differs from that of subsequent editions.]

To describe a Cambridge supper party among gay young men is a business as little suited to my taste as to my powers. The higher classes ought to know pretty well what such things are like; and the working men are not altogether ignorant.....But I must say, that I was utterly disgusted; and when, after the removal of the eatables, the whole party, twelve or fourteen in number, set to work to drink hard and deliberately at milk punch, and bishop, and copus, and grog, and I know not what other inventions of bacchanalian luxury, and to sing, one after another, songs of the most brutal indecency, I was glad to escape into the cool night air, and under pretence of going home, wander up and down the King's Parade, and watch the tall gables of King's College Chapel, and the classic front of the senate-house, and the stately tower of St. Mary's, as they stood, stern and silent, bathed in the still glory of the moonshine, and seeming to watch, with a steadfast sadness, the scene of frivolity and sin, pharisaism, formalism, hypocrisy, and idleness, below.

Noble buildings! and noble institutions! given freely to the people, by those who loved the people, and the Saviour who died for them. They gave us what they had, those mediæval founders: whatsoever narrowness of mind or superstition defiled their gift was not their fault, but the fault of their whole age. The best they knew they imparted freely, and God will reward them for it. To monopolise those institutions for the rich, as is done now, is to violate both the spirit and the letter of the foundations; to restrict their studies to the limits of middle-aged Romanism, their conditions of admission to those fixed at the Reformation, is but a shade less wrongful. The letter is kept – the spirit is thrown away. You refuse to admit any who are not members of the Church of England; – say, rather, any who will not sign the dogmas of the Church of England, whether they believe a word of them or not. Useless formalism! which lets through the reckless, the profligate, the ignorant, the hypocritical; and only excludes the honest and the conscientious, and the mass of the intellectual working men. And whose fault is it that THEY are not members of the Church of England? Whose fault is it, I ask? Your predecessors neglected the lower orders, till they have ceased to reverence either you or your doctrines; – you confess that, among yourselves, freely enough. You throw the blame of the present wide-spread dislike of the Church of England on her sins during "the godless 18th century." Be it so. Why are those sins to be visited on us? Why are we to be shut out from the universities, which were founded for us, because you have let us grow up, by millions, heathens and infidels, as you call us? Take away your subterfuge! It is not merely because we are bad churchmen that you exclude us, else you would be crowding your colleges, now, with the talented poor of the agricultural districts, who, as you say, remain faithful to the church of their fathers. But are there six labourers' sons educating in the universities at this moment? No! The real reason for our exclusion, churchmen or not, is because we are *poor* – because we cannot pay your exorbitant fees, often, as in the case of bachelors of arts, exacted for tuition which is never given, and residence which is not permitted – because we could not support the extravagance which you not only permit, but encourage, because, by your own unblushing confession, it insures the university "the support of the aristocracy."

2. From *The Life and Letters of Benjamin Jowett, M.A.*, Master of Balliol College, Oxford, by Evelyn Abbott and Lewis Campbell (2 vols.; London: Murray, 1897).

[These extracts are taken from Vol. II, 58-61 and 296-9.]

On June 11, 1874, a meeting was held in the Victoria Rooms, Clifton, to promote the foundation of a local College or University [at Bristol]....Jowett was asked to speak second, and he spoke for the Colleges and the part which they had taken in the movement.

The project, he said, did not emanate from the Universities. Yet it was also true that many persons both in Oxford and Cambridge had desired to extend the borders of the Universities. They wanted to place them really, as they were nominally, at the head of the education of the country. They did not like to see their benefits confined to the upper hundred thousand. As much as twenty years ago a scheme for teaching and examination in the large towns, somewhat similar to this, had been put forward by a distinguished person, brother of the present Warden of New College. Looking about to find ways in which these views could be carried out, they were told that the city of Bristol was already establishing a College designed to meet the wants of the locality. The two schemes met in one; they thought that by the union of the two something better could be accomplished than either could effect singly. They at Oxford desired to show their good will by a moderate contribution of money, and having spent all their lives in education, they hoped that their experience might be of some service.

In the words of the resolution, the College was to be established "for those who wish to pursue their studies beyond the ordinary school age." These words, he supposed, applied to two classes of persons – first, to regular students who, though they could not afford a University education, could carry on their studies at home; and besides that, to another class which had at least equal demands upon their sympathies, those who could only carry on their studies by the use of the few hours which they could spare early in the morning or late at night, while they were at the same time earning their livelihood. In any of their large towns there were thousands of such persons with a taste for knowledge, with a zeal for improvement, but yet without the opportunity of education. Was it not almost denying a man bread to deny him knowledge if he had the wish for it? They often spoke of the wealth of a country, but was there not something much worse than this in the loss of the intelligence of the country? They could not bring this class to the Universities, and therefore they must take the Universities to them.....

The College [at Bristol] was opened and the first Professors appointed in 1876. When giving evidence before the University Commission in October, 1877, Jowett was able to say that he was completely satisfied with the result. "During the past session there had been more than three hundred students paying fees, of whom about half were women.".....

[Nearly a decade later:] For some time past the fortunes of University College, Bristol, had been declining, and as it was now becoming doubtful whether the institution could be carried on, a meeting was called by the Council of the College at Clifton (March 3, 1887) to support an appeal to the State for aid. Jowett was unable to be present, but he wrote a letter to the *Times* urging that assistance should be given by the State to local Universities.

In order to disarm the opposition of the economists he pleaded: (1) that the sum required was not large, and would be help given to those who are helping themselves; (2) that any State grant might be proportioned to the amount of subscriptions raised in the locality; (3) that no new principle was involved: the Government were only doing for England what they had already done for Ireland, Scotland, and Wales; (4) that the country as a whole was taxed for education, and therefore that all classes, in proportion to their needs, should have a share of the benefits for which they pay; (5) that a grant for the maintenance of University Colleges was likely to produce far greater results than any grant of equal amount applied to elementary education.

To the objection that such Colleges, if they were needed, would be self-supporting, he answered that the needs which they supplied were not such as appealed to the humane or religious feelings of mankind; and that many persons are jealous of giving good education to the poor.

"Their popularity," he wrote, "is not in proportion to their usefulness. Nor can their usefulness be properly developed unless the means at their disposal are considerably increased. The benefits which they confer on the places in which they are situated, and generally on science and literature, are of many kinds. They bring the higher education to the doors of those who cannot leave their homes in search of it. They become the centres of educational hope and interests to a whole district, and, if provided with a library, they are the best sort of clubs. They nourish a germ of science or literature in the artisan or man of business. They may have even kindled in the minds of one or two the spark of genius. In every large town there are many hundreds who have abilities above the average, but their gifts are thrown away because the means of education are not provided for them. The seed of national intelligence is, of all treasures, the most precious; and to let it be scattered by the wayside is, of all wastes, the saddest and the worst. It is this seed which we would fain preserve and cherish, that in another generation it may produce fruit in literature, in science, in business."

Secondary education in all its various forms was now occupying Jowett's thoughts. During his Vice-Chancellorship the Oxford branch of the University Extension system had been put on a new footing, largely through the labours of the present Bishop of Hereford, then President of Trinity College. Jowett presided not only at the first meeting of the new committee, but at every one of the first seven meetings. And the arrangements made at these meetings, though of course they were not all due to him, were of the very greatest importance in securing the success of the system. The Lecturers who have been the backbone of the movement were then appointed, travelling libraries were instituted, courses for co-operative societies were arranged, prizes were first offered, and, at his special request, lectures were given in Oxford. In April, 1887, a conference on University Extension was held at Oxford, to which Jowett invited the Bishop of London, and the guests were entertained at luncheon in Balliol Hall. His sympathies were altogether with the movement, though he wished to see it supported by something of a more solid and enduring nature.

In proposing the health of the guests at the luncheon he spoke of the duty of the State towards secondary education, and maintained that we must not trust to existing endowments for the progress of higher education among the middle classes. No principle of political economy prevented a Government from doing for its subjects what it could do for them and what they could not do for themselves; and the expense of higher education was far beyond the means of what may be termed the lower half of the middle class. He pointed out that nearly every civilized country in the world already provided education, both primary and secondary, either free of cost or at a very trifling cost; and suggested that, whatever might be the natural commercial disadvantages of England compared with other countries, it was possible they might be much more than compensated by the spread of education. He concluded with an apology for his "speculations."

"They are quite outside the purposes of the conference," he said, "though connected with it. Whether any large scheme of secondary education is adopted by the State or not, the University Extension Lectures are the best preparation for it. They prove the need of it; and though their twenty thousand students are not much more than one in a thousand of the whole population of England, still to a considerable extent they supply the need of education which is felt for every man who desires to have it, and in the degree to which he is able to receive it."

3. An extract from Sir James Mountford's *British Universities* (London: Oxford UP, 1966), 24-5:

[T]he *University Extension* movement.....was inspired by the missionary zeal of James Stuart, a young mathematical Fellow of Trinity College, Cambridge. He had the idea of "a sort of peripatetic university of professors which would circulate in the big towns", and hoped that by this means permanent university establishments in the provinces might be made possible. After a successful course of lectures on gravitation which he gave in 1867 to audiences composed mainly of schoolmistresses in Leeds, Liverpool, Sheffield, and Manchester, he rallied support for a bolder plan, and by 1873 had induced the University of Cambridge to organize courses in English literature, political economy, and mechanics in Nottingham, Leicester, and Derby. By 1875 more than one hundred courses were being given by a group of lecturers under the Cambridge auspices. In 1876 London began to organize extension lectures of its own, and Oxford followed in 1878. It would be difficult to over-estimate the seminal importance of this movement. It had a direct and unmistakable connexion with the establishment of the university colleges in Sheffield, Nottingham, and Reading; it was in the front line in the battle for better education for women; and the provision which all universities now make for adult education through their departments of extra-mural studies is essentially a continuation of the work James Stuart began.

4. An extract from Harold Pollins' _The History of Ruskin College_ (Oxford: Ruskin College Library, 1984), pp. 9, 11, 12:

This "College of the People" or "Workman's University" was intended to be different. It was to be a residential college for working men. They could spend a year there or they could come for shorter periods.....While workers' education was not new the idea that they should undertake full-time study was quite novel.....

The founders were two young Americans, Charles Austin Beard, aged 24, and Walter Watkins Vrooman, aged 29.....They came together no earlier than the autumn of 1898 and by the beginning of December the new scheme was being publicised.

.....Mrs. Vrooman was a rich woman and she supported her husband's various schemes: almost all the money for the first year's operation came from her. The founders, released from that problem, were busy drumming up support, addressing meetings in many parts of the country, trying to interest in their scheme trade unions, trades councils, co-operative societies, church organisations and Ruskin societies. They were so successful that on 22 February 1899, no more than five months after the Americans had arrived in Britain, a grand inaugural meeting was held in Oxford Town Hall.

Appendix G: Divorce in Jude the Obscure.

In late Victorian England, divorces were regulated by the Matrimonial Causes Act, 1857, and by subsequent Acts of Parliament that modified it. The crucial part was this:

> It shall be lawful for any Husband to present a Petition to the said Court [the High Court of Justice], praying that his Marriage may be dissolved, on the Ground that his Wife has since the Celebration thereof been guilty of Adultery; and it shall be lawful for any Wife to present a Petition to the said Court, praying that her Marriage may be dissolved, on the Ground that since the Celebration thereof her Husband has been guilty of incestuous Adultery, or of Bigamy with Adultery, or of Rape, or of Sodomy or Bestiality, or of Adultery coupled with such Cruelty as without Adultery would have entitled her to a Divorce à Mensâ et Thoro [from bed and board, a separation], or of Adultery coupled with Desertion, without reasonable Excuse, for Two Years or Upwards..... [1]

Since this did not cover all the circumstances which might lead couples to seek divorce, collusion sometimes took place between the couples. Collusion, however, was unlawful (section XXX of the 1857 Act made this clear), and, if detected, would result in the dismissal of the divorce petition.

In *Jude the Obscure*, the divorces of Jude and Arabella and of Phillotson and Sue involve elements of collusion and deception which, if known, would have rendered the petitions invalid. In the case of Fawley *v.* Fawley, there has been "agreement between the par-

---

1   "An Act to Amend the Law Relating to Divorce," 28 August 1857; 20 and 21 Vict., Cap. 85, section XXVII. See *A Collection of the Public General Statutes, Passed in the Twentieth and Twenty-First Years of the Reign of Her Majesty Queen Victoria, 1857* (London: Eyre and Spottiswoode, 1857), 642. (William A. Davis's article, cited later, misquotes the Act, omitting the phrase "or of Bigamy with Adultery,".) Before this legislation, divorce in England, whether by private act of Parliament or by appeal to the Court of Arches, was very difficult and expensive.

ties": Arabella has asked Jude for a divorce "in kindness to her", and he has agreed. In addition, Arabella has married bigamously in Australia. Jude knows this, but conceals the fact; a concealment which might well have been sufficient, had it been discovered, to invalidate his petition. In the case of Phillotson *v.* Phillotson, deception is involved. Phillotson is led to believe that Sue has committed adultery with Jude, at a time when it has not by then been committed. When Sue, after the separation, visits Phillotson during his illness, she implies during their conversation that adultery has taken place. Phillotson becomes a figure of scandal when it is believed that he has condoned the adultery. Although the divorce proceeds without legal difficulty, Sue remarks to Jude: "Well – if the truth about us had been known, the decree wouldn't have been pronounced."

In a lucid essay on this topic, William A. Davis Jr. points out that one of Hardy's friends was Sir Francis Jeune, who, in the 1890s, was President of the Probate, Divorce and Admiralty Division of the High Court of Justice. Davis remarks:

> Jeune was a skilful judge, and with his acumen combined with the intervention of the Queen's Proctor, his court became the scene for a number of case dismissals based on unlawful collusion and condonation.[1]

Hardy, therefore, was well informed. In addition to his attendance at police courts and law offices, and his study of divorce reports in newspapers, his friendship with Sir Francis afforded ample opportunities for consideration of the flaws in the operation of the divorce laws. What Hardy was implicitly advocating was made explicit in the "Postscript" to the 1912 "Preface" to *Jude*: "[A] marriage should be dissolvable as soon as it becomes a cruelty to either of the parties....." Gradually, the law was changed in the spirit of Hardy's recommendation, though progress was slow. In 1891, the number of divorce decrees in England and Wales together was 369. By 1911, the total had risen to 580: still a remarkably low figure, compared with later results.

---

1   William A. Davis, Jr., "Hardy, Sir Francis Jeune and Divorce by 'False Pretences' in *Jude the Obscure*", *The Thomas Hardy Journal* 9:1 (Feb. 1993): 62-74 (quotation, 69).

In 1923, however, a new Matrimonial Causes Act made the permitted grounds for divorce the same for women as for men, and subsequent legislation extended the grounds. By 1931, the figure was 3,800. The Divorce Act of 1969 at last recognised the concept of divorce by mutual consent. In 1971, the total increased to 74,000. Thus one may partly trace, in Lawrence Stone's words, "the erosion of the old religious and social beliefs by the advancing tide of secularism and individualism".[1]

Valerie Cromwell points out that Lord Penzance's Matrimonial Causes Act (1878) had given magistrates' courts the power to grant a separation order with maintenance to a wife whose husband had been convicted of aggravated assault on her, and this power was widened by successive acts.

> In the ten years between 1897 and 1906, 87,000 separations and maintenance orders were granted by magistrates' courts. Thus, by the end of the nineteenth century, two very different remedies for matrimonial difficulties existed in England. The more affluent could obtain divorce and judicial separation by means of the centralized divorce court; the poor with no chance of obtaining a divorce could get separation orders from local magistrates' courts.[2]

Lawrence Stone concurs, noting that the passage in 1878 and 1879 of Acts for the Maintenance of Wives, which allowed a battered or deserted wife to obtain a temporary maintenance order from a local magistrate, resulted in "an avalanche of applications". In England and Wales between 1900 and 1904 the total was 14,700.[3]

Although *Jude the Obscure* gives the impression that in late Victorian England it was not very difficult for such people as Jude to obtain a divorce, the statistics suggest otherwise. Subsequently, from 1920 onwards, it was provided that poor persons and undefended cases

---

1 Lawrence Stone, *Road to Divorce: England 1530-1987* (Oxford: Oxford UP, 1990), 435-6, 391; see also Valerie Cromwell, "The Changing Role of Women in Modern Britain", *The Forum Series* (St. Louis, Missouri: Forum Press, 1979), 5.
2 Valerie Cromwell, "The Changing Role of Women in Modern Britain", 6.
3 Lawrence Stone, *Road to Divorce*, 386, 439.

might be heard in provincial courts and not in London alone: a provision which reduced the costs. The Legal Aid and Advice Act of 1949 enabled needy petitioners to receive financial subsidies. In the period 1951-4, the average annual number of petitions for divorce or nullity rose to 33,132; by 1974, the annual number of divorces was 131,000.[1]

---

1 Valerie Cromwell, "The Changing Role of Women in Modern Britain", 13. See also: O. R. McGregor, *Divorce in England: A Centenary Study* (London: Heinemann, 1957); Olive Anderson, "The Incidence of Civil Marriage in Victorian England and Wales", *Past and Present*, 69 (1975): 50-87; Lawrence Stone, *Road to Divorce*; and Joan Perkin, *Women and Marriage in Nineteenth-Century England* (London: Routledge, 1989).

Appendix H: Map of Wessex Appended to the 1895 Edition of Jude the Obscure.

Hardy drafted the map for the first "Collected Edition" of his works (1895-7); the draft was revised by Edward Stanford; and the revised version appeared as the endpaper to the 1895 edition of *Jude the Obscure*, from which the following reproduction is taken. Names of towns which are in block capitals (e.g. SOUTHAMPTON, PORTSMOUTH) are non-fictional; otherwise, names of towns and villages are fictional. As Hardy explained to Bertram Windle in 1896 (*Collected Letters*, vol. 2, 131-3), "South Wessex" corresponds to Dorset, "Outer Wessex" to Somerset, "Lower Wessex" to Devon, "Mid-Wessex" to Wiltshire, and "North Wessex" to Berkshire; "Shaston" is Shaftesbury, "Alfredston" is Wantage, "Marygreen" is Fawley. In the "General Preface" (dated 1911) to the Wessex Edition, he augmented the list.

The map reproduced here has done much good, clarifying the movements of characters and emphasising the importance to Hardy of a known terrain; but it may have done some harm, by suggesting too immediate a correlation of the imaginative world with the geographical specificities of nineteenth-century England.

While being ready to assist readers in relating the fictional places to real places, Hardy was understandably keen to emphasise the differences between fact and fiction. In the "General Preface" to the Wessex Edition, he declared that his description of locations was "done from the real – that is to say, has something real for its basis, however illusively treated.....[N]o detail is guaranteed.....the portraiture of fictitiously named towns and villages was only suggested by certain real places, and wantonly wanders from inventorial descriptions of them....." Again, there is a typically guarded reference in *The Later Years of Thomas Hardy*, 49:

Lord Rosebery took occasion in a conversation to inquire "why Hardy had called Oxford 'Christminster'." Hardy assured him that he had not done anything of the sort, "Christminster" being a city of learning that was certainly suggested by Oxford, but in its entirety existed nowhere else in the world but between the covers of the novel under discussion.

Hardy's response is partly evasive. He was obviously right to say that while Christminster was "suggested by Oxford", the fictional city through which Jude and Sue walk differs from the historical city in being an imaginative location with uniquely fictional data. On the other hand, Christminster is far more like Oxford than it is like, say, Cambridge. Not only is its geographical location precisely correspondent with that of Oxford, as the "Wessex" map emphasises, but also the alumni recalled in detail by Jude and the narrator (notably Jonson, Addison, Wesley, Johnson, Gibbon, Ken, Peel, Shelley, Newman, Arnold, Browning and Swinburne) are specifically *Oxonienses*; and its Tractarian movement is explicitly cited. Yet the changes made to various place-names do introduce a fruitful ambiguity into the reader's response. What happens is that the historical Oxford becomes a shimmering presence that moves into and out of imaginative focus. When it moves out of focus, it is displaced by our recognition of "Christminster" as a *representative* locality: representative of wider forces in the cultural and social world. The disguises, though often transparent, become at such times relatively opaque as the general thematic significances of the narrative press upon us. The very name "Christminster", after all, bears the etymological meaning "monastery devoted to Christ"; so it serves (as the name "Oxford" could not) to remind us of both Jude's aspirations – the educational *and* the religious. It keeps the name of Christ before us, and thus emphasises the hypocritical lack of charity and love which Jude finds in the supposedly Christian society; and it particularly emphasises the cruel irony that sometimes the workman who meets rejection and scorn reminds us (however briefly and fleetingly) of Jesus Christ, the carpenter's son.

Thus, as a realist and craftsman of literature, Hardy was right to make clear that he was using known historical locations; while, as a creative writer with the artist's ability to invest topographical facts with general significances, he was also right to affirm his prerogative to transform them. The "Preface" to *Jude* declares that the novel seeks "to give shape and coherence to a series of seemings, or personal impressions". What is important but harder to specify is the complex process engendered in the reader by fiction which so often invites an identification of a fictional with a real locality while also offering a distinctive totality of vision unique to the creative imagination of the author himself.

The effects of the recurrent use of a "Map of Wessex" in so many editions of Hardy's works have been very diverse. One effect has been to proclaim Hardy as "The Author of Wessex" – to emphasise a coordinating territory of the fiction. The reader's attention is visually drawn to the ways in which, though his novels and tales may differ markedly from each other in many respects, there is a common grounding to most of them provided by an environment derived from nineteenth-century geographical realities. Repetition and overlapping of locations in successive works of fiction can have a cumulative imaginative effect. While reading one novel we may carry over into the imagination information derived from a previous novel with a similar or overlapping setting. Furthermore, as location is linked to location, and as characters sometimes recur, there may be generated the sense of a meta-fictional territory, one closely related to reality and from which all the completed works of fiction may be regarded as only a selection. ("Meta" means "beyond". Various writers, including Conrad and Kipling, achieve a meta-fictional effect by their use of the same characters and the same places in different works.) The reader's imagination is prompted to extend the literary hinterland.

Repetition of the map may, however, make that territory seem too static. The Wessex of the novels is a region undergoing change and disruption. The map shows no railways, but repeatedly in the novels the railway is a crucial agent of change, affecting distant rural localities and binding the provinces more and more to an economy directed from London. The absence of London from the map may encourage some readers to think too much of "rural Hardy" and to forget the ways in which the metropolis and urbanisation impinge on the lives of the characters. In *Jude the Obscure*, Sue has lived and worked in the city for two years before going to Christminster; Arabella worked in industrial Aldbrickham before meeting Jude; and the metropolis has sent forth the architect who arranges the devastation of the ancient church at Marygreen. Jude and Sue inhabit a world of telegrams, rapid rail travel, and the speedy dissemination of information and ideas by newspapers, books and magazines. The contrast with *Under the Greenwood Tree* makes evident that the story of Wessex unfolded in the main sequence of Hardy's works is a sombre story of the gradual erosion of the rural communities and their traditions by the growth of a modern urbanised civilisation. Deracination — uprooting (of various kinds) — is a pervasive theme of *Jude the Obscure*.

Another effect of that Wessex map, then, is to encourage the kind of reader who enjoys both mental and touristic nostalgia. Coach and train excursions may be made to "Hardy country", and hotels and restaurants may exploit the literary connection. The tourist industry and the publishing trade thus aid and abet each other. Certainly, knowledge of *Jude the Obscure* will make Oxford more interesting for a visitor, and a knowledge of Oxford will make *Jude the Obscure* more interesting. On the other hand, cultural tourism may obscure the fact that the power of this novel lies largely in its texture: in its vivid embodiment of Hardy's determination to address problems of sexuality, class, inequality and moral hypocrisy which are not confined to one limited geographical location. We come closer to Hardy's imaginative territory by reflecting on the literary verve of his indictment of social injustice than by walking the streets of Oxford, book in hand, seeking to touch the very stones of his Biblioll College. As the novel's first epigraph reminds us, "The letter killeth, but the spirit giveth life"; and the "Map of Wessex" may sometimes have deflected attention from the spirit to the letter, from the sensitively intelligent to the mundanely topographical. If, however, you think of obvious contrasts between the static terrain that the map presents and the mobile ideological battleground that the novel depicts, then the hallowed "Map of Wessex" may become appropriately replete with irony. If the map suggests provincial localisation, the territory of the novel's ideas remains contrastingly extensive and perennial.

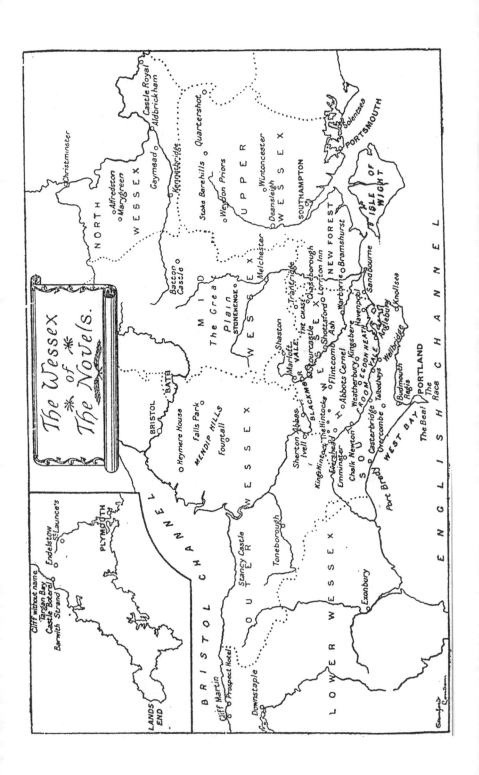

Select Bibliography

Bibliographies:

Draper, Ronald P., and Martin S. Ray. *An Annotated Critical Bibliography of Thomas Hardy*. Hemel Hempstead: Harvester Wheatsheaf, 1989.

Gerber, Helmut E., and W. Eugene Davis. *Thomas Hardy: An Annotated Bibliography of Writings about Him*. De Kalb, Illinois: Northern Illinois UP, 1973.

____. *Thomas Hardy: An Annotated Bibliography of Writings about Him: Vol. II: 1970-78 and Supplement for 1871-1969*. De Kalb, Illinois: Northern Illinois UP, 1983.

Purdy, R.L. *Thomas Hardy: A Bibliographical Study*. Oxford: Oxford UP, 1954; corrected reprint: Oxford: Oxford UP, 1968.

Weber, Carl J. *The First Hundred Years of Thomas Hardy, 1840-1940*. New York: Russell & Russell, 1965.

Autobiographical and Biographical Material:

Björk, Lennart A., ed. *The Literary Notebooks of Thomas Hardy*. Vols. 1 and 2. London: Macmillan, 1985.

Hardy, Florence Emily. *The Early Life of Thomas Hardy 1840-1891*. London: Macmillan, 1928.

____. *The Later Years of Thomas Hardy 1892-1928*. London: Macmillan, 1930.

____. *The Life of Thomas Hardy 1840-1928*. London: Macmillan, 1962.

Millgate, Michael. *Thomas Hardy: His Career as a Novelist*. London: The Bodley Head, 1971.

____. *Thomas Hardy: A Biography*. Oxford: Oxford UP, 1982.

____, ed. *The Life and Work of Thomas Hardy, by Thomas Hardy*. London: Macmillan, 1985.

Orel, Harold, ed. *Thomas Hardy's Personal Writings*. London: Macmillan, 1966.

Purdy, R.L., and Michael Millgate, ed. *The Collected Letters of Thomas Hardy*. Oxford: Clarendon Press, 1978-88.

Taylor, Richard H., ed. *The Personal Notebooks of Thomas Hardy*. London: Macmillan, 1978.

Critical and Scholarly Studies and Collections:

Brooks, Jean R. *Thomas Hardy: The Poetic Structure*. London: Elek, 1971.

Boumelha, Penny. *Thomas Hardy and Women: Sexual Ideology and Narrative Form*. Brighton: Harvester, 1982.

Chase, Mary Ellen. *Thomas Hardy from Serial to Novel* [1927]. New York: Russell & Russell, 1964.

Cox, R.G., ed. *Thomas Hardy: The Critical Heritage*. London: Routledge & Kegan Paul; New York: Barnes & Noble; 1970.

Cunningham, Gail. *The New Woman and the Victorian Novel*. London: Macmillan, 1978.

Draper, R.P., ed. *Hardy: The Tragic Novels: A Casebook*. London: Macmillan, 1975; Basingstoke: Macmillan, 1991.

Eagleton, Terry. *Criticism and Ideology: A Study in Marxist Literary Theory*. London: New Left Books, 1976; London: Verso, 1978.

___. *Walter Benjamin or Towards a Revolutionary Criticism*. London: Verso and N.L.B., 1981.

Garson, Marjorie. *Hardy's Fables of Integrity: Woman, Body, Text*. Oxford: Oxford UP, 1991.

Gatrell, Simon. *Hardy the Creator: A Textual Biography*. Oxford: Oxford UP, 1988.

Gregor, Ian. *The Great Web*. London: Faber & Faber, 1974.

Guerard, Albert. *Thomas Hardy*. Cambridge, Mass.: Harvard UP, 1949.

Higgonet, Margaret R., ed. *The Sense of Sex: Feminist Perspectives on Hardy*. Urbana, Illinois: University of Illinois Press, 1993.

Ingham, Patricia. *Thomas Hardy*. Hemel Hempstead: Harvester Wheatsheaf, 1989.

Langbaum, Robert. *Thomas Hardy in Our Time*. Basingstoke: Macmillan, 1995.

Lawrence, D.H. "Study of Thomas Hardy." *Phoenix* [Vol. 1]. London: Heinemann, 1936.

Miller, J. Hillis. *Thomas Hardy: Distance and Desire*. Cambridge, Mass.: Harvard UP, 1970.

Millett, Kate. *Sexual Politics*. New York: Doubleday, 1970; London: Virago, 1977.

Morgan, Rosemarie. *Women and Sexuality in the Novels of Thomas Hardy*. London and New York: Routledge, 1988.

Pinion, F.B. *A Thomas Hardy Dictionary*. Basingstoke and London: Macmillan, 1989; revised ed.: 1992.

Watts, Cedric. *Thomas Hardy: "Jude the Obscure."* London: Penguin, 1992.

Widdowson, Peter. *Hardy in History: A Study in Literary Sociology.* London and New York: Routledge, 1989.

___. *Thomas Hardy.* Plymouth: Northcote House, 1996.

Wright, T.R. *Hardy and the Erotic.* Basingstoke: Macmillan, 1989.

Articles on *Jude the Obscure* appear frequently in *The Thomas Hardy Journal*, the organ of the Thomas Hardy Society (UK).

broadview literary texts

"This is a series in which the editing is something of an art form."
The Washington Post

"Broadview's format is inviting. Clearly printed on good paper, with distinctive photographs on the covers, the books provide the physical pleasure that is so often a component of enticing one to pick up a book in the first place.... And, by providing a broad context, the editors have done us a great service."
Eighteenth-Century Fiction

"These editions *[Frankenstein, Hard Times, Heart of Darkness]* are top-notch—far better than anything else in the market today."
Craig Keating, Langara College

The Broadview Literary Texts series represents an important effort to see the ever-changing canon of English literature from new angles. The series brings together texts that have long been regarded as classics with lesser-known texts that offer a fresh light—and that in many cases may also claim to be of real importance in our literary tradition.

Each volume in the series presents the text together with a variety of documents from the period, enabling readers to get a fuller, richer sense of the world out of which it emerged. Samples of the science available for Mary Shelley to draw on in writing *Frankenstein,* stark reports from the Congo in the late nineteenth century that help to illuminate Conrad's *Heart of Darkness;* late eighteenth-century statements on the proper roles for women and men that help contextualize the feminist themes of the late eighteenth-century novels *Millenium Hall* and *Something New*—these are the sorts of fascinating background materials that round out each Broadview Literary Texts edition.

Each volume also includes a full introduction, chronology, bibliography, and explanatory notes. Newly typeset and produced on high-quality paper in an attractive Trade paperback format, Broadview Literary Texts are a delight to handle as well as to read.

The distinctive cover images for the series are also designed (like the duotone process itself) to combine two slightly different perspectives. Early photographs inevitably evoke a sense of pastness, yet the images for most volumes in the series involve a conscious use of anachronism. The covers are thus designed to draw attention to social and temporal context, while suggesting that the works themselves may also relate to periods other than that from which they emerged—including our own era.